The Healer

Erin-Leigh Mclauchlan

Erin-Leigh Mclauchlan

July /08

"The Healer," by Erin Leigh Mclauchlan. ISBN 978-1-60264-183-9 (softcover); 978-1-60264-184-6(hardcover).

Published 2008 by Virtualbookworm.com Publishing Inc., P.O. Box 9949, College Station, TX 77842, US. ©2008, Erin Leigh Mclauchlan. All rights reserved. No part of this publication may be reproduced, stored in a retrieval system, or transmitted in any form or by any means, electronic, mechanical, recording or otherwise, without the prior written permission of Erin Leigh Mclauchlan.

Manufactured in the United States of America.

To my sister Heidi, the co-creator of this story and the
reason most of it was written down.

To my husband Andy, my very own Tren-Lore
and the love of my life.

To my mom, who taught me that punctuation and
grammar should have a place in my "vision" and to my
dad, who showed me the importance of stories.

Thank you all for your unconditional
love and support.

Chapter One
Monsters in the Darkness

Fear assaulted my senses until they were nothing but raw and bloody wounds, ready for the infection of details. It was my fear that made me notice how gradually darkness seeped into the air. Had the taint of terror not been in my veins, night would have leapt from obscurity. I saw every moment of the slow deterioration of light and it brought forth ragged sobs. I imagined monsters in the darkness. I pressed myself against the side of my mother's bed and reached up to grasp her hand. It was cold and stiff. I closed my eyes. I did not want to see the darkness or the monsters. Let them come, but I would not see them. It was better to be blind.

My body tensed as I heard footsteps in another part of the house. It was the soft tread of monsters. I heard words but my mind would not make sense of them. Fright reached cold fingers down my throat and I choked on my tears. I was shaking and my breath came in short gasps as the sounds of monsters became louder and louder and then stopped just as they reached my mother's bedroom door.

There was a terrible moment of silence and then...

"Mother!"

The scream was mine and escaped before fear had a chance to strangle me. My eyes snapped open and I cried hysterically, screaming for my mother to wake up, clawing at my face in wild fear. The floor was stained with jagged shadows that stabbed at the walls. Two black figures advanced through the doorway. A final surge of terror overwhelmed me and I fainted.

I awoke to find myself surrounded by the warmth of soft blankets. The haze of sleep lingered and I lay without stirring or opening my eyes. The sound of soft female voices filled my ears and the repose of slumber let me listen without puzzlement.

"Kara's last letter asked for my help. I could not come quickly enough to save her, but I will not fail her child."

The declaration was made with quiet passion but the reply was full of patient reason. It reminded me of my mother speaking calmly to someone who refused to take their medicine.

"Namin, listen to me. You cannot take Lara. You can scarcely spare a moment for the children you already have. Not a day passes where you are not fleeing from anger and hate."

The rejoinder came swiftly. "She has the gift, Sophie. She will share in this life I lead. There is no use in trying to hide her from it."

"She is just a child. Let her face these realities when she is older, when we are certain she is a Healer. For the time being, I can take her into my care and keep her from harm."

Silence followed.

"You are right."

"Then it is decided. Lara is in my care."

The words washed upon my consciousness like the soothing embrace of sun-warmed water, and I sunk once more into sleep. When I next awoke, everything was silent. The sun glowed pink and warm on my closed eyelids. It was only a dream, my mind whispered in consolation. It could not have been real. Mother was never sick. It could not be real. I opened my eyes to reassure myself and was met with a sight that tensed my body into rigid knots of fear.

I sat up with a jerk. The window on the far wall, the chest of drawers across from the bed, and the table placed an arms span from where I cowered, were all obscured by one glaring detail. This was not my room! This was not my house! My mother was not here! Suddenly the door opened. A plump woman, humming softly, entered the room. The fear that had been about to leap at me with bared teeth retreated, and lay growling with sullen unease.

The woman's soft features took on a look of surprise as her kind brown eyes met my gaze. "I did not expect you to awaken so early, Lara," she said.

Speech had deserted me and I remained crouched, the blankets caught tightly in my unyielding fingers. I stared dumbly at her.

"I am Sophie Grim," the chubby woman said as she absently smoothed tiny wisps of graying brown hair back into the bun perched upon her head. "You may call me Sophie." There was a moment of silence as Sophie studied me, finally asking, "Are you hungry?"

I nodded. The very thought of food made my stomach ache painfully with longing. It had been two days since I had last eaten; two days since I had cowered in the doorway of my mother's room, a piece of dry bread grinding loudly between my teeth. It seemed so much longer.

"Well, come with me then, child." She held out her hand, and with considerable hesitation, I abandoned the bed and crept toward her.

I took Sophie's hand tentatively. It felt very much like my mother's. I wrapped my fingers around the back of her warm palm.

Sophie led me out of the room and down a narrow hall that ended in a flight of stairs. As we descended, the common room presented itself as a large, nearly deserted area, full of round tables. A woman sat at one of the tables, a book spread before her. Her brow was creased in concentration but at the sound of our approach, she looked up. Her gentle, serene face was framed beautifully by a rich brown mane of hair that tumbled over her shoulders. The color looked like the freshly turned earth in the garden behind my house. I absently fingered the ends of my own disheveled locks.

She smiled as we neared her. "Good morning, Lara."

I returned her greeting with silence.

"This is my sister, Namin," Sophie said as she guided me to a chair. "She trained to be a Healer with your mother."

I recalled the name instantly. Namin was Mother's dearest friend. They had trained together at Telnayis. Some of my favorite stories revolved around the adventures they had at the ancient Healer's school. If anyone knew where Mother was, it would certainly be Namin.

"Where is my mother?" I demanded.

Sophie and Namin exchanged a meaningful glance and Sophie replied, "Let me order you a morning meal, and then we can talk about that."

I nodded and watched as Sophie bustled out of the room. Namin quietly shut her book.

"How old are you now, Lara? Eight Springs?" asked Namin.

"Nine Springs," I responded in a barely audible voice, and then added out of sheer habit, "but it is nearly my last Spring Year."

"Nine!" Namin exclaimed. "Why, it will be your tenth Spring Year before you know it! And then your first Summer Year! Can you imagine being eleven whole years old?"

I smiled with shy pleasure. The approach of my first Summer Year was a subject of great excitement.

Sophie returned and set a glass of milk, a piece of buttered bread, and a bowl of porridge before me. I hesitated a moment, but my hunger quickly overpowered my dislike for porridge. I spooned the tan-colored gruel into my mouth.

"Did you arrange the carriage?" Sophie asked Namin.

Namin nodded and reached over to tuck a napkin into the front of my dress. "We can leave as soon as Lara is finished with her meal."

Sophie turned to me. "Have you ever heard of Caladore, Lara?"

"Yes," I replied quietly, my mouth full of porridge and my eyes trained on the bowl. My mother had told me stories of the magnificent castle that bore our country's name and had risen from the ashes of Kalamorian, last of the nine great cities built by the Ascendants.

"Sophie lives there, and you can stay with her if you like," Namin offered.

I shook my head, my hands now moving to the piece of bread. "I want to go home with my mother."

Sophie and Namin glanced at each other, and then both turned their full attention to me. "Lara dear, your mother was very sick," Sophie began in a soft voice.

Suddenly the bread seemed dry in my mouth. It tasted of memories I could not think about. I dropped the remnants of the slice back onto the plate.

Namin spoke in gentle tones. "She wrote to me the moment she knew she had contracted Elvin Fever. The message reached me too late, and I could not come in time."

Sophie leaned forward, her hand moving to cradle mine. "Do you know what happens to people when they die?"

The words were so ingrained in my memory that they tumbled from my lips without the prompting of thought. "At the moment of death a body may be reclaimed by the earth, but the spirit infuses a new born child. The spirit lives again with virtue and vice but without memory."

"Part of the Healer's doctrine," Namin murmured. "Kara taught her well."

"Do you understand what that means?" Sophie asked, her fingers tightening slightly on my hand.

I nodded.

"Your mother's sickness claimed her body, but her spirit is safe." Tears were in Namin's eyes. "Take comfort in that."

"Your mother has died, Lara."

I did not know who had spoken that last sentence. A nauseating wave of knowledge had broken upon my mind, and my consciousness fought to keep it at bay. Something was devouring my thoughts, keeping my mind from comprehending the words I had just heard. I sat without moving, staring fixedly at my piece of half-eaten bread. Sophie rose and gathered me into her arms. Namin stood as well. Her face was contorted by the effort it took not to cry. She led the way from the room.

"You poor little dear," Sophie murmured into my ear. "You need not worry; Sophie will take care of you. Everything will be all right. I will love you like your mother, darling, just like your mother."

The sentence reverberated in my mind. Just like your mother ... my mother. I tightened my grip around Sophie's neck and buried my face in the soft material of her dress. Just like my mother.

* * *

The carriage was small, and I was seated snugly between Sophie and Namin. The first part of the journey was spent in silence. When Sophie had first placed me in the carriage, comprehension had been out of my grasp. Sleep had come swiftly. It was sometime in the late afternoon when I awoke. I sat up and looked about uncertainly. Sophie was leaning against one side of the coach with a folded cloak serving as a pillow. Her eyes were closed and she was snoring softly. Namin had one of her feet tucked under her and a large book balanced on her lap. She glanced up at me.

"Did you have a nice sleep?"

I nodded.

Namin grinned and inclined her head toward her sister. "Sophie is just resting her eyes."

I glanced at Sophie and then back at Namin. It was obvious to me that Sophie was sleeping. People who were resting their eyes did not snore. Namin seemed to think her remark was amusing, so I smiled uncertainly back at her.

When Namin returned her attention to the book she was reading, I let my eyes wander through the inside of the carriage and eventually out into the expanse beyond the window. The land slipping by was not an unfamiliar sight. It resembled the terrain that surrounded the little house outside of Ekrin where my mother and I had resided. Something deep inside me flinched at the memory, but I could not think why I should feel this way.

My gaze shifted quickly to Sophie as though the sight of her was a salve upon a healing wound. The uneasiness subsided and I returned my attention to the window.

The landscape warranted consideration for only a moment longer. I smiled at the speckling of bright flowers peeking out of the grass, and then began to pick at a loose thread on the hem of my skirt. I swung my legs absent-mindedly. My boots made a nice rhythmical thud against the seat. Sophie snorted softly and shifted into what I assumed was a more comfortable position.

Without looking up, Namin asked, "Would you like me to tell you a story?"

I stilled my legs and turned my attention to her. Stories were almost as good as playing outside. "Yes, please," I murmured.

Namin closed her book and looked up with a smile. "I should warn you before we begin that I am not very good at this. Sophie got all the talent as far as storytelling is concerned. You would not know it to look at her now, but when we were young, she would tell tales that would frighten me half to death."

"I do not like scary stories," I told her solemnly.

Namin laughed. "Neither did I, when I was your age. What type of story would you like to hear?"

"The one about Sankwin and the Elves," I entreated, squirming with anticipation.

"Very well," she consented, rubbing her forehead in thought. "Let me see...that is a very old story, Lara. The last time I heard it I was probably in my fourth Summer Year. I must have been at Telnayis. Let me see ... Sankwin was ... was ... a boy like any other boy, until he met some Elves."

I wrinkled my nose. "That is not how the story starts."

Namin poked me in the ribs. "Oh really? Well, if you know how it starts, *you* can be the storyteller and *I* will listen."

I giggled and twisted to escape her tickling.

Sophie awoke with a start. "What? What is happening? Is everything all right?"

"Yes, Sophie, everything is fine," Namin replied soothingly.

Sophie sighed and absently smoothing her hair into place, murmured, "Thank the Ascendants. Traveling is so hard on my nerves."

Namin was looking out the window. "You will not have to suffer much longer. I think I can see Caladore."

"Would you like to have a look, Lara?" Sophie offered.

I climbed onto her lap and sat with my forehead pressed against the windowpane. In the distance, the rolling ground had gathered itself into a large hill. A wall sat on the slope like a giant crown, and a castle rose from within the protective circle. It was impossible to distinguish any details from our position, but this did not prevent me from staring greedily. I thought sights such as this only existed in imagination.

"That is where you live?" I asked Sophie incredulously, my breath making fog on the glass.

"It is, and there is nowhere else I would rather call home."

"What do you do there?" In stories, the only people who lived in castles were royalty. Sophie seemed very nice, but she did not look much like a princess or a queen.

"I am Head of the Kitchen," Sophie proclaimed proudly.

I thought about this as I blew deliberately on the window and drew a tiny cooking pot in the mist that appeared. I had never heard any stories about people who were Head of the Kitchen, but maybe Sophie knew some.

Soon the carriage was climbing the hill that led to the open gates of the castle. I held my breath as we passed through the giant turrets that flanked the entrance. Beyond the massive walls, a tall tower rose like a giant tree, growing straight through the cobblestone courtyard. The carriage came to a halt and Namin was the first to climb out. I sat uncertainly and stared at the view the open door had just provided. Swarms of brightly dressed people milled about. The loud babble of the crowd was as shocking as cold brook water on a hot summer day.

"Come on, Lara," Namin coaxed. She extended her hand invitingly toward me.

"Go on," Sophie prompted.

I crawled over the seat and hesitantly lowered myself down. Behind me, Sophie grunted as she made her way out of the carriage. The driver was already waiting outside with a battered bag. He set it next to Sophie. The two sisters exchanged a few words, but I was too enchanted by the sights before me to hear their conversation.

First, the sharp snapping of flags in the wind drew my attention. Atop each turret that linked the huge outer walls was a blue flag bearing a dragon insignia. The blue of the flag reminded me of the cloudless sky on a sweltering summer day. Out of this azure blur flew a massive silver dragon. His open mouth showed rows of jagged teeth, and I imagined him roaring a challenge to some unseen enemy.

Next, my attention focused on the large crowd of finely dressed people that populated the courtyard. Some were dancing to the elegant music being played by a group of minstrels, while others stood in groups discussing issues that gave them cause to frown or laugh. Many sat contentedly at the beautifully carved tables that speckled the courtyard. Servants were close by with trays of food and pitchers of wine. It looked like a very enjoyable party.

Sophie squeezed my hand. I returned my attention to her and Namin. "This is the end of our journey, little one," Sophie informed me, "but Namin is going to continue on toward Karsalin."

I nodded, even though I had no idea what Karsalin was.

Namin stooped and hugged me tightly. "Everything will be fine." She stood quickly and hugged Sophie. Then, without another word, she climbed back into the carriage. I waved to her as the coach rumbled away from us.

"Well, there is no use standing here like fools," Sophie declared. She picked up her bag and began to lead me through the tangles of people. "It is Prince Tren-Lore's Summer Year today. King Kiris, the Ascendant of Sovereignty preserve him, has been planning this party for weeks."

A little shiver ran through me. It was so exciting to think that there were real princes and kings. We soon reached a set of stairs that rose slightly to meet the inner wall. Two massive wrought iron doors barred our way. The same dragon from the flag was imprinted in the metal. Two guards flanked the image. They both smiled as Sophie and I mounted the stairs.

"Good day, Lady Grim!" one called, raising his hand in greeting. "Who accompanies you today?"

"This is Lara. She will be staying with me."

The guards welcomed me to Caladore as the large doors were swung open. The world behind the inner walls was green and lush. The space between the wall and the actual castle of Caladore was filled with the most magnificent gardens I had ever seen. Sophie and I walked along a wide path lined with flowers. I pulled on Sophie's hand as I twisted this way and that, attempting to take in the entire scope of the garden. The castle loomed in massive grandeur before us, but we turned left down a small side path.

"This is the quickest way to the kitchen," Sophie explained. "No need to go in the front doors."

I could see that before us the path gave way to a circular cobblestone clearing. Standing in the middle of this clearing was a sight that made my mouth open in surprise. "Sophie!" I cried in excitement. "What is that?"

"What?" she laughed as I tugged harder on her hand, urging her to walk more swiftly. "The dragon fountain?"

"Yes. Is that what it is?" I demanded.

I stared in awe. At first, I had only been able to see the grand head and the tips of the wings, but as we approached, the rest of the carved body was revealed. The statue was huge but wonderfully lifelike. It was as though a sorcerer had cast a spell upon a real dragon and turned it to stone. The creature was in the middle of the fountain and appeared to be wading through the water. Water sprayed into the sunlight from around its feet. I felt goose bumps rise on my arms. It was as if the lore of the dragons had suddenly become reality. "It is wonderful," I breathed as Sophie and I stopped and tilted our heads back so we could see the entire statue.

"I have always rather liked it, too," she agreed. Sophie shaded her eyes from the sun. "There are few who even take notice of it any longer. It is fairly old now, built about the same time Prince Tren-Lore was born."

I was reluctant to leave the statue, but Sophie drew me away and we entered the castle through a small side door. It was cooler inside. We climbed several flights of stairs before entering a hallway. On the left side of the passageway was a door, which Sophie opened.

She led me into a room full of bright sunshine. It was a large chamber with west-facing windows. Shelves lined the adjacent wall and were filled with all manner of bowls and jars. There was a table off to one side and giant barrels marked with words I could not read. Sophie took me through another door into what she called the main kitchen.

It was so vast that it made the chamber we had just been in look tiny. A long table claimed the middle of the room. Against the surrounding walls were ovens, counters, shelves, basins for washing dishes, and many long windows that had an excellent view of the party. I was most impressed, however, by the fireplace. It was so huge I could have walked into it and stretched my arms above my head without touching the top. Sophie's room was off the kitchen and contained two beds, a rocking chair nestled by a small table, and a full length mirror in one corner.

Sophie placed her bag on the table, and with a great sigh, sunk into her rocking chair. "It is lovely to be home. There are simply too many worries on the road."

I stood uncertainly in the doorway. I was struggling with a pain that was growing inside me. I wanted to be back in the little house my mother and I shared. I wanted to look around and have my eyes find only familiarities.

"Now," Sophie said, turning her attention to me, "you may sleep in the bed by the window. We will have to get you some new clothes and a chest to put them in. Perhaps a chair for around the table, and...."

Sophie continued on this line of thought as she began to unpack her bag. I climbed upon my new bed. There was some comfort to be taken in the knowledge that something in the room was mine. I watched silently as Sophie plucked a few dresses from her bag and, folding them neatly, returned them to the dark recesses of the chest at the foot of her bed. When the bag was empty, she put it under her bed and took a clean white apron off one of the pegs in the wall.

"I had best check on things down at the celebration," she chuckled, tying on her apron. "Something is probably going wrong as we speak."

Upon our return to the courtyard, Sophie directed me toward a group of children playing on the outer fringe of the party.

"The other servants' children," she told me in explanation. "Enjoy yourself, dear."

I hesitantly left Sophie's side. She had disappeared into the crowd when I looked back. Reaching the children, I stood warily on the outskirts of their group. I had never had any friends. The parents of Ekrin kept their children away from me. They whispered things about that evil Healer's daughter. The children themselves were not so kind. To find myself alone in their presence was to be caught in a hail of rocks and cruel names. Mother said it was because they were afraid; that they did not understand the art of Healing. I could not comprehend this explanation. They were certainly afraid when they came to my mother, begging for help, but it was their sicknesses they dreaded, not her. Why, then, should the very people my mother saved from their fears be the same to cast aspersions on her in public?

"Hey!" someone yelled.

I started, and my attention returned at once to the situation at hand. To my surprise, I found that the game had stopped and a girl, who looked to be about my age, was walking toward me.

"Who are you?" she demanded as she stopped before me, her arms folded across her chest.

"Lara," I replied cautiously. "Who are you?"

She studied me with large brown eyes. The group behind her milled about restlessly.

"Flock," she finally answered. "Why are you here?"

I frowned at her. "Lady Grim is caring for me."

Flock paused. Her eyes squinted as she considered my explanation. "Do you want to play Pandels and Laowermings?"

I had heard the stories about Pandels and Laowermings, but could not imagine that a game could be made from the tales. From what I had heard, they were nasty little creatures that chirped and twittered at night. Their song was intended to lure children from their houses and into the forest. Once there, the Pandels and Laowermings would gobble up the unsuspecting adventurers.

"How do you play?" I asked in trepidation.

"You do not know how to play?" she exclaimed in scorn.

"Would I have asked if I knew how to play?" I replied, and glared at her angrily.

Some of the children behind her laughed. She whirled, her chestnut curls bobbing wildly. The group was silenced by her furious stare. She turned back to me. "You can be the Pandel. Rathum is the Laowerming." She gestured over her shoulder to a short boy with unruly red hair and a copious number of freckles. "You and Rathum have to try and catch the rest of us. If you do, we become Pandels and Laowermings too."

I agreed to this and soon found myself involved in the game. At first I enjoyed myself. At the start of each game, however, Flock informed me that I had to be the Pandel again, and by the end of the fourth game I was so tired of this role that I quit and went to find Sophie. My search for her did not go well. I wandered unnoticed through a maze of brightly dressed nobility. I was jostled a great deal and heard uninteresting fragments of conversation.

"The cloth was beautiful. I told my tailor I would take..."

"It would make quite an alliance. Just the other day I was saying..."

"He was very rude to us, and in our own home. Why he..."

After an exhaustive hunt, I decided I would go back to the kitchen and wait for her there. I was in poor spirits as I slipped through the crowds and made my way into the castle. Caladore was nothing like the stories I had heard. The inhabitants of this magnificent castle were pale copies of the heroes I had imagined. Their clothes were beautiful but not spectacular, and their discussions were ordinary instead of intriguing. It was quite a disappointing realization.

* * *

I sighed in frustration as I turned yet another corner and found myself in yet another corridor that did not look familiar. Unlike the other halls I had ventured down, this one had no doors or diverging passages. It was long and straight and ended in what looked like a balcony. I moved forward on a quest to satisfy my curiosity about what lay at the end of this hall. Lining the walls were tapestries. As I walked, I examined each one.

The first tapestry illustrated two saplings growing together in soft moss. Their young branches were entwined. The second depicted silver ivy weaving itself about the body of a young woman. The next was a simple blue flower against a flaxen background. The fourth was a resplendent red flower, but curling up its stem was a dark green serpent. The next tapestry made me cringe. Woven into the surface was a picture of a dragon with a sword buried deep in its heart. Blood pooled around the dragon's body. The creature had such a look of agony on its face that I hurried on. The following pictures were just as unsettling. One depicted a giant labyrinth made from a black and thorny hedge. The barbs were stained with blood. On another, the Ascendant of Eternity held a baby in one hand and a skull in the other. The last tapestry was more to my liking. It showed a wall covered in green ivy, and just visible through the foliage, a door. It was slightly ajar. As I tried to decide if the door was being opened or closed, I stepped out onto the balcony.

Below me I could see the inner courtyard, silent with green perfection, and the outer courtyard, full of carousing people. Dark clouds had gathered on the horizon while I had been lost in the castle. Thunder rumbled in the distance. To combat the early dusk that had been summoned by the impending storm, several bonfires had been lit. The wind carried the scent of rain and wood smoke.

"You know, I am fairly sure that not one of them has any idea what they are celebrating."

I let out a startled cry and turned swiftly. The person who had spoken was a boy. He wore a gray cloak that made him hard to see against the backdrop of the stone wall. I had walked right past him without noticing his presence.

"I... I..." It was hard to collect my thoughts over the pounding of my heart. "I... thought they were here for the prince's Summer Year."

The boy grinned wolfishly. "Then you know more than they do. They are here to flaunt their wealth, plot and scheme."

I was struggling for a reply when the soft thud of footsteps drew my attention. Walking down the hall was a tall figure dressed so splendidly that I lost any hope of making an intelligible response. The figure was soon on the balcony. He was a tall young man, whose golden blond hair and handsome features matched his rich attire. He took no notice of me, but rather turned immediately to the boy.

"Ascendants curse you! You never did have any manners," the young man snarled as he shoved a silver crown, similar to his own gold one, into the boy's hands. "Get down to the courtyard. Now!"

"You are not King yet, Yolis," the boy retorted as he pushed himself away from the wall.

Thunder growled overhead, and the wind caught the younger boy's cloak. Fingers of air pulled it back to reveal that he too was clad in exquisite clothing. Imprinted on the front of his rich blue tunic was the dragon I had seen on Caladore's flags. His hose were made of thick black material and his boots were soft deer hide, studded with silver.

"No," Yolis replied, "but Father is, and he wants you down in the courtyard."

"Fine," the boy muttered, and put the silver crown on. It glinted in his short, ruffled black hair.

Anger marred Yolis' face as he turned and strode from the balcony. The dark-haired boy hesitated, and then followed. My amazement was so intense that my feet seemed to have taken root in the uneven stones beneath me. I stared after the retreating figures. If their father was king, that would make them princes! Their clothes, expressions, and tones, were what stories were made from. I stood frozen, even after the echoes of their footsteps had died away. My mind was reveling in the thought of imagination come to life.

Fanfare sounded from far below. As the brassy music melted into the evening air, I turned and leaned eagerly over the edge of the balcony wall. A man in a dark red cloak was standing on the stairs that led to the inner courtyard. A little girl was held snugly in his arms, and standing on either side of him were the two boys I had just encountered.

"Noblemen of Caladore! Gentle Ladies! I present to you, King Kiris, Prince Yolis, Prince Tren-Lore and Princess Nahanni!"

I could not tell who had made the proclamation, but it caused a ripple of bowing and curtsies. King Kiris began to speak. I strained my ears to hear his words.

"It is a proud day for Caladore. My-"

Suddenly the king's voice was lost in a deafening crash of thunder. It ripped through the air, shaking torrents of rain from the ominous clouds. A cry rose from the people below. In a unified mass, they moved toward the inner wall. The doors were opened and everyone hurried toward the castle. In only moments, the entire courtyard was deserted except for the dark-haired boy I now assumed must be Prince Tren-Lore. I was in awe as I watched him. I could hardly believe that I had spoken to a prince. He walked down the stairs and stopped at the bottom step. Spreading his arms, as though welcoming the rain, he raised his face to the sky.

"Lara!"

I jumped and spun to find Sophie standing at the entrance to the balcony.

"I have been looking for you everywhere. Come inside at once. You will catch your death of cold standing in the rain."

Reluctantly, I did as she bid me and we walked hand in hand back to the kitchen.

"Sophie," I began, as we entered the large room, "why did Prince Tren-Lore stay in the courtyard after everyone else left?"

"The prince has his own ways," Sophie replied simply, and guided me toward the fire. "Sit here and warm yourself. I will get you something hot to drink."

"His own ways!" one of the women laughed. "Sophie, the boy is wild and King Kiris does nothing about it."

"If you ask me," began another, "His Majesty simply does not have the heart to discipline the poor child now that his mother is de-"

Sophie placed a kettle over the fire and interrupted the discussion. "It is not our place to criticize King Kiris."

"Certainly not, of course not," they all agreed, and the subject was quickly changed.

One of the ladies took up a description of the rain-drenched nobles as they hastily departed from Caladore and escaped the shame of being seen by their equally rain-drenched peers. This was apparently a very amusing subject, for it sent them all into gales of laughter.

Sophie surveyed my clothing as she handed me a plate of meat and cheese. "Nearly dry?"

I nodded as I bit into a piece of cheese.

"Good. Eat this all up, and by that time the water will be ready," Sophie instructed as she picked up another stick of wood and pushed it into the fire. Humming, she turned and bustled off in another direction.

I watched as the newly excited flames licked at the bottom of the kettle. A chair scraped beside me, and I looked up to find Prince Tren-Lore seating himself.

"Hello," he said as he removed his crown from his wet hair.

I nearly choked on the meat I had in my mouth, but managed to reply, "Hello."

Prince Tren-Lore was grinning as he undid his cloak and tossed it on the floor. "What a storm!"

17

"I liked the thunder," I murmured, and stared shyly at the fire.

"Me too," he agreed, and threw his crown on top of his cloak. "My name is Tren-Lore."

I looked up and met stunningly blue eyes. They were deep azure, the color of the sky just before a storm. "I am Lara."

He nodded with practiced courtesy. "I am pleased to make your acquaintance, Lara."

Sophie returned to take the kettle from the heat, and to my astonishment, she did not seem the least bit surprised to see Tren-Lore sitting before the fire.

"Hello, Lady Grim," he greeted Sophie politely.

"Hello, child," she chuckled, and lifted the kettle from the flames. "I suppose you will be wanting something to eat?"

Tren-Lore smiled. "And maybe some hot berryroot cordial for me and Lara?"

Sophie looked shrewdly at Tren-Lore. "Does your father know where you are?"

"No, he will be too busy with Nahanni to even notice I am gone. She is deathly afraid of storms, you know."

"Very well," Sophie nodded. "Berryroot cordial it is, but then you had best return to the royal chambers. We would not want King Kiris to worry." Sophie returned shortly with another plate of meat and cheese and two steaming mugs of red liquid. "It is very hot," she warned, "mind you do not burn your mouths."

I hesitantly tasted this new drink. To my delight, I found that it was delicious. I swallowed deeply and burned my tongue and the top of my mouth.

"I am going to build a fort," Tren-Lore told me abruptly.

"Really?" I asked in interest, slowly lowering my cup to my lap. "What will it be like?"

Tren-Lore began to describe the plans he was making, and I listened intently. His ideas were grand and he spoke with an excitement I found contagious. Our conversation made the time pass so quickly that our drinks were soon gone and the windows revealed nothing but gray dusk.

I jumped as the door swung open and an impressive figure strode into the kitchen. He was taller and much older, but I thought immediately of Prince Yolis when I saw him. There was stunned silence for a moment, a quiet so absolute it seemed to forbid even the slightest movement, and then suddenly everyone broke into a flurry of curtsies and warm greetings for King Kiris.

"Great Ascendants!" Sophie exclaimed. "I forgot entirely. My apologies, Your Majesty, I should have sent him up to the royal chambers long ago. I hope you were not concerned."

"No." The King smiled warmly. "I thought he would be here, and when Tren-Lore is in your company, my good Lady Grim, I never have cause for concern."

Sophie swept a curtsy. "Your Majesty is too kind."

"Not kind, merely truthful," King Kiris replied, and held out a hand to his son. "Nahanni, Yolis and I are about to play Questkon, if you would like to join us."

"Wonderful!" Tren-Lore replied enthusiastically, and leapt from his chair. He paused and turned to me. "It was nice to meet you, Lara."

"Do not forget your crown," King Kiris reminded.

The smile that had creased Tren-Lore's face was abruptly gone. "I wish I could," he grumbled, and unceremoniously scooped cloak and crown into his arms and strode from the room.

King Kiris frowned and, bidding a polite farewell to the ladies, followed his son from the kitchen. After the royal pair had left, Sophie hurried me to bed. She handed me one of her sleeping gowns and laughed when it pooled around my feet.

"We will see about getting you a new sleeping gown tomorrow," she promised, pulling back the covers on my bed. "Climb up here now."

I crawled onto the unfamiliar bed and Sophie tucked me in.

"Sleep well, child," Sophie said, and snuffed out the candle.

"No!" I cried and sat up suddenly. The darkness summoned memories I had no wish to recall. In the void of night, my mind filled the blank darkness with the stiffness of my mother's hand, with the cold stone floor, the terror, the grief I could not – or would not – understand. "No, Sophie! It is too dark!"

Sophie fumbled with her flint and tinder and relit the candle. She beheld my tear-streaked face with puzzlement and compassion. She set the candle on the small table between the two beds and seated herself beside me.

"There now, child," she soothed, smoothing my hair from my forehead until I relaxed and lay back. Sophie's soft fingers continued to stroke my brow and she began to sing softly.

It was a song I knew. My mother sang it, and indeed, as sleep enveloped me, it was my mother's tender touch and sweet voice that lulled me into slumber.

Chapter Two
Tren-Lore

T houghts of Tren-Lore were with me even before my mind had fully escaped its sleep induced muddle. I lay for a time puzzling over him. He was so real; earnest and forthright, yet a person worthy of the grand tales of imagination I had heard. I liked him, I decided as I threw back my blankets. I emerged from the room clad in the same clothes I had worn the day before. Sophie and a few other ladies were setting the long table.

"Good morning, child. Climb up on this chair." Sophie patted the back of one seat. "We will be breaking fast in a moment."

I did as she bid me, and soon the table was encircled by merrily chattering women passing plates of steaming food from hand-to-hand. Sophie had seated herself on my left and, to my dismay, Flock sat on my right.

"Are you coming to sanctuary, Lara?" she asked as she distastefully sniffed at a slice of freshly baked bread.

I glanced uncertainly at Sophie, and she nodded quietly before turning back to her conversation.

"Yes," I told Flock, nibbling on a piece of apple.

"Then you can sit with me," she stated imperiously. "Sanctuary is *so* dull. You will need the company."

"Oh, Flock, you can be so dramatic!" said a pretty young lady in an exasperated tone.

"You just like sanctuary because Prince Yolis is there," Flock retorted. Turning to me, she announced in a whisper meant for everyone to hear, "Prince Yolis is the same age as Kella, and she is smitten with him."

Kella reached across the table and gave one of Flock's curls a sharp tug. "Be quiet."

"Mother!" Flock cried. "Kella is being mean to me again."

One of the women talking to Sophie stopped abruptly in mid-sentence and glared at the two girls. "Flock! Kelladyn! You will both behave this instant or I will smack both of your behinds."

"But Mother!" Flock whined.

Kelladyn looked indignant. "I am in my Seventh Summer, Mother," she said in a clipped tone, tossing her chestnut curls over her shoulders. "I do not appreciate you mentioning my behind in front of-"

"Enough!" their mother ordered sternly, and then continued her interrupted discourse with Sophie as though nothing had happened.

The sisters continued to bicker quietly throughout the meal. I was greatly relieved when Sophie informed me we would be leaving for sanctuary early so we could purchase a few things down in Cala. I was smiling widely as I swept from the kitchen, hand in hand with Sophie. Not only did this remove me from the presence of the quarrelsome Flock and Kella, it also excused me from dishes, a task I did not relish.

Cala presented itself as a sparkling city whose wide streets were lined with ancient trees. Sophie guided me into several shops. Pushy merchants showed Sophie pieces of cloth and various other items she apparently needed. It seemed to me that a large amount of coin changed hands before Sophie hurried me into the carriage. She was juggling several packages and fretting about being late for sanctuary.

Despite Sophie's concern, we arrived with plenty of time and joined the throngs of people pouring through the massive arched entrance. I strained to see the interior of the building. There were so many bodies pressing in on all sides that I could only make out the grandly vaulted ceilings. The congregation eventually spilled into a large room. The walls were made of a shining stone that reflected the crowd perfectly. Sophie led me to a row of seats near the back.

"Sit here and do not stir until I return," she told me sternly. "There is someone I must say hello to. I will be back in a moment."

With that, she was gone. I was alone to marvel at the walls, which made the chamber look twice its actual size. The royal family was standing at the front, engaged in conversation with a few richly dressed nobles. I swiftly noted that Tren-Lore was missing from the family. I puzzled at his absence as my eyes roamed about the room and found the familiar figures of Flock and Kella amongst the throng. I smiled as I watched Kella straining to catch a glimpse of Yolis. Suddenly, from somewhere deep within the sanctuary, a bell tolled. I jumped slightly, and everyone hurried to find seats. Moments later, a priest appeared on the dais at the front of the sanctuary. All noise ceased.

I rose onto my knees and twisted in my seat, searching for Sophie. I could not see her anywhere. A thin woman in gray, seated behind me, gave a condemning look as her thin lips silently formed the words, "Sit down!" Her raised eyebrows added the exclamation mark. I immediately did so, my cheeks warm with embarrassment. The priest had begun to speak, but I only heard the words indistinctly over the clamor of worry in my mind. Where was Sophie?

"This month we gather to celebrate The One. It is our most sacred of ceremonies, for it was The One who created us. I know the story of creation is familiar to all of you, but let us search the classic tale for new meaning. As you listen today, reflect upon how the lessons in this story may be applied to your own life. When The One created us, he took a piece of his own spirit and infused it into each one of his new creations to give them life. The One set his new creations upon the earth and bid them enjoy what they would. All was well for a time, but eventually the people became greedy. They claimed land that was intended for all to use. They formed large groups that took up arms to slaughter each other in a quest to have more than their fellow man. The One saw this and cried in grief and horror. He knew now that vice was a beast that would stalk his people as long as they lived without rules to guide them."

I caught movement in the corner of my eye, and not wishing to incur the wrath of the woman behind me, I discreetly glanced sideways. To my immense surprise, Tren-Lore was walking down the aisle. His eyes met mine and he smiled. He slid into the seat beside me and whispered a greeting.

"Calling upon all his strength," the priest continued, "The One brought into existence nine Ascendants to preside over fire and sky, rock and water, plants and animals, sovereignty, unity and eternity. He charged the Ascendants with the governance of his creations. It was his final act, for having given so much of himself, he ceased to exist."

"Why were you late?" I asked softly.

He jerked his head toward the exit. "Follow me."

I was caught in a moment of indecision, but as Tren-Lore stood and grinned boldly at the thin lady who had scowled at me before, I forgot all my concerns in a great rush of amusement. His behavior was obviously outrageous to her, and yet, she did not dare to give the prince the kind of nasty look she had used on me. He led me from the room and into the main corridor from which the nine other houses of worship could be reached.

"I got a horse for my Summer Year!" he told me as he strode through the huge hall.

I tried to match my gait to his confident one.

"You see, I am training to be a knight, so Father got me a charger. That is why I was late. I was practicing my riding this morning." His expression was determined. "I need to have excellent horsemanship so I can be top of my class."

I watched Tren-Lore with admiration, having no doubt in my mind that he would be an excellent rider and top of his class. He said nothing more until we were outside the sanctuary and nearing a knobby tree that grew close by. Tied to the tree's lowest branch was a large black stallion.

The beast stamped angrily at the ground as we approached.

"I named him Storm Wing, after the first dragon Lord Rayn ever spoke to," Tren-Lore informed me. Sticking his hands in his pockets, he watched the stallion yank viciously on the reins that tethered him to the tree. "Have you heard any of the Lord Rayn stories?"

I took a step back from the cantankerous horse. "I heard the one where Rayn leaves his life as a nobleman to learn the lost tongue of the dragons ... Your father gave you *this* horse for your Summer Year?"

"I picked him out myself," Tren-Lore told me happily. "That is just the first one - of the Lord Rayn stories, I mean, not horses. I could lend you the other books if you would like."

My silence drew Tren-Lore's gaze. My shame made it difficult to respond. Until that moment, the fact that I could not read had been of no concern. Suddenly, it seemed I was lacking a vital skill. "I do not know how to read," I finally muttered.

"I can teach you," he offered easily as he reached out to stroke Storm Wing, only to be rewarded with an angry snort. "It is not hard. I wish learning to fight with a sword was half as simple as learning to read."

"Is sword fighting hard?"

Tren-Lore's countenance abruptly grew dark. "Yolis does not think so, nor do most of the boys we are training with. I am fine as long as I can fight with my right hand, but I am doomed the moment I have to use my left."

"You need to be able to use both hands?" I asked in surprise.

He nodded grimly. "I practice when I can but .... Lara ..." His voice was suddenly aflame. "If I teach you how to read, would you practice sword fighting with me?"

The idea struck my mind with the violence of an arrow meeting wood, and then, like the vibrations of the quivering shaft, sent ripples of excitement through my body. "That would be wonderful!" I breathed.

He grinned and slapped me on the shoulder. "Great! We will need somewhere secret to practice. I can bring the swords. Can you come tomorrow?"

I was about to answer in the affirmative when the turbulent sound of many voices speaking at once filled the air. Tren-Lore and I both turned our attention to the sanctuary and found the congregation spewing forth from its wide doors. "Sophie!" I gasped in horror, only now realizing the promise I had broken to the kindly woman. I turned quickly back to Tren-Lore. "Where should I meet you?"

His deep blue eyes reflected the energy of the moment. "Tomorrow at noon. Outside the kitchen."

I nodded, and without even bidding him farewell, I darted toward the sanctuary. I arrived at the seat I had been sitting in only an instant before Sophie. To my relief, it was she who had to apologize for her absence during sanctuary. I said little on the ride back to Caladore, for I was too preoccupied with my visions of the coming day. I was going to learn to read and swordfight with a boy who seemed to be made of legends!

The rest of the day was full of work that kept my hands busy but allowed my mind to wander. While Sophie measured me for my new garments, I imagined grand duels in my head. I washed dishes with Flock and envisioned myself bent over giant leather-bound books and unrolling aged parchments.

When at last it was time to retire, I slipped into my new sleeping gown and crawled into bed. I was eager for slumber to hasten the evening away, but sleep would not come. At first, it was my anticipation that kept me awake. Then, it was the strange sounds of the castle: a faint thud echoing from deep within the walls and the hooting of an owl alarmingly near my window. I pulled the woolen blankets up around my chin and squeezed my eyes shut.

Sophie was sitting in her rocking chair, sewing by the flickering light of a single candle. I reminded myself of her presence to lull my fears. Instead of imagining the adventures I wanted to have with Tren-Lore, I thought of home. I was back in the small house my mother and I shared. I was cuddled in my warm bed. The smell of the fresh bread that had been made that morning still lingered in the air. My mother was sitting by the fire, mending a piece of my clothing. Her chair creaked rhythmically against the floor as she rocked back and forth. Tears slipped from the corners of my eyes, and grief welled up inside me. I cried silently until the soundless tears brought weariness and I fell asleep.

The sun was just rising in the sky when I awoke, but Sophie's bed was already deserted. A new dress lay across the chest that now sat sedately at the foot of my bed. I smiled as I climbed out of bed and pulled it on. The cloth felt soft against my skin. After inspecting myself in the mirror and finding my new attire much to my liking, I ventured forth into the kitchen. Sophie was bustling about, already preparing food for the day. She was quick to set me to work helping get the morning meal on the table.

The morning passed with agonizing slowness. With every moment, I realized how much I disliked chores and desperately wished that noon would come swiftly. I helped prepare the midday meal, and then, in the commotion of sending out food to the rest of castle, I slipped into the antechamber unnoticed and out into the passageway.

Tren-Lore was leaning casually against the wall, awaiting me. "Good afternoon," he said with a grin, and then proceeded down the corridor. In a few dozen paces, he had led me to a flight of stairs. Tren-Lore glanced at me. "Want to race?"

I did not reply, but rather sprang up the stairs as fast as I possibly could. He shouted an exclamation that echoed with surprise and amusement before he bounded after me. We ran up and up the winding flight of stairs until we collapsed on a huge landing. The air smelled as though our gasping breath was the first breeze to stir there in quite some time. The landing was circular and housed six doors. Dust-covered tapestries hung next to each entrance.

Tren-Lore avoided the doors and walked confidently up to one of the hanging rugs. The delicate stitching depicted a dragon. The creature's wings were spread as though it were about to take flight. Tren-Lore drew back the tapestry to reveal a door. He pushed it open, and I followed in amazement, holding the tapestry for him, so he could enter the room. I tried to release the rug and follow him into the dark room, but fear battered against me. A faint sickness pushed its way into my stomach. From that darkness, memories rose that I shied away from. I unconsciously stepped away from the threshold.

Suddenly, light tumbled into the room and the memories retreated with the blackness, remaining only in the corners of my mind as shadows of recollection. Tren-Lore had thrown back the shutters of a large window and revealed a room nearly the size of the kitchen's antechamber. It had a fireplace, a rickety bookshelf standing adjacent, and a dilapidated table pushed against the wall opposite the window. Two swords stood in one corner.

"I come here a lot. It makes a good escape."

I agreed fully and thought how nice it would be if I could spend my days hidden in a secret room, avoiding chores and Flock.

"Here." Tren-Lore picked up one of the swords and handed it to me. "The blades are dulled, so we need not worry about hurting each other too badly."

The sword was a bit too heavy to handle with ease, but I hefted it eagerly. Tren-Lore was a patient instructor and I learned the basic moves quickly. Once he was satisfied that I could defend myself from his attack, he started his own practice. He began with his sword in his right hand, and I only withstood a few blows before he had the blunt end of his weapon pointed at my chest.

"Do you yield?"

I smiled boldly at him and replied defiantly, "No."

I swung my sword awkwardly at his legs. It was not graceful or any of the standard attacks Tren-Lore had shown me, but it served my purpose. Tren-Lore leapt back, and I met two more of his assaults before the young prince struck my blade so soundly it made the hilt vibrate painfully in my hands. I dropped it instantly.

"Do you yield?" he persisted breathlessly.

"Of course I yield. I do not have a sword."

Dismay and then mirth flashed across Tren-Lore's face. He chuckled, and withdrew his blade. "That was not a very noble answer, Lara. Next time try something like, I yield, or, I grudgingly accept my defeat," Tren-Lore suggested teasingly. "Do you want to try again? This time I will fight with my left hand."

"I want to try too," I agreed.

After taking a moment to catch our breath, we began again. The results were startlingly different. Tren-Lore was not nearly as good a swordsman when he used his left hand. To his surprise, as well as mine, I could fight as easily with my left hand as I could with my right. Neither one of us was very good, however. The fight became a clumsy and drawn-out affair. It ended when I swung at Tren-Lore, and in the same moment he moved to lunge at me. My blade met his forearm, inflicting a bloody wound. We both stopped and Tren-Lore looked at the injury in surprise.

"I did not think they were sharp enough to draw blood!" He grimaced as he slowly flexed his hand. A wry smile was quick to replace his expression of pain. "Perhaps we should work on reading at our next meeting. I may not be able to hold a sword tomorrow."

"I am so sorry, Tren-Lore!" I gasped.

He laughed as he drew my sword from my grasp and leaned the two weapons against the wall. "I am only joking. I have endured far worse."

I caught his arm in my hands and used the cuff of my sleeve to dab away the blood. "I have nothing to bind it with, or I would."

"Maybe it will scar." He looked at his arm reflectively. "That would look pretty good."

I laughed and released his arm. It was just then that I noticed how low the sun had sunk. I promised Tren-Lore that I would meet him in the secret room tomorrow and hurried toward the kitchen. When I reached the cheerful room, it was buzzing with the preparations for the evening meal. The carefully ordered madness allowed me to slip back into the kitchen without being noticed. I had almost reached the door to the room I shared with Sophie when one of the ladies caught my arm.

"Flock needs some help with dishes, Lara."

I sighed and silently joined Flock at the washing basin. I picked up a cloth and took the soapy bowl she handed me.

"Where did you go this afternoon?" she asked.

"I . . ." my voice dwindled into silence, and I suddenly demonstrated an all-consuming interest in drying the bowl in my hand.

I knew instinctively that it would not be a good idea to tell Flock about my secret meeting with Tren-Lore. It would not be a good idea to tell anyone. I had heard enough stories to know that princes were not supposed to befriend girls who worked in a kitchen.

Flock paused, her hands half immersed in the sudsy water. She looked at me suspiciously. "Where did you go?"

I grabbed the partially washed plate from her grasp and busily dried it. "I went exploring," I told her without meeting her gaze.

"You did not!" She pulled her hands from the water and assumed an indignant posture, one hand on her hip, the other letting the wet rag hang at her side. "Tell me where you went. Now."

"No," I retorted, and watched as fury bloomed in her face.

"Flock!" Sophie's tone was sharp and carried over the din in the kitchen. "You are letting dish water drip all over the clean floor. Finish washing those dishes. We need them for dinner."

"Yes, Lady Grim," Flock replied sullenly, and turned back to her work. "I do not want to know where you went, anyway," she continued in a soft, vicious tone. "You are going to be in such trouble when Lady Grim finds out! Sneaking out for the whole afternoon!"

This comment worried me considerably. I did not want to make Sophie angry, but I desperately wanted to meet Tren-Lore tomorrow. It was a relief to find that Sophie did not seem upset with me. In fact, she did not even comment until she was tucking my covers around me at bedtime. "Did you have a nice afternoon, dear?" she whispered.

I paused a moment in shock, and Sophie, seeing my expression, smiled conspiratorially. I nodded hesitantly and Sophie patted my cheek. She left the candle lit. Her skirts rustled gently as she left the room. I closed my eyes, and as puzzlement over Sophie's kindness faded to thoughts of learning to read, I fell asleep.

Chapter Three
In the Ranks of Healers

My last Spring Year arrived just after I had marked two entire months of living at Caladore. Sophie planned a lavish party and invited all the children I played with during feasts. Though Tren-Lore had not been invited, he showed up anyway, making Sophie smile fondly at him and causing me to feel as though I would burst with happiness. The party was held during the evening. The tables were laden with jugs of berryroot cordial, and so many sweets and cookies that when I saw the platters piled with treats, I ran to Sophie and hugged her wildly, exclaiming, "Oh, thank you, Sophie! Thank you so much!"

Sophie had surprised me with a gift earlier that day. When my guests arrived, I was already wearing the pretty blue dress she had sewn for me. Flock stared at me in envy. I saw her eyes dart to my ruffled cuffs and I could not help smiling even more widely. I was particularly proud of how nice my cuffs looked, and knowing that Flock was jealous of them made me like them all the more.

Rathum greeted me with his typically meek "Hello", but then stood before me staring at the floor and clearing his throat. "You...ah....my mother said to tell you that....you look ... ah, very nice." The spreading pink coloration of his skin clashed horribly with his red hair, but I could not have liked him more at that moment.

Tren-Lore gave my new dress a quick glance and said scornfully, "You look like a girl."

I grinned at him. How utterly wonderful, and unbelievable it was to have a friend such as Tren-Lore. "I hope so," I replied quietly, so as not to call attention to the fact that Tren-Lore and I were talking.

He returned my smile and punched me on the shoulder. "Joyous Spring Year, Lara."

"Thank you," I replied, absently rubbing my shoulder, "Would you like some berryroot cordial?"

"And a tart," Tren-Lore responded promptly.

Flock was approaching us, a look of extreme interest on her face. For her sake, I dropped a curtsy to Tren-Lore and said loudly, "I will return with your cordial and tart in just a moment. Will there be anything else?"

It was the kind of thing I had heard Sophie say while she was serving, and I thought my rendition of it was quite convincing. Obviously Tren-Lore thought so too, for he was staring at me in absolute shock, his blue eyes suddenly somber with confusion and unease. I looked pointedly to the side and he followed my gaze to find Flock striding toward us. Instantly comprehending what I had been doing, Tren-Lore's expression cleared and his smile returned. "No, thank you. That is all for now," he replied in such a regal voice that it was my turn to be surprised.

Sparing him one last look, I moved toward the table where the pastries had been laid out. I trusted that Flock would be watching me, and so I swung my arms as I walked, drawing extra attention to my lovely cuffs. I wondered absently how long Flock had been watching me talk to Tren-Lore. Maybe she was jealous of that, too. In my mother's stories, girls were always "green with envy". I covered my mouth with my hands and giggled at the thought of seeing Flock with green skin.

* * *

Flock's skin had failed to turn any shade resembling green the night of my last Spring Year. I was sure a verdant blush was about to spread its way across her cheeks, however, as my afternoon absences from the kitchen continued to be tolerated. A month had slipped away already. I had developed a routine that I did not intend to change, no matter how unfair Flock felt it was.

The morning would be spent doing chores, but the moment the noon hour arrived, I would make a stealthy retreat up to the secret room, where Tren-Lore and I practiced swordplay and reading. As the strength of our friendship grew, the formality of our exercises lessened. They typically dissolved, because we lost ourselves in jokes and laughter. When evening crept upon Caladore, I was once more in the kitchen and subject to a thorough questioning from Flock. I was growing braver in my replies to her, however. On one occasion, I had smothered a grin and assured her calmly that I had no idea what she was talking about, for I had not even left the kitchen that afternoon.

It was this comment which had truly sparked her wrath and provoked her into maintaining an increasingly vigilant watch. That midday, as I moved toward the kitchen door, I could feel Flock's eyes on my back, and I was not surprised to hear her penetrating voice inquire loudly, "Why is it that she does not have to do any work, Lady Grim?"

Sophie sighed audibly and held a broom out to me. "You can sweep the floor, Lara."

I took the broom from her and shot the grinning Flock a scathing look. I had just begun to sweep the stone floor when Flock sidled up to me and whispered in a spiteful voice, "I guess you will just have to stay this afternoon and work like everyone else."

I glared at her. "If everyone else does as little work as you, I might just decide to stay every afternoon."

Unable to find a response to this, Flock stuck out her tongue and marched over to the bread dough she had been assigned to knead. She set about working it vigorously, as though attempting to prove how hard she really did work. Her efforts were lost on me, as I had my own job to do and needed to complete it quickly. Tren-Lore would be expecting me. I hurriedly finished sweeping and, leaning the broom against the wall, hastened towards the door. I was not quick enough. Flock rose in her seat, about to voice an outraged cry, when Sophie cut her off. "Are you nearly done with that dough, Flock?"

"But Lady Grim, she is-"

"Hurry up, child," Sophie interrupted, not heeding her objections. "That bread needs to be ready for this evening's meal."

I smothered a laugh as I ran through the antechamber and out into the main hallway. I was smiling widely as I proceeded to the secret room. Tren-Lore was already running through exercises when I arrived. He was stripped to the waist and sweating profusely. His chest had several deep bruises on it, and his eye was black. He paused when he saw me, wiping sweat from his forehead. "Flock?" he asked between breaths.

I nodded and went to pick up my own sword. "What happened? I mean, how did you get those bruises?"

"We are practicing hand-to-hand combat in training," he replied shortly, and assumed a ready position.

"Who did you fight?" I asked in shock, my eyes moving from his bruises to a deep gash just at his hairline. I had not noticed it when I had first entered. His pallor suggested that it had bled a great deal.

"Yolis," he stated flatly, his face suddenly expressionless. "Are you ready?"

I was hesitant to take a fighting stance. "Should you be sword fighting today?"

"Yes," he snapped, and feigned a lunge.

My guard was immediately up, and my blade struck his in a defensive block. We fought furiously. I was cross with him for his curt reply, and he seemed to be driven by an anger unrelated to me. We battered at each other. Tren-Lore and I abandoned many of the formal moves we were trying to master in exchange for awkward, but more vicious attacks. I was still not a match for him. Soon, he had his blade leveled at my chest. We were both breathing hard and glaring at each other.

"Switch hands," I told him.

He looked surprised for a moment. It was usually Tren-Lore who uttered this familiar command. He did shift his sword to his left hand, however, and we began again. As always, this battle was much longer. We directed blow after blow towards each other, until we were both gasping for air. Suddenly, Tren-Lore staggered back and fell! His sword clattered to the floor. He lay motionless. I gasped and rushed to kneel at his side. "Tren-Lore?"

His face was very pale and he opened his eyes slowly. "What happened?" he asked faintly.

"You passed out. I think you must have lost too much blood from your cut."

His hand found the gash on his forehead. He winced as his fingers grazed it. "This has been a very bad day." He pushed himself to a sitting position, his face set in a determined expression. "There is nothing for it. I will simply have to practice harder. I have to be top of my class, Yolis or not."

I frowned at him in concern. Why did he have to push himself so hard when he was injured? I hated seeing Tren-Lore like this. I wished there was something I could do to make him feel better about what had happened. I wanted desperately to be able to fix everything for him, to take away his pain. "You *will* be top of your class. We will practice, but just not today. You should rest." I reached over and lightly touched his cut. "This needs time to heal." It was an unconscious gesture, but the instant I touched his skin, I felt a strange, soft tingling sensation run through my hand.

Tren-Lore stared at me in shock.

"Why are you looking at me like that?" I asked, suddenly very aware of myself.

His hands were both on his head now, feeling the place his wound had been. "How did you do that?"

I gasped as he removed his hands. The skin was healed, as though it had never been injured. I was suddenly cold with panic. "I never meant to! I do not even know how!" I cried, and leapt to my feet.

I remembered my mother performing such feats. This was a Healer's ability, and an irrefutable sign that would forever place me in their ranks. Tren-Lore would never want to be my friend now that he knew. Tears blurred my vision, and my mind flashed images of the angry people of Ekrin and all the children who had rejected my friendship.

I had wanted so much to be friends with Tren-Lore, and now that would be impossible. I turned and ran.

"Lara! Lara! Wait!" Tren-Lore yelled after me.

His words did not slow the pace of my feet. I could not go back to the kitchen. The thought of facing Sophie and Flock was too much to bear. I could not possibly explain to them why I was upset. Neither one even knew that Tren-Lore and I had been spending time together. I sought solace in the inner courtyard's garden. Hot anguish spilled down my cheeks, and when at last the spring within me had run itself dry, I sat for a time in silence, calmness returning.

My arrival in the kitchen went unnoticed by all but Sophie and Flock. They noted my presence, but neither commented. Flock's silence, I guessed, was intended to be punishment for our quarrel that day. I had no idea why Sophie tolerated my daily absences. It did not matter. Her patience would not be tested any longer. Tears stung my eyes again, but I blinked them away. My days would be spent working in the kitchen instead of playing at knight and scholar with Tren-Lore.

* * *

Tedious chores were now the pillars which supported each day. Sophie watched me with concern, as I often wore an expression of despondency. My adventures with Tren-Lore had occupied my thoughts to the exclusion of all else. Their absence was very much like the darkness I feared. It was a void that allowed too many disturbing thoughts to grow.

"Flock, get some more water from the well," one of the ladies ordered. "You can take Lara along to help you."

Flock smiled and grabbed a water bucket from beside the washing basin. She liked being sent for water. She usually managed to turn the simple task into a leisurely outing. I followed her from the kitchen, two pails in hand. In no hurry to get back to her work, Flock ambled along, humming and swinging the buckets she held. She seemed perfectly happy. Envy twisted my stomach into a tight knot.

As though reading my mind, Flock suddenly said, "You do not like living here, do you?"

Her question caught me off guard, and I stumbled over several nonsensical words before Flock interjected. "Well, you should appreciate training in the kitchen. It is a privilege not everyone has. Kella and I are both grateful for such an excellent opportunity."

I could not help but smirk. Grateful was not the word I would have used to describe Flock and Kella's attitude. Lazy would have been my descriptor of choice.

"Of course, not just anyone can train to work in the kitchen. You have-" Flock stopped suddenly, and her speech ended just as abruptly. Her hand flew out to grab my wrist. "The prince!" she gasped in breathless excitement.

"What?" I demanded in confusion, trying to remove my arm from her grasp.

"Look!" she hissed, her eyes transfixed on the hallway before her.

Prince Yolis was striding down the corridor toward us. He was magnificently dressed, and had a bow slung over one shoulder. A quiver of arrows bristled from behind his back. He had one of the shafts in hand and was toying with it.

"Good day, Your Highness," Flock said loudly. "It is a great honor to see you today."

I made a face at this greeting, but Flock did not notice. Her attention was completely upon the handsome Yolis. He looked up, and I thought absently that it was little wonder Kella fancied him. Flock must have shared her sister's feelings. She curtsied so low I imagined her knees scraped the ground. I was in the midst of giving a polite little bob when Flock yanked sharply on my arm. Losing my balance, I stumbled forward. Yolis reached out and caught me by the elbow. I could feel my face burning with embarrassment. Swallowing hard, I glanced up at the first Prince of Caladore. He was not even looking at me. His gaze was upon Flock, and his icy blue eyes did not seem to match with the rest of his charming appearance. They were cold and calculating. "Are you Kelladyn's sister?" he asked, absently tensing the arrow he held.

Flock's surprise was so obvious that I nearly laughed aloud. Flustered, Flock pushed one of her curls away from her face. "Y-yes, yes, I am."

"Well," Yolis said, sinking the arrow back into its quiver, a grin playing on his lips, "tell Kelladyn that I enjoyed her company immensely last night." And with that, he brushed past us and walked away.

"Does Kella know the prince?" I asked Flock as we proceeded down the corridor again.

She was frowning. There was nothing Flock hated more than discovering she was not privy to the complete inner workings of the entire castle. "She must," Flock replied vaguely. She absently chewed on her lip as she considered this surprising bit of news. "But that does not make sense."

We stepped outside and were immediately awash in a glorious wave of golden sunshine. It was a beautiful day. A soft breeze swirled my hair about my face. The air was deliciously sweet with the heavy scents of summer. We strolled along the edge of the castle. The exquisite royal gardens stretched to our right and the archery field was just beyond the well. A single archer stepped forward from a group of men, and slowly raised his bow. I came to a halt and stared intently. I was almost certain that the archer was Tren-Lore.

Tren-Lore's arm tensed, but no further movement was visible as he released his arrow. It must have been a good shot, for there was a dignified round of applause from the group. I watched Tren-Lore in awe, the old feeling that he was more legend than boy returned swiftly. I found myself grinning.

"Lara!" Flock shouted indignantly from the well. "Get over here and help me!"

At her loud cry, Tren-Lore glanced sharply in our direction. He looked at me and Flock, and then turned away. Someone handed him another arrow. Once again, he fitted it to the string. Thinking that he had not recognized me, I moved to help the struggling Flock draw water from the well. The bow sang as Tren-Lore released his second arrow. I watched in surprise as the shaft sailed over the mark, landing between the target and the well.

"I am going to get that arrow for them," I told Flock, and set off at a run, not giving her any time to object.

A man in uniform started to move out of the crowd, but Tren-Lore stopped him. The two exchanged a few words, and then the young prince jogged towards me. He arrived just as I had plucked the arrow from the ground. I handed it to him.

"Thanks," he said warmly. "Listen, about the other day. I -"

In a flash of white-hot panic, I abruptly remembered that Tren-Lore knew I was a Healer. "It was no trouble," I said shrilly, and turned quickly to leave.

He caught my arm and held it firmly. "I do not care if you are a Healer, Lara. Well, I care..." He grimaced at his own awkwardness and raked his fingers through his hair. "What I mean is... I think Healers are admirable. My mother thought so, too. I know some people do not like them but I do *not* share their ignorance."

He never failed to surprise me! After a few moments in which the wind played between us, I smiled broadly at him.

He punched me in the shoulder, grinning. "Is everything good, then?"

"Very good," I replied.

Someone was calling Tren-Lore's name from the group. He glanced over his shoulder, and then back at me. "Meet me in the stables tomorrow at noon, all right?"

I nodded and we both turned and walked in opposite directions. When I returned to Flock, she was staring at me with interest. "What did he say to you?"

"He thanked me," I replied easily, as I began to lower the bucket back into the well. "Take hold of this rope, we need to pull it back up."

She wrapped her fingers around the rope and we both heaved. "He said something else," Flock persisted between the efforts of drawing water. The bucket came to the edge and we pulled it over.

I wiped my forehead with my sleeve and met her curious gaze. "Fine, he said thank you very much."

"Lara!" she protested, carelessly slopping the water into one of our pails. "Tell me right now!"

I dropped the bucket into the well and heard the satisfying splash. "No," I refused, and gave the rope a tug.

Flock shot me a look of poison and sullenly began to help me draw our second bucket. "I am not speaking to you until you tell me!" she threatened.

"Good," I replied spitefully.

True to her word, Flock did not say anything more as we filled the pails and proceeded back to the kitchen. I found this punishment to be most enjoyable.

The next day could not have come quickly enough. Indeed, when at last I slipped from the kitchen, I felt as though I had endured the passing of ages. I found the stable without too much difficulty. Tren-Lore was waiting for me. He was dressed in a tunic and hose that bore testament to many rough adventures.

A girl who seemed to be slightly younger than me was standing beside Tren-Lore. She was garbed in a beautiful blue dress, and her golden hair cascaded around her shoulders and down her back. Her opulent attire and blond tresses marked her as one of the royal family. I was instantly sure that she was Princess Nahanni. I stood hesitantly in the doorway, watching as Tren-Lore saddled a small chestnut mare. The princess was maintaining a steady stream of one-sided dialogue, and Tren-Lore was visibly irritated.

"Nahanni!" Tren-Lore finally exclaimed, turning on her. "Would you stop to take a breath at least?"

She smiled brightly at him, and I marveled at how pretty she was. "I am taking breaths," Nahanni replied with feigned innocence. She played absently with the ends of her golden locks.

Tren-Lore did not appear to be softened by his sister's winning smile. He frowned at her. "I told you that if you were-"

Nahanni, who had just noticed my presence, interrupted cheerfully. "She is here," she sang, and gestured to the entrance. "Hello, Lara!"

I clasped my hands behind my back. I felt slightly intimidated by Nahanni's presence. "Hello," I replied softly.

Tren-Lore turned from the mare and smiled. "Hello, Lara. This is my sister, Nahanni." He rumpled the girl's smooth hair.

Nahanni hit his hand away. "It is nice to meet you, Lara."

I murmured a similar greeting and returned the princess' merry smile with an unsteady one of my own.

"I thought we could go for a ride today," Tren-Lore told me, returning his attention to the horse he was saddling. "Come over here and I will show you how to mount."

I stared at him in surprise. Riding? We were going riding? I crossed the stable, feeling as though a great vat of emotion was stirring within me. Trepidation, excitement and happiness all sloshed together in a great wash of sensation. As Tren-Lore began to patiently instruct me, Nahanni maintained a light-hearted monologue that chronicled the events of her morning. I found that I could not help but like her. Tren-Lore, on the other hand, frequently told her to be quiet.

When I was able to climb into my saddle with relative confidence, Nahanni mounted her own white mare, and with a lump of sugar, Tren-Lore managed to persuade Storm Wing that he really did want a rider. Taking hold of my reins, Tren-Lore led the group from the stable and out into the courtyard.

When I had first arrived, noble people had filled the space. Today, it was quiet except for a few merchants bringing supplies to the castle. The guards at the gate saluted as we rode through the massive entrance. Nahanni kicked her horse forward. A cloud of dust rose on the dry road as she pounded ahead, the sun glittering in her hair. I felt envious of the ease with which she handled her horse.

"Sorry she had to come," Tren-Lore apologized as he shaded his eyes and watched his little sister trotting away. "She saw me leaving and threatened to tell our father if I did not take her."

I smiled and gently stroked my horse's neck. "I do not mind in the least. She seems very nice."

"Nice like a Pandel," Tren-Lore scoffed. He shook his head as Nahanni turned her mount and came back towards us. "The secret room is getting too hot to practice in. I thought that if you learned how to ride, we could work outside, away from the castle. I could even show you where I am going to build my fort."

I laughed. "*When* are you going to build your fort?" He had been talking about it for some time, but Tren-Lore's ambitious pursuit of military excellence did not allot him much leisure time.

"Soon," he insisted with a grin. "We..." his words faded into a stern frown as Nahanni and her mount thundered around us in a tight circle and headed back down the road. "Nahanni!" Tren-Lore shouted after her. "Stop that! You will tire your horse!"

She slowly drew in her reins and waited for us to catch up to her. The young princess looked vexed. "Yolis lets me do that when we ride together," she told Tren-Lore in an irritated tone, glaring at him as her horse fell in step with ours.

Tren-Lore's face was suddenly expressionless, and his voice was hard. "Well, I am *not* Yolis."

His reaction startled me. It seemed to disconcert Nahanni as well, for silence settled over our group. It prevailed for several uncomfortable moments, until Tren-Lore returned his attention to me, his happy countenance apparently regained.

"Because of the heat, formal training will be completed in a fortnight or so, and it does not start again until autumn. That gives me lots of time to build the fort and do some practicing."

"What about your lessons?" Nahanni objected, leaning over in her saddle to pluck a bright yellow flower that was growing along the roadside. "Father hired a tutor for you."

"End him," Tren-Lore cursed. "I am not interested in lessons."

Nahanni looked outraged by her brother's use of this curse. I had to admit that part of me shared in her sentiment. The thought of ending someone's spirit, of preventing them from returning in another life, was rather ghastly. Still, if Tren-Lore felt that it was necessary...

Nahanni was obviously on the brink of telling Tren-Lore exactly what she thought of his swearing. To keep the peace, I quickly changed the topic. "Is that Cala?" I pointed to the outline of buildings just visible in the distance.

"Yes," Tren-Lore replied, and Nahanni launched into a high-spirited story about Cala. I breathed a sigh of relief. The two of them did not get along any better than Flock and I.

We did not get to see Cala in any more detail, as we soon veered off the road and into a field of tall grass and wildflowers. We stopped when we were fully out of sight of the castle. Tren-Lore and Nahanni dismounted, and I slipped clumsily out of my saddle. My instruction began, but ground to a halt again as Tren-Lore and Nahanni quarreled over the style of riding I should learn. The young prince won eventually, and I was taught to ride sitting astride the horse rather than sidesaddle. After this defeat, Nahanni lost interest in my lessons and wandered off to pick flowers. The day seemed to melt away under the heat of the sun, and before I knew it, a flushed twilight fell.

Tren-Lore drew in his horse beside me. "We had best head back now," he said, and tightened his reins again as Storm Wing pranced restlessly. "Come on, Nahanni."

The princess did not answer. I looked around and found her curled up on the ground. She was sleeping soundly. The wreath of flowers she had woven was still clutched in one hand. Tren-Lore swung off his mount and paced toward his sister. It was hard to discern Tren-Lore's expression in the ruddy light, but he seemed to be smiling. Reaching Nahanni, he affectionately nudged her with his foot. "Wake up."

She groaned and sat up, rubbing her eyes.

"Come on," Tren-Lore repeated as he placed one foot into his stirrup and swung onto Storm Wing's back. "We are leaving."

Nahanni staggered to gain an upright stance, and after several feeble attempts to mount, she slumped against her horse's side. "Tren-Lore, I am too tired," she whimpered.

"Nahanni," he sighed. Cantering over to her, he grabbed her by the back of the dress. Tren-Lore hauled her into his saddle and seated the little princess before him. He wrapped one arm around his sister and grabbed the reins of her mount with his free hand. Giving Storm Wing a small kick, he set off at a walk toward Caladore. I followed gladly. I would have followed Tren-Lore anywhere.

* * *

"You are in trouble now," Flock hissed with smug satisfaction. She whisked past me with a large stack of dirty dishes. They were the only remnants of the dinner I had just missed.

"Lara," Sophie's voice sounded from across the kitchen, "would you join me in our room, please?"

Sophie met me at our chamber door and ushered me inside. The door closed with a final-sounding thunk. I perched on the edge of my bed, hands beneath my legs, chewing on the inside of my lip. Sophie smoothed her hair, and then allowed her hands to rest on her ample hips. She gave me an appraising stare. "I brought you to Caladore so you could be happy, and if these adventures that you go on make you happy, then so be it. I will not hinder you. But if you miss dinner again, young lady..." Her stern words hung unfinished in the air.

Perhaps Sophie was not entirely certain what she would do if I was once again absent for dinner. Perhaps she knew that my mind had already leapt ahead to think of a dozen horrible punishments that frightened me a great deal more than any threat she could have made.

I hung my head. "I am sorry, Sophie."

Sophie threw her hands up in the air, a cross smile creasing her plump cheeks. "Oh, Lara! Must you look so pitiable? In the name of the Ascendants," she muttered as she moved to sit beside me. "I am too soft-hearted. I am not angry with you child, I was just worried. You need not feel so badly." She gently took my chin in her hand and tilted my face so that she could look into my eyes. "Mind that you are home for evening meal every night after this. Do you hear?"

"Yes, Sophie," I replied obediently.

She patted my cheek. "Good girl. Now let us see if we can get you something to eat before it is all put away."

I slipped my small fingers around Sophie's hand as she rose. She led me from the room, and for a brief moment, I felt safe and loved. It was as if I belonged to her entirely, as though her hand was the one I had been reaching for since memory's birth.

* * *

I fell asleep quickly that night, and disturbing dreams came just as swiftly. I was digging in dark, black dirt. My fingers were desperately clawing through earth in a frantic search to find something. Faster. Deeper. There was blood but no pain, no pain though my fingers bled. At last! I grasped at blue cloth and yanked it from the earth. I pulled it over my head and down over my chest. It was Tren-Lore's tunic, the dragon bright upon the front.

"Lara."

The voice was my mother's. I looked down into the hole I had made, and Sophie's face was staring up at me. It was deathly white against the raven earth. Her lips parted, cracking into a black abyss.

"Lara! Save me, Lara!"

I was digging again, tearing at the dirt around her, but more and more kept spilling in, until Sophie's face was covered. I was screaming, ripping soil away until suddenly my nails meet flesh. My mother's voice came again.

"Lara! Save me, Lara!"

I could not stop my fingers. I dug and dug until my nails were gory with dirt and blood. Sophie's skin was tearing away in strips to reveal my mother's visage. She was dead, with eyes that saw nothing, and suddenly she was lying on her bed and I was at the bedroom door, and still she stared at me. I scrambled backwards, pulling the tunic over my eyes. I was trying to scream, but no sound would come.

"Mother," I finally managed to whimper.

I sat up suddenly, tearing myself free from the dream but not the terror that still coiled around me. My sleeping gown was clammy with sweat and my fingers were twisted painfully around my blankets. Sophie was at my side in a moment, a ring of light wavering around her as the newly lit candle shook in her hand.

"It is all right, little one. It was nothing but a dream. Sophie is here now." She set the candle on the table and held her arms out to me. I clung gratefully to her. Slowly, she rocked back and forth, whispering softly in my ear.

Tears streamed down my face. "I will not think about it. I will not think about it," I sobbed. I held onto Sophie as tightly as I could and did not let sleep weaken my grip until the moon had almost faded from the sky. It did not seem to matter to Sophie, though. She cradled me in her arms and tried with all her might to wash the dream away.

Chapter Four
Rebellion

Tren-Lore and I stood before a massive river with the forest crowding around us on all sides. "Venst," Tren-Lore named the tumbling body of water. "Out there is where I intend to build my fort." He pointed to an island parting the river.

I squinted at him through the bright sunlight. "But how do we get out there?"

Shaking his head, he tethered Storm Wing to a thin tree trunk. The horse watched with an expression of disapproval as Tren-Lore waded down into the rushes that grew on the river's bank. He glanced back at me. His face was creased in a grin, and the glimmering summer light danced on his rumpled hair. I crumpled up my face in a doubtful expression. "Have some faith, Lara," he laughed.

"I have faith!" I protested, and hastily tied my reins to a low-hanging branch. I followed him into the tall grass with as much confidence as I could muster. "I was just curious about what you were doing."

My curiosity was soon satisfied as Tren-Lore revealed a small boat bedded amongst the reeds and mud. We clambered into it, and as Tren-Lore rowed, I bailed the water which was so eagerly filling our vessel. We traveled in this solemn way for only a few moments. The lure of the warm river was too much. Soon we were shouting and splashing, and had forgotten about rowing and bailing.

Our small boat had meandered a fair way down river before I noticed the receding island. Staggering in the still-swaying boat, I sat down heavily and pointed at our distant destination. "We should start paddling again."

"Rowing," Tren-Lore corrected teasingly.

I stuck my tongue out at him, and he made a face in return.

"This should be fun," he commented wryly as he resumed his seat and took hold of the oars.

As Tren-Lore strained against the current, I frantically sloshed water from the heavy craft. We eventually arrived at the island, both quite wet but in adventurous moods that prevented our sopping clothes from dampening our spirits. We had both been anticipating this moment.

It had been just over a month since Tren-Lore had finished his formal training, but the sweltering summer days had been so full of our own practice and fun that somehow we had not yet managed to come to the island. We lost no time in exploring our surroundings, and deliberated long and loudly about the various spots where the fort could be built. Tren-Lore decided that when we came next time, he would bring swords, and after catching my skirts on a great many thorns and branches, he promised to bring some old clothes for me as well.

"End this!" Tren-Lore muttered as he helped me free my dress from a particularly stubborn snag. "I promise that you will have more fun tomorrow. You must hate having to bother with these useless skirts."

"Are we coming tomorrow?" I asked in surprise. "What about your lessons? I thought...well... should you really miss another one?"

Tren-Lore had not been to a single lesson for nearly two weeks, and I was worried he would get in trouble if his disobedience was carried any further. His fingers finally pulled my hem free of the bramble, and he straightened.

"No," Tren-Lore said, sucking a cut on his finger, "I have decided that I have no interest in any sort of enforced academic pursuits. I want to learn how to fight. What is the use in knowing Tolrem's exports or the political policies of the Renarii? When am I ever going to use that?"

He smiled mischievously. "I think I will leave all that interesting learning to our future king, Yolis."

* * *

Despite Tren-Lore's decision to leave the academics to his brother, our plans went awry. The next day, a young man dressed in the blue and gray of Caladore's uniform brought bad news. "I have a message for Lara," he told me when I answered his demanding knocks upon the kitchen door.

I looked at him sharply. Surely this was all some confusing joke. "Who?" I asked in surprise.

The man repeated himself as he absently straightened the bottom of his coat. In a daze, I informed him that I was the person he was seeking. The messenger looked skeptical and handed me a folded piece of paper. I thanked him, but he had already turned to leave.

I turned the parchment over in my hands and I noticed that the red wax seal had a dragon insignia imprinted in it. Knowing it must be from Tren-Lore, I eagerly ripped it open and read the note.

Lara,
Father is angry that I have missed so many lessons. He is making sure I go to them today. Meet me in the stables after dinner. I still need to practice tonight.
T.L

I struggled over a few words, but soon had managed to read the entire message. Feeling rather proud of myself, I slipped the paper into my pocket and returned to the main kitchen, where everyone was eating breakfast. I slid into my chair, pondering what lie I could tell Sophie so that I could leave after the evening meal was finished.

"Who was at the door, Lara?" Sophie asked as I sat down beside her.

I looked up at her in surprise. I had been so busy thinking of a fib to tell Sophie later that I had not bothered to contrive one for the dilemma at hand.

"It was....ah....Rathum from the stables. His father was wondering if....if we had any....ah...." I cast a desperate glance about the room, and my eyes settled upon a large bowl of freshly dug carrots, waiting to be washed. "Any carrots to spare."

Sophie paused, her fork nearly at her mouth. Her gaze followed mine, and she arched an eyebrow in a way that suggested she did not believe me.

"Carrots?" she repeated.

"Oh, yes," I replied, my mind taking a firm grasp on the tale. "He is trying to train two new colts, and he would like some carrots to give them as rewards. He would like them after dinner is finished, if that is possible."

"Well, I am not going!" Flock's muffled declaration came through a mouthful of egg. "Lara can go. I hate the stables."

Kelladyn leaned forward across the table, a smug expression stretched across her face. "If Lady Grim tells you to go, then you will just have to trot off to the stables like a good little girl. And stop talking when you have food in your mouth. It is perfectly revolting."

"*You* are perfectly revolting!" Flock retorted, her spoon clattering to her plate.

"Be quiet!" Kella snapped as her brown eyes darkened in anger.

"I can go if Flock does not want to," I said quietly. My offer was enough to silence both Flock and Kelladyn.

Sophie gave me an appraising stare, and then nodded. "Very well. You may go when the evening meal is done."

I smiled brightly, making a mental note to tell Tren-Lore how skillfully I had lied. "May I stay to see the colts?"

"If you like," Sophie said, "but mind that you are back in this kitchen before it gets dark."

Flock's original look of surprise had slowly changed to uncertain suspicion. I knew enough of Flock to guess she was now worried that this outing to the stable was more than a simple chore. Her meddling nature would not prevent her from missing such an event, but it was not in her personality to volunteer her services without punishment or reward acting as a catalyst. At last, her indecision broke. "Maybe I should go, too," she suggested.

51

Sophie took a sip of her tea before answering. "No, Flock, I think one person is quite enough."

* * *

The stable was dim and warm. I stood in the entrance a moment, letting my eyes adjust to the dark before entering. Tren-Lore arrived shortly after I had finished saddling my horse. He did not even offer me a greeting, but instead, bridled Storm Wing and swung up onto his back. Tren-Lore was angry. I could see it in his face, and his mount must have sensed it too, for the usually churlish Storm Wing was at last obedient.

"Come on," Tren-Lore said shortly, and cantered from the stable.

I followed him out past the castle walls and onto the open fields surrounding Caladore. We rode until the castle, and even Cala, was far to the east. Tren-Lore said nothing the entire time. It was an uncomfortable ride; not only because of Tren-Lore's silent brooding, but also because of the pace he kept. It was fast and hard. Each jarring fall of the horse's hooves beat into me. At last he drew rein. It was an abrupt action, which caused Storm Wing to rear in angry protest.

He looked at me and held my gaze for a moment. His blue eyes were serious. "I am not going to any more lessons." His voice was dangerously quiet, and I knew he meant exactly what he said. "They are a waste of my time."

This startled me. I had not considered that the source of his anger might be his lessons. I had assumed that it concerned Yolis. I sat uneasily in my saddle, feeling my mare's ribs expand with heavy breaths. "What happened?"

Tren-Lore sighed and slipped from Storm Wing's back. "You can never tell anyone this," he said in low tones.

I nodded and dismounted, leaving my horse to graze. We walked to the top of a small crest before we sat. Tren-Lore stared off into the distance. The castle of Caladore loomed against the horizon.

"This will all be Yolis' someday. He is to be king, and for that my father is proud of him." Tren-Lore laughed.

"Proud of him for something that he had nothing to do with."

I picked at the grass. I was not sure what I should say. I thought it might be nice if I told him that his father was proud of him too, but I did not really know if King Kiris *was* proud of Tren-Lore. Maybe that was not what Tren-Lore wanted to hear anyway. I was still struggling for a reply when Tren-Lore saved me by continuing to speak.

"I do not envy Yolis his birthright, although he finds that very hard to believe. Most of the time, I wish I were not even a prince. But I hate it that my fa-" He stopped abruptly, and his expression seemed to say that he regretted even voicing part of the thought he had cut off. "What I mean is... I need to do something I can be proud of. I need to be more than a useless title. I want to be a Sanysk."

In the moment of surprise that followed his declaration, I looked at him as if I had never really seen him before. My lips parted with words slain by shock. In my mind, the Sanysk had never stepped past the boundaries of make-believe. Perhaps I had not wanted them to be real. The one and only story I had heard about them had been glorious and desperately sad, all in the same breath. My memory of this event was so strong that the moment my mind touched upon it, I felt as though I were being pulled back through time.

It had been a cold winter's night, and the fire crackling in the hearth was the only light in our little house. I was sprawled on the big rag rug that was spread before the fireplace. My head was resting on one arm, and my other hand absently moved along the twisted cloth. Mother was sitting nearby and the story that she wove that night involved a young man who was part of the warrior elite; the League of Sanysk. Even knights fell before these masters of battle, and the tale was full of high adventure, grand deeds, and an ending that allowed cold sorrow to twist and bind itself about me.

The young Sanysk, so guilt-ridden over all the lives he had taken in battle, allowed himself to be mortally wounded in a duel. I had cried at this and insisted that he could not be dead. My mother had drawn me onto her lap and rested her cheek on my head. With a soft hand, she had smoothed my hair back from my face in an attempt to comfort me, but she would not change the ending.

"How would you have him live?" she had asked quietly.

"A Healer," I had insisted, "a Healer could save him."

She had held me even tighter at this. "My darling, my darling," she had murmured. "It is not a Healer's job to take away death, but rather, to give life. Sometimes we must accept that people die."

I jolted back to the present to find Tren-Lore watching me with a wary expression. The light had begun to fade slightly, and in the summer twilight he had a look of feral unease. It was as though he felt a predator was about to attack and was torn between fleeing and staying to face the danger. I did not like to see Tren-Lore like that, and yet, I was once again lost for words. It was an exciting goal, and at the same time it alarmed me. I did not want Tren-Lore to be killed as the young man in the story had been.

I smiled as brightly as I could, memories still echoing within me. "I never knew that the Sanysk were real," I said in a desperate effort to banish his unnerved countenance. "My mother told me a story about them once."

He seemed to consider me for a moment, and then relaxed. "Will you tell it to me?"

I related the tale to him, but was unable to keep my anxiety to myself. "Please do not die!" I implored, my hand catching hold of his sleeve. "Please do not become like the boy in the story."

"First, I actually have to *become* a Sanysk. Then -"

I waved my hand at him dismissively. "Of course you will become a Sanysk." I had absolute conviction that Tren-Lore could accomplish anything he chose to set his will to. "But when you do, you must-" I stopped and stared at him. His eyes were full of silent mirth, and his mouth was curved in a smile. "What is so funny?" I demanded.

He refused to say anything, and I continued to insist on an explanation, until at last the dispute was settled with a small scuffle on the ground that concluded with me sitting atop Tren-Lore, with my knees firmly planted on his chest.

"I let you win, you know." Tren-Lore grinned up at me.

I ignored him. "Tell me what was so funny," I said sternly, although I was smiling as widely as he was.

"Fine," he said. "I think you have been spending too much time with Flock. You looked exactly like her when you interrupted me."

I opened my mouth to voice my outrage at such a comparison. Before I could, he dug his fingers into my ribs and I crumbled into a heap, shrieking with laughter. His comment, along with his tickling, sparked another fight, which ended in both of us laying side by side in breathless exhaustion.

"Lara?" he panted.

"What?" I replied as I gasped for air.

"Will you help me practice to become a Sanysk?"

Of course, I thought. I was slightly surprised that he even asked. I rolled onto my stomach and gave him a disbelieving look. "Was I helping you practice before?"

He nodded.

I collapsed onto my back, spreading my arms above my head as my breathing slowed. "Then nothing has changed."

Silence swelled to fill the gap between my last remark and Tren-Lore's next question. "Do you want to hear the story *I* know about the Sanysk?"

I settled myself more comfortably on the ground. "Sure."

Tren-Lore was a very good storyteller. He was expressive, and his vocabulary ranged from crude fighting terms to elegant, descriptive language. I listened to him with my eyes closed, letting his voice enchant my mind so that it danced with the images in the story. He, too, told a tale about a young Sanysk, but this man's adventures were twice as spectacular and the battles he engaged in were glorious. His conscience had no cause to plague him, because his noble nature would only permit him to slay the most treacherous of villains. He ended his days sitting hand in hand with the fair maiden whose affections he had won, and basking in the glory of his heroic deeds.

I thought it was an excellent story. I sighed and opened my eyes. "That was – oh, no!"

Tren-Lore sat up, staring at me in concern. "What is wrong?"

"Look how dark it has gotten! Sophie is going to be so mad!" I scrambled to my feet and ran towards the horses. "Come on!" I yelled at him.

I leapt onto my horse's back, and despite my trepidation about Sophie's fury I could not help but smile.

"Nice mount," Tren-Lore commented as Storm Wing stomped irritably, backing away from his rider.

I pushed my hair out of my face and grinned broadly at Tren-Lore. "I know."

Kicking my horse hard, I spurred the mare into a gallop. Tren-Lore and I raced the ever-deepening dusk back to Caladore. We thundered into the stable, and I jumped out of my saddle.

"Go," Tren-Lore said. "I will take care of the horses."

I hastened to the door, but Tren-Lore stopped me with a remark I found puzzling. "Thank you," he said.

I turned to stare at him. The young prince was standing in murky shadows, a bridle in hand, his giant warhorse looming behind him. What did he have to thank me for?

"I will see you tomorrow," I promised, and raced from the stable.

I fell three times in my mad dash to the kitchen. The first was an inconsequential stumble. The hem of my dress caught under my foot, but pulled free before it sent me pitching forward. That was an activity I saved for the second time. Thankfully, I caught myself with my hands and only lost a few strides before regaining my footing. Gathering the troublesome skirts in fingers and palms that had been scraped by sharp little stones, I hurried on. The last fall came on the stairs up to the passageway leading to the kitchen. One side of my dress had escaped my grasp, and I stepped upon it. There was the sound of ripping cloth, and my shins struck the stone steps with an agonizing impact.

"End this!" I swore angrily, unshed tears tightening my throat.

I winced as I got up. I took the last few stairs more slowly in comparison to the rest of my journey. My arrival to the kitchen was labored. I was limping and had to grit my teeth so that I could stand the feel of my raw palms pushing open the door. I froze in the entrance as my gaze fell upon Sophie. She was sitting in one of the chairs in the outer room. Her arms were crossed and her expression was controlled in a way that made me cringe.

"Where have you been?" she demanded.

"I.....I was, I mean, I went...."

Apparently, Sophie was not really interested in an answer to her question, for she cut me off with an angry exclamation. "What did I tell you? You were to be inside this kitchen before dark! And your dress!" Sophie rose from her chair and came towards me. "In the name of the Ascendants, what have you done?"

I stared at my shoes, tracing each scrape and scuff with my eyes. "I tripped," I muttered.

"You cut your hands, too!" she exclaimed as she took my hands and turned the palms up. "What will people think of you running around at all hours of the night, coming home looking as though a Laowerming tried to eat you?"

I frowned and jerked my hands away from her. "The sun *just* set, Sophie. It is not that late." I had been prepared for some anger, but now I felt that Sophie was being unreasonable and unfair! I had not broken the rule by very much, and I felt her remark about my appearance was hurtful. She should try running in a dress, I thought grumpily.

"Look out that window, young lady." Sophie pointed, and her other hand went to her hip. "Is it dark?"

I glared into the floor. "Yes," I replied bitterly.

"Then it is late!" She paced to the inner door and opened it. Drawing an audible breath, Sophie exhaled in a great sigh. "For the next week, I do not want you to leave this kitchen. Is that clear?"

I looked at her in outrage. "That is not fair!" I cried.

Sophie looked tired, but her expression was stern. "Go to our room, Lara. I want you in your sleeping gown and in bed by the time I come to clean your hands."

Ignoring the pain in my legs, I stomped into the kitchen and did not even have the presence of mind to be thankful that Flock was not there. How would I stand not seeing Tren-Lore? How would I stand *seeing* Flock?

"Sophie does not understand anything!" I muttered furiously to myself as I pulled my sleeping gown over my head. "She is unfair and mean and horrible and I hate her!"

* * *

Sophie was uncompromisingly grim the next day, and I harmonized with her negative mood by being as cantankerous as I could possibly be. By the time the evening meal was set upon the table, the worst of Sophie's bad mood seemed to have passed. She talked cheerfully with the other ladies around the table and even directed a few kind comments toward me. My heart would not be softened, and I crossed my arms and scowled at my plate.

The few women who had been in the kitchen during my confrontation with Sophie did not hesitate to discuss the incident over dinner. The ladies all laughed over the story and made remarks to Sophie about discovering the trials of children. Flock did not miss a chance to add her own barbed comments that tore at my pride. No one seemed to notice her nasty remarks, and I grew more and more furious with every passing moment.

Flock took a sip of her milk and caught my gaze over the rim of her glass. Her eyes shone with mockery. "What is the matter, Lara?" Flock asked in a sickly-sweet imitation of sincere concern.

In a flash of scarlet anger, born not from that one comment but from its addition to the many other remarks she had made, I swung my leg as hard as I could and kicked her in the shin. Flock screamed and scrambled away from the table. Her chair fell to the stone floor with a resounding clatter. She shrieked, "Lara kicked me!"

"You deserved it!" I yelled at her before the entire kitchen exploded into noise.

I met Sophie's gaze from where she had risen near the end of the table, and my breath caught in my throat. I swallowed hard and watched as Sophie moved toward me. The sound of female voices was swelling to a deafening pitch as each person tried to express emotions ranging from irritation to confusion. Sophie was at my side, pulling me toward our room, and Flock's cries rang above the clamor. "My leg! I will never walk again!"

"What did you do?" Sophie's aggravation was clear as she shut the door to our room and leaned against it, running her hand over her hair.

I balled my fists at my side, tears of fear and outrage making hot lines down my cheeks. "I am not sorry!" I sobbed, and threw myself upon my bed. "She was mean to me all day, and I wish I could have kicked her harder!" I declared in a voice that was considerably muffled by my pillow.

"When you have calmed yourself," Sophie's voice sounded strained, "there will be dishes that need doing. The rest of us will be serving at the garden party. I would like everything clean by the time we get back."

My only response was resentful sobbing. Sophie sighed, and I heard the door open and close. I rolled over onto my back, feeling wet emotion slip down my cheeks and into my hair. I brooded about the injustice of the situation, and then allowed my inner turmoil to swell once more. I would be miserable if I could not spend my days with Tren-Lore. And Flock! The heat of anger served to dry my tears. I never wanted to see her again! And I *did not* want to do the dishes!

I lay until the sounds in the kitchen had ceased. Slipping off the bed, I ventured forth, taking some comfort in the fact that everyone would be away serving, and I could do my penance in private. As I opened the door, I beheld Flock sitting by the hearth. Her foot was propped up on another chair and her arms were crossed. She looked incensed.

"Why are you here?" I exclaimed in dismay.

Usually, all of the servants' children were allowed to play quietly in an area slightly removed from the party. Flock reveled in these chances to order a large group of children around.

She spared me a look of absolute venom, and then redirected her gaze to the smoldering fire in the hearth. "Mother says I am too injured to go down to the garden," she replied icily.

This struck me as immensely funny. "You have to stay?" I blurted out, laughing uproariously. I came over to where she was sitting, shoved her foot off the chair and sat down.

"Oww!" Flock wailed as her face contorted in irritation rather than pain.

I sighed as my laughter died and, leaning forward in my seat, grabbed a piece of wood from the pile near the hearth and tossed it in. "Stop pretending," I told her.

"Sophie said you have to do all the dishes," Flock remarked smugly and stretched her feet toward the small flames crawling from under the new log, "and you need to get some water for washing, too."

I made a face. I hated hauling water by myself. It was such an awkward job. Settling myself more firmly in my seat, I folded my arms across my chest. "If I have to get water, you are coming with me."

"I will not be able to take a single step this entire evening, not after you kicked me so brutally." Smugness stretched Flock's lips into a mean little smile.

I was about to ask her if she wanted another kick, but was interrupted by a rapping upon the outer door. Interest straightened my posture. I sat for a moment of brief excitement, listening to the echoes die away. Flock made the first move to rise, but I leapt to my feet before she could get up. "I will get the door," I informed her, and then added delightedly, "I mean, since you will not be able to take a single step this entire evening."

Before she could object, I grabbed a candle off the main table and hurried into the dark outer chamber. There was no fire in this room, and the dark seemed to have poured through the windows and drowned the chamber in blackness. My heart began to beat wildly against my ribs. I held my candle high and stepped into the darkness. Walking through the dancing shadows, I hastened toward the door. Reaching it, I gently grasped the handle with my still-healing hand and pulled.

The ruddy light from the torches in the passageway scorched the darkness with a red glow. I felt the tense muscles of my body relax, and then my heart leapt once again. It was not fear that made my blood surge, however, but surprise. Tren-Lore stood in the entrance. Not only was his appearance entirely unexpected, but he was dressed so finely that I took a step back. It was hard to believe that I even knew this boy who was so obviously a prince. He was garbed in rich green cloth, and a gray dragon was stitched upon the front of this tunic. The sturdy leather boots he usually wore were replaced with ones of soft doe hide, studded in silver. His crown glinted in his ruffled, raven hair. I was torn between shouting a happy exclamation and bobbing a curtsy, as Sophie had taught me.

"So, did you kick Flock really hard?" he asked in a jovial tone, sticking his hands in his pockets.

I laughed in relief. The Tren-Lore I knew was suddenly restored. I set the candle down upon a barrel near the door. "How did you know about that? Kicking Flock, I mean."

Tren-Lore shrugged. "I was looking for you at the garden party and Flock's sister told me that you had kicked Flock, and Sophie was making you stay up here for the entire night."

I leaned against the doorframe and frowned. "I have to stay in the kitchen for the entire week. I got in trouble with Sophie last night. She was very angry when I came in after dark."

"But it was barely dusk," Tren-Lore objected.

"I know!" I agreed, throwing my hands in the air. "That is what I told her, but she still said that I had to stay in for a week. Flock was teasing me about it, so I kicked her."

Tren-Lore grinned into the floor. "I wish I could have seen that," he said wistfully. "I brought you something to make your imprisonment more enjoyable."

"You brought me something?" I raised my eyebrows at him. "What?"

"This," he replied and produced a book from under the folds of his cloak. The binding was deep brown leather, and the gold letters across the front seemed to glow in the white light of my candle

"Rayn," I read hesitantly aloud.

Tren-Lore handed it to me. "It is the first of the Lord Rayn books. He becomes a Sanysk in this one. I think this is my favorite, although I really like the fourth one, too."

"Thank you," I breathed, my fingers wrapping carefully around the soft leather cover.

* * *

I was seated in Sophie's rocking chair with one of my feet tucked under me. Over the past few days, I had often made time to retreat to our room so that I could read about the adventures of Rayn. I had pulled the chair close to the window. The last sigh of daylight brushed the pages of my book and made it easier to read. I needed every advantage I could get. *Rayn* was more challenging than anything I had previously tackled, and I struggled over words in every sentence. I read most pages twice, first to figure out the actual words, and second to comprehend the content. My endurance for this type of struggle was almost equal to the patience I had in learning to swordfight. As much as I enjoyed these activities, however, they both left me raw and bruised in pride, and forbearance.

"End this," I muttered angrily, after several unsuccessful attempts at combining a series of letters that did not seem to want to form any kind of intelligible word. I snapped the book shut and strode to my bed, where I shoved the offending piece of literature under my pillow. "This is stupid," I grumbled to myself. "Why would I ever need to know words like that? Who talks like that?"

Throwing myself back into the chair, I pushed my toes hard against the floor to cause a sharp rhythmic tottering motion. Yet, as my frustration faded, I found my mind drawn back to Rayn's adventures. He had just fled his father's manor. A half smile flickered across my face. The idea of running away was quite complimentary to my state of mind. I took a moment to imagine myself running away. Flock would be so jealous, and Sophie would cry because she was sorry that she had been mean to me. Still, I thought, I would choose the kitchen over the dragon's lair that was sheltering Rayn.

A vision of Rayn flashed behind my eyes. He was stumbling toward a cave hollowed deep in the ribs of a mountain. There was snow, mounds of snow, and screaming wind that battered him. At last, he gained entrance to the cavern. The air prickled with the heat inside the cave. Suddenly, the earth was shaking under his feet. Smoke began to drift up from the bowels of the cave and puddle on the ceiling. Then... but from that moment on, the scene in my head ended against an abrupt wall of unread literature. I did not know what happened next.

I inhaled sharply in irritation and held my breath pensively. I could feel both the comfort of that needed oxygen and the tension that came from caging it in my lungs. Rayn must have felt the same way...relieved, and yet afraid of what would come next. A dragon, I thought, as I exhaled noisily. I was sure that in the next part, Rayn would face a dragon. Of course, he would not show his fear. Rayn was very brave. And rather handsome, my mind added, to which my mouth replied with a secretive smile.

I slowly allowed my chair to stop rocking. After a moment's hesitation, I got to my feet and moved swiftly toward my bed. It did not matter that I could not read that particular word. I would just skip over it and find out what was going to happen to Rayn. My anticipation made my chest tight with excitement. Slipping my hand under my pillow, I made a mental note to ask Tren-Lore what bowels were. I had heard my mother use the term, but it was in reference to people and not caves. My fingers discovered the soft leather book almost at once, and I was about to pull it from its hiding place when my door swung open. This startled me considerably, and I leapt back from the bed as though something had just bitten me.

Flock stood in the entrance, her usually wide eyes narrowed in suspicion. "What are you doing?" she asked.

"Nothing," I protested a little too vigorously. "What do you want?"

Flock took a step into the room and I unconsciously took a step back. "What are you hiding?" she demanded.

Recovering slightly from my surprise, I managed a laugh. "I am not hiding anything." I moved back to the bed and smoothed the blanket to an unwrinkled finish. "I was straightening my bed. Why are you so interested? Do you want to help?" I turned to face her with an expectant expression.

At the prospect of chores, Flock's interest evaporated immediately. "Sophie is about to tell a story. She wants to know if you would like to listen."

"Really? I did not know Sophie told stories!" I exclaimed as I walked toward the door.

Flock turned to lead the way from the room. "Oh, yes," she replied in a knowledgeable tone that irritated me, "but not very often."

We joined the group which had gathered around Sophie. She had brought a chair close to the hearth, and the soft lighting made her look much more youthful than she really was. She reminded me of her younger sister. Just then, it occurred to me that Namin had told me that Sophie was a very good story-teller. I wanted to lean over and tell Flock that I had known as much, but Sophie was already beginning her tale.

"After The One ceased to exist, the nine Ascendants each built a great city. Grand castles were constructed to rule over the cities. Whole countries rose as the namesakes of these magnificent palaces. The countries were prosperous and happy under their creators' rule, but there were also those whose spirits withered in such an atmosphere. Those who fed on chaos and lawlessness found themselves to be gaunter than even the lowliest of beggars. These misguided creatures complained that living under the rule of the Ascendants was to become a group of slaves linked together by chains, rather than a group of people linked together by their own humanity."

The door of the kitchen thudded shut, and everyone jumped. It was like being pushed into water, a sudden change of substance and surrounding. The story had been living around us, and suddenly we were all back in the kitchen with the young Prince of Caladore walking through the door. There was a general murmuring, but no one was really surprised to see him. Tren-Lore visited too often to be an exciting oddity.

Sophie smiled at him and continued to speak. "Soon the voice of one discontented became the voice of many. Finally, their protests were thunderous enough to shake the grand castles. These Discontents formed armies and began to attack the cities."

Tren-Lore sat down quietly beside me, and we exchanged a look of silent greeting before both of us turned our entire attention to the story.

"The Ascendants charged their people with the monumental task of destroying these Discontents and saving the great cities. Most of the citizen heeded the cry to war, but there were others that slipped noiselessly away into the countryside and did not return."

"The Barlems," someone hissed in a tone that held both malice and fear.

"Battles raged for ten years, and one by one, the Ascendants retreated from the earth. In the beginning, they protected their cities and ended the spirits of those who attacked them. The Discontents were not to be stopped. 'What good is it to live another life such as this?' they cried. 'Another life in another body will still be a life lived under the oppression of this rule.'

Hearing such reasoning, the Ascendants knew that they could not continue as they had been doing. The destruction of so many spirits would lead to the annihilation of a large piece of The One. They would not do this, and so they left their people and their cities... but not entirely. Before they retreated, they chose a few from among their followers. Only to these men and women would they speak, and through them, the rest could hear the words of the Ascendants. It was two of these chosen that helped to end the battles."

It was late when Sophie finished her story. The tale had chronicled the fall of eight of the great cites. By the time the young priest and priestess who championed Sophie's story made their valiant stand at Tolremorian, the fire in the kitchen had been reduced to glowing embers. There was a moment of silence when she finished, and then everyone rose slowly. They thanked Sophie in voices that were muted with weariness. Each made their way slowly out of the kitchen.

Sophie came over and laid her hands on my shoulders. "Time for bed," she murmured.

I was so tired that I could not even find the energy to protest her decision. Giving Tren-Lore a weary smile, I allowed Sophie to steer me toward our room.

Chapter Five
The Barlem Prince

"Lara!" Tren-Lore exclaimed in exasperation. "Put down that book and come and train with me."

I looked up. Tren-Lore was leaning against his practice sword, looking bored.

"If you remember, there were two parts to our deal, Tren-Lore. I was going to help you train, and you were going to teach me to read."

Tren-Lore slashed easily at an imaginary opponent. "And I did. You are on book three-"

"Four," I corrected.

"Four, then." He melted from one practice form to another. "My point exactly. You are reading voraciously, and I have to go back to formal training tomorrow. I need more practice."

"Fine," I relented.

I closed my book and set it on the pile of wood that was heaped at the bottom of four closely spaced trees. This was the spot we had chosen for the fort, but it had yet to become anything more than a place for reading and sword fighting. Picking up my sword, I came forward and made an informal thrust at Tren-Lore's chest. Tren-Lore blocked with a force that made the muscles in my shoulder ache and my cheeks crease in a grin. He had nothing to worry about. None of the boys he was training with would be able to beat him, but that did not mean that *I* could not try. An entire summer of fighting with Tren-Lore had given me both skill and strength. Although I never came close to beating him in a fair fight, I endeavored to find ways that might provide me with an advantage. We practiced until my arms shook from strain. When Tren-Lore finally allowed us to stop, he had won all the battles. I had managed, however, to trip him twice and divert his attention with a pretend wolf sighting.

"Good fight," he said, clapping me on the back.

I grinned at him and wiped the sweat out of my eyes with the back of my hand. "Thanks. You, too. None of those boys are going to beat you tomorrow."

* * *

The next day, Sophie sent me to collect the last of the potatoes. The warmth of the sun on my back and the beauty of the autumn trees slowed my steps. I had just paused to examine an anthill when the sound of shouting came to my ears. I straightened and listened hard. The voices seemed young, and a backdrop of metallic clangs made me forget my purpose. Leaving my basket beside the anthill, I hastened toward the noises.

Deep within the gardens, the carefully plotted flowerbeds and shrubs gave way to a large circular area crowned in massive trees. A group of boys stood about the perimeter. They ranged in height, and I presumed age, but they were all dressed in identical garb. Their blue tunics and gray hose differed only in the degree of griminess that encrusted them. Within the ring of bodies, two boys were battling one another.

Curious about the fight, I endeavored to improve my vantage point. I chose a tree that stood at least twenty paces from the circle of boys and, leaving my shoes at the bottom, I took hold of the lowest branch. By pushing with my feet and pulling with my arms, I was able to sling myself over the bough. It scraped painfully against my stomach, but I ignored the sting and righted myself. I continued my climb into the heights of the tree.

The yelling from the group below thoroughly drowned any noise my ascent may have made. When at last I had settled myself near the top, I leaned over and peered down through the burgundy leaves to the green grass below. My shoes looked much smaller than when I had slipped them from my feet. Ant shoes, I thought. One of my fingers was absently exploring the holes I had put in my stockings. Sophie's displeasure at this crossed my mind, and I may have gone on to consider Sophie's horrified reaction to the great height at which I was perched, or even her anger at my much-delayed return to the kitchen, if I had not received such a jolt of recognition. I suddenly realized that the boy who was sparring was Tren-Lore!

The fight continued only moments longer. The young Prince was quickly victorious, and the group of boys exploded into cheers. An adult I had not noticed before emerged from the crowd. He clapped Tren-Lore on the back and said something I could not hear. After allowing the noise to continue a moment longer, the man raised his hand for silence. It was granted instantly. "Our young Tren-Lore did well today. Why did he win his fight?" the man asked in a voice that was both gruff and doting.

"A special favor from the Ascendant of Sovereignty," someone called, and the group laughed.

"Think so, do you?" the man paused and considered them. "Why else?"

"He was stronger," a short boy with brown hair grunted.

The sound of agreement rippled around the circle.

"Really? Then let us see how far his strength gets him. I want one of you from the older group to come fight him. The rest of you watch to see if it is his strength that keeps him in the battle. Any volunteers?"

There was no answer. My heart was like a heavy fist in my chest, pounding against my ribs and vibrating my whole body with anticipation.

"I will fight him," declared a clear voice.

From out of the circle stepped a tall blond boy. I inhaled audibly as I realized that it was Yolis who had accepted the challenge. My mind wildly attempted to guess at the emotions Tren-Lore must have been feeling. Fear? Anger? Determination? If it had been me, I would have been terrified. I had always felt Yolis was slightly

threatening, but to face him with a sword in his hand
would be too much. Tren-Lore was a good fighter, though,
much better than me, I reminded myself.

"You can do it, Tren-Lore," I muttered under my
breath. As Yolis and Tren-Lore faced each other, my
anxiety grew. Yolis was much taller than his brother.

"Begin," the man bellowed.

The group of boys exploded into shouts. Without
thinking, I added my voice to the noise of the throng. Yolis
made the first move, striking quick and hard at Tren-
Lore's head. I gasped, and Tren-Lore ducked and lunged,
his sword aimed at Yolis' stomach. Yolis blocked, and the
blades ground along one another. Freeing his sword, Yolis
swung again. Tren-Lore leaped aside and lashed out. Yolis
only just deflected this side strike and stumbled back a
few steps as Tren-Lore's assault continued in a flow of
attack thrusts. My throat was hoarse from yelling. Yolis'
blade crunched against his brother's, and Tren-Lore
staggered under the power of the blow. The next blow
struck Tren-Lore on the arm, and the right sleeve of Tren-
Lore's tunic turned black with blood.

"It will not be a deep cut, it will not be a deep cut," I
told myself over and over again. "The blades are too dull."

"Enough!" the man was yelling.

Yolis was advancing. Tren-Lore grabbed his sword in
his left hand and met the attack. I could barely stand to
watch. With my hands over my eyes, I peered through my
fingers at the scene below. Everything was deathly quiet.
The man was running toward the brothers. "Yolis! Stop!"
he ordered.

Yolis kept advancing. His sword arched upward. I
tightened my fingers over my eyes to obscure the sight but
could just make out Tren-Lore raising his sword to meet
the attack.

"I said stop!" the man repeated sternly.

There was more silence and I slowly removed my hand
from my face. Tren-Lore was still standing and Yolis was
before him. Although I could not see it, I imagined the look
on Tren-Lore's face. It was rage and hard resolve. It would
not always be like this. When Tren-Lore was a Sanysk.... I
was angry for him, and my thoughts became a tumble of

scalding, rushing ideas and images. The man was talking to both brothers. Was he reprimanding Yolis? I certainly hoped so!

He turned to address the group. "Do you still think his strength kept him in the fight?"

No one replied.

"It was his determination. He was not willing to lose...no matter what the cost! Practice is done for today," he told the group.

No one moved as Tren-Lore and Yolis stood facing each other in silence.

"Nice fight," Tren-Lore said with a carefully controlled edge of sarcasm in his voice.

To my outrage, Yolis slapped Tren-Lore on the back. It was merely the imitation of a friendly gesture, and it made Tren-Lore stumble forward slightly.

"I thought so too," Yolis replied, loudly enough for everyone to hear. "Excellent persistence. The very quality I was hoping to bring out in you. The scratch did not hurt too much, I trust." Tren-Lore did not reply, and Yolis continued in a voice that had the pretense of being brotherly. "If you keep practicing, one day you might be as good as me. Father will be proud when I tell him you are following in my footsteps. What do you think?" He turned to address the group. "How about a round of applause for Tren-Lore's valiant efforts?"

The tension in the group seemed to have been dispelled by Yolis' words. They cheered as though they had not been witness to the disturbing scene that had preceded Yolis' pretty speech. I was furious. It was so obvious that he was lying. Why did the rest of them not see it?

The circle crumbled and the boys dispersed in different directions. Some came to congratulate Tren-Lore, and three of the taller students gravitated toward Yolis. The four of them ambled off the field together. Tren-Lore's friends gradually drifted away, and he was left standing by himself, sword still in hand. It reminded me of the first day I had come to Caladore and Tren-Lore had been standing in the rain. He always seemed separated from everyone else. I eased myself onto a lower branch, and then slid a couple of feet down to the next bough.

Yolis and his friends were talking in boisterous voices as they walked. Their conversation filled my mind as my body made the difficult descent. "You heard about that?" Yolis was laughing. "She is good fun, but that is the only thing her kind is useful for. With her there are no dull balls to attend, and no lady-like objections. It is the ideal combination."

"How did you convince her?" one of the boys demanded.

"The usual promises: eternal devotion, love, and riches. It does not take much, and when she grows tiresome or contradicts me... well...."

The group exploded in pleased exclamations, but by this point, concentration deafened me to their clamor. I had nearly lost my balance, and teetered for an agonizing moment before I regained my footing. Clutching the trunk more tightly, I slithered down the last few feet and landed on the springy grass.

Quickly brushing myself off, I ran toward Tren-Lore. He glanced at me as I approached, but his expression did not give way to surprise. It remained fixed in a rigidly controlled look that appeared to be devoid of emotion. I knew Tren-Lore well enough to realize that this lack of expression was the same as crying might be in someone else. He was angry, I surmised. His fingers were wrapped so tightly around the hilt of his sword that his knuckles were white.

"You fought wonderfully," I said, nervously moving my shoulders so I could draw my arms up into my sleeves and catch hold of the cuffs with my hands.

"Tomorrow we start mounted combat," he replied without focusing his gaze on me.

I licked my lips and watched him uneasily. "Your training group?" Silence was my answer and I shifted my weight from foot to foot. "Tren-Lore, are you all right? Can I look at your arm?"

He turned to me then. It was disconcerting to look into a face and eyes that told you so little. "No, you and I start mounted combat tomorrow," he said. "Meet me in the stables at noon."

I nodded, and he walked away from me, still carrying the sword. Then, it was I who was alone on the field, and in that solitude I made the unfortunate realization that I was going to be in a lot of trouble with Sophie. Turning, I ran back to the tree and shoved my feet inside my shoes. I retraced my steps as quickly as I could. I found my basket still sitting by the anthill. There were no ants outside now. They had probably been smart enough to finish *their* work on time, I thought bitterly as I dashed toward the vegetable garden.

* * *

Pushing up my sleeves, I sunk my arms into the soapy water and followed this customary activity with my customary sigh. I hated doing dishes.

"What did you do to your arm?" Flock asked, taking firm hold of my elbow and twisting my arm to get a better look at the yellowing bruise running the length of my forearm.

Removing my arm from her grasp and frowning, I handed her a cup to dry. "Nothing," I told her.

"You did something," Flock insisted, and set down the cup without properly drying it.

"You missed some soap," I replied, pointing at the cup with a dripping finger.

"Lara," she said in a strict tone, and pointed her finger at me. "What happened?"

Not wanting Flock to draw my bruise to the attention of anyone else in the kitchen, I decided to pacify her with a lie rather than antagonize her with silence. "I slipped on the stairs," I told her, and with a dull thud set a scrubbed pot on the counter.

"Oh." Flock seemed vaguely disappointed with this uninteresting answer. She picked up the cup and dried it more thoroughly. "Well, your arm looks terrible."

I shrugged and continued washing the dishes. Personally, I did not agree. I was proud of my bruise. In fact, I was fond of all the bruises I had gained while learning mounted combat. They were battle wounds, and I had received them with honor. For all the times I had been knocked, or simply fallen out of my saddle, I had never once cried. Tren-Lore did not have nearly as many bruises as I did, but he did have some. I smiled into the sudsy water. I had unhorsed him twice, but it was Storm Wing who knocked him out of his saddle most frequently. It was still beyond me why he wanted to ride such a disagreeable animal.

Unfortunately, our recent practice sessions had been replaced by studying. Tren-Lore had not attended a single lesson since the night he told me that he wanted to be a Sanysk. This had been a constant battle between Tren-Lore and his father, but King Kiris had finally won. He had informed Tren-Lore that unless he passed his exams, he would no longer be practicing to become a knight.

Tren-Lore was valiantly attempting to memorize everything that he should have been learning over the course of the summer, but to further challenge him, his concentration was diluted by excitement. His cousin Myste was coming from Jacinda in two days. As soon as I was done with the dishes, I had planned to slip out of the kitchen and see what I could do to keep Tren-Lore's mind on his work.

I looked up to discover that Flock had wandered away. Her damp dishcloth lay limply on the counter. There were no more dishes to be cleaned, but a large pile of wet pots and pans sat piled beside me. I withdrew my hands from the murky washing water and wiped them on my skirts. My eyes searched the kitchen. I found Flock standing on the outskirts of a conversation her sister was having with Olyanne, another young serving girl.

"Flock," Sophie called from across the kitchen, "the dishes are drying themselves, and that, I believe, is your job."

I smiled and watched as Kella whirled about to find her little sister standing there.

"Flock!" Kella cried in outrage, "What are you doing? Ascendants end you! I wish you-"

"What did you just say, young lady?" It was Flock and Kella's mother. Her inflection made it seem as if she did not approve, but her facial expression was bland. She never even stopped stirring the stew. "Both of you get back to work."

Flock hesitated for a moment, but in the end, decided not to push her mother into a rare but actual rage. Flock stalked back to the washing basin. "It was just getting interesting!" Flock huffed and snatched up the dishcloth. "Kella was telling Olyanne about this man she knows and if Sophie," she hardened her voice as the name formed in her mouth and threw a resentful look at the kindly woman, "had not interrupted me, I think... well, Kella was talking about meeting him last night. I think she was about to tell Olyanne that he kissed her, but now I will never know."

I hefted the washing basin with a quiet grunt. "You could just ask her."

Flock gave a look which was clearly meant to inform me that I knew nothing at all about anything!

"I am going to dump the washing water," I told her, and did not wait for a response. I highly doubted that Flock was even going to make one. She would be too absorbed in speculating about her sister to spare me an answer.

My deliverance from the kitchen was cloaked beneath the menial task that was disposing of the washing water. After I dumped the heavy basin, I slipped into the outer chamber to replace the washing tub, but did not linger. I bounded up the stairs to the secret room where Tren-Lore was waiting.

A cheerful fire was burning in the hearth, but the room was filled with an autumn chill. Tren-Lore had the window open and was leaning on the sill, staring out at the brightly changing landscape beyond. His books sat neglected on the floor.

"It is freezing in here," I said, and went to kneel by the fire.

"Do you want to go for a ride?" he asked without turning around.

I grinned and leaned over to grasp one of the books. "You should be studying," I told him, and flipped the book open to an arbitrary page. "Please count in the Old Tongue used in the time of the Ascendants. Start at one."

"Morian, dore, eckwin, sar – Lara, I know this," Tren-Lore assured me. "The weather is just right for riding. We could go out to-"

I flipped to a new page. "In what year did King Witfel discover Tolrem?"

Tren-Lore laughed. "My Great Uncle Wit founded Tolrem in the 200th year after the Drawl. He and my grandfather signed treaties and Caladore and Tolrem have been allies ever since."

"And what is the Drawl?" I asked, holding my finger over a little note at the bottom of the page that gave a definition of the Drawl.

"It was when the Ascendants left because they thought we were all idiots," Tren-Lore replied impertinently. He was leaning against the windowsill, grinning with an irritating confidence. He knew this answer was only a shadow of the definition, and he was waiting for my reaction. It amused him to see how far my patience would stretch.

"No," I frowned at him and read aloud from the page, "the Drawl occurred when the Discontents de-"

"I know this stuff, Lara," Tren-Lore interrupted, his grin transforming from irritating to pleading. "It is wonderful outside. Could we please go for a ride?"

I met his beseeching gaze directly. "Tren-Lore, you know what will happen if you fail these examinations."

Tren-Lore turned and snapped the shutters closed. "I promise that I will not fail these tests. Besides, half of the people in these history lessons are relatives of mine. I think that should give me an edge. Could we please stop studying and go for a ride?"

I hesitated only momentarily, and then nodded. It was very difficult to say no to Tren-Lore and it gave me a nice feeling to know that my opinion meant something to him.

"Fine," I consented, and dropped the book to the floor.

Tren-Lore offered me his hand and hauled me to my feet. "What part are you at in *Rayn*?"

"Oh, it is so good!" I exclaimed as I wiped my dusty hands on my dress. "Rayn is defending the dragons against the Renarn."

"That is a great part," Tren-Lore agreed as he strode toward the door. He caught hold of the handle and heaved it open. He let me leave first, and I pushed aside the tapestry and headed for the stairs. Tren-Lore caught pace with me in a moment.

"Did they really do those terrible things to dragons?" I asked, glancing sideways at Tren-Lore as we thundered down the stairs. His forehead was creased with a scowl.

"Yes," he said darkly. "Most countries treat dragons that way. Caladore is one of the few exceptions, and from what I can gather from the old books, dragons are also sacred to the Barlems."

This surprised me. The only thing I had ever heard about the Barlems was that they were a mysterious and violent people. No one knew exactly where they lived, or in what conditions they lived, but everyone knew that above all else, they enjoyed killing. I would not have thought they would make an exception for dragons. I remembered the night Kella had told us about her friend's friend. The fire had been dying. I had wanted to flee from the encroaching darkness, but had been held by Kella's words.

"A Barlem leapt out of the bushes at him," she had whispered. "He never had a chance. When they found him, he had been run through at least a dozen times, and his horse and dog were dead, too."

I had run from the room, ignoring the taunting comments that Flock threw after me. I had wanted to escape the dark more than anything, but Kella's story had frightened me, too. I had nightmares that night about Barlems. I could not imagine them being kind to anything, least of all dragons.

"The Barlems like dragons?" I asked in a puzzled tone.

Tren-Lore jumped the last four steps and landed hard. He turned and waited for me to catch up. "I would not say they *like* dragons," he replied as I came to the bottom of the stairs, and we started off down the hall. "They respect them like we do. We respect them for their fighting prowess." He scratched at his cheek in thought. "From what I understand, they respect dragons because they have never been under anyone else's rule. That is the same type of freedom the Barlems believe in."

We reached a side door that led out of the castle and this time, I heaved it open. The sun was bright outside. It warmed the air, making the breeze smell of earth and leaves.

"Did you ever think that maybe King Kiris is not really your father? Maybe he found you when you were a baby?"

Tren-Lore squinted at me. "What?" he said in utter confusion.

"Well, it is just that you and the Barlems seem to share the same ideas about not obeying anyone. Maybe you are really a Barlem prince, and Pandels and Laowermings carried you off when-"

I shrieked suddenly as Tren-Lore caught me around the neck and pulled my head down. He proceeded to grind his knuckles painfully across my forehead.

"Stop!" I shouted. I was crying with laughter and pain.

"A Barlem prince?" he repeated, his voice a mockery of anger. "A what, Lara?"

I jabbed my elbow into his stomach, and he grunted as the air in his lungs escaped. His grip around my neck loosened and I ducked, turned, and then tackled him around the waist. We fell to the ground in a heap and rolled about in the dirt until we were both completely winded. We struggled to a sitting position and pressed our backs against the cool stone of the castle. I could not help grinning. I was not thinking about how much fun Tren-Lore and I had, or even what a wonderful friend he was. I was merely living in the moment, and the moment demanded that I be happy without question. Just be happy, that was it; no thought attached and no explanation necessary.

"We should..." Tren-Lore did not seem able to finish his thought for want of breath.

I knew what he was about to say. The same thought had just occurred to me. We were sitting in a fairly visible spot, and it would be much too easy for someone to see us. "We should go," I said, finishing his sentence.

He grinned at me and hit me on the shoulder. "Exactly."

We scrambled to our feet and moved toward the inner wall. Tren-Lore threw back his head and spread his arms. "What a fabulous day!" he declared without breaking step. "I can hardly wait for Myste to come!"

I smiled at him. The sun danced in his rumpled hair, and his clothes were covered with dirt. He was the perfect picture of everything a hero should be. I believed with unwavering certainly that Tren-Lore's presence in the story of my life would transform my insignificant tale into one of grand adventure and important deeds.

Chapter Six
Myste

The kitchen was a dizzying swirl of activity. Women were bustling in every direction, and the air was filled with all sorts of delicious smells. I was sitting in the very hub of the madness, my legs tucked under me as I leaned over the large bowl on the table. I grasped the wooden spoon in both hands and moved it through the heavy cake mixture. Myste had arrived today, and a banquet was being prepared in his honor. I had not been able to slip away as I usually did. In the quagmire of work that needed to be waded through, I had suddenly become a vital part of the kitchen staff. I felt particularly slighted by this turn of events. The very day I most wanted to leave was the day when I could not go.

"Are you finished with that, Lara?" Sophie asked as she came up behind me.

I pulled the spoon out of the mixture and watched as globs of batter fell back into the bowl. "Yes," I muttered.

Sophie took hold of the spoon and scraped it along the edge of the bowl. "Thank you, dear."

I squirmed in my chair so I was facing her. "Sophie, can I go out and-"

"I am sorry, child," she replied before I had even finished my sentence. Taking the bowl in one hand, she smoothed her hair with the other. "There is simply too much to be done. We cannot spare you. It will be the

Ascendants' hand if all of this cooking gets finished before tonight. Benya!" she cried suddenly. "Just a little salt will do!" With that, she hastened off again.

Another one of the ladies passed by and dumped a mound of potatoes in front of me. "Chop these up, would you, Lara?"

I scowled and went to get a knife.

This pace continued until dusk. Sophie then informed us that the food was to be transported into the banquet hall.

"Not to the garden?" I blurted.

"Really, Lara!" Flock sighed as she swept past me with her chin tilted at an angle meant to denote superiority. "It is far to cold to have celebrations outside!"

"Can you see anything with your nose that far in the air?" I snapped.

Flock made a face at me, and I stuck my tongue out. Kella told us we were immature as she handed over baskets full of bread to take up to the banquet hall.

When the food was in place, Sophie chose the women who were to stay with her and serve. Everyone else was dismissed. I walked slowly back to the kitchen and dragged my feet on the floor to emphasize how disappointed I was with the outcome of the day. There was no one in the kitchen when I arrived, and I slumped in a chair by the fire and pouted. Everything had been ruined. I had planned on meeting Myste and spending the entire afternoon having fun with him and Tren-Lore, but instead, I had been washing dishes and chopping vegetables all day. Life was not fair.

Unfortunately, this line of thought had limited entertainment value, and I was soon tired of sulking. Abandoning the fire, I went to my room and crawled onto my bed. I pulled the fifth volume of *Rayn* from under my pillow and opened it to the page marked with a ribbon that Nahanni had given me the last time we had been riding.

"Lara does not want that girly ribbon!" Tren-Lore had protested.

I had agreed hesitantly. Later, though, when Tren-Lore was trying to avoid being bitten by Storm Wing, I had taken the lovely pink ribbon from Nahanni and thanked her with a quiet profuseness.

I fingered the silky ribbon as I began to read. Soon I was lost in Rayn's adventures with the hardships of the day far behind me. I was so absorbed, in fact, that I did not hear the kitchen door open.

"Lara?" called a voice.

"Oh!" I cried, and my muscles tensed. My eyes turned to the door, and for a breathless moment, I expected Sophie to come into the room and find me reading. Then she would know that –

"Lara, are you here?"

I let my breath out in relief. The voice was Tren-Lore's. I slipped the book under my pillow and bounded from the room.

Tren-Lore was standing in the middle of the kitchen, and beside him stood a boy I assumed was Myste. He was slightly taller than his cousin, and had curly brown hair that was even more disorderly than Tren-Lore's. He was dressed in wonderfully rich clothing that mirrored the quality of Tren-Lore's own garb.

Tren-Lore had one of his fingers between his collar and his throat. "I think I am choking," he muttered to Myste as he pulled at the material around his neck.

"Consider yourself fortunate," Myste replied with a grin. "At least you will die soon. I will have to wear this all night."

Tren-Lore laughed and took his hand from his collar. "Well, there is that," he conceded.

Myste chuckled as he irreverently seated himself on the table. He sat easily, swinging his legs and surveying the kitchen. "Do us both a favor, would you, Tren-Lore? Undo a top button. I would rather you died a little further into my visit. We have not had any fun yet, and I have not even met..." his words faded into a silent smile as he noticed me standing in the doorway to my room. "Lara, I presume."

Tren-Lore turned and matched his cousin's grin. "I thought you might be here."

"Lucky it is only me you found," I mumbled, and nervously brushed at the wrinkles in my dress. It always made me uneasy to face people who were dressed in such finery.

"I was willing to chance it." Tren-Lore shrugged. "I did not think anyone would be at work when they did not have to be. Lara, this is my cousin, Myste. Myste, this is my best friend Lara."

Myste caught my gaze and held it. "Lovely to meet you, Lara."

I could feel my cheeks grow hot with a blush. I was uncomfortable with such formalities. "Ah, yes." I tore my eyes away from his and sought the familiar sight of Tren-Lore. "It is...ah...nice to meet you too," I stuttered, and curled my toes hard in my shoes.

Tren-Lore glanced momentarily at Myste. His look was appraising, but his expression did not reveal what he was surmising. "We are going swimming," he told me. "Do you want to come?"

"Now?" I exclaimed. "But it will be so cold."

Tren-Lore nodded. "But you are coming, right?"

I wavered in mute indecision. Slipping out of the kitchen at night to go swimming in the river was appealing; however, the idea of plunging myself into freezing water was not as tempting. Still...

"All right," I consented. Now that the decision was made, I felt exhilarated.

"We have to get changed, so we will meet you in the stable as soon as we can get there," Tren-Lore said, and moved toward the door. "Come on, Myste."

Myste leapt off the table. "Good-bye, Lara."

I looked up in surprise. Tren-Lore and I did not typically exchange such formal partings, and the fact that someone was offering me one was rather unexpected.

"Come on, Myste," Tren-Lore repeated with a sigh of exasperation.

"Good-bye," I replied, and watched as Myste smiled and turned to leave with his cousin.

As the two passed into the outer chamber, Tren-Lore shouted, "Try not to be seen, Lara!"

"Of course," I yelled back and scampered into my room.

I knelt beside my bed and stretched my arm beneath it. My hand met only chilled stone. I winced. If the floor was this cold, what would the river be like? My speculation went no further, for my fingers touched upon something soft. It was the clothing Tren-Lore had given me for our summer adventures. I eagerly pulled them from their hiding place. They would be nice and light for swimming.

"Try not to be seen, Lara," I whispered as I crept down the torch-lit passageways leading out of the castle.

Tren-Lore's advice seemed a remarkable understatement now that I was in actual danger of being spotted. A young girl caught sneaking around at night while dressed in boy's clothing with a guilty expression on her face would certainly have some explaining to do. Especially to Sophie, I thought with a grimace. There was suddenly an unexpected sound from down the corridor. I froze, and my breath caught. I stared blindly into the dimness before me. My mind exploded with ideas of escape, and the force pulled my limbs in all directions, effectively rendering me motionless. The dull thuds were coming quickly, one after the other. The person had already rounded the corner by the time I decided that the best alternative would be to press myself against the wall and hope that I did not draw undue attention. My hands felt clammy and blood thundered in my ears. As the figure got closer, I realized it was Yolis!

Please do not notice me, please do not notice me, I intoned silently.

"You!" called Yolis' strong voice.

One part of my mind, which seemed to be detached from the situation, wondered briefly if Tren-Lore would sound like that when he grew up. The other part was incoherent with dread. I had been caught!

"Boy!" he called again.

I looked up suddenly, staring wildly about, searching for the person he was addressing as 'boy'. Certainly it could not be me!

"Yes, you boy," Yolis continued, stopping a few feet from me. "Are you familiar with any of the kitchen wenches?"

I stared at Yolis in amazement. He thought I was a boy! I had not been discovered after all!

"Are you deaf, boy?" Yolis snapped. "I asked you a question?"

"I ... I ..." I suddenly realized that I had not curtsied to the prince. I immediately made to do so but caught myself just in time. I awkwardly transformed my bob into a bow. "I know them well, Your Highness. I ... often sneak into the kitchen .... for scraps."

Yolis was frowning at me as he absently straightened the cuffs of his ornate sleeves. "Yes, well, do you know a girl named Kelladyn?"

I nodded and stared at my feet. I did not want to meet Yolis' gaze. It was too penetrating, too forceful. I wondered silently why Yolis was interested in Kella.

"And do you know where she is right now?" he demanded.

I knew exactly where she was. Kelladyn had made sure that everyone in the kitchen knew where she would be: settling into a chamber of her very own. It was a right Kella had only recently been granted.

"She is spending the night in her room. It is on the second f-"

"I know where it is," Yolis said as he brushed hurriedly past me.

I waited until he turned the corner, and then set off at a run. I wanted to put distance between myself and the scene of my narrowly averted disaster. Tren-Lore and Myste were waiting in the stables when I arrived. I burst noisily through the door and stood panting for breath.

"What happened?" Tren-Lore asked shrewdly.

I gulped in more air. "I ran into ... Yolis. He was ... looking for Kelladyn."

Tren-Lore leapt up onto Storm Wing's back. "Flock's sister? That is strange," he mused and absently patted Storm Wing's neck as the horse snorted angrily. "Your horse is over there." Tren-Lore pointed to Paence, the brown mare I usually rode.

Paence was standing as far away from Storm Wing as she could. Translated from the Old Tongue, her name meant good sense. I thought she was living up to her moniker very nicely. Why Tren-Lore chose to ride a horse like Storm Wing was beyond me.

"Thank you," I replied, and crossed over to Paence. I leaned heavily against her side, waiting for my breathing to become more regular. "Why do you suppose Yolis would be looking for Kella?"

Myste mounted his own horse and shifted in the saddle. "Maybe he likes her," Myste suggested.

Tren-Lore squinted in thought. "Maybe. But he has been courting the daughter of some duke for the past couple of months. He seemed pretty focused on her."

"Perhaps he focuses on girls the same way you focus on your studies," Myste suggested.

I laughed and mounted Paence. Tren-Lore looked as though he was trying to be irritated, but I suspected he was actually quite amused by his cousin's barb.

"Who told you about my studies?" he asked, a smile tugging at the corner of his lips.

"Nahanni has been filling me in on all sorts of interesting details," Myste replied.

Tren-Lore laughed and kicked Storm Wing into stride. "And did she tell you I was going to pummel her later?" he asked as Storm Wing cantered from the stable.

Myste shook his head and nudged his own horse forward. "No, I do not believe she mentioned that. Lara," he asked, glancing at me, "have you heard anything about this?"

"Nothing," I replied with a wide smile.

We passed from the stable and out into the courtyard. The air had the calmness of evening, and a full moon tempered the darkness that would have otherwise conjured images of the past. We were let through the gates without question. Apparently my depiction of a serving boy was just as convincing as my Lady in Waiting. Once free from the castle walls, we talked loudly, our voices rising into the night sky. Myste told us the story of his trip to Caladore. It detailed his encounter with a band of bumbling thieves who were very fond of crude sayings and ale.

"I swear, I swear!" Myste protested, holding up his hands. "That is exactly how it happened!"

Tren-Lore was laughing so hard, he was barely sitting straight in his saddle. "It did not! Not one word of that is true." Tren-Lore looked at me. "Lara, tell Myste what a liar he is."

I glanced at Myste and found that he was already looking at me.

"Lara believes me, Tren-Lore," Myste replied, and winked at me. "You are the only one who has not had adventures with pirates."

Tren-Lore's laughter was ebbing. He rubbed ruefully at his ribs and grinned broadly at his cousin. "Pirates? I thought it was bandits."

"No, it was pirates," Myste assured him with a smirk, "You should listen more carefully when I am lying to you."

* * *

The sting of the cold water came like the bite of thorns. The three of us shouted and cried, waving our hands frantically in the air and pausing every now and then to stand motionless, torn between the warm shore and the inexplicable urge to wade more deeply into the river. Tren-Lore was the first to plunge his entire body into the black depths of Venst.

"Come on," he called, sending a spray of water toward us. "It is not that bad once you get used to it."

Myste turned to me, a look of skepticism upon his face. "People only say that when it really *is* that bad and there is no hope of *ever* getting used to it."

I rubbed my hands together and tried to stop my teeth from chattering. Tren-Lore's figure was just barely discernable. He was standing waist deep in the river. His hair was a spiky mess, and the water that clung to his body shimmered under the caress of moonlight. He looked wild and grand. Like an Aquara, I thought.

I suddenly remembered a story my mother had told me. It had been a favorite of mine, and the characters still walked firmly in my memory. I could picture the young man as he crouched on the soft banks of a babbling brook. He leaned forward and let the water flow into his cupped hands. He and his love, Quara, had run away from families that would not allow them to be together. They were lost and had not had anything to eat or drink in several days.

The young man drank deeply, gratefully, and thanked the Ascendant of Water for the gift. Suddenly, it felt as though he was drowning, he could not breathe for the water he had just consumed filled his lungs and throat. Long ago a Sorcerer had placed a curse upon the brook, and all who drank from it perished. The young man clutched at his throat and toppled forward into the water. Quara heard the splash and rushed to the brook, but it was too late! His body was already sinking into the expanding depths. Without thought, she dove into the water.

She swam down into the cool silence of the suddenly bottomless brook. She swam and swam, but no matter how she struggled she could not reach him. He was always just before her. The curse would not allow him to be saved, but she would not abandon him. She vowed that she would die rather than relent. Her chest felt tight with the crushing emptiness of suffocation, and her vision began to fade. When at last she passed from consciousness, her hand was still stretched toward her love. Her lips parted and her body instinctually drew breath. It was a watery breath that should have meant her end, but it did not.

The Ascendant of Water had been grateful for the young man's faith, and was touched by Quara's devotion to him. The Ascendant changed Quara and her love so that their bodies were formed of water. Removed from a world that would tear them apart, they were free to love each other for all eternity. So came to be the Aquara, I heard my mother's voice say, the mythical people who preside over running water.

It was Tren-Lore's voice, and not my mother's, that I heard next. He was yelling goading insults at me and Myste. I shook off my imaginings, and after listening to a few moments of his well-aimed slander, I was forced to dive in after him. The water broke over my head, and when I came to the top I was breathless with the cold. I barely had time to recover from the shock of the frigid water before Tren-Lore lunged toward me and knocked me back under.

We only swam for a few moments, but it was long enough to ensure that we were all chilled to the bone. With shaking hands, Tren-Lore pulled blankets from his saddlebags and tossed them to us. Wrapped in the blankets, we rode slowly home. Anything more than a walk created a breeze that was unbearable against our wet skin. My lips were quaking so badly that I could not even begin to speak. It seemed the others were suffering similarly, for only a few labored remarks were exchanged during our return journey.

It almost seemed a dream when at last I found myself under the thick quilt of my own bed. Thankfully, no one had been in the kitchen to see my haggard arrival. Sophie and the other ladies were still serving at the banquet. Shivers continued to wrack my body, but they were growing less and less frequent. I stared absently at the candle burning on the nightstand and thought about the evening. It had been worth it. An adventure with Tren-Lore was worth almost anything. I could understand why Tren-Lore had been so eager for Myste to arrive. Tren-Lore's cousin was certainly a lot of fun. Pulling the covers tightly around my chin, I smiled to myself as I thought of Tren-Lore's happiness that night. I fell asleep shortly after and did not hear Sophie return.

The next morning began in the usual way. Sophie woke me up and I helped prepare breakfast. After the food had been readied for the others in the castle, the kitchen servants sat down to eat. Flock made remarks about my hair, which had dried into an unfortunate mound of lumps and crinkles. I retaliated with my own insults, and eventually Sophie and Flock's mother had to put an end to our bickering. The older women talked over the success of the banquet, and Kella remained remarkably quiet. She ate with a silent smile upon her face, but added nothing to any of the conversations.

When the meal was finished, I returned to my room and tried to brush my hair flat. The familiar noise of the kitchen was soft in the background. Sunlight filled the room and tumbled over the bed I had forgotten to make that morning. Humming to myself, I dragged the comb through my disheveled hair and pursed my lips in critical thought as I examined the results. There were none. What did Flock know anyway? My hair did not look *that* bad. I dropped the comb on the table and licked my palms. I pressed them to my scalp and tried to flatten the more obvious bulges. My hair was undaunted and sprang back into place. I frowned. Flock was right. It did look like a Pandel's nest. I hated Flock.

"Sophieee!" I called, scowling into the mirror.

The kindly woman bustled into the room and I watched her reflection survey me with a small smile. "Yes, dear?"

I pulled vainly at the bottom of my unruly locks. "I need your help," I told her.

She chuckled and came to sit in her rocking chair. Reaching over, she picked up the comb and dipped it into our washing basin. "Come, sit," she instructed.

I knelt with my back to her and she pulled the comb through my hair. She hummed contently to herself, and I listened, trying to place the tune. I had heard Sophie humming often enough that I was beginning to distinguish a pattern. There were five distinct songs that she hummed. I did not think I had ever heard anyone else sing them.

"Sophie?" I asked, tilting my face back so I could just see her.

"Hmm?" she replied, and straightened my head.

I stared forward and felt the water from her comb twist through my hair. "When you hum, are you humming songs?"

"Yes, old songs, from when I was a young woman."

My mother had loved to sing and I had heard many songs from her lips. Once she had told me that the girls at Telnayis had taught her the tunes, and that the songs had their origins in many faraway lands. My mother had never sung any of Sophie's s... I felt a sudden pain in my chest, deep and cutting. I yanked my mind away from the comparison and concentrated on Sophie, on the familiar details of the room, on the presence of sunlight, on the sounds of the kitchen and on the warmth of Sophie's legs against my back.

"I have never heard them before," I told her when I calmed.

"No." She paused and when she spoke again there was an odd tightness to her voice. "You would not have. They are gone from the memories of most. Disappeared across the sea."

This answer did not make much sense to me, and I wrinkled my brow in confusion. "Why do you remember them?"

"Because I love them," she said quietly.

"What do ..." I began.

"There now," Sophie interrupted and, placing the comb on the table, rose suddenly. "Your hair is fine."

"Sophie ..." I began again, but she cut me off once more.

"Your bed is another matter, however. It needs to be made, and once you are done that, you and Flock can start on the morning dishes."

She stepped around me, and I watched her leave the room. That had not been like Sophie at all. I resolved to tell Tren-Lore about it and see what he thought.

I had just finished tucking in my sheets when the sound in the kitchen came to a sudden halt. I stood up straight and stared forward, listening hard. There was not even the clink of dishes. What was going on?

"Welcome, Your Majesty. Our kitchen is honored by your presence." It was Sophie speaking. She sounded shocked. No, puzzled was more like it.

It could not be Tren-Lore. He dropped in too frequently for anyone to even take notice of his presence. The King would not have warranted such a tone in Sophie's voice. Perhaps Yolis? I moved toward the door, but before I reached it, a familiar voice responded to Sophie's greeting, "I was wondering if there was anything I could do to help?"

My mouth opened in surprise. "Myste?" I exclaimed under my breath and rushed forward to see.

My guess had been correct. Myste was standing in the entrance, his hands at his sides. He was dressed in a fine red tunic, and his thumb was absently rubbing the silver ring he wore on his index finger. It seemed a gesture he was not even aware of. He smiled warmly at the astonished servants.

Sophie set a plate she was carrying on the table. It was the only sound in the room, and everyone gave a little start and scowled with momentary displeasure at the dish that had taken their attention from the strange situation unfolding before them.

"That is very kind, Your Highness, but not necessary," Sophie assured him and ran her hand over her hair. "You need not worry yourself about us."

"I would like to learn, though," Myste persisted, and took a hesitant step into the kitchen. He looked around, but his gaze rested finally upon me. "If none of you would mind too much, that is."

"You *want* to work?" Flock blurted, and was hushed by several women. I had to admit that I shared Flock's sentiment. Why would Myste volunteer to do chores?

Sophie clasped her hands before her and smiled at Myste. "If that is what you would like, I am sure there are a few things we could teach you. You can help Lara and Flock with the dishes."

A dark ripple of disapproval ran through the serving women. "Sophie!" one of them hissed. "You do not really intend to make royalty wash dishes, do you?"

Sophie turned to the group. "I am not making him do anything. If the boy wants to help, he can help. I am sure that Lara and Flock will not object."

"He can wash," Flock offered, and held out the ratty dishcloth.

Myste grinned, and Sophie beckoned to me. I came forward and stood by her, glancing swiftly at Myste from across Sophie, and then at the floor. I traced a crack in the stones with the tip of my shoe. I felt as thought I had returned to the moment in which I had just met Myste.

Sophie clapped her hands briskly. "Back to work. The noon meal is swiftly approaching." Suddenly, the noise in the kitchen resumed and everyone hurried off to find the work they had abandoned. Sophie put a hand on my shoulder. "Lara, can you show his Highness what needs to be done?"

I nodded and smiled briefly at Myste. "The washing basin is over here," I told him. We moved away from Sophie, and I reminded myself that this was the same boy I had been swimming with last night. "Why do you want to help?" I asked in a great rush that swept away my nerves.

He shrugged. "Tren-Lore is training and I could not play dolls with Nahanni for one moment longer. It would have been an offence to my manhood. The kitchen was the natural place to retreat to, being such a natural haven for men and all."

* * *

By the time Myste left the kitchen that day, he had mastered doing the dishes. To Flock's great irritation, he had even discovered the joys of towel snapping. I suspected that her grievance was not with the immaturity of his newfound skill, as she loudly professed, but rather in the fact that he was not using this skill to harass her. It was me that he foolishly chose to focus his attacks upon. He would have been assured victory had he done battle with Flock, for she had little to no towel-snapping capabilities. I, on the other hand, was proficient with the towel, and Myste eventually threw down his weapon and with a broad grin, declared me the irrefutable champion.

To my great surprise, he returned the next day as well, and the day after that and the day after that, until Myste's arrivals in the kitchen were expected as part of the daily routine. He was always close by my side, even if we were working on separate things, and his presence made the eagerly awaited afternoon come quickly. Myste's mind was that of a scavenger, finding humor in the remains of situations and comments and tearing from them the meat of mirth. I laughed a great deal when Myste was in the kitchen. His wit may not have been the sole reason for my laughter. One sunny afternoon, Tren-Lore had betrayed the ticklish state of my ribs. From that moment on, Myste had delighted in making up outrageous excuses to get close enough to me so that he could jab me in the side. In an Ascendant-sent mercy, I discovered that Myste had a similar weakness and I was quick to use it in my defense.

I yelped as Myste's fingers dug into my ribs. The spoon I had been holding fell from my grip and sank from sight into the brown sludge that was supposed to be a stew. I glanced down in dismay. How was I supposed to get the spoon out of that great mess? End Myste! I whirled about and found his standing a few feet away.

He scratched ruefully at his cheek and leaned slightly to his left so he could see the pot behind me. "I do not expect the spoon will add much to the taste."

I opened my mouth and then closed it again, torn between laughter and outraged exclamations. I finally settled on the later. "Myste!" I shouted and dove at him. He jumped back and caught me by the wrists. We struggled as he tried to keep my hands away from his own ribs. "You Barlem!" I cried in outrage, twisting in his grip. "I do not need help making it taste bad!" I pulled sharply away and one of my hands came free. I thought briefly that I really needed Tren-Lore to teach me hand-to-hand combat.

Myste released my other wrist and dodged out of the way, putting a table between the two of us. I put my hands on the smooth wooden surface and bent my knees, ready to spring either way.

"Come on, Lara," he protested with a grin and mimicked my stance. "Maybe it will catch on." He assumed a pompous expression. "Really, boy," he said in mock scorn, "there are not nearly enough spoons with my stew."

I burst into laughter and darted around the table. He retreated with playful slowness, backing away from me with his hands held in a gesture of benevolence. "Think this over, Lara. Do you really want to-"

I leapt at him, and his sentence remained unfinished, lost in the thunder of shouts and laughter. There was suddenly a sharp crack upon the table. It was only inches from us, and Myste and I froze in our struggle.

"That is quite enough," Sophie said, holding ready the damp towel she had just snapped at us. She was trying to look stern, but her eyes were dancing with amusement.

Myste and I released one another and both turned to stare at Sophie in shock.

"Lady Grim..." Myste began in bewilderment. "I... whoa..."

Sophie burst into laughter. "I am not the Head of this kitchen for no reason, young man."

Myste bowed deeply to her. "I am sorry, Lara, but I think Lady Grim is the new towel-snapping champion."

I kicked sideways at Myste, and he capered out of my way. "Be quiet," I told him with a grin. "Does Namin know you can do that?" I asked Sophie. I would never have suspected that such talent lurked behind Sophie's domestic demeanor.

"Oh, yes," Sophie chuckled, clasping the towel before her. "Now, my dear children, I will retrieve the spoon from the stew if you fetch me some water from the well."

Myste and I agreed and went to gather the buckets from the outer chamber.

"Wear warm cloaks," Sophie called after us over the noise of Flock's complaints.

"I *never* get to go for water," she whined.

Myste grabbed one of the fur-lined cloaks off the pegs in the wall and handed it to me. Winter had fallen heavily upon Caladore. Icy drafts of air leaked from chinks in the stones, making it nearly impossible to keep the castle warm. Roaring fires blazed in every hearth, but even this was not enough to banish the permanent chill that seemed to have settled in the rooms and halls of Caladore. Compared to the temperature outside, however, the castle was as warm as a dragon's lair.

"Did Tren-Lore say what we are doing today?" I asked Myste as we trudged down one of the corridors.

Myste was whistling to himself and swinging his buckets as he walked. "No," he replied, and thumped one of the pails into my backside.

I furrowed my brow and gave him my most disapproving gaze. "Quit it."

"What?" he asked innocently, and hit me again.

I stopped and clenched my fingers tightly around the rope handles of my buckets. Myste could be very irritating at times. "Quit hitting me. You already ruined my stew."

He smirked and rubbed his nose with the back of his hand. "I had nothing to do with ruining your stew." He began to back away from me. "You had that nicely in hand before I tickled you."

I gasped in indignation and Myste took off at a run. I chased him, but had trouble keeping up because of my weighty cloak. The door that led from the castle was stiff with the cold and hard to open. I had just caught up with Myste when he managed to force his exit. We burst out into the snow-covered garden. The wind howled in protest and tried to push us back into the castle. Undaunted, I swung my bucket at him and caught him soundly in the side.

"Ouch! Lara!" he protested, ducking as I tried to hit him again. "You have been spending too much time with Tren-Lore." He grunted as my pail struck him again. "Lara! Really! I never hit you that hard!"

I started laughing at his irate expression, and in the lull of my attack he grabbed me about the waist and threw me over his shoulder. The next thing I knew, he had dumped me in a snow bank. The shock of the snow against my skin was enough to numb even my mind. I lay there for a moment and then began to giggle. Myste was out of breath. He ruefully rubbed at his shoulder. "You are pretty tough," he consented, and offered me a hand. I took it.

His fingers were warm against mine. He hauled me to my feet and I stumbled forward, putting my hand on his chest to steady myself. We were so close that I could feel the warmth of his body. The wind blew at my hair and cloak so that they swirled around us. Myste was looking at me, and I met his gaze. His eyes were deep brown, full of life and fun, but there was seriousness there. His eyes were not at all like Tren-Lore's. You could read emotion in Myste's gaze.

"We should get the water," I told Myste, and took my hand from his.

* * *

It was nearly a month since the day of his arrival, and Myste was wreathed in serving women. He had a natural ability for cooking, and learned so swiftly that soon he was baking dishes with smells and tastes that were delicious enough to lure the women of the kitchen away from their own work. Myste was often ringed in a circle of women, all expounding upon the excellence of his latest creation. He certainly seemed to enjoy their praise, but at times I wondered how much it really meant to him.

"Delicious!" one of the ladies murmured through a mouthful of the pie Myste had just made.

"Such a talented child!" another sang, and the rest of the group harmonized with various forms of agreement.

This acclamation came dimly to me as I scooped another glob of lard out of the tub before me. I smudged it onto the sides of the large pan I was greasing and smiled. I was thinking of Tren-Lore and the fight he had described to me last night.

It had been the final mounted combat session held that year. Tren-Lore's instructor, Hazar, had designed it in a tournament style. That morning the fury of a blizzard had been unleashed upon Caladore. The wind howled and battered against the castle, while the temperature became so cold that it cracked the stiff leather armor the boys wore. Hazar had told them that the conditions were not ones he would have chosen, but reminded them that battles would be fought even if the sun did not come out. It was a reality the boys should learn to accept. Tren-Lore and I agreed that this was very true, and named various situations in which Rayn had been forced to fight when the conditions were less than ideal. The boys had fought through Hazar's tournament and faced both the cold and each other. Tren-Lore endured, and in the end was the champion of his age group. I had been very proud of him, and Myste had even managed to forgo his usual jokes and congratulate his cousin with sincerity.

I glanced up to see what Myste was doing. The ladies still surrounded him and were all clucking with delight. One had asked him what spices he had chosen, but Myste had failed to answer her. When I looked up, I found that his entire attention was upon me. He seemed oblivious to the gabbling women. His thumb was moving against his ring but the rest of his body was still, as though he were in deep thought. Our eyes met for only a moment, but his gaze was intense and full of emotion that I could not name. Myste looked away quickly. He mumbled a reply to the inquiry about spices while a flush grew on his cheeks. Was he blushing? I frowned in puzzlement. That was not like Myste. Why had he been watching me, and why was he blushing?

I puzzled this for only a few moments and then dismissed it. The only lingering effect of the entire incident was the bad mood Myste had been thrown into. He did not even attempt to engage me in his usual banter as we walked up to the secret room after lunch. I was slightly concerned by this, but when I saw Tren-Lore, all my worries vanished. He was sitting on the floor of the secret room binding fur to his boots with strips of leather. He was clad in one of his dirtier tunics and a pair of ripped breaches. He grinned as we entered, and I knew immediately that adventure lay before us.

"We are going hunting for dragon eggs," he declared.

"Well, that sounds like a safe way to fill our afternoon," Myste remarked sarcastically. He sunk into a chair by the fire, twisting his ring around his finger.

"It will hardly be dangerous at all," Tren-Lore told him. "Dragons hibernate in the winter."

"I hate winter," Myste muttered, and stretched out his hands toward the flames.

Tren-Lore jerked his head toward a book on the table. "I brought the sixth volume of *Rayn*," he said to me. "A boy in my class says there is a dragon's cave along Venst."

"The riverbank?" I echoed as I moved over to the table. "But dragons do not like the water."

"I know," Tren-Lore agreed, and began to work on his other boot. "I told him that dragons hardly ever live by running water."

I frowned at the contradicting facts. "Of course not. They are too smart to take the chance. A dragon would die if it accidentally swallowed an Aquara. Thank you for bringing this," I said as I hefted the thick book.

"No problem," Tren-Lore replied easily as he tied the last knot on his boots and stood up. "I told Gare exactly the same thing, about the Aquara that is, but he insisted that he had seen the eggs this fall. I think we should go and check it out."

I nodded, but had doubts about the validity of Gare's story. I did not think there would be any dragon eggs to find. I leaned against the wall and flipped through the novel, relishing the sight of so many words but feeling sad at the same time. It was the last book in the series. Its length only prolonged the painful reality that I would have to close the book and leave Rayn in its pages. Still, I was happy that the novel was as long as it was.

"Why do you hate winter?" I asked Myste absently as I set the book back on the table.

He grunted and leaned over to grab a piece of wood from the pile near the hearth. "It is just so cold," he complained, and shoved the log into the fire.

Tren-Lore smiled at his cousin and picked up a fur cloak from a pile of clothes dumped in the corner of the room. "I have noticed that about winter. Very cold. Not at all like summer."

Tren-Lore and I exchanged grins as Myste turned to look at us. "You can both stop snickering at me."

"Snickering!" Tren-Lore objected, and opened his mouth in a silent expression of indignation. "We were not snickering...we were scoffing."

Myste rolled his eyes. "Fine, but the winters in Jacinda are not like this. They are much warmer. You can forget it if you think that I am going to wade through waist-deep snow looking for dragon eggs that neither one of you believes are even there. It is just too much senseless excitement for me."

Tren-Lore pulled the heavy cloak around his shoulders and knotted the ties. "Are you sure?"

"Yes," he said resolutely, and turned back to the fire, crossing his arms. I thought he looked a little sad. "You and Lara have a good time."

Tren-Lore frowned and glanced briefly at me, and then back at Myste. He made no reply to his cousin. I pushed myself away from the wall and came slowly over to the pile of winter clothing. I grabbed a piece of fur and began to strap it over my right boot. Myste had not been himself today. Perhaps he missed Jacinda and his parents. I knew what it felt like to be homesick, but dwelling on the problem had never made me feel any better. Brooding in front of the fire certainly would not help him. If Myste knew what was good for him, he would come with us and take his mind off the matter. I looked over at Myste's slouched figure. The fire gave him a ruddy glow. "Myste, please come," I beseeched. "It will be lots of fun."

Tren-Lore knelt down beside me and worked on binding fur to my other boot. Myste glanced at me and for a moment I thought he looked hopeful, but his features were quick to crumble into an expression of despondency. "No thank you, Lara," he replied glumly, twisting his ring.

I clasped my hands dramatically before me and smiled brightly. The gesture reminded me of something Nahanni would do. "Please, please, please. I really want you to come."

Apparently the princess' charm worked for enchantresses other than herself, for Myste hesitated but finally agreed to come. We found the cave, but as Tren-Lore and I had suspected, there were no dragon eggs. It was a very nice cave, however, and we played out the story in which Rayn had to heal a dragon after it had swallowed an Aquara. It was a great deal of fun, and Myste, having emerged from the murkiness of his bad mood, delivered a very convincing performance as a dragon in agonizing internal pain.

Chapter Seven
The End of Stories

With no regard for Myste's dislike of the cold, winter fell even more heavily on Caladore. Tren-Lore, Myste and I spent a great deal of time in the secret room. We sat around the fire and wrapped ourselves in blankets until we appeared to be poor travelers garbed in patchwork cloaks. Tren-Lore and Myste taught me how to play Questkon, and many hours were spent in ruthless gaming. We also worked on training skills with Tren-Lore. Myste was very impressed with my sword-handling ability and often told me how skilled I was. Tren-Lore's reply to my skill was usually, "All right, try it with your left hand, then."

For me, the period of time in which the sun of my happiness was at its peak was when we roasted narkanytch, and Myste and Tren-Lore told stories. I had never eaten narkanytch before but King Kiris had purchased an entire bag from a traveling merchant and Tren-Lore had pilfered them for us. They were small cubes of hardened sap taken from trees that grew only in the Renarn. When toasted over the fire, they softened into a sticky and delicious goodness. Around the warm fire, there was no worry of chill or competition. There were just three friends telling tales and laughing.

"So Tren-Lore told him that we were the sons of a farmer from the next village," Myste recounted as he methodically turned his narkanytch over the low flames.

"So then," Tren-Lore's voice leapt into the story, "the man said he would call off his dogs if Myste and I promised to help him in his fields." Tren-Lore's narkanytch was perilously close to the fire, but he was so involved with the story that he took no heed.

I laughed through my mouthful of toasted candy and shifted so I was sitting cross-legged between the two boys. "But what about the lunch everyone was attending?"

"Exactly," Myste nodded. He examined his narkanytch, and then extended his arm so that one side of the sticky treat was more fully exposed to the heat of the flames. "When we did not show up, everyone went looking for us."

"Really?" I asked in disbelief, licking each of my fingers. I could not imagine King Kiris looking for Tren-Lore. Half the castle would be employed in a constant search for Tren-Lore if his father still had such an attitude.

"Oh yes," Myste assured me. "Tren-Lore was not such a renegade in his youth. His disappearance was actually cause for concern then. So the entire royal family, even Grandmother Seridia, I think..."

Tren-Lore waved his narkanytch in the air, trying to put out the fire that had unsurprisingly crawled from one of the logs on to the surface of the candy. He glanced at his cousin, an expression of sudden revelation upon his face. "You are right, she was!" The flames took a steadier hold on the poor narkanytch. "I remember her complaining about her knees after they found us. Ah, cursed thing. Go out." He brought the narkanytch close and blew on it. The fire died, leaving a black shell on the candy.

Myste stared at his own perfect narkanytch, a crooked smile of wry amusement playing across his lips. He continued the story. "So the entire royal family was out looking for us, and Tren-Lore and I were squatting in some farmer's field picking weeds. It must have been the Ascendants' work that Aunt Sage found us. She was probably the only one who would not have turned us over her knee and spanked us then and there."

I giggled at the thought of Tren-Lore and Myste being spanked.

Myste removed his narkanytch from the fire and pointed his finger at Tren-Lore. "Your mother was always great that way. She would..."

Tren-Lore turned to me abruptly. "Do want my narkanytch?"

His face was emotionless, and I knew immediately that reminiscing about how wonderful his mother had been was causing him pain. My mind recoiled from this realization. I did not know how he was feeling. I could not know, would not know. I met his gaze with defiance.

Myste was watching us both with a sudden caution. His thumb was unconsciously turning the ring on his finger. He cleared his throat, and Tren-Lore and I were suddenly back in the moment.

"Here, Lara, have mine," Myste offered, holding out his stick. "You might as well eat a piece of coal if you eat that thing Tren-Lore roasted."

The tension shattered, and Tren-Lore grinned first at his cousin, and then at me. "We shall let the lady decide."

"Very well." Myste nodded. His face had become somber. "Whose shall it be, Lara? My perfect narkanytch-"

"Overly perfect," Tren-Lore interjected, and leaned back so that he was sprawled on the floor, feet facing the fire. His roasting stick was in his hands, and he stared contemplatively up at his narkanytch.

Myste spared him a quick frown. "There is no such thing as overly perfect," he replied. Myste returned his attention to me. "So, your choices are my perfect narkanytch or Tren-Lore's piece of coal."

I grinned and lay back next to Tren-Lore. It was not a difficult choice. I wanted Tren-Lore's simply because he had made it. I reached up for his narkanytch, and without a word he tilted his stick so I could take it.

* * *

On warmer days we went outside, and with breath that looked like dragon smoke, we trudged through the snow, finding our entertainment in digging forts, snow fights, and sledding. I came to look forward to the evenings, for the ladies of the kitchen would take turns telling stories. Everyone would gather about the fire, and with steaming mugs of berryroot cordial in hand, we would listen breathlessly to the wondrous tales. When spring came, cold no longer drove the women of the kitchen to huddle around the hearth during the evenings. It was the end of stories, and the end of Myste's visit. Both events saddened me, but Myste's departure was hardest of all.

It was the day before Myste was set to leave. The three of us were sitting in a line on the table in the secret room.

"What if King Kiris finds out you left?" I asked, pursing my lips in worry.

Myste looked across Tren-Lore to where I sat. "Then I can explain to dear Uncle Kiris that since I did not attend my welcoming party, I thought it might be bad form to attend my farewell party."

Tren-Lore laughed and shook his head. "We will not need to explain anything to him, because there is no way he will notice that we are not there. With the royal family of Hemlizar here and the nobles to deal with, Myste and I will be the least likely people to be on his mind."

The king of Hemlizar and his family had arrived unexpectedly the morning before. They were traveling through to Nara Vit, and had been caught in a thunderstorm that had forced them to seek the solace of Caladore. King Kiris had given them a warm welcome and invited them to stay for the celebration being held the next day. They had graciously accepted his offer.

"So let us all meet at the dragon fountain about..." Tren-Lore paused in thought and stared briefly at the ceiling. "About five songs into the party. We can go from there."

"The dragon fountain, then." I nodded and leapt off the table. I could not stay long that day, because the preparations for the celebration required every hand in the kitchen. I had managed to slip away on the ploy of dumping the washing water, but already the time which had elapsed since my departure would have been enough to empty eight washing tubs.

Hurrying back to the kitchen, I thought eagerly ahead to that night. Instead of attending the party, we were going to the riverbank for a bonfire. I could scarcely wait! I leapt down the last few stairs and bounded along the hallway to the kitchen. I burst through the inner door and grabbed the washing basin. Hastening into the main kitchen, I replaced the washing tub and was set to work by one of the other ladies before Flock or Sophie had even noticed I had returned.

* * *

A group of servants' children was gathered on the outskirts of the garden, and only a trickle of noise from the party could be heard. Flock was standing on a marble bench, and her voice rose loudly over the group.

"We are going to play Barlem's Hunt. Rathum." She pointed at him. "Quarin, annndddd..." She pressed a finger to her cheek as though she were seriously considering her next choice. "Lara. You three are Barlems. The rest of us are going to hide. I will shout when you can come and find us." She leapt from the bench, and her chestnuts curls sprung wildly. "Cover your eyes," she ordered us.

Rathum and Quarin exchanged a helpless glance, and then turned to do as she had bid them. I frowned at her, but put my hands over my eyes. I thought that Flock probably liked playing dictator more than she liked playing any of the actual games she decided upon. Rathum and Quarin were soundless beside me. I wondered if they had left. I did not understand why any of us listened to Flock's bossy commands. I parted my fingers slightly and through the crack, I could see that they were still there.

I shifted from one foot to other, scuffing my feet on the gravel path. I wanted Flock to give the signal. As soon as she did, I would make my way to the dragon fountain under the guise of hunting for the others. Then, Tren-

Lore, Myste and I could be off for our bonfire! What was taking Flock so long? I parted my fingers again and looked about. There was no one in sight. They must all be hidden by now. Why had Flock not called for us? I sighed audibly, and as though imitating my gusty release of air, the soft spring wind stirred my skirts so they shifted restlessly about my legs.

"Bar-lem!" Flock shouted from somewhere far off to my left.

At last! I removed my hands from my face and set off toward the dragon fountain. I arrived to find that Myste was already there. Tren-Lore was nowhere to be found.

"Hello," Myste said as I emerged from the hedges that lined the path.

He was sitting on the edge of the fountain, dressed in a deep red tunic edged with gold stitching. Behind him, the sun was setting in a glorious display of color. The stones that surrounded the fountain were bathed in pink light, and the dragon itself seemed to glow with the final radiance of the daytime's orb. The carved creature's shadow stretched impressively across the ground, powerful wings spread wide, the shadow of its noble head ending nearly at my feet. I stared at the sight in awe, entirely entranced. "Hello," I replied vaguely without taking my eyes off the statue.

Myste glanced behind him, squinting into the sunlight. "It looks very grand."

"Yes," I agreed, and came to sit on the edge of the fountain. "I love this fountain. It seems magical, like it should be part of a story."

Myste muttered an agreement, and for a time neither one of us said anything. The only sound was the melody of leaping water. I curled my toes in my shoes, feeling vaguely uncomfortable in this unusual silence. I could feel Myste glance at me several times.

He cleared his throat. "Ah, Lara, I have something that I want to talk to you - well, tell you about, I guess." He was nervously twisting his ring about his finger.

I looked up at him in puzzlement, and our eyes met. His gaze was full of emotions that I could not even begin to name. I was suddenly very aware of how closely we were sitting, and of the warmth of his knee against mine. I willed him to make a joke or do something to break the tension. "What is it?" I asked with soft uncertainty.

His eyes flickered to my lips as I formed the sounds of my question. It was the briefest of glances, but all at once, I felt entirely overwhelmed. I looked swiftly down at my hands and Myste rose abruptly. It was an instant relief, as though the air of normalcy had rushed back to fill the gap that had been created. I glanced up as he paced before me.

"It is nothing very impor..." he trailed off. "Well, no, well to me it is, but..." He rubbed his hand over his mouth. "But telling you will not really...." He exhaled a long, calming breath and stared at the ground.

I watched Myste in uneasy confusion. A clue to explain his strange behavior could not even be gained from the expression upon his face, for he was standing in the shadow of the dragon and the details of his figure were lost in its shadow. For a shocking instant, my mind suggested that perhaps he was going to declare ardent feelings for me. I dismissed this immediately. Such things were saved for heroes in stories, and this was not a story, nor was Myste a hero. He was simply Myste, my friend, Tren-Lore's cousin.

"Myste?" I asked tensely.

He straightened, and I was once more in his view. He wiped his hands on the sides of his breeches. "Lara," he began, "for what it is worth, I wanted to tell you that I really li-"

Just then the sound of gravelly footfalls came to my ears and I twisted eagerly to see if it was Tren-Lore. Myste stopped speaking abruptly. "Oh, sorry, Myste," I said as I turned back to him. "I just thought I heard Tren-Lore coming. What were you saying?"

He shook his head and gestured to the path, which emerged behind me. "Nothing. You were right. Tren-Lore is here."

"Hello," sounded the familiar voice.

I rose and turned to find Tren-Lore approaching us. I smiled widely, and he grinned wolfishly back at me

"Sorry I am late," he apologized, removing his crown from his head. "Father wanted me to meet the princess of Hemlizar, and it took me a little while to convince Nahanni that she wanted to entertain the princess in my place. Are we ready to go?"

I nodded vigorously, and Tren-Lore led the way from the garden. I fell in pace with Myste, who had not spoken since Tren-Lore's arrival. "What were you going to say?" I asked him curiously.

Myste looked ahead at his cousin, and then back at me. The corner of his lips bent in a mocking smile. "It would not have mattered to you. It was just another one of my jokes. Tren-Lore," he called, "did you bribe or threaten Nahanni into diverting the princess?"

This comment marked the end of Myste's strange behavior. For the rest of the night he was his old self, boisterous and happy, making jokes out of nearly everything that was said. He told us stories that he insisted were true, but which were so funny and impossible that his use of an actual language was the only factor that gave them any hint of reality.

I said good-bye to him that night, as I would not see him in the morning. It was a sorrowful parting, and as I lay in bed that night I felt as though I had rocks of sadness resting upon my chest. I closed my eyes and waited for the oblivion of sleep to chisel away my melancholy.

The next morning I felt much better, and upon meeting Tren-Lore in the secret room, my mood was revived entirely.

He greeted me with, "Let's go to the fort."

I eagerly agreed, and we headed for the stables. It was a glorious day outside and the air was so warm it could have belonged to the fair months of summer. We rode out into the forest and a playful breeze tossed about the sweet smell of flowers. From somewhere in the depths of the woods, a bird trilled a repeated song of happiness. New growth covered the ground and the trees seemed to course with energy that burst from them in a zenith of soft green buds.

"Do you suppose that the fort will have finished itself over the winter?" I teased as we rode into the forest. I stole a sideways glance at Tren-Lore.

He was grinning and shaking his head. "You are as bad as Myste." He tugged at Storm Wing's reins as the horse twisted his neck to snatch a mouthful of new foliage. "And we *are* going to finish the fort this summer."

I smiled into the woods. I was so happy to be outside again, riding through such verdant splendor at the side of my best friend. "I like the new book you gave me," I remarked after a period of contented silence. "Not as good as *Rayn,* but I still like it."

I had finished the last *Rayn* book almost a fortnight ago. I had closed the book and held it against my chest for a while, feeling full of images but empty with sadness. It had been like losing a friend. In many ways, similar to how I felt when Myste left. Tren-Lore had promptly handed me a new novel about a rogue knight and a damsel in distress.

We discussed the new book and reminisced about Rayn's adventures until we reached the river and dismounted. Venst strained against its banks. The rising river had taken the ground that had once belonged only to the trees, and now they stood, caressing the Aquara with their branches. A tree further back had fallen, and stretched out into the water. The river rushed over its top, pulling at its limbs and leaves, making them wave desperately from beneath the sun-dappled surface of Venst. It was breathtakingly beautiful and frightening all at the same time: deadly power masked with such loveliness.

Tren-Lore grimaced at the high water as he tethered our horses. "I wonder where the boat has gotten to."

I was about to suggest that we check downriver when an angry voice cut me off. "What are you doing here?"

We both turned to stare in shock as Yolis came stalking towards us. He was dressed in his usual finery, but the effect of the attractive clothing and handsome face was lost in the torrent of rage his countenance expressed. In a clearing, just removed from the main path, a picnic was spread upon the ground and Kella was sitting amidst the food and dishes. She blushed furiously as she fumbled with the buttons of her dress. I could clearly see her white corset against the green of the forest. Kella and Yolis! I did not have any more time to be surprised, for Yolis was before Tren-Lore and I, looking very threatening.

"Leave," he said in a low voice, his hands clenched at his sides.

I took an involuntary step back. Tren-Lore stood his ground and stared impassively at Yolis. "Fine," Tren-Lore said quietly, "but I am sure Father will be very interested to hear about the lovely outing you two are having."

Yolis took a step forward, but Tren-Lore did not move. The brothers regarded each other in a silence that bristled with hostility.

"Empty threats," Yolis snapped dismissively. "Need I remind you that you too are in the woods consorting with a serving wench?"

"Do not call her that, Yolis," Tren-Lore replied coldly, and then his lips bent into a sharp, close-lipped smile. "Anyway, we were just going for a ride. What were you two doing?"

"Yolis!" Kella protested in alarm. She had come forth from the clearing and was standing a few feet away, gripping one of the trees as though she needed the support. "Make him promise not to tell."

Yolis glanced at her, and back at Tren-Lore. "You shall have his honored pledge," Yolis growled. "I promise."

He lunged at Tren-Lore. With one hand, Yolis grabbed the front of his brother's tunic, and in the next instant he had slammed his other hand into Tren-Lore's face. Tren-Lore brought his foot up and kicked Yolis in the stomach. He tumbled backward, taking Tren-Lore with him. Leaping to his feet, Yolis viciously kicked his brother in the chest. Tren-Lore stifled a cry, and I let out a silent sob of fear. Pulling Tren-Lore to his feet, Yolis punched him in the stomach. Tren-Lore doubled over, and the first Prince of Caladore brought his knee up into his brother's face. Tren-Lore fell to the ground in a bloody heap.

"Please, please stop it!" I pleaded.

Yolis whirled around. "Stay out of this!"

"But you could hurt him," I cried.

"Hurt him?" Yolis laughed harshly. "That is the point."

Seeing that his brother's attention was turned to me, Tren-Lore scrambled onto the tree that had fallen across the river, seeking to put distance between himself and his brother. He balanced there, his hands on his knees, breathing hard. Blood ran freely from his nose, and from a deep cut just above his jaw. Discolored patches marked the bruises that were beginning to form on his forehead and cheek.

"Do you think her parents will send her to work at the sanctuary?" Tren-Lore asked in an antagonizing voice, wiping his mouth with the back of his hand.

Yolis turned sharply. It was the response of a predator hearing the movements of his prey. "End you," he snarled, and leapt at Tren-Lore.

The whole scene seemed to happen so slowly. Yolis and Tren-Lore grappled, and then suddenly Tren-Lore was falling backwards. Yolis grabbed at Tren-Lore's arm, but caught only his shirt. The sound of ripping cloth came just before the sickening crack of Tren-Lore's head meeting a branch that was thrust from the water by the fallen tree. Tren-Lore toppled into the Aquara's abode, and the river swallowed him whole.

There was a moment of absolute silence. All reactions seemed to be battering against a wall of impenetrable shock. We all stared at the river as it crashed against the tree, stared at the very spot where Tren-Lore had just been consumed by Venst. Suddenly, the wall crumbled. Panic broke upon me and I was screaming Tren-Lore's name. I tried to run forward, but something jerked me back.

"Lara, no! You will be killed!" It was Kella's voice, shrill in my ears. She was holding onto my upper arms. "Yolis, do something!"

Yolis sunk to his knees, apparently completely stunned. He gazed at the water, not hearing Kella's words.

"Let go!" I cried, struggling against her. The world around me moved in a blur as I thrashed against her grip.

She was sobbing, telling me over and over again that I would be killed, and hysterically shrieking at Yolis, "Save him!"

"Let – go!" I yelled, and kicked back at her.

My foot connected with something and I was suddenly free. I lurched forward, my fingers sweeping the ground before I regained my balance and started running for the river. The water must have been like winter's touch, but terror dulled my senses. I was in past my waist when suddenly the full wrath of the river's current took hold of my legs and swept them from beneath me. My head went under and all sound ceased. My eyes were open, but it was a moment of oblivion. It was too dark and too cold. I could not see or think. There was pain. I jarred to reality. My fingers were touching something soft. I seized it, and my hand closed about cloth. Kicking hard, fighting against the water and my skirts, I burst into the blinding light of day. The image of gray water and green trees was before me, and someone was grabbing at the back of my dress, hauling me out of the water.

I knelt on the riverbank, gulping air, my left hand still clutching the neck of Tren-Lore's tunic. His face was gray and his eyes stared blankly at nothing. I had seen such a gaze before.

"He is dead!" Kelladyn's shrill words pierced me. "Yolis, he is dead."

Dead. The word hit my mind with a bloody violence that drove me into the past. I crouched in the doorway to my mother's room, the taste of stale bread lingering in my mouth. I watched as she laid motionless, one of her arms hanging limply off the bed. Her face was ashen gray. She was looking at me ... watching me with a gaze that would not waver, with eyes that would not blink. Dead eyes. When had her eyes stopped seeing me? When had she died?

I tried to breathe, again and again and again. I flailed my arms wildly, trying to fling away the horror that clung to me. "No! No!" I screamed. It was such burning horror. "No! She is not! She cannot be dead!" My lungs did not seem to take in air. I fell against the cold mud and brought my knees to my chest. Scalding pain coursed my cheeks, and I tried to expel the agony with helpless noise. My throat constricted and my body shook.

"He is breathing. He is *not* dead. Ascendants curse you, Kelladyn! Why did you say that? Calm her down, and then get her back to the castle. I am going ahead with Tren-Lore."

"No, Yolis! Do not leave me."

There was the sound of horse's hoofs on soft turf, and then the silence of unconsciousness as the world slowly faded to black.

Chapter Eight
Monsters of the Darkness

When I awoke next, I found myself in my own bed. My wet dress had been removed, and in its place was a warm sleeping gown. My back hurt and I dimly remembered colliding with something hard under the water. Probably the tree, I thought dully. I could hear Sophie humming softly to herself in the kitchen. The room was filled with dying light, and the memories that had returned to me on the riverbank filled my mind once more. My pain was great enough that not even tears came. I wanted nothing more than for the darkness to return and fill my being.

The humming stopped. Sophie poked her head in the door. "Oh, you are up, my dear? I will bring you a bite to eat then."

She vanished from sight before I could tell her that I was not hungry. I stared at the wall. I traced the curves of the stones with my eyes. In a few moments Sophie returned bearing hot bread, cold meat and cheese. She handed me the platter.

I looked down at the food in my lap. "I am not hungry," I told her quietly.

"There, now." Sophie sat beside me and brushed my hair back from my face. Her hand was warm. "You have had a hard day. Imagine falling into Venst at this time of the year! It will be a wonder if you do not catch a chill. I absolutely forbid you to play by the river any more. When Kella carried you in here, all limp and wet, well...." She put her hand to her chest and shook her head. "I think my heart stopped, child, I really do. And when I think about what would have happened if Kella had not been there to save you...just stay away from that river."

I frowned and picked at the meat on my plate. Putting a tiny piece in my mouth, I chewed slowly. Obviously, the story Kella had told Sophie was not what had really happened. I had a moment of brief amusement as I thought of Flock's reaction, had she heard the truth about her sister and Yolis.

"That is a good girl," Sophie patted my leg. "You eat that up. I will get you a mug of berryroot cordial to warm you."

She left, and I set my plate on the bedside table. When Sophie returned, I pretended to be sleeping. I heard her quietly set the mug next to my uneaten food. I lay with my eyes closed, surrounded by a darkness that was entirely my own.

The next morning I returned to my life as though nothing had happened. I went about my chores without complaint or comment and maintained a stolid countenance. I did not want anyone to suspect my grief. If they knew, then I would have to explain why I felt as I did, and this would only make the pain worse. The realization that my mother was dead had cut my mind so that it bled with dark emotions. It was a wound that would not stop bleeding, and it felt as though my body had been filled with crimson agony. If I was silent, if I kept my mouth closed, then the pain would remain encased within me and could not gush forth into the limitless void of the world.

A plate tumbled from my hand. It smashed loudly, and everyone in the kitchen turned to look. Not even their stares tore me from the foggy world I was living in. I bent and began to numbly pick up the shards of pottery. Sophie rushed to my side, and gently guided me to my feet. "Come with me, Lara," she whispered in my ear, and then in a louder voice said, "Flock, come pick up this mess."

Flock made a disgusted noise and reluctantly did as she was told. Calmly, Sophie guided me into our room and sat me on the bed. She seated herself beside me, and wrapped her arm around me. "What has happened to make you act this way?" she asked softly.

"Nothing," I mumbled.

"Lara." Sophie sighed and ran her hand over my hair. "Something is obviously wrong. If you tell me what it is, I can help you. But if I do not know, then-"

I leapt to my feet. "Nothing is wrong!" The fear of discovery made my voice sound angry.

Sophie rose, reaching a hand out to me. "Lara, dear, come and sit..."

I did not wait to hear the rest of her sentence. I fled from the room and dashed through the kitchen, leaving a wake of confused women staring after me. The moment I had slammed the door of the outer room I burst into tears. I could think of only one thing. I needed Tren-Lore. He would find some way of making this better.

I had received a note from him yesterday saying that he was completely recovered and returning to training. He had wanted to meet at noon, but I needed him now. It was still morning; he was bound to be down at the practice field. I set off at a run. I was soon in the garden, and the sound of shouting led me straight to the practice field. I beheld a group of boys paired off for sparring. They were all so involved in the exercise that no one noticed me. My breathing was ragged and tears blurred my vision. With a watery gaze, I desperately searched for Tren-Lore. I found him near the middle of the group, fighting with a heavyset boy. Tren-Lore's face was still bruised, but his movements did not appear to be hampered by any of his injuries. He moved with his usual skill, and his expression was one of calm determination. His opponent, however, looked rather harried.

I was lost for a moment. I wanted to call out to Tren-Lore, but I·knew that to do so would draw the attention of the entire group of boys. The folly of my plan was suddenly clear to me. I did not know what to do. All at once, Tren-Lore glanced in my direction. His eyes fell upon me and his arm froze, his blow remaining undelivered. The boy he was fighting stopped too. The boy's chest was heaving, and his arm wavered as he held his sword in a blocking position. "Tren-Lore?" the boy asked tentatively.

Tren-Lore glanced at him. "I am leaving," he told the boy, and dropped his weapon on the ground.

"What?" the boy exclaimed, still holding his sword as though he expected Tren-Lore to come rushing back and continue the fight. "What do you mean?"

Tren-Lore did not reply. He said nothing to any inquires that were shouted after him as he strode off the practice field. I retreated down the path to wait for him. He arrived in mere moments, sweating and still breathing hard. For once the dark blue of his eyes did not shroud his emotions. He was clearly worried. "Let us go to the secret room," he said, and started toward the castle.

I followed him, grateful that he had chosen not to take up the matter of my unexpected arrival while we were so near to the practice field. We walked swiftly through the castle and climbed the stairs to the secret room. It was a relief to enter the familiar chamber. The empty hearth, the table littered with books, the shafts of sunlight cutting through the dusty air: all these things were the cool hand of reminiscence upon the fevered brow of my current turmoil. Tren-Lore shut the door with a soft thud. I turned and we stared at each other. This time his face was unreadable. "Is your mother dead?" he asked quietly.

The shock of his question made my knees weak. I reached out and blindly groped for the wall. Finding the cold stone beneath my fingertips, I slid to the ground and huddled against it. My body heaved with grief. "Yes," I sobbed. "H-how..."

Tren-Lore came and sat beside me, his back against the wall, his elbows resting on his knees. "When you first came to Caladore, I knew something must have happened to your parents, or you would not have had to stay with Lady Grim. But you never said anything, so I never asked. You...well, if you wanted to tell me you would have, right? And then down by the river, I heard you screaming and I just..." His words crumbled into silence and he paused. "My mother is dead, too," he said finally, his voice flat. "She died when I was eight. She drowned."

"Tren-Lore," I sobbed. "It hurts so much."

"I know," he replied in a tightly controlled tone. "But at least you have Sophie."

It was true. I did have Sophie. She was just like my mother.

Tren-Lore moved and awkwardly put his arms around me. He drew me close, and I clung thankfully to him, weeping into the soft material of his shirt. He said nothing, but his arms were warm about me.

* * *

That night I sat silently by the fire, recalling the day's events. I fervently wished that I could take back every action I saw there. Why had I cried like that in front of Tren-Lore? I had been such a girl, so weak and sniveling. Tren-Lore would not respect that. I dug my toes into the bottom of my shoes and wondered how I would ever face him again. The sound of rustling skirts came from behind me. I glanced over my shoulder and found Kella's form emerging from the dimness of the candlelit kitchen. She seated herself in the chair beside me, and I was awash in the smell of lavender.

Kella leaned toward me, tucking her chestnut curls behind her ears. "How are you feeling, Lara?"

"Fine," I replied sullenly, wishing that she would go away and leave me alone.

"Oh, good," she crooned, reaching over and laying one hand on my leg. "Everyone has been *so* worried about you." She was smiling warmly at me, but there was rigidity in her body that would have been akin to someone sitting on pins and needles.

I rubbed my temples. Kella's perfume was giving me a slight headache. "I am not going to tell anyone about you and Yolis, if that is what you are worried about," I said.

Kella's facial features jumped in surprise, and I watched as she visibly struggled to return them to her previous look of demure concern. "Really, Lara." She tucked her hair behind her ears again. "What a suspicious nature you have. I came to see how you were...but since you mentioned it..."

I rolled my eyes. It was like talking to an older and even more transparent version of Flock.

"I am sure," Kella continued, "that you and the prince want to continue your, your ah... friendship in privacy, just as Yolis and I would like to remain discrete about our love for one another." She was smiling at her lap, a blush of pleasure upon her cheeks.

I suddenly remembered the conversation I had overheard Yolis having with his friends that day on the practice field. Last spring the remarks had meant little to me, but all at once they made sense. He must have been talking about Kelladyn. I felt terrible for her. Poor Kella! I had to tell her what I had heard.

"Kella, I-"

"Good, then," she interrupted and rose, smoothing out her skirt and adjusting her bodice. "I am so glad we are in agreement." She patted me on the head. "You feel better now."

As the days passed, I could find no refuge from the grief that permeated my being. I missed Tren-Lore horribly. After that terrible morning of hysterics, I was afraid to see him again. I was afraid that he would not want to see me. I spent most of my time in my room, lying lifelessly on my bed, struggling to understand my mother's death. Sophie attributed my behavior to illness and treated me as though I were suffering from a sickness. She fussed over me and insisted that I drink all sorts of horrible-tasting tonics. My cure was not to be found in medicines, however; it was to be found in Tren-Lore. His message came early one morning, disguised as an order from Nahanni.

"Lara," Sophie had whispered.

My name hooked my consciousness and pulled me up through the heavy waters of sleep. I awakened slowly to the blurry sight of Sophie's figure leaning over me. Rubbing my eyes, I smiled up at her. Sophie's hair was not yet in its customary bun, and wisps of her graying locks were sticking up all over her head. She put a hand to my cheek and returned the smile. "You are looking better this morning."

My smile vanished as reality crushed the merciful oblivion that had been granted to me for those few fleeting moments.

"I am glad to see it," Sophie told me as she pulled my covers back. "Princess Nahanni has summoned you to the royal chambers. She wants you to act as one of her Ladies in Waiting."

I wondered if it was truly Nahanni who had sent the message. Maybe it was Tren-Lore. But if it was him... I pulled my blankets back up around my chin and turned on my side. I did not want to think about it.

Sophie patted my leg. "Come on, now, up you get. You do not want to keep the princess waiting." The kindly woman began to move about the room, preparing for the day. "Poor little dear is probably lonely for some company her own age. Although I am sorry that she chose today of all days to summon you."

I sluggishly heaved myself out of bed. The floor was cold against my bare feet. "Why?" I asked without a great deal of interest.

Sophie finished buttoning her dress. She glanced at me as she moved over to the mirror and picked up one of the hairpins that lay on the table. "Because," she said, both hands working to tame her hair, "if you were feeling better, we could have used you in the kitchen. It is Prince Tren-Lore's Summer Year, and there is to be a party tonight."

* * *

I had never been up to the chambers that housed the royal family, and as I walked down the long hallway that led to the giant rounded doors, I felt quite intimidated. Everything was so quiet. I tried to move as softly as I could. The massive doors were soon looming before me. My fist hovered over the wood, and squeezing my toes in my shoes, I rapped lightly upon the door. My feeble plea for entrance was heard at once. Nahanni opened the door and scooted out into the passageway. The door thudded shut behind her.

Nahanni glanced about covertly, and then leaned forward to whisper, "You are supposed to meet Tren-Lore in the stable. He said that I was to make you swear you would come. Do you swear?" she demanded furtively, her blue eyes wide.

I smiled in spite of myself. Tren-Lore and Nahanni had their disagreements, but when Tren-Lore chose to include his little sister in what he was doing, Nahanni was always eager to perform the task perfectly. Tren-Lore must have impressed upon her the importance of secrecy, for she was being overly clandestine.

"All right," I consented. "I swear."

She nodded gravely and slipped back into the royal chambers. I made my way down to the stables. With each step, a new thought rang through my body. Maybe Tren-Lore still wanted to be my friend? Maybe he had realized that I was not good enough to be his friend and he wanted to tell me in person? Maybe, maybe...

As I approached the stables I could see that he was waiting outside, leaning on the wall near the door. He had the reins of Storm Wing and Paence in his hand. The big warhorse was restlessly pawing at the ground, and Paence was nuzzling Tren-Lore's neck in the hopes of charming some sugar from the young prince. At this first sight of him, happiness bloomed within me, but it quickly wilted into trepidation. What was the purpose of this meeting?

"Joyous Summer Year," I mumbled, staring at my feet.

"Thank you," Tren-Lore replied. "I have a surprise for you."

I looked up at him, and our eyes met. He was grinning broadly and I involuntarily smiled back. My unease was vanishing. Nothing in his gaze had changed.

I reached out for Paence's reins. "What is it?"

Tren-Lore tossed the reins to me and leapt onto Storm Wing's back. "I have to show you."

I stuck my foot into one of the stirrups and mounted Paence. Tren-Lore led the way out of the castle. It felt wonderful to ride again. When Tren-Lore glanced back at me, I was smiling widely. He grinned and nudged Storm Wing into a canter. When we had left Caladore far behind and the forest's edge was coming closer, Tren-Lore slowed Storm Wing to a walk. I reined in Paence as well.

Tren-Lore glanced at me. "I missed you, you know," he said simply.

"I am sorry!" The words burst from my mouth and all at once I was explaining everything. I explained how I had been ashamed of my behavior, how I thought that he would not like me anymore, how I could not stop thinking about my mother, how Sophie had explained my behavior with sickness, and most of all, how sad I felt. When at last I slumped in my saddle, spent and silent, I felt as though I had unbound the wound that had been bleeding within me. The scarlet pain had spilled forth, but it was not as endless as I had imagined. I felt drained but more at ease than I had felt in a long time.

The river was before us now, and I was abruptly reminded of what Tren-Lore had told me about his mother's death. I looked down at my saddle. "I... I am sorry about your mother."

Tren-Lore slid off Storm Wing's back. I could see the muscles in his jaw moving. He was clenching his teeth. For an instant, I thought that perhaps I should not have said anything. "So am I," he said finally. "Come on," he beckoned to me. "The boat is over here."

"The boat!" I exclaimed, and eagerly dismounted. I was growing more and more curious about the surprise Tren-Lore had for me. I tethered Paence next to Storm Wing. The giant warhorse was already ripping at the leaves around him. The mare gave me an imploring look. I patted her neck in amusement. "Maybe he will grow on you," I told her, and then turned to hurry after Tren-Lore.

He was sitting on the edge of the old boat. It was run up on shore and even more battered than it had been last summer. I wondered if it was even going to float.

"Get in, and I will push us out." Tren-Lore stood and moved aside so that I could clamber into the rickety vessel.

I pulled my skirts up around my knees and climbed over the edge. I felt the boat shift sluggishly to one side. "Where did you find it?" I asked as I settled myself at one end.

"Down river," Tren-Lore grunted. He pushed the boat into the water and leapt in. "Way down river."

"Is it going to sink?" I asked pleasantly. Water had already seeped through my shoes, and my toes made a funny squishing noise as I pressed them into my stockings.

Tren-Lore reached down and grabbed a small bucket from the bottom of the boat. "That depends on how good you are at bailing?"

"The very best there ever was," I told him, and held my palms out in a gesture of helpless perfection. "I am the Mortex of bailing."

Tren-Lore laughed and tossed me the bucket. "All right, Mortex, start bailing then."

I leaned over and scraped the bucket along the bottom of the boat. "I will start bailing when you start paddling." I glanced at him through my eyelashes, a goading smile upon my lips. He hated it when I interchanged the words 'paddling' and 'rowing'. As he had gravely explained to me one day last summer, they were entirely different movements. Tren-Lore noticed my teasing expression and raised his eyebrows at me. I tried to look innocent as I met his gaze, but I am sure I did little to conceal my true mirth.

He leaned back and grabbed hold of the oars. His face was creased in a broad grin. "Fine, you bail and I will paddle." He set about rowing, and I waged a diligent war against the intruding Aquara. The creak of the oars and the scrape of my bucket were the only accompaniment to the music of the rushing river. "My mother laughed a lot," he said suddenly.

I stopped bailing for a moment and looked up at him. The wind ruffled his raven hair, and his blue eyes were focused on the far riverbank. I doubted he was even seeing the green and blue matted shore. He had a far-off look, as though he walked in some other realm, where fiction was reality.

"And she smelled like wild roses and she loved the rain. Father would always have something that he needed to teach Yolis or do with Yolis," Tren-Lore said, pulling hard on the oars, 'so they would be locked away in the castle, but Mother always wanted to be outside. We would go exploring together all the time. She knew so much about plants and animals. And in the middle of summer, when the nights grew warm, we would sleep on the ground under the stars. She said it reminded her of what was important. After she died, I slept outside for a fortnight. Doing the things that we did together comforted me. I guess it still does." He laughed in bitter amusement. "Everyone thought I had lost my mind, but sleeping outside reminded me of her. It made me feel like there was still part of her with me. And it helped *me* realize what was really important. After that fortnight, things were never the same again."

As he finished speaking, I realized that I was still poised with my empty bucket in hand. I scooped some more water from the boat and splashed it over the edge. I could find nothing to say, but I did not feel that Tren-Lore really expected a reply.

He paused in his rowing. "What was your mother like?"

My throat clenched, and my eyes burned with unshed sorrow. I stared hard at a crack in the bottom of the boat. I studied the water seeping through, tried to concentrate solely upon the moving shimmer of translucence through which the wood's image changed and curved.

"She told me wonderful stories," I said, the words escaping quickly before they could be strangled by the grief gripping my throat.

Tren-Lore began to row again. "Would you tell me one? But only if you want to."

"Yes," I sniffed, looking up at him, "I want to tell you." Wiping my cheek with the back of my hand, I told him the tale of the Sorcerer Mortex and the weather spells. I had nearly completed the story when our boat bumped up against the shore of the island that was to be the future home of the fort. I looked about in perplexity. "What type of surprise is this?"

"The type that is not a surprise if I tell you what it is. Come on." He dropped his oars and began to clamber out of the boat.

124

When we had both successfully gotten out of the boat without falling into the water or crumbling the rickety vessel with our weight, Tren-Lore tromped off into the cool forest. I followed with a great deal of curiosity, holding my skirts up so that they would not snag on any brambles. As we passed the familiar landmarks - a stump into which Tren-Lore had carved an arrow, a tree whose mounded root formed the entrance to an animal's burrow, and the crumbling remains of a small stone structure - I became sure that we were headed for the site of the fort. The usual ring of trees soon came into sight, but something was different. Built in the limbs of the four center trees was a platform. I stopped and stared, my hands covering my open mouth. "A fort!" I cried, beginning to jump up and down. "You actually built a fort!"

He grinned roguishly and held out his hands. "Was there any doubt?"

I laughed and ran toward the circle of trees. Tren-Lore was close behind me. We stopped a few feet away. I shaded my eyes and looked at the platform high in the trees. "It is wonderful! Did you do this all by yourself?"

He nodded. "For you."

For an instant I could scarcely believe that I was living such a moment, standing at the side of such an amazing person. He was my best friend. He had made this for me. I felt like crying again, but this time my tears would have been tears of happiness. "Thank you," I said reverently. This meant more to me than he would ever know.

Our gaze met, and without even looking at his bent lips, I knew he was smiling. "I am glad you like it." He gestured to the fort with a slight bow and extension of his arm. "Well, shall we?"

I nodded eagerly and we ran toward the fort, bounding up to the circle of trees. There were pieces of wood secured to the trunk of one of them. Tren-Lore scrambled up easily and then, lying on his stomach, hung his head over the edge to watch my clumsy progression. "You are very slow," he commented.

"Tren-Lore!" I exclaimed in irritation, trying to keep hold of my skirts and the tree at the same time. "You put on this dress and then see how fast you climb."

He crawled back from the edge, grinning impertinently. "No, thank you."

"Barlem."

"Double Barlem."

I reached up and caught the edge of the fort. Throwing my leg over the platform, I pulled myself up with a grunt. "That does not even make sense. What is a double Barlem supposed to be?" I turned and peered down the way we had just come. The space rushed beneath me until it collided with the brown earth far below. I inched away from the edge.

Tren-Lore's voice came from behind me. "Do you want to finish your story now?"

I turned and sat cross-legged. Tren-Lore was walking the length of the platform. He could take about four paces before he had to retrace his steps. I swatted at a bug that had landed on my arm. "Where were we?" I grimaced as I wiped the dead bug off my hand and onto the floor of the fort. "Oh yes, so even after the Ascendants had warned him, Mortex continued working his spells until a great storm of magic raged in the sky."

"That sounds bad," Tren-Lore replied, and swiveled to walk the other way.

I smiled as I remembered expressing a similar, more sincere sentiment to my mother. Happiness and sad remembrance braided themselves within me. I took a deep breath and tried to recall the words of the story just as my mother had told them to me.

"It stormed for twenty days, and when the rain finally stopped, the people were overjoyed. What they did not know was that it would never rain again. If you travel to the far-off reaches of the south, one day you will find yourself trudging through endless, rolling dunes of sand. You will have come to the Three Sisters. Where once there were three lush forests, there is now only desert. The people of the Three Sisters claim that the Ascendants have forsaken them, and to this day not a drop of rain has fallen from the sky."

"You know," Tren-Lore said as he sat and leaned his back against one of the four rising trunks, "my mother told me that there were actually thirteen Ascendants. She said there were Ascendants for Sorcerers and Sanysk and Healers, and other beings that I had never even heard of."

I squeezed my toes in my shoes and considered this, wrinkling my brow in thought. "Why would the sanctuary ignore the other Ascendants?"

Tren-Lore rubbed at the back of his neck and frowned. "I do not know."

We spent the rest of the day playing Mortex and making grand plans for the fort. My arrival in the kitchen was like the snap of a shutting book. All pretend was suddenly locked away, and I was returned to the real world. It was hot in the kitchen, as the ovens had undoubtedly been blazing all day. The smell of turkey made the air thick with scent, and serving women hurried from one task to another. Flock paid close attention to my return. She must have heard that I had been called to the royal chambers, and watched me out of the corner of her eye as she arranged pieces of carved meat on a massive silver platter. I could tell she was longing to ask me what it had been like serving for Nahanni.

Sophie bustled past me, jugs of milk in her hands. "Lara," she called, "can you ladle the gravy into that large bowl? It is on the counter."

I turned about on the spot, searching the counters for the large bowl she was speaking of. "Where on the counter?"

"Benya can show you, dear," she said, and then was gone across the kitchen.

Benya whisked past me and pointed to the mystery bowl Sophie had been speaking of. I dodged through the moving obstacles that were the preoccupied women of the kitchen, and set about transferring the gravy from the blackened cooking pot to the beautifully decorated bowl it was to be served in. Not for the first time, I marveled at Sophie's gravy. It ran smoothly from the ladle, thick and delicious-looking. If it had been my gravy that was to be served tonight, the dinner guests would have had to chew it or choke on the lumps. Flock was suddenly at my side. She had apparently decided that enough time had elapsed to give me the impression that she was not really interested in my life at all.

"So," she began, setting a platter of meat down with a loud thud, "I heard you were serving in the royal chambers."

"Oh, really?" I replied, dripping gravy on the counter as I moved the ladle between the pot and the bowl. I was not going to volunteer any information to Flock.

Flock glared at me, her hands moving to her hips. "Lara, do not be so coy with me. Just because you served in the royal chambers does not mean you are better than me."

"Of course not," I said easily. The ladle rasped against the metal bottom of the pot. I peered into the dark cooking cavern. I could probably get two more scoops out.

"Kella knew a girl like you once," Flock snapped, her brown eyes narrowing in spite. "She was so full of herself that her whole face swelled up, and it has stayed that way forever. My sister says the girl cries every day because she knows she will never get married. She is just too ugly." Flock hefted her tray and tilted her head to one side, a sour smile stretching her chubby cheeks. "I hope that does not happen to you, Lara."

I picked up my own bowl. "I knew a girl who lied, and warts grew all over her tongue and lips. No one would look at her, and of course, no one would marry her. I hope that does not happen to *you*, Flock."

Flock made an indignant noise and stomped away. It was only the beginning of her bad night, however, for I won twice in Barlems, and for three turns in a row she was a Pandel. I was exceedingly pleased with myself when I tromped back up to the kitchen that night, but as I lay in bed, the blackness filled with memories. I wept until sleep enfolded me in a soft embrace that quieted my mind and I found my mother not in the dark oblivion of night, but in a sun-dappled dream of days that seemed long ago. We walked hand in hand through golden grass. She told me old stories that I had loved.

"Mother," I asked, "will you tell me a new story now?"

She smiled down upon me, and her pink lips parted with a reply that I never heard, for at that moment, I awoke and found the light of day spilling upon me. The sound of Sophie's breathing came softly from the next bed, and birds trilled happily from outside the window.

Chapter Nine
Summertime

I sunk the sewing needle into the material of one of my dresses. I had put another hole in the bottom of my skirt, and Sophie had declared, "Child, if you insist upon being so hard on your clothes, then it will be you who mends them."

I pulled the thread taunt and left a generous amount of space between my old stitch and my new one. It was much faster that way. Sophie poked her head in the door. "How is your mend- Lara!" She hastened to my side and took the skirt from my hands. She frowned. "Young lady, you know that is not the proper way to sew. Small stitches, remember."

I had been sitting on my bed, but at this remark I flopped back and stared up at the ceiling. I linked my fingers over my stomach and felt it heave as I sighed. "It takes so long that way," I whined. "How about I just leave the hole? I really do not mind."

"I do mind," Sophie replied as she picked the stitching out of the dress.

"It keeps me cool," I said in defense of the hole.

"You look like a Barlem child," Sophie countered.

I smiled winningly at her. "But with a hole, there are ever so many lovely breezes."

"Lara!" Sophie exclaimed with a laugh. "What am I to do with you?" She held out the skirt.

I groaned. Sitting up, I reached for the material. Sophie caught my outstretched hand in her own hand. "Ascendants' mercy, look at your thumb!"

I stared at the blackened nail, my mind already dashing toward an acceptable explanation. It would not do to tell Sophie that I had smashed it with a hammer. These days, games were often disregarded because Tren-Lore and I had become engrossed in fort building. We wanted to have all the walls up by the end of the next week. I folded my other thumb into my palm. It bore similar bruises and I did not want to have to complicate my lie. I was not quick enough, though.

"Your other nail, too!" Sophie dropped the skirt upon the bed and I helplessly unfolded my hand and presented it for her inspection. "What did you do?"

I looked everywhere except into her eyes. "Umm, I caught them in a...door?"

Sophie raised her eyebrows. "Both of them?"

I nodded and struggled to keep my expression neutral. Sophie held my gaze in a silent interrogation.

"It hurt like anything. I think my nails might fall off soon," I said, hoping that a brush of colorful detail would give my story the pallor of credibility.

Sophie released my hands. Her countenance seemed mildly amused. "I doubt you will lose your nails, but you will have to be more careful with your thumbs...and your dresses," she added. She turned from me and moved toward the door. "Remember, small stitches."

I took hold of the skirt and slid the needle back into the material. "Medium stitches will do," I muttered to myself, and hummed one of Sophie's songs as I sewed.

* * *

Tren-Lore and I lay side by side, staring up at the canopy of trees and blue sky that was framed by the grandeur of our newly finished walls. Our fingers and mouths were strained red with the juice of the raspberries we had been eating. We smelled of summer sun, water, and happiness.

Erin Leigh Mclauchlan

"A roof would be good," Tren-Lore mused. "What do you think, my dear child?"

I promptly punched him in the shoulder. In the interval between our Summer Years, he had the brief privilege of being three years older than me and had delighted in teasing me about it.

Tren-Lore squinted at me and rubbed his shoulder. "How many days until your Summer Year?"

"Two," I replied promptly. I was very excited for my first Summer Year!

"Two?" Tren-Lore echoed, and looked back up at the sky. He chuckled softly. "The last count I took, it was four."

I shook my head. "No, because -"

"You cannot count today, and you cannot count the day it is on," Tren-Lore recited with a teasing grin upon his face.

I smiled back at him. "Right." Reaching over, I grabbed the last few raspberries from the bucket by Tren-Lore's knee. I popped them into my mouth, chewed the tart granules and asked, "Where are you planning on getting more wood?"

"I am not sure yet." He held up his arms, touching his bruised thumbs and forefingers to make a square. "Maybe we could put a trap door in the roof."

* * *

It was the smell of cooking meat that called me from my sleep, but I lay still, allowing my mind to linger in the pass which led from dreams to day. It was a moment of contentment. The pleasant smell of breakfast filled the air, and the soft touch of the sun warmed my face and arms. I could hear Sophie singing in the other room, and as the verse finished she remarked fondly, "I think that child intends to sleep through her entire Summer Year." My eyes snapped open as Sophie continued, "Will you flip these for me, Thriana? I am going to wake Lara up."

I threw back the covers and leapt out of bed. It was my first Summer Year! Sophie opened the door just as I had pulled on my dress. She stood in the entrance and

132

looked at me fondly. "And how does it feel to have lived eleven whole years?"

"Wonderful!" I declared in a swooning voice.

Sophie held out one of her hands to me. I was reminded of the very first morning we met. It seemed much longer than a year and a bit. It seemed as if I had been reaching for her hand all my life. An unbidden thought flashed into my head. Sophie loved me as much as my mother had, and I loved her in return.

"Come, dear. Breakfast will be on the table soon, and if my old mind has not failed me, there might even be some presents for you."

I had the rare privilege of sitting at the head of the table. Sophie sat beside me as the rest of the kitchen staff, including the highly irritated Flock, worked around us.

"The one in the green wrap is from me," Sophie pointed, "and the other one is from Namin."

I took Sophie's gift first and eagerly untied the bow. I let the cloth wrapping fall away from the box. Barely daring to breathe, I lifted the lid. Soft material concealed what was inside. Drawing back the folds, my heart seemed to falter under the strain of my rapture. Before me lay a doll. Her green eyes stared up at me and her delicate pink mouth curved into a smile. I smiled back. Her body was made of soft cloth and covered with a pretty green striped dress. I loved her instantly, and named her Kara after my mother, a treasured gift from my mother.

"Thank you, Sophie!" I cried, hugging her impetuously. She laughed and patted my back. I placed Kara safely in my lap and took Namin's gift in hand. It was a box much smaller than Sophie's, and I wondered for a brief moment if she had sent me candy. Giving it a little shake, I heard the contents thump softly against the inside. Perhaps one big piece of candy, I thought. I hastened to open the box and rooted through the soft cloth inside to touch upon something that felt like metal. I pulled the object from its box in puzzlement and found a ring captured between my fingers. It was made of silver, and had been wrought to look like a circle of delicate ivy. Sophie murmured something, but the distance between us was too great and I could not hear her words.

My mind had rushed back over the many leagues of distance and time to a summer long ago. The image of our garden was a blur of landscape as I turned my head down to the work my mother was doing. Her hands were in the dirt, and her Healer's Ring, her ivy ring, was verdant around her finger. It was not metal then. It was alive, and yet never wilted or suffered injury. I loved that ring, loved it for its magic, for the way it fit perfectly around my mother's slender finger. One day, she said, I would have a ring of my own.

With a jolt of pain, I was suddenly in the kitchen and Sophie had taken my hand and was leading me to our room. I was crying silently, trying to expel from my body this fresh pain.

"I told Namin," Sophie was muttering, "I told her...too soon...would have been fine without it. I would have known. Lara, darling." Sophie sat in her rocking chair and gathered me onto her lap. She rocked me gently, back and forth. "My girl, my little girl," she whispered into my hair. "Sophie is here."

I clung tightly to Sophie. I was her girl, she was here. Just like my mother, my mother. Slowly my tears stopped and my breathing slowed.

"Do you want me to put the ring away?" Sophie inquired.

My head was pressed against her chest, and I heard the words vibrate within her. I hesitated for a moment, and then my fingers closed around the ring. I could not give it up. This must have been how Tren-Lore felt when he was outside. It made me feel like part of my mother was still with me. "No, I want to wear it."

Sophie straightened in her chair. "Are you sure?"

I nodded, feeling the warm material of her dress rub against my cheek.

"Very well, then," Sophie agreed, "but it is much too big to wear on your finger. Here." She lifted me from her knees and moved across the room. Opening her trunk, she reached in and retrieved a little black bag. She withdrew a delicate silver chain. It winked merrily in the sunshine. "This was given to me many years ago, and now I want to give it to you. You can wear the ring about your neck and not worry about it slipping off your finger. You must remember that if you are going to wear this ring, it needs to be against your skin."

I bobbed my head in compliance, but not understanding. "Thank you," I said with a slight waver in my voice, and took the chain from her.

* * *

That night, the kitchen was full of children. All greeted me brightly, some of the girls hugging me in a giddy overflow of energy.

"Hello, Lara!"

"Joyous Summer Year, Lara!"

The entire evening was glazed with awe. It was hard for me to believe that all these people were here to celebrate my Summer Year. It was such a stark contrast to my life in Ekrin. It was Tren-Lore's presence that meant the most to me, however. After everyone had eaten as many cookies as they possibly could and a comparison had been made on the varying levels of berryroot stains that brightened our tongues, Sophie sent us out to play games in the garden. Tren-Lore and I slipped away before the Flock-directed fun could begin.

We ambled along the gardens and eventually settled on the edge of the dragon fountain.

"I have something for you," Tren-Lore said.

"Something for me?" I echoed in confusion.

Evening was encroaching upon the day, and the dragon's shadow enveloped us both. Tren-Lore reached to the back of his belt.

"What is it?" I demanded, my toes curling in anticipation.

The object was in his hands now, and looked very much like a dagger. He held it out to me. Reaching for it, my fingers brushed against his warm skin and then took hold of something cold. It *was* a dagger! I pulled it loose of its scabbard and held it up out of the dragon's shadow so that the last glimmers of sunlight could slide down the silver blade. The hilt was a black-hued metal that bore the inscription, *Solrium Vallent.*

"It was my mother's," Tren-Lore told me.

My grip loosened instinctually. I held the dagger with careful reverence. "Oh," I breathed, "Tren-Lore, you should keep it."

"No," he replied, his blue eyes meeting mine in a gaze that was perfectly readable, clearly full of affection. "I want you to have it."

My eyes felt hot with unshed tears. The earlier incidents of acceptance had merely been leading up to this climax of belonging. The gesture was profound. Not only was Tren-Lore giving me something that had belonged to his mother, but the gift also had the weighty significance of a centuries-old tradition. It had begun when the war against the Discontents was at its bloody apex and loyalties were crumbling as quickly as the grand walls of Kalamorian. So in this time of uncertainly, when warriors did not know who to trust, two young men exchanged blades, saying with this gesture that they gave their swords, their very lives, to one another and would fight side by side until death or victory. Generations later, this ancient gesture still retained its significance.

"Thank you," I whispered, and clutched the dagger to my chest. "I...thank you!" I threw my arms about him. For a moment he was stiff with surprise, but the instant passed and he returned my embrace with a reassuring tightness. We drew apart slowly. The slightest of smiles played on Tren-Lore's lips, and his brow creased in an expression that almost looked like puzzlement, but not quite. I did not know what to make of it. I let my hands slide from his arms. "What?" I demanded, searching his eyes for a clue to his thoughts.

He shook his head, and his smile broadened. "Joyous Summer Year, Lara."

I grinned. "Should we go see what the others are doing?"

"Definitely." He pushed himself up from the fountain.

We strode down the path together and I ran my finger down the carving on the hilt of my dagger, feeling the strange words under my touch. "What does the inscription mean?" I asked suddenly.

"What?" Tren-Lore started.

"The inscription, solrium vallent, is that how you say it? Well, what does it mean?"

Tren-Lore shook himself. "Oh. Umm, well..." He raked his fingers through his hair. "My mother told me that it was part of the Old Tongue, and that there was no direct translation. The closest she could come was 'self hero'."

I made an unintelligible sound that was meant to denote a perplexed sort of comprehension. Letting my eyes wander about the shadowy garden, I tried to deduce the meaning of such an engraving.

Understanding my utterance as well as he would have understood a spoken question, Tren-Lore commented, "I think it has to do with depending on yourself, or maybe being your own hero."

I tucked the dagger into the waist of my skirts and pulled my bodice down over it. My mother's ring moved against my skin, feeling warm and familiar. Both the ring and dagger felt as though they had always been part of me, although the message upon the dagger was foreign. My mind held the two words apart as contradictions. In stories, heroes were the people who saved others, not themselves. I was about to ask Tren-Lore what he thought of this, when a voice shouted jovially from a few paces behind, "Barlem on Lara and Prince Tren-Lore!"

We both whirled about to find the dim form of Rathum standing triumphantly in the middle of the path. Tren-Lore and I glanced at one another. His countenance was mirthful, but he was trying to hide that from Rathum. He leaned closer to me and remarked under his breath, "I told you that you were a Barlem."

"Come on," Rathum exclaimed, and gestured for us to follow him, "Flock and a few of the others still need to be caught."

He set off at a run, and I glanced over my shoulder at Tren-Lore. "Double Barlem," I said and bounded after Rathum.

"What does that even mean?" he yelled after me, his tone rich with amusement.

I did not answer him, but heard the quick tread of his feet as he followed Rathum and me down the path. Our laughter and shouts filled the garden with a tangible excitement. It seemed as though the remnants of the day lingered forever, and when at last the darkness came and Sophie called us in, we returned to the castle sweaty but smiling. The night air was warm with cheer, and for the first time since my mother's death, the darkness held only the slightest breath of fear.

It was the beginning of a summer full of reckless abandon. For those few brief months, Tren-Lore and I escaped entirely from the obligation of chores and lessons and practices. A few days after my Summer Year, Tren-Lore's father received a message from the king of Hemlizar.

"They want us to come for the summer," Tren-Lore told me over the pounding of our hammers on the partially constructed roof. "It is intended to repay Father for taking them in last spring."

I stopped hammering and wiped the sleeve of my shirt across my sweaty forehead. The roof was proving to be an exhausting part of the fort's construction. I looked at Tren-Lore, feeling considerably perturbed. I did not want him to leave for the summer. "So," I began, trying to keep my voice neutral, "you are leaving for the rest of the summer?"

"No," Tren-Lore replied firmly.

I smiled in relief and returned to my hammering. "What about your father?"

"He is..." Tren-Lore paused, considering his word choice, "not pleased. But he does- err! End this!" Tren-Lore's hammer had made contact with his left thumb. He dropped the hammer and nursed his thumb for a moment. Finally, he remarked, "Father does not usually press matters like these. He lets me go my own way."

And so he did, for at the end of that week, King Kiris, Yolis and Nahanni all clambered into a coach set for Hemlizar, while Tren-Lore and I headed down to the river for a swim. With the royal family gone, there was not nearly as much work to be done in the kitchen. So little, in fact, that Sophie gave many of the women free time and said that Flock and I could do as we liked during the summer. Flock went to live with her Uncle and Aunt, and I ran wild with Tren-Lore. His father had not renewed the services of Tren-Lore's tutor, and the steward King Kiris left in charge of the castle, was given instructions not interfere with Tren-Lore's plans. Tren-Lore and I were completely free, and neither one of us could remember being happier.

We usually devoted our morning to working on the fort or practicing swordplay. When the heat of the afternoon sun fell upon us, we retreated to the river and the cooling touch of the Aquara. We fished and swam and sprawled on the grassy banks, telling stories and dreaming of the future. Tren-Lore usually joined us in the kitchen for supper. Sophie liked Tren-Lore and was delighted with this turn of events. We grew careless about hiding our friendship and would often burst into the kitchen together, talking loudly about the events of the day. Sophie never remarked upon this, until one day when we tumbled into the kitchen, sunburns and dirt darkening our faces, the smell of the fish that we had caught and eaten for lunch clinging to our clothes.

"Ascendants help me!" Sophie exclaimed in an exasperated tone. Her hands were on her hips as she stood near the middle of the kitchen, surveying us with motherly disgust. "Child, I can stand many things, but your smell is not one of them. Go and bathe."

I began to protest, and Tren-Lore started laughing.

"You too, Tren-Lore." She shooed us both out of the kitchen and into the hallway. "Tell your steward to fetch the water quickly. Dinner will be ready in a few moments, but we will wait for you. Lara, come with me." She guided me toward the washing chamber. Giving me a wolfish grin, Tren-Lore bound up the stairs that led to the royal chambers. "How are we ever going to get a comb through that Pandel's nest you call hair?" Sophie demanded. "I swear, child, one day I will just cut it all off."

I clutched at my hair and looked at Sophie in horror. "No, Sophie, I promise I will start brushing it!"

"That is what you said last week. I will be a happy woman when autumn comes and there is work to keep you busy again." She was trying to look stern, but I could see her brown eyes dancing as she opened the door to the steamy washing chamber and hurried me inside.

Sophie may have been happy when the heat of summer dissolved into the relaxing warmth of fall, but Tren-Lore and I had mixed emotions. We hated to give up our summer freedom, but with the return of the royal family, it was inevitable. Still, there was Myste's annual visit to look forward to.

It was nearly a week before he was due to arrive. The autumn smells of earth and falling leaves had filled the castle and given the air a refreshing scent. I hummed and swung the empty water pails at my side as I walked toward the well. I was just in the midst of wondering how well the fort would survive the winter, when Myste stepped around the corner! I gasped and stopped in my tracks, for a moment doubting that the vision before me was even true. The buckets slid from my grasp and clattered against the stone floor. "Myste!" I cried, covering my open mouth with my hands.

"Yes!" he replied with a teasing grin. Obviously he had intended to shock us with his early appearance, and he seemed to be enjoying my reaction very much.

"I thought you – oh, stop laughing," I snapped with warm fondness.

"Or what? Will you beat me with one of your pails? Oh, wait...you very well might, and the bruises from my last pail-beating are just fading. Very unsightly. All-"

I burst into happy laughter and caught him in a fierce hug. "I have missed you! Does Tren-Lore know you are here?"

We broke apart from one another. He was taller than last year, but nothing else appeared to have changed. He stuck his hands in his pockets and smiled at me. "Yes. I gave him a rude awakening this morning. I had some exciting news to tell him."

I was sure that any tidings which prompted Myste to arrive a week early had to very exciting indeed. I raised one of my hands. "Wait one moment." I grabbed the buckets from the ground and turned back to Myste. "All right, what has happened?"

We walked along the corridor together, and Myste disclosed his news. It proved to be nothing short of thrilling. In the coming spring, the Lord of Knights was to visit Caladore. I had only heard of such a person in the *Rayn* books. Yet again, I was struck with wonder at the surreal events which surrounded everything Tren-Lore did or dreamed of. I listened with rapt attention as Myste explained that the Trials were held randomly, depending upon the need for new knights. It had been seven years since one of these great tests of fighting skill had been held. Any young men past their second Summer Year from the countries of Nara Vit, Hemlizar, Tolrem, and of course Caladore, could be included. Those young men wishing to become knights would travel to Caladore and compete in the Trials. Based on what the Lord of Knights and his council saw, they would select one hundred boys to receive the formal training that would lead to Knighthood. And eventually to the League of Sanysk, I added silently in my heart.

Chapter Ten
On the Edge of the Future

T he training began at once. The summer of freedom took us into a winter of discipline. Myste's father and mother had high hopes for him, while Tren-Lore was as determined as ever. I was as eager as either of the boys, and arrived daily in the secret room ready to provide whatever assistance I could. I helped them practice swordplay and learned quite a bit as I watched them struggle with each other during the hand-to-hand combat sessions. On warmer days, we took the horses outside to practice mounted warfare. Military strategies were discussed, and every now and then we stole some time to play Questkon.

"It is hands-on practice," Myste justified to the frowning Tren-Lore.

* * *

It was a particularly cold day, and not even the blazing fire in the giant kitchen hearth was enough to warm the air. Mild headaches had been plaguing me for the past month, but the pain had peaked that morning in a throbbing agony that made me miserable. I moved about my tasks slowly. Myste had arrived just before the afternoon meal was to be set upon the table.

"So she has not written to me in a fortnight," he said in an agitated tone. Taking the spoon from my grasp, he stirred vigorously at the soup I had been making.

I sunk into a nearby chair and rubbed my temples.

"When I left, we promised to write every day," Myste continued. "I kept my promise, but she certainly did not. I have only received *one* letter from her!"

"You did?" I asked with as much surprise as I could muster. My head pounded with the noise of the kitchen. It had never seemed so loud. The clang of dishes, the thunk of wood, the gabble of voices and Myste's complaints about Relymar all drove sharp spikes of pain into my head. At least she had written him one letter. When we had talked last, he had been dispirited because she had not written to him at all. In my opinion, Relymar was not worth the adoration Myste felt for her.

"Yes," he began as he banged the spoon loudly against the side of the pot. "I would rather that she..." Myste trailed off as Sophie whisked up behind me and set a huge stack of bowls upon the counter.

"Lara, dear – oh, hello Myste!" Sophie said pleasantly. "Lara, will you ladle the soup into these bowls? There should be twenty-two there. Get an extra one for Myste."

I felt entirely overwhelmed. I did not think I could handle filling twenty-three bowls with soup. My emotions must have been clear upon my face, for Myste said quickly, "I can do that, Lady Grim. I do not think Lara is feeling well."

"Not feeling well? Perhaps you should go lie down." Sophie put one of her hands on my forehead.

I pulled away. "No, Sophie, I am fine. It is just a headache."

If I had to go lie down, I would not be able to meet Tren-Lore in the secret room, and I wanted to help him and Myste practice.

Sophie patted one of my cheeks. "As you like, child." She left and Myste gave me a penetrating stare, absently twisting the ring upon his finger.

"Are you sure you are all right?"

"Yes," I insisted, taking my hands away from my temples and folding them in my lap. I inhaled a long calming breath. The pain seemed to subside slightly. "What did the letter say?"

Myste said nothing for a moment, his eyes roaming about the kitchen without resting upon any one thing. "She..." He cleared his throat. Grabbing some of the bowls from the counter, he turned his back to me and began to fill them. "She said that she did not want me to write her any more and, ah..." He cleared his throat again. "And when I got back to Jacinda she did not want me courting her."

"Myste, I..." my voice faded into uncertain silence. I did not know what to say to him. I rose to my feet, and coming to stand beside him, awkwardly patted his back.

"Well, End her!" He slammed one of the bowls back onto the counter, splashing soup over the wooden surface. "I do not need her, and she obviously does not need me. I am sure her winning personality will serve her well." Myste's sarcasm was cutting and as finely honed as his humor.

He said nothing more on the matter, but rather expressed his emotions through bitter verbal attacks on everything around him. I had to admit that I found him slightly intimidating when he was in such a foul mood, and therefore, said nothing more as we filled the rest of the bowls and set them on the table. Lunch was a quiet affair. I wretchedly ate my soup, feeling both my own physical pain and Myste's emotional distress. After Flock's careless chatter had earned her a well-aimed and caustic remark from Myste, the ladies of the kitchen had been slightly subdued. They murmured quietly amongst themselves, sensing, I thought, the animosity Myste was capable of at the moment.

It was a relief to escape from the kitchen. Myste said nothing as we climbed the stairs to the secret room. I rubbed at my eyes and neck, desperately searching for a way to alleviate my nasty headache.

"I am sorry that I acted the way I did," he said finally, as we approached the circular landing. "I can be a real Barlem sometimes. Can you forgive me?"

I smiled weakly at him. "Of course."

His expression was suddenly concerned. "Is your headache still really bad?"

I nodded, and he put one of his arms around me. "I told you that you were not thinking enough. Now you have brain rot."

I laughed in spite of myself, and Myste pulled back the dragon tapestry. I opened the door and we ducked into the secret room, Myste's arm still around me. Tren-Lore was already at work practicing fighting stances. He glanced at us when we entered, looked away, and then looked back quickly. His expression changed ever so slightly that I do not think anyone but I could have noticed. It was a darkening in his eyes, a slight clenching of his jaw. Tren-Lore was not pleased about something.

"We should forget training for today," Myste suggested, taking his arm from about my shoulders and going to put another log on the fire. "We could get some berryroot cordial, a few blankets, tell stories like we did last winter. Just do nothing."

Tren-Lore glared at him with a surprising amount of anger. "Nothing? Myste, we do not have the time to do nothing. We only have two more months until the Trials."

I knew at once that this was not the time for Tren-Lore to be contradicting Myste. His mood was too volatile. Something needed to be said to distract them. "I was thinking that -"

"Why are you being so serious?" Myste demanded, cutting me off. He turned slowly from the fire and added spitefully, "Yolis is taking these tests, too, and he is not practicing half as much."

Tren-Lore's face was suddenly hard and expressionless. This was one of the few things Myste could have said that would have really upset Tren-Lore. I stood uneasily by the door, watching the scene unfold. I should have tried again to soothe their tempers, but the pain in my head was too fierce. Everything seemed too great an effort. Even my ring felt heavy about my neck.

"No one is making you stay," Tren-Lore said, his tone ominously low. "Leave if you want."

I squeezed my toes in my shoes. Nothing good was going to come of this. I reached up and pressed my temples, struggling for something to say. The boys could still be calmed if I could–

"I do not know why you are even worried," Myste replied, and then added maliciously, "You are going to pass anyway. Your father is King, remember?"

I inhaled sharply. The situation was entirely lost. Tren-Lore dropped his sword and dove at Myste. Wrath had driven technique from their minds, and they rolled about the floor, battering each other with their fists.

"Stop it!" I ordered, and pushing myself through the pain of my throbbing head, leapt forward and took hold of the back of Tren-Lore's tunic. "Tren-Lore! Myste! End you both!" I heaved against Tren-Lore's weight.

He suddenly let go of Myste, not because of my strength, but by his own volition. I stumbled back, and he staggered to his feet. Myste rose without haste. His eye was reddened, and he held his sleeve up to his bleeding nose. Blood ran freely from Tren-Lore's mouth and a bruise was forming around his eye. The two exchanged one last silent look, and then Myste turned and left the room, slamming the door behind him. I winced. The noise drove into my mind like a wedge of wood under my nail. I turned wearily to Tren-Lore, pushing vainly at my temples. End this cursed headache.

Tren-Lore's face was so emotionless that I knew the things Myste said must have hurt far more than any of the blows he had dealt. Tren-Lore wiped at the blood running down his chin. I wanted nothing more than to comfort Tren-Lore, to take away the sting of Myste's words and the pain of Tren-Lore's injuries. I admired him so much. How he found the courage to face all he did was beyond me. It seemed a strength born in tales of old that should not be possible in the real world. I came and gave him a hug. He held me tightly against him, and I longed to be able to take away his pain, to heal all his injuries. My head was thundering with the sound of my own heartbeat, and my ring seemed hot against my skin. Blinding light suddenly filled my vision, and I could vaguely feel my knees giving way beneath me.

"Lara?" Tren-Lore's voice was coming from above me.

I opened my eyes slowly. He was kneeling over me. For a moment I could not remember where I was. The cold of the stone floor was seeping through my dress, and the ceiling did not look familiar. My hand wandered to my head, as though my fingers remembered something that my mind did not. As I touched my brow, I recalled everything that had happened. I remembered the terrible headache, the mean letter Myste had received, his horrible mood, and then the fight. I sat up abruptly and stared at Tren-Lore in amazement.

"What happened to your bruise?" I exclaimed, my fingers touching my own eye.

He laughed in relief. "I should like to know the same thing. The cut in my mouth is gone, too. I think you must have Healed me accidentally."

"I do not have a headache anymore, either," I said in wonderment. Had I Healed myself?

Tren-Lore offered me a hand and helped me to my feet.

* * *

When next I saw Tren-Lore and Myste together, it was as though nothing had happened. I assumed they must have talked about their differences, or perhaps found that beating each other had expressed their grievances sufficiently. Either way, I was glad for the peace. As the date of the Trials approached, we could not afford the distraction. My headaches were beginning to return, but not with the strength of the last one. I did not mention them to Tren-Lore or Myste, as I felt that they needed to concentrate entirely upon their training.

On the day that marked one week before the Trials, the air was filled with newly awakened warmth.

"I like Caladore so much better in the spring," Myste declared as the three of us tromped into the secret room.

The boys went immediately to their swords and I threw open the shutters, letting a playful breeze into the chamber. Leaning out over the windowsill, I watched dozens of people hurrying about in the courtyard. As of late, the castle felt rather like an anthill of royal visitors.

You could not walk down the corridors any more without having to stop and curtsy to someone. It was scouring away what little patience I had, and exposing the grave irritation that lay beneath. The sound of clanging metal drew my attention from the expanse outside and focused it upon Tren-Lore and Myste.

"Myste, you are leaning too far forward," I told him as I circled the outskirts of the fight. "Watch your footing, Tren-Lore."

The improvement was incredible. I was no longer a match for Tren-Lore with my right or left hand, and when he and Myste fought, Tren-Lore almost always won. There were times when Myste was able to triumph, but it was only if Tren-Lore was fighting with his left hand. It was still one of his weaker points, although fairly negligible when coupled with Tren-Lore's other talents. The only help I could be to the boys now was as a watchful bystander who pointed out minor points that could be improved upon. I could not function in this task for long today, because Sophie needed me in the kitchen. I commented upon their performances for only a moment longer and then took my leave.

After curtsying my way back to the kitchen, I threw open the inner door with great irritation. I hated having so many nobles cluttering up Caladore. There was work waiting for me, and I set about chopping carrots with a fierce vigor. Flock glided over to me.

"Hello, Lara," she said in a sickly-sweet tone. Taking a piece of carrot from the pile I had made, she brought it to her mouth and bit down with a sharp crack.

"Do you mind?" I snapped and pushed the pile away from her. "I am not cutting these for your enjoyment."

She chewed loudly on her carrot and leaned against the counter. "Sorry. So, are you still sure you want to go to the Trials? It will just be a lot of cooking for sweaty men."

Flock had been a mixture of fake friendliness and slippery cajoling ever since she had found out that Sophie was taking me with her to the Trials. Once the Lord of Knights arrived, the boys would be split up into twenty groups of twenty and taken out into the wilderness surrounding Caladore. There were to be many important people accompanying these groups. Some were judges; some were interested knights, and others, like King Kiris or Myste's parents, were merely family members whose rank warranted their invitations. Members of the kitchen staff were to go with the company so that meals could be prepared for these prestigious participants and spectators.

King Kiris had asked that Sophie and her team accompany his group. Sophie, not feeling right about leaving me alone in the castle, had invited me along. I was overjoyed with the turn of events! It meant that I would be near Tren-Lore during the Trials. Flock, however, was less than thrilled. She was going to be left behind in Kelladyn's care and had been trying vainly to change her fate.

"You do not really want to go," Flock assured me. "It might seem like fun, but it is really going to be grueling work, night and day. Although..." She gasped as though she had just been struck with a brilliant idea. "*I* would be willing to go in your place if it would spare you that suffering. I am not one to mind a little hard work, you know."

I snorted in wry amusement, and Flock continued haggling with the type of desperation and deceit found only in a merchant trying to sell a three-legged horse.

"Let me help you, Lara. Not only will I go for you, but I promise to do the dishes all by myself for an entire month."

I scooped up the pile of cut carrots and dumped them into a bowl. Hefting the bowl, I started toward the stew boiling over the fire.

"Wait, wait!" Flock cried after me. "I can make things even better..."

I laughed. "No, thank you." I dumped the carrots into the huge pot. There was nothing that Flock could do to make things better. They were perfect exactly the way they were. In only six days, I would see Tren-Lore take his first step toward becoming a Sanysk.

* * *

I awoke early on the day of the Trials, indeed, far earlier than Sophie or even the sun. I lay for a time, clutching Kara and wondering what the day would hold. When at last I thought that I could not stay still a moment longer, I crept from bed and went out into the dark kitchen. I pulled open the shutters on one of the long windows and stared out at the gray dawn, thick with mist from the rain that had fallen the night before. It was hard to believe that this day had arrived so swiftly. All our practice and all our dreaming had been in preparation for this day; this quiet, sleepy day that did not even seem to know how important it was.

There was a soft thud from somewhere behind me, and I turned to find the inner door slowly being pushed open. I had only a moment to be alarmed before I realized that it was Tren-Lore who was slipping into the kitchen.

"What are you doing here?" I whispered.

"I had to see you before everything began. I wanted – is that a doll?"

I was suddenly aware that I was holding Kara. I thought briefly of hiding her behind my back, but realized immediately that it was too late for that. My face felt hot with the blush that was undoubtedly reddening my cheeks. "Ahh, yes. It was a present from Sophie for my Summer Year."

He regarded me silently, surprise clearly demonstrated by his countenance, and then slowly a smile creased his face. He reached out and took her from my hands, turning her about to examine her dress. "What is her name?" he asked.

I was utterly shocked. I thought Tren-Lore would be scornful of such girlish playthings. "Kara," I replied. "I named her after my mother."

He nodded and gave her back to me. "I like her little boot lace things."

I giggled. Such a compliment sounded so strange coming from Tren-Lore. "Are you nervous about today?"

He rubbed at his jaw and considered my question. "In a way, I suppose, but I think Myste is more nervous. He was awake practically the entire night. He is certain that he is going to be impaled and die over the course of eight agonizing days."

"Eight?" I echoed with a grin.

"That is what he tells me." Tren-Lore pulled out a chair, and I did likewise. We sat next to each other, elbows side by side on the long kitchen table. "How he plans to be impaled upon blunt wooden swords, I do not know. He really has nothing to worry about. He is going to do fine."

"So are you," I said softly.

He let silence return to the room, and I watched the first touches of sunlight creep over the window ledges. I savored the feeling of sitting next to my best friend. For nine days he would be surrounded by other people and entirely removed from me. Soon the Lord of Knights would come, and a sequence of events would begin that would change Tren-Lore's life forever. My stomach clenched with excitement and nerves.

"It seems like ages since I first met you," Tren-Lore said without warning. "It seems like we have always known each other. I came down here because I was thinking of how different things would have been if you had not come to Caladore. I wanted to thank you for everything. For practicing with me and...for being my best friend."

Slowly, a smile spread over my face. "Thank you for being my best friend, too."

There was a pause, and then he cleared his throat. "I will see you at the Trials." Tren-Lore pushed back his chair and stood. He seemed taller than before, and golden streaks of sunlight fell upon his form, leaving bands of luminance about his neck.

"The Trials," I agreed, and watched as he turned and strode from the kitchen.

Sophie awakened shortly after Tren-Lore had left, and the rest of the serving women slowly began to fill the kitchen. It was much earlier than they usually began work, but there was a great deal to be readied for the afternoon departure. The kitchen was filled with a tangible excitement. I imagined that if I opened my mouth and tasted the air, it would be sweet with glorious anticipation. Flock and I kept wandering past the windows, hoping to catch a glimpse of the Lord of Knights galloping up the wide road that led to Caladore. The ladies of the kitchen were quick to call us back to our chores, saying, "When he comes, you will not need your eyes to know. There will be fanfare the likes of which you have never heard. It will be like the day of King Kiris' coronation. There was such trumpeting! Why, the whole castle rang for a month!"

Flock and I washed and dried the breakfast dishes with an uncommon fervor, and did not even stop to exchange our usual morning barbs. We were united in our excitement and both strained our ears for the tumult of sound the ladies had described. It began as a long clear note that quivered in the air, and then exploded into an enormous melody of joyous heralding. Flock and I both screamed in giddy delight. Flock dropped the cup she had been washing as we rushed to the window.

Far below us came a parade of horses and riders who bore the snapping flags of Caladore, Nara Vit, Tolrem and Hemlizar. The trumpeters marched after them, leading the way for a magnificent man seated on a prancing stallion. He was dressed all in black with an ornate cloak of silver rippling off his shoulders. We were too far away to distinguish many details, but I was immediately sure that he was the Lord of Knights. Flock agreed wholeheartedly. Riders in full armor followed on carefully curried, prancing horses. The sun caught the bright metal and made it glitter with a dazzling brilliance.

The group behind the knights was dressed in an array of colors. Their horses cantered without worry of maintaining lines or positions. These riders were followed by a second group of knights. Trailing far in the distance was a lone horseman. I stared at him with curiosity. There was enough distance between him and the Lord's party that he might have been a solitary traveler who just happened to be on the same road by chance. It was hard to keep the man in focus, as he seemed to disappear against the background of the road. I watched as he reined in his brown steed and slowed the animal to a walk. Then, to my surprise, the rest of the party slowed their pace to match his.

"I think you were wrong, Lara," Flock said, and pointed at the man. "He must be the Lord of Knights."

I shook my head, but made no reply. I did not know who the man was, but I was sure that he was not the Lord of Knights.

"All right, ladies," Sophie called above the noise, "those who are coming must gather what we need and make their way down to the courtyard. Our store wagons are waiting there. The rest of you have a lovely week. Benya, take good care of my kitchen."

Benya laughed and slipped an arm about Sophie's chubby waist. "Rest easy, Sophie. We will keep everything just as you left it."

Chapter Eleven
In League with the Sanysk

I strained my neck in all directions, trying to look past the familiar figures of the Caladore servants and see the exotic people who were standing all around me. The outer courtyard smelled of horses, and the air reverberated with the sharp clip of hooves on cobblestone and the gabble of many people. Sophie held my hand tightly so that I would not be tempted to wander away into the crowd. It was probably best that she did, for I must admit, I was very tempted to do just that. From my vantage point, the only thing I could see was King Kiris standing atop the steps leading to the inner courtyard. Two people were standing with him, and I stretched up on the tips of my toes to get a better look.

"That is Lord Tren and Lady Jacinda, Myste's parents," Sophie explained. "Lord Tren is King Kiris' brother and Prince Tren-Lore's namesake."

I watched Myste's parents as they talked with King Kiris. Lord Tren clapped his brother on the back, nodding his head in vigorous agreement, and Lady Jacinda's dark glossy hair fell across her tanned face as she laughed. Reaching up, she swept her shiny locks back over her shoulder and turned her head to say something to her husband. Her lips were a deep red color, and she smiled even as she spoke.

"She is beautiful," I murmured to Sophie.

Sophie straightened her bonnet, and then reached down to straighten mine. "Lord Tren certainly thinks so," she agreed. "He named his castle after her."

"How romantic," I sighed.

"How foolish," Driana said from behind us. "Imagine naming a great hunk of rock after your wife."

"Look!" I cried and pointed to the stairs. At the same time, fanfare overtook the noise of the throng. The man in the silver cloak was climbing the stairs.

King Kiris held up his hand, and all sound ceased. "Good people of Caladore, respected guests," he said in a loud voice that reached everyone's ears. "I have the privilege of opening the Trials and introducing to you, the Lord of Knights."

A great cheer rose from the assembly, and the Lord of Knights bowed deeply. When all had quieted, he began a very long speech which contained many words but little information.

I shifted from foot to foot and stared about. The tense excitement in the group was unraveling as more and more dull moments slipped away. "Is he almost finished?" I whined, and Sophie hushed me.

"The child is right, Sophie," Driana sighed. "I wish he had just said, 'You will all be split up into twenty groups of twenty and will face nine challenges, each in honor of one of the Ascendants.' There. Done."

The Lord of Knights seemed unaware of his audience's growing boredom and continued to talk for some time more. When at last he had called the names of the boys in each group, and the servants, knights, priests, priestesses and guests had all been organized accordingly, it was well past noon and my stomach was growling. Sophie gave me a piece of bread and some cheese from the store wagons, and I walked along beside her, chewing contently and feeling very grateful to be free of the Lord of Knights' dull ramblings.

The group we were traveling with was made up of an array of important people. This included three of the knights who would be judging the performance of the competitors, four priests, five priestesses, King Kiris, and ten other nobles that I did not know. Marching behind these riders were the competitors themselves. They were all dressed in identical gray tunics and breaches, and while I knew that Tren-Lore walked somewhere amidst the group of boys, I could not distinguish his form from the others. Myste had been placed in another group. I had been a little disappointed about this, but for the most part, my happiness burned too strongly to be dampened.

When the parties had left the gates of Caladore, each went their separate ways. Twenty bases would be set up in the Caladorian wilderness. From there, the teams would complete the Trials.

We were moving north, staying on the outskirts of the forest and angling toward the mountains. It was only until I became too tired to walk any more and Sophie lifted me into the back of a wagon that I noticed the strange traveler riding behind our party.

His mount walked with a slight limp, and the rider himself did not look in much better shape. His hair was shaggy and hung about his shoulders. His shirt and breaches were made of battered leather. It seemed as though the colors of the earth, trees and roads had been stained upon his clothes and cloak. I fancied that he had slept on the ground, adventured through forests, and treaded dusty tracks for so long that the hues of those places had become indelibly imprinted upon his attire.

When at last we set up camp, it was at the foot of the mountains. Dusk was falling and the air was cold. To our left lay the forest, and a mountain river held our right. It was between the trees and the Aquara that we camped. While the boys pitched the tents, all of the kitchen servants set about making dinner. I relished cooking outdoors. I felt just like Rayn when he had first run away from his parent's home. Even the headache that was beginning to build in my temples did not diminish my enjoyment. We served the meal on the tables that had been erected near the river, and everyone ate together. King Kiris, priests and priestesses, kitchen staff, stable hands, guards, knights, and nobles: we all populated one long table.

Tren-Lore and the other boys in the Trials occupied a table of their own, and already the conversation was filled with joking voices and laughter. Friendships seemed to be forming quickly, and I felt a stab of jealousy at the thought of Tren-Lore jesting amongst the others at his table.

"My dear girl, would you pass the chicken?" asked a friendly voice.

I looked up and found that it was King Kiris addressing me. He was garbed in simple clothing and his head was not adorned with his crown, but I did not need this token to remind me that I was speaking to a king. I took hold of the platter and held it out to him. My hand shook slightly. My intimidation was two-fold, for not only was he royalty, but he was Tren-Lore's father. I felt that by just looking at me, King Kiris would be able to learn of the secret friendship I had with his son.

King Kiris took the chicken from me and said thank you. There was no mention of Tren-Lore, and I released a silent breath of relief.

A knight garbed in scuffed leather armor rose from our table and addressed the competitors. "Men," he said, "when your bellies are full, I suggest you take to your tents. Morning comes swiftly in the wilderness, and you will all need to be rested for the Trials tomorrow."

"Yes, Winmaris," I heard a few boys murmur.

I scraped the last of the meat and gravy from my plate and smiled as I chewed. It was so strange to hear the knight, Winmaris, referring to Tren-Lore and the other boys as men. Some of the boys started heading for their tents. Many remained, however, lingering over their meals and conversation. My headache was quite painful by this time, and I found the bright lights of the lanterns and the spikes of laughter amidst the talk very painful.

"May I go look at the horses?" I asked Sophie.

She did not hear me, as she was deep in conversation with one of the knights. I decided to slip away rather than interrupt her. Leaving the table and chatter behind, I dodged through the tents and over toward the horses. It was a relief to be surrounded by the quiet darkness. It was like bathing my senses in cool water. A rough stable yard had been built near the back of the camp, and I leaned on the uneven bars of the fence and watched the horses.

One of the stallions ambled toward me. He was limping, and as he neared and revealed his dull brown coat, I became sure that this was the steed of the loan rider. I held out my hand to him. He came and nuzzled my palm. His dark watery eyes met mine and I smiled.

"Sorry, no sugar." I stroked the coarse hair on his muzzle. "My name is Lara. Who are you?"

Unsurprisingly, the horse did not answer but continued to look at me with a kind gaze. I scratched his ears. He shifted his weight from his left foreleg and held it up off the ground. I took one of my hands away from the horse and squeezed the bridge of my nose. "My head hurts," I told him, "but probably not as much as your leg. It must really hurt for you to hold it up like that."

He nickered softly, his hot breath brushing my cheeks. I felt very sorry for the poor old creature. It was an empty feeling, a helpless pity, and I wished very much that I could fill the void with the passion of action. I cupped his chin in my hands. It seemed so unfair that an innocent animal should suffer in pain. I wanted to sweep away his agony. I wanted –

I gasped and closed my eyes against the white light that suddenly consumed my vision. I could hear my heart drumming in my ears, could feel the rush of blood in my body. My ring burned against my skin, and heat rushed down my arms and into my fingers. I could feel it flowing into the horse, but I could not let go. And then, as quickly as it started, it stopped. The light shattered into darkness and I felt vaguely sad to have lost it. My knees buckled underneath me, but someone caught and steadied me.

I stood staring into the night. My brain seemed to have been wiped clean of the knowledge of what I had been doing. Soon, however, my mind had made sense of things again. I knew where I was, what I had been doing, and realized that the headache which had been plaguing me was now gone. What I did not know was who was holding onto my upper arms. I turned slowly and looked up into strange amber eyes. They stared back, unblinking. It was the lone rider.

"Who *are* you?" I murmured.

"I assume that my name would not suffice as an answer to your question." His voice was deep. There was a long scar running from the middle of his cheek and across the corner of his mouth. I watched it move as he parted his lips to speak. "I am a Sanysk." He reached up and touched two silver bands about his neck. They were glowing softly with a silvery light. "And you are a Healer."

I stepped back from him in surprise, my back hitting the fence. "No," I said with instinctive panic.

A memory struck me like a bolt of lightning. A furious Ekrin man from long ago was shouting, "We should burn down your house while you sleep and rid this town of filth like you! Leave while you still can, you dirty Healer!"

"No! I am not!" I cried. "Why would you say that?"

"I am not one of those," he said gravely. "I am of the old belief that still holds the Triad sacred. I appreciate what you did for Quell, even if you did not mean to. I have not seen him looking so spry in many years."

I did not understand most of what he had said, but I had the distinct impression that he did not mean me any harm. I turned to look at Quell. The horse had moved off into the corral but as I gazed at the stallion, he came cantering toward me, tossing his head in the air and kicking up his feet. I watched him with a feeling of great wonder.

"Did I do that?" I asked.

"Yes," said the man simply.

"What was wrong with him before?" Quell was in front of me now and stretching his neck over the railing. He nudged my shoulder with his nose and whinnied happily. I giggled and patted his cheeks.

"It was a battle many years ago, when we were both much younger," the man explained. "Quell injured his leg, but he had so often saved my life that I could not take his. I cared for his leg, and in time he was whole again. I think that injury plagues him now in his old age."

As he had been speaking, a fact lost in the flood of my panic was slowly surfacing. The loan rider had said he was a Sanysk! I whirled about to face the tall man once again. I was so excited, I thought I would have to jump up and down on the spot or explode with all the energy humming inside me.

"You are a Sanysk!" I exclaimed, and felt a hot blush upon my cheeks as soon as the words sprang from my tongue. It was a silly thing to have said. "I mean, well, of course you are a Sanysk, you just told me that. What I mean is, well, what I mean...I just have never met a Sanysk before. My friend Tren-Lore wants to be a Sanysk, and we are always training together. Do you know Lord Rayn?"

"No," the Sanysk said gravely, "Lord Rayn died before my time. I think he would have been a very good person to know. Is your friend Tren-Lore in the Trials?"

I nodded vigorously. "Yes."

The Sanysk considered me for a moment. It was the type of stare that made me feel as though he could read every one of my thoughts and knew things about me that not even I was conscious of. Strangely, it was not a gaze that I wanted to look away from. I did not feel as though I would mind if this man knew every single one of my secrets.

"What is your name?" he asked, looking down at me.

"Lara," I said, squeezing my toes in my shoes.

"Draows," he said in return and bowed deeply to me. "Would you like to ride with me tomorrow and watch your friend in the Trials? Quell would be happy for a chance to fulfill the debt of thanks he owes you, and I would be glad of your company. I am curious about you, little Healer. I have many questions I would like to ask."

I accepted his invitation without thought of what Sophie might say.

"Meet me here tomorrow morning at sunrise, and we will ride out together," said Draows.

I promised that I would be there, and ran back to our tent on feet that were swift with exhilaration.

"Guess who I met?" I shouted as I burst into the tent I was sharing with Sophie.

Sophie was sitting on her pile of blankets. She had her arms crossed, and her face was set in a stern frown. Even these gestures were not enough to make her look threatening. A straight-backed chair or the room to pace restlessly would have suited her purposes better. As it was, bedrolls and soft blankets surrounded Sophie.

"Where have you been?" she demanded, smoothing her hair back. "I was very worried."

I leapt upon my mound of quilts. "I told you that I was going to see the horses. You will never guess who I met!"

"Young lady," Sophie said, struggling to her knees, "you did not tell me anything of the sort!"

"But I did, Sophie. You were talking to one of the knights and I told you. I do not think you heard me but I did not want to interrupt you, so I did not bother telling you again."

Sophie was on her feet now, though she had to stoop because of the tent's low ceiling. One of her hands was on her hip, but her shoulders were so hunched that she looked like a lumbering Barlem. She struggled with the low-hanging roof, pushing vainly upon it with one hand while still trying to maintain her stern gaze. "Lara, you should-"

"You always tell me that interrupting is rude!" I blurted out in my defense, and then clapped my hands over my mouth, realizing that I had just interrupted her. "Sorry."

Sophie's stern facade cracked with creases of laughter, and despite herself, she began to chuckle. She sat back down and shook her head. "What will I do with you child? Now, who have you met?"

I told her about my meeting with Draows, omitting only the part in which I Healed Quell. It seemed too personal a thing to tell even Sophie.

"I suppose you can go," she consented with a stifled yawn. "It is an honor that I would not have you miss." Sophie pulled the last blanket up on her bed. "I will be stiff tomorrow. Bones as old as mine were not meant for sleeping on the ground."

* * *

I was awake and slipping from the tent far too early to find out how vigorously Sophie's bones had punished her for the night spent on the ground. The sky was filling with the ashen look of first light and most of the camp was still sleeping. A few of the boys were wandering about, and I saw Winmaris down by the river, splashing water on his face. None of the kitchen staff had awakened yet. We had received orders last night that the competitors would not need feeding in the morning, and that King Kiris and his people would be having a late breakfast. I could not have slept any longer though, even if I had wanted to. I was far too excited.

Draows was not yet at the stable yard when I arrived. I climbed up onto the top railing and sat there swinging my feet and watching for him. I tried to imagine what Tren-Lore would say when he found out that I had met a Sanysk. Quell soon discovered that I was waiting there and came to stand beside me. The sun had just begun to tint the sky, and camp was now full of gray-clad boys moving about. I wondered what Tren-Lore was doing at that very moment.

"Good morning," said a deep voice.

I gasped in fright and nearly fell backwards off the railing. Draows caught me by the arm and steadied me. His approach must have been utterly silent, for there had been not so much as the snap of a twig to alert me to his presence. He nodded to Quell, and the horse nickered softly at him.

"Good morning," I replied a little sheepishly as I slid off the fence.

In a few long strides, Draows reached the gate and lifted the latch. Quell trotted out of the corral and stood patiently before his master. Draows held out his hand to me. I came to where the two of them waited. Draows lifted me up onto Quell's back, and then leapt up himself. I was not surprised that Draows rode without a saddle. A saddle would have seemed too bulky and awkward for the lithe Sanysk.

"What is your mother's name?" Draows asked as we rode away from the camp and across the river.

This question startled me, and I twisted my fingers nervously in Quell's mane. I did not answer for several moments and instead stared out at the rolling land before us. "Kara," I said finally, my voice wavering with pain.

"I am sorry, Lara," Draows said, his words a low rumble, "but be comforted, for I sense that there is much of her in you."

I let go of Quell's mane. Tears were blurring my vision and rolling softly down my cheeks. It was a calm pain, though, not at all like the raging grief of before. "Did you know her?"

"No. Our paths never crossed, although I heard much about her. She was a very great Healer. There were few with her power or bravery. Not many Healers could weather the storms of fear and hate that darken the people of Caladore. I had not heard of her death. It is sad news, indeed."

I reached up and dried my cheeks with the cuff of my dress. I furrowed my brow in confusion. "How do you know she is dead if you have not heard?"

"Lord Rayn had many powers that were not written of in his books. A Sanysk is taught to hear both spoken and unspoken words. The grief in your tone spoke as clearly as tidings from Ekrin."

I was surprised once again. He did know a lot about my mother. I thought for a time about what he had said. I had always believed that my mother was wonderful, but to hear others say that she was powerful and brave was a new experience. I had faced the opinion others had of my mother, and it was always in a defensive posture. Draows spoke of her with respect, spoke as though many people shared his feelings. The idea stood in my mind, not yet part of my own thoughts, but there nevertheless.

Draows guided Quell left, cutting around two little hills. "Shall we speak of more cheerful things?"

I nodded.

"What of Tren-Lore?" asked Draows. "How is it that the prince of Caladore stumbled upon such a worthy friend?"

I laughed in amazement. "You really know a lot!"

He chuckled softly. "I am afraid that in this case, my wisdom is nothing more than a guess, though a safe wager it was. Tren-Lore is the only boy in the Trials with such a name. Now, what is the story of your meeting?"

I thought back to the day I had first met Tren-Lore and what luck it had been, both in our meeting and in his choice of me as his friend.

"It was Tren-Lore's Summer Year," I began, "and his father had planned a big celebration and invited all the nobles. Tren-Lore does not really like things like that, so he slipped away from the party. He was on the balcony watching everything from above when Yolis, his brother, found him. Yolis was in a terrible rage and made Tren-Lore return to the celebration. It started raining and everyone ran inside, but Tren-Lore stayed. He is like that. Sophie – that is the woman who takes care of me – well, she has this expression about having enough sense to come in out of the rain, but sometimes I think it is the people who do not come in, that make the most sense."

"Very true," Draows replied, and for a time he said nothing more. "You seem to have only told one side of the story," he commented finally.

"Oh," I waved my hand dismissively, "my side is not very interesting. I just got lost and then wandered onto the balcony."

Draows paused. "I see. Have you and Tren-Lore been friends ever since?"

There were yellow flowers growing all around us on long waving stalks. I leaned over and grabbed one. "Yes," I replied as I righted myself, flower in hand. "He taught me how to read and write, and I helped him practice sword fighting."

"You are one of the more interesting people I have met in a great while, Lara. A sword-fighting Healer whose best friend intends to be a Sanysk. Rare, indeed."

"Why is it rar-" I realized just then that in my fit of excitement I had told Draows that Tren-Lore wanted to be a Sanysk. The flower dropped from my fingers. "You must promise not to tell anyone that Tren-Lore wants to be a Sanysk. It is a secret."

"I promise," Draows replied in a sincere tone, and then answered my unfinished question. "It is rare because the Triad was broken only a few years after the Drawl. There is little love between the Healers, Sanysk, and Sorcerers. They mistrust one another a great deal. I add to my promise a vow to tell you the tale before we part ways. Look." He pointed, and my gaze followed his extended arm to a large, flat piece of land that was encircled with small hills. "There is the place of the first Trials."

Chapter Twelve
The Trials

Quell, Draows and I stood upon one of the small hills that provided a good vantage point from which to see the pool of boys and horses that had collected in the basin of land. I searched for Tren-Lore, but could not distinguish him from any of the other gray clad competitors.

"What will they have to do?" I asked. There did not seem to be any organized challenges for the boys to overcome.

"Well," said Draows, rubbing the stubble on his cheeks, "the Trials open with a tribute paid to the Ascendant of Fire. The Trial will undoubtedly involve fire, though the use may be symbolic or realistic."

I looked up at him, mouth agape. "You mean that you do not know what the Trial will be?" He seemed to know everything else.

A smile tugged at the corners of his lips, and for a moment the scar that ran across his mouth was disturbed. "I mean exactly that. I did not want to know. There are times that anticipation becomes a poor companion, and I long for the lively fellowship of surprise."

Before I had a chance to consider this explanation, I was interrupted by an abrupt silence. The presence of noise suddenly seemed inappropriate as a reverential hush fell over the group below us. A woman had ridden into the dell. She was draped in long white robes and sat proudly upon an ivory horse. She was not beautiful, for her nose was crooked and her face continued into her neck without the interruption of a jaw line, yet there was something about her that made me stare in awe. Perhaps it was her obvious power. Perhaps it was her awareness of that power. I did not know for sure, but something made her so riveting that I hardly even noticed the other two women riding behind her. Both were wearing similar robes dyed to a deep blue color.

"She is the Head Priestess for the Ascendant of Fire," explained Draows in a murmur, "and they are the priestesses that serve under her."

He bowed deeply to her, just as all the competitors did. I found myself bobbing a curtsy, though I doubted she had noticed us standing atop the hill.

"I speak for the Ascendant of Fire," said the Head Priestess in a ceremonial tone "and today I bring a test to challenge your ingenuity. The Ascendant of Fire is perhaps the most willful of all the Ascendants. Flames bring comfort and defense, but they can also bring fear and destruction. If you are clever, the Ascendant of Fire will reward you. If you are foolish, however, peril and heartache shall be yours. Are you prepared for your first Trial?"

"Yes!" cried the group in a tumble of voices.

"Very well," said the priestess. "Imagine this. You are a band of knights that have been caught in this valley." She raised a hand that was lost in her cavernous sleeve and gestured to the hills around them. "The enemies are approaching from every side. All will be lost if you are forced to attempt an uphill battle. Your only chance is to enclose this dell in a circle of flames so that no enemy may pass. To aid you, I give you only those resources which you have at hand. Make yourselves ready in thought, and then the bodily effort shall begin. A beginning and eventually an end will be signaled."

The priestess turned her horse and walked it slowly up one of the hills that was directly opposite our vantage point. The other women followed. There was silence in the group below us, and I tried to imagine what Tren-Lore was feeling. Was it anxiety or excitement? Probably a mixture of the two, I thought. My own mind was already gnawing at the problem and endeavoring to spit out a solution of some kind. There was nothing in the dale that would serve as firewood. The grass would burn for only moments, and would not be enough to hold back an attacker.

"They are going to need wood," I said to Draows in a low voice.

"Agreed," he responded. He shielded his eyes from the light of the newly awakened sun and gazed out over the countryside. "There," he replied quietly and tilted his chin to a finger of forest that crooked over some larger hills no more than a league away.

I stared at the vague green of the trees, hoping that Tren-Lore has also noticed them. Time dripped by like water melting off a block of ice. Each moment seemed to stretch and dangle until at last it plunged downward into the past. My stomach was beginning to twist with apprehension. When would it begin?

"In the name of the Ascendant of Fire," said the priestess, and all eyes were suddenly upon her. It was starting at last! "I open the Trials and bid you all to the challenge of flames."

A great clamor rose from the tangle of boys as everyone began talking at once. I winced. It was clear that if someone did not take the lead they would all sink in a swamp of endless suggestions.

"Stop!" someone shouted. "Everyone stop talking!"

"We need wood," continued another voice, a familiar voice. It was Tren-Lore, speaking with calm authority.

I gasped and covered my mouth in excitement. Tren-Lore mounted Storm Wing so that the crowd could see him.

Another boy swung onto the back of a tall gray horse. "Tren-Lore is right. Gura," he called, "run to the top of one of the hills and see if there are any trees nearby."

"Right away, Dayr!" one of the gray-clad boys replied, and set off up the hill.

Tren-Lore turned Storm Wing in a quick circle, surveying the dell. "We will need to uproot a strip of the grass all along here," he indicated a wide ring a few feet up from the base of the hills, "or else we will set ourselves on fire, too."

"There are woods!" bellowed Gura from the top of the hill. I tore my eyes away from Tren-Lore and looked across at the newly appointed scout. "They are probably a league off, maybe more."

A worried ripple of words ran through the group. "That is too far! It will take too long! We cannot walk all that way carrying wood!"

I turned my gaze to Tren-Lore, waiting for an answer. He and Dayr had reined in their horses close to each other and appeared to be talking. At last, Tren-Lore said, "Those of you who have horses, come with me, and everyone else do as Dayr tells you to do."

The young prince spurred Storm Wing through the crowd, and a little more than half the group leapt upon their mounts and followed Tren-Lore out of the small valley. I watched him lead the party, and my ears heard Dayr giving orders to the remainder of the boys.

I looked up at Draows to discover his reaction to the events that had just occurred. His eyes were moving from Tren-Lore's party to the boys below us. His face was unreadable. At least Tren-Lore already had one of the skills of a Sanysk, I thought with silent amusement.

Dayr and his group worked diligently, but their tedious labors could not hold my attention for very long. I watched the horizon for signs of Tren-Lore's return. I was tense and my heart seemed to be shaking my whole body with the ferocity of its pounding.

"I was always glad that I was in the battle rather than at home awaiting news of victory or defeat. Waiting is a weary pastime," said Draows as he absently ran his hand along Quell's side.

"You could tell me the story about the Triad," I suggested with a flare of hope. My focus was swept from the Trials and was instantly upon Draows.

He settled himself on the ground. "Very well," he said.

I sat down across from him and shifted so that the grass would not poke me through my skirts.

"I assume that you have heard tell of the Drawl. Now," Draows looked out across the dale, "if you were to ask the priestess to tell you this story, she would give a rendition very similar to the one you have already heard. But there is more to the story... much more. The Discontents were not alone in their abhorrence of the Ascendants' rule. Some of the Ascendants also believed that the people should be free to govern themselves. The two powers rallied their people around them, and bitter strife ensued. They pounded down the gates of the great cities, set them ablaze, and pulled down their grand walls in a thunderous rumble of destruction."

I shivered, though it was not cold. Draows' voice was rich and swelled and dipped over the words in a way that made images rise in my mind. I could see great battering rams booming against huge wooden doors and fire leaping from within tumbling stone walls.

"The legend is that the Ascendants left because they could not stand to destroy any more spirits – any more of The One. This is not true," Draows continued. "During the entire battle, not a single spirit was destroyed, but carnage of the flesh was immense. They say so much blood was spilt that the earth oozed with gory mud that would not dry for days. And then, one dawn, the Ascendants looked out upon their lands." Draows swept his hand out and I followed his gesture with my eyes. "They were black with people."

I tired to imagine what these fertile grounds would have looked like, scarred and stained, blood drenched. I wondered briefly if Sophie would approve of Draows telling me this tale.

"So driven to ire were the Contented and the Discontents, that standing upon the battle field was every man, woman and child from both groups. They were senseless with vehemence that the Ascendants had kindled and fed. If the two sides had warred it would have meant the end. The Ascendants knew this, and so they convened high in the mountains."

"Those mountains?" I inquired, staring north at the looming pinnacles of rock.

Draows slung one of his arms over his bent knee and looked at the mountains with a type of fondness. "I always liked to think so. In my younger years, I went exploring there, hoping to find the Ascendants' meeting place." He shook his head, and his expression seemed one of wry amusement. "I nearly froze to death."

My mind instantly made the connection between Rayn and Draows' adventures. I turned to the Sanysk in excitement. "That is just like Rayn!"

"So it is," he chuckled, looking slightly surprised but rather pleased. He scratched at his cheek. "Now, I fear that have led this story quite astray. Shall we return?"

I nodded eagerly, clasping my hands in my lap.

"The Ascendants departed into the mountains to take council or continue the conflict with one another. No one knew the exact purpose for which they went, but they were never to return again. As you know, they left priests and priestesses and, as few remember, they also formed the Triad. The members of the church were to be their mouths - spreading the words of the Ascendants, pronouncing worthy men as the kings of the countries that would need to be rebuilt. The Triad was to be their limbs. The power of Magic, Healing, and Battle was given to men and women whose natural characters lent themselves to such skills. Alone, such powers are forces to be reckoned with, but together..." Draows paused, and there was a look of wonder and sadness in his dark eyes. "The Triad had such power. When the Healers, Sorcerers and Sanysk stood against the impending war, they came as a blinding light that annihilated the dark battling that had been raging for so many years. They restored harmony."

"Yet soon they grew restless. The Sorcerers became great philosophers and withdrew from society, preferring thought to action. The Sanysk took another path and went out in search of new combat. The Healers dwelled among the people and tried to cure them of their ills. In time, though, each group began to forget the unity that had bound them into a whole. Hostility began to build within the groups. The Sorcerers prized lofty musing and solitude over all else. To the Healers, care of others was most important, and to the Sanysk, the battle was everything. You can see, Lara, how these different philosophies would have grated upon one another. Each group was afraid of the other because they no longer shared understanding. I wish it were not so."

"But you and I get along!" I protested. "It seems-"

Just then, the sound of running horses came to my ears and my protests were swept from my mind. Tren-Lore had returned!

The boys were riding in pairs. They held crude litters between them, piled high with stacks of deadfall. Dayr's group turned to the oncoming riders, shouting approval. I leapt to my feet, and Draows stood up next to me.

"They did well," he said as I jumped up and down next to him, cheering for Tren-Lore.

* * *

The next day Draows and I set out together. We rode high into the mountains and Draows told me about Ulmorian, the Sorcerer dwelling that lay on the other side of the steep ridges of rocks. He said that it was the ruins of one of the great cities, and the only contact the inhabitants had with the outside world was the news brought to them by the Atalium. This astounded me. I had heard so many stories about these beautiful, winged men who delivered messages from the Ascendants. I had always considered them to be creatures of myth.

"You mean they are real?" I breathed and looked about, half expecting to see Elesbrium swooping down from the sky. "That is incredible! It is like magic in the real world!"

"Or the reality of a magical world," remarked Draows softly, and Quell whickered as though in agreement.

We arrived at the place of the next Trial only moments after this discussion, and I surveyed it with fear. There was a deep crevasse in the mountain terrain, and over it was stretched a plank of wood. My throat was immediately tight with dread and I leaned back against Draows' hard chest, recoiling from the thought of walking on the makeshift bridge.

It was even worse than I had feared. The Priest of Sky informed the boys that they were to fight one of the knights while standing on the plank.

"This Trial is to test your endurance and bravery," the priest told the group. "You must resist the knight's onslaught for as long as you can. By this I mean that if you take a step back, your turn is over and you do not get to continue the duel."

There was a great deal of nervous chatter rippling through the crowd. It did not appear that many of the boys even wanted to start this Trial, let alone continue it. I could not say that I blamed them.

"There will be a rope tied about your waist," the priest said. "If you fall, it will probably hold you."

"Probably?" I echoed in an alarmed whisper.

I did not want Tren-Lore to go out on that plank and face a full-fledged knight. It was pure agony watching each boy as they walked out over the crevasse and did their best to maintain their balance and defend themselves at the same time. Most boys stepped backward before they lost their footing. A few wavered, but always retreated rather than plunge into the fissure. I had my hand over my eyes and watched most of competitors through the slits made by my fingers.

When Dayr fought, I watched with bated breath. He lasted longer than many of the boys, but as Winmaris' blade caught his and slid down to the hilt, I knew that Dayr would either have to step back under the pressure of the blow or fall. His face contorted as he strained against the knight's strength. He staggered finally, and his right foot moved out behind him to compensate. He caught the edge of the plank and his leg slid off, pitching him sideways. Winmaris leapt forward and caught him by the arm before he could fall. He steadied him, and Dayr stood hunched for a moment, looking as though he could not breathe. I could scarcely find air myself, for my chest felt as though it had been crushed by the fear of the moment.

"I do not like this Trial at all!" I said fretfully, wishing it were over.

Draows began to reply, but his words were abandoned as the Priest of Sky called Tren-Lore's name.

"Oh!" I gasped, my voice wavering. I closed my fingers over my eyes but was forced to open them again after only a moment. It was worse *not* knowing what was happening to him.

He was standing upon the plank, facing Winmaris. They both held their swords in the ready position. Tren-Lore was watching his opponent and did not, like many of the boys before him, spare a glance for the emptiness beneath him. He looked calm and grim with determination. Tren-Lore was facing the situation with the bravery of a hero in a story, but I was shaking with fear.

"Begin!" shouted the Priest.

Tren-Lore made a quick low strike, but Winmaris blocked. The knight returned the blow. The ring of their colliding blades sounded over and over again. Neither one took a step back. My mouth was dry, and I curled my toes so hard that they began to cramp.

Winmaris swung his blunted sword sideways, and Tren-Lore twisted to stop the blow. Their blades never met. Winmaris suddenly withdrew his arm and thrust forward. The knight's sword glanced off Tren-Lore's hasty block, but it was enough to push Tren-Lore off balance. He teetered, and for a breathless moment I waited for him to take a step back to regain his balance. The moment never came. Tren-Lore never moved his feet. He toppled sideways over the edge of the plank.

"Tren-Lore!" I screamed, and leapt from Quell's back.

I rushed forward as the rest of the group did the same. I pushed my way through the gray-clad bodies until I was at the brink of the chasm. Falling to my knees, I peered over the edge and felt my limbs flood with a liquid relief. Had I been standing, my legs surely would have given way beneath me. The rope tied to Tren-Lore's waist had held. He was suspended from the metal loop that had been driven through the middle of the plank. As Winmaris hauled him up, I could not decide whether I felt like cursing or crying.

"End me, but that took some nerve!" declared Winmaris, clapping Tren-Lore on the back. "Good for you, my lad."

Tren-Lore did not reply. He was smiling, but it was a rather fixed smile. He looked as though part of him realized he had done the only thing that would have allowed him any sort of victory, while another part was horrified that he had just let himself fall. I imagine that my expression nearly mirrored his. I was so proud of his courage, but so shocked by what had just happened.

I returned to Draows with unsteady steps. He was standing beside Quell, and neither horse nor rider seemed the least bit concerned. There were even traces of a smile upon Draows' lips. I began to wonder if perhaps the rope had been sturdier than the priest had led us to believe.

"Would you like to go back to camp?" Draows asked.

"Yes," I sighed in relief. My nerves could stand no more of this Trial, even if I knew the safety of the boys was ensured.

Draows helped me onto Quell's back, and then mounted as well.

"Did you know?" I demanded suspiciously as Quell trotted away from the site of the second Trial. "The rope, I mean. Did you know that it would hold?"

"No, I merely suspected," replied Draows. "I have seen enough Trials to know that the lives of the competitors are never placed in jeopardy. From the start of the challenge, I doubted that the purpose was to determine skill or balance. Pitting relatively untrained boys against a knight does not reveal very much about their potential. It was, as Tren-Lore guessed, a test of sheer courage. They wanted to see if the boys would face great fear rather than retreat. The rope was perfectly safe, but it was important to create the illusion of danger."

* * *

The next morning, I realized with a start that it was Tren-Lore's Summer Year. I counted the days out on my fingers, but the date was confirmed. Tren-Lore was fourteen years old and I probably would not even be able to bid him so much as a Joyous Summer year.

I listened without great interest as the Priest of Rock declared, "A rock endures all things. Let us see what you can endure."

The boys spent the day engaged in hand-to-hand combat, while those who were not competing watched and cheered. I was silent. If Draows noticed the change in me, he did not say. For the first time since I had come to Caladore, Tren-Lore was spending his Summer Year without my company. I felt as though he were slipping into a realm of grand deeds where I could not follow.

Spirits in the camp were high, and dinner was a festive affair with much laughter and many toasts to the feats of the day. Tren-Lore's Summer Year warranted a lengthy and off-key song from his fellow comrades. I sat quietly for the most part. My head was starting to hurt again, and I was in a generally bad mood. I missed Tren-Lore and felt as though a million leagues separated us. As dinner passed, I cultivated my garden of negativity until dark thoughts were sprouting everywhere.

I slipped away from the table without telling Sophie. Glancing back, I felt bitterly neglected when no one noticed my departure. My eyes ran over the vivid portrait of gaiety. Sophie, Winmaris, and another knight were laughing together. Beside them sat Draows. The Sanysk was not absorbed in the company around him, however. He was leaning back in his chair, a goblet in his hand and a contemplative expression upon his face. His gaze met mine. He nodded shortly and then returned to his musings. I went back to my tent for a good cry.

The next day found me in better spirits. In the early morning hours, Draows and I wandered out onto the rolling plains and made our way up one of the distant swells to secure a good vantage point from which to watch the Trial of Water. The young sun warmed our backs and I told Draows about the fort Tren-Lore and I had made. He seemed particularly impressed by the trap door in the roof. That discussion was quickly forgotten as a group of boys from our camp began their march downriver to confront, and hopefully best, another group of competitors. They looked more like tiny gray figurines moving against a board of green and blue than real people. It was like a game of Questkon whose pieces had been enchanted. An image of Tren-Lore, Myste and I playing in the secret room popped unbidden into my mind, and I could not help but wonder how Myste was faring.

Draows and I sat side by side as we watched, and he told me riddles to pass the time. I was still pondering one of the more difficult ones when the fifth Trial began. It was held in the forest, and to the dismay of the competitors, the warm morning sun had given way to gray clouds and rain. Draows and I took shelter under a large tree and watched the boys labor with their task of building a shelter that was both large enough to house them all and yet still defendable from enemy attacks. As in the first Trial, Tren-Lore and Dayr led the group. No one questioned the orders the pair gave, and the party worked with the skill of a team who was becoming aware of the varying abilities of each member.

"Is it a crow?" I said in response to the still-unanswered riddle Draows had posed for me. I rubbed at my temples, trying to crush the pain that was dwelling within my skull.

Draows shook his head and stooped to pick up a small leaf from the ground. He turned it over in his hands. "You are getting closer."

"An eagle?" I guessed again as I watched Tren-Lore and several other boys struggling to lift a heavy log from the forest floor.

"Closer still," said Draows, tucking the leaf into a pouch at his belt and shaking the rain from his cloak.

* * *

The following day brought more rain, and the Priest of Animals pronounced his challenge through a beard that dripped with water. The boys competed in mounted combat even as the clouds growled above them. Tren-Lore lost only one of his five fights, and the other horses learned to fear the cantankerous Storm Wing. He was quick to bite or kick whenever he had the chance, and I felt that perhaps Tren-Lore had not made such a bad decision when he had chosen Storm Wing as his Summer Year present.

The day after the sixth Trial, the rain finally ceased and the group set off early in the morning. They were bound for Caladore, where they would be meeting another group. One of the parties was to attack the outer walls of Caladore while the other would act as the defenders. I had wanted to go, but the pain in my head was so fierce that I was forced to tell Draows that I would not be able to tolerate the ride.

"Do you have a Healer's ring, Lara?" he asked.

"Yes." I drew the ring out, and Draows reached forth and caught it between his fingers.

My shadow was upon his form, and through the imposed darkness, I noticed that the silver bands around his neck were glowing.

I stared at them in awe and scarcely heard him mutter, "It is as I thought." He released the ring. "You are on the brink of your powers. See how your ring is turning green."

This tore my attention from the bands around his neck. "My ring is turning green?" I looked down to find that the sculpted ivy was tinged with a verdant blush that had a soft radiance to it. "What does that mean? Why is it glowing?"

"It glows because we are near one another, and your power is flowing freely within you. When a member of the Triad comes close to another member and uses their power, the marks of their trade begin to glow. My bands," he touched his neck, "your ring, and the wrist plates of a Sorcerer. Your ring is green because it is coming to life as more and more Healing powers fill you. That is why you have such a terrible headache. Until you learn to control your energies, pain will continue to plague you."

Had it not have been for the pounding within my head, I would have been very impressed by the light produced by the uniting of members of the Triad. As it was, it was difficult to concentrate on anything other than the pain.

"How do I control it?"

Draows looked down at me with sympathy in his eyes. "Unfortunately, my knowledge in such matters is no greater than what I have already told you. Only another Healer can teach you to control your powers. I will speak to Lady Grim about it when I return from today's Trial. For now, take this." He reached into the pouch at his belt and withdrew the leaf he had found yesterday. "Crumble this into hot water and drink it slowly. It should help your headache."

"Thank you," I replied, and carefully took the leaf from him.

He put a hand on my shoulder. "I shall see you at the evening meal."

* * *

The Trial in honor of the Ascendant of Sovereignty took much longer than anyone expected, and Draows did not return for dinner. Indeed, none of the party that had ridden out that day came back in time for supper. They all arrive in camp long after dark. They were tired but full of stories. Everyone gathered about the fire as the tales were told, and I curled up next to Sophie and laid my head in her lap.

I was soon asleep and dreaming about gardening with my mother when I heard Sophie's voice whispering, "Lara, Lara. Come, child, wake up. You are getting far too big for old Sophie to carry back to the tent."

Reality and dreams wound about my mind in tendrils of foggy confusion. "What?" I tried to say, but it came out as more of a tired moan.

"Can I be of assistance, Lady Grim?" asked another familiar voice.

My eyes fluttered open, and I saw Draows standing before me. The light of the fire leapt across his lean figure and ragged hair. His face was consumed by darkness. Had I not known what lay beneath the hard exterior I would have been frightened, but as it was, I smiled sleepily at him.

"Oh, no," replied Sophie. "Do not trouble yourself."

"It is no trouble," Draows assured her in deep tones as he lifted me effortlessly from the ground. I rested my head against his shoulder, and with the comforting scent of leather and Quell's dusty mane filling my nostrils, I fell back to sleep.

I was pulled from slumber early the next morning by the shrill cawing of a crow. Heroes in books were never awakened by the horrible squawking of birds outside their tent, I thought in brief irritation. The crow had reminded me of Draows' riddle, and I lay for a time searching for an answer.

My skin hangs in a balance; measure and weigh
I have a fear of the prized; a joy for the bane.
A Dweller of Earth; a Dweller of Sky
I have infinite worth, with no bond or tie

If I could only understand the meaning of the first sentence, perhaps that would lead me toward a solution. I shook my head. The pain was returning to my temples and I found it was hard to concentrate. Pushing back my blankets, I went to reheat some of the water that I had steeped the leaf in. My headache ebbed, and I was able to help with breakfast and watch the Trials without too much pain.

The Priestess of Unity proposed one of the more interesting challenges. The boys worked in pairs. One was blindfolded and held a wooden sword. The other had to stand out of the way and yell instructions to his partner. The boy carrying the sword could not move unless his partner told him to. Two blindfolded competitors faced one another, but as the priestess emphasized, it was 'a test of trust rather than skill' and she urged the boys to choose their partners wisely.

Tren-Lore and Dayr were immediately at one another's side. Jealousy cut deep as I saw this, but when they were called to fight, I knew that they were a perfect match. No matter what instruction the other shouted, his partner moved without hesitation, and at the end of their turn, a cheer exploded from the boys. The Priestess of Unity was smiling, and one of the young priestesses who stood behind her was whistling, the tips of her index finger and thumb in her mouth.

* * *

On the last day of the Trials, I was torn between happiness and sadness. I would be glad to return home, but I was loathe to abandon the company of Draows. When we had broken camp, the group separated into two sections. The competitors and those involved in the judging traveling south toward Jacinda, while the rest of us were bound for Caladore. There was no word as to why this was so, but I contented myself with the assurance that I would find out in good time.

"Good-bye, Draows," I said, having to choke back the tears that were rising in my throat. The tall Sanysk was standing before me, the wind playing in his hair and a solemn expression upon his stubbly face. "Good-bye, Quell," I added and ran my fingers through the horse's mane. "Thank you for letting me ride you." Quell nuzzled my ear, his breath hot upon my cheek and neck. "Are you sure that you will not tell me the answer to the riddle?" I pleaded one last time.

"No," replied Draows with a fond smile.

"But what if I do not see you again?" I protested. "Then I will never know what the answer is!"

"Our paths will cross again," he said with calm assurance, and then he bowed to me as he had done on our first meeting. "I look forward to that day."

* * *

It was a dull journey home without the company of Draows, yet when we plodded through the outer gates, I looked about in relief. It was good to be home. As Benya had promised, everything was just as Sophie had left it, and I climbed gratefully into my bed and fell into a dreamless sleep.

Fanfare awoke me the next day and I sat bolt upright. Sophie's bed was empty, and I leaped off mine and ran to the window. There was a flood of boys in the outer courtyard, and the Lord of Knights stood on the outside steps.

"You have all shown a great deal of skill and talent," bellowed the Lord of Knights. "Caladore, Nara Vit, Hemlizar and Tolrem can all feel proud to have such skilled and talented young men."

I chewed on my lip with impatience. I had forgotten how lengthy his speeches tended to be.

"You may all leave here today – or stay, if you live here, knowing that you are a credit to your country."

There was a restless groan from the crowd, and the Lord of Knights paused as though realizing for the first time that his audience was not pleased with him.

He cleared his throat. "Ah yes... well, without further ado I will read the names of those selected to receive official training for the rank of knight." He unfurled a long paper before him. "Aldart, son of Meyner...."

The list seemed to go on and on, but I waited breathlessly, every now and then hearing familiar names.

"Dayr, son of Xolyar...Gura, son of Gurat.... Myste, son of Tren..." With that I gave a little shout of happiness, but my ears really strained for one name alone. I endured name after name, blood pounding in my ears, my hands sweaty with anticipation and wild hope. And then at last - the names that began with T! I leaned out of the window as far as I could.

"Talis, son of Ofem," called the Lord of Knights, "Teban, son of Telan; Thendal, son of Polz; Trazom, son of Pelfam; Tren-Lore, son of Kiris..."

I let out a whoop of joy that brought Sophie rushing into the room. "Sophie," I screamed with unbridled exultation, "Tren-Lore is going to be a knight!"

Chapter Thirteen
Ivy Rings

I met Tren-Lore and Myste in the secret room the day after their return. They were already waiting when I entered, both of them sitting on the rickety old table in the corner. They hopped down as soon as I burst through the door. I ran to them, and first hugged Tren-Lore and then Myste. It was so good to be in Tren-Lore's company again.

"Guess who I met!" I demanded as I took a step back to view both of them. They were tanned from the summer sun, but other than that, nothing appeared to have changed.

"What?" Myste exclaimed, a teasing smile upon his face. "Tren-Lore and I risk being impaled and dying over the course of eight long and agonizing days, and we do not even get so much as a 'congratulations, burly heroes'. Really, Lara, where *are* your manners?"

I laughed. "Congratulations, burly heroes. Now, can I tell you who I met?"

"Please do," Tren-Lore replied, and smirked at his cousin. "Anything is preferable to hearing Myste refer to us as *burly*."

Myste punched Tren-Lore, who retaliated by catching him around the neck and wrestling him to the ground.

"A Sanysk," I said calmly over the noise of their wrestling. "I met a Sanysk."

This statement brought an abrupt end to the scuffle. I was suddenly the focus of their attention. We spent the entire afternoon sitting in the dusty secret room exchanging stories about the Trials. I told them all about Draows, and they related every detail about the last challenge.

"So the Priest of Eternity said something about his Ascendant bringing the cycle of life into being," Myste explained.

Tren-Lore continued. "He said that it was us who gave the cycle meaning. Then he told us that we were going to have a race to Caladore from Jacinda, and the first forty people there would be the winners. They were not really looking for how fast you could complete the race. They wanted to see how you conducted yourself during the race."

"Some of the boys rode their horses to death." Myste shuddered as though images still plagued him. "And others were so quick to leave friends behind that you would never have guessed that they had fought and worked side by side."

The talk soon turned from what had happened to what we wanted to happen next. The fort had to be visited; there was swimming and fishing, and an exciting plan for camping. When I returned to the kitchen that night, I was smiling broadly and did not even protest when one of the ladies asked me to help Flock set the table.

"Hello, Flock," I said in cheerful greeting. I was too happy to fight with her. Everything was exactly as I wanted it. I was home, and Tren-Lore and I were going to spend the rest of the summer together.

Flock looked at me suspiciously, her eyes squinting as she tried to deduce what I was plotting. "Hello," she replied cautiously.

Sophie came by and set a plate of freshly cut bread on the table. I inhaled deeply, feeling grateful to be back in the kitchen.

"Lara," she said softly to me, "I have a little matter I would like to discuss with you before the evening meal. Meet me in our room as soon as you are finished with those bowls."

I nodded, and Flock gave me a sidelong glance through her curls. Her mouth was twisted into a spiteful smile. "You-are-in-trou-ble," she sang softly as she lifted a plate from the pile she was carrying and set it on the table.

I put my last bowl on top of the plate Flock had just put down. "She is probably going to tell me to keep my eye on you. Someone has been stealing kitchen supplies, you know."

Flock glared at me, and I smiled and turned toward our room. Apparently, my good mood did not hinder my sharp tongue. I did wonder why Sophie wanted to talk with me, though. No one was actually stealing. It had turned out that Benya had just been putting dishes in the wrong cupboards. I could think of nothing that deserved a reprimand from Sophie. Perhaps it was a surprise, I thought with a flicker of hope.

Sophie was sitting in her rocking chair. She was smiling, but the rest of her face seemed to be hardened by an emotion she was trying to conceal.

I stopped in the doorway. The warmth of my optimism was swept away. I felt cold with dread. Something was not right. "What happened?"

"Nothing, dear," Sophie replied. "Come sit down. I have some news for you."

I walked wearily into the room, as though at any moment this 'news' was going to leap out at me. Sitting on the bed, I pushed my fingers under my thighs and tapped my toes nervously on the floor. "What kind of news?" I asked slowly.

"Well," Sophie ran her hand over her hair, "I had a talk with that nice Sanysk, Draows. He says that it is time you received some formal training."

I let out an explosive breath of air that I had not realized I was holding. "Is that all? He told me that, too."

"But that means, Lara, that we are going to have to move for-"

"Move!" I blurted in outrage. "I do not want to move!"

"For a time, just for a short time!" Sophie held up her hands in a calming gesture. "Only for a few years, while

Namin trains you. We will have to go live with her in Karsalin. It is about six days' ride from here."

"Is there no one closer?" I protested. My eyes were hot with anguish, and I felt as though I were choking on my grief. I did not want to leave Tren-Lore, Myste, or the familiar little room I shared with Sophie. I did not want to leave Caladore. I was happy here, and I was afraid that I would not be able to find that happiness anywhere else.

Sophie shook her head. "No, Namin is the best we can do. Oh Lara, darling, do not cry!" Sophie came and sat next to me, and put a comforting arm around me.

I buried my head in the front of her dress and continued to sob. "It is not fair! I do not want to move. I do not care if I become a Healer. I do not want to go! Everyone will hate me like they hated my mother!"

"Hush, child," Sophie murmured. "No one hated your mother. They were afraid of her power, afraid and very foolish for it. You have a wonderful gift, and Namin can teach you how to use it. You will like it at Namin's. She has three daughters, and one about your age." Sophie smoothed my hair. "Come, Lara, stop your tears. Things are not as bad as you think."

"Yes they are!" I cried, and flung myself face down into my pillow.

Sophie patted my back. "We can talk about this later." She rose, and I heard her walk quietly from the room.

I wept until sleep crept to my bedside and with an unperceivable touch, slowly smoothed my jagged breathing and calmed my agitation.

* * *

As the next few weeks passed, Sophie spent her time packing our things and making arrangements for a carriage and driver. She began training Benya to take over as Head of the Kitchen, and she wrote to Namin to tell her we were coming.

I spent my time moping. It was hard to enjoy Tren-Lore and Myste's company when I knew that the moments I had to spend with them were so fleeting. Myste did his best to cheer me up with a variety of jokes and capering. It helped a little, but when at last a final good-bye was necessary, not even Myste had the heart for jesting.

We were all in the secret room, and the sun was lancing the old stone walls with pink and crimson rays of light. I looked about fondly. The rickety table and old bookshelf had never seemed so dear. For the moment, any smudge of pain or unhappiness that had marked the past was wiped clear. It seemed like a haven, and I longed to return to it - to remain safe and surrounded by my friends. I looked up at them, only to discover they were watching me. Myste's countenance was solemn and Tren-Lore's face was unreadable. I straightened and sniffed, trying to compose myself.

"Farewell, Myste," I said with only a slight waver in my voice. "I will miss you."

"Good-bye, Lara." He gave me a firm hug. "I will miss you, too."

We stepped back from one another, and I turned to Tren-Lore. My resolve cracked. I began to cry, but it was not a sadness that could be expelled with tears. Cold sinews had twisted about my ribs. It hurt. The mere thought of leaving Tren-Lore was physically painful.

"Good-bye!" I sobbed and threw myself into his arms.

He hugged me for some time, as though he were reluctant to let go. "Good-bye," he replied finally.

* * *

The evening meal was a lively affair. The women of the kitchen had planned a little party, and there was an array of delicious food and drink to choose from. Everyone toasted Sophie and me.

"Sophie, Lara, may your journey be a safe one!" said Benya, and raised her glass.

"Indeed!" declared Sophie. She tipped her cup back and drained it. Sophie was very worried about the trip. She had been twittering constantly about dangers on the road, bandits, and the quite probable chance that the horses would run wild.

"May your welcome in Karsalin be warm!" cried another woman.

"And your departure from Caladore swift," Flock muttered under her breath. She was bitter that I was being lavished with so much attention.

I wanted no part of that attention. I did not care to hear another word about leaving, not from Flock, not from anyone. I rose from the table quietly and slipped from the kitchen. I wandered aimlessly for a time and eventually made my way up to the secret room. This was probably the last time my feet would tread upon these stones. When I arrived at the top, I did not enter directly. I stood and stared at the dragon tapestry. In the torchlight, the dragon looked so lifelike. The dark eyes seemed to be staring at me, and its scales seemed to glitter.

I gasped suddenly. Scales! Of course! *My skin hangs in a balance; measure and weigh.* Scales were used for balancing different weights.

"A dragon!" I blurted. "The answer to the riddle is a dragon. They are afraid of water. That must be the prize, and they love fire. That is the bane. Of course." I smacked my forehead. "I should have thought of it before."

Grinning, I grabbed the tapestry and drawing it back, I threw open the door. As I stepped into the secret room, a surprising sight greeted me. A fire was crackling in the hearth, and Tren-Lore was standing in the middle of the chamber. He had a sword in hand and he was flowing through attack moves with a fierce intensity that stayed any words of greeting I may have had for him. I watched him moving with a warrior's ease. The flickering firelight glittered off the silver dragon insignia that branded the corner of his tunic. His hair was a spiky mess, and his jaw was clenched with effort. For the first time I noticed how handsome Tren-Lore was.

"What are you doing here?" Tren-Lore asked me suddenly, though I had not realized he knew I had entered.

I shook off my cloak of private thoughts. "I did not want to be in the kitchen. I do not feel like celebrating the fact that I am leaving." Walking over to the corner, I hefted one of the swords. I felt the familiar weight pull at my arm. "Can I help you practice?"

He stopped moving abruptly and looked at me. His face seemed sad. He nodded.

We assumed ready positions, swords in our right hands. I made the first move, a low thrust that he blocked easily. He returned the strike, and I stopped his blade just in time. We fought for only moments before I was backed into a corner with Tren-Lore's sword leveled at my chest.

"Switch hands," I said. The words felt like an enchantment, summoning up the past.

We sparred time after time, until we were both breathing hard. Sweat made a cold path down my spine as I struggled to defend myself against Tren-Lore's latest attack. Our initial smiles had faded as our concentration increased. I was lost in the fight, and it seemed that with each blow I deflected, my unhappiness lessened. Tren-Lore struck over and over again, and I blocked with a fierce determination. My arm was shaking and I was gasping for air, but I forced myself to continue.

Tren-Lore's sword flashed down at me and I blocked high. Our blades crashed above our heads, and at the same instant, with the same force, his stormy blue eyes met mine. Grief and fear were in his gaze. He too had been giving life to his emotional battle, but his sadness was not to be defeated with strength or a weapon. He threw his sword to the ground, and I let my arms fall slowly to my sides. The hilt of my sword slipped through my stiff fingers. It clattered on the flagstones as Tren-Lore grabbed my upper arms.

"Lara." His voice was ragged and desperate. "Lara, swear that nothing will change. Swear that you and I will always be the same."

We shared this fear. Both of us were terrified that we would lose each other, lose friendship such as we had never experienced before. I felt deeply connected to him at that moment. Tren-Lore was my best friend. He was dreams come to life, dreams of heroes, dreams of friendship.

"I swear it in blood," I said solemnly. "We will always be the same."

Tren-Lore released my arms, and we drew our daggers. He put his blade to the inside of his hand and slid the sharp metal across it. I did not even hesitate. The oath was more important than the pain I knew was coming. I cut my palm without wincing and then watched as the blood began to run into the creases of my skin. Tren-Lore held up his hand and I pressed my fingertips to his, my palm to his palm. It was warm with his blood.

"Dore kavens, dore bellads, morian penent," Tren-Lore murmured.

I recognized the verse immediately, though I would not have been able to recite it myself. It was the Old Tongue and from the final *Rayn*. It was the promise Rayn and his best friend Solra had made to each other. There, in the final chapter of the seventh novel, they faced their last peril together. They fought and fell, but the oath, *two bodies, two blades, one blood*, linked their spirits for the next life and the lives thereafter.

"Morian penent," I whispered.

* * *

The next day dawned with the promise of summer heat. We had been up before the sun rose, and now we were awaiting our coach outside the palace walls. I had cried myself to sleep the night before, but by morning my tears had boiled into wrath. If it were not for my Healing powers, I would not have to leave Caladore. I had never asked for such ability, and I did not want it. To further aggravate me, my head was beginning to throb with a headache. I had run out of the elixir I made from the leaf Draows had given me, and so I was forced to suffer.

"End this," I muttered, and pressed my fingers to my temples.

"What was that, young lady?" Sophie asked warningly. She was looking down at me with arched eyebrows.

I pulled my bonnet down over my eyes and kicked angrily at a stone on the ground. "Nothing," came my surly reply. I was doing my very best impression of Storm Wing.

"You will see that this is not as bad as you are making it seem," Sophie assured me as I watched her hands nervously smooth the front of her dress.

I did not reply, and we stood in silence until the noise of the coach upon the road came to our ears. The carriage pulled up in front of us and the driver clambered down from his high perch.

"Good morning to you ladies," said the man. He swept his hat from his head to reveal a shining bald scalp. "I am Terrel, your carriage driver."

"I am Lady Grim," replied Sophie, putting a hand on my back and adding, "and this is Lara."

"Nice to make your acquaintance," Terrel said as he shoved his hat back onto his head. "Now, let us get this luggage onto the carriage so we can be off."

With a grunt, he hefted Sophie's heavy trunk onto the back of the carriage, then helped Sophie and I up into our seats before slamming the door shut behind us. We could hear him whistling as he climbed up in front. With a jingle of the reins and an inaudible call to his team, we jerked forward.

"Oh, my!" Sophie put her hand to her heart. "Ascendants preserve us."

I turned around in my seat and watched Caladore fade into the distance. I imprinted the castle's proud gray walls and snapping blue flags in my memory. This was the second home I had left behind. Suddenly my tears returned. I leaned against the side of the rocking carriage and wept silently.

* * *

Our journey was a weary one, but Sophie made things easier by telling me all the stories she remembered from her youth. We sang songs together, and when I was not sighing with boredom, complaining of headaches, or staring mournfully at the cut across my palm, I had a fairly good time. Each night we stopped at an inn, and every morning we set off before dawn.

As the sun fell on the last day of our journey, we pulled into the courtyard of an inn that was larger than the others we had stayed in. It was a pleasant looking two-story building with torches flanking the entrance. The lower windows glowed warmly and a happy harmony of voices floated out into the dusk.

Terrel opened the carriage door. "The Jolly Bard," he declared with a smile, removing his hat and bowing deeply. The flickering torchlight danced on his bald head. "This is one of the best inns this side of Caladore," Terrel continued. "It is about as warm and friendly as can be."

"And clean, I hope," Sophie comment dryly. Taking Terrel's hands, she gingerly descended from the carriage.

"That too, my dear lady," he replied as the corners of his eyes creased in amusement.

I scrambled out of the carriage before Terrel could offer me his assistance, and we all started up toward the inn. I fell in step with Terrel and we began talking of the road ahead, and the length of the journey tomorrow.

"We should get to Karsalin before the old sun gets to setting," said Terrel.

I groaned. "That long?"

Terrel laughed and clapped me on the back. "You know, Lara, I have never once been a passenger, and I never intend to be one. Terrel, I say to myself, why would you be sitting when you could be doing? Tomorrow you come and sit up front with me, and the trip will not seem so long."

I agreed eagerly, and that night my sleep was disturbed by the anticipation brewing inside me. I was already awake when a light knock sounded upon the door. I threw back my covers and padded over the cold floor. I opened the door and found Terrel standing on the other side.

"Now tell me truthfully Lara, were you sleeping?"

"No," I replied earnestly. "I have been awake for a long, long time. I was too excited to sleep."

He laughed jovially. I did not think it was the sound of humor so much as an expression of happiness. "Wonderful! I shall await you and the good Lady Grim at the coach."

I nodded and closed the door. I tiptoed to Sophie's bed and leaned over her. "Sophie," I whispered, "Sophie." There was no response from the sleeping woman. "Sophie!" I said in a louder, more insistent voice.

Her eyes snapped open and she sat up straight in bed, looking about wildly. Her gaze finally settled upon me. "By every Ascendant there ever was!" Sophie declared. "Do not do that to me!"

"I am sorry," I replied, leaping onto my bed and jumping up and down with unbridled energy. "Terrel just came and he says it is time to leave and he is waiting for us at the carriage and he invited me to sit up front with him today."

Sophie rose stiffly from her bed. "He did, did he? Well, I suppose that will be all right, if Terrel does not mind. I swear," Sophie muttered and knuckled her lower back, "those mattresses are stuffed with rocks. Lara, stop jumping on the bed."

Complying as best I could, I made one last grand vault off the bed and ran to get dressed. I was done far before Sophie, and sat in a chair watching as she fussed over her hair. I could not help but smile to myself. By the end of the day, no matter how carefully she pinned it up, tendrils would always escape, spoiling her carefully created look of sternness. Terrel was waiting by the carriage when we left the Jolly Bard. He helped Sophie into the carriage, and I clambered up beside him. We were soon off on the final leg of our journey.

"Now," said Terrel, as he gave the reins a tug to the left, "how old are you, Lara?"

"In..." I paused, trying to figure out how many days there were until I turned twelve. "In fifteen more days, I will be in my second Summer Year."

Terrel chuckled. "Plenty old enough. Here, my girl, take the reins." He held them out to me, and I stared at him in disbelief. "There now, just take hold of them and give them a little shake. We will make these beauties canter and give your dear Lady Grim something to complain about."

I smiled at him and hesitantly reached for the reins. The leather was hard against my fingers, and my heart beat wildly with fear and exhilaration.

"Get a nice, strong grip. Do you have them? Now, give them a shake and yell *yah*!" Terrel instructed.

I moved the reins slightly and repeated the utterance as he had told me.

"Oh, Lara, you can do better than that! Louder now, girl, from the belly!" He patted his own stomach and laughed heartily. "Say it like you mean it."

"Yah!" I shouted and snapped the reins.

The horses jolted into a trot, and Terrel whooped in encouragement.

Perhaps it was this increased speed or Terrel's company, but the little town of Karsalin seem to leap from the very ground we were treading upon. I felt as though I was about to burst with energy as we clattered down the cobblestone streets. We drove through the town and left the last few houses behind. Far in the distance, I spotted a cheerful little cottage perched on a small hill overlooking the town. We headed in that direction.

When we arrived, Terrel helped Sophie from the coach, and I hopped down off the seat. I landed with a thud, earning me a disapproving look from Sophie. "That is very unladylike, Lara!" she scolded, shaking a finger at me.

Terrel laughed, and I smiled shamelessly. Sophie looked quite exasperated but did not say anything.

After fetching our trunk, Terrel tipped his hat. "It has been a true pleasure traveling with you, Lady Grim," he said in a sincere voice. The quick wink he gave me seemed to indicate contrary feelings.

I covered my mouth so I would not laugh out loud. It was not a pleasure traveling with Sophie, no matter who you were.

Terrel turned to me. "And Lara, you drive like you were born to it. I will miss you on the way home." With that, he clambered up into his seat and after calling loudly to his team and flicking his reins, he and his coach were gone.

Sophie looked at me, the expression on her face the preamble to the scowl she wore when she was angry with me. "Driving?" she echoed. "Were you-"

Just then, the door of the cottage burst open and out ran two young girls. "Mother, Mother!" cried the girls, "They are here!" Sophie was suddenly surrounded by two brown-haired girls who were hugging her wildly and crying, "Auntie Sophie, Auntie Sophie!"

I stood to one side, watching them and feeling very out of place.

"Lara!" declared a voice, sounding very happy and very familiar.

Namin was coming out of the house, wiping her hands on a dishcloth. "Hello," I said with a shy smile.

A bearded man with an unlit pipe clenched in his teeth accompanied a short, brown-haired girl out of the cottage. I would not have considered the girl to be pretty, but there was something that made her very striking. Her jaw was strong and her eyes wide. She was wearing a very pretty green dress with her long hair twisted in a knot at the base of her neck.

"Hello!" Namin replied. She caught me in a warm embrace, and then held me out at arm's length. "Look how tall you are getting! Sophie, what have you been feeding this girl?"

Sophie chuckled and turned to give her sister a hug. "Nothing that you have not been feeding your own children. Where do they find the time to grow this much?"

Everyone was laughing and talking at once. Amidst the clamor, I was introduced to Namin's husband, Rolias. He had a booming, jolly voice and insisted that I call him Uncle Rolias. I was also introduced to Namin's three daughters. Dyradan, clad in green, was a year older than me. She was followed by Lilock, who was in her eighth Spring, and Garidet, who was only five Springs old.

As Namin ushered us inside the house, Dyradan was at my side asking me about Caladore, while little Garidet slipped her hand warmly into mine. My feelings of alienation ebbed. Perhaps Karsalin would not be as bad as I had feared.

* * *

That night we had a marvelous dinner and I laughed so hard that my sides hurt. After everyone had eaten their fill, Namin called the girls into the kitchen to help with the dishes.

"Sophie," she insisted, "sit by the fire and relax with Rolias. And you," Namin gazed sternly at her husband, "no smoking."

"But Namin," Rolias protested as he and Sophie pulled their chairs close to the hearth. "What is a man if he cannot enjoy smoking his pipe before the fire?"

"He is a man who can enjoy smoking his pipe outside," she replied with a fond smile, and ducked into the kitchen. "Come on, girls."

"Outside!" scoffed Rolias, and put his pipe into his mouth.

"Father!" cried Lilock, leaping to the side of his chair. "Mother said that-"

Rolias waved his hand at her. "I heard her, I heard her. I can sit with an unlit pipe in my mouth if I want to."

Dyradan burst into laughter and rolled her eyes. "Father, you are so silly."

Rolias reached over and tickled Lilock. "Go help your mother!" he said over his daughter's squeals of laughter.

Dishes were not nearly as dull as they were in Caladore. Namin taught us a song she said the girls at Telnayis sang when they were on dish duty. We were nearly at the end of the dishes when we were finally able to give a mistake-free rendition. As Lilock tossed Dyradan the final pot, the last stanza echoed confidently about the kitchen.

Fast with that plate, quick with that spoon!
Scrubbing we can do without, rinsing makes us swoon!
Spots are never noticed, eating soap is not so bad!
Dishes must be hurried when outside awaits a charming
lad!

Dyradan banged the pot into the cupboard. A resounding clang marked the end of dishes and the end of the song.

That evening I enjoyed myself so much, I forgot about the circumstances that had brought me to Karsalin. The night felt like an island of time which lay clear from both present and past. After dishes, the girls and I went outside to play. I could feel nothing but happiness amidst all the laughter and games. When Namin and Sophie called us inside, however, I was quickly reminded of my woes.

"Here, Lara." Namin handed me a glass full of a purple liquid. "Drink this before you go to bed. It will prevent a headache from awakening you in the night."

I stared at the glass and then hesitantly took it from Namin. "If I am a Healer, why can I not Heal myself?" I muttered bitterly.

"The entire idea of Healing is adding extra energy to a depleted source. If your life energy is low, you have no way of adding to it. You may, of course, regain it over time, just as all people do when they heal naturally. But enough of that. Tonight is for sleeping, and tomorrow we will start training." Namin bent to kiss my cheek. "Off to bed with you now."

The idea of being trained as a Healer terrified me. I felt sick with dread. Placing the glass to my lips, I drank in the memories. I remembered being shunned and scorned because my mother was a Healer. I remembered the public aspersions and hate, the secretive knocks upon our door that heralded people who felt ashamed at seeking the help of a Healer. I felt desperately alone and lost. I wished that I was back in Caladore. If only I could run up to the secret room and find Tren-Lore waiting for me. We could practice and talk, and he would include me in his world and save me from this shame. I began to cry. They were tears of homesickness, loneliness, and fear of the future. I lay stiffly on the edge of the bed with my back to Dyradan, muffled sobs shaking my body.

"Lara?" she whispered, not wanting to awaken her sisters who were sleeping in the bed next to ours.

Quiet sobs were my only reply. Rolling over, Dyradan gently placed her arm around my shoulders and snuggled up to my shuddering back. She did not offer any other consolation, but her simple gesture of comfort soothed me. It eased my pain, and after some time, I drifted off to sleep with Dyradan breathing warmly on my neck.

When I awoke the next morning, Dyradan was laying on her back with one arm flung across my throat and the other dangling off the bed. I eased away from her and tiptoed from the room, the unhappiness of last night still staining my mood.

Namin was sitting in the kitchen with an open book before her and a cup of steaming liquid upon the table. Cheerful morning light danced along the floor and counters. She looked up as I entered the kitchen, and tucking her long earthy-colored hair behind her ears, she smiled warmly. "Good morning, Lara." Namin lifted her mug and sipped from it. "Would you like some tea?"

I shook my head and came to sit in the chair beside her. I pulled my knees up inside my sleeping gown and wrapped my arms around myself. "Namin," I began uncertainly, curling my toes into the hard wood of my chair, "do I have to train to become a Healer? I really do not want to."

Namin put down her cup and looked at me in concern. "At the very least, I must teach you to control your powers. You cannot live your entire life with a headache. Beyond that..." she paused and pursed her lips. "I will not force anything on you."

"Good," I declared in relief and let my legs slide to the floor. "Perhaps I will have some tea."

Namin rose and went about making me a cup of tea. "How much do you know about Healing?" she asked as she poured steaming water into a carved wooden mug.

I rested my elbows on the table and tried to remember everything I had learned. "Life energy...no..." I was attempting to recall the exact words my mother had taught me. "Each person is filled with an energy that gives them life, but most cannot bring this energy under their control. Healers are able to channel their life energy to help others."

"You would have done well at Telnayis," Namin chuckled and set my tea before me. "I could never manage to quote the Healer's doctrine directly."

I smiled under her praise. "I do not remember the rest of it exactly, but I know that Healers have more life energy than most people, and the bigger the wound, the more energy it takes to Heal it."

"Very good," Namin said as she resumed her seat. "Now you need to understand that it is the excess of life energy which causes your headaches. Imagine it as a wind. Similar to most people, young Healers experience life energy as a gentle breeze which blows through the body. As Healers age, however, the breeze gathers strength, building into a veritable storm. To stop your pain, Lara, you must learn to calm your energy."

"All right," I muttered sullenly as I wrapped my hands about the warm mug. "How do I do that?"

My training began as Namin explained about learning to sense my own life energy and using my mind to calm it. My Summer Year found me able to control my energies for short periods of time, but as more and more days slipped past, I was eventually able to consistently calm my energy without much thought.

When the headaches finally ceased, Namin approached me again, asking if I wanted to learn more. "You have your mother's power, Lara. You could do so much if you were to receive more training."

"*I* am going to be a Healer when I grow up," little Garidet told me, as though this would persuade me to learn more.

The power had not been passed to either of her sisters, and it was Garidet's fondest dream that she would be the daughter who was gifted as a Healer.

"We shall see," Namin replied, patting her hair. "Lara, what do you think? Would you like more training?"

"No, thank you," I replied quickly, squeezing my toes in my shoes.

With my headaches gone, I felt no desire to learn more. I was safe from the scorn of others and quite content to spend my days with Dyradan. Healing held no interest for her, and she often told me I was better off without it. Dyradan focused her attention upon boys, dresses, and different ways to do her hair. Under her influence, I soon became involved in the social circles of Karsalin. I could not say that I enjoyed her company as much as Tren-Lore's, but I did like her very much, and she certainly introduced me to some interesting new aspects of life.

* * *

Dyradan and I were ambling along the streets of Karsalin on an errand for Namin. She had asked us to go to town for some meat. Dyra and I had agreed without hesitation. Myrrancy, the boy Dyradan fancied, worked in his father's butcher shop in Karsalin. We often went walking in the hope that we might see him. Dyradan's nightly prayers were directed only to the Ascendant of Unity, and were pleas to arrange some sort of chance meeting between herself and Myrrancy. Today it looked as though her prayers would be answered.

"Does my hair look all right?" Dyradan asked, patting the pile of brown curls she had wound about the crown of her head.

I examined her closely and nodded. "You look beautiful, Dyra." I was sure Myrrancy would be suitably impressed.

She smiled brightly. "Good." Turning purposefully, she walked toward the butcher shop.

I followed close behind her. A bell tinkled cheerfully as we entered the store. The heavy smell of meat assaulted my nose and I looked about at the hanging fowls and large barrels pushed against the walls. For all of the times I had sauntered past it, I had never actually been inside the shop. Except for Myrrancy, who was slicing meat, and his friend Rion, we were the only people in the store. Both boys looked toward the door when the bell heralded our arrival.

"Hello, girls," Myrrancy greeted us warmly, although his eyes were focused only upon Dyra. "What can I get you?"

Dyra was grinning foolishly. "Mother sent us to get a slice of meat."

"Wonderful!" replied Myrrancy with a broad smile. "Meat is wonderful!"

It was all I could do to keep from laughing. I had never seen two people so pleased about meat. I could only imagine what Myste would have said if he had witnessed the scene.

"Is she brewing up another potion to poison us all?" Rion asked, absently pushing his ear-length sandy brown curls out of his eyes.

I glared at him. "No, but if she does I will make sure you get some." I had not liked Rion from the moment we had first met. He mocked everyone with a mean-spirited joy and thought he was the Ascendants' gift to the world.

Dyra gave me a look that was meant to implore my silence, and then turned to Rion with a stiff smile. "It is for dinner."

Rion ignored her entirely. His attention was upon me, and his mouth was crooked with spiteful enjoyment. "Or is the meat for you, Lara? I heard you are a Healer, too."

"She is not a Healer," Dyradan insisted, and at the same time Myrrancy leaned over the counter and told Rion to stop it.

I did not know how to reply. It was as though Rion had slid a sword through a chink in my armor. I stood in cold horror, the blade of his words running painfully through my body.

"I have to go," I said abruptly, and turning swiftly, fled the shop.

"Nice work, Rion," I heard Myrrancy say sarcastically.

Rion's reply came just as I shut out the butcher shop and everyone inside. "I was just teasing her. She should not take everything so seriously."

I stalked away from the shop with my back rigid, my head held high and a grim expression on my face. Fury gradually seeped into my body, pushing out the original shock I had felt at his comment. I wished I was a Sorcerer, or a Sanysk, or any other being that would allow me to exact revenge upon Rion.

When I arrived home, I would not tell Sophie or Namin why I was back so early, or why I was in such bad spirits. Instead, I stormed out to the garden and sat with my back against the cottage, staring at the fallen leaves skittering across the ground. I missed Tren-Lore more than ever. I longed for his company daily, but it was at times like these that I felt his absence most keenly. I wept for a time, and then sat with my forehead pressed against my bent knees.

Why would anyone want to be a Healer? What drove them to embrace such a curse?

Suddenly, amidst the clamor of my contemplation, there was a loud thud from somewhere in the garden. I looked up, wiping my eyes with the back of my hand. The garden was silent again. Nothing moved, save the strange plants Namin grew in her yard. They swayed on their stiff stalks, and a few copper-colored leaves floated down from the large tree to my right. I could see nothing that might have caused the noise.

I sniffed and scrambled to my feet. The cold seemed to have seeped through my clothes and laid itself across my skin. I stepped toward the door and reached out my hand for the sturdy wooden handle. My fingers touched it but did not take hold. Laying a step away from me was a small bird, its soft white feathers marred with dirt and blood. The bird's black eyes looked wild with fear as I knelt beside it. One of its wings beat against the ground, while the other lay still.

I covered my mouth in a gesture of pity. "What happened to you, little one?"

I looked about the garden for a cat before noticing the greasy smudge left upon the kitchen window. The bird let forth a feeble sound that returned my attention to it. Blood was coming from its sooty beak and its downy breast was heaving. Its eyes had lost that look of fear, and once again, I was caught in an empty gaze. I stumbled back, trying to get away from those blind eyes.

It felt as though the night had leapt upon me. I was surrounded by memories, a thousand images, and a million whispers, all reminding me of the past. The pain and horror of my mother's death returned, and I felt as though I was still crouched in that doorway, still paralyzed by that absence of sight. My chest was tight and I gasped for air, trying to clear my vision, trying to return myself to the present. I dug my fingers into the earth and clung to reality, forcing myself to shut out the blackness of those memories.

"You are not going to die," I said, addressing both past and present.

I crawled forward and gathered the bird into my hands. It was still warm with heat and blood. There was no thought of Rion or any of the cruelty I had endured in Ekrin. There was only my determination; my desire to change the course of events. I took a steadying breath and consciously prevented my mind from calming my life energy. I expected to see the familiar blinding light, to hear my heart pounding in my ears, to feel my Healer's ring burning against my skin. I wanted the heat to rush down my arms and leap from my fingertips into the tiny bird's body. I awaited all of this, but nothing happened. Nothing changed. My ring, my body: all remained cold. No heat came. Another drop of blood dripped from the bird's beak into the creases of its snowy feathers. Why was it not working? I tried again. Still nothing.

"Namin!" I screamed at last. "Namin!"

In an instant, the door burst open and Namin rushed out. In one stride she was kneeling beside me.

"Heal it!" I demanded.

"Oh, Lara, we usually do not heal animals."

"Heal it," I repeated, my voice ragged with desperation. "I have to save her."

There was a pause, and then Namin reached out and took the bird from me. Her green ivy ring was bright against the white feathers. Namin closed her eyes, and for a moment I could see no change. I gathered my own ring up in my hands and held it against my lips, willing the bird to be Healed. Suddenly, its lifeless wing fluttered slightly against Namin's palm and its eyes cleared until they were once again black pools of life. The bird watched me for a moment, and then emitted a joyful, surprised twitter.

I felt happiness swell within me, and relief loosened my tense muscles. Namin smiled and gently tossed the bird up into the air. Wind immediately caught beneath its wings and it disappeared over the garden wall, leaving behind only a lingering trail of song. Namin had given it life. Namin had been able to save her from death. I needed to be able to do that.

"I want to learn," I said quietly, and enclosed my ring tightly in a determined fist.

"What?" Namin exclaimed, and looked at me uncertainly.

I met Namin's gaze and saw hope and love in her eyes. Hers was the gaze of life. I had stared into the eyes of both life and death and realized that Healing could give me the power necessary to banish that cold, unseeing stare. If I was a Healer, I could conquer death and only experience life and light. I could be in a world without darkness.

"I want to learn to become a Healer," I said.

Chapter Fourteen
Talents

"**W**ell," said Namin at the start of our next lesson, "we will have to begin teaching you to read. Much of what you will need to know comes from our ancient writings." She reached for a ragged book with a scuffed leather cover. "This is the first book they had us read in Telnayis," she said.

My eyes ran over the simple text and the large print. I thought ruefully how much I would have liked to have had a book such as this when I was learning to read. There was not one difficult word on the first page. No mention of bowels or any other obscure references to perplex the mind.

Grinning mischievously, I stretched my arm over the table and picked up one of Namin's heavier books. "Karhine," I read aloud, "is derived from a small bush that grows in the southern regions of Caladore and Renarn's wooded areas. When dried, the leaves may be used to alleviate pain." I looked up at Namin, and to my great satisfaction, noted that her expression was one of surprise.

"That is marvelous, Lara!" she exclaimed, pulling the book toward her so that she could see the passage I had read. "Where did you learn to do that?"

I smiled with pleasure, thinking of Tren-Lore and all the time we had spent together as he taught me to read. It had been such fun. I opened my palm and looked at the pale scar running across it. I missed him very much.

"Lara?" Namin prompted.

I was jolted from my musings and realized that I had a very difficult question before me. How would I explain my knowledge of reading without telling her about Tren-Lore?

"Ah...where did I learn?" I repeated, stalling for time. "I... ahh ... a friend taught me."

Namin's lips bent upward and her rosy cheeks creased pleasantly. "He must be quite the friend."

I turned quickly back to the book. "I did not say he was a boy," I protested weakly.

"You did in every way but words," Namin laughed with conspiratorial pleasure. "Is he handsome?"

I felt my face flush as the words reminded me of my thoughts on the night before I left. The image of Tren-Lore standing in the secret room was before my eyes, as clearly as though I had stepped before a mirror that reflected only memories. His sword was in hand, and firelight danced upon his disorderly hair.

"I...I do not know. He is just a friend."

"Very well," said Namin, as though she knew something I did not, "but perhaps someday you will tell me more about him."

I chose not to elaborate on my friendship with Tren-Lore, and we returned to Healing. Soon we were engrossed in herb lore. Namin said that having the ability to channel life energy was important, but she wanted me to understand the properties of plants, be able to set broken bones, and know how to bind wounds *before* using my powers.

As these topics became familiar to me, so did Karsalin and the little cottage I shared with Sophie, Namin and her family. I began to feel very much at home. A daily pattern of living slowly established, and I felt like a young sapling sending out an ever-increasing number of roots into the moist fertile soil. I drew sustenance from awakening every morning to the sounds of Namin and Sophie laughing in the other room. After breakfast, Namin and I would lock ourselves in the kitchen. Amidst the pale winter sunshine, Namin's numerous stacks of books, and the copious jars of strange herbs and mixtures, I eagerly absorbed all she could teach me.

My love for Healing grew steadily, but it was a passion that I kept close to my heart. I was careful to conceal this aspect of myself from Dyra, Myrrancy, Rion, and Elanyn – the company I most generally kept. With Namin, however, I was voracious in my hunger for new knowledge.

"When will I actually learn to Heal?" I demanded one day.

Winter was at its coldest point, and we had all been locked in the cottage for days on end. The air smelled faintly of wood smoke, and our after-lunch session seemed to have dragged on forever. I was feeling frustrated and tired, and the noise of Garidet, Lilock, and Dyra spilling from the other room made part of me wish that I could join in their fun.

"You *are* learning how to Heal," Namin replied, shutting the book we had been studying. "A good tourniquet, the right diagnosis, these are as important to our art as channeling energy. Use your knowledge rather than your powers whenever possible, Lara. But if you must, always remember that it is a Healer's job to give life, not to take away death. There will be some people you will not be able to save."

I shook my head resolutely. "If I learn enough, and if I have enough power, there will always be a way."

Namin reached over and took my hand in hers. The expression upon her face was the same as my mother's when I had protested this familiar part of the Healer's doctrine.

"No," Namin said quietly, 'sometimes people are beyond our reach. When you Heal someone, you are giving them a piece of your energy. If that person's energy is too eroded by injury or age, you will not have enough life energy to save them. You could die trying."

I yanked my hand away from Namin's grasp and stood up abruptly. I did not want to believe that. If I had been able to Heal when I was younger, I *would* have saved my mother. Nothing would have stopped me, not the Healer's doctrine, not anything!

"Perhaps giving your life for someone else's is worthwhile! Perhaps sometimes it *should* be a Healers job to take away death!"

Namin looked sad. "Even if you wanted to, you would not be able to. By some magic that lies within us, or by some feat of the Ascendants, you will simply not be able to Heal someone who has lost too much of their life energy." She paused, and the shadows of the coming night darkened the air around us. "I tried, Lara. Once, when I first became a Healer, I tried. It was like trying to channel through a stone wall. The energy would not leave my fingers."

I did not reply, but rather turned and walked resolutely from the kitchen. I did not care about Namin's experiences. I would be different. I would be able to cure death.

Despite these small disagreements, by the time the evening dishes were done and Namin had pulled her old ragged chair to the hearth, peace was restored to the house. We gathered about Namin as she told us stories from ancient Healer's lore or from one of the many books she had read. Garidet often pleaded for tales about Sophie and Namin's youth, but I liked to hear the stories about when my mother and Namin had been at Telnayis together. By the time Namin finished her stories, we were all more than ready for the comforts of bed.

The two younger children usually fell asleep quickly, the peace of their mother's stories wrapped about them like warm quilts. Dyra and I were not so swift to find slumber. We would talk long into the night. We complained about Rion and how mean he could be at times. She speculated about what kissing Myrrancy would be like, and I asked how she thought she would breathe with her face pressed against his. Our voices would eventually grow languid and soft as weariness numbed even our lips. We would drop off to sleep, the sound of quiet breathing creating a peaceful rhythm in the still room.

* * *

Spring was breaking over Karsalin and as we sat eating dinner, a warm breeze twisted through the window and stirred the herbs I had hung from the rafters. I inhaled deeply as the scent of rosepyr filled the kitchen. I silently listed its uses in my head. Rosepyr could be used for treating infection of the bowels, sores of the mouth, and in small doses could be used to elevate weariness, but only for short amounts of time. I smiled and stabbed another piece of meat with my fork. Putting it into my mouth, I chewed contently.

Dyra leaned over, a slice of bread halfway to her mouth and mumbled, "Myrrancy wants us to meet him at the Cleft after dinner."

I nodded.

"Where are you going after dinner?" Namin inquired pleasantly as she took a sip of her milk.

"To see boys!" Lilock giggled.

Dyradan swallowed the bite of bread she had just taken and looked down the table at her sister. "They are just our friends." She turned back to Namin. "Mother, may we go?"

"I do not see why not," Namin replied.

"But be back before dark," Sophie added.

"That is Sophie's favorite rule," I told Dyra when at last the dishes had been finished and we had fled the house. "Once Tr- once I was playing outside and I got back only a little bit after dark. She made me stay in the kitchen for an entire week!"

"That is nothing," Dyra began as we started the hike up to the Cleft. "Once..."

She proceeded to tell me a very funny story about a similar incident.

When we arrived at the Cleft we were laughing so hard that we had to lean on each other for support.

"Hello!" shouted Myrrancy, and raised his hand in greeting.

Myrrancy was standing near the back of the Cleft with Rion and few other boys. A group of girls stood giggling a few feet away from them. This was a popular spot for the older children of Karsalin. It was one of the few places in Karsalin that boasted a stretch of level ground, and the sheer rock walls that rose on either side provided protection from the elements, as well as the prying eyes of adults.

As soon as Elanyn spotted us, she hurried to Dyra's side. Elanyn was very shy and uncertain around boys. She only felt comfortable if she had an army of female companions to help her stage the onslaught of conversation. "What are you laughing at?" she asked nervously, catching a piece of her black wavy hair to put in her mouth.

I winced. I liked Elanyn, but that was one habit I had difficulty tolerating. "Just a story Dyra was telling me about when she was in trouble with her mother."

"Oh." Elanyn looked relieved. She always worried that if anyone was caught in merriment, it would inevitably be at her expense. She turned to Dyra. "Guess what I heard? Jaylie said that she heard that Myrrancy was going to ask you to the dance."

Dyradan's eyes gleamed and her face flushed. "Really? Where did she hear that?"

I left the girls to their plotting. The dance was months away, and I could not see a point in speculating about something that was so far in the future. I was much more interested in the few scraggly-looking horses that the boys had brought with them. Not having seen many horses since I left Caladore, I went to have a closer look at the animals. I smiled at Myrrancy as I approached, and deliberately walked past Rion without acknowledging his presence.

"Hey, Lara," he jeered, "we heard you laughing a league away. Do you always snort when you laugh?"

The boys snickered.

I shot Rion a withering glance. I did not snort when I laughed. I took a deep breath and summoned up my best Myste-like comment. "Do you always sound so stupid when you talk?"

The group responded with rough delight, and Rion grinned shamelessly at me. I did not return the smile. Instead, I turned my attention to the horses. I walked among them, letting my fingers run along their coarse coats. There was not a great need for horses in the small mountain town. The paths the people traveled were generally too narrow and treacherous for horses.

"Where did you get them?" I asked, stopping to rub the muzzle of a shaggy gray mare. I suddenly felt a pang of homesickness. I wished vainly that it were Paence's warm breath that was caressing my palms, or Quell's ... or even Storm Wing's angry huffing.

"My father," Fremer said proudly. Fremer was a short, stocky boy with flaming red cheeks. "He traded them for some of our goats two days ago. He is going to use them to haul ale down to the Jolly Bard. The man who sold them to us said they were the finest animals this side of Karsalin."

I raised my eyebrows and had to close my lips tightly against the comments that were flooding my mouth. If only I had Storm Wing there to show them. Then they would have known what a fine animal really looked like. That would have made Rion think twice about teasing me again.

"All right," Myrrancy declared, "everyone get to your horses." He put a hand on my shoulder. "You might want to go stand with Dyra and Elanyn. You do not want to get hurt."

I looked at him, my face crumpled with confusion. "Why? What is going on?"

Myrrancy hauled himself up into his saddle. "We are racing," he explained.

"So get out of the way," Rion added, and clumsily spurred his horse between Myrrancy and me. "This is better left to men."

I scoffed. "Then you had better get out of the way, too."

"Lara!" called Dyra from the side of the Cleft. "Come on!"

I looked over at her and Elanyn. They were sitting on a small outcropping of rock on the left hand side of the Cleft. The girls were bathed in the pink luminance of the setting sun and made a striking image. They gestured for me to join them at their vantage point. I remained where I was and returned my gaze to Rion and Myrrancy. They were both sitting awkwardly in their saddles, and I was reminded of when Tren-Lore had first taught me to ride.

"Let me ride one of those horses. I bet you anything I can beat all of you."

Myrrancy looked startled, but Rion seemed interested. "What exactly are you willing to bet?"

I shrugged. It did not matter what I bet. Tren-Lore had taught me all I needed to know in order to beat these mountain boys. "Anything you like. It does not matter to me."

"All right." Rion's green eyes met mine. "If you lose, you have to kiss me – on the mouth," he added with a mischievous grin.

Kiss him! My mind screamed in shock and apprehension. He would pick the very thing that would disgust me the most, I thought bitterly. I struggled to maintain my composure. I could not let Rion see the impact his remark had made upon me.

"Rion, come on," Myrrancy protested, but Rion made no reply to him.

"Well, Lara?" he asked, checking the sideways steps of his mount with a hard tug on the reins.

I swallowed hard and reminded myself that the bet did not matter. I would not have to kiss him because I would not lose. "Deal," I agreed with a short nod, "but if *I* win, you have to pull all the weeds from our garden." It was a chore Dyra and I had been dreading since the snow began to melt.

"Lara! Rion!" Myrrancy's brow was furrowed. "Come on. We do not even have a horse for her to ride. Lara, do you really want to do this?"

Rion leaned down from his saddle and held out his hand. I took it. His palm was warm and we shook firmly.

"Fremer," Rion barked as he straightened in his saddle, "give Lara your horse."

Fremer responded to Rion's order with a dumbfounded, open-mouthed stare. "B-but they are *my* horses," he finally stuttered.

"Exactly. You can ride them whenever you like. Lara needs one right now." He looked at me and smirked. "She thinks she can beat us."

Incredulous shouts rose from the group, and as Fremer dismounted and I swung up into his saddle, I heard Dyra and Myrrancy voicing protests. I did not look at them, but instead concentrated on getting my horse into the line that was forming. Dyra could yell as loudly as she wanted, and my heart could pound as hard as it could, but I would not be deterred. I was going to win this race!

When everyone had jostled into place, Fremer stood at the side of the line and, inhaling a great breath of air, cried, "Ready!"

I tensed in my saddle, gripping hard with my knees.

"Set!"

I spared a quick glance at Rion. He looked nervous.

"Go!"

I dug my heels into the flanks of my horse, and the animal moved forward in a canter. There was not the surge of speed I had felt in Paence or seen in Storm Wing, but I was quick to turn the lope into a gallop. My body remembered the motion and I moved smoothly in time with the animal's gate. I glanced to my left and saw that Rion was just behind me, but steadily falling back. My blood was surging and the sound of hooves against packed dirt resounded in my ears. They struck over and over again, and suddenly I was drawing in rein. The race was over. I was alone at the end of the Cleft for a moment before the others came thundering up around me. They were all shouting enthusiastically and clapping me on the back.

"Incredible!"

"Where did you learn to ride like that?"

"That was great, Lara!"

Dyra, Elanyn and Fremer were running from the other end of the flat piece of land. They were cheering excitedly. Rion caught my gaze and gave me an appreciative grin. It was the first time I had been surrounded by so much praise, and while I smiled outwardly and tried to respond to everyone's exclamations, I felt distracted. My eyes searched the crowd. I almost felt as though I were part of a story almost, but something kept the moment from slipping into the realm of tales. I suddenly realized with a jolt of pain that the person I most wanted, the hero I needed to complete the story, was leagues and leagues away.

* * *

That night when Dyra had fallen asleep after rejoicing about not having to pull weeds this spring, I crept from our chamber and made my way through the dark house into the kitchen. I lit a candle and set it upon the table. I rummaged about until I found a quill and paper. The scratching of my pen upon the parchment seemed loud in the slumbering house, but I was soon so lost in recounting the events of the day that I did not notice the sound or the passage of time. It was only when the candle sputtered from life and returned me to the darkness of night that I decided to draw the letter to a close. It had felt so good writing to Tren-Lore. It was as though the words had created a spell that could remove the barriers of distance, if only for a short time. I scrawled the last line in the dark, trusting that my hand would be able to form the letters without the aid of my eyes.

Morian penent, I wrote, and then padded off to bed.

My letter lay under my pillow, forgotten for the better part of two days, when suddenly there was a knock upon the door. Namin and I were the only ones in the house, and I scampered away from the table to answer the call. Perhaps it was Rion, come to fulfill our bargain. It was not Rion standing on our doorstep, however, but a man dressed in the gray and blue uniform of Caladore. Mud splattered the front of his tunic, and he looked as though he had been traveling for many days.

"I have a letter for someone called Lara," he said, wearily rubbing at his eyes. "The people in town told me she lived up on the hill."

"I am Lara," I told him in wonder.

"Then this is for you." He held out a folded piece of parchment.

The red wax seal bore a dragon insignia. I gasped and grabbed it from him. The message was from Tren-Lore! I clutched it to my chest. "Thank you!"

The man smiled. "If you would like me to bear a message back to Caladore, you can find me at the inn. I depart for home in the morning."

The letter hidden beneath my pillow came suddenly to my mind. "Wait here," I cried and dashed off to my room. I returned triumphantly, flushed with excitement. "Here!" I said and handed him the message. "Please give this to Prince Tren-Lore."

With a bemused expression, the messenger took the proffered paper and bowed slightly before turning to leave. When he had gone, I immediately opened Tren-Lore's letter. I stood in the entranceway, my eyes devouring the familiar script.

Dear Lara,

How is Karsalin? I have been thinking that the mountains of Karsalin are probably the same mountains Rayn got lost in when he ran away from home. Are there any signs of dragons there?

I smiled at this, for I too had been wondering if there would be any dragon caves gaping at me from the mountainside. The closest I had come, however, was the dragon insignia on Tren-Lore's letter. Either these were the wrong mountains, or the dragons had fled the rocky peaks in the days between Rayn's life and mine.

Dayr, Myste and I have been very busy with training. To Myste's surprise, he has yet to be impaled and die over the course of eight long days. By the way, he sends greetings. The practice is hard, but Dayr and I have been doing lots of work outside of class. Dayr wants to be a Sanysk too.

Jealously stabbed me. It was as though Dayr was taking my place. I chewed on my lip, feeling rather disquieted. As I read on, my anxiety ebbed.

I am reading a book about a Healer right now. It is good, but not as good as the books about Rayn. Still interesting, though. I will send it to you when I am finished with it. How is your training going? Are there lots of Healers in Karsalin?

I went out to the fort yesterday. It looks great. The winter does not seem to have done it any harm. It was hard to get over to the island though. Trying to bail and "paddle" at the same time is not easy.

I laughed fondly.

I wished you had been there. Dayr and I went camping about a fortnight ago. Myste said that it was still too cold to sleep outside and he was probably right. It is getting much warmer everyday now. Myste is very pleased so he says he will come with us the next time we go. It is strange to think that we do not have much more time for things like that. This summer we will be leaving for training in Tolrem. Then, neither one of us will be at home.

In a way, I am excited to leave. Father decided that Yolis' training as a knight would end when the rest of us went to Tolrem. Father says Yolis needs to train for his kingship more than his knighthood. Leaving home will not be very sad, since it means leaving Yolis behind. Besides that, Caladore is not the same anymore. It has not been the same since you left.

My lips parted in a quiet expression of happiness. I was not replaced. He felt my absence as I felt his.

Morian penent.
Tren-Lore

I read the letter again and stood staring at the last words of our pact.

"Lara?" called Namin's voice from end of the hall. "Are you all right?"

I grinned at her and curled my toes. "I am wonderful! A letter came for me." I gestured behind me at the door. "It was a messenger knocking. He brought me a letter from – from my friend."

"The same friend that taught you how to read?" she asked with a smile.

I nodded, and after carefully folding the parchment, ran my finger over the dragon insignia.

"Lara, I am Sophie's younger sister. Keeping secrets from her has become a habit for me. If you want to tell me about this friend of yours, I promise I will not say a word to her... and I will bake you some cookies."

"What?" I exclaimed, looking at her in puzzlement.

"Please tell me about this mystery boy!" she pleaded suddenly, her visage as a woman crumbling away into juvenile curiosity. "I am dying to know."

I blinked rapidly in surprise, and then laughed.

"Come," Namin said, holding out her hand. "We can make some cookies. You can tell me your secrets, and I will tell you mine."

It was in this way that Namin became my confidant. In placing such trust in her, I was rewarded by being the first to know that Namin was going to have a baby.

* * *

The next knock upon our door heralded the arrival of Rion, who had finally come to pull the weeds from our garden. I sat outside with him as he worked. I enjoyed the warm glow of the sunshine that fell around me, I enjoyed the smell of the fresh spring air, and I even enjoyed Rion's company – a little bit. He was, after all, still Rion. He began the afternoon by telling me some jokes he had heard in his father's tavern. I laughed in spite of myself.

"So, where did you learn to ride like that?" asked Rion as he pulled out a handful of spiky gray weeds.

I stared off at the mountainous horizon surrounding us. Somewhere in the far distance I knew that the proud castle of Caladore stood, its dragon flags snapping smartly in the wind. I wondered if my message had reached Tren-Lore yet.

"A friend of mine taught me. When I lived in Caladore, there were always lots of horses around. Fremer's horses look like mules compared to the animals we had in Caladore."

Rion laughed and tugged on some deeply rooted grass that was sprouting in the garden. "Fremer sort of looks like a mule himself."

It was a very mean thing to say about Fremer, but nevertheless I found my lips twitching with amusement. I covered my mouth with my hand. It was always that way with Rion. Without considering it, he bombarded the people around him, jabbing and slashing with a dagger of comments. I could feel both edges of his blade, the cold hurtful side and the wickedly funny side. I was never quite sure if I should reprimand Rion or laugh along with him.

* * *

Warm winds began to blow in from the south, and the taste and feel of summer was soon licking at our faces and rustling the newly green leaves. My third Summer Year arrived, and Namin and Sophie arranged a party, inviting all of the girls and boys that Dyra and I were friends with. It was a wonderful day, but I found that I could not enjoy myself fully. I felt Tren-Lore's absence most sharply.

Time moved on without Tren-Lore, and soon the dance was only days away. It was Dyra's primary preoccupation. She spent days sewing her new dress, and every word that tumbled from her mouth seemed to be about either Myrrancy or the dance. With an Atalium-like knowledge, Elanyn had correctly predicted that Myrrancy would ask Dyra to the dance.

I was more concerned with the garden. Namin had let me decide what was to be planted this year, so I felt a special bond with the rich soil and the germination of the seeds. I spent a great deal of time studying the plants as they matured and memorizing their uses. Garidet would often accompany me. As I lost myself in my learning, she would play quietly in another corner of the garden.

On this particular day she worked diligently, transplanting tiny flowers from one spot to another and encircling them with pebbles. Her soft little voice rose musically in the sweet summer air.

"This is ilatoly," she said happily to herself or some imaginary listener. "No, no, do not cry. It will grow fast, and then we can make your cut all better."

I smiled at her from where I was kneeling in the garden. I had been examining the berries growing on a Fire Leaf shrub, but now I let my mind drift back to a few days ago. A cut on Garidet's foot had become infected, and I had treated it with ilatoly. Namin had been proud of me and had promised to begin more intensive training so I could utilize my powers.

I caressed the secret thought that soon I would be a Healer. Surprisingly, it brought me a great deal of pleasure. I absentmindedly scooped some of the deep brown earth into my hand and let it tumble through my fingers. The gesture was familiar. It was not because I had done it many times before, but because I had often seen my mother perform the same act. Memories filled my mind like sunlight. For an instant, I was blind to the present. I could see my mother kneeling on the warm dirt, her long hair falling over her shoulders. She smiled at me as she leaned forward and took a handful of earth, and allowed it to trickle through her fingers to the ground between us. Her hand was different from mine, though. She did not have the thin scar across her palm, and she wore her Healer's ring on her index finger.

I grabbed at the chain that hung about my neck. Like a sleeper awakened from a dream by their own voice, my movement had returned me from the past. I withdrew the ring and held it before me. It was a soft green, a pale facsimile of the solid lush green color of my mother's ring. I wondered if I had grown enough to be able to wear it.

Abruptly, there was a sound at the gate which led into the garden. I looked up and saw Rion strutting toward me. My heart leapt. It was fear, I told myself. I did not want him to know that I had a Healer's ring, and hastily dropped it down the front of my dress. The smile I greeted Rion with suggested that perhaps the surge of blood I felt upon seeing the handsome young man had causes other than fear.

"Eating worms again, Lara?" he quipped as he stopped before me.

I was beginning to believe that Rion was of some sarcastic religion that did not believe in the word hello. The first words to escape his lips were always teasing comments. The frequency of Rion's visits had increased since he first came to weed the garden. Now, he was visiting on an almost daily basis. He never failed to have some sort of barbed remark to greet me with. We had developed a strange friendship, and from one day to the next, I could never be sure if I liked him or not.

"End you," I replied with playful viciousness and wiped my hands on my skirts.

Rion laughed in delight. "What would Sophie say if I told her you talked like that?"

My mouth crooked in a half smile. "Probably the same thing your father would say if I told him you were stealing apples from old Gregor's orchard."

"You had better not," Rion replied as he came to sit on the band of wood edging the garden, "because then you would be in trouble, too."

"I would not." I sat next to him, feeling very aware of the distance between us. We were so close, yet there was part of me that felt as though even that small distance was as far away as the sky from the earth. "*I* was only watching. *You* were stealing."

Rion turned to face me. His green eyes glittered with anticipation, and I could tell that he was ready to argue. Just then the door burst open and Dyra leaned out.

"Garidet, Lara." She stopped as she noticed Rion. "Oh, hello. Sophie wants you two to come inside and help with the evening meal."

Garidet rubbed her muddy hands onto her skirt and skipped inside.

I nodded. "I will be there in a moment." Dyra closed the door and I looked back at Rion. "Would you like to stay and eat with us?"

He smirked and shook his head. "No, you would probably try to poison me with rat tails and prickle weed."

My jaw clenched, and suddenly the lovely summer day was shredded by my rage. It was such a typical Rion remark. He did that to everyone, prying and clawing into cracks of sensitivity. As of late, his jabs had been without that personal bite, and I had begun to believe he was exempting me from his torture. I had secretly hoped that perhaps he liked me enough to spare me.

"Why do you even bother to come over if you are going to say things like that?" I stood up abruptly. "And prickle weed would not make you sick, you idiot!" I kicked dirt at him and stalked away.

"Lara!" Rion protested. "I was just teasing. Lara, come back!"

I ignored him and marched across the yard toward the door. I had just laid my hand upon the handle when Rion shouted desperately, "Lara, wait!"

He said it with such sincerity that I stopped and turned to face him. He was standing where I had left him, his sandy blond hair falling into his eyes. He pushed it off his forehead and scowled.

"Look. I came..." He clenched his fists, and then relaxed his hands again. His cool demeanor slowly returned. "I came to ask if you would go to the dance with me."

I stared at him in shock, for a moment forgetting that I had been moving or that an answer was required of me. He wanted me to go to the dance with him! I had wanted him to ask and he had! But he had also just mocked me for being a Healer.

"So, will you or not?" Rion persisted, beginning to look a little less confident than before.

I was at a loss for words. I thought of saying, 'No, I would rather go to the Dance with Elesbri and never be seen again'. I thought of saying something demure like the maidens in the stories I had read. 'Why Rion, I thought you would never ask. Go and fetch your steed so we may ride off together'. I thought of a plethora of things to say, but instead ended up stuttering, "A... Ask me tomorrow."

Rion's mouth opened, and surprise seeped into his expression.

I turned and went into the house. It was hot inside, and Sophie was sitting before the small cooking fire turning a roast on a spit. Namin, Dyra and Lilock were at the table shucking corn.

"Are you going to ask Rion in for dinner, Lara?" Sophie asked pleasantly as she looked up from the meat.

"No," I replied grumpily. "Maybe tomorrow."

Sophie chuckled and smoothed back her hair. "What did he say this time?"

"Nothing," I snapped. I did not want to tell Sophie he had asked me to the dance. It seemed embarrassing, and not the kind of thing you talked over with adults who would not understand. "He said nothing at all." I caught Dyra's eye in a silent demand for an immediate conference.

Namin saw the look and quickly said, "Dyra, can you and Lara fetch your father from the upper pasture? Dinner is nearly ready."

"I can go!" Lilock volunteered, half rising from her seat.

Namin put a quieting hand on her daughter's arm. "No, sweet, you stay right here with me. Run along, you two," she responded good-naturedly.

I thanked Namin silently in my heart. "We will be right back," I promised aloud as Dyra and I scampered from the kitchen.

"Take your cloaks," Sophie called after us. "The evenings are still cold, and you do not want to catch a chill."

"Oh, Sophie!" Namin declared with a laugh. "They are in their third and fourth Summer Year, and certainly old enough to judge if they need a cloak."

Ignoring Sophie's advice, we left our cloaks draped on the pegs by the door and hurried out of the house.

"What happened?" Dyra demanded the moment the door thudded shut.

"He asked me to go to the dance and I told him...well, I told him to ask me tomorrow."

Dyra's eyes grew wide, and she giggled. "I bet he was not expecting that. Rion usually gets exactly what he wants, exactly when he wants it. What are you going to say tomorrow?"

I bit my lip. "I do not know."

Chapter Fifteen
Poison

D yra and I lay next to each other in bed, whispering about the Rion dilemma.

"Well," Dyra asked in a voice only half awake, "would it bother you if he went to the dance with another girl? What if he was there with Elanyn instead of you?"

I made a face. I did not like to think of Rion with any of the other girls in the village. I had to admit to myself that I was secretly proud of the fact that I was the only girl Rion actually talked to, instead of just teasing. I crossed my arms behind my head and stared up into the darkness. "But he is rude and mean and...Dyra?" I asked softly, noticing suddenly that her breathing had the heavy sound of sleep.

She did not answer, and I sighed. He is rude and mean but I still like him. It was hard to admit, even to myself. Rion made me laugh, and there was something about his green eyes and mischievous smile that I found attractive. When I was with him, I felt as though people forgot the rumors they had heard about me. I was granted a type of anonymity under the cloak of Rion's reputation. I gave all these arguments their due consideration, but in the end it was Dyra's final comment that decided the matter. The image of Elanyn standing next to Rion, chewing on her hair, was too much. I decided to accept his invitation.

So it was that I found myself getting ready with Dyra on the night of the dance. She was breathless with anticipation and anxiety. She pinned her hair up in seven different ways before deciding that she would wear it down.

"I am so nervous!" she moaned, leaning close to the mirror to examine her face with a critical expression.

"Why?" I asked in puzzlement.

I was sitting easily on the bed watching her exhaustive preparations. To me, this evening seemed like nothing but fun. It was enjoyable knowing that Rion had picked me over all the other girls in the village, and that I would have his attention for the entire night. It seemed like a situation which required the relish of anticipation rather than the corrosiveness of anxiety.

Dyradan began to answer me, but her voice faltered as Lilock bounded into the room.

"Myrrancy and Rion are here," she squealed. "Father is talking with them in the entrance."

Dyra looked stricken. "*Father* is talking with them! Does he have that silly unlit pipe in his mouth?"

Lilock nodded, and I laughed aloud.

"It is not funny, Lara," Dyra snapped and hurried from the room with Lilock at her heals. "Why is Mother letting him make fools out of us?" she demanded.

Rousing myself from the bed, I made my way to the entrance. Rion and Myrrancy were standing side by side, listening to Rolias' booming commentary about sheep. Rion was wearing a green tunic that I had never seen before. His hands were shoved in his pockets and he appeared to be bored. Myrrancy, however, was making every attempt to look interested. He was standing rigidly, his head bobbing in agreement like an apple floating in water. Namin was just coming down the hall, followed by a blushing Dyra.

"Rolias," Namin called. "Myrrancy and Rion did not come to talk with you. Come away from the door."

Rolias glanced back at his wife, and then returned his gaze to the two boys. "Right, right," he grunted, taking his smokeless pipe from his teeth. "You have fun, then. Take good care of our girls."

"We will, sir," Myrrancy replied with a solemn expression.

Rion had just noticed my presence. He caught my eye and grinned wickedly. I smiled back. How grateful I was that Rion was not as serious as Myrrancy!

After donning our cloaks, we all set off down the hill. Myrrancy and Dyra were awkward and said little, daring only brief glances in each other's direction. Dyra giggled nervously at the slightest comment. Rion gave them both a withering look and, grabbing me by the arm, pulled me ahead of the bashful couple.

"Guess what I brought?" He pulled a flask out of his cloak. "I took it from my father's tavern. I am going to pour it in the berryroot cordial and make the dance more interesting."

"Rion!" I gasped, looking around as though someone would leap out from behind a bush and discover us. "You cannot do that!"

Rion unscrewed the cap. "Why not?" he demanded rebelliously, and took a swig from the bottle.

I frowned at him. "Rion promise me that you will not do that!"

He grinned at me and took another drink. "Why?"

"Because -" I began loudly and then glancing back at Myrrancy and Dyra I lowered my voice. "Because it is not right to put things in people's drinks when they do not know about it. Promise me you will not do it." Rion began to protest again, but I interrupted him. "Promise, or I will go home."

Rion's smiled faded slowly, and he seemed to consider me for a moment. "All right," he finally consented, and tucked the bottle back into his cloak.

As soon as we entered the large town hall, a group of girls rushed up. A pack of boys surrounded Rion and Myrrancy, and we were swept apart. Most of the boys gathered at one end of the hall and the girls stood at the other. The adults mixed together in the middle, talking and dancing.

The girls were all eager to hear every detail of the walk from the house to town, and Dyra provided a rousing story composed mostly of what she wished she had said, rather than what she had actually said. She was just describing the way she had wanted to hold Myrrancy's hand, when the very subject of her discussion began to walk slowly toward the giggling group. He looked as though he was being pulled backward and pushed forward at the same time. When at last he stood before us, there was an expectant silence and he cleared his throat. All eyes were upon him, and a blush was spreading down his neck and back into his ears.

"Ah....ah.... Dyradan, do you..." he trailed off and stared at his shoes for a moment. Then all at once he blurted as quickly as he could, "Do-you-want-to-dance?"

She beamed at him and nodded, her hair sliding over her shoulders and partially covering her face. The two of them set off to the dance floor, and the group of girls burst into a titter of comments.

"I cannot wait for their wedding!"

"Dyra said she is going to kiss him tonight!"

"My mother says that kissing makes you pregnant!"

I rolled my eyes. "And if you put your tongue in a boy's mouth you will have twins," I muttered sarcastically and went off to find Rion.

"Really?" I heard Elanyn exclaim. "Lara, is that true?" she called after me.

I did not answer and instead concentrated upon finding my way through the labyrinth of people. I had just dodged out of the way of an arguing couple when I saw Rion, Fremer and two other boys standing a few feet away. They were huddled around the table where the large bowl of berryroot cordial sat. Rion was dumping the contents of his flask into the red cordial. I was standing before them in five quick steps. Rion looked at me, and for a moment I thought he appeared a bit chagrinned, but as his lips crooked into a smile, the expression was entirely lost. He tucked the bottle back into his pocket. "Want a drink, Lara?"

I stared at him, feeling both hurt and angry. "You promised."

Rion glanced at the other boys, and then turned his gaze back to me. "I did not. And anyway, if you had your way, Healer, we would all be poisoned by now."

I drew in a sharp, quick breath.

"Yes, Healer," one of the boys jeered. "Leave us alone."

My cheeks were hot with wrath and embarrassment. I turned quickly before anyone could see the tears that were blurring my vision and making the lights and colors run together. I pushed my way through the crowd of people. The pain of their remarks had sent my self-control into convulsions. I could feel tears burning down my cheeks. My breath was coming in noisy gasps. I covered my mouth with my hand and burst out into the cold night air. How could Rion have said that? Why had he even asked me to this stupid dance? I longed to be back in Caladore with Tren-Lore. I stumbled down the stairs and sat on the bottom step, weeping into the folds of my dress. I hated Rion, and I was ashamed of my love for Healing, of even wanting to be a Healer. I took a deep breath and tried to calm myself. Looking up into the darkness, I sniffed loudly. The only light came from the town hall's window and illuminated patches of ground on either side of the stairs. Long grass with tiny white seeds grew there. I recited the properties of the plant, trying to soothe my injured spirit.

"C-cattle's L-long St-stem is used for feeding cows and sheep." My voice kept breaking as I tried to catch my breath. "It will cause severe vomiting in humans and is considered to be among the most poisonous of the grass..." My mouth fell open with the realization of wicked possibility. "If it was up to you, we would all be poisoned by now," I mimicked under my breath and got purposefully to my feet. "Not everyone, Rion, just you."

I leapt into the tall grass and stripped a stalk. The seeds were delicate and crushed in my hand. Turning, I marched back into the hall, my left hand clenched in a fist of grim determination. Rion and the other two boys were no longer milling about the table. Fremer was still standing there, shifting from foot to foot. I did not know if it was a nervous gesture or his interpretation of dancing. I did not give the thought much consideration, because my focus was upon the four cups sitting on the table behind Fremer.

"Which cup is Rion's?" I demanded of Fremer.

"Lara!" Fremer looked surprised. "You – Healers – well I am sure you are good – if you are a Healer, of course." Fremer stared at the floor, his round face growing red. "Namin Healed my Gram, you know, and I, well.... I am sorry for what Rion said."

At the moment I was still too filled with anger to appreciate Fremer's sweet words. "It is not your apology to make," I replied impatiently, glancing about to ensure that Rion was not returning. "Which cup is Rion's?"

Fremer lifted his head, his brow furrowing. "Why?"

I clenched my teeth in frustration, and steadily met his gaze. "Fremer, which one?"

He glanced at the table and then pointed. "This one. Why? What are you going to do?"

I was reaching for the cup before Fremer had finished his sentence. My fingers opened and the white powder spilled into the cup. Fremer was objecting, and I found my lips parting, and words slipping out. "What do you care? He is horrible to you anyway." The words did not seem to be part of me.

The red liquid devoured the poison, and I stared at the cup, suddenly very aware of the magnitude of what I had just done. Part of me was very glad, but another part was starting to recoil in horror.

"Changed your mind?" asked a taunting voice.

I looked up. It was Rion. He was grinning. The same grin that had seemed so charming a few hours ago now made me want to hit him. My fury returned and I was suddenly part of the moment again, out of the reach of any thoughts of consequence or morality.

"Going to have a drink with us after all?" He reached for his cup.

I was nodding. Fremer's eyes were huge, but his lips were pressed so tightly together that they looked as though they were sewn shut.

Rion was smiling. "Good. When you left, I almost thought you were mad at me." He laughed at the idea, and my chest felt tight with suffocating rage. He thought he could say whatever he pleased to me! "What should we drink to?" Rion asked jovially.

"Your health," I replied, the words slipping over my tongue like cold scales.

"To my health!" Rion echoed, and in one swift movement he drained his cup.

My mouth opened in amazement. The situation had lost any feeling of reality. Rion was still talking, but I could not make sense of his words. My mind was staggering with victory and fear. All at once, Rion was silent and everything became dreadfully real again. He doubled over, clutching at his stomach and moaning in pain. "What is happening?" Rion groaned.

"I poisoned you," I told him through a haze of my own disbelief. "Just like you said."

Rion fell onto his knees. "You poisoned me? Why-" He never finished his question.

Fremer and I leapt back as Rion began to wretch violently. The music stopped suddenly, and it seemed as though everyone was rushing toward us all at once. I was pushed out of the way and Dyra was quickly at my side, clutching at my arm, entirely bewildered. Regret filled me. At that moment I would have given anything to have been as confused as Dyra.

"We have to go," I said urgently.

On the way home I told Dyra what I had done. I ended the tale by sobbing, "I am sorry that it was me who poisoned him, but I am *not* sorry he was poisoned!"

"Oh, Lara!" Dyra breathed. She did not seem to be able to find anything else to say. "Oh Lara...what are you going to tell Sophie and Mother?"

A new dread filled me. "Do we have to tell them?" My voice was panicked.

Dyra looked at me, and her expression was one of agony. "You had better do it before they find out from someone else."

* * *

Sophie was furious. "I can not believe you would do something like this! I do not care what he said to you; there is no cause, just no cause!"

Even worse than Sophie's reprimand, however, was Namin's silence. It hurt more than anything else. Namin looked sad and said only, "Go to bed, Lara. I will talk to you in the morning."

I lay in bed that night sobbing into my pillow. What a mess everything had become. I dreaded the rising of the sun. I would have to face Namin and Rion...

"H-he is probably s-saying horrible things about me – me at this very m-moment!"

Dyra rested her head on my shoulder and rubbed my back. "That is if he can talk at all through the vomiting."

I laughed despite my tears, but my happiness flickered like a weak flame and I found myself once more surrounded by dark thoughts. "Ev-everyone is going - going to hate me now!"

Dyra was ominously quiet for a moment. I knew that she thought I was right.

* * *

Namin faced me from across the kitchen table the next morning. It had been a silent breakfast, and everyone had left quickly when they had finished eating. Namin and I were alone. I stared at the table, running my fingernail up and down a crack in the wood, feeling wretched and guilty.

"Lara," Namin's voice seemed like winter water – calm and chill. "Sophie and I have talked about this, and we have decided that you will be confined to the house for two months. You will also go and apologize to Rion today."

I was about to object when she added the last part of her sentence. It was so terrible that it snatched the suddenly unimportant protest from my mouth.

"I will also cease training you as a Healer."

I gasped, breathing in pain. Namin would not train me as a Healer! I would not be able to save anyone! I would never be able to save her! This knowledge was my own brand of poison, and as it spread throughout my body I felt tears filling my eyes. My hands shook.

Namin did not appear softened by my reaction. "If you were attending Telnayis, you would be discharged from the school immediately, so consider my actions as Ascendant-sent kindness. I may choose to reevaluate my decision in a month or two... depending on your behavior."

I sobbed in agony. I would have given anything to have made a different decision last night. "Do you hate me, Namin?" I found myself asking through my tears.

Namin smiled sadly. "No, Lara, I do not hate you."

I cradled my head in my hands, and tears continued streaming down my face. "But – but everyone else does!" I wailed.

"You can work to make this right," Namin told me quietly.

When the time came to apologize to Rion, the reaction of his mother was enough to make me believe that things would never be right again, no matter what I said or did. We arrived at Rion's house late that afternoon, and Namin knocked upon the door while I curled my toes hard in my shoes and tried to fit the right words into an appropriate apology. Rion's mother opened the door with a smile, but her eyes narrowed to tiny slits when she beheld Namin and I standing on her stoop.

Namin put her hands on my shoulders, keeping me from retreating back the way I had come. Tears were already filling my eyes. I was not brave enough to face this foe. I wished that I was more like Rayn, whose spirit was as hard as the steel of his sword. I wished that I was Tren-Lore, who would have found the right thing to say. I wished that I was any hero in any tale rather than my frightened self.

"Lara has come to apologize to Rion," Namin said.

I saw the muscles in Parsi's jaw twitch, and her fists clenched at her sides. "How dare you! Get off my doorstep! I want nothing to do with you, Healer!" she yelled. "You take your little Pandel and leave before I set our dogs on you!" Turning abruptly, Rion's mother slammed the door.

Namin and I stood staring at the barred entrance for a moment. Namin muttered something under her breath that sounded very much like a curse, and grabbing my hand, she pulled me back onto the street. Namin was moving very quickly, each sharp stride a testament to her unspoken anger.

"I want to go home," I wept quietly, stumbling as I tried to keep pace with Namin.

"We are going home, Lara," Namin replied in a strained voice.

No, I thought in my head, I want to go home. I want to be back at Caladore with Tren-Lore to take the lead. It was obvious that left to my own devices, I would make nothing but bad decisions. I longed to be wrapped in his adventures again, to slip into the background of his story and be swept up in his grand plans.

Chapter Sixteen
A Thousand Unfurled Possibilities

I passed my two months of confinement quietly, focusing all my attention upon work. I helped Namin take care of the children and aided Sophie with the household cleaning and cooking. My fourth Summer Year came and went without much ceremony, but yielded an unexpected, yet special gift. Namin deemed that I was ready to start training again. I threw myself into learning with an all-consuming vigor.

When my punishment was finished, Dyra tried to convince me to come and socialize with our old friends again. I refused, believing that everyone despised me. I was too afraid to face such hatred, so I took solace in the childish games of Lilock and Garidet. I often joined them in their play, though I was growing more inclined to just sit and watch. The doll Sophie had given me for my Summer Year had an honored place on the shelf in my room, but I scarcely took her down anymore. Such play did not hold the same appeal as it once had. The little girls often demanded stories, and in this task I was always eager to oblige.

"Tell us about the last battle of Lord Rayn," Garidet demanded from where she sat at my feet.

"No," Lilock whined, "I want to hear something new. Lara, tell us about when you beat the boys in the horse race."

I furrowed my eyebrows and shook my head. "If I am going to tell a story, it has to be an interesting one."

"That *is* inter-" Lilock began to protest, but I interrupted her.

"Lord Rayn knew that the battle was hopeless..."

Namin, however, was the greatest comfort of all. We talked and laughed a great deal, and she prepared me for the delivery of her new daughter. Healers, she told me, only bore girls.

Sometime near the middle of winter I received a letter from Tren-Lore, along with the new book he had promised me in his last message. This served to raise my spirits for some time, and every night before I went to bed I read a passage from the book and a piece of his letter. I had most of his message memorized, but it was the line at the end of one of his paragraphs that occupied my thoughts most often.

There is no winter in Tolrem. Tren-Lore wrote. *Yesterday it was unbearably hot here, and I was thinking how nice it would be to be back in Caladore where it is freezing cold. Me and you and Myste could sit in front of the fire in the secret room and roast narkanytch. Or burn them, in my case. I miss winter. And I miss Caladore, but most of all I miss you.*

Before winter had drawn to a close, Namin insisted that it was time I start treating people other than members of her family. I reluctantly went with her to Karsalin, and every day we visited someone new who needed our help. Some seemed genuinely happy to see us, but others looked as though our visit was nothing more than a necessary evil. I wondered, as I treated them, if they knew what I had done to Rion. Did they secretly hate me for what I was capable of? Did they fear I would do the same thing to them?"

It was to my great relief when Namin's pregnancy put a stop to our daily visits and I could once more remain safely in the house. Namin was calm about her impending labor, I was nervous but tried to appear calm, and Sophie was obviously agitated and had no hope of being mistaken for a calm person.

"Lara," Namin had called from the next room.

"Ascendants' grace!" Sophie exclaimed, dropping the bowl of sugar she had been carrying. It smashed on the floor, and Sophie cried above the clatter, "It must be time! It is time!"

"Lara, check to make sure Garidet has her mittens on," Namin continued. "She is playing in the garden, I think."

I grinned at Sophie, and then looked pointedly at the spray of sugar that spread across the kitchen floor. "I think I left the broom in the closet."

Sophie put a hand to her gray hair and shook her finger at me. "Do not be smart with me, young lady. Go and check on Garidet."

I laughed and went to do as I was asked.

Later that evening, I was sitting before the fire. The room was flushed with the dancing light of the burning wood, and I had to squint to see what I was writing. With a large book balanced on my lap, and a piece of paper spread across its hard cover, I was composing a letter to Tren-Lore. I hummed softly to myself as I paused to think of what I should write about next. I had been working on the letter for over a week, and even though I was running out of things to report, I was loathe to bring it to an end. Writing to Tren-Lore made me feel less alone.

I had just set the quill to the parchment again when Sophie rushed into the room. "It is time, Lara," she said swiftly.

I looked up at her in confusion. I was still enveloped in my own thoughts, and Sophie's words did not make sense in that context. "Time?" I repeated.

Rolias was suddenly behind her and laid a calming hand on her shoulder. "If you need me, I will be smoking my pipe outside. Lara, you had best go tend to Namin's labor."

"Labor!" I cried in shock and leapt to my feet, sending the book and paper to the floor. I looked desperately at Sophie. "What should I do?"

Sophie's own expression of panic dimmed, and she smiled at me with a motherly reassurance. "You know what do to, Lara. Just stay calm and keep your wits about you."

"Right," I agreed, running my hands over my hair and exhaling a long, soothing breath. "I know what to do. All right, I need you to stoke the fire and boil some water. Ask Dyra to keep Garidet and Lilock from underfoot."

Sophie nodded, and her eyes filled with tears.

My mouth opened in dismay and I hurried to her. "Sophie, what is wrong?"

"Nothing, nothing." She wiped the moisture from her eyes. "I am just proud of you, child." Sophie laughed. "I had best stop calling you that. You are certainly not a child any more, but I cannot seem to rid myself of the notion that you are still my little girl."

"Oh, Sophie," I breathed, tears forming in my own eyes. My love for her filled me with warmth, and I hugged her tightly. "I *am* your little girl."

We held each other for only a brief moment, and memories leapt around me: the way she still left a candle burning for me on my nightstand and still worried if I did not wear my cloak, her habit of humming softly to herself, her secret ability to snap towels, and her empty threats to cut off all my hair if I forgot to brush it. These were the mundane details of our time together that made Sophie so dear to me. I remembered how my hand had fit so perfectly into hers, and how much I had needed her on those first dark days. It was very clear to me just how much I still needed her. Just like my mother. My mother.

"I love you, Sophie," I whispered.

She squeezed me. "I love you too, Lara."

We held each other one breath longer, and then broke apart.

"Go care for Namin," Sophie said. I nodded and left the room, feeling completely awash in emotions.

When I opened Namin's door I found her lying on her bed, straining with the pain of contractions. She was moaning, and I felt as though I had collided with a wall of fear and was stumbling back from the blow. Gripping the door frame, I steadied myself and went inside to help

Namin. The night became a blur, and I do not know how many hours passed when at last Namin groaned, "Something is not right." She twisted against the agony that seemed to be ripping her apart.

I looked at her, and our eyes met. I shook my head and replied, "No, everything will be fine. Your baby will be fine." It was a statement of defiance. At that moment I felt ready to battle with any of the Ascendants to change the destiny of this baby. "Push, Namin. Everything will be fine."

We struggled together, and at last I held a tiny baby in my shaking hands. I removed the umbilical cord that had been wrapped around her neck. She was not breathing, but I could still feel the life energy within her---only an ember, but still glowing. I was transfixed, entranced with the sensation of life. My mind could think of nothing else, and I did not even realize that my control over my own life energy had ebbed until a burning wash of power poured from my hands to fill the little body before me. Her tiny lips parted and she drew a shaking breath. She opened her eyes, stared up at me, took another breath and began to cry.

"Everything is fine," I repeated, my voice sounding as though it belonged to someone else.

Before long, Namin was laughing with joy and calling for Sophie and her family to come and see the baby. When everyone had crowded into the room, the baby had stopped crying and was snuggling against Namin's warm body. I was standing next to her, my mind unable to comprehend what had happened. The sun was rising outside and the glory of the morning bathed the infant. It was not only the dawn of a new day, but also the dawn of a new life.

Namin looked up at me and smiled. There was happiness in her face such as I had never seen. "I shall name her in honor of a great Healer," Namin murmured.

I nodded and stared at the baby in wonder. She was so tiny, and I could not begin to fathom all that the world could give to her, and all that she might give to the world.

"I shall name her Lara," Namin resolved softly.

I tore my eyes away from the baby and gazed at Namin in disbelief. I felt my knees giving way.

Sophie caught me by the arm and steadied me. "There now, child," she murmured, "time for bed. You have had a hard night." Sophie guided me from the room, and together we walked to my sleeping chamber. I stood before the washing basin with a dazed patience, and Sophie rinsed my right arm. "Give me your other hand, Lara," Sophie said

It was only then that I realized I had been clutching my ring. I uncurled my fingers and looked down at the Healer's band. The ivy that had once looked as though it was made of a light green metal now appeared to be fashioned from a living plant, growing in a perfect, unbreakable circle.

Sophie gently took my hand and helped me to wash.

"It is still too big, though," I muttered in a voice slurred with weariness.

"We shall see," Sophie replied as she tucked my blankets tightly around me.

"It is. I know it is," I insisted, and then fell asleep, too tired to say another word.

* * *

Just as I was becoming accustomed to the idea of this new life in our midst, Elanyn and a few of the other girls came to visit. They wanted to see the baby, and Sophie invited them in, setting a platter of cookies and a pot of tea upon the table. I was filled with trepidation about seeing them again, but the girls all greeted me so warmly that I was soon at ease. We spent the first afternoon of many sitting in the kitchen and talking over the events of the town. No one mentioned Rion, though part of me wished that someone would have some tidings from him.

Sometime that spring, Namin began teaching me how to channel my life energy. We started by reading the section in the Healer's doctrine pertaining to giving life rather than taking away death. I made a face at this familiar adage and held back the words that were pushing against my closed lips. I would not voice my true opinion

and risk Namin postponing this training any longer. I
wanted to learn how to channel my life energy. I wanted
that more than anything. Outwardly, I wanted to learn
how to channel so that my training would be complete and
I would be a full-fledged Healer. In the darkness of my
mind, however, alternative motives dwelt. I was not even
fully conscious of them. I could feel them as a longing to
change the past, and if I had tried to articulate them, it
would have been like trying to explain a void, to explain
the feelings of loss, the absence of something I had only
been able to replace in a reality of my own construction.

The training, however, did not go well. Everything else
had come so easily, but I struggled vainly to channel my
life energy. I could feel the power surging through me, but
I could not release it. I devoted my attention almost
entirely to this one accomplishment. Only the letter Tren-
Lore sent me from Renarn, the visits of the girls, and the
needs of baby Lara could distract me. Yet, my Fifth
Summer Year arrived with no progress.

"I hate this day!" I exclaimed as I stomped into our
room and slammed the door. I threw myself onto my bed
and lay squinting at the ceiling, willing it from existence –
willing everything from existence.

Dyradan was sitting in front of the small mirror in our
room, carefully applying mashed berryroot to her lips. It
turned them a lovely shade of red, and according to Dyra
kept them very soft. Dyra turned in her chair. "Lara, forget
about Healing for one night. Come to Rion's party."

I laughed bitterly. "I would be more welcome in a
Sorcerer's camp."

"That is not true," Dyra assured me, and rising, came
and snuggled up next to me on the bed. "All the girls want
you to come, and Myrrancy says that Rion is not even mad
any more. No one cares any more, Lara."

Sighing, I continued to stare at the ceiling. "I am not
going," I told her resolutely.

Dyradan wrapped her arms around me and squeezed
me in a hug. "Pleeeease," Dyra pleaded. "Please, please,
pleeeease. Come for me, Lara. Nothing is as much fun
when you are not there."

I felt my resolve fracturing. My steady upward gaze broke. I sat up, and Dyra did the same. I looked at her with a forehead creased in concern. "Are you sure that no one cares any more?" I wanted to ask specifically about Rion, but could not seem to bring myself to say it.

Dyra's face was very solemn, and she reached over to slip her hand into mine. "I am sure. No one even remembers."

Pursing my lips, I inhaled deeply, madly hoping to find courage in that intake of air. "All right," I said finally. "I will go."

This answer was greeted by a wild squeal from Dyra, who bounded off the bed, pulling me with her. She helped me get ready and even insisted that I, too, put some berryroot on my lips. I reluctantly agreed and found that the taste of cordial on my tongue reminded me of Tren-Lore. I fondly remembered the first day we had met. Tren-Lore had requested that Sophie make berryroot cordial for us, and we had talked about his plans for the fort. I could never have imagined that the grand visions of youth would ever have come to fruition, and I had certainly never dared to hope that we would become best friends. I missed Tren-Lore so much that my chest ached.

"I am going to ask Mother if you can borrow her cinnamon scent," Dyra declared. "She never wears it anyway."

My pain ebbed and then disappeared entirely as I turned my attention to the situation at hand. "No, I do not n..." My protest crumbled into silence when Dyra ignored me and ran gleefully from the room.

She returned a few moments later with a small rounded container in hand. "Mother says you can have it," Dyra told me as she set it down on the table in front of the mirror.

"Really?" I asked in wonder, and came to examine the treasure. It was carved out of a deep burgundy wood and was very beautiful.

Dyra smiled. "You can thank her later." She twisted the lid off the container, and the room was suddenly filled with the wonderful smell of cinnamon. "You only need a tiny little bit."

I hesitated for only an instant, and then brushed my finger against the clear jelly-like substance within.

"Rub it on your wrists and neck," Dyra instructed.

I did as I was told, and we grinned at each other.

"Ri-" Dyra began, but quickly stopped herself. "We, um, we should go."

* * *

The party was being held at the Cleft, and Rion appeared to be the most popular person there. This was probably because the get-together had been Rion's idea and it was his father's ale that filled everyone's mugs. Dyra and Myrrancy disappeared together shortly after we arrived and I found myself standing beside Elanyn, nearly ready to join her in some hair-chewing of my own. One of the boys from town, whose name I did not remember, came by and handed us both a cup of ale.

"This is the first party I have ever been to," Elanyn confessed as she took a sip of her drink and grimaced, "but do not tell anyone that."

I looked down at the mug in my hand. I felt uneasy with the entire situation.

Elanyn swallowed a large mouthful of ale and declared weakly, "It is not so bad if you drink it really quickly."

I nodded in agreement, but did not move the mug any nearer to my mouth. It tasted awful, that much was clear, and I felt wretched and guilty just holding it in my hand. What would Sophie say? Elanyn continued to talk, and with a few more gulps, had finished her drink. I wavered for a moment and then silently handed her mine.

"You do not want it?" she exclaimed, her words sounding slightly slurred.

"No," I replied, "you can have it."

She took it, and I felt slightly better. Elanyn choked back the contents of my mug even faster than she had her own. Her talk grew less and less nervous until she delightedly slung her arm about my shoulders, and grinned foolishly, announcing, "The more you drink...." She paused as though thinking. "The better it tastes." She sounded as though her words were being shredded by her teeth. "You know who I like?"

Elanyn started in on a detailed list of all the boys she was smitten with. Despite my best efforts to stop her, she pointed openly to the males in question, more often than not, alerting them to the fact that she was talking about them. I winced in embarrassment, and by the time I had convinced her to move away from the center of the party, she had obtained and finished yet another drink. Elanyn was hanging on to me for support as I guided her halting steps toward the outskirts of the crowd. She was now tearfully describing all the reasons why none of the boys she liked would ever feel that way about her.

"None of them are nice enough for you, anyway," I whispered to the sobbing girl.

Rion, Myrrancy, Dyra, and Fremer were standing only a few feet away, and I did not want to draw their attention.

"No," Elanyn wailed. "I am going to be an old maid!"

My hopes for remaining unseen were dashed. Dyra and everyone else in the small group turned around. Rion's gaze met mine for only an instant, but the visual contact felt like the smack of cold river water and the blazing heat of the summer sun. I stared at the ground, feeling as though I were as drunk as Elanyn.

Suddenly, Dyra and Myrrancy were at my side, and Dyra was crooning, "What is wrong with Elan? Oh, poor Elan, are you all right?"

"Here," I said, shoving Elanyn into Myrrancy's arms. "You two can take care of her. I am going home." I obviously had no place at the party. If I was not drinking, there was no point in being there. Rion certainly did not want me there, and I could not stand to watch Elanyn humiliate herself any further.

Dyra grabbed my arm. "No!" she protested. "You have to stay!" She stumbled forward and hugged me. "Everyone wants you to stay. Myrrancy wants you to stay and Elan wants you to stay and Rion wants you to stay." She pulled away from me, and before I could stop her she demanded, "Rion, tell Lara you want her to stay."

I did not wait to hear Rion's reply. I fled before he had a chance to say anything. Once I had escaped the noise and light of the party, I slowed my steps. I should never have come. I should never have chanced seeing Rion again. He had probably been on the verge of telling me to leave, anyway. Well good, I thought, trying to harden myself with anger. I did not want to stay at that stupid party either. I did not belong there, and I did not want to belong there. The shroud of my own inner ranting prevented me from hearing the quick footfalls that were coming from behind me until the runner was nearly upon me. I turned sharply. The moon was full, and by its light I could make out the form of Rion coming toward me. He stopped as he reached me and bent with his hands on his knees, trying to catch his breath. I stared wordlessly at him.

Finally, he straightened and looked at me. "Hello, Lara," he said. Apparently, my stunned mind noted, he was not of that sarcastic religion after all. "I was thinking that...well, it is pretty dark, and well...can I walk you home?"

I felt as though my heart had stopped for a moment, and then the dam of blood burst within me and I reeled under the ferocity of my own pounding heart. Rion wanted to walk me home! That did not seem like the gesture of someone who hated me. I nodded, not trusting myself with words.

We walked in silence for a time, and I was painfully aware of my every movement, conscious of even my own swallowing. It seemed abnormally loud. I gripped the inside of my cloak and tried to think of something to say. Should I ask him if he was still mad? Should I apologize for poisoning him? I decided on the latter.

"I am --" I said just as he blurted out, "Lara, what-"

As our words collided, we both stumbled back into silence. I felt a blush burning my cheeks. I was thankful for the darkness.

"About that night," Rion bravely tried again. "I am sorry for saying those things about you. I deserved to be sick."

"Yes, you did." The comment slipped off my tongue before I realized how wrong a reply it had been. I winced, thinking bitterly that the girl in the book Tren-Lore had sent never said stupid things like that. Rion laughed, and the fire on my cheeks grew more intense. "No, *I* am sorry. I never should have done what I did -- no matter what. I am truly sorry."

"So are we even, then?" Rion asked.

I glanced at him and found that he was already looking at me. I smiled. "Yes."

"Good." Rion pushed his hair out of his eyes and grinned roguishly. "None of the other girls are half as much fun to torment."

I chose not to retaliate to this barb, and instead took it as the compliment I knew Rion had intended it to be. Rion slowed his pace and then stopped altogether. I stopped beside him and drank in the night. The air smelled of summer, and stars twinkled in the cloudless sky. A warm breeze flowed between us like thick black syrup. The moment was entwined with an enchantment that banished speech from our mouths and left only a silent understanding. Our gaze met, and then slowly Rion leaned toward me. I closed my eyes. His lips brushed gently against mine. I felt alive with sensation, filled with the warmth of summer and the excitement of a thousand unfurled possibilities. Rion was kissing me. Rion!

As we drew apart, I could not help but smile at the surprised expression on his face. I was sure that it matched my own bemused countenance.

He grinned slowly. "So, do I have to ask Rolias' permission to court you?" Rion asked.

"No," I replied. "You have my permission, and that is all you need."

Chapter Seventeen
That Lovely Girl with Rion

N amin laughed when I related this response to her and told me she thought it was the perfect answer. Dyra, however, was still perturbed by it three weeks later.

"He should ask *someone's* permission," she insisted as we strolled down to Karsalin to meet Rion and Myrrancy.

"He did ask someone. He asked me." I kicked at a stone on the road. "Besides, Rolias is not my father. It would be silly to ask him."

Silence followed my reply, and then at last Dyra asked quietly, "Lara, what happened to your father?"

I squirmed inwardly. I remembered making the same inquiry. It had been when I was very young. My mother had stared off into the distance, and tears had stood in her eyes. Before that moment, I had never seen her cry.

"I will tell you the story when you are older, Lara. I want you to understand, and right now you cannot possibly. He loved you, though, when he was with us. Remember that, at least."

That was all the explanation I had ever received. I shrugged uncomfortably. "He died," I fibbed.

"Oh," murmured Dyra, clearly sorry she had asked.

I brooded about the subject until we met up with Myrrancy and Rion. My dark and serious thoughts were quickly banished. With Rion, everything was about laughter and teasing. He grabbed my hand in his and we set off up the road, bantering back and forth while Dyra and Myrrancy followed, whispering shy compliments to each other.

We passed the autumn and winter in a similar fashion. It seemed that Rion and I were always hand in hand, always laughing. That is, when I was not irritated with him. Rion had a fantastic talent for making remarks that would hurt my feelings and make me mad.

"Just leave," I snapped one winter day, pulling away from him and storming out of the room.

"What?" he demanded, his hands held out in a gesture of helpless innocence.

"Leave!" I yelled, and slammed my chamber door.

Yet, I never stayed angry for long. Soon I would be reaching for Rion's hand again, and he would grin at me and perfection would be restored. Rion was my champion. He had the power of infection. If he held an opinion, it seemed that soon the entire town would be influenced by it. I was no longer 'that Healer girl'. I was no longer a necessary evil. People welcomed me into their homes when I came to care for them. I was 'that lovely girl with Rion'.

Thankfully, Rion was also my diversion. I still was not able to channel my life energy, and had it not been for the distracting force of his company, I would have bashed myself upon the rocks of my own incompetence. Namin said that it would come in time, but I saw the way her mouth tightened around the corners. She did not know why I could not consistently channel my life energy.

* * *

Honey-colored sunlight poured through the windows and dripped over Lilock, Garidet and me. The younger girls were both sprawled on the floor playing dolls, and I was sitting in Sophie's rocking chair. I was mending a torn seam in an old dress of mine. Garidet had grown during the winter and needed new clothes for spring.

"Look," said Lilock, holding up two dolls and mashing their faces together. "I am Lara and Rion." She made horrible sucking noises.

I raised my eyebrows, but could not prevent my lips from turning up at the edges. I concentrated upon my stitches. They were small and close together, tightly binding the cloth.

Garidet dropped her doll and came to rest her head against my knee. "Are you going to marry Rion?"

"Certainly not," I replied lightly, as though I had not spent many moments dreaming about that very subject.

I tied the last knot on my mending. The seam was as good as the first day Sophie had sewn it. I fondly ran my fingers along the soft cloth. It had been one of the first dresses Sophie had made for me. There was a dark stain on the cuff, and I touched it gently with my finger. It was Tren-Lore's blood, I remembered suddenly. It had been the first time we had fought with swords, and I had cut him with a lucky blow. My hand tightened over the cloth, and I had to battle with the irrational urge to fold the dress up and keep it forever.

"Who *are* you going to marry, then?" Lilock asked.

"Oh," I replied with a whimsical smile, "probably some hairy young Barlem, or perhaps a grumpy old Sanysk." Lilock groaned, and I gestured for Garidet to stand up. "Let us see if this dress fits you."

As it happened, the dress fit perfectly and Garidet wore it through the spring and into the summer, even though she had grown again and the sleeves were already too short for her. It seemed, in fact, that everything was sprouting madly. Lilock was beginning to talk about boys, and baby Lara was tottering around the house, putting everything she could find into her mouth. Even Rion seemed to be growing in his feelings for me.

"Well, now," Rion declared as he caught hold of baby Lara and lifted her away from the burning candle she had been reaching for, "that would not be a good idea, would it?"

The infant smiled at him, and I found myself mimicking the expression. I loved to see Rion care for her.

"Here," I said, holding out my arms. "I will give her to Namin. It is far past her bedtime."

Rion rested the chubby baby in my arms and leaned closer to kiss me. "When I marry you, I want to have lots of children -- a whole house full of them."

I laughed shakily, not sure if he was joking. It was as though all my imaginings had suddenly materialized, and when faced with the reality of them, I found myself a little frightened.

"I should go," Rion said. "It is getting late." He kissed me again and left.

Even though he was no longer present, his words seem to hang in the air. 'When I marry you...' I tried to imagine spending the rest of my life with Rion – being 'that lovely girl with Rion'. How safe it would be. And yet, a slight feeling of discontent registered in my consciousness. Still feeling perturbed, I went to find Namin. She was alone with a large book spread before her. She did not look up when I entered. She had not mentioned it to me, but I knew that Namin had begun to search her books for the cause of my inability to channel.

"Namin?"

She looked up and smiled. "Oh, hello. Is it getting late?"

"Yes," I replied and came to sit with her at the table. I bounced baby Lara on my lap. She squealed with delight, but Namin's concentration was upon me, rather than her daughter.

"What is the matter?" Namin asked, her long hair sweeping the pages of her open book.

I sighed. The *idea* of marriage and children had filled my head with a light and giddy happiness, but the reality of it seemed to weigh heavy upon me. There were many aspects to these concepts that I had not considered until this moment. So many things could go wrong. There was so much possible pain. I looked at Namin with a steady resolve. "What happened to my father?"

Namin's eyes widened slightly, and she pursed her lips. "How much do you know?"

"Nothing," I replied.

Namin closed the book before her and began to tell the story of my parents' past. It was a tale I had never heard, and I listened with tense readiness, snapping up every word that dropped from Namin's mouth.

"Well," she sighed, "his name was Raven. He was a merchant. Your mother met him in the summer, and when she returned to Telnayis that fall, he came to visit her all the time. He was always appearing with flowers or sweets, or something of that sort. Naturally, we were all madly jealous. We all thought Raven was so handsome and romantic. He courted her for... well, for only a few months. Your mother said it was love at first sight. Then one day, he asked her to marry him. We were all so excited for them. But..." Namin stopped as though she had come to a cliff, a sheer drop-off in the story, and did not want to plunge over that edge.

I gathered baby Lara more tightly into my arms.

"But," she continued, "he left her two years after they married. He left a note saying that he felt trapped in their marriage, and that being a father and a husband was too much for him." There were tears standing in Namin's eyes.

I could find nothing to say. The story hurt in a way I could not explain. I had never known a life that included my father, and I had never known my mother when she had been with him. Yet something in me grieved for what had happened, for what could have been and never was, for the tiny, painful spike that had been driven into my basic understanding of love.

On the day of my Sixth Summer Year, I was awakened by a rapping on the outer door. Still in our sleeping gowns, Sophie, Namin and I stumbled to the entrance and discovered a messenger wearing the grey and blue uniform of Caladore. He produced a battered envelope with my name scrawled across the front, and a white scroll addressed to Lady Grim. I eagerly took the letter and bounded out to the garden while Namin and Sophie were thanking the messenger.

Choosing a particularly sunny spot on the outside step, I held the letter in hands that shook with excitement. Everything was quiet; perhaps the earth was still caught in slumber, or perhaps it was holding its breath in anticipation, waiting for me to open the letter from Tren-Lore. I carefully broke the red dragon seal and pulled the letter from its envelope. The ink was slightly faded, but Tren-Lore's familiar writing was still clear enough to read.

Dear Lara,

This letter may be a little worse for wear by the time it reaches you. I am training in Hemlizar right now, and there is no one who is willing to deliver a letter to Karsalin. You would like it in Hemlizar. Not because they do not deliver letters to Karsalin – what an articulate mood I am in today!

I laughed. I could picture Tren-Lore grimacing as he realized that his explanation was none too clear. I was sure that this was a letter Tren-Lore would not have shared with Myste.

The culture here is extremely story-oriented. I have some great stories to tell you when we get back. When are you coming back? The reason this letter has taken so long to get to you is because in Hemlizar, there are all sorts of tales about fiendish beasts who live in the mountains. People avoid going up there at all costs. I had to send your letter to Caladore and have one of our messengers deliver it to you.

It is hard to believe, but training is almost done. We just have to complete our final exams, and then we will all be returning home. That is all Myste talks about. He is the only one who is not completely consumed with exams and can actually think about what will happen afterward. I do not sleep much anymore. Training for these tests is more important than anything. I want to finish first.

I could almost hear Tren-Lore's voice as he said this. It was a phrase I had heard him utter many times. I smiled fondly. I knew that no matter what trials Tren-Lore faced, he would overcome them and finish first. That was just the way Tren-Lore was.

I wish you were here to practice with me.
Morian penent.
Tren-Lore

It was the shortest letter he had ever sent me, and the most disjointed. He was tired and under a huge amount of pressure. He did not say it directly, but I could tell. Even as he wrote, he was probably thinking about his next battle. In spite of everything, he had taken time to write to me. I read it once more and then went back inside. I slipped quietly into our sleeping chamber and slid the letter under my pillow. I padded barefoot down the hallway toward the kitchen, where I could just hear Sophie and Namin talking in hushed voices.

"Oh, Sophie, waiting is no fun. I say that we give it to her now," Namin said impatiently. "Then she can wear it tonight at the party Rion is hosting in her honor."

Curiosity flared within me and I curled my toes in delight. What were they planning to give me? I paused and listened eagerly, a remorseless eavesdropper.

"She cannot wear it tonight," Sophie's voice protested.

Wear what? I wondered.

"She would look like an overdressed fool," Sophie continued. "Besides, we should wait for everyone else to wake up."

"Fine, she does not need to wear it to Rion's party, but it is not fair to make her wait until everyone wakes up." Namin's voice had a tone of youthful wheedling.

Sophie chuckled. "You mean it is not fair to make *you* wait until everyone wakes up."

By this time, my curiosity was a raging inferno that demanded to be quelled. I burst into the kitchen. "What are you giving me?" I demanded.

Sophie and Namin were sitting at the table, cups of tea in their hands. They both looked up at me and laughed.

I pulled up a chair and plunked myself into it. "Well?"

Sophie shook her head in amusement and rose from her seat. She shuffled from the kitchen.

"Oh, good!" Namin rubbed her hands together. "Lara, you are going to love this."

I waited impatiently and soon Sophie returned carrying a large box. She was smiling so widely that her soft face was as creased as crumpled paper, and her eyes were full of warmth. She set the box before me.

"A fitting present for a girl of Six Summers," she said as she resumed her seat. "Well, go on." She waved her hand at me. "Hurry up and open it, child."

Namin laughed in delight. "And you wanted to wait!"

I was driven off my chair and onto my feet by the excitement leaping about inside me. I yanked the top off the box. The inside was filled with a deep red cloth. I pulled it free of its confinements, and the cloth tumbled and unfolded until its lengths nearly touched the floor. I gasped. It was a beautiful gown, with a full skirt and cream ribbons that laced up the front of the bodice and cuffs.

"This is amazing!" I cried, clutching the dress to me. "Thank you so much." I hugged Sophie, and then Namin.

"You can wear it if you are ever back in Caladore," Sophie told me, and I nodded, not really paying attention. "That message I received...it was about that. Benya and her family are moving away, and King Kiris would like me to return to Caladore immediately."

At this I looked up sharply, the dress in my hands entirely forgotten. "When?"

"In a week or so, but that does not mean you have to come with me. You have Namin and Rion here, and if you-"

And at home, I had Tren-Lore! The thought of seeing him again brought tears of happiness to my eyes. At home I had Tren-Lore, and Myste and Sophie! It was the best Summer gift I could ever have received. I dropped the dress on the table and threw my arms around Sophie. "We are going home!" I said in a voice resonating with joy.

When I looked up, Namin was crying. She laughed as she saw that Sophie and I were staring at her in concern. "It is just that I will miss you both so much. You must promise to write to me. Lara, you must keep practicing your channeling."

Namin's tears reminded me of my own reasons for sorrow, and I too began to weep. Leaving Namin and her family behind was a sobering thought. And Rion – leaving him would be desperately hard.

Sophie reached across the table for her sister's hand and put a comforting arm around my waist. "There now," she murmured. "Do not cry. We will see each other again."

* * *

"Lara, you look positively ancient," a familiar voice declared as Dyra and I walked into the tavern. Rion had convinced his parents to close it for the night so he could have my celebration there. He pushed his way through the crowd and kissed me. He tasted of ale. "All those Summer Years must be catching up with you," he teased.

My eyes were suddenly stinging and blurring with grief. I was beginning to realize how hard it would be to leave Rion. I had not planned to tell him tonight, but I desperately wanted to be comforted. "We need to talk," I told him.

The taunting expression upon his face flickered, and for a moment he looked concerned. "All right," he answered as he led me to a storage room at the back of the tavern and closed the door behind us. "What is so urgent?"

I began to cry. "I am leaving."

Rion looked shocked. He opened his mouth, but no words came out. Finally he stuttered, "W-what?"

I wiped tears from my cheeks with the back of my hand, thinking that 'what' did not provide the comfort I had been seeking. "Sophie got a message from Caladore. They need her at the castle."

Rion's face was suddenly relieved. He pushed his hair out of his eyes, and his smile returned. "Do not do that to me, Lara."

"Do what?" I asked in bewilderment.

He laughed and slung an arm about my shoulder. "Come on, Lara. There is no real problem here. Sophie has to leave, but you do not. You can stay here with me. I was talking to my father, and he says that in a few years if we want to get married, we can live above the tavern."

I made a skeptical face. Living above a tavern was not a future I had envisioned for myself. I pulled away from

Rion, suddenly angry with him. He had not bothered to discuss any of this with me. "I *want* to go home."

It was now Rion's turn to look puzzled and irate. "But I thought...Lara, I thought this was your home. I thought we would have a future together."

I curled my toes in my shoes and pulled my hands up into my sleeves. This conversation was not going well at all. "I do want to have a future with you." I was lying, but I could not bear to tell him the truth. I had not wanted this to turn into a conversation about our relationship. I had simply wanted to be comforted. Obviously, Rion was not going to be the savior I had been searching for. "Look," I told him, "we will talk about this later."

Rion stared at me, searching my eyes for something. His mouth was a hard line. "It is not Karsalin you want to leave, is it? You want to leave me."

I took a step toward him, my hand outstretched. "No, Rion, that is not it at all."

It was as though he had not even heard me.

"You *are* leaving me," he said in low, mean tones. He turned and stormed from the room.

"Rion!" I yelled after him. He did not respond. I sunk to the floor and sat with my head in my hands. "You are not going to cry," I told myself sternly. "End Rion. You can deal with him later." I took a deep breath and stood up, pushing my hair back from my face. I straightened my shoulders and returned to the party, making a silent vow to enjoy the company of my friends on one of my last nights in Karsalin.

Dyra was quick to find me. Taking my arm, she pulled me off to a corner table where she and some other girls were sitting. They all shouted my name in a jovial greeting, and I was pushed down into a chair and given a detailed account of exactly what the girls thought of each person at the party. Everyone around the table was convulsing in laughter, but all I could manage was a vague smile. I kept craning my neck, looking for Rion. His anger ate at me until at last I could stand it no longer.

"I will be back in a moment," I said, abruptly interrupting a comical remark being made by one of the girls.

Without waiting for a response, I rose and went in search of Rion. At last, after slipping through tangles of people, I saw Rion standing by the bar, three of his friends surrounding him. His back was to me, and I hurried toward him. I stopped abruptly when I heard my name. "Lara?" Rion repeated. "I am done with her. I could only stand being with someone like her for so long."

I felt cold wash over my body, and I started to shiver uncontrollably.

"I want a girl who is gorgeous and knows how to keep her mouth shut. And really, can you actually see *me* living the rest of my life with a Healer?"

His words felt as though I were pressing my flesh onto freezing metal. My mind was numb.

"We are finished." The voice must have been mine, for Rion turned around, looking as thought he had just swallowed a mouthful of Cattle's Long Stem.

"Lara!" he exclaimed.

"Finished!" I slashed my hand through the air to emphasize the word.

I fled the tavern. How stupid I had been to allow Rion to court me in the first place! I felt as though I could finally see, after a year of blindness. The compliments he had paid me, the kind gestures: they had all been a lie. His talk of our 'future together' made me want to spit in rage.

When I returned home that night, I shut myself in my room and ignored the soft knocks on my door. I did not want to see Sophie or Namin, or anyone else for that matter. I do not know where Dyra and her sisters slept that night, but it was not in our chamber. At first I was too angry to cry, preferring to pace and mutter wrathfully instead. How dare Rion say those things about me! How dare he! I had been fooling myself all this time. I hated him!

Slowly, as the darkness of night became more complete, grief blanketed me and I sat upon my bed and wept. I mourned the death of our relationship, and of my own persona as 'that lovely girl with Rion'. I began to see all the reasons Rion might have had for behaving as he did. He was right, a dark piece of my spirit cried. I was ugly and I talked too much, and I was a Healer. This thought struck me with the force of a battering ram, and my remaining composure shattered.

Weeping shook my whole body, and my control crumbled entirely. I rolled over onto my stomach, tears hot on my cheeks and cold on my neck, my head ringing with pain. I clutched my pillow to me and felt the rough texture of paper brushing against the skin of my hand. It was Tren-Lore's letter. I pulled it out, and as I held it, memories flowed over me like cool water. There was the gentle touch of Venst on lazy summer days. There was the sound of Tren-Lore's voice and the smell of the kitchen. There was the sight of the dragon fountain against a setting sun.

"It does not matter," I whispered, and stared fixedly at the letter before me. My breathing calmed. "It does not matter because I am going home." My muscles relaxed, but my fingers remained tight around the letter. It did not matter, because I could flee from this place and return to Caladore and Tren-Lore. I closed my eyes and found sleep pulling me toward dreams.

"Back to Caladore," I murmured as my mind stepped over the threshold of waking and into a realm that had the hue of heroics and grand old tales. "Back to Tren-Lore."

Chaos prevailed for the next week. Everything was packed, and then unpacked and repacked when we found something we had forgotten to stow in our bags and trunks. There were people to say good-bye to, and a carriage and driver to be arranged. Messages needed to be sent to inform Caladore of our return, and Namin suddenly remembered dozens of things she needed to teach me. As well, it suddenly seemed as though each moment needed to be spent with the utmost care. Our days with Namin's family were numbered. I tried to enjoy my time, but it was difficult because the wound inside me was slow to heal.

Some moments, I despised Rion and was glad to be through with him. At other times, I missed him terribly. I felt embarrassed for being foolish enough to involve myself with him, and I felt as though it was he who had been foolish in daring to be with me. I fought against a prevailing fog of despair that made me choke on hopelessness and doubt. Had I done the right thing? Would I ever find another boy to love me? Through all this, however, the knowledge that I was returning to Caladore sustained me.

* * *

"I have been thinking," Namin began, as we finished the morning dishes together, "that perhaps wearing your Healer's ring would help to focus your energy." She handed me a plate to dry. "You are Six Summers old; it must fit you by now."

I dried the plate vigorously and frowned. I did not want to wear my ring. It was the last thing I needed. People were quick enough to loathe Healers without a visual reminder to prompt them. Perhaps, I thought bitterly, instead of the ring I should wear a big wooden sign around my neck declaring myself to be a Healer.

"I will put it on next time I try to channel," I promised, and hoped that this compromise would satisfy her. It was our last day in Karsalin, and I did not want to argue with Namin.

"Try it on, Lara. It would do my heart good." Namin tapped her fingers on the washing basin, and then took the cloth from my grasp and dried her hands with it.

I sighed and fumbled at the nape of my neck to find the clasp on the chain. I undid it and pulled my ring free from the chain. They both rested in my palm: the shiny silver chain, and the ring, a calm deep green.

"Sophie's necklace!" Namin gasped. "I wondered what happened to it. Sophie never wore it after Jerran left."

I frowned in confusion and closed my hand over the ring. Had Sophie some secret love I had not known about?

"Who is Jerran?"

Namin's brown eyes widened in surprise. "I thought you would know." She paused, began a sentence, and then stopped again. She sat down at the table. "Perhaps it is not my place to tell you."

"Namin," I said sternly, and came to sit across from her. I leaned my elbows on the table and held her gaze.

"You cannot very well say something like that and then not explain."

She bit her lip, until all at once her resolve broke. She leaned forward, her voice hushed. "All right, I will tell you."

I grinned.

"But-" She held out her hand. "But only so you can understand how special the chain is, and know how much Sophie loves you."

I settled myself more comfortably in my seat, deeply curious to hear the story behind Jerran.

"When I knew Jerran best, he was only a child, a kind-hearted little boy whose family lived in the same town as ours. When I left for Telnayis in my Second Summer Year, he and Sophie were only friends. When I returned, a girl of Eight Summers, they were in love with each other. He was a wonderful man, Lara. He and Sophie were married in the spring. That chain was his wedding gift to her."

I was stunned. I had never imagined Sophie as a married woman. She had always been just Sophie. My surprise spread like rings in water. I had never considered Sophie's past. I had simply accepted her as I had first come to know her: Sophie, my gentle caretaker, Lady Grim, independent Head of the Kitchen. It never occurred to me that Sophie's tale did not begin when my story intersected her own.

"I used to love to visit their house." Namin sighed and rested her chin on her hands. "It was always such a happy place. Sophie and Jerran always seemed to be laughing and singing. I have not heard Sophie sing since he left."

The words frightened me. They reminded me of my own parents' story, and I desperately hoped that Jerran had not left Sophie the way my father had left my mother. "Where did he go?" I demanded.

"He was a sailor, one of the finest in Caladore's fleet. The King at the time, who would be your friend Tren-Lore's grandfather, was planning a voyage to see what the seas held beyond Tolrem. So, four years after Sophie and Jerran's marriage, three ships set sail to explore the outer reaches of the sea. The King had assigned his best mariners to the mission. Of course, Jerran was Captain of the flagship. Sophie was so proud, and everyone assumed that in a few months the ships would return bearing tidings of exciting new places." Namin stopped suddenly, and her eyes glazed with tears. She stared out the kitchen window. "The ships never came back. No one knows what happened to them."

I felt a great emptiness, as though sadness had eaten a hole inside me. It was so unfair. Poor Sophie. I wanted to leap from the table and go to comfort her, even though her wound would be long healed. Yet, I thought, perhaps it was not. My own agony over Rion clung to me with a firm grip, and I could scarcely imagine the feelings associated with losing your husband.

"She is still in love with him." Revelation made my tone soft.

Namin returned her gaze to me. "Yes, I think so. There was a time, before I had met Rolias and after Jerran had left, when Sophie and I were both living at home. After our father died, Mother pleaded with Sophie to take a new husband so there would be someone to provide for the family. She refused. I clearly remember when Mother first suggested it. Sophie smashed a cup on the floor and stormed out of the house, yelling that she was still married to Jerran."

My mind could not conjure the image. Sophie did not smash cups on the floor.

"That was when King Kiris came to her aid. He had just come into power, and regretted the foolish mission his father had sent the men upon. He personally sought out the families of each crewmember to see if he could help in any way. When he came to Sophie, she told him she needed a job. He told her he needed a new Head for his kitchen." Namin laughed suddenly and rubbed her eyes. "This is all beside the point. You were supposed to try on your ring."

I was still so absorbed in this new revelation about Sophie's character that I did not have the presence of mind to object. I slipped the ring on my finger.

"It is a perfect fit," Namin said.

I looked down at the green ivy encircling my finger. How did everything become so muddled? What contaminates plunged perfection into despair? My mind flashed with the complications of life. So much suffering was possible, and I had only brushed against the torment which Sophie and my mother had suffered. It terrified me. I pulled the ring from my finger. "It is too big," I muttered, slipping it back on Jerran's chain and hiding it once more in the folds of my dress.

Chapter Eighteen
The Return Home

The ride home was a solemn one. I had said my farewells and departed in tears from Namin and her children. I laid my head in Sophie's lap and wept as we drove out of Karsalin. She stroked my hair and remained comfortingly silent. My sadness, however, was balanced against my anticipation to be at home again, and as we drew nearer to Caladore, my spirits rose in accordance.

"Sit down, child!" Sophie chided as I leaned over her and pressed my hands to the window. My heart was pounding and a smile was creasing my cheeks. We were nearly home!

"Lara!" Sophie protested again, trying to move me from my precarious position, half on and off her lap. "You are crushing me."

I scarcely heard her, for just then, the coach crested a hill and the castle of Caladore was revealed. "Caladore!" I cried, and involuntarily pushed even closer to the window.

"Ascendants' Mercy!" Sophie declared as my knee accidentally hit her in the stomach. "Lara, sit down!"

I did as I was told. We could now see Caladore from both sides of the coach. I felt charged with excitement, full of the energy of a thunderstorm. It was hard to even sit still. I was home! I was going to see Tren-Lore! "Oh,

Sophie!" I gasped. "I just want to jump out of the coach and run all the way home!"

She glanced crossly at me and smoothed her hair. "Well, you can rid yourself of that notion, young lady. You will sit in this coach until it stops."

I did not bother to reply and instead gazed breathlessly ahead. The details of the castle were now becoming clear, although to my unease, they seemed slightly different. The gates were barred, and there was no sound of people from within. The walls seemed to loom ominously overhead, their gray stone seeming almost black. Soldiers manned the watchtowers and the flags hung limply, obscuring the dragon. I frowned.

The coach drew to a halt and a man's voice bellowed from the wall, "Who goes there?"

Our driver yelled an answer, and Sophie and I turned to look at each other in confusion.

"What is this all about?" I asked Sophie.

Sophie shook her head, but did not say anything. An order to open the gates was issued, and after a pause, the gates slowly grated open. I tried to ignore my disquiet and concentrate on the fact that I was home. We drove through the gates, and the carriage stopped just outside of the large doors of the inner wall. I climbed easily from the carriage and while the driver helped Sophie down, I stared around the empty courtyard. Sophie arranged to have our baggage delivered to the kitchen and she and I climbed the steps leading to the massive iron doors.

The guards looked grim. "What is your business here?" one of them demanded gruffly.

"I am Lady Grim, Head of the Kitchen" Sophie replied.

The sentinels glared at her as though something sinister lurked beneath Sophie's plump and graying exterior.

"We do not have any orders to admit a Lady Grim," the guard replied.

Sophie arched her eyebrows at him. "Well, I would check your orders again."

"Go away, woman," the other guard growled. "Stop wasting our time."

I looked over at Sophie and found that her cheeks were flushed with anger. I thought she might be ready to start smashing cups, but I did not think this approach would garner an expedient entry. "Listen," I said pleasantly, stepping forward and ignoring the creak of armor as the guards tensed, "I know you are only trying to do your jobs, and we do not want to cause any trouble. Please take a message to Prince Tren-Lore asking him to come down and give you authorization to admit us. He knows who we are, and I am sure he would be more than happy to straighten this mess out. There are only, what, three flights of stairs down from the royal chambers?" I smiled at them, as though this was not the threat we all knew it was.

The guards blanched, and I tried to imagine what they were thinking. Were they conjuring images of Tren-Lore in a rage over being dragged into such trivial affairs? I sincerely hoped so, even though I knew that would not be his reaction at all.

"Very well," one of them grunted and abruptly yanked the door open.

I led Sophie past the scowling sentinels and into the garden. As the doors banged shut behind us, I sighed in relief.

Sophie was muttering irately, "I never thought I would live to see the day...Something is simply not right!"

I silently agreed, but as I turned my gaze upon the sprawling green landscape, I found it difficult to keep worry in the forefront of my mind. This, at least, did not appear to have changed. I savored each step we took along the familiar course, and when at last we turned left down a small side path, I ran ahead to find the dragon fountain. I stared up at it, embracing it with my mind, letting my eyes caress each familiar detail. I was home!

Sophie came up beside me, and for a moment we both stood and smiled up at the fountain. Then, turning, we hurried toward the small side door and I threw it open. We entered the castle and I breathed in deeply, savoring the familiar scent of dust and sun-warmed rocks and the ever-so-faint smell of bread. I bounded up the stairs following the scent, with Sophie coming behind more slowly. I arrived at the kitchen door and dashed inside, nervous about what I might find. I paused and slowly looked about; a visual demand to the room to reveal its changes. It did not appear that anything had been altered. The table, shelves, barrels of water and grains – everything seemed to be the same.

"Thank the Ascendants," Sophie's voice said from behind me. Apparently, she too had feared what transformation might have occurred in her beloved kitchen.

We walked together through the antechamber and entered the main kitchen. The sound of many voices, the clinking of dishes and the aroma of bread all seemed to wrap themselves about us. As we closed the door, everyone glanced up from their work, and surprise temporarily crippled the sound within the kitchen. All at once noise leaped back into the room and everyone was talking and rushing toward us.

"Sophie! Welcome home! I just do not know how you managed to travel so far. If it were me..."

"Look how tall you have gotten, Lara! Why, when you left you were only..."

"How was your trip? Did you have any trouble with the Renarn? We heard just yesterday that..."

And then, all at once, I found myself caught in an ecstatic hug that almost knocked me over.

"Lara! Oh, Lara, how I have missed you!" exclaimed a dramatic voice.

I staggered back from the demanding grip and stared at a person I did not recognize for a moment. She had a curvaceous figure that was clearly displayed by the bodice of her dress. Her brown curls were piled intricately on the top of her head, and her lips were bent upward in a fairly decent imitation of sincere happiness.

"Flock!" I declared, and grinned at her. "It has not been long enough!"

She grinned back with malicious delight. "You look terrible, Lara! Are you getting too much sun?"

* * *

Even before our trunks arrived, Sophie had been absorbed back into the kitchen. There was a banquet being held in the garden that night, and the kitchen was in its usual state of carefully controlled chaos. Sophie bustled off to taste the huge pot of soup that was cooking over the fire and was adding spices before I could hang up my cloak.

"Help Flock cut up those potatoes, would you, Lara?" one of the women asked as she swept by bearing a large platter of roast duck.

I chuckled with wry amusement. Flock would have to be the first person I worked with! I seated myself across from her and took up a knife.

Flock's mother rustled past us with a small bowl of carrots in her hand. She glanced at her daughter, looked toward her destination, and then stopped abruptly. Her eyes narrowed as she surveyed Flock once again. "Young lady!" she declared, coming up behind Flock. "If I have to tell you one more time..." Slamming her bowl to the table, she grabbed the top of Flock's bodice and pulled it up, so that suddenly her daughter's neckline was modest rather than revealing. "Keep it that way." She picked up her bowl and swished past us.

Flock glared after her, and once she was certain her mother was engaged in other matters, she took hold of the sides of her dress and tugged it back down. "Much better," she declared. "Mother is so silly. Now, what news have you heard? Probably nothing. Well, you need not worry. I can catch you up on everything that has been happening in Caladore."

Apparently, nothing important was happening in Caladore that did not include Flock. She proceeded to tell me all about Leffeck, the very rich and handsome young man who was currently courting her, the gifts he had given her, and her suspicion that he was going to be the man she would marry.

I shrugged and viciously sliced a potato in half. "It is your mistake to make."

Flock stopped her knife in midair. "Well, that kind of talk will certainly not win you a husband. Kella started talking like that, and she is still not married."

My eyebrows rose in shock. It was hard to imagine Kelladyn speaking negatively about boys or anything pertaining to them. Perhaps, I thought as I turned around to look for her, Kella's involvement with Yolis had not ended as she had hoped.

"Oh, she is not here," Flock informed me, waving her hand dismissively. "Mother sent her to live with our aunt."

"Why?" I asked, throwing a handful of sliced potatoes into the bowl on the table.

Flock looked down suddenly. "She just did."

I held Flock in a scrutinizing stare, but she did not meet my gaze. Obviously she was not willing to discuss this topic any further. It was this unwillingness that made me deeply curious. Flock was always glad to talk about any subject, as long as she was the center of attention. This uncharacteristic silence was very puzzling. I decided not to push for any more information. Rather, I would ask Tren-Lore when I saw him next. When would I see him next? Was he even home yet?

"Is Prince Tren-Lore still away on training?" I asked Flock, and she looked up eagerly, apparently relieved at the change of topic.

"Yes," she tossed some potatoes in the bowl. "He came back about a month ago, but he left again last week. I heard he was going back to Hemlizar to visit the princess. Apparently, he has fallen in love with her, or so I have heard."

I had to struggle to keep my face from displaying my disappointment and shock. It felt as though I had suddenly swallowed a great wash of freezing river water. Tren-Lore was not here, and this news about the Hemlizar Princess...if it was true, why had Tren-Lore not told me? This occupied my thoughts until we had finished preparing and moving the food down to the garden.

Sophie spared a moment to go to our room and dig out a clean dress from the trunk that had been brought up. I followed her into the chamber and was happy to see that everything had remained as we had left it. Someone had even been kind enough to dust. I crawled up onto my bed and watched as Sophie got ready. My mind was still brooding over Tren-Lore.

"Such a mess," Sophie muttered to herself. "Everything will have to be put in order. Oh, here, Lara," she said suddenly, holding up my new red dress. "You might as well wear this."

I scrambled across the bed and took the gown from her. At last, a chance to wear my dress! I was so thrilled with this turn of events that I managed to forget I had been upset about Tren-Lore. The expression upon Flock's face when I emerged from our room was enough to put a permanent smile on my lips. This dress was ten times better than ruffled cuffs!

* * *

Tables had been arranged outside, and the garden was awash in summer twilight. Musicians were playing softly in the background and the air had the scent of flowers and fresh growing things. People were standing in small clusters, and servants wound between them offering drinks and food. Sophie said that she did not need my help, and so for a time, I sat on the outskirts of the party watching the elegant guests talk and laugh. I tried to imagine what grand topics they were discussing. When I grew tired of this, I wandered off toward the dragon fountain again.

"Hello," I said quietly when I had reached the statue.

My only reply was the soft sound of moving water. I walked all around the basin of the fountain, finally settling myself on the edge farthest from the path. I stared up at the dragon. Somehow, it seemed older than when I had last seen it. The fading light made the stone appear more finished and smooth, but at the same time it added shadows to the dragon's face and wings that made it seem dangerous and powerful.

"Excuse me," said a voice from behind me. "Is there a party being held in the garden?"

I turned slowly, finding it hard to tear my attention from the dragon statue. "Yes, there..." my words dissolved into the dusk as I beheld the figure before me. Standing only a few feet away was Tren-Lore!

He looked shocked, and he stared at me as though I were not really there. "You have no idea how many times I have had this dream," he said as his face creased into a grin.

I leapt to my feet, uttering a cry of joy. Running to him, I threw myself into his arms, and he swept me up in a hug. We held each other as though we never intended to let go.

"Oh, Tren-Lore," I mumbled into his shoulder, "I missed you so much." We broke apart and I reached up to touch his cheeks. They were rough with stubble. "You are so tall!"

His hair was cut shorter than before, but it was still ruffled and disorderly. His tunic, pants, and cloak seemed to blend into the surroundings, and reminded me vaguely of someone or something I could not place. The only things he wore that did not allow the eye to effortlessly glide over him were the dragon clasp that held his cloak about his neck and the sword at his belt.

"You look..." Tren-Lore's smile widened, and he laughed. "You look incredible."

I looked down, feeling a blush on my cheeks. "Thank you." I shook myself and turned my eyes back up to Tren-Lore. "Why are you here? I thought you had gone to Hemlizar to visit their princess."

Tren-Lore chuckled. "One of many rumors, I am sure." He glanced around the dragon fountain and down the path toward the castle. "So, is the party in the garden?"

I nodded. "If you want to avoid it, we can go in through the kitchen entrance."

Tren-Lore clapped me on the shoulder. "I am glad you are back." We started off down the path. "Do you want to go to the secret room? I can tell you why I was really in Hemlizar, and you can tell me everything you were leaving out in your letters."

I was suddenly reminded of his last letter and the mention of exams. I glanced over at him. "How did your tests go?"

Tren-Lore scratched at his jaw and shrugged.

I laughed and slipped my arm into his. "First?" I could tell he was trying not to smile, but it was to no avail.

"Yeah." His face broke into a wide grin. "I am now officially a knight."

I felt warmed with pride. I had known he would be first. "And now?"

"Indeed," he replied. His voice was soft and mysterious. He grabbed the door and heaved it open. "Want to race?"

I shoved past him and sprinted up the stairs.

"Lara!" Tren-Lore exclaimed.

I heard his feet pounding up the steps behind me. My mirth prevented me from making an effective escape, and Tren-Lore's hand caught hold of the back of my dress. His grip spun me around, and for a moment, we were standing face to face in the narrow hallway, so close that our bodies brushed together.

"You are such a cheater," he laughed.

I grinned up at Tren-Lore and felt warmth surge through my body as our eyes locked. I had forgotten the weight his gaze held. I had also forgotten how handsome he was.

Tren-Lore cleared his throat and stepped away. "Do you happen to remember Draows?" he asked suddenly.

"Of course," I replied, and turned to continue up the stairs. Draows was not someone I could easily forget. "Why?"

"Because it was him I was meeting in Hemlizar. I met him while I was there for training, and then about eight days ago I received a message asking me to return. He gave no explanation, but I was not about to question Draows' motives. It turns out that it was a Council of the League. Do you remember that part in *Rayn*?" Tren-Lore asked excitedly.

I nodded vigorously. I knew exactly what part he was talking about. The Council of the League had been one of my favorite moments in the book. I had loved the description of the Sanysk lounging about a long table in the middle of the woods.

"It was exactly like that," Tren-Lore continued. "I even got to meet Adewus! He is the Head of the League! Dayr and a few other men I know were there, too. Adewus said he wished to train me but Draows said that he had been

269

with me at the Trials, and therefore, deserved to be the one to complete my Sanysk training. So, it was decided that Adewus would train Dayr, and Draows would train me."

I stopped and turned around, my mouth open in shock. "What?" I demanded, and my voice rose with excitement. "What? You are training to be a Sanysk! How dare you not say anything until now." I hit him in pleasant outrage. "I always knew you would be a Sanysk. I knew it! When does your training begin?"

"In four days." Tren-Lore rubbed the spot where I had struck him. "Seriously, Lara, our hand-to-hand combat teacher would have loved you. When we were training-" Tren-Lore stopped abruptly and shook his head. "It seems like the only thing I do is train, and then when I am not training, I talk about training. Now that Draows is coming, I am sure it will only get worse. Do you suppose our training will ever be done?"

"Our?" I echoed teasingly as we started up the stairs again. "I am done. It is only you who insists on torturing yourself."

"Are you done with your training?" Tren-Lore's tone was intrigued.

My hand went involuntarily to the ring around my neck. I imagined that I could feel its warmth through the material of my dress. I wondered if I would have the ability to channel, if I had the courage to wear it. "Well, almost. I still do not have control over my life energy."

Tren-Lore wanted a full explanation of this, and by the time we had made it to the secret room, I had stumbled through a description of what exactly Healing and channeling entailed. Tren-Lore threw the shutters open, and a pleasantly cool breeze wafted through the window. The interior of the secret room was filled with books. There were small turrets of literature rising from the floor and table. The bookshelf was laden with leather-bound novels and rolls of parchment. A stack of wood was tossed carelessly in one corner.

I stepped over a pile of papers and smiled. "Read any good books lately?"

Tren-Lore chuckled. "Quite a few, actually. I have several that you should read. When I got home, you were not here, and Myste and Dayr had left and there was no training to do, and I was sort of, well..." He rubbed the back of his neck. "I had no idea what to do with myself."

"Well, I can keep you busy now that I am back." I picked up a book from the table and turned it idly in my hands. The cover read, *Herbs of Caladore* by *Sir Emdridge Eraklerst.* I held it up to Tren-Lore.

"Are you learning about this?"

He winced and slid to the ground, his back against the far wall. "I am trying to, although I think Emdridge Eraklerst finds herb lore just as confusing as I do."

I put the book down. "I could teach you about this. Namin taught me all about herbs and plants. Why do you want to know?"

Tren-Lore rose and moved over to the hearth. He grabbed a few pieces of wood and went about lighting a fire. "I thought it seemed useful. I have been reading all the old records in Caladore's library, and I am finding references to something called Forest-wisdom in the early documents." Tren-Lore struck his flint and tinder together and sent a shower of sparks down upon the kindling. "It seems the Sanysk used to know all about the properties of plants, but in the recent records there is no mention of it at all. I think it may have something to do with the breaking of the Triad."

"Well," I said, my lips bending up at the corners, "I can teach you."

The embers that had been suckling upon the wood suddenly burst into flames and danced cheerily in the fireplace. Our figures were awash in the comforting glow of firelight, and I came to sit beside him.

"So, what did Rion say when you told him you were coming home?" Tren-Lore asked as he pushed another log into the fire.

I started. The very sound of Rion's name seemed strange, as though he were a character mentioned in a book that he did not belong in. "He – well..." My mind touched upon the branded image of Rion and his friends at the tavern. His words rang in my head. *I am done with her. I could only stand being with someone like her for so long. I want a girl who is gorgeous and knows how to keep her mouth shut. And really, can you actually see me living the rest of my life with a Healer?* Tears filled my eyes, and I numbly relived the scene for Tren-Lore. By the end of the tale I was sobbing hopelessly.

Tren-Lore put a comforting arm around me. He was silent for a moment, and then asked, "Do you want me to beat him senseless?"

I laughed in spite myself. "No," I sniffed and sat up, wiping tears from my cheeks.

"Lara, listen," Tren-Lore said, and I looked up at him. Firelight danced across the tips of his spiky hair, and his dark blue eyes were stern. "What Rion said is not true. There is nothing wrong with being a Healer. One of the first things that attracted me to you was that you did *not* keep your mouth shut, and if he thinks that you are not gorgeous, then he is blind."

His words wound about me like a spell of comfort. "Thank you," I murmured. We were both silent for a moment, and I reached across Tren-Lore to add another piece of wood to the fire. "So, what about you? Is there any truth to this rumor of you and the princess of Hemlizar?" A very large part of me hoped that it was nothing more than idle gossip.

Tren-Lore leaned back with his hands behind his head. "When I was in Hemlizar we spent some time together, but it was nothing serious. Areama is very much a product of her courtly life."

I fought back a feeling of relief, and the conversation turned to other topics. Tren-Lore told stories from Hemlizar. A particularly chilling tale involved the belief that in all shadowy places dwelt Disanima, shapeless creatures that could slip inside you as you breathed and devour your spirit. This was enough to make me pleasantly afraid, but when our talk turned to the explanation for the changes in Caladore, a true fear took hold of me.

"War?" I repeated Tren-Lore's words in horror. "Could this dispute really lead to war?"

We were both standing at the window, and I stared out into the darkness trying to mentally overlay the quiet landscape with marching armies and glaring torches.

Tren-Lore shifted beside me. "It could. Yolis would like it to." I did not have to see Tren-Lore's face to know that his jaw was clenched and his expression angry. "My brother believes that Caladore is stagnating and needs to expand her borders. It is really nothing more than two farmers bickering over property lines, but Yolis would be perfectly willing to see it escalate into full-fledged war."

Chapter Nineteen
Double Edged Swords

"I simply must dry. If I wash those dishes, it will ruin my nails," Flock insisted, and threw the washing rag at me.

"I am not washing," I told her again and threw the cloth back at her. "I washed all the dishes last night."

Flock grabbed my hand and pressed the rag into it. She closed my fingers over the material and patted my fist. A patronizing smirk flashed across her face. "And what a fine job you did. Trust me, Lara, you are meant for w-" Flock stopped in mid-sentence, her attention suddenly taken by a knocking upon the door.

We both turned toward the sound.

"I will get it!" Flock volunteered.

Just to be ornery, I replied, "No, I can get it."

Flock glared at me, and Sophie declared, "*I* will get it." She disappeared through the inner door and returned a moment later with a piece of parchment in hand. "Lara, you are needed in the royal chambers. Princess Nahanni would like you to wait on her."

I grinned at Flock and handed her the washing cloth. "I am sure Leffeck will love you, even if your nails are ruined."

Her lips parted as though she were trying to say something but could not find the words.

I waved a cheerful good-bye. "Have fun," I told her, and fled the kitchen before her surprise turned to rage.

I made my way up to the royal chambers with some hesitation. I had only been there once before, and I was not entirely sure if I remembered the route. After taking several wrong turns, I finally found myself in the hall leading to the massive oak doors. I hurried toward them, feeling sure that it was Tren-Lore and not Nahanni who was responsible for the summons. I rapped upon the door, and after a few moments Tren-Lore opened it.

"Do you want to go riding?" he asked.

"Of course," I replied.

Rathum was working in the stables that day. He mumbled a shy greeting, but he and Tren-Lore talked easily as they brought Paence and Storm Wing from their stalls. I laughed in delight as Paence whickered a greeting to me. I leaned my cheek against her muzzle and rubbed her ears. To my surprise, I found that my fingers still remembered how to saddle a horse, and as Tren-Lore and I rode out of the stable, I felt as though I had never been away from Caladore. It could have been a day four years ago, except for the silent outer courtyard. There was not a single merchant or visitor to be seen.

"Yolis convinced Father that permitting goods to be delivered to the castle made us more vulnerable to a possible 'Renarn infiltration'," Tren-Lore scoffed. "No one enters without direct orders from Father or Yolis."

The outer doors were thrown open at our approach, and the posted guards saluted formally but still smiled at Tren-Lore with an easy friendliness. Tren-Lore reined in Storm Wing and greeted the two men warmly. He introduced me to Ryth and Quarin.

"Nice to meet you," Ryth replied with a nod.

Quarin grinned at me and leaned heavily on his spear. "Yes, Lara, very nice to meet you."

I was not sure, but I thought that Tren-Lore gave Quarin a brief, but warning look. He kicked Storm Wing into a canter and we clattered past the two guards. As the huge gates grated closed behind us, I drove my heels into Paence's flanks and the mare surged forward. Beside me, Storm Wing neighed fiercely and leapt into a gallop. The sweet summer air blew past my face as we tore wildly across the countryside. An intoxicating feeling of exaltation filled every inch of my body, and the ground seemed to melt from under Paence's pounding hooves. How had I lived without this sensation? We drew rein as we neared the forest, and Storm Wing stamped and snorted, protesting the end of the race.

We spent the rest of the day wandering through the forest. I began to teach Tren-Lore about the plants that grew among the trees, and we talked and laughed and filled the woods with our noisy energy. By the time we got back to the castle, it was dark. We parted at the massive castle doors and I hurried back to the kitchen. I was half-afraid that Sophie would be waiting there for me, ready with a scolding and punishment. My trepidation was unfounded, however, for Sophie merely smiled at me and asked me about my day. I told her it had been wonderful.

* * *

Sunshine danced across the floor and flecked the table with golden patches. I hummed softly to myself as I folded cloth about a wedge of cheese. I fetched a loaf of bread, some apples and dried meat, and put them all in the pack resting before me. I rolled up my cloak and stuffed it into the bag as well. It was early in the morning and the kitchen was still deserted. Sophie was asleep. This made things much less complicated. I had told her the night before that I was accompanying the princess on an overnight pilgrimage to the sanctuary in Cala. I would have been hard-pressed, however, to explain why I needed so much food, or why I was dressed in Tren-Lore's old clothes.

My heart leapt as I thought about the day ahead. How wonderful it was to once more be part of Tren-Lore's adventures. I missed Namin and her children, but I had to admit that they did not compare to life with Tren-Lore. It was like comparing reality to the loveliness of myth. I tied the pack shut and smiled in satisfaction. I heard the soft creak of the door opening and turned to find Tren-Lore standing in the entrance.

"Come on," he whispered, and jerked his head toward the door.

I came without question. I knew where we were going. Draows was coming today, and we had decided to meet him on the road and then ride back to Caladore with him. I slung my pack over my shoulder. We left the kitchen quietly and were soon swinging up into our saddles. They were laden with provisions for the overnight stay we anticipated.

Tren-Lore bowed his head to me. "After you." He gestured to the door.

I dug my heels into Paence's sides, and she surged forward. Storm Wing and Tren-Lore were close behind me. We flew through the courtyard and out of the gates, our passing sounding like thunder in the silence of the sleeping castle.

"That green plant there." I pointed to the small shrub growing along the road. "What is it called and what is it used for?"

"It is called..." Tren-Lore leaned back in his saddle, squinting up into the sky, searching for answers. He thought for several moments, and then replied confidently. "It is called onitary and it is used for treating infections of the blood."

"And," I prompted, shading my eyes from the bright sun on the road.

"And for seasoning rabbit," Tren-Lore laughed.

"Very good," I replied, and shifted to a more comfortable position in my saddle. "Emdridge Eraklerst would be proud of you."

We continued to talk in this manner for some time, interrupting the discussion of idle topics to identify plants. Soon, under the caress of sunlight and summer air, we were too relaxed and lazy to even continue conversation. We walked our horses in contented silence. Words seemed unnecessary. It was enough to simply share the moment and be at Tren-Lore's side.

We had a late lunch under a large, gnarled tree. Sitting in the shade with our backs to the road, we unpacked the food I had brought. The cheese was a little warm and mushy, and the apples were bruised, but our hunger made us blind to these flaws.

"When do you suppose we will encounter Draows?" I asked, my words considerably muffled by my mouthful of bread.

Tren-Lore swallowed the piece of apple he had been chewing and leaned back against the trunk of the tree. "Soon, I would think."

I took another bite of bread. I was anticipating the meeting with Draows as I would have looked forward to my Summer Year. We had only spent a short time together, but over those brief days, I had become extremely fond of him. I also wanted to know if my answer to his riddle was correct. I wondered briefly if he would even remember the riddle, but decided that Draows did not seem as though he forgot anything.

"He will be very surprised," I said, and we grinned at each other. "That is, if it is possible to surprise a Sanysk."

"It is, in fact," remarked a deep voice from behind us, "entirely possible."

Tren-Lore's hand went instinctively to his sword and I gasped in fright, my fingers fumbling for the dagger Tren-Lore had given me. I glanced quickly over my shoulder, and instead of finding the stranger I had expected, I beheld a familiar figure. It was Draows, and behind him stood Quell. They both looked as though they had stepped out of the past and into the shadow of our tree.

My grip loosened from my dagger. I had not worn it in Karsalin, and was slow in drawing it. Little good it would do me, I thought as I marveled at how quietly Draows must have moved to come upon us entirely unnoticed. Tren-Lore and I scrambled to our feet.

Draows smiled broadly and held out his hand to Tren-Lore. "Well met," he said as they caught each other by the forearm and shook hands. "And the Healer Lara," Draows continued as he turned to me. "You travel in good company, Tren-Lore." He bowed to me with a grace that belied his rough exterior.

"Is it a dragon?" I asked, even before the Sanysk had fully righted himself. Suddenly realizing that I should have returned his greeting instead of bombarding him with questions, I quickly stuttered, "I – um, sorry, hello. Would you like something to eat?" I gestured to the food spread across the ground.

While the scar across Draows' face was undisturbed by any hint of a smile, his amber eyes seemed amused. "My answer to both questions is the same. The riddle is indeed about a dragon, and yes, I would very much enjoy some food. Quell and I did not break fast."

We all returned to the picnic and let the weather and other such unimportant things dominate our conversation. It was decided that we would make camp there tonight and return to Caladore in the morning. Draows began instructing Tren-Lore that night, and I listened with silent interest. The Sanysk talked about the ethics of his League and its leader Adewus.

"There are three rules which you must abide by. If you do not live by these rules, Adewus can strip you of your bands of rank. The first is that a Sanysk is never to attack the defenseless."

Tren-Lore nodded intently.

"The second," Draows continued, shadows dancing across his face, "demands that a Sanysk always declare his intentions for battle."

Tren-Lore frowned. "What exactly does that mean?"

Draows stared into the fire. "It means different things to different men." His voice reminded me of the growl of a wolf. "For some, it is the means to a wicked end. They believe that as long as a warning of intended action is given to an opponent, a Sanysk can then commit any foul deed he wishes."

My mind immediately made sense of this chink in their doctrine. "So if I was to warn an unarmed man that I was going to kill him, I could argue that I was still following the rules?"

Draows inclined his head slightly. "Precisely. It is my belief, however, that the Ascendants first created this law to prevent the Sanysk from becoming merciless killers. A Sanysk is not bound to fight for his native land, though once he makes a vow of loyalty, he must fight until victory or death. As prince, you may be more inclined to be loyal to your country, but as a Sanysk, you are not obligated to fight for Caladore if you do not choose to do so."

This was rather astonishing news for me. I had never considered the freedom that being a Sanysk would bring to Tren-Lore. If he was feeling similar emotions, they certainly did not show upon his face. He did not reply, and the Sanysk did not seem to require a response. I was not content, as Draows was, with Tren-Lore's silence. As we lay in our sleeping rolls that night, I asked Tren-Lore about the dilemma.

"I hope that Caladore never comes upon such dark times that it is necessary for me to make that choice." Tren-Lore shifted beside me, folding his arms across his chest. "But if it does...well...I will fight that battle when I come to it."

I fell asleep with Tren-Lore's words in my mind and the quiet evening sounds of the world whispering in my ears. I awoke to the clang of metal and the smell of smoke and cooking meat. Sitting up, I stretched and rubbed at my back. It may not have bothered Lord Rayn to sleep on the ground, but my muscles felt as though they were tied in knots. I looked about our campsite. It was late in the morning, and the fire had been left unattended. Meat dripped and sizzled from the skewer above the flames.

Tren-Lore and Draows were over by the tree, and it appeared that Tren-Lore's second lesson had begun. The men had their swords in hand and were both stripped to the waist. They must have been practicing for some time, as they were both sweating and Tren-Lore was breathing hard. As I threw back my blankets, I could not help noticing the way the muscles in Tren-Lore's back and shoulders moved as he blocked a thrust from Draows. Rion never had muscles like that.

"No," Draows said in a patient tone and lowered his blade. "Resist the instinct to block my attack. Step away from the blow, and then strike. Here, I will show you."

They took ready stances as I walked quietly to the fire to examine the meat. Kneeling, I stirred the coals, keeping a close eye on Tren-Lore and Draows.

Draows held out his left hand and beckoned Tren-Lore with two crooked fingers. "Attack me."

I was thankful I was not facing Draows. For all I knew of his kind spirit, I would still have found it unnerving to face that hardened expression and those knowing amber eyes. Tren-Lore lunged, and I knew enough to appreciate the form in his precise motion. Against any other opponent it would have forced a retreat, but rather than raising his blade and staggering back under the power of the blow, Draows stepped sideways. The movement was as quick as a gasp of breath, and in the time it would have taken to exhale, the Sanysk had his sword inches from the side of Tren-Lore's neck.

"You cannot defend against something you do not expect." Draows lowered his weapon and laid a friendly hand on Tren-Lore's shoulder. "Remember this as you do battle. The better you become at predicting and being unpredictable, the more deadly you will become."

"And the more likely you are to come home alive," I added under my breath.

Draows sheathed his sword and stretched his arm across his chest. "Very true, Lara."

I felt a faint blush brighten my cheeks. I turned hurriedly to fetch some bread from the packs. How in the name of the Ascendants had Draows heard me say that?

* * *

"I can hear nine sounds," I told Draows, and he nodded and turned to Tren-Lore.

"Eleven," the prince replied, and fought against Storm Wing's demanding jerk upon the reins. The stallion snorted angrily. He hated to walk. "Why, how many do you hear?"

"Thirty-one," said Draows.

I shook my head in wonder. We had played this game four times during the journey home, and Draows could always hear far more than me or Tren-Lore.

"Try to find a balance between your inner thoughts and your concentration on the outside world," Draows advised in deep tones. He touched the scar upon his cheek. "This is the cost of becoming too involved in my own musings. I did not hear my enemy as he approached me. It is not a mistake I have made twice."

We spent the remaining trip in silence. I assumed that Tren-Lore was doing as Draows had instructed, but such close attention was not for me, and soon my mind had wandered onto new topics. I worried about how much I would see of Tren-Lore now that he had begun his training. When I had been in the midst of *my* training, I had virtually excluded everything from my life that was not Healing. Biting my lip, I hoped that Tren-Lore did not become as monopolized as I had become.

To my great relief, my fears proved not to be rooted in reality. I began to think that Tren-Lore was really training to be a Sorcerer, for he seemed able to create time where there should have been none. We spent time talking and playing Questkon in the secret room, and we even made a few excursions to the fort. I continued to teach him about herb lore, and I helped him with his practice.

I would lunge at Tren-Lore and he would attempt to dodge rather than block. The lithe movement was not easy for him to master, but he never once stormed away from the task as I had done when I had been trying to learn to channel. His frustration was expressed by a tightening of his jaw and an increased determination to get it right. I admired him a great deal.

I was not the only person who thought highly of Tren-Lore. A letter arrived from Myste some time in mid-winter, and Tren-Lore and I bounded up to the secret room to open it. Myste's verbal and written styles were so similar that as Tren-Lore and I sat upon the table, his letter between us, it felt as though I could almost hear Myste's voice.

My dear Tren-Lore and my dearest Lara, (Yes, it is true, Tren-Lore; I like her more than you.)

I am afraid that this year I will not be coming for my annual visit. I have seen far too much of Tren-Lore over the past couple of years and would have to kill him if we spent any more quality time together. I am joking, of course. If I fought Tren-Lore, I would not even be able to scratch him, let alone mortally wound him.

I smiled as I read this and thought briefly that the difference between Myste and Rion was that Myste teased because he was fond of you, while Rion teased because he was fond of being cruel. Stupid Rion.

So, Myste continued, *you will just have to enjoy your freezing cold winter all by yourselves. And while it would be lovely to spend time with the two of you, life is so excellent right now that it would be hard to tear myself away from such an existence. I think knighthood was designed by the Ascendant of Unity. Now that I am a knight, I practically have to beat the women off with a stick. Luckily I, with all my training, am now an expert in all manner of beating, bludgeoning and kicking.*

I laughed as I read this, and Tren-Lore grinned in wry amusement.

I am rather busy right now with keeping everything in Jacinda running smoothly. It is harder than usual, what with the tension between Caladore and the Renarn, but I still do not know how my father stands doing this everyday. This type of responsibility is not for me. Perhaps I will run away and go live in the forest. Then I would only have to worry about freezing to death, starving to death, being eaten by Pandels (to death), losing my spirit to Disanima or getting shot by Elves. It would be much more pleasant than running this courtly gauntlet everyday.

Well, I do not really have much more to tell you. Lara, I hope Karsalin was nice and that being back is good too. Tren-Lore, I have no doubt that you will be the best Sanysk since Lord Rayn. I send you my wish of good luck in not impaling yourself and dying over the course of your training. Take good care of him, Lara. I miss you both.

Myste

Despite Myste's absence that winter, the season was full. When I was not helping Sophie in the kitchen, I was with Nahanni, Draows or Tren-Lore. The princess and I had become fast friends since my return, and occasionally

Draows and I would go walking together to discuss Healing and mythology. Tren-Lore and I continued our friendship as we always had, scarcely aware of a world outside of each other.

Tren-Lore looted the library for several new books about herbs, and despite my best intentions, I found myself too busy during the day and too tired in the evening to read them. The books sat in a stack next to my bed and gathered dust, as did many of my other intentions. I was so involved with Tren-Lore and everything else that was happening around me that it was easy to forget about practicing my channeling. My ivy ring hung unnoticed around my neck, save for the occasional brush of guilt. If Namin knew I was not practicing... She did not, I reminded myself. Besides, I had more important things to do. Tren-Lore needed me to help him train.

* * *

Spring seemed to leap upon Caladore. One day the landscape was bound in icy ropes, and the next it was free of winter. The melting snow rushed into Venst, and the mighty river overflowed, uprooting trees along its banks and flooding small towns near the water's edge. The river water must have seeped into the ground, for the land around Caladore seemed filled with the same wild frenzy. Growth burst from the earth and green covered the trees. Hunting was better than even those in their Winter Years could remember it ever being, and the fisherman brought in bushels of silvery-scaled javins. This raw power had infected Tren-Lore as well, and one day under the warm spring sun, he beat Draows in a fight.

"It will not be long before he triumphs in every match," Draows told me as we ambled through the long grass outside of the castle walls. His deep voice held no trace of resentment. Rather, his words seemed to resonate with quiet pride. "He has more talent than I, and though the League would be loathe to admit it, more talent than any of the men who are now calling themselves Sanysk. He may very well be the next Lord Rayn." Draows smiled at me. He knew this comparison would please me.

I beamed back at him. I appreciated that Draows shared these compliments with me, for I would never have heard them otherwise. Tren-Lore was too modest to relate such extravagant compliments.

"Tren-Lore is certainly more determined than I ever was at his age, and I never had such a friend as you." Draows regarded me solemnly. "He draws much of his strength from you and your aid."

I wrapped my fingers around a stalk of grass and pulled it free. I studied it intently, trying to conceal how pleased I was to hear this. I probably need not have bothered. Even if I had shrouded myself in a cloak of darkness, Draows still would have been able to guess my reaction.

"I am ill at ease, though, Lara."

"Ill at ease?" I repeated the words and my hand tightened around the rough grass. I looked to him for explanation. Was something wrong with Tren-Lore? Did the Sanysk know something about the Renarn that I had not yet heard?

Draows was walking with his head lowered, his eyes following the faint footprints of a deer. He looked up at me briefly. Pieces of his long hair fell across his eyes, and faint lines creased his forehead. "It is ironic, certainly, that I should have such a worry. A friendship between a Healer and a Sanysk is nearly unheard of. The members of the Triad usually hate one another without even the luxury of an introduction, but I am concerned that you devote too much of yourself to Tren-Lore and his quest. Are you making time to practice your Healing?"

My right hand clenched the grass I had been holding. The fingers of my left hand lay across my chest, covering the spot where my Healer's ring rested. The lie I wanted to tell him would not leave my mouth. It twisted around my tongue, and I could find nothing at all to say. I could not deceive Draows.

"You have not been practicing," he surmised, and was silent for a time. He stared out at the horizon and I glanced furtively at him, trying to guess his mood. "I cannot force you to practice," he said finally. "It is your gift to do with as you please."

"It is my curse," I snapped.

"All swords are edged on both sides," said Draows solemnly.

I threw my grass to the ground with angry force. I was not in the mood to be agreed with.

Draows stopped and turned to me. He laid one hand on my shoulder. "Each of us walks our own path, and it is not for me or for anyone else to dictate this journey for you. I will say one thing further, and then I shall say no more on the subject. By learning to Heal, you pay tribute to your mother." He gently touched my cheek. It was a paternal gesture, and it startled me enough that I raised my eyes to him. "I told you before that there is much of her spirit in you. Honor that part of yourself, and you honor your mother."

The Sanysk did not wait for my response, and instead continued along the deer's trail. I did not follow him. I stared after him until he was out of my sight, and then I sunk down into the grass and put my head in my hands. Draows was right. I should practice. I owed my mother that. If I had known how to channel, I might have been able to save her. I should wear my ring and I should practice. Struggling to my feet, I took the ring off Jerran's chain and slipped it onto my finger.

I set off for Caladore, but with each step fear crept inside me like a Disanima. I could not stand the treatment the ring would win me: the whispers, the black bird-like attention, the sharp glances, and the barely concealed hate. I remembered the threats of the people in Ekrin and the helplessness of being entirely ostracized, of having no one to go to for help. And then, there was the way Rion had mocked me and used my Healing against me. The betrayal of Rion seemed the most vicious of all. These painful experiences gnawed at my stomach, until at last I stopped and tore the ring off my finger. I could not wear it. I put the ivy band back on its chain and as I slipped it under my clothes, I felt immediately relieved. I would practice, I decided, but in secret, and I would not wear the ring.

I arrived in the antechamber of the kitchen feeling better about the whole situation. As I opened the inner door to the kitchen, sound smashed into me and I stared about, trying to understand what was happening. Flock was standing in the middle of the kitchen, and nearly the entire staff surrounded her. A few of the older women were standing off to one side, but even they were smiling widely. Everyone was talking at once, and Flock was beaming at each group. If the Ascendants had created her for only one thing, it certainly had to be the center of attention.

Seeing me standing there in confusion, Flock cried, "Lara!" She waved to me as though there was a chance I might not notice her. "You will never guess, Lara!" The crowd parted as she hurried to my side. "Leffeck has asked me to marry him! I am betrothed to be married!"

I stared at her, and then everyone else in the kitchen. Flock was getting married? Irritating, obnoxious, insincere Flock was getting married! How could she be getting married? I tried to seem happy, but it was difficult. "That is wonderful," I told her with a grimace-like smile. "Congratulations."

If Flock noticed my contorted expression, she did not give any indication. "Thank you," she gushed, and hugged me to her. Then she was off and back to the group, loudly declaring, "Now of course, it will be a long engagement. Only peasants rush into marriage, and Leffeck is quite wealthy. I think it could be as long as a year, or maybe even a year and a half."

There was an appreciative murmur from the group of women, and amidst the torrent of Flock's bragging I managed to make it to my room without being noticed. I closed the door and gratefully cut out the din. I crawled onto my bed and lay with my arms crossed behind my back. I would not have traded places with Flock for all the books in Caladore. Adoration and agony were one, connected as an animal is connected to its tail. I wondered if Flock realized what a dangerous creature she was trifling with. My mother, Sophie, myself: we had all suffered because of it.

"It is not worth it," I decided in a soft tone. "I am not going to chance getting hurt that badly."

After this resolution, my mind wandered from one topic to the next, and then at last, stumbled into slumber. I awoke to Sophie's hand on my back.

"Lara, darling, wake up. Supper is nearly ready."

I groaned and rolled over, throwing my arm across my forehead. Sophie sat on the side of my bed and smiled down at me.

"Flock is getting married," I said aloud. I wanted to taste the words and see if that would give them reality.

"Yes, she is, and she will be better off for it." Sophie smoothed her hair back into its bun. "She is still fairly young, but it will keep her out of trouble. Ascendants know her sister found nothing but unwholesome ways to fill her time."

My curiosity about Kella was sparked once again. "Whatever happened to Kella?"

Sophie hesitated, as though considering several different responses. Finally she said, "I am not one for gossip, Lara. The only fact I know is that she was sent to live with her aunt. I have heard rumors that she was with child, but I do not put much stock in rumors."

The image of Yolis and Kella down by the river flashed before my eyes. I shuddered, trying to imagine how Kella must have felt if pregnancy really was the reason for her banishment. I wondered if Yolis was the father, or if Kella had acquired a new love in the interim of my stay in Karsalin. In any case, if the rumor of her pregnancy was true, then that meant the father of her baby had abandoned her. It was just another example of why following your heart was a dangerous decision. Your heart was the type of guide that would most likely get you lost in the woods, and then leave you to be eaten by Pandels.

I frowned. "I do not ever want to fall in love. Love is nothing but misery."

Sophie chuckled and patted my arm. Her skin had the softness of age. "Love can also be a joy. You may very well learn that one day, if you meet the right man."

I looked at her skeptically. It was hard to believe that Sophie really believed that after everything that had happened with her and Jerran. "I doubt that, Sophie. My mind is made up."

"We shall see," Sophie replied, and pushed herself from my bed. "Come on then, dinner is waiting."

The evening meal was a jovial affair, with many toasts made to Flock's bright future. I derived a great deal of amusement from watching the ongoing war between Flock and her mother. Flock would pull her bodice down and her mother would yank it back up again. When the dishes were finished I went straight to my room, planning to study a little before falling asleep. I would show Draows that he was not entirely right. Undressing quickly, I pulled my sleeping gown over my head. I slipped between the soft blankets of my bed and fell back against my pillow with a sigh. The stack of books sitting on the floor was waiting for me. Eventually, I summoned the will to reach down and grab *The Study of Herbs*. It was too heavy to hold comfortably, but I persevered and read, *The study of herbs is a complex and deeply interesting process. Throughout this book we will examine...*

Unfortunately I never discovered what it was we were going to examine, for the book slid from my fingers and I fell to sleep.

Chapter Twenty
The Reality of It All

I was dreaming of Namin. She was standing before me with her hands full of blue leaves. She shook them at me.

"Why are you not practicing, Lara? Your mother would be disappointed."

"I want to, but I am afraid," I protested, Namin's likeness shifted to become Flock talking about her wedding, and then all at once, Draows was before me, shaking me and calling my name.

Someone was shaking me. I felt it vaguely through the veil of my dreams. I groggily opened my eyes. I had expected to see the bright light of day, and Sophie's face hovering over me. Instead, I found myself enveloped in the shadows of night. Moonlight shimmered across the room to illuminate the tall figure of Tren-Lore. I glanced over at Sophie, but she was snoring softly, one of her arms nestled under her head. He gestured towards the doorway. I climbed out of my bed and followed him from the room.

"What are you doing here?" I winced at the creaking of the door as I eased it closed behind us.

"You have to see the sky," Tren-Lore whispered, and then turned and walked out of the kitchen. He moved like a shadow and his passing made no noise.

I grabbed my cloak off a peg on the wall and hurried after him. Tren-Lore led me down the passages of the castle to a wooden door. It swung inward on soundless hinges to reveal a seemingly endless, dark corridor. Tren-Lore entered without hesitation, but I stood in the entrance feeling afraid and rather foolish. I was too old to be afraid of the dark.

Tren-Lore stopped and held out his hand. I knew without benefit of sight that the mark of our pact remained on his palm.

"Come on," he whispered.

I reached out and slipped my hand into his. His skin was warm against mine, and I stepped over the threshold. He led the way to a flight of stairs and we began to climb. The steps seemed to go on forever, one after the other until I could no longer guess how high we were. I imagined that we were trapped in an enchanted tower and the stairs had no ending. This made me smile. At this moment, it sounded like a rather nice fate. The stairs were not infinite, however, and soon Tren-Lore halted. Our hands slid apart, and I felt strangely regretful.

There was the deep shuddering of a door long unused, and then Tren-Lore and I were soaked in starlight. I could clearly see that we were standing before the entrance to one of the six turrets that guarded each corner of the castle. I moved swiftly forward and leaned against the edge of the wall. It was the perfect vantage point to observe the beautiful celestial display, as well as the castle surroundings. The gardens rushed out to meet the inner walls, the deserted courtyard lay sleeping, and outer walls kept a silent vigil. In the distance, I could even see the shadowy outline of Cala and the mountains starkly silhouetted against the horizon.

"It is so beautiful." My voice was almost as soft as breath.

Tren-Lore grinned. "I thought you would like it." He inhaled deeply. "It smells wonderful out here."

"Yes," I murmured distractedly, "it does." My thoughts had returned to the matter of Flock.

Tren-Lore eased himself to the ground and rested his back against the wall. "What is wrong?"

I made a face and came to slouch next to him. The entire day had seemed full of things that were wrong. "Flock is getting married," I told him.

"To whom?" he asked.

I shrugged. "Someone named Leffeck."

Tren-Lore chuckled and rubbed at his chin. "Poor girl."

"I know!" I declared. I was trying to make my voice sound light with trivial disapproval. "I have no idea why she wants to get married. I never want to get married."

"Really?" Tren-Lore shifted so he was facing me. "Never?"

"No," I replied, and then repeated myself in the hopes of hardening my spirit to the idea. "Love is a curse and I want nothing to do with it."

"Oh," said Tren-Lore and turned again. He stared up into the sky and was silent for a moment. Though I knew him better than anyone else, I could not have begun to guess what he was thinking. "My pity for Flock is not based on the fact that she is getting married. I feel sorry for her because of who she is marrying. Have you ever met Sir Leffeck?"

I shook my head.

"Well," Tren-Lore began, a wolfish smile creasing his cheeks, "they certainly will make an.... interesting couple."

I could not let Tren-Lore escape with such a cryptic response, so I demanded a more in-depth explanation. I was soon laughing so hard my sides hurt and Tren-Lore was fully engaged in a colorful description of the 'charming swine' that was Leffeck. My mirth soon wiped away any traces of sadness that may have been lingering within me. Tren-Lore and I sat happily at the top of the turret and talked until the stars retreated from the sky.

The first light of dawn found me slipping quietly back into my bed. I fell asleep almost immediately, and slumbered peacefully until Sophie woke me late in the morning.

"You must hurry, dear." Sophie spared a quick glance at herself in the mirror. Giving her hair one final pat, she turned to me, her hands unconsciously smoothing the skirts of her dress. "They will soon be expecting you in the royal chambers."

I crawled wearily out of bed, feeling as though my head was filled with sand. I dressed and stumbled up to the royal chambers. I found a few servants scurrying about, cleaning the grand rooms.

"The princess instructed me to wait here until her return," I told them as an explanation for my presence in the royal chambers.

"You can help us while you wait," a skinny older woman informed me, and handed me a soft dusting cloth. "Be quick and quiet about it. Prince Tren-Lore is still sleeping."

Had the other ladies not been present, I would have charged into Tren-Lore's room and given him a rude awakening. If I had to suffer, so should he. Stifling a yawn, I lethargically went about my task. As soon as the cleaning had been completed, and the other servants had left, I flopped wearily into one of the soft couches. I had intended only to rest for a few moments, but when I opened my eyes again, Tren-Lore was sprawled in the chair across from me. He was dressed in his nightclothes and was eating bread with dark red jam on it. He had a book in hand and his countenance was intent. As I stirred from my sleep, Tren-Lore looked up.

"Good afternoon," he said cordially. "Would you like some bread and goolsberry jam?" He nodded to the plate next to him.

I pushed myself into an upright position and stared speculatively at Tren-Lore's bread. "What is goolsberry jam?"

Tren-Lore held up the bread and looked at it with an expression of great fondness. "Marvelous stuff. They eat it in Tolrem all the time. Myste says that it tastes like bitter death, but I quite like it."

"All right," I agreed bravely.

Tren-Lore leaned over to hand me a piece. I bit into the bread, trying to ignore the chunky appearance of the jam. Bitterness stabbed at the back of my mouth, but as I chewed through the lumps, the taste became sweeter.

"Not bad," I consented and took another bite.

Tren-Lore inclined his head in approval, and for a time we ate in silence. As I chewed I looked around thoughtfully. The royal chambers seemed decidedly empty. "Where is everyone?" I inquired through a partially full mouth.

"Well," Tren-Lore mused, and took another piece of bread from the plate. "Nahanni went down to Cala today to distribute food to the poor. My father is busy with some matters of state and I am sure that Yolis is with him. They usually spend their time together." Tren-Lore's face was carefully controlled, but it was obvious to me that Tren-Lore was bothered by the amount of attention King Kiris paid to Yolis.

"When are you practicing with Draows?" The question was meant as a salve for my friend. A reminder of Draows was a reminder of everything Tren-Lore was determined to do. He was more than his title, and he did not need the fawning of the court or his father to convince him of his worth.

Tren-Lore raked his fingers through his hair. "There is no practice today. Draows is not here."

"Not here?" I glanced out the window as though I would be able to catch a glimpse of Draows riding Quell away from the castle. "Where did he go?"

"He did not say where he was going, or when he would be back."

I leaned back against the sofa and smirked mischievously at Tren-Lore. "How irresponsible of him. You know, Draows reminds me of you in so many ways."

Tren-Lore chuckled and hurled the cushion from behind his back at me. "Be quiet, Lara."

I caught the cushion and held it before me like a shield. Tren-Lore rose. "Where are you going?" I demanded "Or are you going to wrap yourself in a cloak of Sanysk-like mystery and not tell me?"

Tren-Lore stooped and picked up his empty plate. "First," he began with a solemn expression, "I will put this plate away. Then," he continued, "I am going to get dressed."

"You do that," I replied mockingly.

Tren-Lore made a face at me. "Barlem."

I stuck out my tongue. "Double Barlem."

* * *

Tren-Lore was in the midst of his balancing exercises when Nahanni burst into the royal chambers. Her cheeks were glowing with excitement. Every time Nahanni entered a room, I was struck by her beauty. There was something about her that reminded me of sunlight.

"I have the best, most excellent idea!" she pronounced and slammed the door behind her.

Tren-Lore, who was still attempting to balance on his left foot, smiled at her. "And what would that be?"

Nahanni swept past him, and with a solid shove, pushed Tren-Lore off balance. "Draows is gone and you have been practicing too much. Lara, I have already told Lady Grim that you will be accompanying me to Cala. I think we should all go to the Festival of the Four," she decided as she disappeared down the hallway that led to her chambers.

"The what?" I asked, turning to Tren-Lore, who looked vaguely irritated.

"Every ten years these four men who claim to be Sorcerers come to Cala. They goad people into giving them room and board in exchange for some cheap tricks," Tren-Lore replied.

Nahanni returned to the room, a lovely blue hat in her grasp. "You make it sound so dull," Nahanni chided. "It is really very exciting, Lara. The whole town is decorated, there is lots of food and drinking, and The Four do magic for any who ask."

"How do you know it is so exciting? You have never even been to it," Tren-Lore pointed out.

Nahanni ducked past her brother and faced her reflection in the large gilded mirror upon the wall. "A very reliable friend told me all about it," she answered lightly as her fingers moved deftly through her golden hair. She braided it quickly, her head tilted to one side. "I think we should all go. Me, you, Lara, and Zander."

"Zander?" Tren-Lore repeated, and he and I exchanged questioning looks. "Is he Lord Mambar's son?"

"Yes," Nahanni replied defensively. She tied a ribbon about the ends of her hair. "Is there a problem with that?"

Tren-Lore held up his hands defensively. "No. I was just wondering why Zander was suddenly being included."

Nahanni turned from the mirror. "Because," she said, reaching up to pat Tren-Lore's cheek, "it is not nice to exclude people."

I grinned at this response. Only Nahanni would dare to patronize Tren-Lore like that.

"Well, come on," the princess insisted. "Zander is waiting for us in the stable." She grabbed hold of my hand and swept me from the room. Tren-Lore followed us, and Nahanni chatted pleasantly about her day as we made our way down to the stable. I truly believed that Nahanni was energy personified.

* * *

The day was warm and the dust from the road rose around our horse's legs. Nahanni and I rode in front, while she told me everything she knew about The Four. I listened absently. I was actually more curious about Zander. Lord Mambar's son had proved to be a very handsome young man who was slightly taller than Nahanni and had sandy brown hair that curled around his ears. He had greeted us all with a wide, genuine smile. Tren-Lore had scowled at him, and Nahanni had flushed with pleasure. I was fairly certain she was smitten with him.

Unfortunately, Zander and Tren-Lore were now cantering behind us. After exchanging the customary remarks that courtesy demanded, they had both sunken into silence. If they had been engaged in their own conversation, I would have asked Nahanni about Zander. As it was, however, I satisfied myself with a resolve to question her later.

When we arrived in Cala, we found it decorated with elaborate care. I twisted in my saddle, trying to see everything at once. Poles had been driven into the ground along the main road, and braided pieces of colorful cloth were draped between them. In front of every house was a pot of fresh flowers, and many people had donned bright costumes. As we approached the center of Cala, we were forced to dismount and lead our horses. Small children darted through the throng, dogs barked, and the call of merchants rang clearly in the air.

We reached the town square just in time to see four men in long black robes climbing onto the large platform assembled near the middle of the square. All of the men were clean-shaven and their faces were youthful. One of them raised his hand, and abruptly the noise stopped. I noticed the silver bands of a Sorcerer on his wrist. In the bright sunlight of the square, the metal shimmered with a luminance of the Triad. They were real Sorcerers.

"Name the magic and it shall be performed," one of the men pronounced, and I winced slightly as people began to bellow suggestions.

The Four listened for a moment, and then signaled for silence. "Brothers, what say you to flowers?" the shortest Sorcerer demanded.

The other three nodded. Joining hands, they formed a circle with their backs to the crowd. The Sorcerers did not move. They remained this way for quite some time, and the shuffle of feet and the rustle of voices indicated a growing restlessness. Suddenly a cry arose from the crowd, "The ground! Look at the ground!" Everyone turned their eyes downward, and a general exclamation of surprise echoed off the buildings. Small daisies were springing by the hundreds from the cracks in the cobblestones.

Zander stooped to pick one and handed it to Nahanni. She smiled delightedly, but Tren-Lore looked at Zander sharply.

"What was that?" he whispered in my ear.

"You know perfectly well what that was," I replied with a smile. "She *is* in her fourth Summer Year."

Tren-Lore frowned at Zander, but he was too enthralled by Nahanni's smile to pay attention.

We spent the first part of the morning strolling about the town. All the shops had stands set up to display their wares, and women were wandering through the crowds giving away wreaths of flowers. Large pavilions had been set up on the streets to serve drinks and food and perhaps tempt visitors with games of skill and chance. After we had looked at all the merchants' wares, Nahanni and I collapsed in exhaustion on some of the cushions that were set up in the shady corners of the tent for resting.

"Lara!" a voice squealed from some distance away. "Lara! Over here!"

I sat up and looked about the crowd, absently pushing my crown of flowers off my forehead. Finally, my eyes settled upon Flock. She was ruthlessly shoving her way through the masses of people. Following daintily behind her was a short, stocky man. He was dressed elaborately, with his long, brown hair tied at the nape of his neck. I groaned and waved weakly to Flock.

When she reached us, Flock noticed Nahanni sitting next to me. Flock gasped in pleasure, "Good day, Your Highness." She curtsied deeply. "Leffeck, can you believe who is here ... Princess Nahanni!"

I rolled my eyes. Nahanni hardly needed an introduction.

Leffeck's lips puckered in a simpering smile and he bowed gracefully. Nahanni nodded to him, her blue eyes wide. She was obviously slightly overwhelmed by Flock and Leffeck's reaction.

"And this is Lara," Flock told him. "She is a girl from the kitchen. You remember, I told you all about her. Well Lara, this is my dashing Leffeck."

Leffeck looked down his nose at me, and after a short sniff of disapproval, inclined his head so slightly that I thought I might have imagined it. "How lovely to make your acquaintance," he drawled.

"Leffeck and I are looking for tapestries for the house he is going to build me. Did you know Leffeck was building me a house, Lara? It will be lovely. Seven sleeping chambers, and a huge kitchen. Perhaps you can come and work for me someday."

The only thing that stayed the malicious retort that burned across my tongue was Nahanni's hand on my arm. She pointed into the crowd to where Tren-Lore was striding toward us. The town's people parted to let him through, and he thanked them as he passed. When he saw who we were talking to, his face took on a look of endless amusement.

"Flock! Leffeck!" he declared, grinning wickedly. "I hear you are getting married. Well, that is just wonderful! You both deserve each other." He winked at me.

I pressed my hand to my mouth and tried to suppress my laughter. My eyes were stinging with the effort, and it was hard to keep my breathing even. Flock glanced at me, and then back at Tren-Lore. Her mouth tightened slightly and she raised her chin. She realized the true meaning of Tren-Lore's statement, but Leffeck seemed oblivious.

The short little man bowed floridly to Tren-Lore. "Your Majesty honors me greatly."

"Now," said Tren-Lore cordially, "if you will excuse us, I would like to take these two ladies to the dance."

Not to be outdone, Flock turned to Leffeck. She grasped his arm. "Leffeck, you simply must ask me to dance."

He jerked his arm away from her demanding grip. "Unhand me, woman, and try to contain yourself!" Turning back to Tren-Lore, he smiled calmly. "Of course Your Majesty. I hope you enjoy yourself. Come, Flock. I am tired of these..." he waved his hand vaguely in the air, "festivities."

He turned gracefully and began to pick his way gingerly through the crowd. Flock glanced once at us and then hurried to follow her departing husband-to-be.

Nahanni shook her head as she watched the two retreating figures. "Poor Flock," she murmured quietly.

I chose to believe that Nahanni pitied Flock's intent to be married, though her true meaning may have been closer to Tren-Lore's sentiment. Nevertheless, I took in her words like sustenance that could strengthen my spirit. Even Nahanni recognized that marriage was a plague. It was not something I wanted to be part of. It did not matter if I was a Healer and exiled from the love of a man. Why would I want that anyway?

* * *

The dance was being held in the main square, and we made slow progress through the dense crowds that surrounded the dancing couples. We finally made it to the edge of the circle and could clearly see the dancers. Each one was wearing a mask meant to depict Atalium. The women's masks were covered with light red feathers, while the men's were dark green.

"The Atalium do not actually have feathers, do they?" I had to speak loudly to be heard over the tumultuous music. It had a quick beat and the dancers changed partners frequently, creating a swirl of colors and stomping feet.

Tren-Lore shook his head. "Not from what I have read."

The tempo of the music increased and swelled until it concluded in a powerful crescendo. Masks were torn away, and with much laughing the partners embraced passionately, and in some cases, quite drunkenly. I was suddenly reminded of Rion and the sensation of his kiss. The thought smote me and left my self-esteem bruised. I frowned. Forget Rion, I told myself severely, and took a mask that was being offered. I put it on defiantly.

Nahanni assumed her own Atalium visage with some reluctance. "I am not sure that I want to do this," she protested as a masked man caught hold of her hand and pulled her into the throng.

The stranger glanced back over his shoulder and flipped his mask up for a moment. Zander's smiling face was revealed. "I will not let you out of my sight. I promise," he told her solemnly.

Nahanni continued to protest meekly, but trailed after him with no hesitation.

Tren-Lore's jaw clenched. "He is really beginning to get on my nerves. Who invited him, anyway?"

The first notes of music were beginning, and someone grabbed my hand and pulled me into the dance. "I think it was Nahanni," I yelled back to Tren-Lore and chuckled at his disgruntled expression.

The dance was quick: two steps left, two right, spin and change partners. The world blurred into a smear of colors, and by the time the music began to build to its conclusion, I was laughing, out of breath, and so dizzy I could barely stand upright. The swift notes tumbled over one another as they rushed toward the ending of the song and exploded into a harmonious finish. One of my hands was held firmly by my partner, so I used the other to tear away my mask. My laughter stopped abruptly as I saw whose fingers were entangled with mine.

"Tren-Lore!" I exclaimed.

He was breathing hard, but grinning. "Hello Lara."

Everyone around us was caught in each other's arms, embracing with an Elesbri-like enthusiasm. Smiling at me fondly, Tren-Lore reached out and tucked a stray piece of my hair behind my ear. Bending forward, he kissed me on the cheek.

Suddenly the crowd surged forward in panic, and I stumbled backward. My hand slipped from Tren-Lore's and I fell painfully to the ground. People were screaming something about the Renarn. I clambered to my feet and saw men mounted on warhorses charging into the droves of dancers. Swords flashed in the sunlight. I did not know if the weapons were Caladorian or Renarn.

"Tren-Lore!" I screamed over the din, but was not heard.

I could not see him anywhere. I turned and ran. It seemed everyone was running in different directions. I knew men on foot would be no match for mounted warriors. I joined a large group of people who took shelter in what seemed to be some sort of storehouse. Two men barred the door, and for a moment, the silence of suspense hung over the crowd. My heart was pounding with fear and I curled my toes into my shoes. This could not be real. This could not be real. Things like this did not happen. Everyone stood still, mothers hushed their frightened children. There was nothing but deathly quiet. When no sound came from outside, people began to move again. No one spoke above a whisper.

I looked about, but could not find Tren-Lore. I felt like crying in fear. Smoothing my hair away from my face, I drew a calming breath. The air was hot and my throat was dry. I silently prayed that Nahanni and Zander were safe – that Tren-Lore was safe.

There was the muffled sound of someone groaning, and the quiet, fearful sobs of children. Glancing at our company, I realized for the first time that many of them had been injured. I took action without stopping to think about it. This was what I had been trained to do.

Soon I was standing beside a young man whose arm had a bloody gash running from the length of his shoulder to his elbow. It was a deep wound, and through the red flesh, white bone was visible. Ripping a strip of fabric off the bottom of my dress, I bound it with a comforting instinct that meant I did not have to fully realize what I was doing.

"Are you a Healer?" His voice was soft with pain and fear.

I met his gaze, but did not reply. "I have stopped the bleeding, but when we get out of here you will need further attention."

I moved on to the next of the wounded. I worked without contemplation, letting something deep inside me tend to the injured. Dragging my sleeve across my sweating brow, I knelt beside a burly man sitting on the floor, his mangled leg stretched before him.

"Bunch of cowards!" he muttered in a voice as loud as he dared. He sucked breath through his clenched teeth as I tended to his wounds. "I fought." He jabbed his thumb into his chest. "I fought, and the rest of you ran! End all of you!"

"There was nothing else to be done," I told him quietly, and began to bind his calf.

"Nothing else!" he spat. "We could have-"

"She is right," Tren-Lore's voice said from behind me.

I felt my muscles loosen in relief at the sound of his voice. It was all I could do to continue bandaging the man's leg. I wanted to throw myself into Tren-Lore's arms and hold him against me until I was sure he was real.

"If we had stayed, they would have slaughtered us. We will retaliate," Tren-Lore assured him grimly, "but we will do it when the odds are more even. In the meantime, keep your mouth shut."

The man looked quite daunted by Tren-Lore's authoritative tone, and his haughty berating of everyone else ceased immediately.

When I tied the finishing knot around his ankle, my hands were shaking. The gore I had seen was beginning to seep into my awareness. I turned to Tren-Lore, my eyes searching him for any injuries.

"I am fine," he said, and held out his hand to me. "Are you all right?"

I leaned heavily on his arm. My knees felt rather weak and my stomach was churning. "I feel a little ill. I...I have never seen anything like this before. Once Dyra cut the bottom of her foot on some glass and I had to stitch it up. She was bleeding, but not like this. She bled on the carpet and Sophie tried to get the stain out but never could." My thoughts were wildly fleeing from the butchery I had just tended to, and words were spilling from my mouth. "Do you remember when I cut you the first time we were sword fighting? The dress still has the stain, but Garidet has it now, though. I -"

"Lara." I felt as though Tren-Lore was calling me from a great distance. His voice was firm, and I stopped talking, my mind clearing slightly. "Lara, calm down. Everything will be all right. I feel sick too, but it will pass. All of this will pass." He helped me to the floor and waited until the panic slowly subsided. "I have to go help the others for a moment, but I will be back. Will you be all right?"

I nodded mutely and watched as he strode back into the group. His walk was purposeful. He moved with a power that belonged to heroes in stories, and I felt calmed. Tren-Lore could handle this. When he returned, he settled himself a few feet away from me and I watched as he methodically ground a nick from the side of his sword. My eyes lingered on the blood splattered across his gray tunic. I knew he was a knight, and training to be a Sanysk, but the fact that he could actually kill someone had never occurred to me. The blood smeared across his shirt was the mark of his trade. It was what he had been trained for. My fingers touched my own dress. It was stiff with blood from the wounds I had tended. I yanked my hand away, startled by the sensation, and quickly turned my gaze to the floor. Soon, however, I found myself staring at Tren-Lore again. I purposefully avoided looking at his tunic, and instead studied his face. His brow was creased, and his eyes were lowered over his task. There was dirt on his cheek and his mouth was set in a critical frown as he turned his blade over in his hands.

"You have dirt on your cheek," I observed. It was really an unimportant statement considering our circumstances, but I took comfort in the triviality.

He looked up, revealing those unreadable blue eyes of his. "What?"

"You have dirt on your face. Right here." I gestured to the spot on my own face.

He wiped the side of his face with the back of his hand. "Is it gone?"

"Wrong side," I laughed. The response felt wrong, as though sometime between the dance and now, my humor had been beaten down and caged.

He grinned and tried again. "How is that?"

"No, you only made it worse."

Tren-Lore got to his feet, and sheathing his sword, came to sit across from me. Wordlessly, I began to rub the dirt from his cheek. Just as I drew my hand away, my eyes met his.

"I was worried about you when we got separated," Tren-Lore told me, not breaking his gaze.

My heart was pounding. His eyes were the dark blue of a rain-filled sky. "You know me," my voice trembled slightly, "I can take care of myself." We were so close. I could have leaned forward just a little and our lips would have brushed together.

"Yes," Tren-Lore agreed softly and absently touched the spot where the ash had been, "but sometimes we all need someone to take care of us." There was a thudding noise from behind us, and Tren-Lore looked away suddenly. A faint blush colored his cheeks and he rose quickly "Ah, I mean..." He cleared his throat. "I mean, what are friends for?"

I was not given the opportunity to respond to this comment. A rolling boom shook the building, and suddenly there was only the present. The warmth of our closeness vanished in an icy surge of fear.

There was yelling from outside. "Ram it down. One, two, three." Another thundering blow made the door shudder and groan.

"Arm yourselves with anything you can find!" Tren-Lore shouted, and his sword hissed from its sheath. "Just as we planned: ten of you at each side of the door, and the rest facing it!"

The men moved at Tren-Lore's command, and at the same moment the door burst inward, sending a shower of splinters into the air. Men charged into the storehouse, shouting in guttural Renarn accents. People were shrieking and bodies hurtled at each other. I stood fixated in revulsion. I did not know what to do. People were being cut down and trampled in the tangled, raging mass. A man staggered and fell by my feet, his hand still clutching his sword even in death.

"No! Ascendants, someone help us!" The desperate, almost hysterical voice broke my transfixed daze.

I followed the sound and found a woman standing with a child in her arms. In front of her was a man desperately trying to ward off their attacker. He was being beaten down with each blow of the Renarn's sword. Another strike and the man staggered and fell to his knees, his sword falling from his hand. I did not pause to think. Scrambling, I grabbed the blade from the dead man before me. The Renarn raised his weapon and I charged toward him, a scream rising from inside me.

The large man whirled about just in time and met my attack with a strength that made me feel as though every bone in my arm had been shattered. I cried in pain and the blade clattered to the floor. The Renarn stared at me in a moment of shock, and then, with the abruptness of snapping wood, he bellowed in rage. I dove for my sword. Grabbing it with my left hand, I raised it just in time to block his attack.

He roared and lunged at me again. My body remembered the long hours of training I had spent with Tren-Lore, and instinctively I jumped aside. I felt his sword slice the fabric of my dress, but there was no pain.

The blade had not touched my flesh. The Renarn, entirely off balance now, toppled forward. His heavy form fell upon me. I hit the floor with a force that pushed the breath from my lungs.

"Get off of her." The voice was low and threatening. "Now."

It took me only a moment to identify the speaker.

With surprising agility, the man leapt to his feet, swinging his sword in a wide arch. His opponent had moved, and the blade sliced through air. Tren-Lore was behind the Renarn. He leveled his sword at the man's back.

"Put down your weapon," Tren-Lore ordered.

The man whirled about with a mad howl and slashed desperately at Tren-Lore. The blow nearly caught him in the face, and he stumbled back, his expression one of shock and dismay. The Renarn raised his blade again, but Tren-Lore was ready this time. He moved so quickly that the Renarn never had a chance to deliver his blow. Tren-Lore plunged his blade into the man's chest.

I squeezed my eyes shut, but I could still hear the sounds of the Renarn man's death: the dull rasp of metal against bone, the thud of the body falling to the floor, the scratching and scuffing upon the wood as the man convulsed. The fighting seemed to subside as I stumbled away. Falling to my hands and knees, I vomited repeatedly until there was nothing left in my stomach and my throat burned.

There was a gentle touch upon my back. I gasped, recoiling in terror, but the voice was soft. "Thank you for saving us."

I turned. It was the woman and her child. She reached down and touched my face. "Is there anything I can do to help you, to repay you?"

I shook my head. "No," I mumbled. "I did nothing. It was Tren-Lore. He saved us."

The woman said something else to me, but I was not listening. I rose, and on feet that seemed to move without my bidding, I walked wearily back to Tren-Lore. He was still standing in the very place from which he had killed the Renarn. Tren-Lore's face was emotionless and he was staring at the Renarn's body.

"He was not supposed to do that," Tren-Lore muttered. "In books..." His voice was broken with grief. "He was not supposed to do that."

* * *

Tren-Lore, Nahanni, Zander and I took a room in Cala that night. Nahanni and Zander attempted some small conversations, but both Tren-Lore and I were as silent as death.

"We will go get food," Nahanni said. She was trying to be brave, but fear lay beneath her words. Zander slipped his hand into hers and they left quietly.

I crawled on one of the beds and lay on my side, my knees drawn close to my chest with my right hand resting away from me. The pain and swelling led me to believe that I had fractured a bone in my wrist. Tren-Lore had helped me splint it, but the binding did little to relieve the pain. Tren-Lore seated himself in the chair by the window and stared out at the night with the unreadable expression I had seen many times before.

"When did you start doing that?" I asked in a barely audible voice. It was a question I would not have ventured if I had not been numbed and frozen by the horrors of the day.

Tren-Lore turned to look at me. "Doing what?"

"You get this blank expression on your face when you are angry or hurt."

Tren-Lore's countenance was weary. "If no one knows what you are thinking, you can feel exactly what you like without ever having to suffer the consequences."

"Consequences?" I echoed weakly.

He looked away from me and studied the darkness outside. For a time he did not respond, but when at last he did speak, his voice was controlled and without warmth. "I think it began after my mother drowned. My father was destroyed. He locked himself in the council chamber and did not come out for months. Sophie was only allowed in to deliver food. Yolis' tutor took care of him, and Nahanni still had her nurse. Before, my mother had always protected me from the court, but now I was left at their mercy, and that is akin to being left in the care of wolves. They leapt upon the slightest show of emotion and fed upon my pain. It was all a great drama for them. I learned defenses quickly."

Tears rolled silently down my cheeks. I cried for my own sorrows and for Tren-Lore, for what I had seen today and for the deeds that had been done - for the reality of it all.

Chapter Twenty-One
Enter the Princess

The group that had traveled to Cala the day before bore little resemblance to the group that returned to Caladore. We did not speak. Tren-Lore was the image of a battle-worn warrior. His face was dark with grim thoughts and stubble. There was a faint scratch across his cheek, and his clothes were black with blood. Nahanni's eyes were red with tears and Zander was slumped in his saddle. I cradled my arm against my body and tried not to think.

When I returned to the kitchen, Sophie nearly crushed me in a hug. I held my arm away from the embrace and let the kindly old woman hold me in her shaking grasp.

"Lara, I thought, I thought...I did not know what to think. Thank the Ascendants." She held me out at arms length. "Is your wrist all right?"

"Fractured, I think." I was thankful that Sophie had not asked what had happened. I did not want to relive it.

I moved slowly through the kitchen that day, seeking tasks to occupy my mind. When night came, however, the dark left me with no distractions. Memories bombarded me with a terrifying intensity. My body convulsed with sorrow, and Sophie held me as though I were a small child. She stroked my hair until I was soothed and sleep slipped upon me. I did not slumber for long. Nightmares hunted me, and I fled from them into the waking world. Again and again this happened, until morning came.

The day did not dawn with hope. Just as the sun was rising, Caladore troops marched forth from the castle. They were bound for Rang, the Renarn town that had spawned both the farmers who had begun the dispute and the troops that had attacked Cala. Tren-Lore went with them. The only way he had time to say farewell was in a quickly scrawled note delivered by an irritated gardener who told me that this was not his job.

Take care of your wrist. Do not worry about me.
Morian penent.
T.L.

There was no other word from him for the next three weeks. The days dragged by, and I felt ill in both body and mind. The pain in my wrist subsided, but I was aggravated by my constant state of trepidation and turmoil. I worried about Tren-Lore. What if he was wounded? What if he was killed? Part of me wished that I was with him, so I could tend to any injuries. Another part, however, flinched at the idea. I did not want to see any more of what I had witnessed in Cala.

Nahanni did what she could to keep me informed of the latest developments. Had it not been for her, I am sure I would have been driven mad by the wild rumors Flock was spreading.

"The Renarn keep bears and use them in battle. Yes, bears, Thriana, like in the forest. If you are not going to listen, then go somewhere else. Leffeck says that three Caladore soldiers had their heads torn off and..."

I slammed the kitchen door on the sound of Flock's voice. It was a gloriously warm morning, only a few days after my seventh Summer Year, and yet I hardly took notice. I had just received a summons from Nahanni. I knew this meant she had news, so I hastened to the royal chambers.

A servant opened the door, brushing past me as he hurried out into the hall. He had a letter in hand and was muttering nervously to himself. Closing the door behind him, I wondered what had agitated him. Not foul tidings, I hoped. Perhaps that was what Nahanni had to tell me. I stared at the floor in panic, my mind leaping irrationally to Flock's story about the bear.

I was saved from any further imaginings by the sound of footfalls. I looked up just in time to see a tall, blond man stride into the room. He was dressed in rich black clothing and his hands were full of papers. He studied them intently, his face creased with worry. His troubled expression only added to his already extremely handsome features, and I felt the irrational urge to go and comfort him. He glanced toward the door and stopped abruptly.

I could feel myself blush deeply as I realized that I had been staring. I curtsied to hide my reddening face and hoped that he would continue on his way.

When I had righted myself, he was still standing across from me. His eyes slid over me, and a half-smile crooked his lips. "Lara?" he asked tentatively.

My brow creased in confusion. "Yes?" How did this man know my name?

The man laughed and tossed his papers down on the small table next to him. "You have no idea who I am! Well, how kind of you. I am glad not to be equated with my unpleasant, adolescent self." He grinned wickedly. "Yolis, Prince of Caladore, at your service."

I inhaled sharply, surprise hitting me like a punch in the stomach. *This* was Yolis! This could not possibly be the same boy who had been down at the river with Kella. He was so polite and so...so incredibly good-looking.

"And what prompted your homecoming?" Yolis inquired, graciously smoothing over the rut in the conversation that my shock had created. "You and the good Lady Grim were gone for some time, were you not?"

"Yes, we... we spent four years in Karsalin, Your Majesty." My words were faltering and I twisted my thumb and forefinger about the binding on my wrist. "Duty required us to return."

"And may I assume that it was duty that brought you to this fortuitous meeting?" He caught my gaze for a brief moment and my heart surged. His words were casual, but his eyes seemed to speak of different things.

311

"Yes. The princess summoned me," I replied, looking at everything except him.

"If I am not mistaken, it is usually a duty toward my brother that brings you here." The pleasant gloss in Yolis' voice was suddenly lost, and his tone was rough. "The princess is not here. Your talents would be more valued in the kitchen."

I curtsied again and fled the royal chambers. I stomped down the stairs, feeling irritated that I had climbed all those steps just so I could climb back down them. Why had Nahanni summoned me and then left? When I arrived in the kitchen I had worked myself into a foul mood, and to make things worse, I discovered that Sophie had just received notification that there would be a banquet held in two days. She was not given a reason for the sudden celebration.

"Perhaps it is to honor all of our fallen soldiers," Flock speculated, and crumpled her face into an expression of grief. She blinked rapidly, trying to conjure tears. "Oh, those poor, poor men."

I glared at her. "If you are determined to weep, I can poke you in the eye."

Flock's hands went to her hips and she gasped in indignation. Sophie intervened before a fight truly got underway. She set us at separate tasks. Flock was sent to the garden to pull carrots, and I was given a huge bowl of apples that needed to be cut up. I retreated to the antechamber and set about my work. I was still irritated and I sliced the apples too vigorously. The edge of the knife met the skin of my thumb. I yelped and dropped both the apple and the knife. I was sucking on the small cut and feeling thoroughly vexed when the door opened and Nahanni entered.

I removed my thumb from my mouth. "Where were you?"

The young princess winced. "I am truly sorry about that. I had to run and do something. Yolis was just being a Barlem. He was not supposed to send you away." She pointed toward the inner door. "I am going to tell Sophie you will be spending the rest of the day with me. Will you go down to the stables and tell Rathum to get our horses ready?"

"Very well," I agreed, pushing back my chair and standing. "Did you get any news today?"

Nahanni smiled suddenly. "Yes, but I will tell you later. You will be quite surprised." She bounded into the kitchen without another word.

I stared after my young friend. Something was going on, but I did not know what. Perhaps she had arranged for a Renarn bear to eat Flock. I laughed at this thought and turned for the door. Grabbing the handle, I threw it open and stopped suddenly, my hand still wrapped around the cool metal. Leaning against the opposite wall was Tren-Lore! His clothes and face were grimy and his hair was a dark mess, but he looked unscathed.

"Hello," he said calmly, grinning at me.

I remained motionless for an instant longer, and then I began to laugh. It was the expression of happiness, of wild relief, and indignation. "Nahanni, she...she..." I turned and stared back at the inner door, and then turned around again. "She planned this. She knew you were coming home and she did not tell me!"

"We can do something to get even with her." He was laughing too. I wrapped my arms around his neck, and he pressed me close to him. He was warm and smelled faintly of wood smoke and horses. "Do not be too hard on her. She only knew of my return a short time before you did."

I withdrew from the embrace with a soft reluctance, my hands running down his arms, prolonging the sensation of our contact.

"The rest of the army should be back tomorrow, but I wanted to be at home. I..." His voice faded and he looked down at me. His gaze was searching, and I felt as though he knew my very thoughts, knew that I had been thinking of him nearly every moment we had been apart, knew that as we hugged my heartbeat had quickened.

"Thank you, Lady Grim!" called Nahanni pleasantly, and the inner kitchen door swung open. Tren-Lore and I both stepped away from each other. "All right," declared the princess, "everything is taken care of. Now, to the royal chambers to change, and then off to the river we go."

I raised my eyebrows. "Are we going swimming?" I asked as Nahanni slipped her arm into mine.

"Yes," she replied, and bent her head down so it rested briefly on my shoulder. "Were you surprised, Lara?"

"Pleasantly so," I chuckled.

We spent the afternoon swimming in the warm river water. The bindings on my arm were uncomfortably wet by the time twilight crept from under the rocks and roots of the trees. Darkness was all around before we had even lit our fire. We were forced to stumble about the forest searching for wood. Our laughter and voices resounded in the blackness, and soon we had collected a large pile of deadfall. Tren-Lore lit a fire with deft skill and we sat upon the banks of Venst, our figures glowing with the luminance of dancing flames and happiness.

Tren-Lore would not tell us much about the battle, but he did reveal that Rang had been taken and was being held. This infringement upon Renarn land, however, made war impossible to avoid. Both sides were readying their troops. King Kiris was attempting to make an agreement with Hemlizar to secure an alliance. The king of Hemlizar was due in Caladore in two days' time, and it was for him and his family that the banquet was being held.

* * *

I stared at the deep gold flags of Hemlizar. The crowd around me leaned forward to see the royal family as they were grandly led into Caladore by their flag bearers. Trumpets roared and the onlookers clapped and whistled.

"Oh!" Flock cried, grabbing my upper arm in a talon-like grip. "I am so glad King Kiris allowed us come and greet them. Look how beautiful Princess Areama is! When Leffeck and I are married, I want a dress just like that!"

I studied the girl in question, trying not to feel jealous. Flock was right, she was beautiful. She reminded me of the princesses that I had conjured in my imagination, sparked by my mother's stories of the ancient days before the Drawl. Areama's hair was white gold and shimmered down her back in loose ringlets. A sparkling crown encircled her head and dipped down her brow in a gentle

V. Areama's skin was cream-colored and flawless, untouched by any sign of worry or sun. The princesses' stunningly red lips parted in a charming smile as she waved gracefully to the cheering throng. She seemed perfect.

My finger went absently to the bridge of my nose, which was presently peeling from the sunburn I had acquired down at the river two days ago. Tren-Lore's words were suddenly echoing in my head. *When I was in Hemlizar we spent some time together...* Pain sprouted inside me. Its vines grew swiftly. After spending time with Areama, it must have been awfully hard for Tren-Lore to return to my dull, plain company. In comparison to the princess, I must have seemed like twilight to her brilliant sunshine. Exactly how much time had they spent together? Seeing her now, it was difficult not to believe Flock's story that Tren-Lore had been in love with her. What man could resist her stunning beauty? The part of my mind that was not engaged with wild assumptions reprimanded me sharply for my musings. It did not matter if Tren-Lore was in love with her. He was my friend, and I would be happy for him no matter what.

I attempted to stop thinking about the whole situation. I turned my eyes to the steps leading toward the inner wall. Draows, King Kiris and his three children were all standing on the stairs. Draows had returned only yesterday, and his explanation for his sudden disappearance had been vague at best.

"There was a grave matter that needed my attention," he had told us. "A sword which was placed in the care of the Sanysk has been stolen. It is a grievous blow to any hope that may have existed for reuniting the Triad."

"A sword?" Tren-Lore had echoed.

"What does the Triad have to do with this?" I had asked, but Draows would say no more.

Tren-Lore and I had speculated on what this could mean, but we had come to no conclusions. I studied Draows. The tall Sanysk was presently standing next to Nahanni and her family. Both King Kiris and Yolis appeared pleased by the day's events, as did Nahanni. She was very obviously excited and looked quite radiant. In contrast, the expression on Draows' face was unreadable, leaning neither toward happiness or dissatisfaction. Tren-Lore also appeared quite stern, with his hands shoved in his pockets and a grim expression upon his face.

The two families greeted each other with bows and curtsies. My mouth hardened into a frown as Areama said something to Tren-Lore that brightened his countenance. His inaudible reply made her laugh gaily, and her lovely hair slipped over her shoulders to cascade charmingly around her face. I turned abruptly and made my way back to the kitchen. I very nearly slammed the door, but then thought better of it. There was no reason for me to be so annoyed. I inhaled deeply, and by the time the rest of the servants had returned, I was ready to give a strong performance as an untroubled person. In truth, I was deeply vexed by my reaction to Areama. What was wrong with me?

We worked diligently throughout the day, and as evening approached, we began to move the huge platters of food into the banquet hall. Sophie appointed a few of the 'most suited' ladies to stay and serve the guests, and shooed the rest of us out of the grand hall. I begrudgingly returned to the kitchen and wandered about aimlessly for a time. Finally, I slumped into a chair by the window and resolved to sulk. Sophie had refused to let me serve at the banquet and had effectively foiled my plans. I had secretly hoped to be there so that I could observe Tren-Lore and Areama together. I was not about to admit this to anyone, though, least of all myself. Aloud, I grumbled about my talents being overlooked. "I am excellent at serving banquets. This is so unfair!" I muttered angrily.

I was fully involved in a serious bout of self-pity when a rather heartening idea occurred to me. What was preventing me from just going to have a quick look? A smile swept over my face as the answer presented itself to me. Nothing! Absolutely nothing! I got to my feet and made my way to the banquet hall.

Guards were posted at the main doors, but I passed by them with a sweet smile and a simple lie. "I have a message for Lady Grim."

The men nodded and let me pass. I strode purposefully down the wide hall that led to the grandly carved banquet entrance. When I heard the doors swing shut behind me, I slowed my steps. I crept silently forward. The inner doors were partially ajar, and I peered through the crack. I did not divert my attention to anything but the head table – specifically Areama, who was sitting beside Tren-Lore. She had one hand on his arm and was leaning close to whisper in his ear. As she drew away, she was laughing. His answering smile smote me like a blow from a sword.

Music was beginning to play, and Tren-Lore rose to his feet. He offered his hand to the princess and helped her rise from her seat at the table. She was very tall, almost as tall as Tren-Lore, and her frame was slender. Her scarlet gown made my red dress look like something worn on cleaning day. The rich material swished as she walked elegantly onto the dance floor. I tore myself away from the door, just as Tren-Lore pulled her into his arms to dance. I was unable to watch any more.

I stormed back to the kitchen, filled with inexplicable anger and despair. This time I did slam the door behind me. I slammed it as hard as I possibly could, and then went directly to my room. I felt like someone had just slapped me across the face. For a time I would not allow myself to believe that I knew the reason for my emotions. I paced back and forth, struggling with a truth that I did not want to accept. Finally, I threw myself upon my bed and began to cry. I had to admit that perhaps I was fonder of Tren-Lore than a friend should be. The worst part of the whole situation was that he was obviously enamored with Areama.

I was an unpleasant mixture of fury and pain as the days passed. Tren-Lore forwarded a message saying he would not be able to see much of me until the Hemlizar royal family left. I tore the letter up and wept bitterly. I suspected it was not the Hemlizar family that held his attention so completely, but rather the Hemilzar princess.

I was not alone in this assumption. It seemed that Tren-Lore and Areama were frequently the topic of many conversations. I tried to ignore the gossiping women, but the regularity with which they kept council made this impossible to do.

As I was washing dishes, I heard about how Tren-Lore had looked at Areama.

"The look of love, and there is no mistaking that!"

As I was chopping vegetables for the soup, I heard about the balls they had been attending.

"Did you know that she refused to dance with anyone but Prince Tren-Lore?"

And as I sat miserably at the dinner table, moving the food around on my plate, I heard about what a perfect match they would make.

"The Ascendants arranged it! Those two were meant for each other. It is just like one of those romantic tales."

I stabbed my fork into a piece of potato, my eyes stinging with tears. In seven days, I had not even seen Tren-Lore once. It had taken only seven days to replace me entirely. I kept my head lowered, trying to hide the tears that were rolling freely down my cheeks. I felt ill with grief. I stood abruptly. "I do not feel well," I muttered, and threw down my napkin.

Sophie looked concerned and rose, coming toward me to put her hand to my forehead. I tried to protest. I wanted to flee. I wanted to huddle under the blankets of my bed and block out the world. I just wanted to be alone and cry.

"You do feel a little warm," she conceded with a frown. "You had best go to bed and -"

Sophie's words were eclipsed by the sound of the kitchen door banging open. The clatter of dishes and voices stopped as everyone turned to see why Flock had made such a dramatic entrance. She had been having dinner with Leffeck that night, and was back surprisingly early.

"You will never guess!" she squealed. "Prince Tren-Lore and Princess Areama are getting married!"

Chapter Twenty-Two
An End

This was the end of everything. The pain of this thought pulled at me, tore me apart until I was scarcely able to breathe. I was losing my best friend - the only hero I had ever known. Once Tren-Lore was married, he would not stay in Caladore. He and Areama would leave for their own castle and that would be the end of our friendship. That would be the end of any hope I might have had for a deeper relationship with Tren-Lore. But what hope had I truly ever had? A bitter sob escaped my lips and I rolled over, smothering the sound in the cloth of my pillow.

I must have fallen asleep, for when I opened my eyes again, the room was black as pitch. The candle at my bedside table was no longer burning, and though I could not see anything, I had the strong and terrifying sensation that I was being watched. My heart twisted inside my chest and my mouth felt dry.

"Who – who is there?" I managed to whisper hoarsely.

The response that came made my emotions change with the swiftness of a fickle wind. Initially, I was bombarded with a gale of fear that transformed into gusty relief, and then howled again with rage. My voice hardened. "What do you want, Tren-Lore?"

There was a pause before Tren-Lore replied, "Come with me ... down to the garden. I want to talk to you."

Reluctantly, I threw back my blankets and climbed out of bed. I walked across the room with a stiff, perfect posture. I strode past Tren-Lore and grabbed my cloak off the hook on the wall. Slipping on my shoes, I led the way from the kitchen. We walked in uncomfortable silence, only the noise of our steps broke the quiet.

The night was filled with soft creaking and chirping. As a child I had believed the noises to be the song of Pandels and Laowermings, but I did not believe that any more. Or rather, I tried not to believe that any more. A cool breeze swirled my cloak about my bare ankles. I shivered. A full moon lit the garden with an eerie luminescence. The tall trees reached out their spindly arms and stretched their shadows across the neatly trimmed grass. I wandered forward into the shadow-drenched garden. I did not know what to say to Tren-Lore. It seemed as though a dozen thoughts and emotions were battling with each other, and none had yet been victorious in gaining the forefront of my mind.

With a few quick strides, Tren-Lore caught pace with me. "What is wrong?" he asked in a worried tone.

"Nothing," I murmured without looking at him. Seeing him so near to me only reinforced the fact that in a short time he would be gone, and I would be forgotten.

Tren-Lore seized my upper arm and forced me to stop. "Lara, what is wrong?"

I could not tell him what was wrong. *Well, you see, Tren-Lore, I am miserable because I just realized that I like you as more than a friend but you are in love with someone else, and now I have to pretend that I am happy for you, but trying to do so is like trying to grind rocks between my teeth.* The words sounded horrible, even in my mind and panic began to rise in me. I felt like an animal cornered by hunters, facing a front of bristling spears.

"I do not want to talk about this!" I tried to pull away from him, but he tightened his grip on my arm.

"Talk about what?" Tren-Lore demanded.

I could feel a lump forming in my throat, but I forced myself to look up at him. "I was very pleased to hear about your marriage to Areama." The words drove pain through the very core of my being.

Tren-Lore stared at me in shock, apparently struggling for something to say. "My – my marriage? I am not getting married!"

My response was irrational and spurred by a lack of sleep and desperate grief. His words seemed to ring with untruth. If he was not enamored with Areama, then why had he spent so much time with her? Why were so many people talking about them with such certainty? Why had he forgotten about me? I wanted to hit him.

"Well, you certainly have been very distracted by her!" I yelled.

Tren-Lore took a step back, holding up his hands in defense. He seemed bewildered. "Well, I do like her, and Draows said it was important for me to make a good impression on her father. This alliance with Hemlizar is very important."

"Draows!" I cried, feeling utterly betrayed. Turning on my heel, I stalked towards the entrance. Tears were beginning to blur my vision.

Tren-Lore leapt after me and grabbed my hand in his. "What are you so angry about?"

I was sobbing now and I tried vainly to twist from Tren-Lore's grip. I did not want him to see me crying. I did not want him to leave. I did not want everything to come to an end. "You like her more than me."

The words startled both of us, for I had not meant to say them, and I do not think Tren-Lore had expected to hear them. His fingers tightened around my hand and I stared at the grass beneath my feet, wishing that a crack would suddenly open in the earth and swallow me whole. Why had I said that?

"What?" Tren-Lore asked, and his voice seemed strangely unsteady.

"You like Areama more than you like me." I looked up at him, tears still slipping from my eyes.

Tren-Lore reached out and gently wiped the dampness from my cheek. "Lara, I do not like Areama more than you."

"I do not believe you," I protested, pressing my toes into the bottom of my shoes. "How could you not favour her?"

Tren-Lore regarded me sternly. "Areama is a nice person and I like her well enough, but she is certainly not you."

"No," I sniffed, 'she certainly is *not* me. She is beautiful and wealthy and graceful *and* of royal blood."

"And you are beautiful and intelligent and funny and courageous." Tren-Lore's face creased in a grin. "Trust me, Lara, I...I like you much more than her."

I shook my head and turned my gaze downward once again. It seemed impossible that Tren-Lore would think so highly of me.

He caught my chin in his fingers and made me look up at him. His deep blue eyes were full of caring, and excitement. "Do you want me to prove it to you?" he asked softly.

My heart leapt and I could say nothing. Reality seemed to have slipped away from me. There was no breath, no time, no thought. There was only Tren-Lore. His fingers brushed against my cheeks and lingered for a moment. I could not help but respond to his touch. I stepped toward him, reaching up to slide my arms around his neck. I could feel the warmth of his body against mine, feel his chest rise and fall with every breath. He bent forward slightly and our lips touched. It was like a whisper of lightning, a rumble of thunder far in the distance. I closed my eyes and he kissed me again, and this time I was caught in the power of a storm that ebbed and flowed and tasted of the wild energy of earth, of enchantment, and of happiness. I felt drowned in wonderful sensation, lost in a moment I had never believed would come. When at last we broke apart, we were breathing hard and grinning.

"Well," I said breathlessly, "that was not exactly the argument I was expecting, but you did make quite a convincing case."

Tren-Lore laughed. "And it is not an argument I ever made to Areama ... or one I ever intend to make."

* * *

I scratched lazily at my hair and pulled one sleeve of my sleeping gown down from around my elbow. I slowly crawled from bed and stumbled out of my chamber the next morning. I was hoping to convince Sophie to let me take a few slices of bread back to bed. I did not feel like facing everyone this morning. I wanted to cocoon myself in the warmth of my blankets and relive last night. It still did not seem completely real.

"Sophie, can I..." My words faltered as I saw that Sophie was not alone.

Tren-Lore was sitting at the table with a steaming mug of berryroot cordial. Sophie was chatting away to him as she bustled around the kitchen. He listened with a contented expression upon his face. His hair was in spiky disorder and his tunic was blue: both qualities that made him especially handsome that morning. He grinned when he saw me, and a surge of remembrance made me giddy.

"Good morning," I said to both Sophie and Tren-Lore. Suddenly, returning to bed did not seem so appealing.

Sophie turned, and her eyes grew wide as she beheld the clothing I was wearing. "Lara!" she practically screamed. "Ascendants' sake, child! Get back to your room and do not come out until you are properly clothed. Are you trying to shame me to death?" She herded me into our room with outraged cries that dwindled into sharp scolding. "Of all the days to wander around half-naked!"

I could not help but laugh. My sleeping gown covered me from neck to ankle. I was hardly half-naked.

"This is not funny, young lady!" Sophie shook her finger at me and I tried to straighten my lips into a serious line. "Prince Tren-Lore does not come to visit very often any more, and he will get the wrong impression of you. I do not want him thinking that I have raised some Barlem wild-woman."

It was terribly hard to keep myself from bursting into laughter. Where was Sophie coming up with these expressions? I pulled a dress over my head and was thankful to have a few moments for concealed grinning. Today, nothing could dampen my spirits. When I had attired myself in a fashion that met with Sophie's approval, she allowed me to leave the room.

"Thank you for the cordial, Lady Grim," Tren-Lore said as he stood up from his seat. "It was delicious as always, but I really must be on my way."

Sophie beamed at him, and I could not help but mimic the expression. Tren-Lore bowed to her swiftly, and as he turned to leave, he winked at me. I smirked and winked back.

"I am going to serve at the royal chambers," I told Sophie, and before she could say anything to detain me, I hurried from the room.

Tren-Lore was waiting for me. "Do you want to come and practice?" he asked. I nodded, and we started down the hall together. Tren-Lore glanced at me. "What was Sophie saying to you while you were getting dressed?"

I chuckled and reached out to run my hand along the smooth stone wall. "A number of very interesting things. My favorite, though, was when she told me that you were going to think I was a 'Barlem wild-woman'."

"Well, the dear Lady Grim can set her mind at rest. I do not think you are a Barlem wild-woman." He paused, and I could almost hear his words before he said them. "I think you are a double Barlem wild-woman."

"Oh, be quiet!" I exclaimed, and hit him playfully on the shoulder.

He lunged at me, and his fingers dug into my ribs. I screeched with laughter and shoved him away. "Truce!" I cried, still half bent over to protect my sensitive ribs.

Tren-Lore nodded and extended his hand. There was the familiar scar across his palm. "Truce," he agreed.

I smiled and reaching over, entwined my fingers with his. Holding Tren-Lore's hand seemed to be the most natural of all actions, and yet, the strangest. We had spent so long being friends that this addition to our relationship felt very different... and very pleasant. I could not help grinning.

So it was that we arrived at the practice field hand in hand. Draows was sitting upon the ground, his wrists resting on his bent knees. He squinted up at us and began to laugh. "Let it never be said that the Ascendant of Unity acts swiftly. I am glad for both of you!" He rose in one fluid motion. "It is an end to much blindness." Drawing his sword from its scabbard, he nodded at us. "Valena fayr alleneth. Come Tren-Lore, let us fight."

Tren-Lore unsheathed his own sword. As the two men sparred, I sat at a distance and watched. Half of my attention was taken by the fight, but in some corner of my mind I was pondering the meaning of Draows' words. I knew them to be of the Old Tongue, but I did not know what they meant. I decided that when I had time, I would find out.

Later, when Tren-Lore was finished with his practice, he and I set out to visit the fort. The air shimmered with heat and the breeze smelled sweet with summer scents. We crossed the river in our old boat and were so wet when we reached the other side that we decided to complete the job and go swimming. After cooling ourselves under the touch of Venst, we tromped up to the fort.

"I still think it creaks more than it used to," I insisted as I clambered up the footholds fixed to the tree.

Tren-Lore scrambled into the fort after me. "I think you are imagining it," he told me, "but I suppose it could. Things do change."

I smiled suddenly, his words prompting a realization of new possibilities. I took hold of his collar and kissed him impetuously. He looked surprised as I drew away from him, but the expression passed quickly. He slipped his hands around my waist.

"This is so strange," he said with a roguish grin.

"I know," I replied with a laugh. It was comforting that he shared my sentiments. I was about to tell him this, but Tren-Lore's lips were upon mine again and I forgot what it was I had been about to say.

* * *

This feeling of novelty or oddity - I was not sure how to describe it – waned with each day, and when the Hemlizar royal family left, I felt even more confident about my relationship with Tren-Lore. King Kiris and the Hemlizar ruler could not agree on the details of an alliance, so he and his family returned to Hemlizar without signing a treaty. I did a little dance of joy in the kitchen. Areama had left, and everything was perfect!

When autumn's peaceful cool fell upon Caladore, I found it hard to believe that there had been a time when the feel of Tren-Lore's kisses had been unknown to me. As with everything that Tren-Lore was involved in, our relationship seemed magical and story-born. We spent as much time together as we possibly could. The pleasure of these moments was unrivaled by anything I had previously experienced. It even sustained me during our frequent separations. On most days, Tren-Lore was needed to help with preparations for the war, in addition to his regular Sanysk training. Draows was beginning to teach him tracking techniques and survival skills. All of the knowledge he had gained about plants and herbs was finally put to use, and Draows was suitably impressed. He encouraged Tren-Lore to pursue his interest in Forest-wisdom.

"It is not every Sanysk," Draows said, "who has the benefit of a Healer's company."

I was flattered by Draows' kind words, and above all, I wanted to help Tren-Lore. When he and the Sanysk disappeared on their week-long excursions into the wilderness, I revived my interest in the long forgotten books stacked at my bedside. I learned a great deal about medicinal plants, and even attempted to practice channeling. Unfortunately, it ended as it always did. My mind was inevitably drawn back to dark memories and a desperate longing to change what had happened. The energy would just not flow from my fingers. Why could I not do it? Why did I even bother trying? I knew that answer, and it made tears spring to my eyes. If I could channel, if I could have channeled, I would have been able to save my mother from death.

"End this," I snapped, and pushing away the plant that I had tried to channel into, I laid my head on my arms and cried.

* * *

I rejoiced when the world swept a white cloak of winter about itself. The snow and howling storms froze any ambition Caladore and Renarn had for battle. Until the time when the wrappings of winter were shed, each country's troops were confined to their homes. Tren-Lore was safe, and the time he and Draows spent away from the castle lessened. This was my first reason for mirth. My second was the return of Myste.

He arrived the day of the first snowstorm. Tren-Lore and I were so filled with anticipation that we stationed ourselves in the main entrance. We both wore heavy cloaks to keep the chill of the castle from seeping beneath our skins, and had diverted our minds from the cold with an involving game of Questkon.

"An assassin!" I cried in indignation, and Tren-Lore nodded, an irritating grin upon his face. Since he and Draows had been studying strategy, Tren-Lore had been nearly impossible to beat. "How dare you! He is a Sorcerer; you do not just go around assassinating Sorcerers. That is as bad as... well, it is just underhanded!"

"Take a chaos card," Tren-Lore instructed me calmly, leaning his elbows on the table.

I stuck out my tongue at him. "I know, thank you very much." I snatched one up and winced. It was a ten. I might as well give Tren-Lore the game. I had been about to place the card on the table when Tren-Lore twisted in his chair.

"Myste is here," he said, and a few moments later the inner door burst open in a flurry of snow and wind.

A figure garbed in a fur cloak staggered in. "What a lovely raging blizzard we are having!" Myste's disgruntled voice announced as two servants heaved the huge inner doors shut. Tren-Lore's cousin threw back his hood to reveal a bearded face and curls wet with melting snow.

The doors boomed together, and the wind screamed and pried at the chinks in the entrance. I shoved the chaos card back into the deck and stood up, smiling. It was wonderful to see Myste again! I had missed him and his caustic humor.

"We arranged it especially for you," I told him.

"And I did not think to get anything for you!" Myste declared with false dismay, his mitt-clad hand moving to his cheek. "I promise to send you a nice plague for your next Summer Year."

I laughed and bounded forward to hug him. He had grown since I had last seen him, though he was still a bit shorter than Tren-Lore and the addition of facial hair added age to his face. I reached up tentatively and touched the close-cut hair of his beard. "Very manly."

Tren-Lore came forward to stand beside me. He shook his head. "I tried to stop him," he said.

"But naturally, I ignored him entirely," Myste replied. "Sir Goolsberry over there has notoriously bad taste."

Both men grinned, and then caught each other in a rough hug.

"It is good to see you," Tren-Lore said, clapping Myste on the back.

"It has been much too long," Myste agreed as the two cousins broke apart. "Now," he said, "what is this Tren-Lore told me about the two of you?"

* * *

That winter was a season from the past. I felt as though our childhood selves had been roused from some long sleep to enliven our spirits with a new energy and joy. We lounged before the fire in the secret room, played games, and talked endlessly as the days slipped away. The subjects had changed, but there was just as much laughter and teasing as there always had been. We told stories and talked about love and dreams and ideals. We discussed books and reminisced about the past as we roasted narkanytch. We allowed ourselves to forget about the war and look to the immediate future – a future that involved the delightful scheme we had concocted.

The scheme in question involved a small cottage on the royal family's land. We first heard of it in a story Tren-Lore told us one blustery winter evening.

"It was dark before we made it there," Tren-Lore said in a soft, eerie voice. "It was one of those nights that seemed cold enough to freeze even sound. The trees looked black and their bark seemed twisted into faces. I remember riding past this fallen tree and being absolutely sure that I saw something move in the darkness beneath it."

"Disanima," Myste whispered and wiggled his fingers, making claw-like shadows on the roof.

"So," Tren-Lore continued, "the cottage finally appeared through the woods and my father went toward it. Mother followed, carrying Nahanni in her arms. It was the Ascendants' work that Nahanni was sleeping, or she would have been crying in fright. Yolis went next, and I was last and probably the most reluctant. To me, the entrance looked like a gaping mouth and the windows like black eyes. When my father forced open the door, it swung in with this horrible screaming noise."

The wood of the fire snapped, and I gasped in fright.

"No one had been there in more than ten years," murmured Tren-Lore. "It was like midnight inside, and as we stepped over the threshold a terrible sound rent the air... It was the sound of screeching voices."

I sat up, my heart beating hard in my chest and my hand upon Tren-Lore's upper arm. "Voices?"

Tren-Lore shook his head. "Well, not really. It was only owls."

I collapsed back on the floor in relief. All at once the fire seemed to dance more cheerfully, and the shadows in the room receded like Disanima creeping away.

"One of the windows had been broken, and a family of owls had started living there," Tren-Lore explained as he stretched his legs out and propped them up against the pile of wood near the hearth. "I guess we startled them."

Myste made an owl shadow on the ceiling. "We should go there," he said, moving his hands so the shadowy figure flapped its wings.

I creased my face in a show of disdain. "It sounds scary. Why would we want to go there?"

"It was only scary that night," Tren-Lore replied from beside me. "It was usually a lot of fun. Myste, you were there once, right?"

Myste nodded. "With Grandmother. It is fun there. She let me eat whatever I wanted. I ate more honey that week than I have eaten during the rest of my life."

Tren-Lore and I laughed, and thus began our discussions about a journey to the cottage. At first, it only included the three original plotters, but soon grew to encompass Nahanni and Zander. We became weavers of lies, spinning reasons for our impending absence. King Kiris, Sophie, and Lord Mambar all received different explanations. Draows was the only recipient of the truth and he, like the rest of the adults, agreed to give us reprieve from our responsibilities.

Chapter Twenty-Three
Sir Puff Puff and other Secrets

T he day of our journey dawned cold and clear. It was a jolly company that rode away from the castle. We made directly for the forest, our breath pouring from our mouths as though a fire were smoldering in our bellies. I would not have been surprised if by some feat of magic this were actually true. This was an adventure! This was a gathering of all my friends and a chance to be together without the worry of duty or discovery.

Some time after lunch, Tren-Lore taught us a song that he had learned from Draows during one of their excursions. It had simple lyrics and a rousing rhythm. We sang loudly, savoring the fact that the trees provided our only audience.

An unknown road I follow now
Through grass and brook and under bow.
For dragon's mouth or mountains gate
I wander hither to my fate.
I seek not glory or glittering stone
But only a story to call my own!
So an unknown road I follow now...

And so the song circled back on itself, and we repeated it over and over again until we caught the first glimpse of the cottage. I pushed Paence forward, and as we skirted a large group of trees the cottage came into full sight. I was surprised. The sinister description Tren-Lore had originally given of the place had rooted in my mind, but the image I was presented with was quite the contrary. It was a small stone cottage with a gently sloping roof and a friendly door. Snow dripped from the eaves and partially covered the windows that flanked each side of the entrance. The right window was boarded up and reminded me of a bandage on a scraped knee.

We all dismounted in snow that was nearly up to our knees.

Tren-Lore dug a rusty key out of his pocket and tossed it to me. "I am going to put the horses in the stable," he said. "See if you can get the door open."

"All right," I agreed, and handed him my reins. Myste did the same, and Storm Wing snorted in protest, pulling back his lips as though he were preparing to bite the two other horses pressing close to him.

"Stop it, Storm Wing," Tren-Lore told him gruffly.

The huge charger huffed angrily, but did as he had been ordered.

"I will help you, Tren-Lore," Zander offered. He took hold of Nahanni's reins. The princess smiled at him and gently touched his cheek. Tren-Lore was already striding around the side of the cottage, and with a quick grin, Zander hurried after him. "Is Storm Wing named after the first dragon Lord Rayn talked to?" Zander asked as he caught up with Tren-Lore.

I smiled. Zander admired Tren-Lore a great deal, and Tren-Lore, despite his best efforts, was beginning to like Zander. I waded through the snow toward the door, thinking that this demonstration of Lord Rayn knowledge was one of the best things Zander could have ever done. I finally managed to fit the key into the keyhole, but the latch would not open the door.

"Hurry - up – Lara." Myste's voice was broken by the chattering of his teeth.

"The door is stuck," I told him. I set my shoulder to it and heaved. The hinges must have been stiff with rust and frost, for they would not move.

Myste and Nahanni added their strength to the struggle, and just as Myste was declaring that he hoped wolves came and ate us before we froze to death, the door burst open and we all tumbled into the room.

"I will make a fire!" Myste volunteered eagerly. He made directly for the fireplace along the back wall. There was a large pile of dry firewood waiting, and tearing off his fur gloves, Myste grabbed some kindling and tossed it onto the grate. He soon had a roaring blaze burning, and was kneeling by it with his hands outstretched and his cloak pooling around him. There were several seats arranged in front of the hearth, but Myste would not stray far enough from the heat to sit upon them.

Nahanni and I removed our mittens and tossed them on the dining table in the middle of the room.

"Come on," Nahanni said, slipping her warm hand into mine, "I will show you the cottage."

It was a small building, and despite the frigid temperature and stone walls, it gave me a sense of cozy warmth. There were six small sleeping chambers that opened directly off the main room. Each room housed a large bed with quilts that Nahanni said had been made by her mother.

"She made one for each of us," Nahanni said as we leaned into one of the sleeping chambers. "Mine," she said, pointing to a beautiful blanket draped over the bed, "has a sun on it. Mother always used to call me sunshine. Tren-Lore's has a dragon, and I think Yolis has a castle on his." Nahanni led me down a small corridor and into a kitchen full of windows and light.

There were dried herbs hanging from the beams of the roof. I identified them quickly as rezylarath and teraroot. Cupboards lined the walls, and a small table sat in the center of the room. Resting upon its rough surface was a dish full of shiny rocks. Nahanni leaned over and picked one up. She smiled, but her eyes seemed sad. "There is a brook a little way from here. It eventually flows to join Venst, but the waters were never deep and swift like Venst. We had a boat that we played in and Tren-Lore, Mother and I would go swimming all the time. We always kept an eye out for pretty rocks." She looked up at the dried herbs, and then out the window. "It is strange being here, Lara. At home it does not even seem as if my mother was ever there, but here, it seems as if she will be back in a moment."

The sound of the door being shoved open made both of us jump. We looked at each other for an expectant, breathless instant, and then Tren-Lore's voice declared, "Could you sit any closer to the fire, Myste?"

"Possibly," we heard Myste reply, "but it would do me more harm than good."

Nahanni and I giggled nervously, both feeling slightly foolish for our lapse of reason. Nahanni dropped the rock back into the bowl and we made our way down the hallway to the main chamber. How nice it would be, my mind thought wistfully, to be in a place that made you feel so close to your mother. To this my memory responded with the speech Draows had given me about not neglecting my Healing. I shook my head and tried to divert my attention.

Zander was tossing our gear inside, and Tren-Lore was stooping to dump an armload of freshly chopped wood upon the floor. As he straightened, he saw me and grinned. This was all the distraction I could have asked for. I smiled back at him, and the warmth of my fondness swelled within me until there was no room for anything else.

As we unpacked, disorder spilled out into the cottage, and for a time it was strewn with food, clothing, bedding and games. It took us quite a while to regain control, but when everything was in its place, the shutters had been opened to let the sunshine in, and the blanket of dust had been swept away, we collapsed before the fire.

There was talk of going outside to explore and a discussion on the topic of supper, but in the end, we resolved to remain inside and eat narkanytch for dinner. A better plan could not have been made, and it was an evening of much laughter and merriment. We talked for ages until, like the candles scattered through the room, our conversation melted and the room became peacefully silent and dark. One by one the members of our company retired to their beds, until it was only Tren-Lore and I left.

We lay on the couch together. My head rested upon his chest, his heartbeat faint in my ears. He smelled of the wood he had been chopping and I smiled in weary contentment. I stared into the twisting flames of the fire. I felt, not for the first time, that through my contact with Tren-Lore I had passed into the realm of stories.

"And then a Sorcerer came and laid a spell upon them," I murmured in sleep-softened tones, "and time was frozen forever."

Tren-Lore wrapped his arms around me. "That would be nice," he replied. His voice was deep and quiet, like winter night.

When I awoke, it was morning and I could hear Nahanni, Zander and Myste talking softly in the kitchen. I sat up and looked down at Tren-Lore. He was still asleep, and his face was relaxed. Slumber had made his raven hair into a mess of spikes, and his tunic was wrinkled. I gently touched the small dragon insignia stitched onto the corner of his shirt. He did not stir, and so I bent over him and kissed him gently. As I drew away, he opened his eyes and I was held in a calm gaze that had the depth and color of the sky, and the power to make me feel beautiful, loved, and special. He reached up and tucked my hair behind my ears.

"Good morning." He smiled, and I leaned forward and kissed him again.

"All right you two," a teasing voice proclaimed, "that is quite enough of that.

I laughed and looked up to see Myste standing in the corridor, a long wooden spoon in hand.

"Come on," he insisted. "Breakfast is ready."

I clambered off the couch and Tren-Lore sat up, stretching his arms over his head.

Myste shook his spoon at his cousin. "Move, boy, my eggs are getting cold."

I grinned in wry amusement and hurried toward the kitchen. Behind me, I could hear Tren-Lore and Myste exchanging barbed remarks. "You know," Tren-Lore said, "sometimes you really remind me of Sophie."

"Well, sometimes you really remind me of a dirty old goat," Myste retorted, "but I never tell you that, do I?"

I could tell Tren-Lore was trying not to laugh. "I have no idea why I even like you," he replied finally.

Myste chuckled with good humor. "My mother says the same thing about me all the time."

* * *

After the delicious breakfast Myste had prepared with a talent I could never hope to rival, we all donned our heavy winter wrappings and went out into the snow-laden world. The brook Nahanni had mentioned provided steep banks that were perfect for sliding down. This recreation quickly degenerated into playful fighting, and soon we were all knocking each other into the deep snow and yelling war cries we had read in books.

We returned to the cottage when our feet felt like blocks of ice and our cheeks were pale with frostbite. Myste built up the fire and we all sat upon the couches, pursuing various forms of entertainment. I was reading a book on the plants of Hemlizar, and Tren-Lore was frowning over a novel written in the language of the Renarn. As part of his training, he was mastering several different languages, but it was a rather challenging task. Zander and Nahanni were holding hands and whispering quietly to each other, while Myste was composing a letter to the girl of his latest affections. When the fire had burned down to a mass of hot coals, we set about making supper. Under Myste's guiding hand, it turned out to be a lovely meal.

"Just as good as Sophie would have made," Tren-Lore declared with a smirk.

After we were finished eating, we returned to our places around the fire. Myste went to grab extra blankets from one of the sleeping chambers, and Tren-Lore opened a bottle of wine we had brought. Tren-Lore had just finished pouring the last of the wine when Myste emerged from the room with a pile of blankets in one arm and something else clutched in his other hand. He was grinning like a wolf, and his delight was so evident that I was half surprised to find that his tongue was not lolling from his mouth.

"Look who I found!" Myste declared as he climbed over the back of the couch.

I leaned forward, trying to discern what it was he was referring to. Tren-Lore put the wine bottle down with thud. For a moment the strange thing held in Myste's grasp was obscured as he struggled with his wealth of blankets. Nahanni took the extra quilts from him as he reclaimed his seat. Resting in his lap was a small dragon made of cloth and stuffed with something soft.

"Now, Tren-Lore," Myste began, his fingers gently petting the top of the creature's spiky head, "correct me if I am wrong, but was this or was this not an old friend of yours?"

We all turned to look at Tren-Lore. He seemed torn between irritation and amusement. Finally, he nodded gravely. "His name is Sir Puff Puff, and he is, indeed, a very old friend of mine. I thought I had lost him years ago."

We all burst into laughter. Myste tossed the stuffed animal to Tren-Lore, and grinning, Tren-Lore caught it. I chuckled, amused by the endearing image of Tren-Lore with Sir Puff Puff.

"To Sir Puff Puff!" Myste said, raising his glass in salute.

We all did the same. The wine had been made from berryroot, and while it was not as sweet as the cordial, it was still quite excellent. Tren-Lore put his arm around me and I leaned against him, cuddling Sir Puff Puff and sipping at my wine.

"I guess," Myste consented, as he leaned back against the couch, "everyone has something like that, some sort of secret love or hidden talent. Remember how Grandmother could fit her entire fist in her mouth?"

Tren-Lore coughed, choked by the combination of laughing and swallowing at the same time. Nahanni looked astonished, and I giggled skeptically, mentally adjusting the image I had of Tren-Lore's grandmother to include a mouth stretched with the breadth of a fist. The painting in the royal chambers had certainly never suggested such a talent.

"Could she really?" I demanded of the smirking Myste.

He shrugged, scratching absently at his beard. "Like I said, Lara, everyone has a hidden talent. I am sure even you have some concealed skills you are not telling us about."

I stiffened. I knew that Myste was only teasing, but I could not stop the cold blade of fear that had slid between my ribs and robbed me of my breath. I felt attacked and vulnerable, and my lips parted in a defense of words that would not come. Tren-Lore must have felt my muscles tense or instinctively understood my discomfort, for he came swiftly to my rescue.

"Myste," Tren-Lore began, and my body felt fluid with relief, "get the Questkon board." His voice reminded me of Draows'.

Tren-Lore may not have been wearing the silver bands of the Sanysk, but he was very much part of the League. I wondered, as I sat up and grabbed the deck of chaos cards, when we had all grown up so much? Tren-Lore was in his ninth Summer Year and on the brink of Sanyskhood. Myste was beginning to take command of Jacinda, Nahanni had fallen in love and I... well truth be told, I was exactly the same girl who had come to Caladore. I was still hiding from the fact that I was a Healer. I blanched at the thought. It made me feel ill and feverish. Tren-Lore glanced at me, concern flickering across his face.

"Are you all right?" he asked quietly.

I slipped my hand into his and savored the feeling of his warm skin. I was not the same girl who had come to Caladore. Tren-Lore had changed me. He had turned my fictions into reality. He had taught me how to ride, how to read, and how to fight. He had chosen me as his best friend, and then he had chosen me over Areama. I smiled at him and leaned over to kiss his frowning mouth.

"So long as I am with you, I will always be all right."

* * *

Morning light streamed in through the kitchen windows, and I hummed as I kneaded the bread I was making. Tren-Lore was standing beside me, chopping dried meat with a warrior's precision.

"Tren-Lore," I objected as I pushed my hair out of my face with the back of my hand. I frowned critically at his work. "No one is going to be able to swallow that. Cut it into smaller pieces."

He hacked off another large chunk and grinned at me. "Mezra rew garshneth flarick."

"And what does that mean?" I demanded with an arched eyebrow. I had heard enough of the Renarn's guttural language to recognize the origin of the words, but I did not have any idea what the sentence translated to.

Tren-Lore grabbed me around the waist and pulled me close to him. "I am still learning, but I tried to say you have flour on your face." He stooped and kissed me, his fingers coming to rest on my cheeks. The touch was strangely powdery and I pulled away, gasping indignantly.

"You Barlem!" I shouted in mirthful outrage, and rubbed at the flour Tren-Lore had just smeared across my cheeks.

He laughed and picked up his knife again. "I warned you," he replied teasingly, as he resumed hewing the meat as though it were a ferocious enemy. Wrenching his blade free, he lifted it for another stroke and then stopped, his knife wavering in midair. "Actually, I may not have warned you at all. My Renarn is still not very good. The Renarn word for flour is very similar to a rather nasty curse word."

I giggled at this and turned back to my bread. I pushed down hard and felt the soft dough give and move under the pressure. It would be lovely if it could always be like this. I indulged myself in a flight of fancy and imagined that the cottage was really the home I shared with Tren-Lore. I pictured us eating breakfast before the fire. I did not know what we were talking about, but we were laughing and happy. Suddenly, there was a rap upon the door. It was Draows with an important message from the League of Sanysk. They needed Tren-Lore to –

The image within my head vanished as an abrupt sound awakened me from my daydream. Tren-Lore cursed and his knife clattered to the kitchen floor. I turned quickly to find blood splattered on the counter. Tren-Lore was holding his left hand by the wrist and staring at the gory slash across the top of his hand. His face held an expression of disbelief, and for a moment, we both stood without moving.

My mouth opened in shock. Hysterical laughter and panicked words battled for command of my tongue, but from somewhere within me a strong voice demanded nothing less than a Healer's composure. *Find something to stop the bleeding. Decide if it will need to be stitched.* I grabbed the dishcloth from the table and pressed it against Tren-Lore's hand.

"Hold you wrist as tightly as you can. I have to check to see how deep the cut is."

"It could be worse," Tren-Lore quipped grimly, and did as I had instructed. "I could have been impaled and died over the course of eight long days."

I smiled vaguely, but my attention was too complete to be laid aside by the frivolity of humor. If he had cut deep enough, tendons could have been severed. A needle and thread would be of no use in correcting an injury such as that. Taking a deep breath, I peeled back the cloth. His hand was a bloody mess, and the whiteness of tendon and bone glared up at me. I reapplied pressure.

"Do not try to move your fingers," I told him sternly. "You have severed the tendons across the top of your hand." The calm of my own voice surprised me, for already my mind was leaping ahead to the shattering ramifications of losing dexterity in his left hand. How would he hold a sword? How would he become a Sanysk?

His fingers remained still, and my own hands began to shake. I tore my gaze away from his hand and looked up at him. Tren-Lore's blue eyes were darkened with fear. The muscles in his jaw tightened as he clenched his teeth. "What does that mean?" Tren-Lore demanded. "Can you fix it?"

I nearly choked on the words. "No. It means that you will lose the use of your hand."

I could feel his hand shaking violently. In the same moment, we both conceived of a new future that held none of the dreams of our childhood. We had worked too hard for it to come to this! My sight blurred with tears. It could not end like this! I did not want it to end like this! The air in the kitchen felt as though it had caught fire. My skin was burning and my head was filled with white heat – light. The storm that had been trapped inside me raged uncontrollably and energy poured from my fingertips and into Tren-Lore. The ring about my neck pulled down upon me and I staggered to my knees. For a moment I could see nothing. I blinked and then blinked again, each brush of my eyelids bringing me closer to sight. I began to perceive the floor, the glistening red blood, and the grooves in the stones. I had used my power! How was it that I could not channel it upon command, but that it would come unbidden?

"Lara?"

The familiar voice drew me past my bemusement and returned my thoughts to my prior worries. Tren-Lore! My head jerked up and I beheld him kneeling before me.

"Your hand?" I demanded.

He held it up to reveal unmarked skin. He flexed his fingers. "Healed." There was a trace of wonder in his face. "How are you?"

I felt a smile creeping across my lips and I laughed in relief, pressing my palms briefly to my temples. "Oh, Tren-Lore, I have no idea. I think I am fine."

"And," someone remarked, "in the possession of quite an extraordinary hidden talent."

We both turned sharply to find Myste standing in the doorway. His expression reminded me of a poorly constructed puzzle. The various emotions playing across his face did not fit together: confusion and comprehension, happiness and pain.

"You could have told me, Lara," he said as he entered the room and pulled a chair out from behind the table. He sat down and regarded Tren-Lore and I.

I felt anxiety frothing within me. What would Myste think of me now? I scrambled warily to my feet, involuntarily bracing myself for the cruel words that might be coming. Blindly, I reached behind me and Tren-Lore's fingers caught mine. "I..." my voice faltered as I debated the wisdom of telling Myste the truth. "I was afraid," I finished. "There are many people who...who would hate me simply because I am...because I am..." I curled my toes and struggled with the word.

"A Healer," Myste finished, "and a pretty good one, from what I can see. Lara, I have nothing against Healers, and even if I hated them like Barlems I would still feel the same way about you as I always have."

Tears of gratitude sprang to my eyes. It was hard to believe that I had such a friend. I regarded Myste with a fondness that was impossible to verbalize. Such warmth of feeling could not be contained in words. "Oh!" I declared and began to cry. "What a day this has been and it is only morning! And...and our breakfast is ruined now, too." I was a mess of emotion and entirely overwhelmed by the rapid transition from one feeling to the next. Tren-Lore gathered me in his arms, and I wept into the soft material of his tunic.

Myste chuckled. "I am sure breakfast was delicious before someone went and bled all over it. Trust a Sanysk to cut his hand off with a kitchen knife."

I laughed in spite of myself and wiped the dampness from my cheeks. Myste's chair scraped against the floor as he stood up. "First, we need to clean up, and then I will exercise one of *my* many talents. It is not as dramatic as Healing, but it will put food in our bellies. Tren-Lore, where is my spoon?"

That was the last comment Myste made about my Healing abilities. In a gesture of mercy, he never mentioned the subject again and my curse remained hidden.

Chapter Twenty-Four
The Question of the Two-Headed Beast

I t was difficult to return to life at the castle. Our time at the cottage had been so lovely. Existence in Caladore seemed a poor substitute. It was unpleasant - I scowled at Flock, who was already scowling at me – and it was lonely. I only saw Tren-Lore once a day, and after the leisure of the past week, the time we spent together now felt rushed. He had his duties and I had mine, and ever in the distance loomed spring. When the weather broke, the troops were sure to be leaving for war. Sighing, I took the soapy dish Flock handed me and rubbed it dry.

"Stop huffing, Lara," Flock snapped. "I hate doing dishes just as much as you, but you do not see *me* complaining."

This was blatantly untrue. Just a few moments ago, Sophie had told Flock to stop complaining. Had the dishes not been at their end, this comment would have warranted a verbal brawl. As it was, I had the more attractive option of escaping the kitchen on a mission to dump the washing water. I grabbed the tub and supported it against my hip.

"I will be back in a moment," I called to Sophie.

Sophie looked up from the stew she was making. "Put on a cloak, dear."

I turned and shifted the basin so I had a better grip on it. "Sophie," I protested, "it is not so cold that I need a cloak to merely step out the door."

Sophie raised her eyebrows and caught my gaze in a warning look. I looked back at her with calm persistence, and Sophie shook her head.

"Very well, child." She smoothed her hair into place and returned her attention to her cooking pot. "Do what you think is wise."

I smiled and swept from the kitchen. My cloak remained hanging on the peg by the door. I was feeling quite excellent about my little victory until I laid my hand upon the icy handle of the outer door. Heaving it open, I was greeted by a blast of freezing air. I made a face of disgust. My hands and ears were already burning under the frigid lashing of the wind. Grimacing, I dumped the washing water as quickly as I could. It splashed against the frozen earth and splattered the front of my white skirts.

"Oh, end this!" I declared in exasperation and stalked inside, slamming the door behind me.

I stomped up the stairs, the washing basin knocking against the side of my leg and my teeth chattering uncontrollably. Why did Sophie always have to be right about everything? I was so engaged in my brooding that I did not notice who was walking down the corridor toward me.

"Lara!" declared the delighted voice of Tren-Lore.

I looked up, and despite my black mood I could not help smiling. "Hello," I replied, my lips still quivering with cold. "What are you doing down here?"

Tren-Lore gestured behind me to the stairs leading to the lower levels of the castle. "Father wanted me to spend today supervising the servants who are counting swords in the armory."

"Counting swords?" I repeated skeptically.

The young prince shrugged. "Assessing weaponry, counting swords, it is all the same thing. I have more important things to do, and my presence was unnecessary. The numbers will be the same whether I am there or not."

I shook my head in fond amusement. Some things never changed.

"But," he continued, "I *should* make a brief appearance, at the very least. Myste and I will meet you in the secret room tonight."

We kissed each other in parting. He strode toward the stairs and I turned toward the kitchen. I smiled down at the floor, the sensation of Tren-Lore's kiss warming my whole body. The marks on my dress no longer seemed important, and I did not mind if Sophie was right. Everything was wonderful. I looked up and my footsteps faltered. Standing at the end of the passageway was Yolis. He regarded me for a moment, and then turned with such ferocity that it almost seemed as thought he was upset or angry. I frowned in brief puzzlement, but did not give the matter much consideration.

* * *

"My bones do not ache so much, but my heart hurts, Lara." Sophie eased herself into her rocking chair one night on the brink of spring. "Warm weather agrees with my old body, but for the sake of those boys I wish it would not come."

I pulled a brush through my hair and regarded Sophie from where I was sitting on my bed. Her bun was in disarray and there were lines of worry creasing her already wrinkled face. More than anything else, however, she looked tired. I imagine I had a similar appearance about me. Lately, the kitchen was a place of turmoil. The army would need an incredible amount of provisions, and the effort had consumed the kitchen and spread into two nearby chambers. As noise and steam rose through the air, we toiled side by side with women from Cala who had come to supplement the regular servants. It was grueling work, and Flock was not the only one to complain bitterly about it. It did not really bother me, though. It kept my mind engaged, and this prevented the knot in my stomach from becoming any more twisted and tight.

It was during the evenings that I was most bound by worry. I had nothing to occupy my thoughts. Previously, Myste, Tren-Lore and I had spent a few hours each night in the secret room. Like the blossoming warmth outside, their responsibilities had grown until they no longer had time for even these brief meetings. I tried to fill my time with reading. I even attempted to practice channeling, but it was to no avail. My mind would turn to the possible injuries Tren-Lore might suffer on the battlefield - to the possible death that might be waiting there for him, and I would have to close my eyes and bring my concentration to something else. I felt trapped in an unseeing gaze and confronted by an enemy that had always defeated me in the past.

"Foolishness," Sophie muttered.

I jumped slightly, realizing that I had been holding the brush poised against my hair but I had ceased to move my hand. How could thoughts become so consuming?

"What is foolishness?" I asked as I set the brush upon the table and pulled back my blankets.

Sophie rocked slowly and stared out the window. "War," she said. Her chair creaked softly against the floor. "War is foolishness. Nothing more than a bunch of boys squabbling over a piece of land."

Slipping under the covers, I settled back and sighed. I did not want to agree with Sophie. I wanted to believe that the battle would be grand in purpose and deeds. I needed to believe that Tren-Lore, like all good heroes, would return unscathed.

"Sophie," I yawned sleepily and drew my rough woolen blanket around my chin. "Tell me a story."

Sophie laughed and picked up her mending from the basket next to her. "You have not asked for a story in a long time."

I closed my eyes. "I want to hear one now. One with a happy ending."

"Very well," Sophie's warm voice murmured. The soft sound of her rocking chair became a constant rhythm. "When the world was young and the Ascendants still roamed upon it..."

I heard no more, for the familiar noises of my childhood were soothingly peaceful and I lapsed into sleep. I was awakened the next morning by a resounding clap of thunder. It startled me from slumber and I sat up straight in bed. My first thoughts were wildly panicked and composed of fragmented fears. Tren-Lore was injured! We were all trapped! The Renarn were battering down the gate! Slowly I calmed and began to realize what had awakened me. Rain lashed against the windowpane, and the wind roared in a mad rage. A thunderstorm had darkened the skies of Caladore. Spring had arrived.

There was an uneasy feeling in the air that morning. Even the comforting scent of freshly baked bread did nothing to soothe me. I glanced toward the window and once again saw the confirmation of spring spattering the glass, running down the window like blood. I was not the only one suffering through gnawing anxiety. Other women were casting apprehensive glances outside, and nearly everyone wore an expression of grim knowledge. The sound of thunder smashing overhead made us all jump.

"In the name of all things eternal!" Sophie exclaimed, and laid a hand to her chest. "I might as well put a pot on my head and bang against it with a spoon. What a terrible racket!"

Thriana leaned against the window and shook her head. "I do not think anyone from Cala will be coming to help us today. There are not many people who would dare to brave this storm."

Flock placed a platter of cheese upon the table with a thud. "Leffeck says that storms like these happen when the Ascendants are angry. He says that it means something bad will happen." Her brown eyes were wide with conviction.

"I was unaware that the Ascendants were in Leffeck's close circle of friends." My words were clipped with irritation. I added a plate of fresh bread to the breakfast setting and then crossed my arms in front of my chest. "How is it that he believes he is privy to the inner workings of nature, and why do you feel the need to repeat him? We are all worried enough. You do not have to make it worse."

Flock's hands went to her ample hips, and her bosom heaved indignantly. "I always said you had the manners of a dragon! Do try to hold your tongue, Lara. You have no right to criticize your betters."

The soft sounds of work faded away as the women of the kitchen turned their attention to our squabble.

Everyone looked as though they had been petrified by a Sorcerer's spell – fully enchanted by the prospect of something new to gossip about. I did not care. If they wanted a diversion, I would give them one. The tension in the air had been making my spirit stiff and sore, but Flock's comment was like heat on aching muscles. I was ready for a fight.

"I fully agree," I retorted sharply, and pressing my palms on the table's surface, I learned toward her. "I do not have any right to criticize my betters, but since you and Leffeck are certainly not in that category..." The level of my voice was escalating as my anger grew. "I feel perfectly comfortable telling you that Leffeck is a-"

"That is quite enough," Sophie interrupted.

At the same moment, the kitchen door was thrown back. It slammed against the wall, and thunder growled overhead. I whirled about and found Myste standing in the entrance. His hair was plastered to his forehead and his clothes were dark with water. He was out of breath. Even if this situation had been entirely typical, Myste's expression still would have told me that something was wrong. I felt myself growing cold with fear. The ladies of the kitchen were murmuring in surprise, but Sophie stepped forward calmly.

"Can we help you, Your Majesty?" she asked, her hands smoothing her white apron.

Myste twisted his ring about his finger. He was nervous, but when he spoke his voice was commanding. "Lady Grim, I must ask for the services of one of your staff. I need Lara to come with me immediately."

Sophie nodded in concurrence. "Of course, Sire." Her countenance was as puzzled as the rest of the ladies surrounding me, but Myste's tone did not invite questions.

I glanced briefly at Sophie. She looked worried, and I tried to smile comfortingly before I hurried after Myste. He was waiting in the outer chamber, my cloak in his hand.

"You have to leave right now," he whispered, pushing the garment into my hands. "Tren-Lore and Draows – they rode out a few moments ago."

"What?" I gasped. Tren-Lore had gone to war, and I had not even been able to say good-bye. I grabbed Myste's arm. "I have to go after them!"

"I know," he replied quickly. "They are riding along the eastern road to Ekrin."

Pulling my cloak over my shoulders, I dashed out the door, still fastening the clasp as I went. Myste and I hurried down to the stable, and as we ran, Myste told me what had happened. A messenger had arrived that morning. King Kiris had read the letter and then summoned Tren-Lore and Draows to him. Moments later, they were striding out the door. Myste came with them all the way down to the outer walls and Tren-Lore rapidly explained everything that he could.

"Apparently, Renarn assassins were seen passing over our eastern border this morning," Myste told me. "Draows and Tren-Lore are going to intercept them before they reach the castle. The troops are going to be called out in a day or two. He told me to go to the kitchen and tell you good-bye, and morian penent."

I swung up onto Paence's back and something Draows had once remarked upon suddenly returned to my memory. *I was always glad that I was at battle rather than at home awaiting news of victory or defeat. Waiting is a weary pastime.* It was an extremely weary pastime, as I had well learned, and not one I was willing to endure without a proper farewell. I needed to know that if Tren-Lore never did come back, I had at least said good-bye to him.

I leaned down and kissed Myste on the cheek. "Thank you," I said solemnly, and then whirling Paence around, galloped out into the rain.

The storm screamed around me, its wrathful tantrum of wind and rain stinging my skin and making it hard to see. I bent forward and gritted my teeth. On and on I rode, until Paence's steps slowed with fatigue. There was no one on the road before me, and I could not force Paence to continue at this pace for much longer. My pursuit had been in vain. Above us, thunder smashed and lightening illuminated the gloom for a moment. I cried out in surprise. Ahead on the road, I caught a glimpse of two figures. They were garbed in cloaks that seemed to melt into the background, as though they had been dyed using the very colors of the earth. Sanysk cloaks!

"Tren-Lore!" I yelled, and dug my heels into Paence's flanks. As though sensing my desperation, the mare surged forward with renewed vigor. "Tren-Lore!" I shouted again. I was counting on the sharp hearing of the Sanysk. The sound of my voice was being torn away by the howling wind.

Both riders turned. There was a pause, and then one of the riders kicked his horse toward me. It was Tren-Lore and Storm Wing. The stallion breathed life into his name, galloping forward as though he moved on the very gale itself. Horse and rider were approaching fast, and then a deafening peal of thunder rolled in the sky. Paence flinched, and Storm Wing reared in an angry challenge. The wind caught Tren-Lore's cloak, and for it moment, it flared behind him like wings. His sword was clearly visible and his hair was a mess of sharp spikes. He looked grand and threatening. Reining Storm Wing in sharply, Tren-Lore drove him forward with a demanding kick. I pushed Paence back into a gallop, and the distance between us closed in a swirl of water and wind and pounding hooves.

When Tren-Lore was before me, I grabbed him by the collar and kissed him. The frail constraints of language could not have held the violence of emotion I needed to express. He was everything to me. He was my best friend, my hero, my hope. I pulled away from our embrace and looked deeply into his eyes.

"Bye," I said simply.

His expression was one of mild bemusement. He looked at me as I had looked at him all those year ago. His gaze held the wonder of a child who never thought they could be lucky enough to see the enchantment of story come to life in the real world.

"I love you, Lara," he said.

Part of me had longed to hear these words, had longed to taste them on my own tongue, yet such a desire seemed reckless. I believed that their very utterance would result in grievous repercussions. I feared that Tren-Lore's words would be enough to rent the earth beneath our feet. I pressed my shaking fingers to his lips. Tears filled my eyes.

"Do not say that," I whispered. "You shall curse us all."

There was silence between us. Tren-Lore's face was unreadable.

"Morian penent, then."

"Morian penent," I repeated, "and farewell."

He reached out and touched my face. His hand was warm against my damp cheek. "Farewell," he replied.

I swallowed back the cry of anguish that was building in my throat. I did not want him to go. I wanted to be able to tell him that I did love him. I did not want to be so afraid. Perhaps I would have told him all these things if he had stayed but a moment longer. Perhaps I never would have. Tren-Lore turned Storm Wing, and casting one last glance at me, he galloped back to Draows. I nudged Paence into a walk and began the journey back to the castle. I did not hurry this time.

"Flock is wrong," I told Paence. Pushing my wet hair out of my face, I looked ahead at the bent trees and the torrents of rain. "The Ascendants are not angry, they are in pain."

* * *

I did not go directly to the kitchen upon my return. I went first to the secret room, where I could be alone with my thoughts. I made a fire and let the heat dry my dress and hair. What Tren-Lore had just said, and what I had *not* said, were paramount in my mind. I did not hear the door open. I did not notice Myste's presence until he laid a hand upon my shoulder.

I turned to him slowly, as one dazed by a blow to the head. "Is love a curse?"

Myste's brow furrowed. He rubbed at his mouth, perhaps attempting to conceal the look of surprise and consternation that was so clearly expressed in his face. "Do you think it is?"

I let my knees give way beneath me and I sank to the cold stone floor. The damp folds of my skirt pressed against my legs. "I do not know. My mother and Sophie, they..." My voice faded. The stories seemed to press down upon me and I did not feel as though I had the energy to tell them. "I have been hurt, and my mother, and Sophie too. Love seems to end in pain. Women...women seem to be punished for loving men."

"And men are punished for loving women," Myste added, and sat down next to me. "Love also has its rewards, though. Am I to assume that Tren-Lore told you he loved you?"

I nodded and stared into the fire. "He said he loved me, and I told him to be quiet. I said he would curse us all."

Myste stretched his arms behind him and leaned back. "Good for you. 'I love you too' is so overused. It was about time someone got a little creative."

"You can be quiet, too," I laughed bitterly.

"Fine," he agreed, "but I get to say one last thing. If love was really a curse, then you and Tren-Lore would have been finished years ago. I think you were in love with each other from the first moment you met, even if you did not know it then."

I turned to stare at Myste. My lips parted in shock. I was not sure if it was genuine surprise at this newly unearthed revelation, or if I was merely startled at having the secrets of my heart laid bare.

Myste chuckled and shifted so that he was facing me. "When I was younger, I was crazy about you." His hands caught mine and he smiled at me, his brown eyes warm with affection. "I still am, of course, just in a different way. But back then..." He sighed. "Back then, I wanted nothing more than to court you. To the dismay of my boyish heart, however, you were scarcely aware of my existence. For you, there was only Tren-Lore."

My vision blurred with tears and my throat felt tight as Myste continued. "Tren-Lore told me what Draows said when he found out that you two were together."

I took one of my hands from Myste's gentle grasp and wiped my eyes. Giving a rather hopeless sniff, I mumbled, "I do not remember what Draows said."

"Valena fayr alleneth," Myste said. "In the Old Tongue, it means, love before knowledge. Draows knew, just like I knew, that you were always in love with each other. So there you are. You have lived your entire life tempting this curse to smite you, and yet nothing has happened. If I were you, I would not worry too much about it."

Myste's words were of some comfort, but I continued to think a great deal about what he said. Maybe my understanding of life was not as solid as I had believed it to be. Not only had I missed the full depth of Myste's character, but my understanding of love was transforming into some new two-headed beast. I had come to clearly understand that love brought the possibility of pain. I now saw that it also contained the possibility of delirious happiness as well. For the first time, I was wondering if perhaps it was worth chancing the curse.

A fortnight later, I was still tied tightly in the bonds of this same contemplation. Flock and I had been asked to mash the potatoes. We sat next to each other at the large table in the middle of the room. The spring sun was gaining more strength each day. It flowed through the windows and across the floor in wide bands of light. I was scarcely aware of this lovely sight, and was paying even less attention to Flock's jabbering.

"Leffeck was saying that he thought I looked wonderful in green." She poked feebly at a potato. "Not everyone can wear green, you know. Well, take you, for example. It makes you look like you are going to retch. Although you always look sort of sickly, if you ask me."

"Right," I replied vaguely and bore down hard upon the potatoes.

This response, or lack thereof, seemed to irritate Flock. Her fork thudded as she dropped it on the table.

"Young lady," her mother's voice warned. "Pick that fork up and keep working. We need these done for the afternoon meal... and pull up your bodice."

Flock took up her fork again, but did nothing about the low state of her neckline. "Did you hear that the Renarn tried to cross Venst last night? Prince Tren-Lore's regiment drove them back, and now they are camped there. That is only a little to the south east of the castle."

She dented one of the potatoes. "It is very frightening to think that those hideous Renarn are so close to us. Apparently there was another skirmish this morning, and-"

I leapt abruptly into her sentence. "Are you sure Tr-ah, Prince Tren-Lore's regiment is that near to Caladore? Who told you that?"

Flock put her fork down again and patted her hair imperiously. She was obviously pleased to have won my attention at last. "Leffeck told me, of course. He was one of the first ones informed. You should be grateful to know me, or you would never have heard of this so soon, Lara."

For a miraculous instant, I was actually thankful for my acquaintance with Flock. If Tren-Lore was only leagues away, I could get Paence and ride out to see him! Maybe I could sneak away after lunch! Energy was suddenly humming through my body. The thought of Tren-Lore made me smile. I ceased to consider my previous dilemma. The power of my excitement was enough to batter any deeper thoughts into submission. I could scarcely wait to hear his voice again, feel his touch upon my skin, and confirm that he was not harmed. I mashed potatoes with a new vigor, already trying to decide what lie I could use to escape from the kitchen. In the end, I opted for a tried and true deception.

"The princess sent word that she needs me in the royal chambers," I told Sophie as we cleared away the dishes from the afternoon meal. "I will not be back until late."

Sophie had been bent over the table gathering cutlery, but she straightened to fully reveal her surprised expression. "When did the messenger come?"

I had foolishly not anticipated this question. I dumped a pile of plates into the washing basin, and over the terrible clatter I muttered, "Yesterday."

"Lara!" Sophie scolded, and for a frightening moment I thought she knew I was lying. Rushing toward the washing tub, Sophie grabbed the side with her plump fingers and peered in. "You are going to break every single dish we have!"

I exhaled in relief. Thank the Ascendants that Sophie cared so much about a couple of plates. "Do we have any goolsberry jam?" I asked quietly.

Sophie picked up one of the plates and examined it with a critical eye. "In the outer chamber, I think, second shelf down. Child, you really must be more careful. We do not have so many plates that you can just smash them whenever you please."

Sophie continued to advocate for the gentle treatment of plates. I slipped away just as a few of the other ladies joined in the discussion and began to expound upon the truly vital role that dishes played in the smooth running of a kitchen.

I found the goolsberry jam just where Sophie had said it would be. I put it into a small bag and added a loaf of fresh bread and a flagon of berryroot cordial. Slinging my cloak over my shoulders, I made my way down to the stables.

The sun had just begun its descent from the sky when Paence and I cantered out of the castle and set off across the plains. I hummed as we went and breathed deeply. The air was sweet with the scent of growing things, and the only sound was the song of birds and the chirping of crickets. I was glad that my course did not put me upon the road. Caladore was infected with tales of thieves and murderers that preyed upon travelers. Flock had told a particularly gruesome story involving a family and a group of bandits. The family had been ambushed, taken prisoner and tortured. In the end, they had escaped thanks to the quick thinking of their brave (and according to Flock, incredibly handsome) son.

I doubted the validity of the tale, but just thinking about it made me nervous. I looked about uneasily. The peacefully waving grass now seemed as though it could be concealing danger. Slipping my hand under my cloak, I fingered the dagger Tren-Lore had given me. The hilt was cool to the touch, and I traced the familiar engraving. *Solrium Vallent.* It was a comfort, but I would have rather had the young man from the story riding at my side. My lips crooked in a tiny smile. I would not have minded at all, especially if he was as good looking as Flock claimed.

My journey did not avail a need for any heroics, however, and as the sun was dipping behind the horizon, my destination came into sight. Tents speckled the golden plain, and behind the camp, Venst flowed in a dark blue rush of water. Smoke drifted into the sky and the wind was drenched with the smell of cooking meat. From somewhere within the post, I could hear the clang of a smith's hammer.

I drew Paence in sharply. Two men were galloping toward me from the camp. They both carried bows with arrows trained upon me. I held up my hands so they could see I was not concealing any weapons. Paence shifted beneath me and whickered softly, her teeth grinding at her bit. I thought quickly. They would not believe me if I told them I had business with Tren-Lore, but perhaps an association with Draows might not be so inconceivable.

"My name is Lara," I called. "I must see the Sanysk Draows at once. I am a friend of his and bring important news."

The men stopped a few feet away, but did not lower their weapons. They were both regarding me skeptically. "And are you a friend of Caladore?" one of the men grunted.

My mouth felt dry, and I nodded hastily.

The same soldier glared at me. "Ride before us, woman, and we shall see if you are telling the truth. If Draows does not know you, I shall have your head."

My heart was thundering with fear. Rationally, I knew that everything would be fine, but there was still part of me that could not help but respond to his threat. I rode into camp flanked by the two men who were now gripping their swords. The ground around the tents had been trod into mud, and I stared at the grimy mess feeling that this plan may not have been one of my better ideas.

"Atelm," barked a familiar voice. "What are you doing?"

My chest tightened with relief. "Thank the Ascendants," I murmured and turned to look at the speaker.

He was striding toward us, and at first I was not sure that it *was* Tren-Lore. Without the clue of his voice, I may not have even recognized him. Dried blood and dirt smeared his face and clothing. His hair looked stiff and his tunic was ripped in several places. He looked utterly exhausted but still whole, I was pleased to note. Despite his appearance, I could feel my body warm under a current of adrenaline.

"She said she wanted to see Draows," the man replied, and scratched at his hair. "We wanted to make sure she was not a Renarn spy."

Tren-Lore smiled. "She is no spy. I will vouch for her. Lara, give Paence to Atelm. He will put her in the corral with the other horses, and Radjik, find my cousin and tell him to come to my tent."

I grinned. It was so comforting to be in Tren-Lore's presence. I untied my bag from the saddle and slipped off Paence. I handed the reins to Atelm, who was now looking slightly embarrassed.

"This way," Tren-Lore said to me, and jerked his head toward a nearby tent. I followed him as he pulled back the flap and led me inside. The instant the flap fell closed behind us, we were in each other's arms. To feel the solid pressure of his body against mine was to discover that my worst fears had not come true. My senses confirmed that he was safe and whole and really there. Most convincing was my sense of smell, for had I truly been imagining all of this, I certainly would not have included the terrible odor that clung to Tren-Lore. He stunk of blood and sweat and horses.

I grinned and kissed him. "You smell horrible."

He laughed. "Nice to see you, too." The shadow of a frown darkened his expression. "What are you doing here, though? Is something wrong?"

I stepped back so that his odor was not so overpowering. Tossing my bag to the ground, I replied, "No. I just wanted to see you."

Our eyes met for a moment, but he looked quickly away. Though he was trying to conceal it, Tren-Lore was exceeding pleased with this explanation for my appearance in camp. I curled my toes in delight.

"If I do stay, you will have to get washed. I hardly recognized you." I licked my thumb and grinning mischievously, rubbed at a spot on his forehead just above his eyebrow.

He pushed my hand away. "Lara! Quit it." His face creased with disgust.

I giggled and shook my finger at him. "I can stand many things, child, but your odor is not one of them. Go and bathe."

He laughed and grabbed a rough towel off a barrel in the corner of the tent. "Did Sophie say something like that to us once?"

"Yes, she did." I held open the tent flap for him. I had been quoting Sophie with fond playfulness, but I was serious in my demand.

Tren-Lore knelt beside his pack and pulled a paper from his grimy pocket. He folded it and stowed it carefully inside. "A letter from Dayr," he explained to me. "Apparently, he and Adewus are not getting along well right now." He continued rummaging through his pack. "Well, this should irritate you properly, Myste"

I stared at him in confusion. "What do you..." The sentence perished before it could be fully uttered. Just at that moment, Myste ducked into the tent. I frowned in a flash of annoyance. The *Rayn* books had never mentioned how disconcerting a Sanysk's foreknowledge could be. I thought briefly that I would have to start listening more carefully.

"Lara!" Myste declared with a wide smile and kissed me on the cheek. The smell of war was not clinging to him. He was as well kept as he had always been. "You are the best thing I have seen all day!" Myste turned to his cousin. "What will irritate me?"

Tren-Lore straightened. He had clean clothes, his towel, and a bar of soap in hand. "The fact that I am going down to the river to have a bath."

"On the contrary, dear cousin, I am delighted. My insistence-"

"Your badgering," Tren-Lore muttered, and Myste snorted indignantly.

"My *insistence* that you bathe was not a personal request. It did not matter to me who convinced you to take a bath, so long as someone did." He sat on Tren-Lore's bedroll and began to push the blankets into a more comfortable formation. "Though I admit it would have been nice to have been the hero that saved the rest of the army from your stench."

Tren-Lore threw his arms in the air, and I wondered how the two men had kept from killing each other during their four years of training.

"The whole army smells just like I do," Tren-Lore replied in exasperation. "While you were bathing, the rest of us were fighting a war."

"Now," Myste continued, entirely ignoring the fact that Tren-Lore had just spoken, "I realize that you might have considered using your formidable scent as a weapon, but honestly, Tren-Lore, how often are the Renarn downwind?"

I pressed my hand to my mouth, but could not help but laugh. Myste grinned wickedly. Tren-Lore gave us a withering look before he strode from the tent. He returned a short while later looking and smelling much more like his old self. I demanded that Myste and Tren-Lore tell me everything that had happened since they had marched from Caladore. By the time they were finished, it was dark and torches lit the tents with a flickering glow. My imagination was a cyclone of grand images. Myste had acted as the primary narrator, and despite his teasing, it was obvious that Myste was proud of his cousin. I had listened with pleasure and awe as Myste had described incidents of bravery and skill.

"I wish I had a story half so good," I sighed.

"You probably do," a deep voice remarked from the entrance.

I jumped and felt Tren-Lore tense beside me.

Myste swore under his breath. "Draows! Do not go sneaking around like that!"

Draows continued looking at me, even as he replied to Myste. "I was not sneaking around. Why are you here, Lara?"

There was something ominous about his tone, and though his expression was as neutral as ever, I flinched under his amber gaze. Was he angry with me? I nervously fingered the hem of my dress. "I...I came to visit," I muttered.

Shadows slid down the long scar on Draows' face. "I see," he said shortly. "Then you will be staying the night. In days such as these, darkness is not our ally. It would be perilous to attempt the trip back to Caladore, even with a whole regiment of soldiers."

I was so happy about the prospect of staying with Tren-Lore that I did not stop to consider the full ramifications of what Draows had said. I was grinning with a force that hurt my cheeks. It did not even occur to me to consider Sophie's reaction to my absence.

"You will wait until light," Draows continued, "and then I shall accompany you home."

Tren-Lore pushed himself to his feet. "I can take her." His face was nearly a reflection of my own.

"*I* will accompany her home," Draows repeated. "I suggest you all have some food. There is a pig roasting over the fire, if such a meal would interest you." With that, he turned and moved silently back out into the night.

Myste pushed himself off Tren-Lore's sleeping mat. Pacing to the tent flap, he looked out after Draows, and then returned his attention to us. "What put him in such a bad mood?" Myste asked in puzzlement. "You would think he had a Pandel down his pants."

Tren-Lore and I laughed, and the tension of Draows' visit dissipated. If he was upset with me, he could tell me all about it in the morning. For now, everything was perfect. "Myste, toss me that pack on the floor." I pointed to the spot beside his feet. Draows' mention of food had reminded me of the provisions I had brought.

Myste grabbed the pack and threw it to me. I scrambled up onto my knees and opened the bag. Tren-Lore and Myste were both leaning forward to see what I had brought. As I pulled the first item from the depths of the pack, Myste made a sound of disgust. "Lara, how could you! Goolsberry jam!"

Tren-Lore took the jar from my grasp and held it with reverence. "You are my favorite person in the whole world."

Myste scoffed. "Are you talking to the jam or Lara?"

"The jam, of course," Tren-Lore replied, and his cousin laughed.

I yanked the jar out of his grasp and punched him hard on the shoulder. "Well, thank you very much, Elesbri! You can consider this a belated gift for your Summer Year."

"Well, Joyous Summer Year to me." Tren-Lore said, absently rubbing the spot where I had hit him and smiling at the jar.

"I will leave you three alone," Myste said, and stepping out of the tent, secured the flap behind him.

* * *

"This was wonderful," Tren-Lore told me. He put the last piece of bread into his mouth and chewed slowly, savoring the taste.

We were sitting on the ground, with a blanket spread beneath us. Our feast of berryroot cordial, goolsberry jam and bread was finished, and I felt tranquil, lulled by food and good company. The tent was warm and the camp around us was finally quiet. It was late now, and I thought that probably only the watchmen still stirred.

"Thank you so much for this," Tren-Lore said softly. "Thank you for coming."

His dark blue eyes met mine, and I smiled at him. The torchlight flickered across his face, and I absorbed every familiar detail. My fingers involuntarily moved to touch his cheeks. I let my hands linger for a moment, and then leaned forward to kiss him. His lips were soft against mine. The kiss was gentle, a fingertip touch on water. He was still looking in my eyes when I drew away.

"I... I-" he stopped suddenly and broke the gaze. "I am so tired," he said, and shifted so that he was lying with his head in my lap. "Every muscle in my body hurts. Draows and I had stopped training, but then yesterday, out of nowhere, he wakes me before dawn to practice."

I frowned. Actual battle seemed like good enough practice to me. Why would Draows suddenly continue with formal lessons? "What were you learning?" I asked.

Tren-Lore rubbed his eyes and grimaced. "Everything. We did everything. I kept asking when we would be finished, and he kept saying that he would tell me when we were done. It got dark, and he still kept pushing me. He did not seem to care that we could not see, or that the wind had picked up, or that neither one of us had eaten since the morning. He just kept barking orders until I fell down."

Soft, disbelieving laughter capered momentarily upon my tongue. "What do you mean?"

Tren-Lore reached over and entwined his fingers with mine, drawing my hand up onto his chest. I could feel his heart beating, could feel the soft rise and fall of his breathing.

"Until I fell down out of exhaustion," Tren-Lore explained. "Draows came and loomed over me and ordered me to stand. I just lay there. I did not even say anything. I do not think I could have. I wanted to. I wanted to get up and tell him that I did not care what he said, that I was not doing any more training today, but I was just too tired and...and it was Draows."

"What did he do?"

"He sort of grunted and told me that practice was done, and then he walked away."

My forehead crinkled in puzzlement. "Why would he do that to you?"

"A test, a lesson, maybe?" Tren-Lore made a frustrated sound. "I do not know. It does not matter. What have you been doing?"

"The same old things," I replied with a fond smile.

He stifled a yawn. "Will you tell me about them?"

I started at the beginning and recounted the washing and the gossip and the biscuits (or rocks as Flock had called them) that I had baked. I told him I had discovered another use for ryalin in the pages of one of the books I was reading, and I complained about the burn I had on my forearm. I told him all this and then lapsed into silence. The tent was filled with the kind of quiet noises that are only discernable to the unoccupied ear: the sound of torches, wind against the canvas walls, Tren-Lore's soft breathing.

I looked down at him. His eyes were closed and a slight smile bent the corners of his lips. The firelight danced along the tips of his raven hair, and his fingers were warm against mine. Tren-Lore, my Tren-Lore. So tired. So brave. How I loved him. Happiness filled my entire body, spilling down my cheeks in the form of tears. I would chance the curse for Tren-Lore.

"I love you," I whispered, though I knew he was sleeping.

To my surprise, his fingers tightened about mine. "I love you, too," he replied.

Chapter Twenty-Five
The Complexities of the Beast

"Get up, Lara," Draows barked, and then let the tent flap drop closed again.

I smiled and snuggled closer to Tren-Lore. Draows was certainly grumpy today, but not even the ire of the formidable Sanysk was enough to spoil my good mood. Tren-Lore loved me and I loved him. This thought was so exhilarating that I had barely slept all night.

"Lara," Draows' voice said warningly. "Move."

Tren-Lore had one of his arms around my waist, and as I slipped from bed, he stirred. "Are you leaving?" he asked without opening his eyes. His tone was still rough with sleep.

"Yes," I replied as I kissed him on the forehead. "Go back to sleep."

His face relaxed, and he shifted so that he was lying on his back. "I love you, Lara."

The words thrilled me, and I smiled brightly. Despite the strife of war and separation, life seemed perfect. "I love you too," I said, relishing the way the words filled my mouth. Glancing one final time at Tren-Lore, I left the tent.

Draows was waiting outside. He wordlessly handed me Paence's reins and leapt upon Quell's back. This silence was more than his usual Sanysk brooding. I climbed into my saddle, sure that Draows was displeased with something. We cantered out of the camp. It was not until we were riding through the rolling grassland that Draows ended his silence.

"Riding out here was foolish. No, it was more than foolish. It was pure idiocy! You could have been killed, Lara!"

I cowered, and it was suddenly hard to swallow. I had never heard Draows raise his voice. He seemed to loom in his saddle, and I was given an abrupt reminder of why such deference was paid to the Sanysk. Beneath the calm and caring was the terrifying power of a deadly warrior. I had become so comfortable in my friendship with Draows that I had forgotten that.

"I could have defended myself," I mumbled, vainly hoping to diffuse some of his wrath.

Draows glared at me, and I was instantly sorry that I had spoken. "This is not going to become a debate about your competence with a blade." His tone had cooled to an icy timber. "I am telling you to question the wisdom of your actions. If the Renarn had captured you, it would have effectively ended this war ... and it would not have ended in our favor. The ransom for your return would have been surrender, and Tren-Lore would have paid it."

A wretched, sinking feeling pulled at my stomach. "I never thought of that."

Draows pulled Quell to a halt and reached over to grab Paence's reins. The mare whinnied in surprise and stopped abruptly. "You *must* start considering such matters. Tren-Lore is going to be a Sanysk, and that means that neither of you has the luxury of walking around in a lovesick stupor. People can be used as weapons just as easily as swords and bows. For Tren-Lore's sake, for your sake... and for mine, try to avoid danger."

This verbal beating stung like the lashing from a whip. I tore my reins away from Draows' grasp and blinked back tears. Lovesick stupor! He could not have chosen a more insulting term if he had tried. I fought against the part of my mind that was shamefully conceding that he was right. My judgment had been clouded. My actions over the past months had been reckless. I was furious with Draows for pointing out a truth I should have recognized on my own.

We said nothing more to each other. The rest of the ride was spent in silence. When we parted ways at the stable door, Draows bid me farewell.

"Good-bye," I said, and felt my anger crumbling under the pressure of my misery. I could not stand Draows being upset with me. "I am sorry." I stared at the ground. If he did not accept my apology I did not want to see the rigidity of his face. "You are right. I was walking around in a lovesick stupor."

"An unfortunate choice of words," Draows said with regret in his voice. "I apologize. I dealt with the situation poorly. Apparently, I am not so calm when facing the mortality of those I care about." Taking a quick step, Draows wrapped his arms around me and held me tightly to him. "I need you to be safe, Lara."

The gesture shocked me and nearly brought tears to my eyes. I would never have presumed to think that Draows cared that much about me, though something deep within me had desperately longed for that to be true. I pressed my cheek against the hard leather of his tunic and hugged him back with all my strength.

When we broke apart, I smiled up at Draows, feeling strangely whole. "Thank you for accompanying me back to Caladore."

Draows nodded formally and his lips bent upward in a small grin. "I suspect that Lady Grim has been awaiting your return. It would be best if you did not prolong that moment any longer."

I gasped and my hands flew to cover my mouth. Sophie! What was Sophie going to say about my absence?

"Ascendants' mercy," I muttered and turning, sprinted across the courtyard.

As my feet pounded up the stairs toward the kitchen, my head rang with sounds and images: Sophie sitting at the main table, her head in her hands, Sophie weeping and sick with fear. This image in itself was hard to bear, but when I added myself to the vision, a dozen horrible endings lunged at me. Sophie was furious. She would not speak to me. The other servants were glaring at me with contempt. Ungrateful. My breath was coming hard as I began the last flight of stairs. Selfish. Four more steps.

Irresponsible. I was before the kitchen door and for a moment I could not bring myself to enter. The dark wood was the only barricade left between myself and the plethora of possibilities. I glanced upward briefly.

"Please," I whispered to whatever Ascendant might be listening and pushed open the door.

There was no one in the antechamber. I wiped my sweating palms on my dress and tried to think. I needed a lie to tell Sophie. Perhaps I could say that- Suddenly the inner door opened. "Sophie!" I yelped and nearly leapt backwards. My heart smashed against my ribs and with irate irrationality, I wondered if Tren-Lore knew just how much trouble he had gotten me into.

"Hello, dear," the kindly woman said as she bustled past me. She stooped to reach something on a bottom shelf and put a hand to her lower back. "Oh," she grunted, "I am too old to bend this way." Selecting a small jar, she stood slowly. "Is the princess feeling better?"

I blinked at her with the wonder of a sleeper awakened by a sudden noise. "The...the princess is fine."

"Good." Sophie smoothed her hair and strode back into the kitchen. "The princess is such a nice girl. I would not like to think of her in any pain."

I followed Sophie and stared in shock at the familiar bustle. There were no accusing faces, no tears, only questions about Nahanni's health. What was going on? I quickly decided that there was nothing to do but play along.

"Yes, the princess is feeling much better." I tried not to make this statement sound like a question. "Is there something I can help with?"

Sophie paused, her finger gently tapping her lip. "Now, let me see. There are vegetables that need to be chopped. Start with that."

"Right," I agreed, nodding in amusement.

Sitting down at the table, I began chopping a carrot into small chunks. Flock glided over and took a seat across from me.

"You are welcome," she said with a devious smile.

I met her gaze with a raised eyebrow. "For what?"

Flock leaned forward onto the table. "Your warm welcome was my doing. I told Sophie that the princess had sent a messenger saying that you were needed for the whole night because she was sick."

My jaw fell open in surprise. Flock had gotten me out of trouble! Flock, who usually went out of her way to make my life difficult, had offered her unsolicited aid!

"You owe me," Flock said in a pert tone. She picked up a carrot and examined it with an expression that struggled to be both uninterested and forcefully disgusted. "You can start by telling me who he is."

"He?" I endeavored to keep my face still and free from expression. Flock was treading too close to the truth.

Dropping the carrot, she reached over and touched the side of my neck. I pulled away and she smirked. "Did a Laowerming bite you, Lara?"

I clapped my hand over the spot she had just touched. I could feel a blush scorching my cheeks. Obviously Tren-Lore's kisses had left their mark. End Tren-Lore! Today was nothing but one challenge after another. My false look of innocence faltered.

"Even without that clue I would have known, and by the way, when you are done with the carrots put on a dress with a high collar." Flock settled back in her chair, virtually swathed in layers of superiority. "It was obvious what was happening. The moment I mentioned that Prince Tren-Lore's regiment was stationed near Caladore, you went into a perfect tizzy, lied to Sophie about a messenger, and finally left, not to return until this morning."

I could barely swallow. Had vapid Flock actually discovered my relationship with Tren-Lore? I should have been more careful!

"I am not as innocent as the old maid Sophie over there," Flock jerked her head toward the kindly woman. "I have sneaked out to visit a few boys myself, and I know what it looks like when I see it. Now, is he a soldier in the prince's regiment? I want details, Lara, details."

The warmth of relief surrounded me as I closed the door on the chilling possibility that Flock knew about my relationship with Tren-Lore. I was more than willing to tell Flock any lie she wanted to hear, so long as she did not know about Tren-Lore. I grabbed another carrot and set about chopping it into unnecessarily small pieces. If I did not have to look at Flock, I would be able to lie more convincingly.

"You are right. He is in the prince's regiment. His name is S-Sarin."

Flock squirmed and rubbed her hands together. "What does he look like?"

"Well..." I began.

All of the carrots had been minced by the time Flock's curiosity had been satisfied. I had lied in such detail that I half felt as though I really did know dear old Sarin – charming soldier, delight of my life. Strangely enough, this cacophony of falsehoods served to quench some of the hostility between me and Flock. There was a definite decline in the number of barbed remarks we exchanged. To my surprise, I was even pleased when Flock invited me to her wedding. She waltzed into the kitchen one sunny morning bearing a basket full of gilded parchment.

"Here you are, Lara," she declared so loudly that anyone not receiving an invitation would realize they were being excluded.

I took the paper from her and turned it over in my hands. Large gold letters spread across the top. *You are cordially invited to witness the Unity of Sir Leffeck and the Lady Flock.* Lady? I looked skeptically at Flock, but she did not seem to notice my expression.

"Bring Sarin with you," she ordered. Flock had been attempting to arrange a meeting for weeks now.

"Oh, well," I held the invitation to my chest, "I am sure he would love to come, if..." If he were real, an internal voice quipped. I smiled. "If he can get leave."

Flock's hands went to her round hips. "Well, see that he does."

"I will," I promised her solemnly and watched as she moved away. I had to admit that Flock had a certain glow about her cheeks and warmth in her smile that had not been there before. It was nice to see people in love.

*   *   *

Flock's wedding was a problem in more ways than one. First, the man who was to accompany me was pretend. Also, it meant that somehow I would have to obtain a present for Flock – something nice enough to settle the score between us.

"Maybe I could bake her something," I suggested to Sophie one evening, a fortnight after the invitations had gone out. I leaned on our windowsill and drank deeply of the sweet summer air.

Sophie chuckled, and I heard her pull back the covers on her bed. "I doubt Flock would appreciate that. I love you very much, dear, but you really are not much of a cook."

"True," I conceded, and pursed my lips. "Maybe I can sew her something." With this genius idea hanging in the air, I left the window open and leapt upon my bed, landing hard on my knees. "I could sew a nice dress with a tight bodice and a plunging neck line."

"Lara!" Sophie scolded, and tried to frown with disapproval. Her frown, however, seemed to be in danger of becoming an amused smile. "You can go down to Cala and buy her something *nice*."

"Flock would think a low-cut dress was nice," I insisted, and leaned over the edge of my bed. I grabbed the book I had dropped on the floor that morning. I had gotten as far as: *Bekwat is commonly found on battlefields*. Hefting the book and righting myself, I settled back in bed. "She would love it. It would accentuate her heaving bo-"

"Read your book," Sophie instructed firmly, tugging her blankets up under her arms.

I pressed the book against my forehead, trying to acquire the answer to my gift dilemma from its pages. Unfortunately, a novel about the healing properties of plants did little to enhance my understanding of what might constitute a nice gift for Flock.

"I have no idea what to get her," I complained.

"You will think of something," Sophie assured me, and closed her eyes, signaling that the conversation was over.

The leather binding creaked as I opened the book and began reading. *Bekwat is commonly found on battlefields*. This reminded me of Tren-Lore, and while I continued to digest the words, I gained no mental nourishment from them. They were meaningless sounds somewhere in the background of my thoughts. I wondered what Tren-Lore was doing at this moment. He was probably somewhere far away, and I was here, lonely and desperate for news or a diversion from the weary pastime of waiting. I sighed, and closing the book, put it back on the floor. I gathered my quilt around my chin and tried to relax, but sleep was a long time coming.

* * *

The stables were quiet and the air heavy with the musky scent of hay and horses. I stood hesitantly in the doorway, peering into the dim depths. It was so unusual to find the stable unattended, even more so because I had arranged for Rathum to be there. In a deferential nod to Draows and good sense, I wanted someone to accompany me on the road to Cala. I had approached the young red-headed man a few days ago and asked him to act in this capacity. He had blushed and stammered that he would be honored. This reaction had made me wince, for I felt sure he now believed I was smitten with him. I shook my head and took a few slow steps into the stables. Sophie was right. I was no better than a wild Barlem woman. "You probably scared him away," I muttered, and then called loudly, "Hello?"

The silence confirmed my solitude. I leaned against the stable wall feeling very irritated about Rathum's absence. The kitchen was busy this week, and it had not been easy finding time away from my duties. A banquet was to be held in two days to celebrate the arrival of Tolrem's troops in Caladore. They would be joining in the battle against Renarn. The ruler of Tolrem, and probably most of his court, would also be in attendance, and thus, a lavish feast needed to be offered.

I exhaled loudly and slid to the ground. I did not enjoy the grueling work in the kitchen, and I was certainly not looking forward to the banquet. It fell on the same day as my Summer Year. The fact that I was going to be eighteen years old was lost in the hail of details bombarding Sophie. She had not even mentioned my impending Summer Year once! I stuck my tongue out at the prospect of suffering through an unacknowledged Summer Year. I dejectedly picked at the golden stalks of straw that littered the floor. I twisted one between my fingers and wondered idly what would happen if I directed my life force toward it.

Nothing, a mean-spirited voice within me replied, nothing at all. A vague feeling of guilt stirred in the pit of my stomach. I had not been practicing at all. Even my attempts at research had been halfhearted. I sensed that Namin, Draows, and my mother would all be disappointed if they knew. I tried to drown the feeling with reason. Keeping abreast of the war situation and making provisions took priority. Yet suddenly, whispering in my ears was a soft familiar voice encased in memory. It was my mother. The vision, which I had forgotten until this moment, returned to me with startling clarity. It had been a dreary autumn day and I had desperately wanted my mother to come and play with me. To my great displeasure, she was turning the earth in our garden. It was an ancient custom she had learned at Telnayis and sprang from a strange old story.

It told of the Lethandree, creatures that slumbered in the form of trees all through the winter, spring, and summer. When the lazy warmth of fall came and the first full moon rose in the sky, the Ascendants shook the mythical forest people from their slumber and granted them one evening of wild merriment. If the fall wind chose to nestle one of the Lethandree seeds in a well-turned garden, great fortune would befall the gardener.

I found this to be a very unsatisfactory tale. The story never said what the fortune might be, and I had never heard of anyone being so fortunate. I had never fully understood why my mother liked it so much, and her observance of the ritual had always puzzled me. "Come and play," I had whined. "Digging is *not* important." She had turned to me then, and her brows had drawn together in a seldom-used expression of disapproval. "Nothing has inherent importance, Lara. We choose that which has priority in our lives." I had frowned back at her, not entirely sure what she meant but certain it was a rebuff.

I realized I still did not understand her message. Scowling, I dropped the piece of straw and pushed myself up. Tren-Lore was hugely important to me, as well as to the entire country. Any simple acts of Healing I might accomplish paled in comparison to Tren-Lore's feats. It did not matter anyway. I exhaled loudly in a display of growing irritation. I had been sitting so long that my feet and legs burned with a painful tingling sensation. Stamping hard on the floor, I tried to return my body to the waking world. As well, I tried to block my mother's message and concentrate on the present. Emotions were threatening to overcome me. I felt cornered by guilt, anger, and sadness. How was it possible to miss my mother and be angry with her all in the same instant?

In an effort to end my disquiet, I took Paence from the stable and left unescorted for Cala. The solid presence of my faithful horse and the hot sun on my head made it easier to muster a defensive calm. I occupied my mind with thoughts of gifts that might be appropriate for Flock and other unimportant issues, until a break in Paence's gait garnered my attention. She seemed to be limping. I drew rein immediately and climbed from the saddle.

"What is wrong?" I asked, gently patting her smooth coat and stooping so I could examine her legs.

No reply was forthcoming, but the answer became clear at once. I crouched on the rough earth of the road and bent Paence's leg so that the bottom of her foot was revealed. The mare's shoe had come loose, and several small stones had lodged under the loose piece of metal. I grimaced in sympathy. It must have been very painful for her.

"Poor Paence," I crooned, and looked about trying to decide what to do about the problem.

It certainly would have been nice if Rathum had been there. In fact, it would have been nice if anyone who knew the slightest thing about shoeing horses had been there. I anxiously bit at my lip. What was I going to do? Why did something like this have to happen just when I had decided to ignore Draows' advice and travel alone? I only needed Renarn soldiers to leap out of the tall grass and the mess would be complete. Adrenaline burned through my body, but I ignored the sensation and tried to think. I needed to help Paence and get back to Caladore. My eyes fell upon a small stick lying amidst the gravel. A plan started to form in my mind. I could use the stick to gently pry the stones from under her shoe.

"All right," I decided, taking some comfort in the company of my own voice. "It is as good a plan as any."

Taking a deep breath and feeling very grateful that I was not about to attempt this on the churlish Storm Wing, I slowly slid the stick between Paence's hoof and her shoe. The mare whickered but did not try to jerk her foot from my grasp. I worked slowly and carefully, not wanting to cause Paence further pain. One by one I removed the obstructions, until the final stone fell free. I smiled in triumph!

It was then that I heard the gritty sound of footfalls. Riders were approaching. My muscles tensed, and I froze as though I were a small animal frightened by a predator. Looking over my shoulder, I could discern five riders. My hand moved to my dagger as I stood up. If I was about to face an enemy, I was going to do it on my feet. The riders were closer now, and the slightest inkling of recognition stirred within me. Could this really be who I thought it was? The first rider reined in before me and leapt from his horse. He gestured to the rest of his party, and they immediately surrounded us.

Yolis smiled at me, bright sunlight dancing on his golden hair and sliding down his lean form. "Good day, Lara."

I felt my heartbeat quicken. There was something in the way he said my name that was disconcerting. It was as though he savored the feel of it in his mouth. I sensed my cheeks flushing and I curtsied to hide the irrational blush. I straightened to face him again.

"Good morning, Sire." I said politely, and despite myself, noticed the definition of muscle beneath his tunic.

"Can I be of some assistance?" Yolis asked, his hand abscntly scratching his horse's ear.

"Ah, um, well, probably." I cursed myself inwardly. Why could I have not thought of something a little more eloquent? "My horse's shoe is loose."

"I see," he said, and in two long strides he was kneeling before Paence.

I sank to the ground next to him. He smelled wonderful, and suddenly I found myself wondering what it would be like to kiss him, to lean against him and feel his arms around me. The idea stabbed at my mind and I felt instantly guilty. Inwardly reprimanding myself for such treasonous musings, I got to my feet and stepped back, leaving a respectable distance between us. I was painfully aware of the guards surrounding us.

Yolis examined Paence's shoe and then stood, absently rubbing his jaw. "I would not suggest riding any further, but your horse will be just fine if she is led." He patted Paence on the neck. "As you are currently at a midpoint between the castle and Cala, one direction does not hold favor over the other, save that if you go to Cala your journey would not be a solitary one."

My eyes widened in surprise. I had not expected such a generous offer, and it would certainly make my trip a safer and more pleasant one. Yet, I could not help but wonder what Tren-Lore would say. I discarded this thought. I was not going to put myself in danger just because of an old grudge.

I smiled at Yolis. "I would be delighted to travel to Cala with you." I realized suddenly how presumptuous this sounded and tried to soften the statement. "If... I mean, if I would not be too much trouble."

"Birds of a feather." Yolis shrugged and handed me Paence's reins.

I took them from him, but my face must have betrayed the confusion I felt over his remark.

Yolis grinned at me wolfishly. "I am nothing but trouble, Lara. We might as well travel together." Catching his own horse's bridle, he began to walk alongside me. His guards maintained a wide perimeter around us, although I felt sure that they were listening to every word we said. "So," Yolis continued, "what is it that set you on the road to Cala?"

Hesitantly at first, and then with growing ease, I told him of Flock, her wedding, and the gift conundrum. Yolis nodded gravely and then proceeded to suggest a number of highly inappropriate, but extremely amusing options. Our conversation grew effortlessly from there. It was easy to forget my prior perception of Yolis. Under the brilliance of his company, the dark shadows of the past slipped away. I was not in the company of Tren-Lore's hated brother, Kelladyn's scandalous lover, or even the High Prince of Caladore. I was with a charming gentleman whose wicked sense of humor made me laugh and whose voice made my blood hot with the sheer pleasure of life. Cala was in sight when I realized that I had not even asked Yolis why he had come to town. Our trip had evaporated as though it was water in the presence of the hot summer day.

"Your Majesty has not yet told me what has brought him to Cala," I said, squinting as I glanced at his sun-bathed figure.

Yolis raised one eyebrow. "And I will not tell you if you keep calling me Your Majesty. Yolis will do quite nicely."

I smiled at him and reworded my question so that it included his name. I was rewarded with an answering grin and the explanation that he had come to procure a sword that had been made for him.

"There," he said, pointing to a building just discernable from our position on the very edge of Cala. "That is our destination. The man who made the weapon for me can easily repair your mount's shoe."

The town was a beehive of activity, and the farther we moved inside, the more crowded the streets became. Everyone was single-minded in their movements, and the narrow streets pitted will against will.

"Out of the way! Out!" a gnarled old woman screeched, and I quickly moved aside and into the path of several other people.

One of the men swore at me, and I parted my lips to return the gesture when Yolis reached over and caught my hand. His fingers intertwined with mine and I swallowed hard, trying to keep Tren-Lore firmly in the front of my mind. Yolis pulled me to his side and marched confidently through the hive of people. The crowd flew from his path, eagerly making way for their future king. His guards and I followed in the wake created by Yolis' importance. We soon reached the structure Yolis had indicated earlier. As soon as we had emerged from the crowd, I withdrew my hand from his, but the gentle brush of his fingers slipping over my skin made me burn with guilt and desire.

The building before us – if it could be called a building – was no more than a roof supported by four huge posts in the ground. Beneath the ceiling was a giant table, scarred with scorch marks and cluttered with iron, tools, and weapons. A large metal block stood to the left of that, and a forge glowed ominously in one corner. A burly man was using long tongs to pull a scarlet piece of steel from the coals. He stopped when he saw us, and returned the metal to its blistering abode.

Wiping at his forehead with a filthy piece of cloth, he nodded to Yolis. "Your Highness," he rumbled.

I tried to imagine the blacksmith bowing, but found it was akin to envisioning a thick tree engaged in the same act.

"I suppose you have come for your sword," the blacksmith surmised. He lumbered over to the table and pulled a long box from the mess. The blacksmith pried open the lid and withdrew a sheathed sword. He handed it to Yolis, hilt first.

The handsome young man took the sword and slowly drew it from its scabbard. It hissed softly and Yolis held it before him, testing the weight. It was a beautiful weapon, the blade burnished silver and the hilt looped with black ivy. It reminded me vaguely of my Healer's ring, and I unconsciously touched it through the soft cloth of my dress.

"What do you think, Lara?" Yolis asked, turning the sword so the glow from the forge bled down the length of the blade.

I held out my hand for the weapon. "May I?" I asked.

Yolis paused for a moment and regarded me steadily. His pleasant countenance did not change, but the subtle break in the rhythm of the conversation made me wonder if perhaps I had surprised him. I rather hoped so.

"Of course," he conceded, and gave me the weapon.

The hilt was cool against my palm and the familiar pull on my arm was innately comforting. It reminded me of younger days when Tren-Lore and I had trained together. The sword was too heavy for me to use with speed, but it was probably perfect for Yolis' strength.

"The blade width is good," I said thoughtfully, "and the grip on the hilt should be improved by the ivy inlay." Holding it straight up, I studied it closely. "The joints are seamless and the weight and balance are excellent." I handed it back to Yolis, whose lips were bent in a mysterious smile.

"Impressive," he murmured, and took the proffered blade. "Excellent work, Lect." He slid the sword back into its sheath. "I have more work for you. The mare's shoe is loose. You have until noon." Yolis tossed the brawny man a gold coin.

With viper reflexes, Lect snatched the money out of the air. "My apprentice will have it finished for you," he grunted and began to rummage through the materials on his table.

My eyebrows rose and a crooked grin tugged at my mouth. I was certainly in the right company if I wanted things done quickly and without protest. Yolis turned to me and offered his arm. I took it, still slightly bemused by his subtle show of power over the blacksmith.

"That means," Yolis remarked, "that you and I have less than half a day in which to complete the monumental task of finding a nice gift for your friend."

I laughed. "We had best begin. Half a day may not be enough."

The shops of Cala were filled with things that would have charmed Flock, but my attention was so ensnared by Yolis' delightful conversation that I touched smooth silks and smelled sweet lotions without even pausing to consider them as gifts. It was not until we were looking at the wares of a young shopkeeper that my concentration was returned to the merchandise before me.

I gasped in pleasure when I saw it, and stared as though enchanted by a Sorcerer. It was a bracelet made of a strange, inky black stone. I picked it up timidly, afraid of breaking it. As I held it, the colors within shifted and changed so that smoky blues and purples tinted the stone.

"You need not worry about breaking it. It is made of feena penent, more commonly known as dragon's blood."

I turned slowly to Yolis. "What do you mean, dragon's blood?"

He leaned against the counter beside me. "I mean that it is made of dragon's blood. Feena penent is a very rare stone created the instant dragon's blood mingles with water."

I regarded the bracelet with wonder. I had never read about anything like this. Tren-Lore would be so shocked when I told him that–

"If you like, I will buy it for you." Yolis' words incinerated my thought. I looked up at him sharply and he continued, "Of course, I will want something in return."

I laughed unsteadily. "And what, pray tell, would a lowly servant have that the Prince of Caladore would desire?"

"A kiss," he said blatantly, and drawing the bracelet away from my grasp, he toyed with it. "What do you think? Is this bobble worth a kiss?"

By the Ascendant of Eternity! By every Ascendant there ever was! I could not believe he was standing there so casually proposing this. He had seen me and Tren-Lore in the corridor. He knew about us, and yet he was asking to kiss me! What audacity, what nerve! I should have told him just what I thought of his offer and stormed out of the shop. I should have, but somehow I could not move. My feet were planted and my head was nodding.

"Is that a yes?"

"Yes," I replied, scarcely able to speak.

Yolis straightened his posture, and with a quick step he was standing before me. Taking my chin in his hand, he turned my face up. Yolis was smiling slightly, and his eyes were such an overwhelming blue. My knees felt weak at his mere proximity. I closed my eyes and waited in anticipation for the feel of his hand on the small of my back. I waited breathlessly for the kiss I had imagined when I saw him earlier that morning. My eyes snapped open in surprise as his lips brushed my cheek. I must have looked shocked, for he chuckled.

"What were you expecting, Lara?" he asked teasingly. "Any more of a kiss and it would not have been a fair trade."

"Fair?" I echoed, my mind unable to pull together coherent words of my own.

He absently touched the end of my hair as it tumbled over my shoulder. "Indeed," he said in a hushed tone. "The only thing I could give you to make such an exchange fair would be my heart, but I doubt you would want that."

"Why?"

"Because, my dear, you already have my brother's. What would you do with another?"

With that, he turned and went to purchase the bracelet.

Chapter Twenty-Six
Fever

Yolis and I arrived back at Caladore late in the afternoon. I had my bracelet on my wrist and clever remarks upon my tongue. Yolis was laughing when we stopped in the middle of the courtyard and he leapt from his saddle.

"Thank you for the lovely day in Cala," he said, offering his hand.

I took it, though I did not need help dismounting, and slipped from my saddle. "The pleasure was entirely mine," I replied and smiled brightly up at Yolis, feeling very pleased at the eloquent response I had managed.

His gaze was not there to meet mine. He was looking past me, and his grip on my hand tightened so slightly that I doubted my own senses. Turning slowly, I discovered what, or rather who, it was Yolis was staring at. Tren-Lore was striding toward us, his sword swinging at his side. His controlled expression made shivers run down my spine.

"Tren-Lore," I gasped silently, and shook my hand free of Yolis'. "What are you doing home?" I called to him and pressed my eyes shut as I realized how terrible that sounded. It echoed painfully in my thoughts, nearly the hideous equivalent of 'you were never supposed to find out about this'. My mind staggered as the repercussions of my behavior that afternoon slammed into my consciousness.

Stomach churning, I forced myself to stay calm. I had done nothing wrong. Yolis had helped me when I was in need, and then we had enjoyed each other's company. There was nothing wrong in that. Tren-Lore was before us now, but his countenance was so dark that I did not dare embrace him.

Yolis nodded cordially. "Good to see you home, Tren-Lore. To what do we owe the pleasure of your company?"

"Lara's eighth Summer Year," he replied tersely, not sparing Yolis a glance. He directed his full attention toward me. "We have to talk."

Yolis stuck his hands in his pockets and smiled at his brother. "Problems, Tren-Lore?"

It felt as though the tension was pulling the air taunt. I was caught by invisible sinews, unable to move or draw breath. What was Yolis thinking? It was clear by Tren-Lore's absolute lack of expression that if he was pushed much farther, the situation would end in violence. I had witnessed such a confrontation before, and it had nearly ended in Tren-Lore's death. Suddenly everything seemed dark and fear snapped the bonds that were holding me still. Reason would have informed me that if a fight had occurred, it would have ended with polar results. I was deaf to rational thought, however, and just wanted to escape.

"Come on," I urged Tren-Lore, taking hold of his upper arm and pulling him away from Yolis.

We walked in silence up to the secret room and my clamorous mental debate filled the void. It had not been evil to ride to Cala with Yolis. It had been the sensible thing to do ... the safe thing. Yet the feelings that had burned within me suggested nothing short of treachery. Reaching the landing, we entered the secret room. It was dim and the door closed behind us with a resounding thud. I hurried toward the table and taking up flint and tinder in hands that shook slightly, I set about lighting the candles in the room.

"It really is not as bad as it seems," I began, but both Tren-Lore's expression and the twisting of my own stomach told me that it was. Setting one candle down, I moved to the ones sitting near the hearth. I needed to banish the oppressive darkness. "I was going down to Cala to get a wedding present for Flock. She is finally getting married to Leffeck." I paused, giving him time to comment on this event. Tren-Lore ignored the opportunity for a friendly response. As my shaking hands lit the candles on the table, shadows seemed to chew at the walls like dragon's teeth. Inhaling deeply I continued, "I got them a charm to hang in their house. It has the symbol for the Ascendant of Eternity carved into it. Flock will hate it." I laughed weakly, but Tren-Lore's expression did not soften. I cleared my throat. "So anyway, I was riding to Cala by myself, but Paence's shoe was loose and I had to stop. Yolis was on his way to Cala too, and so when we met on the road, I thought it would be safer if I traveled with him."

"And then you spent the day together?" Tren-Lore asked in icy tones. He threw open the shutters, and the candles I had just lit were snuffed out by a cold breeze. Daylight flooded every corner of the chamber.

I made an indistinct noise of consent and began straightening a long forgotten pile of books.

Tren-Lore stepped forward and caught my wrist. "Lara, stand still and talk to..." His fingers had closed around the cold stone of the feena penent, and as his voice faltered, he looked down at my wrist. "Where did you get this?" He sounded as though he did not really want to know.

I felt like crying. "Yolis bought it for me." I tried to make my voice casual, as though the gift meant nothing to me.

Tren-Lore's face was no longer unreadable. He looked furious. "You let him buy you jewelry? What else did you let him do?"

"Nothing," I muttered. I tore my hand from his grasp. Turning from him, I took a few quick steps to the window. Guilt oozed over me until I could scarcely breathe through the slime of my own actions. Tren-Lore was quiet, so quiet that I glanced over my shoulder to ensure he was still in the room. He was standing completely still, staring at my back. He looked ill.

How could I have allowed Yolis to kiss me? Worse yet, how could I have hoped for more than the chaste brush on the cheek? And why, of all the people of Caladore, had it been Yolis who had sparked such feelings within me? Tears stung my eyes. At that moment, I despised myself as much as I had despised the evil duke who had betrayed Lord Rayn. I curled my toes and turned, hoping to lie smoothly and put an end to his suspicions. The moment my eyes fell upon him, any deceptions I might have created were lost. Tren-Lore looked dazed. His black hair was a rumpled mess, and he was losing the battle to keep his face expressionless. His hands were clenched, and his blue eyes were dark with pain.

"Oh, Tren-Lore!" I cried, and ran to him, throwing myself against his chest. "He only kissed me on the cheek. I let him, but if I could, I would take it back! I am sorry! I am so sorry!"

Tren-Lore's arms remained at his sides. "I have to go," he said, and stepped away from me. Turning, he walked from the room.

My knees buckled, and I crumpled to the floor. I pulled my knees to my chest and sobbed. I had hurt Tren-Lore. I felt so alone. Despite the sunlight tumbling through the open window, an intense darkness seemed to have filled the secret room. It was the blackness of memories, of another life long ago when stories were just stories, heroes were found only in fiction, and monsters stalked you in the darkness. I tore the bracelet from my wrist and shoved it into my pocket, later to be hidden in the deepest depths of my trunk. My body shook, and I cried until I had exhausted myself and only the pain of regret remained to torture my mind. Deciding that there was no point in lying on the cold stone floor, I heaved myself up with one hand and then staggered to my feet. Upon my return to the kitchen, I was greeted with a great clamor of concern.

"She is back!" Thriana shouted. "No need for a search party."

"Perhaps we should have a party," I heard Flock mutter sarcastically. "Hooray! Lara has returned!" Flock straightened her bodice with a sharp little yank and then crossed her arms, her bottom lip protruding in a very slight pout.

"Lara, we had given you up for dead!" one of the women declared, and was quickly hushed by another servant who looked meaningfully at Sophie.

The kindly woman's expression had relaxed in a look of relief and she came through the crowd of women to hug me. The embrace was comforting, and I vainly wished that I could lay my head in Sophie's lap and tell her all my problems. As we drew apart, her face crinkled with concern.

"Have you been crying, dear?" she asked.

Rubbing at my eyes in irritation, I sniffed to prolong the time I had to concoct a lie. "When I was riding to Cala, Paence threw a shoe. It...it was very trying." Not a very good deception, but it would have to do.

"Well, I can imagine!" Sophie agreed and put a comforting arm around my shoulder. "Traveling is such tricky business. You never know when disaster will strike! What you need is some food and some hot cordial to put everything right."

Unfortunately, food and berryroot cordial did not have the power to restore my emotions, but they did settle my slightly shaky muscles. As I was washing up my dishes, Flock sidled over and took up a cloth as though intending to dry the bowl I had just cleaned. "So...what really happened?" she asked without making any move toward the bowl. Apparently, the cloth was just a prop to enhance her performance as a helpful member of the kitchen.

I scrubbed vigorously at my mug. If only I could have taken the rough cloth to my conscience and scoured it clean as easily. "I had a fight with Sarin."

"Is that all?" Flock exclaimed and dropped the towel back on the counter. "Leffeck and I fight all the time. It is nothing to worry about. Besides, this Sarin of yours does not sound like he is Ascendant-sent or anything. He is always away, he never buys you anything, and everyone knows that lowbred men are uglier than a Barlem's behind. I say leave him. What do you need him for anyway?"

I swallowed hard, but did not reply.

She rolled her eyes at me and snapped, "Oh, Lara, stop being so dramatic." With that, she flounced away and loudly declared that she was leaving for the night and could not possibly do one more stitch of work.

Tears were blurring my vision again and I fumbled blindly for the drying cloth. Flock was wrong. I did need Tren-Lore. I needed him as my champion and I needed the realm in which he walked. That night I tossed and turned, pulling and kicking at my blankets until they were a twisted serpent in my bed. I wept silently, and my pillow felt damp and uncomfortable. I turned it over with violent force but the other side was soon wet as well. I briefly considered interrupting Sophie's soft snoring, but immediately dismissed the idea. Even Sophie, with her dread of traveling, would not believe that a lost horseshoe had caused me such extended grief.

I was exhausted the next morning and my heart ached, but at least all my tears had been spent. As I whisked eggs for breakfast, I tried to think of what to do about the mess I had created with Tren-Lore. My mind was muddled and I felt slightly dizzy. I could not hold thoughts in my head, and the pool of yellow muck that I was stirring made my stomach churn. There was a light knock on the inner door and everyone paused to look at the entrance. A blond head peeked around the corner, and Nahanni smiled cheerfully at everyone.

"Good morning," she sang merrily. "Lady Grim, would you mind too terribly much if I stole Lara for the day? I am having a new dress made, and I could use her help."

Sophie chuckled. "Not at all, dear. You have a nice day," the elderly woman said as she slipped a loaf of bread into the oven.

Thankful to be relieved of my job with the nauseating eggs, I quickly fled the kitchen.

"I thought you might need to talk," Nahanni told me softly as we walked towards the garden.

For an instant I wanted to crush the beautiful young woman in a hug. It was such a relief to be able to talk to someone at last. "How much do you know?" I asked.

Nahanni pulled the outer door open and stepped out into the sunny day. I followed, shielding my eyes from the light. It seemed abnormally bright, and my head started to ache immediately.

"Well," she began, the wind twisting her golden hair. "I know that you and Yolis went to Cala together and he bought you something and kissed you."

"Only on the cheek," I said quickly.

Nahanni ran her hand along the tops of the tall flowers we were passing. Their sweet scent made my stomach churn. "If it had been anyone else besides Yolis, it would not be so bad," the princess sighed, "but you know Tren-Lore and Yolis."

I nodded glumly. I pointed to a bench a few paces away. "Can we sit? I am not feeling very well. I slept terribly last night."

Nahanni and I sat next to one another in the quiet garden, and the princess leaned her head against my shoulder. She took my hand in one of her own. "I am sure everything will turn out, Lara. Tren-Lore loves you too much to stay mad for long."

And I love him, I thought. It was as if that day in Cala had caused a strange, temporary severance between my heart and my body. "Did he mention me at all last night?"

Nahanni laughed and sat up straight. "Oh yes, you caused quite a little stir last night. Tren-Lore came storming into the main room in the royal chambers where Yolis, Father and I were playing Questkon, and he grabbed Yolis by the collar, and without saying anything, punched him right in the face. A huge fight ensued, sending all the servants into hysterics, and making Father furious. They even broke a chair." She told me with wide eyes. "A nice one. The whole thing was really very worrisome. They usually hate each other much more subtly."

I knew Nahanni was trying to be funny, and I attempted a smile, but could not find the energy. "Is Tren-Lore all right?"

Nahanni pulled her legs up onto the bench and crossed them under her. She exhaled gustily. "Tren-Lore is fine. Nothing worse than a black eye, but Father has sent a message to Draows to tell him what Tren-Lore did. I cannot image that the League will really approve. Yolis, though... Father had to summon doctors last night. They say he has a broken arm and a concussion. It was really terrible. I never thought Tren-Lore could do something like that, but I guess he *is* almost a Sanysk."

I leaned forward and let my head drop between my knees. A Sanysk. Nahanni spoke as if the title blotted out the person Tren-Lore had been before. It seemed that she thought of him as a deadly warrior rather than her brother. I felt slightly concerned. I knew two stories about the Sanysk: the frightening one my mother had told me, and the glorious one that Tren-Lore had related. He had decided to create a fate that led him down the path of the latter tale. I knew that if Tren-Lore put his will to something, nothing would deter him for his goal. There was no cause to worry, I told myself, and pushed the emotion away.

Nahanni rubbed my back. "Do you want me to talk to him for you? Or arrange a meeting?"

"A meeting," I mumbled. "That would be good." Maybe Tren-Lore would be more receptive to an apology now that he was calm. I sat up and looked at Nahanni. The blood rushing from my head made my vision black for an instant.

"Very well," Nahanni agreed, reaching over to tuck my hair behind my ears. She smiled fondly at my worried countenance. "It really will turn out, Lara. The Ascendant of Unity would have it no other way. I will tell Tren-Lore to come and talk to you at the celebration tomorrow night."

* * *

Sophie sighed deeply and pulled on my sleeve. "Come on, dear. Up you get. There are preparations to be completed."

"Why?" I muttered, and settled more deeply into my chair by the hearth. My head ached horribly and my body felt weak. "Why does it matter? If the king of Tolrem wants a feast, he can come up here and cook it himself."

"Lara!" Sophie exclaimed, and she raised her finger warningly. "I do not want to hear you talking like that! Now, come and help us."

I pursed my lips in a sour expression. Why should I help any of them? They had all forgotten my Summer Year, and obviously did not care about me at all. I pushed up my sleeves, seeking to battle the heat that surrounded me. It must have been all the turmoil from the wretched preparations, although no one else seemed bothered by it.

"End this all," I grumbled, and watched as Sophie's eyes grew wide.

She leaned in close to me, and her hand gripped my arm just above the elbow. "Young lady," she whispered between clenched teeth. "I have had enough of this attitude. You get out of this chair and do your job before I turn you over my knee and spank you."

This flash of claws from the benevolent Sophie was enough to finally rouse me. I was assigned the loathsome job of peeling potatoes, but I could not seem to find the energy to hurry the task. I assumed that the stress of my fight with Tren-Lore was sapping my strength.

When evening arrived at last, I threw myself onto my bed and savored the feel of my cool pillow against my scalding cheek.

Sophie leaned into the room. "You had best head down to the party. They..." She stopped speaking and frowned. "You are looking a little flushed, dear. Are you feeling well? Perhaps you should stay in bed tonight." She started to come forward with her hand raised so she could feel my forehead.

I scrambled off the bed. "I am fine, Sophie," I insisted, keeping a safe distance between the well-meaning woman and myself. I needed to meet Tren-Lore tonight. I could not afford to spend the night in bed, no matter how badly I felt. I tried my best to smile brightly. "It has just been a long day and I was tired, but now I am fine, even ready to serve." I slipped past her and hurried from our sleeping chamber.

I made my way the garden, gulping the crisp night air like a runner quenching her thirst. I was so hot and breathless that it took a few moments before I could appreciate the beauty of my surroundings. The garden was lit in the soft light of torches and stars. Minstrels were playing in the background, and pairs were dancing. Other highborn people were feasting at tables festooned with elaborate platters of food. King Kiris and a man who vaguely resembled him were standing slightly apart from the party, obviously discussing something of importance.

I sat down on the step, not heeding the disapproving glare one of the other servants gave me. I was too hot and my eyes hurt. I caught sight of Tren-Lore coming towards me. He was wearing a fantastic red tunic with a gray dragon stitched on the front. A silver crown glinted in his raven hair. I suddenly felt too tired for this confrontation, too weak. I needed to leave. I staggered to my feet, catching hold of the side of the rough stone wall for support. Black suddenly filled my view. I held the wall, not daring to move until my vision returned.

"Where are you going?" Tren-Lore demanded in confusion. "I thought you wanted to talk to me."

I stared at him in uncertainty. The air was so hot. The colors of the dancing couples smeared. My legs felt weak. I clutched at the wall, its scent of dusty age filling my nostrils. I could not remember why I was here. The only thing that remained clear in the boiling water of my mind was that Tren-Lore was angry with me.

"You are mad at me!" I cried. "Why would I want to talk to you? I am sorry and that is all I can say."

He threw his hands up in the air. "You do not think I have the right to be angry with you? You betrayed me, and the final knife in my back was that it was Yolis you chose to do it with!"

"It was only a kiss on the cheek. You..." Another wave of dizziness hit me. I stood, wavering for a moment, my forehead pressed against the stone, silently imploring the Ascendant of Rocks for the gift of strength. With some effort, I continued, though the wall received the brute force of my voice and the words were muffled. "You are overreacting."

"Tren-Lore has always been the master of overreaction. I suspect that if there had been an Ascendant for such a skill, my dear brother would have been quite devout."

I slowly lifted my head and found Yolis standing a few paces away. Tren-Lore was saying something to him but the words were too faint to understand. It was so hard to breathe. Suddenly, Yolis was stepping toward me, a splinted hand extended. "Would you care to dance, Lara?" His visage shifted and split, writhed apart like two snakes that had been sewn together in the middle.

I whimpered in fear and staggered away from him. My mind was enclosed in the shadowy world of the Disanima. Everything seemed dim, and I half imagined that I truly had inhaled one of the terrible creatures. It was inside me, gnawing flesh into fiery wounds. I was unbearably hot. I collapsed against Tren-Lore, sobbing. His arms were immediately around me and lifting me up. I laid my hot cheek against the cold cloth of his tunic and closed my eyes to the swirling world before me.

"Get Lady Grim," Tren-Lore's voice ordered, "and a doctor."

I struggled to breathe as the blackness returned in rolling waves that swelled with each ragged intake of air. They crashed into me, forcing darkness into my nose and mouth, filling my eyes. Tren-Lore carried me, bounding up the stairs two at a time. I was vaguely aware that the kitchen looked unusual with colorful decorations and a sign that read, *Joyous Summer Year, Lara.* Before I could reconcile the transformation, my mother's face was leaning over me and her soft hand was on my head.

"Easy, child. Everything will be all right."

Again, something was not as it should be. The voice sounded like Sophie. I tried to speak, but as I parted my lips, dark fingers slipped into my mouth and pushed down my throat, stealing my air and my sight.

* * *

I could hear people talking. The sounds were clear and untainted by the dementia of nightmares. I struggled to open my eyes and ensure that I was not still caught in the depths of hallucination. When I regained my vision, the images were blurry at first, but soon cleared. Tren-Lore and Namin were sitting by the window on two chairs that had been brought from the kitchen. My throat loosened with relief, and tears moistened my eyes. It was not a dream.

"How else was I going to explain my sudden devotion to Lara?" Tren-Lore said, and rubbed at his jaw. "I had to tell my father, or I would have been forced to march out with the rest of the troops."

Tell his father? Tell his father about what?

Namin patted his knee. "I always suspected you were a nice boy. When we were in Karsalin, Lara always spoke of you with the highest regard, although she would never admit that she liked you."

Tren-Lore cleared his throat, and then laughed. "She may never admit that she likes me again. I cannot thank you enough for coming. I know it is not an easy trip from Karsalin."

Namin chuckled and leaned back in her chair. "Elvin Fever is not easy to treat unless you can channel life energy. When I got Sophie's message, I even dashed out the door without my cloak. Garidet, my second youngest daughter, had to chase me down and give me a firm scolding about wearing proper attire. Cloak or no, I would have made the trip a hundred times if I could have helped Lara."

It would have taken a messenger on a swift horse at least five days to get to Karsalin, and the same amount of time for Namin to return. How long had I been ill?

"Tr-" His name stuck in my dry throat. I swallowed hard before trying again. "Tren-Lore." The utterance was so weak that it did not sound like me at all.

He turned immediately and was kneeling at my side in one swift movement. Gathering my hands in his, he bowed his head. "Oh, Lara, thank the Ascendants."

"Lara!" Namin declared in pleasure. Coming to my bed, she leaned slightly forward and placed her hand on my forehead. "Your fever seems to have broken. I will get you something to drink, and then it would be best if you rested." I nodded solemnly, and her rosy cheeks creased with a smile. "Later, I want to have a nice long talk." She glanced briefly at Tren-Lore, and then still wearing a conspiratorial grin, left the room and closed the door quietly behind her.

Tren-Lore and I sat in silence for several moments. When I looked up at him, there were tears in my eyes. "I am so sorry, Tren-Lore. I do not know how you can ever forgive me."

He hugged me, his arms shaking slightly. "I can forgive you because I love you. I love you too much to waste any more time being angry. You do not know how close you came to dying. And when I thought the last words I would ever say to you were born in anger... His voice caught in his throat. "Every time you cried out I thought how stupid I had been. Lara, I want to cherish every moment I have with you."

I began sobbing. He murmured gently to me until I had calmed. When my tears had finally stopped, Tren-Lore straightened. I could see that his eyes were red and encircled with dark shadows. His raven hair was more disorderly than usual, and he appeared incredibly tired.

"You should get some sleep," I told him.

He shook his head. "I am fine. I can stay and talk until Namin comes back."

I smiled vaguely. I was glad he was staying. His presence was comforting, and I had many questions. He answered all of them, explaining that I had been sick for fifteen days, that I had missed the surprise party Sophie had arranged for me, that Namin arrived three days ago, and especially the shock that had occurred when everyone learned of our relationship.

"I had to tell. There was no other way to explain this sudden devotion to you." He grinned suddenly, a wolfish expression erasing some of the weariness from his face. "I wish you could have been there. Sophie was trying to keep herself busy by washing dishes, and I was sitting at the big table in the main kitchen. It was the morning after the Fever struck you, and neither one of us had slept all night. She said something to me about going back to the royal chambers, and I replied that I would probably be staying in the kitchen for a while because I was in love with you. She turned around very slowly until she was facing me, murmured her congratulations and fainted."

I laughed feebly. Sleep was beginning to reclaim my mind, and I closed my eyes, listening to Tren-Lore with a smile upon my cracked lips.

"I told my father about us, and I think he is close to making an official declaration." Tren-Lore lowered his voice in an imitation of his father's. "Henceforth, Prince Tren-Lore will be referred to as 'The Bad Son'. I think he was really counting on the fact that I would marry Areama." Tren-Lore was trying to sound casually amused about the whole situation, but I knew his father's disapproval hurt him.

I tried to think of some way to comfort him, but slumber pulled the thoughts from my mind and tucked them away for later.

"I think I am falling asleep," I mumbled. "Will you stay with me?"

He kissed my hand and held it to his cheek. "Always, my love, always."

* * *

When I awoke next, it was evening. I found that Tren-Lore had pulled a chair next to my bed, but had fallen asleep. His face was relaxed and his expression was free of worry. He looked too youthful to be involved in a war or to be training as a Sanysk. He reminded me of the young boy I had chased dreams with all those years ago. Sophie was leaning over him, pulling a blanket up around his shoulders.

"Poor dear," she murmured. She placed her hand briefly on his stubbly cheek and smiled at him. I painfully turned my head to watch as Sophie walked stiffly over to Namin and sat next to her by the window. "I do not think he has slept since Lara fell ill."

"He is very devoted to her," Namin said. Her words were soft, spoken through a smile.

Sophie sighed and ran her hand over her hair. "I thought their friendship ended after we went to Karsalin, but I was obviously wrong. I suppose it is my fault now that they love each other. The friendship that I turned a blind eye to has certainly developed into something more. I cannot bring myself to feel badly, though. Lara needed someone to take her mind off her grief, and Tren-Lore was one of the loneliest children I had ever met. He pushed everyone away, but for some reason, when Lara arrived..." Sophie's voice was obscured by the fond laughter that danced up her throat. She leaned her elbow against the windowsill and smiled. "I can still remember the two of them sitting by the fire the first night Lara came to Caladore. Her legs did not even touch the ground and she seemed like such a frail little thing, but she succeeded where everyone else had failed. Tren-Lore confided in her and sought her company. Without her friendship, I do not know what would have become of him. "

A breeze moved gently in the room. The sweet scent of summer and the bizarre nature of Sophie's remark worked together to remove the haze of sleep. I had never suspected that Sophie knew about our friendship, but it did explain why she had given me so much freedom. Still, for all that she knew, she was obviously confused about the nature of our relationship. I had certainly needed Tren-Lore... he had never needed me.

"She is like her mother," Namin said. "Kara had steel in her spirit, and so does Lara."

I shook my head and closed my eyes again. Neither one of them knew what they were talking about.

Chapter Twenty-Seven
Of Stories and Heroes

T en days later, I had enough strength to prop myself up on a number of pillows and carry on a conversation without falling asleep halfway through. Nahanni came with a beautiful bunch of flowers and an endless supply of cheerful stories. Sophie and I discussed the fact that I was now in my eighth Summer Year, and as such, was entitled to a room of my own. The thought of being all alone in a chamber made a dull panic rise in my stomach. I promptly told her that I was not interested in a room of my own, and Sophie tried not to look immensely relieved. Namin and I talked extensively about Tren-Lore and indulged ourselves in the delightful task of analyzing his every word and unconscious gesture. Unfortunately, even Flock found time to come and visit.

"It must have been terrible!" Flock said, her brown eyes wide. "Imagine laying here in bed knowing that you were missing my wedding!"

"Oh yes," I replied and fought back a smirk, "that was all I could think of between hallucinations."

Flock's eyes narrowed, and she tilted her head to one side, pressing her lips together in a mean little simper. "Do you know, Lara, that I heard the wildest rumor about you? Leffeck told me that you and Prince Tren-Lore were involved. Can you imagine?" She laughed. "I told Leffeck at once that it could not possibly be true, because you simply do not have the breeding or the looks."

I folded my hands over my quilt and met her gaze. "Actually, Prince Tren-Lore and I are involved."

Flock's giggles stopped abruptly and her mouth gaped, forming a noiseless void of shock.

"We are in love," I told her calmly. Watching Flock struggling with this news, I suddenly regretted that Tren-Lore had had all the fun of informing people about our long-kept secret. The bewildered expression on Flock's round face was possibly the best thing I had seen all year.

Rivaling the perverse joy I took from beating Flock's smug attitude to a pulp was the more sincere pleasure I had from Tren-Lore's visits. He spent much of his time with me, and it was to my great sadness when he was forced to return to the war. Still, I did not have much time to lament, for soon I was well enough to be out of bed and helping with the kitchen duties. Namin took her leave of us, but not before Sophie and I embraced her tearfully and thanked her profusely for coming.

"Keep practicing your Healing," Namin told to me as we hugged, "and take care of Sophie. I do not think she is feeling entirely well."

With that, she was gone and I was left with two tasks, both of which worried me. Channeling never went well, and the idea that Sophie was sick shook the very foundation upon which I stood. I watched her carefully as we worked together and noticed that she moved more slowly than she had before. Her hair was nearly entirely gray now, and she looked tired all the time. I consulted my books and drew upon my knowledge of illness and herb lore. Unfortunately, I could find no cure for old age.

"Sophie," I began one autumn afternoon as we were sitting at the table peeling potatoes. I was not comfortable broaching the subject of her health. Telling Sophie what to do was an extremely uncomfortable role reversal. "I think you need to get more sleep and let me take more responsibility in the kitchen – or let someone else." I added, thinking that I really was not qualified or inclined to increase my workload. "I can tell that you are tired lately, and-"

"Child," Sophie interrupted and reached out to squeeze my hand, "I know that I am not as young as I used to be, and my bones are weary of the Caladore winters but I am fine. I will try to get more sleep." She smiled fondly at me. "But I can still do my duties. Thank you for your concern."

I nodded, and was about to reply when a cry from Thriana interrupted me. "What in the name of the Ascendants? Sophie, come see this and tell me what you make of it."

Thriana was looking out the window, and at her call nearly half of the servants, who were all apparently now answering to Sophie's name, came rushing forward to see what she was so surprised about. I sat at the table for a few moments and watched as the group twittered by the window. I was deeply curious, but tried to focus on my task. I was not going to become a gossipmonger and press my nose to the window in the hopes of gleaning a new piece of information to pander.

"Lara," called Sophie's voice from the crowd, "you should come and have a look at this."

Dropping the potato I was peeling, I leapt so eagerly to my feet that I nearly knocked over my chair. I could feel myself blush, and I quickly glanced about to make sure no one had seen my display of enthusiasm. Luckily, no one had. Moving slowly to the window, as though this would regain some of my lost dignity, I slipped through the crowd of women and gained a position from which I could see what was happening outside. The aged stone around the window framed a very strange sight indeed. A group of Caladore soldiers had just entered the inner courtyard. Within this circle of blue and gray stood two figures. Both were wearing cloaks that made them barely distinguishable from the cobblestones. My body was suddenly filled with a rush of tingling excitement. Those were Sanysk cloaks, and unless I was mistaken, the large black war-horse that was rearing and trying to get away from the soldier that held his reins, was none other than Storm Wing.

"I will be back!" I told Sophie as I turned and pushed past the women. I dashed out the door and took the stairs as quickly as I could without falling. Tren-Lore was home! I had no idea why he had returned, but it did not matter! I was gasping for air by the time I reached the outer exit and was forced to stop and sit down for a moment. My legs shook, and while my heart cried for me to hurry, my body was not yet strong enough to comply. After several deep breaths, I opened the door and rushed out into the chill autumn day. I sped over the collage of brightly colored leaves that covered the path and ran into the depths of the garden. I smiled widely at the dragon fountain as I passed. I was tempted to shout to it that Tren-Lore had returned. The herald proved to be unnecessary. No more than a few paces from the statue, I met Tren-Lore and his group. I stumbled to a halt, my arms extending to balance myself as my feet skidded on the gravel trail.

Tren-Lore's group had been reduced in numbers. Only three remained from the original party I had seen from the window. Tren-Lore stood in the middle, his left leg cast from ankle to knee. An instant of thought was devoted to professional scrutiny, but finding the binding to be well done, I flung aside all concerns and abandoned myself to joy. Not only was Tren-Lore here, but Myste and Draows as well! They were standing on either side of Tren-Lore to support him as he walked. All three men wore similar smiles. I cried in happiness and rushed forward, hugging them wildly and nearly knocking Tren-Lore over.

"You look as though you have spent a week being chased by Barlems!" I declared fondly. I was overjoyed that my boys were home!

"What? This?" Myste glanced ruefully down at his filthy clothes. "No," he replied jovially and grinned at his cousin. Tren-Lore was already scowling. "This is just a bit of hole grime."

"It was a pit, Myste!" Tren-Lore snapped in irritation. "Stop calling it a hole. You make us sound like we got trapped in a dip in the road."

I covered my mouth to hide my mirth from the glowering Tren-Lore.

Even Draows was trying not to smile, but the clean line of his scar was disturbed and his amber eyes hinted at amusement. "It was a trap laid by the Renarn," Draows informed me. "Tren-Lore and his men had the misfortune of stumbling upon it."

"It is an excellent story," Myste chortled.

"And I shall leave you to tell it. King Kiris has asked for my presence." Draows eased himself from Tren-Lore's side. The young man swayed for a moment, but regained his balance quickly. Draows put a gentle hand on my shoulder and squeezed lightly. His silver bands glinted in the afternoon sun. "It gladdens my heart to see you again, Lara."

I smiled at him, feeling as though my world was whole again. With Tren-Lore, Myste, and Draows all safely home, I was embowered in happiness and safety. "It is wonderful to see you, too," I told him.

He nodded and returned my smile. Then turning, he strode down the path, moving with a silent ease that avoided even the crackle of leaves or the scratch of gravel.

"I smell," Myste declared and scratched vigorously at his hair. "So do you, Tren-Lore. We need a bath, something to eat, and then perhaps some narkanytch roasted over the fire in the secret room. Then we can tell Lara about our lovely adventure with the hole."

A short while later, we were all sitting around a cheerful fire in the secret room. We had blankets piled around us to ward off the drafts that seeped through the chinks in the stone walls. Tren-Lore and I were gleefully roasting narkanytch, but Myste refused, saying the flames were too high and the narkanytch would only be burned.

"Draows had been acting strangely the whole week," Tren-Lore told me. He scraped the charred remains of a narkanytch from his roasting stick and made a fresh attempt. "Every morning he had been getting me up before dawn and making me practice until I collapsed."

"Like he did before," I said through a mouthful of half-burnt narkanytch. "I remember you telling me about that when I came to visit you." The sticky candy muffled my words.

"Right." Tren-Lore nodded and absently let his narkanytch dip too close to the flames. Myste reached forward and grabbed the stick from his cousin before the narkanytch could be burnt. Myste set about roasting it with more care, and Tren-Lore continued speaking. "So by the fourth day of that, he and I were not on very good terms. The scouting party we had sent out the night before had not come back, and I wanted to take some soldiers to find out why. Draows told me not to. We ended up having a ... a disagreement."

"Beware the wrath of a Sanysk," Myste muttered without taking his eyes from his task. "It was more than a disagreement."

I pulled my blanket up around my shoulders and frowned. That did not seem very much like Draows. Then again, neither did pushing Tren-Lore to the point of utter exhaustion.

"I took Myste and a few of the other men to track the scouting party." Tren-Lore stopped speaking and groaned. Leaning back on the floor, he pressed the palms of his hands into his eyes. "And that is when I led us into the Renarn trap."

I struggled to visualize this incident. In the stories I had heard and read, traps were usually in the form of ambushes or false allies. "So...it was just a big hole in the ground?"

Myste grinned at Tren-Lore. "More of a pit, really. It was covered over by long sticks hidden with dirt and leaves. They broke the moment you stepped on them. Tren-Lore fell through first, and we all landed on top of him, which I suspect is how he broke his leg. The rest of us were fine, aside from being trapped in a hole for a day." Myste removed his narkanytch from the heat and looked at its golden brown surface in satisfaction. "But it all ended happily. Draows found us before the Renarn did, we were granted a leave, and Tren-Lore..." He stopped suddenly, his narkanytch forgotten. Myste looked as if he had just realized he was about to set foot in dangerous territory. He glanced at his cousin. "Can we – you tell her now?" Myste asked.

I looked back and forth between the two men. The acrid smell of burnt narkanytch flowed down my throat and settled in a heavy lump at the bottom of my stomach. What did they know that they were keeping from me? Had something happened that I was not supposed to know about?

"What is going on?" I nervously demanded.

Tren-Lore was grinning widely, his cheeks creased. "I was going to tell you later," Tren-Lore said, "but now is as good a time as any. Remember when Draows made me do all those practices, and then ordered me not to go looking for the scouting party? Well, he did that because he wanted me to think for myself instead of taking commands from him. He *wanted* me to say no to him. Remember the part of the Sanysk doctrine that says a Sanysk is not bound to fight for any country or person unless he decides to do so?"

I inclined my head slightly.

"Well, being able to live that rule - to choose who and when to fight - is the last step in becoming a Sanysk." His gaze met mine, and my heart quickened. "All that is left is for Draows to present me before the League."

Surprise and excitement jolted my body until it forgot about even breathing. The best my lungs could summon was a gasp. My fingers tightened around the soft material of the blanket. Tren-Lore had done it! He was going to be a Sanysk! I gazed at him in wonder. I was proud of him, so overwhelmed to know him and be loved by him. Tears began to sting my eyes. I floundered for something to say, some suitable way to express my feelings and congratulate him properly.

"Umm..." I could feel the warmth of tears against the skin of my cheeks. "Umm, so... I guess you owe that hole a lot."

If I could have, I would have snatched the word from the air and shoved them back in my mouth. Could I have thought of anything more stupid to say? Before I could truly begin berating myself, Tren-Lore grabbed me around the waist and dug his fingers into my ribs.

"It was a *pit*, Lara!" He laughed as he tickled me unmercifully.

I fell back to the floor, shrieking and helpless against the overwhelming mirth.

* * *

The fire had grown weary and fallen to sleep in its bed of glowing coals. Myste had retired for the evening, and only Tren-Lore and I were left awake in the secret room. We sat side by side, neither wanting the night to end.

"Will you tell me more about the battle across Venst?" I asked, and poked at the slumbering fire with a twig.

"I think it is your turn." He shifted his broken leg so that he could sit facing me. "Weave me a tale of grand adventures, and make sure the hero is a charming young woman named Lara. Try and work in a dragon if you can."

I tossed the small piece of wood into the fire. "A weaver must have thread to work with. None of my stories are worth telling, and I certainly have not come across any dragons lately."

Tren-Lore frowned and shook his head. "Too bad. There are just not enough dragons around these days." He stared up at the languid play of shadows upon the walls. "Do you remember when we went looking for dragon's eggs down by the river?"

I giggled and hugged my knees to my chest. "Myste was not pleased that we were dragging him out in the snow. Do you remember trying to nail that hideous roof onto the fort?"

Tren-Lore grinned and nodded. We continued to reminisce, our talk ranging from the first time we met to our first kiss. We laughed about 'paddling' out to the fort, about double Barlems, and the trials of learning to read and swordfight. Tren-Lore touched upon my Healing, but it was his forthcoming induction into the League of Sanysk that I discussed with enthusiasm. Finally, both of us seemed sated with memories and we sat contentedly in silence. I breathed deeply, taking the perfect moment within myself and holding it there for an instant.

"Lara?" Tren-Lore asked softly.

"Yes?"

"Thank you."

The corners of my lips bent upward in a gentle smile, and with two fingers, I reached out and traced the lines of the silver bands he would soon be wearing. Leaning forward, I kissed him, slowly and softly. He tasted of adventure and magic, of contentment and strength, of stories and heroes.

Chapter Twenty-Eight
The Course to Darkness

I stared out the window in the secret room and sighed. My stomach felt empty. This was my own fault, as I had only picked at the disgusting-looking fish that had been served for dinner. Behind me, I heard the door open. I smiled. Tren-Lore, Myste and a good game of Questkon would be enough to take my mind off my self-inflicted hunger. I turned to find only Myste entering.

"Where is Tren-Lore?" I asked as Myste tossed the Questkon box on the table and pulled out a rickety chair.

"Well, hello to you, too," Myste replied and straddled a chair. "Tren-Lore is not here yet because Uncle Kiris wanted to talk with him."

This news caused a heavy sensation of foreboding to settle around me. "Was it about us? About me and Tren-Lore, I mean."

Myste shook the lid off the Questkon box and dumped the contents on the table. "Yes," he conceded and shifted through the mess of cards. "But it is nothing to worry about. He and Tren-Lore have had several discussions about this, and they always end with Tren-Lore being his old stubborn self. There is nothing his father could say that would make him change his mind about you."

I nodded reluctantly, not unlike a small child who wants to believe what they are being told, but who is desperately afraid it might not be true. I had probably made such a gesture to my mother as she had sat patiently at my bedside explaining that Pandels and Laowermings could not eat me because they were not real.

"Now," Myste said, shuffling the Chaos cards with an air of proficiency, "I suppose you want to be Vrya." Setting the cards down, he tossed me the piece. "I think I am going to be Mortex."

I heard the door open and once again turned toward the sound. Tren-Lore was just entering, and my hand unconsciously tightened around the game piece. The metal bit at my palm, but I hardly noticed the pain. Something was wrong. Tren-Lore was pale and he looked stunned, as though he had just received a blow to the head. I looked quickly for any blood or sign of injury, but found nothing. It was not a physical wound, my heart told me. Tren-Lore's father had said something horrible to him.

"What happened?" My voice was unsteady.

Myste glanced behind him, and seeing Tren-Lore, he leapt up immediately. "Here, do you need to sit down?"

Tren-Lore did not answer, but limped forward and sank into the chair. He swallowed hard before looking at me. "My father said..." It seemed as though he was choking on the words. He stopped, and I could see the muscles in his jaw clenching. "My father said that if you and I do not end our relationship, he will prevent me from becoming a Sanysk. He says he will not have me marrying...marrying a servant. He has already talked to Draows and Adewus."

I had not realized that my hand had opened until the metal figure I had been gripping clanged against the flagstones. The sound seemed to hang in the air. Tren-Lore had not just said that. It could not be possible.

"How can he do that?" Myste exclaimed, anger flushing his cheeks.

"Draows fought against my father's decision, but Adewus agreed." Tren-Lore spoke with a hatred I had only heard when he talked about his brother. "Adewus is head of the League because he embodies the Sanysk in their most deadly form. He does not care about people, and he sees love as a hindrance and a weakness. He has made a pact with my father and will keep me from the League unless I do my father's bidding."

Myste was twisting his ring about his finger as he paced back and forth. "What if you talk to Adewus and make him understand your side?"

"No," Tren-Lore replied, "Adewus has sworn an oath to my father. As a Sanysk, he is bound to his word."

"So, what if you lie to Adewus and your father?" Myste asked frantically. "Tell them you will stop seeing Lara. Once you are a Sanysk, they hold no power over you."

Tren-Lore's gaze met mine, and I struggled to keep my face calm. We would solve this somehow. I wanted to be confident for him, but as he reached out and took my hand I could not help but let fear crease my forehead.

"Adewus can block me at all passes. He can bar me from the League now, and he could strip my bands later if I digressed from Father's plan. Draows warned me about Adewus. He is capable of fabricating stories to justify any decision he deems necessary for the preservation of the League." Tren-Lore drew a tattered breath, the labored inhalation of someone in great pain. His grip tightened around my hand. "I said I choose you over being a Sanysk."

I reeled under the impact of this decision. It struck me with the violence of an axe, the words driving deep to split my spirit into fissures of anguish and shameful relief. Part of me wanted to protest, to scream that it was not right, that it could not end like this. Tren-Lore had to become a Sanysk. Yet if I protested, I risked bringing about another ending that would summon forth darkness and take me from his side forever. My chest was constricting but I tried to hold back the tears. I could not let this happen. Tren-Lore was meant to be a Sanysk, and I could not keep him from that. I would not be able to live with myself if I did.

I staggered to my feet. I could not bear to sit by Tren-Lore and think these thoughts. As our fingers slipped apart, I wondered if this would be the last time I ever felt the touch of his skin. It seemed incomprehensible.

"I have to go," I told him abruptly. I needed to escape before I lost control of the grief welling up inside me. I could not think clearly about the decision while Tren-Lore sat next to me. I fled the secret room. Tren-Lore called after me, but I did not stop.

When I arrived in the kitchen, I ran into my room and slammed the door on the curious, watching servants. I crawled into bed and pulled the covers over my head, creating a false night. It was a dark womb of thoughts that pressed at me from all sides. I could not end my relationship with Tren-Lore, yet I could not let Tren-Lore sacrifice everything he had worked for. He was destined to be a Sanysk, it was his future and I could not stand in his way. I felt as though I were gagging on grief and could not catch my breath. But you love him, a voice within me pleaded, and he loves you. Is that not enough? These desperate words met with a reply that was sure as steel. It is enough. My love of Tren-Lore would give me the strength to do what was best for him. I would sever our ties so he could become a Sanysk, just as I had always known he would be - just as he was supposed to be. I loved him too much to let his story end any other way.

I heard the door open with a harsh, creaking sound, followed by Sophie's soft shuffle as she approached my bed. "What happened?" she asked.

I tore back the blankets. "It is over," I wailed, and anguish ripped through my body, tearing me apart from the inside out. Sophie bent and hugged me tightly, and I mumbled words she did not hear. "If something bad happens, there will be no one to save me."

"Shhh." Sophie soothed and gathered me onto her lap. She rocked me slowly and pressed her cheek to my hair. "Sophie is here."

Even though I was far too grown up to cuddle in Sophie's lap, her arms were strong about me and she held me close until I fell asleep. I awoke early the next morning, and for a moment could not understand why I was laying in bed fully clothed. The memories returned quickly, accompanied by almost overwhelming pain.

The floor was cold on my feet as I slipped quietly from bed. Sophie was still sleeping. I silently changed out of my wrinkled gown and donned one of my older dresses. Its color had always reminded me of dust. In desperate need of something to occupy my mind, I padded through the still kitchen and out into the antechamber. I set about organizing the already organized cupboards, lining up all the pots and jars according to their size. So it was when Tren-Lore found me, struggling to relocate a large barrel to its newly designated spot.

"I think we should talk," he said quietly.

I gave up on moving the barrel and turned fearfully towards him. My heart was beating painfully against my rib cage. I was afraid I would not be able to say what I needed to say, yet I was also sick with the thought that I might be able to force the words out.

Tears were beginning to blur my vision. "You have to be a Sanysk." Grief was burning down my cheeks and stealing my air. "I will not let you choose me. We should not see each other anymore."

Tren-Lore shifted on his crutches and reached out a comforting arm. I could see the white scar of our pact upon his palm. Morian penent, I thought. How I wished things were as simple as they had once been. I lurched forward and hugged him. Feeling the strength and the warmth of his body against mine was almost more than I could bear.

"Lara, I am going to tell Draows that he does not need to present me to the League."

Tren-Lore's resolve panicked me. I could not let him destroy his life like that. With great effort, I forced myself to step away from him. Wiping my eyes with my sleeve, I tried to calm my breathing. It was important that Tren-Lore know I was serious and not just babbling hysterically.

"I will not let you give up being a Sanysk. It is part of who you are, and it is what you love. Even if you did give it up, you would never be happy because...you...it is like..." I was struggling to find a way to explain my thoughts. "Part of you would be missing, and we could never be whole. I would hate myself for taking it from you, and you would hate me for taking it."

Tren-Lore was shaking his head. "No." He uttered the word with power. "I would not hate you. I could not possibly. I love you, Lara. I love you so much it hurts, and I will not let you do this."

I looked up at him defiantly and met his dark blue gaze. I had chosen my path and would not be deterred. For Tren-Lore, I would return to darkness.

"Listen to me," I told him with a calm granted only by the deadening shock of what I was about to say. "I love you, but it has to come to an end. I am sorry."

My stomach was churning and I turned before I could see the impact my words had upon him. I walked stiffly into the kitchen and firmly shut the door. Moving as though caught in a terrible dream that would not let my limbs work properly, I made my way slowly to the counter and took up the washing basin. I sunk to my knees and vomited into the basin until my stomach was as empty and aching as my heart.

* * *

Over the next week, I was lost in a swamp of emotion. The stench of my rotting confidence was sometimes too much to stand and I would often stumble and sink deep into squelching despair. Had I really done the right thing? My decision was certainly not bringing happiness to either one of us, and it certainly was not helping my work in the kitchen.

I was sure that I had broken more dishes than anyone in the history of Caladore, and I could not even laugh at Sophie's outraged shriek, "What has happened to my cupboards? Why is everything arranged like this?"

Despite my irritating reorganization of her cupboards, the kindly woman was my champion. Sophie protected me from the barrage of callers that were suddenly demanding an audience with me. Nahanni, Draows, Myste and Tren-Lore all came knocking upon the kitchen door. I could not bear to face any of them. I had hurt Tren-Lore, and for that I felt too guilty and ashamed to see the other people who loved him. Also, I knew that if my way was blocked by any significant verbal barrier, my resolve would crumble and I would turn from the chosen path. To my great relief, these visits abated after Myste returned to the war, and

Nahanni comforted herself by writing me notes of love and support. I did not know what became of Draows or Tren-Lore.

Time passed with agonizing slowness, and I often wondered how I had previously failed to notice how long the days actually were. To avoid pining over Tren-Lore, I devoted every waking moment to my work. Day after day I rose with the sun, worked until blisters formed on my hands and my back ached, and then fell into a restless sleep that held only dreams of Tren-Lore. On some nights, even the most restless of sleeps eluded me. I would lean against the window and stare out into a blackness that seemed to have become part of me.

There, in those silent evening hours, the darkness shared a secret with me. Only the moon and I beheld the stealthy travelers that rode up to the gate. The gleam of nighttime's orb seemed to be absorbed by the travelers' cloaks but moonlight illuminated their flag. It was emblazoned with a silver S that had two lines running horizontally through the middle of the letter. I knew the mark well. It lay on the title page of every *Rayn* book. It was the sign of the Sanysk. I remembered Tren-Lore saying the only step left in his training was to be presented before the League. This was undoubtedly the League of the Sanysk, and Tren-Lore was about to join their ranks!

A force stronger than reason propelled me from the window and out of the room. I needed to witness Tren-Lore's induction into the League. To be absent would be akin to reading a book but omitting the ending. I grabbed my cloak but left my shoes, as I could move more quietly without them. This proved to be a mistake, for as soon as I exited the castle, I was painfully reminded that winter was swiftly approaching and the ground was freezing cold. Wincing with each step, I passed swiftly down the garden paths and under the dragon fountain. The garden was cloaked in eerie shadow, but I gave no thought to the frightening figures of imagination that could have been conjured in such a setting.

Entirely ignoring the possibility of Pandels, Disanima, or rogue Renarn assassins, I headed to the edge of the inner wall. I had expected guards at the door, but there were none. I breathed a sigh of relief and smiled for the first time in weeks. That was a stroke of Ascendant-sent luck, or perhaps Tren-Lore knew the League approached and had dismissed the door wardens. Either way, I was relieved. I was not sure how I was going to account for my presence. Sleep-walking was about as good as my extremely bad explanations got. Shoving against the door, I opened it just enough to see into the outer courtyard.

The group of Sanysk was already inside the courtyard. They stood in a line, their cloaks hiding both their bands and their swords. Standing across from them was Draows, garbed in a similar fashion, and Tren-Lore, wearing no cloak or sword. He was without his crutches and bearing weight on his leg. At the sight of him, my blood surged and the pain in my feet was forgotten. I crouched low in the shadows and watched with bated breath. I wondered if Tren-Lore was nervous. I would have been shaking if I had stood in his place, but then, I was *not* Tren-Lore. He was presenting a calm demeanor that did not hint at either positive or negative feelings.

"Honored members of the League," Draows said in a low rumble, "I present the next man of our brotherhood, Tren-Lore of Caladore."

A tall man with broad shoulders stepped forward. "I am Adewus, Head of the League, and for this evening our many voices are united in my body."

Adewus! Was this the man who had caused me so much anguish? He was not as I had pictured him – not terrible enough, far too human.

"We accept your judgment, honored brother Draows, and under the watch of the Ascendants who formed our League, I name this boy one of our own. He shall fight with a skill that brings death." As Adewus spoke, another Sanysk bent low and presented the hilt of Tren-Lore's sword to him. Tren-Lore reached out and took it. "He shall hear all. He shall see all. He shall move in silence." Draows wrapped Tren-Lore's Sanysk cloak about the young man's shoulders. "And lastly," Adewus pronounced with such authority that even though he was not speaking to me I felt inclined to obey him, "he shall be a man of honor and keep our doctrine true in all that he does. Welcome, Tren-Lore, honored brother of the Sanysk." Adewus drew silver bands from under his cloak and clasped them around Tren-Lore's throat.

The moment he withdrew his hands, the bands flared with silver light and a collective murmur rippled through the men. In any other group, it would have been a loud gasp of surprise. Adewus tore back the wraps of his cloak to find that his bands were also glowing. In a blur of movement, swords had been drawn.

Adewus growled, "There is a Sorcerer or Healer nearby."

My hand pressed hard against my chest, and I felt my ring burning hot against my skin. I had been a fool to think that silence would be enough to hide my presence. The cold in my feet suddenly spread throughout my body. If I were discovered, what would happen to Tren-Lore?

"Stay, Adewus," Draows said as I rose and stepped away from the door. "Calm yourselves brothers. There is no danger to us. Caladore is merely the home of Healers."

I chanced one more glance and saw swords being sheathed. Everyone had turned their attention to Draows, everyone except Tren-Lore, that is. He was looking in my direction but his expression had not changed. I did not know if he saw me or just sensed my presence. Slipping away from the door, I put some distance between the Sanysk and myself.

"Morian penent, Tren-Lore," I whispered.

I felt better the next day. My sacrifice seemed validated. Tren-Lore was a Sanysk, and I took pleasure from that. It lessened the weight of my pain, but the days seemed just as long and the nights just as restless. I was even happy to hear that the Hemlizar royal family was returning for another visit. All Caladore hoped that this visit would end in an alliance. I only hoped the labor would hinder thought.

The Ascendants granted me this wish, though it seemed more like a mean-spirited joke than the fulfillment of my desires. Two days before a banquet was scheduled to occur, Sophie became ill. With time such a scarce commodity, I ran from my increased duties in the kitchen to Sophie's bedside.

* * *

"Oh, ladies," Thriana remarked from the window, her voice rich with conspiratorial pleasure. "I think Prince Tren-Lore and Princess Areama have rekindled their romance!"

"What!" I nearly shouted and dropped the loaf of bread I had been taking from the oven. Leaving it on the floor, I dashed to the window. I scrubbed hard at the frosty windowpane and stared down at the snowy courtyard. Tren-Lore and Areama were walking arm in arm, and though I could not really tell from my height, it seemed as if they were deep in conversation.

Thriana's face suddenly contorted in guilt. "Sorry, Lara," she said softly. "I had forgotten that you and the prince had...were..."

I turned sharply. "We have too much to do to waste our time staring out the window." This was said not out of irritation with Thriana, but as a way of purging some of the anger that had filled me.

Thriana muttered something under her breath and stomped back to her stew. I did not care what she had said, I was too furious with myself. I snatched the bread off the floor and told myself that I had no right to be mad at him. He could walk with Areama, he could talk with Areama, and he could even fall in love with Areama if he wanted to. He no longer had ties to me. I slammed the bread onto the counter and dragged my sleeve over my cheeks. The dryness was only temporary, for more tears escaped from my eyes.

That night's dinner was quiet, with no mentioned of the bread that had been dropped on the floor. When I brought Sophie her platter of food she chuckled with pleasure. The joyful noise quickly mutated into a hacking cough that shook her body.

"When did you start coughing?" I demanded as I set the tray on the table beside her bed. "Let me listen to your breathing."

"Mercy, child," Sophie cried. "It is just a cough, and I am feeling much better... maybe just a little chilled, though. Be a good girl and fetch me another blanket."

I did as she had asked, but insisted on listening to her breathing. What I heard left me feeling uneasy. Her inhalations were heavy and accompanied by crackling noises – a possible sign of an infection within the lungs.

I withdrew from Sophie and swallowed hard. I was afraid. "Get some sleep." I tried to pitch my voice so that it sounded calm and soothing, like Namin's or my mother's.

Sophie nodded and closed her eyes. I wanted to turn and run. I did not feel able to deal with the situation, yet I had no choice. I would have to face Sophie's illness and continue on by myself. I pressed my fingers to my temples. Oh, I wished there was someone to help me.

Chapter Twenty-Nine
Unlikely Confidants

I pushed my hair back from my sweating forehead and struggled to tip the large kettle into a bowl resting on the floor by Sophie's bed. All day long I had been steeping a mixture of dried leaves in boiling water. The steam billowing forth from this concoction was intended to help Sophie's cough. I hissed in pain as my wrist brushed against the hot metal. I continued to pour and was surrounded by a woody scent that reminded me of summer.

"Be careful, dear." Sophie's voice escaped between her cracked lips before a cough beat her back into silence. The elderly woman whimpered slightly and pressed her hand hard against her chest. Her face was flushed with fever.

I pushed down the spring of emotions that was welling inside me. Indulging in tears was a leisure I did not have. Sophie needed me to be strong. Self-doubt tainted my every thought. If only there was someone else, anyone else to fight this battle for me. I would have felt sure of victory. Now, I dreaded defeat.

"No need to worry," I told her as cheerfully as I could.

I was grateful her eyes were closed, for my expression betrayed my confident voice. I sat on the edge of her bed, and reaching across her, took the glass that was sitting on the small table. It was full of murky water that had been mixed with the bark of a cheren tree. It would dull

Sophie's pain and quell her fever. I slipped my hand under Sophie's head and helped her to take a few sips from the glass. Once again, I had to fight to maintain my calm. It shook me to the core to see Sophie in such a vulnerable state.

"Try and sleep. I have to go serve at the banquet, but I will be back before you know it. Thriana will look in on you."

Sophie made no reply. She was already slumbering. Even in sleep, her breathing was too fast. For every breath I took, she took two. The medicine will make her better, I reassured myself, just give it time. Namin had often said this to me. I had always been anxious for remedies to take effect immediately. Wearily, I stripped off my dress and pulled one of my nicer cream gowns. I caught a glimpse of myself in the mirror and had to stop and stare. The image gave me something of a start. My face no longer had the roundness of childhood, and there was something in my gaze that was less innocent. I knew this change must have occurred some years ago, but I had never really noticed. I sighed and ran my hand over my hair. The past months of grief, loneliness, and worry had certainly not enhanced my appearance. The color had leached from my skin, and dark circles were clearly visible under my eyes. I grabbed a comb and pulled it through my hair. Somehow, tearing ruthlessly through the tangles did not hurt as much as when I had been younger. I tied my locks back into a loose bun and then swept silently from the room.

By the time I arrived in the banquet hall, it was filled with people. Many were seated, while others were milling between the long tables, talking in a rather exaggerated manner to one another. There were so many voices that the multiple conversations melded into a constant hum of noise. My eyes swept over the finely dressed crowd and were drawn, as though by some unmerciful magic, to the head table where Tren-Lore was lounging.

The prince was drinking from a jewel-encrusted goblet while surveying the crowd with a dark expression. His silver bands shone softly about his neck. He was clothed in a fine blue tunic that probably made his eyes look incredible. I harshly reprimanded myself for thinking such thoughts. I forced myself to look at Areama. She was sitting next to Tren-Lore, a beautiful and excruciating reminder that I would never again sit by his side. I scowled at her just as one of the older servants shoved a large platter of buttered bread into my hands.

"Take this," she grunted. "I need to get some air."

I paused only a moment to compose myself, and then began to serve. I tried to concentrate on my job, but between thoughts of Tren-Lore and worries about Sophie, I found this difficult. My arms ached by the time I had finished serving the bread, and yet there was still more to be done. I was immediately summoned to refill the empty ale tankards.

"Girl," a burly man at another table shouted, "we need some of that, too!"

His companions rumbled agreement and pounded their fists on the table. I nodded and hurried toward them, gritting my teeth. It was too bad that nobility had so much to do with birthright and so little to do with manners. After topping off their tankards, I was summoned yet again by a different party. It was some time later before there was a cessation in the demands for ale.

Sighing, I leaned against one of the doors that led into an adjoining chamber. A cool breeze from the room beyond caressed my ankles. Closing my eyes, I tried to quiet my mind. I would serve one more round of drinks, and then I would return to Sophie. It was hard to be so close to Tren-Lore and yet so separated from him. My fingers absently found the scar on my palm and traced the slightly raised line. When I opened my eyes, I jumped in surprise, for standing before me was Tren-Lore! Only a Sanysk could have moved so quietly. He was no longer wearing his cast, so with an easy movement, he took another step forward and settled his hands about my waist. My heartbeat quickened and I felt my cheeks glowing with a blush of pleasure. He looked down at me, and my eyes met his unfathomable blue gaze. It was enough to make my knees weak.

"Lara." His tone was deep and his voice low.

The sound of my name on his tongue was like an enchantment. My resolve crumbled. He pushed open the door I had been leaning upon and we stumbled backwards into the room. I kissed him with the desperation of a drowning person trying to get air. He backed me against the wall and I wrapped my arms around his neck. We kissed with a passion that made my whole body shake. I loved him so much. He felt so good against me. In a flash, reason overcame my heart. I loved him so much that I could not let him lose everything he had worked so hard to gain.

"No." I shoved Tren-Lore away from me. He lurched backward, and for the first time since the start of our encounter, I realized that he was drunk. "We cannot do this."

Tren-Lore gained his balance and glared at me. "You are driving me mad!" he shouted, and I took a startled step backward. "Why, Lara, why do you have the right to decide? Does what I want matter at all? I have thought about this for months, and either way we lose. Either way, we are going to be miserable, so why do we have to be miserable by ourselves?"

He was making too much sense. I did not want my decision questioned. It had been hard enough to make, and I was too tired to rethink it. Circumstances had progressed too far to turn back now. It was a mess, and there were no right answers. Unable to verbalize any of this, I pushed past Tren-Lore and fled the banquet hall. I could not think about this any more. Just outside the kitchen, I ran into Thriana, and even in my haste, her pale face and wide eyes were enough to bring me to a sudden halt.

"What is wrong?" I demanded, cold fear making me sick.

Thriana burst into tears. "Sophie. Sophie is...she is...I should have come to get you sooner."

What had happened? The world seemed to spin with horrible possibilities. What had happened? I dashed past Thriana and into the kitchen. I do not remember crossing the floor to our room or opening the door. My memory had skipped from Thriana's weeping to the sight of Sophie lying upon her bed, her skin ashen, lips slightly blue, and breath coming in quick gasps. She opened her eyes at the sound of my entry.

"Lara," she rasped, and made a feeble gesture for me to come closer.

I rushed to her side and took her hand in mine. Her skin was burning with the heat of an intense fever. With my other hand, I twisted and grabbed the glass of water at her bedside. I held it to her lips, but she turned her head away.

"No, child."

She began coughing and I dropped the glass. The shattering sound came to my ears as only a vague detail. I fumbled for my Healer's ring. I gripped it in one hand and put my other hand on Sophie's chest. I tried to channel my life energy, but could not bring it under my control. I needed to stop Sophie from dying, and I could not bring it under my control!

Sophie weakly moved so she was once again holding my hand. She squeezed it. "I love you, Lara. You... you are the daughter Jerran and I never had. I have always been so proud of you."

"Sophie!" I cried and threw my arms around her. I was sobbing. "Please do not go."

"There, child," she murmured as though sleep were slowly taking hold of her. "You will be fine. Just remember that Sophie loves you. Just remember what a remarkable girl you are."

"I love you, Sophie." My voice was breathless with grief.

I felt her fingers tighten slightly and then relax. The rapid beating of her heart faltered, and then stopped.

"Sophie?" She did not respond to my cry. "Sophie!"

I sat up. Her eyes were closed, and she looked as though she slept. I needed to wake her. I needed her to open her eyes and see me. I shook her and yelled her name and then in desperation, I tried channeling again. I let my life energy consume my flesh, burn down my arms and into my fingertips, but it would not pass into Sophie's body. It was like channeling into rock, into the ground - into a grave. I wretched my hand away from her and lurched backward, falling hard against the floor. Broken glass cut my hands but I could feel no pain. I was disconnected from what was happening. It could not be real. I wiped my bloody palms on my dress. Rising slowly, I turned and walked from the room. My mind and body did not seem to be communicating with one another any more. I wanted to laugh hysterically at the strange feeling.

I left the kitchen, and my feet took me along the familiar path to the secret room. The corridors were dark. This could not be real. I must be lost in some black dream. Even this thought did not upset me, and I continued the climb. When I reached the landing, I drew back the dragon tapestry and pushed the door inward. It opened silently, and to my bemusement I found that there was already a fire burning in the hearth. Two people were sitting before it. It was Tren-Lore and Areama. They were kissing. They drew apart slowly, and as Areama smiled at him, I gently pulled the door closed on the surreal scene.

"Why are your bands glowing?" I heard her ask.

He did not answer immediately, but just before the door and frame fit solidly together he replied, "They glow because I am happy."

I moved back down the stairs, gazing forward blankly. It could not be real. I finally slumped against the wall of the passageway and sat with my arms wrapped around my knees, not thinking, just existing. I do not know how long I stayed like that, but I was awakened from this deadened emotional state by a quiet voice that was both familiar and new.

"Lara?"

I looked up. My head felt too heavy to move easily. Yolis was kneeling before me. His countenance was confused and worried.

"What are you doing here?" He noticed my hands and looked alarmed. "What happened to your hands?"

I furrowed my brow and tried to remember. As understanding began to creep back into my mind, I wanted nothing more than to forget again. I began to cry, and the battle between expressing grief and drawing breath shook my body and fractured my words.

"I fell on glass after... Sophie - is dead. Tren-Lore and Areama – Tren-Lore and Areama were kissing in – were-"

Yolis drew me to him. His arms were strong and I sobbed into the front of his fine tunic. He rubbed my back soothingly. "It hurts now, Lara, but everything will be all right in the end."

I did not believe him. This *was* the end, and everything was worse than I had ever imagined it could be. Sophie was gone. Tren-Lore had betrayed me by showing Areama the secret room. It had been ours, and now he was there with her. I shook my head. It would never be all right again!

"I promise it will be." I could hear Yolis' heart beating within his chest. The pace was steady and firm. "I will make sure everything turns out. Now, come with me to the royal chambers and we will look after those hands."

His demeanor calmed me a little, and all at once I did not feel so alone. "Thank you," I mumbled into his shoulder.

He laughed slightly. "Any time."

He got to his feet and I tried to mimic his movement, but found that it was too much effort. My legs were stiff from huddling in the passageway for so long. Slumping back against the wall, I began to weep with despair. I had been defeated so entirely that I could not even gain a victory over such a little feat as this. Yolis made no comment, but rather stooped and picked me up. He carried me to the royal chambers and set me down in a large chair before the fire.

"Get a bowl of warm water and some bandages," he ordered a servant.

She nodded but her eyes were on the bloody marks I had left upon Yolis' tunic. "Right away, Your Majesty."

Yolis pulled up a seat across from me. "Apparently Lord Bizim and his wife are having quite a bit of trouble with their roof." He gently took one of my hands and began to pick the shards of glass from my palm.

I accepted the pain without comment. It was good to feel something other than grief.

"Lady Bizim has decided that the Ascendants sent Caladore such a mild winter for the sole purpose of vexing her. With every thaw, she is driven from her bed by the icy water that leaks through her roof."

Yolis continued to tell me stories of a similar nature. I knew he did not care about the tales any more than I did, but somehow he must have known that I needed something to think about that was entirely removed from my normal life. I clung gratefully to his words. They were the only things between me and the pit of dark memories that were just a few faltering steps behind.

Yolis stayed with me the entire night and eventually, just as the sky was lightening to the soft navy darkness of dawn, I fell asleep, my head leaning against his shoulder. I awoke only a few hours later in a bleary state of confusion. I felt as though I had been practicing mounted combat with Tren-Lore and had fallen from Paence at least a dozen times. I rolled onto my back and moaned. My hands hurt the most, and as I held them up before me, the agony of memory returned. I had not been practicing with Tren-Lore. He had been with Areama in the secret room. I had failed to save Sophie. She had died! Perhaps if I had done something different - if I had tried to Heal her earlier – perhaps then she would not have died. I sat up and pushed back the blanket Yolis must have tucked around me.

"It is my fault," I realized aloud, and guilt smashed against me. "It is my fault."

I could hear footsteps coming from the other room, and then Yolis appeared in the doorway. He had changed his clothing, and had I not known, I would not have suspected that he had been awake all night. His handsome features were unmarred by shadows of weariness.

"It was not your fault," Yolis assured me. In a few long paces he was sitting beside me again. He put his arm around me and I thought briefly what unlikely confidants desperate times breed. "What could you have done?" Yolis continued, caressing my cheek with two of his fingers.

"I could have Healed her."

I felt Yolis' muscles tighten, and his hand paused. My mind was dulled to all sensations but grief. Neither fear nor prudence had prevented me from uttering such a telling sentence. Yolis cleared his throat and stroked my face again. "There is no one who has triumphed when their opponent is death."

"Heroes do," I said quietly. I was thinking of Rayn and all the times he had snatched people from the brink of death.

"Lara, darling," he laughed, "you are not a hero. You cannot expect that of yourself. I am sure you did all that was humanly possible. Sometimes people just die, and we must accept that."

In my memories I heard my mother and Namin saying nearly the same thing. It is a Healer's job to give life, not to take away death. The words did not comfort me, for in my heart I did not believe them. I certainly was neither a hero nor a Healer. I was a failure. I hated myself.

Yolis, however, did not seem to share this loathing. I could not understand why he was so kind to me. For the next two days he let me stay in a room within his wing of the royal chambers, and never once complained about the fact that his tunics were always wet with my tears at the end of our conversations. He even had the message I wrote to Namin delivered by his swiftest messenger.

I am sick as I write these words, I had scribbled. *Sophie came down with an illness which turned into what I think was an infection in her lungs. I did what I could, but it was not enough. I failed her and I failed you. I am sorry. Sophie has died and I could not save her. Prince Yolis has arranged for Sophie's burial in only a few days.*

The funeral was held in the huge sanctuary in Cala, on one of the coldest days that winter had yet conjured. The Temple of Eternity was already filled with people when Yolis and I entered. I scarcely saw them. Sophie was lying upon a pallet in the middle of the room. The scene was all too familiar. It picked at the scabs of memories which had never fully healed, and I bled with fear and grief that was nearly ten years old.

"I cannot do this," I said, and tried to flee. Yolis slipped an arm around my waist and turned my body so that it was close to his. "There is strength in numbers," he said softly, his breath warm against my neck. "I am right here beside you. Everything will be fine."

I hesitated, but gradually allowed myself to be guided into the temple. The crowd parted for Yolis, and soon we were before Sophie. People were quick to stand beside us, and soon a circle had formed around the pallet. Wider circles were forming around our smaller one, and soon everyone had taken their place in the formation that was meant to denote the eternity of life. I was afraid to look at Sophie. I stared straight ahead, although this sight was not comforting either. Nahanni, Tren-Lore and Draows were standing almost directly across from me. Draows caught my eye and inclined his head slightly. Nahanni's expression was kind and sympathetic but Tren-Lore was staring at the ground.

The Hemlizar royal family had left that morning. He was probably missing Areama. End you, Tren-Lore, my mind snarled. It was bad enough that he had been kissing her, but in bringing her to the secret room, he had defiled our friendship. He had betrayed everything that was special about it. For the first time in my life, I hated him. Until the Priest of Eternity began speaking, this anger sustained me, but his talk of Sophie's death left no room in my mind for wrath. There was only a pain so consuming that if Yolis not had his arm around me, I would have crumpled to the ground. It seemed too much to bear. The ragged sounds of my grief echoed loudly in the sanctuary. I laid shaking fingers over my lips to keep the noise within, but it would not be contained. The priest reached out and touched my arm. His hand was cool, and I felt as though he was infusing me with Ascendant-sent calm.

"Take comfort," he said. "Somewhere she is coming into a new life."

I nodded and brushed the tears from my cheeks. She was not entirely gone. In a way, she was not really dead. I stepped toward the pallet and looked down upon her. For once, her hair lay smoothly on her head, and though her skin had a waxen quality to it, I could still pretend she was sleeping. Her face was at last calm and content, so different from all the times she had rushed to complete her tasks in the kitchen, and for all the moments her brow had creased in worry over me.

"Thank you," I softly whispered, and stooped to kiss her forehead.

With that, I turned and Yolis caught hold of my hand. We walked together from the temple, and I took some solace from knowing that Sophie's spirit was already beginning a new life. Somewhere a mother was holding a baby in her arms; oblivious to the marvelous spirit her child had been gifted. But I knew. I knew and I wept.

Chapter Thirty
First I Lost Myself in Him

I padded softly out of my chamber the next morning. Yolis was sitting at the table in the dining room with maps spread before him. Sunlight was streaming onto his form and glittering against the bottle of wine at his side. I raised my eyebrows. Had he been up all night, and was this the remnant of his evening libations, or had he just begun drinking? I considered returning to my room to avoid disturbing him. I firmly stopped myself. I was not going to make an excuse to delay my departure from the royal chambers. I had already stayed longer than was proper. I would have to return to the kitchen – though the very idea made me ill – pack my things, and return to Namin's.

I cleared my throat. "Yolis?"

He turned and smiled at me, and the expression was pure Atalium. It made his face so utterly attractive that I felt my heartbeat quicken. Lara, I scolded myself, this is not the time for giddiness.

"Good morning," he said, and gestured to the chair next to him.

I sat and folded my hands in my lap. "I want to thank you for everything you have done over the past few days. I could not have endured it without your help." I unclasped my fingers and fidgeted with the folds of my dress. I did not want to continue with the speech I had prepared. I wanted to change it just a little. Instead of telling Yolis that I was leaving, I longed to ask him if I could stay forever. "But...but I have abused your hospitality long enough. I will be returning to the kitchen to pack my things, and then I will be going to Karsalin to live with Sophie's sister."

Yolis regarded me for a moment, and then took a swig from the bottle of wine. He held the liquid in his mouth for a moment and then swallowed. "You cannot leave," he informed me calmly. Leaning forward, he handed me the bottle. "I enjoy having my hospitality abused far too much to let you go." His gaze met mine as he said this, the cool blue depths suggesting that this comment had a double meaning. "But aside from my own pleasures," Yolis continued, "traveling is simply not safe. An alliance has been made between Caladore and Hemlizar. My father led our army out of Caladore this morning. They will converge with Hemlizar troops in a few days and make a final stand against the Renarn. Unfortunately, it has been my observation that final stands tend to be rather messy and ironically lengthy."

Tren-Lore had returned to war! My grip tightened around the neck of the bottle, and I struggled to keep myself from becoming alarmed. It did not matter what happened to him. It would serve him right if he was run through. Even as I thought these things, I knew I did not believe them. I was as afraid for Tren-Lore as I had always been. Hefting the bottle, I put it to my lips and drank deeply. As I set it down, Yolis continued, "I suppose you could return to your chamber in the kitchen, but that might be rather difficult." He drew the bottle from my grasp and took another draft. "The memories would be hard to live with at first."

I nodded, tears filling my eyes. The memories of both my mother's and Sophie's deaths were shadowy fingers that stretched forth from a terrifying darkness in my mind. They tried to take hold of me and crush me in their grip. Thus far, I had eluded all but the cold brushes of flickering recollection, but in the kitchen I would not be able to escape for long.

"I wish I could forget."

"Then you shall." He spoke with confidence – a sorcerer of the mind who could command the elements of memory.

I believed in his power, for it was I who had given it to him. I was willing, eager even, to lose myself in him, to give up my old life and let him wrap me in his existence.

* * *

Nahanni was delighted to hear that I was staying in the royal chambers.

"It is going to be wonderful!" she exclaimed. The beautiful young princess was sitting on the floor of my room, helping me unpack my things. "I am so glad you are here. It helps me keep my mind off the war. I am so worried about Father. I wish he would have sent Yolis and stayed to handle the affairs of the castle himself. But Father said that it would hearten the troops to see their king, and he has never been able to resist a good fight. He is like Tren-Lore in that way, I guess." Nahanni drew a small wooden container from my trunk and looked at it inquisitively. "What is this?"

I grunted and pushed myself off the floor. I had been shoving my books about herb lore beneath my bed. I could not even bring myself to study them any longer. I did not deserve to. I had failed utterly, and even the letter I had received from Namin could not convince me otherwise. I was weak. I would not attack again. Retreat was my best option. Brushing my dress off, I turned to look at what Nahanni was holding. I frowned. A small jar made of red wood rested on her palm and I could not think of what it might be.

I shrugged. "Open it."

Nahanni did, and the scent of cinnamon filled the air. The smell rushed me through years of memory, right to the instant when Dyra and Namin had given me the perfume. When I had returned home from Karsalin, I had not bothered wearing it. It had seemed foolish when I knew my days held adventures that would inevitably coat me with sweat and dirt.

"Rub some on your wrists," I told her.

Nahanni did so, and sighed with pleasure. "Lara, you are a fool not to wear this everyday! I would bathe in it if I could. It smells magnificent." She held her wrists to her nose and inhaled deeply. "I must see about getting some." Placing the little container on the table that rested beneath a gilded mirror, she eagerly rummaged through my trunk again. Not even the dreary chore of unpacking could hinder Nahanni's cheerful spirit. "And who are you?" I heard her croon from the depths of my trunk as she withdrew my doll, Kara.

My cheeks felt suddenly hot. Nahanni would think it was silly that I still had a doll. End it all, even I thought it was silly, but I could not bring myself to part with her. "It was a present from Sophie," I explained quickly. "I just keep it because she gave it to me."

Nahanni was straightening the doll's slightly wrinkled dress. "She is beautiful. My father gave me a doll for every single one of my Spring Years, and I still have all of them. Sometimes," she laughed a little and fiddled with the ends of her golden hair, "if it is really storming at night, I still sleep with my favorite one. You probably think that is silly." She looked up at me tentatively.

"No." I shook my head. "I do not think that at all."

This mutual confession gave me a feeling of warmth. It helped to dull the cold ache that had been with me since Sophie had – I pulled my mind away from the thought. I did not want to ruin the sensation by thinking about such dark things.

Had Yolis been there, he would have agreed with me. He would often say as much. It was best to keep your mind on other things, always moving forward and definitely never looking back. He talked of the future, he joked, he danced me about the royal chambers, and he presented me with gift after gift. One of these presents was a book, and during the evenings, I would sit before the fire and read it.

Though this routine had been established for nearly a month now, I was no more than half finished. I dropped the book in my lap and stared forward at the twisting flames in the hearth. The story was just so boring. There were no dragons or stunning duels on cliff edges. It was pages and pages of two idiotic people swooning about their love for one another. So, as it always did, my attention wandered from the book and I thought about Tren-Lore and Areama. My mind boiled with cruel images that had become familiar conjectures. Tren-Lore's lips upon her neck, her fingers in his hair, his voice murmuring how beautiful she was, how much prettier she was than me. I imagined him telling her that he had never really loved me.

"Should I leave you and your thoughts alone?" a deep voice asked teasingly.

I snapped from my visualizations like a person jerking their hand away from scalding water. I scrambled to my feet and turned to face Yolis. He was standing behind me, looking as he always did, very handsome and well dressed. "No, I was just...just thinking about the book you gave me."

"Really," he mused in a tone that suggested he did not believe me. Taking the book from my grasp, he tossed it into the fire.

I gasped. It seemed like an offence against the Ascendants to treat a book so poorly – even a story as bad as that one.

Yolis slipped his hand around my waist. "Now you can quit thinking about it." His other hand had settled on my hip. We were standing close to one another, the heat of the fire between us. "You are an attractive woman, Lara, but when you smile, there are few who rival your beauty. I would be doing myself a disservice if I encouraged you to ponder things that made you frown."

He looked down at me, and in that moment of silence, I knew what he was thinking as clearly as if he had spoken the words. He wanted to kiss me, and for reasons born of passion and spiteful logic, I shared in his desire. I wanted to kiss Yolis. I wanted to kiss him until I knew that I had hurt Tren-Lore far more than he had hurt me. I slid my arms around Yolis' neck and smiled. It was a formulated gesture that had little to do with my own happiness and everything to do with Yolis'. He grinned at me, and my heart quickened with a sudden and irrational fear. There was something in that expression that seemed...I struggled for the word. As Yolis' mouth met mine I knew the adjective I had been searching for - hungry, ravenous. He kissed me with an aggressive passion I was not accustomed to. Tren-Lore had never kissed me like that. Breath and thought were taken from me. I felt as though I were being consumed, felt sure that when Yolis drew away there would be nothing left of me.

But when he broke our embrace, I was whole. My legs were a little shaky and my lips felt bruised, but nothing outwardly had change. Inside, I felt like Quara after the Ascendant of Water changed her from flesh to liquid. I did not feel like myself. My actions had been purely basic in motivation, and part of me had enjoyed it.

"Now, come along," Yolis said. "I fear that this evening time is not our friend. We are already late for the play."

As Yolis had predicted, we did arrive late. The play had already begun, but still he led me to the front row and we slipped into seats directly before the stage. At first I tried to concentrate upon the play, but it was uninteresting and my curiosity about the audience promoted distraction. This was the first function I had attended with Yolis, and I wanted to see what his social circle looked like.

Pretending to stretch, I glanced about the theater. It was populated by nobles, clad in ornately beautiful garb. None of the men looked quite as good as Yolis, but next to the women, I was hideously underdressed. I slouched a little, trying to hide the red gown Sophie and Namin had given me. It was much too plain for such a grand event. I glanced at Yolis, suddenly feeling insecure. Was Yolis embarrassed to be seen with me? I had to do something about my appearance.

"Yolis," I whispered, "could...do you think I could have a new dress made?"

He leaned close to me. "I think you could have ten new dresses made, if you wanted to." His lips brushed hot against my neck. "I will send for the dressmaker tomorrow."

"Thank you," I replied softly, and smiling, turned back to the performance. My uneasiness was ebbing. Things would soon be right.

An actor in a huge hat was just declaring, "I shall not stand such slander, nor shall I sell this plot of land! No, not this plot of land!"

I slid down in my seat and rested my chin on my hand. Oh, for Ascendants' sake, I thought, sell the plot of land and stop talking! This inward quip made me smirk, and for an instant I wished that Tren-Lore were there to share the joke.

* * *

Yolis was relaxing in a comfortable chair, his long legs stretched out before him, his eyes following my every move. I was modeling one of my new dresses for him.

"What do you think, Your Majesty?" the plump dressmaker mumbled. She was holding several pins between her pursed lips.

Yolis studied me. "Lower the neck line. She is not serving as a priestess for the sanctuary." He grinned wolfishly and winked at me.

The woman bobbed her head and went about making the adjustments. Out of the corner of my eye, I caught Gormek, one of Yolis' advisors, entering the room. Gormek's stout body was not used to quick movement, and his face was red with excitement and exertion. He bowed quickly. "I have a favorable report from the front, Sire. Prince Tren-Lore defeated -"

"The other room," Yolis ordered, and Gormek fled like a mongrel fearing punishment.

I had turned sharply at the mention of Tren-Lore's name, and one of the pins had dug into my side. I hissed in pain and pressed my hand to my ribs. I wanted to ask Gormek what had happened, but he had already left.

Yolis stood and inclined his head. "You look lovely, darling." I was startled by the endearing term. He had never used such a name before. "Have as many dresses made as you want. I will join you for dinner."

Nahanni arrived shortly after Yolis had departed. She had been with Zander and was filled with giddy happiness. I let the princess and the dressmaker convince me that I needed twelve new gowns. We had a delightful afternoon together, and the royal chambers were filled with the forgotten sound of laughter.

Alone in my room later that night, I sat despondently upon my bed, staring at the first of my new gowns. I could take little pleasure in it. Hanging beside the new gown was the old red dress Sophie and Namin had lovingly made for me. That one simple dress was worth so much more than anything Yolis might commission for me. I missed Sophie terribly. My room was so silent and empty without the comforting sound of her breathing. Hugging my pillow to my chest, I cried myself to sleep.

I dreamt that I awoke in my room in the kitchen. It was so dark. The candle Sophie had always lit for me was gone, and I was alone. The floor was icy cold as I moved slowly from bed. I felt sure that I would find Sophie in the kitchen. I pulled on the handle, but the door would not move.

"Sophie!" I called, and yanked harder.

There was rustling and scratching in the back of the room. Terror struck. Monsters were coming.

"Sophie!" I screamed. The monsters were at my back. I could sense them, but could not make myself turn and face them. "Sophie!" I pounded desperately on the door. "Sophie! Mother, save me!"

"Lara."

My own name ripped me from my nightmare – away from the monsters, away from the darkness. Yolis was leaning over me.

"It is all right, Lara," he murmured, and gathered me into his arms. "You were having a bad dream."

I sobbed into the warmth of his sleeping shirt. "I miss Sophie so much!" I felt empty, devoid of the presence of Sophie and Tren-Lore. I missed them both so much.

"Do not think about it," he told me, and kissed the top of my head. "I know how much it hurts, but if you keep your mind from it, the pain will fade."

"I am trying," I wailed. The grief was too much for me, and I knew I would never overcome it. I did not have the strength to face it, and therefore, would have to continue this hopeless flight from memory.

"Shh, darling." He stroked my hair and talked softly to me, but I would not be consoled. As though in desperation, he began to sing quietly. It was a children's song that promised peace at night and happy days to come. He sang with uncertainty at first, presumably recalling words from the past, but soon his voice was stronger and I calmed, entirely enchanted by the soothing tune.

When I awoke the next morning, Yolis was asleep next to me. His arm was slung over my stomach and he was snoring softly. Being careful not to wake him, I inched from bed. Yolis muttered something and rolled over, kicking the covers off his feet. I stood for a moment and watched him. Shafts of sunlight were falling through the window. They cut across Yolis' lean body and made his skin seem as though it was glowing. I was suddenly filled with fondness for him. He had done so much for me. He had been so kind. I owed him a great deal. From now on, I promised myself, I would make a greater effort to do things that pleased him.

Grinning, I softly opened the door. I knew just where to start. Breakfast in bed would be a nice surprise, and if I had heard it once from Benya, I had heard it a million times. Food is the way to a man's heart. With some hesitation I asked one of the servants if she might possibly – if it was not too much trouble, of course – maybe go and get some breakfast from the kitchen. I still felt uncomfortable giving orders. The servants were my equals, and I could not bring myself to command them as Yolis did.

"Of course." She smiled and bobbed a curtsy.

Out of habit, I returned the gesture and then winced as I realized how strange it must have looked. "Well... umm... thank you." I stumbled over the words, not able to think of the proper thing to say.

The girl merely nodded and turned. If she thought that I had the sense of a Barlem, she did an admirable job of concealing it. She returned a short while later with a silver platter mounded with fried eggs, a slice of meat and toasted bread. The meal smelled delicious, and I wondered which of the ladies in the kitchen had made it. After an awkward monologue of gratitude, I took the tray from the girl and hurried into my room.

Yolis opened his eyes at the sound of my entrance and yawning, stretched his arms above his head. "Lara, you are the sweetest girl this side of Caladore." He patted the bed and I sat next to him, the tray settling between us. "We should do this every morning," he decided, picking up a fork to try some egg.

So it was that breakfast in bed became our routine. Yolis would awaken me every morning with a lingering kiss and our morning meal on a silver platter. Then, with the help of several servants, I would don one of the new gowns; have my hair intricately piled upon my head, and rub cinnamon scent into my wrists. It was a rather boring process, but I endured it as another challenge in my quest to please Yolis. He certainly seemed to appreciate my efforts, for his kisses grew more frequent and his compliments more fervent. Beautiful, gorgeous, perfect: words he often murmured into my ear, each a salve upon my wounded ego.

After my morning preparations were completed, Nahanni spent time preparing me to endure the wilderness of court. Nahanni was the Draows of social survival skills. Her countenance was naturally endearing, and when she was practicing the niceties of the court it was impossible not to be entirely charmed by her. She knew just the right behavior for each situation, and I did my best to emulate her.

It was in the afternoons that my ability to mimic the charming princess became most important. I would usually spend this time with the ladies of the court, sipping tea and nibbling upon pieces of gossip. I felt it would please Yolis if I could gain the acceptance of this group, so I tried very hard to be as pleasant as Nahanni. This was difficult, however, because part of Nahanni's allure was in the easy way she spoke. In contrast, I was so nervous that I rarely had anything to add to conversations, and even if I did, I often stumbled and tripped over my words. I dreaded making a remark that might reveal I was a servant of the kitchen rather than a lady of noble blood.

"These are simply delicious tarts!" Lady Rose-Mary declared one day as she waved her tart about in the air. "Really, they are just perfectly delicious!" Crumbs sprinkled the carpet and I pitied the servant that would have to clean it up later. "Now, who is going to divert us with our next story?"

For an instant I considered telling Rose-Mary the origin of the tarts. I knew that Sophie had created the recipe a few years ago, and the tale was really very amusing, although not appropriate to tell in the presence of noblewomen. They would not care about something as menial as baking.

"You tell us another one, Rose-Mary," prompted one of the ladies.

"Yes," I agreed, "you tell them so nicely."

As Rose-Mary began telling her story, I felt some of the tension leave my body. If Rose-Mary was talking there would be no opportunity to turn the conversation toward me or my history. Yolis had created me a vague, but somewhat illustrious lineage, and I did not want anyone asking too many questions. I had reached a point where I thought most of the noblewomen had come to accept my presence. Lady Jizabelle was the exception, however. She took every opportunity to snub me or make unpleasant inquiries about my personal life.

"Do not worry, Lara," Rose-Mary had whispered to me one day a few weeks ago. Jizabelle had been particularly cruel to me that afternoon, and I was blinking back tears. "It is nothing personal. She does that to anyone who has the audacity to exist."

I tried to keep this in mind when Jizabelle's next onslaught occurred later on that month. Fear slid into me like cold steel as Jizabelle's attention turned to me. She glared over the rim of her teacup. I curled my toes hard and raised my chin.

"I was thinking, Lara, that it must be terribly hard for you to be left in the prince's care while your family is away. I heard that he is overly fond of his ale." She paused to click her tongue and shake her head. "Too much drink can make a man perfectly nasty."

I frowned, struggling to find a way to defend Yolis and not incur any more of Jizabelle's wrath. "Oh no," I replied meekly, staring at the pattern stitched into my dress, "the prince rarely drinks. My stay at the royal chambers has been very agreeable."

I glanced up at Jizabelle to find that one of her eyebrows was arched indignantly. She glared at me and pursed her lips. "And when do you expect your stay to end?"

* * *

Yolis laughed when I related the conversation. We were lying before the fire, exchanging the details of our days.

"Irony at its best," he decided, and bent to kiss my neck. "I happen to know that Lord Vanya is more in love with a tankard of ale than he is with our dear Lady Jizabelle. In fact, he was recently so drunk that he was apparently unable to tell the difference between his wife and a buxom serving girl. They dismissed the girl only a few weeks ago. I suspect Jizabelle did not appreciate the forthcoming addition to their family."

I covered my mouth and struggled not to smile. It was terrible that the girl had been turned out when she was pregnant, but part of me delighted in the fact that Jizabelle had been embarrassed.

Yolis pulled me closer to him. "Tomorrow at tea..." His words were interrupted as he stooped even lower to kiss the line of my collarbone. "I want you to casually mention how hard it is to find good help these days. Let Jizabelle know that you and I are not to be trifled with."

I chuckled and we grinned at each other. "I think that would be an excellent idea," I told him.

This prediction proved to be an understatement.

"Yolis!" I called, as I burst into his study the next day. He looked up from the papers he was studying. "You will never believe it! I did what you told me, and Jizabelle's reaction was extraordinary."

He rubbed at his chin, a wolfish grin playing upon his lips. "Was it, now?"

I sighed in contentment and recalled the way the room had fallen silent when I had casually made the inquiry. Had I been sword fighting, my form would have been perfect and my aim deadly. Jizabelle knew she had been delivered a social blow. She pursed her lips until they were leached of color, but she said nothing. The other women realized what had happened. They glanced at me from under lowered lashed. A new combatant had just marched onto the battlefield, and they were trying to decide just how powerful I was going to become. I had smiled at all of them and silently thanked Yolis.

"It was wonderful." I leaned across his desk. "And amazing." I kissed him. "And incredible." We embraced again. "And...and... insurmountable."

"Insurmountable?" Yolis repeated in a voice that was more of a growl.

He pulled me forward onto his desk and his papers fell, scattering across the floor, completely forgotten. Yolis' attention was entirely upon me. I clung to him and tried to concentrate on how handsome he looked that day and how he had saved me. I struggled to ignore the discomfort of the hard desk pressing into my back, and successfully quelled the part of me that wanted to cry. I told myself to concentrate only upon Yolis. My focus had to be him. If I thought of Tren-Lore, Sophie, or my old life where there was no one to depend upon, the pain became too great. My need for Yolis was as fundamental as my need for air. I sacrificed myself just to keep breathing.

Chapter Thirty-One
A Dangerous Alliance

Yolis and I were sitting inside the royal chambers, deep in conversation. Outside the birds were joyfully twittering about the arrival of spring and a cheerful breeze was playing at the windowsill. We were oblivious to the beauty around us as we schemed. Shortly after I had made my first strike against Lady Jizabelle, Yolis and I discovered that an alliance between us was equally beneficial. My growing knowledge of courtly intrigues combined with Yolis' political insights provided a surprisingly complete picture of the happenings in Caladore. I thought more than once of how jealous Flock would be if she had known I was privy to such knowledge.

"Have any of the ladies mentioned Renarn, aside from general war gossip?" Yolis casually asked as he took a bite of his dinner. He followed this with a swig of wine and an expectant gaze.

"Umm...yes. I think so." I tapped my fork on the surface of the dining table and tried to recall who had mentioned Renarn, and why they had done so. This information was obviously important to Yolis, and I desperately wanted to be of service to him. "It was Lord Yarith's wife. She had a beautiful dress and she said the material came from Renarn."

Yolis leaned back in his chair. "Interesting. My spies tell me that one of my nobles has been involved in trades with the Renarn. Perhaps Yarith does not understand that we are actually trying to *win* this war. I think I will have Gormek pay a visit to Yarith's estate this evening."

I poked at the meat on my plate. Yolis' words made me uneasy. What was going to happen to Lord Yarith? I considered asking Yolis, but thought better of it. If I expressed my concerns, he might doubt my loyalty to him and stop confiding in me. Yolis and I were extremely close in some aspects, but in others... I winced. I had been struggling to find a common intellectual ground to share with him. This exchange of information was the best I had been able to do. I did not want to jeopardize it, but my stomach twisted at the thought of Yarith in peril because of something I had said.

"There is no danger to Yarith's life," Yolis said quietly. It seemed that my inner struggle was clear upon my face. "He will be dealt with, but it is nothing you need to concern yourself with." He pointed at my plate. "Eat some more."

I did as he said and tried to take comfort from his reassurance. Yet, that night I slept poorly. I dreamt that Yarith and his wife were dead. Yolis and I were standing in a crowd of people, and no matter which way we turned we could not escape.

"Well done!" someone cried, and clapped me on the back. Yolis turned me to my left and tried to push me forward, but I ran into a tall nobleman who bowed and expressed his admiration. "I could not have killed them better myself." Yolis pulled me right, and I was confronted by Flock. She scowled at me. "I could have murdered them if I had wanted to."

"No!" I exclaimed. "I did not murder them! It was just-"

Yolis yanked me about before I could explain, and I tumbled into the throng. I was suddenly face to face with Sophie. She looked angry. "Young lady, I am very disappointed in you." And then it was Namin I was talking to. "It is not a Healer's job to give death, Lara."

"I know!" I cried and closed my eyes. "I know, I know."

People pressed close around me, and their breath hissed in my ears. You did it. You killed them. Well done. Well done. I tried to push the people away from me, but they caught at my clothes, my hair, and I could not get away.

"Help me!" I screamed, and all at once Tren-Lore was standing before me. I reached out for his hand, but he stepped back and drew the gorgeous Areama to his side. "Please, Tren-Lore," I whimpered.

People in fine clothes surged toward me, and Tren-Lore was obscured in a mass of soft cloth and false smiles. I was forced to my knees. The sound of Tren-Lore's name tore my throat and woke me up with a start. I sat up in bed, sweating and staring about wildly. The room was filled with the gray light of stirring dawn, and Yolis was still sleeping beside me. I looked at him closely. He usually awakened me from my nightmares, and it was odd that his sleep remained undisturbed. Untangling myself from the blankets, I crept from bed.

I summoned my Ladies in Waiting and ignored the guilt that contaminated my thoughts. Their expressions were still bleary with recent slumber, and they moved lethargically. Had our roles been reversed, I would not have been pleased.

"I apologize for beckoning you so early," I told them. "It could not be avoided. Kath, I want you to inquire about Lord Yarith and Lady Helanna. I fear something may have happened to them last night."

The young girl's eyes widened and she curtsied quickly. "Yes, my Lady," she murmured as she hurried from the room.

I turned to the other women. "My purple dress will do for today, and I will need to wash my hair."

Kath returned just as I was on my way to Nahanni's wing of the royal chambers.

"What news?" I demanded. Please, I prayed silently, please let them be fine.

"Lord Yarith is in the dungeon, my Lady. Rathum, a stable hand, said they brought him in last night. Rathum said there was talk of treason."

I nodded shortly. "Thank you, Kath. You did well. That will be all." I waited until the young girl had left, and then I sunk to the floor in relief. Yolis had been good to his word and not harmed Yarith. I had no blood on my hands.

After the galloping pace of my heart had slowed to a steadier gate, I pushed myself up and proceeded to my lessons with Nahanni.

The princess and I accomplished little that day. I was so relieved by the good news I had just received that I was practically giddy. Nahanni was always ready to be infected with another's happiness, and shortly after my arrival my silliness had left its mark upon her. Neither of us was in the right state of mind to master the new dance we had intended to work on that day.

"Do you come to many balls?" I drawled in a deep voice. Pulling Nahanni close, I wiggled my eyebrows at her as I had seen one of the overly charming noblemen do.

She giggled hysterically. "Oh yes, I am often in attendance."

"Impossible!" I declared and swept her around, effectively stomping on both her feet. "Please accept my apologies." We both laughed and I tried to compose my face. "Impossible, for I would have noticed a woman of your....extravagant beauty!"

"Kind sir," Nahanni cried in a breathy voice, "I must confess that I am overcome by your charming remarks."

Laughter was making my hands shake, and I could barely stand straight. We whirled about again, but came to an abrupt halt when Zander's voice politely but unexpectedly interrupted, "May I cut in?"

He was standing in the entrance, grinning. Nahanni smiled back at him. The expression that passed between the two made my heart ache. It was obvious they adored each other. I missed being looked at in that way.

"Do you mind if I go, Lara?" Nahanni asked, reaching out to tuck a few strands of loose hair behind my ear.

I patted her cheek. "Not at all."

When Zander and Nahanni had left, I ambled through the halls of the royal chambers and eventually made my way down to the massive room where the ladies met each day to take tea. I slipped past the heavy doors and into the empty room. It was too early for anyone to be there. I stood and gazed out the large window, admiring the greening landscape of the garden. It surprised me that spring had arrived unnoticed. Tren-Lore and I had always tracked the changing of the seasons. This year I had been dead to the warming of the earth.

I seated myself in one of the comfortable chairs arranged about the room. Tren-Lore was in my thoughts. For a time I was glad to relive old memories, but soon these led to newer recollections that were not so joyful. I curled and uncurled my toes in my shoes and wondered what Tren-Lore was doing now. Was he thinking about Areama? Did he still have feelings for me? In my dream, I had wanted to slip my hand into his. Just his touch would have been so comforting.

"It is perfectly terrible!" I heard Rose-Mary's voice inform someone from just outside the room. She pushed open the door and continued speaking as she entered. "No, we have to wait for everyone to get here. Hello, Lara, lovely dress!"

A pale Jizabelle appeared a moment later, and after her, several other women. Rose-Mary continued to talk on and on about her new story, but could not be persuaded to reveal anything more than it was 'dreadfully tragic and wonderfully interesting'. I did not let myself get caught up in the whirl of curiosity. Rather, I stared out the window and thought that I would ask Yolis to go for a ride after our evening meal. I had not ridden Paence in a long time, and it looked so nice outside. Tren-Lore would have been in his glory on a day like this.

"Now that everyone is here, I can begin," I heard Rose-Mary decide. "Although I wish it was not I who was reporting this terrible news. Ladies, King Kiris has been slain in battle."

There was a collective gasp, and someone's teacup smashed upon the floor. I jerked my attention toward Rose-Mary. What had she just said?

"My son was there, and he returned just an hour ago with the tidings. King Kiris has perished, but we have won the war." Rose-Mary viewed our shocked faces with an expression of sympathy.

I leaned forward in my seat, and when she failed to promptly continue with her story, I gritted my teeth. "For Ascendants' sake, Rose-Mary, what happened?"

"Oh yes, well..." Rose-Mary smoothed her skirts and folded her hands in her lap. "It happened last night. Our army was gathered along Venst and preparing for a last charge when suddenly, three Renarn riders came thundering over a nearby hill, bringing with them a sound that shook the very ground."

Jizabelle's plate clattered as she set it down without looking. "What was it?" she demanded.

Rose-Mary looked about furtively, as though the cause of the sound could be lurking nearby. "A dragon," she breathed.

"What?" I gasped. My mind was reeling. A dragon! A real dragon! Everyone was staring at Rose-Mary with gaping mouths.

"My son said it was as big as an inn, and that when it beat its wings the air moved as though compelled by a fearsome storm. To the horror of all the Caladore soldiers, the pursued Renarn men rode directly for them. The dragon followed. The monster blasted fire into the midst of our troops and then landed, crushing dozens of men. Our army was forced to scatter. Soldiers and horses were running in all directions. My son told me that had it not been for the prince, all would have been lost. Prince Tren-Lore stood alone against the beast and saved everyone."

I gripped the arms of my chair with such fierceness that my fingers hurt. Tren-Lore had fought a dragon! None of this could be true.

"My son said that the prince first struck the dragon on the tail, but his blade inflicted no damage."

Of course, I thought wildly, Tren-Lore should have known that. How many times had Rayn said that dragon scales were impervious to ordinary swords?

Rose-Mary continued. "It was enough, however, to gain the dragon's attention. The brute whirled, covering the ground with flames. Prince Tren-Lore had already moved, and running along side the dragon, he slashed at the tender skin where its wing joined its body. The sword cut clean and the dragon screamed in pain. My son said it was the worst sound he has ever heard. The beast snapped at the prince, but once again, he jumped out of the way. Man and beast faced each other, and with an angered roar, the dragon let forth a burst of flames which engulfed Prince Tren-Lore."

My chest was tight with fear. The room had fallen away, and in my mind I was out on the battlefield with Tren-Lore.

"For an instant, the men thought Prince Tren-Lore had been killed. Lord Myste and the Sanysk Draows, who had both been injured by the dragon's flames, tried to take up their swords to charge the beast, but were held back by several men. Then, unbelievably, Prince Tren-Lore staggered from the flames and with a sword heated by the dragon's own fire, rent the beast's belly. The dragon shrieked and slashed its claws across Prince Tren-Lore's armor. The talons cut clean through the breastplate and the prince fell to the ground. The monster's head plunged down at him, but the prince scrambled to his feet, and holding his sword above his head, drove the blade up into the dragon's mouth."

Tears were standing in my eyes. "He killed the dragon?" I asked in soft disbelief. Tren-Lore had always loved dragons. I could picture the young man's face as the dragon fell to the ground. Not even Tren-Lore could have kept his expression controlled. His features would have been contorted with horror, sadness, and pain – incredible pain.

"Before our armies had a moment to regroup, the Renarn came sweeping over the hill. We were ill prepared to receive their attack, and the brute force of the Renarn troops fell upon King Kiris' party. The King – Ascendant of Eternity guide his spirit – was slain, and Prince Tren-Lore was forced to lead the men. My son said there could have been no better leader. The Renarn quaked with fear at the mere sight of him. They faced not only the prince of Caladore, but a Sanysk of the League, a Sanysk who was furious and wild with rage and grief. To face the prince was to face certain death."

Tears were running freely down my cheeks. As desperately as I wanted to control myself, I could not. It was horrible. Tren-Lore had killed a dragon, his father had died, and his power as a Sanysk had been tainted. He was not the boy I had grown up with, or the man I loved. He was a force that inspired terror in an entire army. I pushed myself out of my chair. I could not listen to anymore of this.

"Lara, where are you going?" Rose-Mary asked in concern.

I hurried toward the door. "There... there is something in my eye." I knew that if I had turned, I would have beheld twelve faces, all trying to wear an expression of sympathy and finding it to be a poor fit. Curiosity was the countenance everyone would most easily slip into. Courtly manners demanded that they wait until I was gone to begin speculating about me. I closed the door and paused in the hall, trying to compose myself. Just forget about Tren-Lore, I thought sternly. Forget about him. He certainly forgot about you easily enough. The sound of Areama's voice filled my head.

Why are your bands glowing?

"They glow when I am happy," I mimicked Tren-Lore. The words tasted like poison and spread the heat of anger through my body just as quickly. "End you, Tren-Lore!" I said, and stalked off to find Yolis.

When I located him, my lips parted in surprise. He was crumpled on the floor by the dining room table, his tunic wrinkled and his hair a mess. He almost looked bruised with grief, and yet I could not reconcile such emotion with my knowledge of Yolis. He appeared vulnerable!

Yolis spoke as I entered the room. "I suppose you have heard." His voice was unsteady, and tears stood in his blue eyes.

I nodded. The images of Rose-Mary's story were chewing at the back of my mind. My other thoughts were being devoured and replaced with pictures of the fight. Even as I hesitantly crossed the room, I could see Tren-Lore hewing at the dragon's wing. I kneeled slowly by Yolis. Everything seemed to have a surreal quality about it. It felt like I was dreaming.

Yolis turned and hugged me fiercely. His back was heaving with erratic breath. "My father is dead," he sobbed.

I stroked the back of his hair. Poor Yolis. Poor Tren-Lore. I could see the look of agony on his face as he slashed the magnificent creature's stomach. I knew there had been part of him that would have rather been killed by the dragon's fire than be forced to continue the assault. I closed my eyes against the tears that were blurring my vision.

"I am so sorry," I said softly.

Yolis pulled away from me, and the abruptness of his movement caused me to open my eyes. He grabbed my face and looked at me with a gaze that was hard as ice. "Do you love me?"

I tried to pull away from him, but his grip tightened. The answer he wanted would not come to my lips. Tren-Lore, the battlefield, the dragon, they were all so clearly in my mind – in my heart.

"Do you?" Yolis' fingers were pressing hard into my cheeks. "I am the king now, Lara. King." He yanked me toward him.

I grabbed his wrists, trying to free myself. "Stop it," I told him, my voice strained by the fear constricting my throat.

"If I do not have you completely, then I do not want you at all. You have to be mine completely or I cannot trust you. Do you love me? Do you *dream* about me, Lara?"

I did not know what to do. I was trapped. I was facing an opponent I had never wanted to meet. I pulled back from Yolis, but he would not let go. His fingers were marks of pain on my face. I had to tell him what he wanted to hear, but if I did... How could I ever betray Tren-Lore like that? The pain in my face was unbearable. *He* betrayed *you,* a desperate voice within me cried. Moments of time crystallized in my mind. I could see Tren-Lore kissing Areama in the secret room and driving his sword into the dragon's chest. I owed nothing to Tren-Lore. I owed everything to Yolis.

"I do love you." I recoiled inwardly as I spoke the words but forced myself to continue. "You are in my heart and my thoughts and my dreams. I love you more...more than anyone." The words were deadly, like a sword sliding into flesh. I felt impaled on my own declarations.

Thus, with my vow of loyalty binding me to Yolis, our alliance grew stronger. As much as I feared what life without Yolis would be like, I sometimes found myself wishing that Myste or Draows would come, pound upon my door, and demand that I cease my association with the new king of Caladore. There was no chance that this would happen. After King Kiris' funeral, Myste, Draows and Tren-Lore had all left on undisclosed business. Sanysk business, everyone whispered.

Like it or not, I was privy to Yolis' every thought, and in turn, he expected that I disclose my mind to him. I focused all my attentions upon the intrigues of the court and the social maneuvering of Caladore's nobility so that I would have something useful to share. My ninth Summer Year passed unnoticed. Like the warm summer months, it was no longer important.

* * *

Nahanni and I stood expectantly in the main room of the royal chambers. The princess sighed and shifted from foot to foot. "If they are not here by the time I count to ten, I think we should go to the ball without them," she decided in a grumpy voice. "I am tired of waiting."

I smoothed my skirts and wiggled slightly in my gown so that the plunging neckline became slightly less revealing. "Yolis is talking with Gormek. He said it would not take too long."

"Well, I am sure Zander is just fiddling with his hair. He is such an Atalium when it comes to that." Her cheeks dimpled with a smile. "But then, I guess he *does* have very nice hair. Perhaps it is worth waiting for."

As it happened, Zander arrived only a few moments later.

"Go," I urged, and directed them toward the door. "There is no need to wait for us." Nahanni opened her mouth to protest, but I interrupted her. "Nahanni, you love dancing and you hate waiting. You might as well go."

She hesitated, and then grinned at me. "Thank you." Kissing me quickly on the cheek, she swept from the room. Zander bowed to me, and then straightened abruptly as Nahanni called from the corridor, "Zander, come on! We have probably already missed three songs!"

"Do you suppose the world will end if we have?" he asked me with a wink.

"Yes, it will!" Nahanni yelled with a teasing, indignant air. "Now come on!"

I laughed as the young man hurried after the princess. Zander and Nahanni always made me happy. Their bliss reminded me of better days. Sometimes I missed those days so much that I felt like crying. Sighing, I turned to find Yolis standing in the opposite doorway. My blood surged hot as I beheld him. His crown glittered in his blond hair and his handsome features were set in an expression of confidence. He was powerful and he knew it.

His eyes slid over me, and I nervously awaited his judgment. "You look lovely," he decided, and in a few long strides was standing before me. As we drew apart from our embrace, he gently touched the Healer's ring that hung about my neck. "Take this off, darling." His voice was soft yet commanding.

I hesitated. I never practiced Healing any more, and I certainly would never call myself a Healer, yet something in me resisted taking off the ring.

"The dress would look much better with the feena penent necklace I bought you," Yolis murmured, "and it would match your bracelet." His lips brushed my throat, and I felt my uncertainty ebbing. His hands moved to the back of my neck and unclasped the chain.

I let him. Even with it, I had failed to save Sophie. I could feel my eyes immediately begin to sting at the thought of Sophie. I was a poor excuse for a Healer, and not fit to wear my mother's ring.

"Trust me," Yolis said as he dropped the necklace on the table. "You will be inundated by compliments the whole evening. Now run and fetch that other bauble."

I did as I was told and arrived at the ball on Yolis' arm. As with everything, Yolis was right. I received more attention that night than I ever had before. Rose-Mary declared that I looked 'perfectly stunning', and any number of noblewomen approached me to simper about the delights of jewelry. I was asked to dance every time the minstrels struck up a new tune, and I even managed to glean a compliment from an unlikely source.

"Lara!" declared a voice that would have been familiar had it not contained the unfamiliar tone of sincere delight. I looked up to find Flock pushing through the crowd. "I am so happy to see you! Your dress is beautiful," she gushed as she grasped my hands in both of hers.

I stared at Flock in disbelief, and for a moment, could find no explanation for her friendly greeting. I was baffled until I gazed into her wide brown eyes and saw a look of desperation. I tried to remember if I had seen Flock at any other balls. I was sure I had not, so I knew she probably felt like an Aquara on land. I knew that feeling all too well.

"Thank you. It is good to see you, too," I told her, and found to my surprise that I meant it. "Where is Leffeck?"

For an instant, Flock glanced to her left and then returned her full attention to me. With a shrill laugh and a flick of her curls, she replied, "You know men, always busy talking about important matters."

I quickly followed her gaze and found Leffeck not far off. Heedless of his wife's proximity, he had his arm about the waist of another woman and was chortling at some joke. I felt my face flush in anger. That laughter, those smiles: Tren-Lore and Areama probably smiled at each other like that. I squeezed Flock's hands in a gesture of sympathy.

She looked at the floor, bright red coloring flooding her face. "Do you know that my cook perfected anagarik pastry?" She laughed again, though it was a sound born of nerves rather than humor. "Remember how it always tasted like salt when we made it in the kitchen?"

I nodded. A request for anagarik pastry had been akin to a demand for mulled river water. Sophie and Benya could never discover the secret to making it taste good.

"How did she do it?" I inquired curiously. Even Myste, with his cooking prowess, had fallen to the enemy that was anagarik pastry.

"Well," Flock began, her shoulders relaxing. The first strains of a new song were beginning, and I leaned close to Flock so as not to miss a word. "It was simpler than any of us expected. She just took-"

A hand slid around my waist and a deep voice interrupted Flock. "Forgive me, my dear, but I must steal Lara from you. I am in need of a dance partner, and no one but Lara will suffice."

Flock curtsied deeply and I was reminded of the day she and I had first encountered Yolis. He had seemed so frightening in those days. Now, he was smiling at me and stooping to brush his lips against mine.

"Come, darling."

To my regret, he drew me away from Flock before she had a chance to reveal the secret of anagarik pastry. "We will talk more later," I called back to Flock. "We must have tea sometime."

I saw Flock part her lips to make a reply, but Yolis whirled me about into the midst of the dancing couples.

"I have an idea," he murmured against my ear. His breath was hot and I could smell a faint scent of the soap his tunic had been washed in. "It is going to make me the most powerful ruler since the Ascendant of Sovereignty. And you, my love, will stand by my side while the world grovels at my feet."

Chapter Thirty-Two
And Then I Lost Him

"Y ou have until the first snow, Gormek." Yolis swung his legs up onto the table and leaned back in his chair. "I want you to find me the most influential and powerful..." he paused and frowned, "villains, for lack of a more accurate term." He casually reached across the table and laid his open hand upon the wooden surface. I slid my fingers into his palm and he closed his grip about my hand. "I want representatives from Nara Vit, Renarn, Caladore, and Hemlizar."

Gormek's small eyes squinted in consternation. "Yes, Sire," he said obediently, though his voice was steeped in confusion. "What am I to tell these gentlemen they are needed for?"

"They need only know that they will be handsomely rewarded."

Gormek nodded, and bowing again, began to back from the room.

"And Gormek," Yolis said in a dark tone, "if I find that you have been indiscreet, or failed me in the slightest way, I will have you killed."

My stomach churned. I wanted to wrench my hand free of Yolis' grasp and shut myself away in my room. It was horrible to hear him talk like that. His plan was bad enough, but this threat made me feel ill. It was nauseating to be so close to death.

The short advisor bobbed his head, and then his stout legs pumped vigorously in a quick retreat.

"He would never betray you," I said quietly. "He barely dares to breathe without your permission."

Yolis chuckled and leaning across the table, kissed my hand. "I know. It is part of the reason I like him so much."

* * *

Autumn was dull. There were few balls, the gossip at afternoon tea had grown stagnant, and Nahanni spent much of her time down at Cala helping the poor.

"Mistress Jolie says she can feel it in her bones that winter is near," Nahanni had told Yolis and me over lunch one day. "She thinks it is going to be bitterly cold this year. There are just so many people in Cala without anywhere to stay or anything warm to wear." The princess' blue eyes were wide with pity. "Jolie has been helping me and Zander find places for the poor to stay, but I am worried it will not be enough."

I delicately wiped my mouth. "I could come and help," I offered.

Yolis swallowed hard and cleared his throat. "Lara, love, I do not think that would be wise. I want you here in case I need you."

Nahanni frowned at her brother, but said nothing. I too remained silent and picked up my fork once again. I stabbed in irritation at a piece of cooked carrot on my plate. I hated cooked carrot, and I was beginning to grow weary of Yolis' controlling manner. It is a small price to pay, I reminded myself. Think of the alternatives. If I left Yolis' protection, I was sure the memories would leap upon me and tear my flesh from my bones. I was not strong enough to keep them at bay. For that, I needed Yolis' commanding presence.

When a letter arrived from Namin a few days later, my fear of leaving Yolis was the farthest thing from my mind.

Dearest Lara, she wrote, *I have been given a lovely surprise, bless the Ascendant of Eternity. We certainly did not expect it, but I am pregnant again, hopefully for the last time. Rolias says that he will have to start sleeping in the garden. Little Lara (not so little any more) is very excited to have a new sister. She told me yesterday that she thinks we should have at least three or four more babies, and that you will need to come and live with us so you can deliver all the new additions she is planning. I cannot tell you how many times I have heard, "Mother, tell me a story about Lara."*

I winced and wistfully thought how nice it would be to have stories that were worth retelling to my namesake.

So, if you could find the time, Rolias, the girls and I would love to see you again. I could really use your Healing abilities in the birth of our new baby.

Guilt filled me and I touched the place on my neck where my Healer's ring had formerly hung. It was sitting in a small box in my room. The verdant color had faded, and I hated to see the dull silver color it had become. I would put it on again, I decided, and go to help Namin. It would be good to get away from the castle for a little while. I would not even bother with a coach. I could just take Paence and ride.

Write and let me know if you can come.
Much Love,
Namin

I folded the letter and pressed it to my chest. I felt more elated than I had since Sophie had died. Already, my mind was compiling a list of things I would need.

"Yolis," I called excitedly.

A muffled reply came from his study. I ran down the corridor and burst into the book-cluttered room. He smiled when he saw me, and rousing himself from his desk, he came to kiss me. I returned his embrace. It seemed as though some long-forgotten energy was awakening within me.

Pulling away from him, I held up the letter. "A messenger just came with this letter. It is from Namin, the woman I lived with in Karsalin." He nodded, and I continued. "Well, she says she is having another baby!"

"Wonderful, dear," he replied, and stooped to kiss me again.

I laughed and gently put my hand on his chest to stop him. "That is not all. She has asked me to come to Karsalin to help with the delivery. I am thinking that I will go in a few days. I am going to take Paence, and I can camp in between inns if I have to." I could already picture the fantastic adventure stretching before me.

"Darling, be reasonable." Yolis brushed a stray piece of hair from my forehead. "You cannot go to Karsalin. The roads are too dangerous, and proper ladies do not ride by themselves."

I grinned at him. "You said just last week that the roads have never been safer. I could always take an escort with me, if you really think it is necessary." I was too excited about my plan to let some minor problems stop me. I would go to Namin's and I would see Dyra and Myrrancy and Rion – Ascendants' sake, I had not thought about him in an eternity. I wondered what he was doing.

Yolis frowned and looked down at me with solemn blue eyes. "If you will not be persuaded with logic, then stay for reasons of the heart." Gathering my hands in his, he kissed each one. "Existence would be but a hollow imitation of pleasure if you were not at my side."

I was touched by his sweet words, but not so overcome that I changed my mind. "Come now," I said softly, and fondly touched his cheek.

I was rewarded with a scowl. He withdrew his hands and leaned back against his desk. The gaze that only a moment ago had been full of tender emotions was suddenly cold and predatory. "You have proven yourself quite capable in taking anything I offer. It appears you fall short when the situation demands you give something back."

It was a calculated attack. If I had been less determined to help Namin, his jaws would have snapped closed upon me and crushed me into submission, but for

Namin, I persisted. She had needed my help with her last birth, and I feared that this delivery might be even more difficult.

"I shall return as soon as the child is born," I promised. "It really will be fine. Please do not take this as a personal insult, because it is certainly not intended to be."

His expression did not change, but his knuckles grew white from clutching the edge of his desk. There was a moment of silence, and then he spoke. "Shall I take this as a betrayal, then?"

A betrayal! I could not help but roll my eyes. How could he even think that? I had done everything I could to demonstrate my loyalty. I pressed my fingers to my temples and drew a deep breath. I felt like yelling at him, but I steadied myself. "This is *not* a betrayal. You are just being dramatic. I am going to go to Namin's, and then I will come back and everything will be just fine."

Yolis had drawn himself up to his full height. "You will not go," he ordered in a low, threatening tone.

My patience bent and snapped into jagged anger. "Yes, I will! I am not Gormek! You do not tell me wh-." My words were forced back down my throat as Yolis suddenly smashed his fist into my face. Metallic-tasting heat filled my mouth. Pain devoured my breath. I staggered backward and fell hard against the floor. Yolis lunged at me. Grabbing the front of my dress, he pulled me back to my feet. Our faces were so close I could smell the wine on his breath.

"Leave, and you will die."

He let me go. I stood unsteadily, my shoulders hunched, staring blankly down at the floor – at my shaking hands. What had just happened? Blood was dripping into my palms. The room was deadly silent and my tongue felt thick in my mouth. I slowly raised my head to look at Yolis. He was staring at me, and for once, his countenance was not controlled. He looked horrified.

I stumbled from the study and retreated into my room. Shutting the door quietly behind me, I knelt before my trunk and desperately began to root through it. I had no conscious idea what I was looking for. Thoughts and feelings about what had happened were beyond my grasp. I pushed past old dresses, *Rayn* books, pieces of fabric, and at last my hand closed upon cool leather. I drew the dagger from the bottom of the chest and held it up before me. *Solrium Vallent.* I traced the inscription on the hilt and my blood-stiffened face cracked into a small smile. Tren-Lore had given this to me. Times had been so simple then.

I sat for some time, staring at the dagger and thinking of different days. Shock slowly bled from me. When my senses began to return, dark red stains had run down the front of my dress, and my nose and lip were swollen, but I had come to a decision. I would go to Karsalin and I would not come back. I could hardly believe my own plan. I packed in silence, hoping that if I was stealthy enough, I could somehow escape the notice of fear and doubt and... and Yolis. I tore off my fine gown and replaced it with an old serviceable dress. My heart was beating hard in my chest. I washed the blood from my face and then drew my Healer's ring from its box. With shaking fingers, I fastened the chain around my neck and secured my dagger at my side. I hefted my pack onto my shoulder and quietly opened the door.

Yolis stood on the other side. It felt like I had walked into a wall. The pain in my face flared. As the surprise in Yolis' face changed to anger, a feeling of cold filled my whole body. I wanted to run, but there was no retreat.

"Perhaps you did not hear me before," he said quietly. Bracing his arms on either side of the doorframe, he leaned toward me. "You cannot leave. You know too much about my plans."

He was right. I did know too much, far more than I ever should have known. I knew his plans, and I knew his mind. I knew that Yolis really would kill me before he would let me go. Tears were stinging my eyes. "I...I promise I will never tell anyone. Please, Yolis, let me leave. I just..." His eyes were blue fire, and I drew back from the door in fear. "I just want to leave."

"Leave?" he bellowed, and his hand flashed out and gripped me by the throat.

I cried out in fear and tried to pry his fingers from my throat. "Let go of me, Yolis." His hand was crushing my words. "Let go!" I kicked at him in rage, but he grabbed the back of my hair and yanked my face toward his.

Our foreheads pressed together, and his teeth flashed white as his lips parted in speech. "I thought you loved me."

"Then you were mistaken." In one swift movement I drew the dagger from my side and pressed the point to his neck. "Let - me - go."

"No," he snarled. Hooking his foot behind my heel, he pulled me off balance. My back struck the floor first, and then my head. The room went suddenly black, and when I regained my vision Yolis was looming over me, my dagger in his hands.

"So I was mistaken, was I?" He spoke in tones of darkness. "I did everything for you. I bought you anything your heart desired. I shared my thoughts with you. I even protected you from your own fears. He looked down at my dagger and turned it gently so the light from my window caught the blade. "I loved you."

"You loved controlling me," I said in a barely audible voice.

He knelt beside me and ripped my ring from around my neck. "It does not matter. Even if your life is not devoted to me in love, it is mine, nevertheless. I own you, Lara, and you will stay with me until I find you have outlived your usefulness. Leave, and I will have you killed." He walked away from me without another word.

I lay on the floor weeping.

* * *

I stayed in my room for the next two weeks, pleading illness. I could not face anyone. My bruises were marks of embarrassment, and I was terrified by what might happen if I were confronted by questions, or worse yet, confronted by Yolis. I spent most of my time sitting by my window. I cried often. It seemed impossible that I was in such a dire situation. I turned in every direction of thought, but could find no escape. Sitting at my window, I watched winter descend to frost the earth and lull the trees into slumber. If I left, I died, and if I stayed, I would inevitably succumb to another form of death.

Yolis came to visit me on the fifteenth day of my confinement. I was sitting at my window and did not turn around. I lacked the courage to even look at him.

"You have been sick long enough," he informed me, and I nodded my understanding. "The noblewomen are starting to ask questions. I want you at tea tomorrow and I want you to be smiling."

I heard his footsteps on the floor, and then felt his presence behind me. My heart was pounding so loudly that I imagined he must be able to hear it. I flinched as his fingers brushed my shoulders and traced the line where my skin and dress met.

"I have been thinking," he began.

I stared forward at the frost building along the edges of the window.

"Even without love, this association is not entirely unappealing. You look very nice on my arm, you are useful at gathering information, and there are aspects of our relationship I can take pleasure in without having to enjoy your company."

I closed my eyes and imagined that the frost was growing to cover the walls. It was gliding over the floor and invading my flesh, rushing to fill me with its numbness.

* * *

When I returned from tea the next day, there was a large group of men lounging around the dining table. I had intended to pass through the room on my way to my own chambers, but stopped in the entrance and watched in fascination. These must have been the men Yolis had sent for. There were several that I might have been uneasy about meeting on a dark street, but most looked like average people. They were talking and laughing with one another. Many were smiling with the congenial faces I had always associated with farmers or merchants. In stories, I thought with bemusement, the villains were always too busy plotting nefarious deeds to sit about and joke with one another.

From the head of the table, Yolis cleared his throat and the noise died away. "I have summoned you for a task that is not to be disclosed under any circumstances. If I discover that you, or any of the men that will be working for you, were unable to maintain my secret, I will have you tortured and eventually killed in ways you cannot even imagine."

"All right," said one of the men, revealing the fact that he was missing most of his front teeth, 'so what is this task that is so secretive?"

Yolis leaned his elbow against the arm of his chair. "Each of you will return to your prospective country and gather a band of men. You will lead this group of men in creating general chaos... murder, rape, pillage." He waved his hand encouragingly.

I clenched my teeth. I could hardly believe that I once found Yolis attractive. He was utterly repulsive now.

"Do whatever you like," Yolis continued, "but ensure that you are not captured. And above all, this is never to be associated with me." Yolis gestured to the man sitting beside him. "Nekadious is my representative in Caladore. He will perform a similar duty, but his work will not be as long-standing as yours. A reduction in Caladore's turmoil does not suggest that your skills are no longer required. You will keep working until I tell you otherwise."

They would keep working, I mused darkly, until the kings of Hemlizar, Nara Vit and Renarn were driven to accept Yolis' aid in quenching the sudden uprising of terror in their countries. The price for his assistance would be an oath of allegiance to Yolis as their Overlord, the promise of tax money, and military support.

"Gormek promised us payment," a man sitting near the end of the table grunted. "What kind of payment are we talking about?"

Yolis chuckled. "How does land and wealth sound to you?"

The man squinted and folded his arms over his chest. "It sounds good, but I am going to need more than just your word. I need something that guarantees I get my payment."

"I will have a contract created for each of you."

"And what if something happens?" the man grunted.

Yolis stared at him menacingly. "Such as?"

"Such as your demise or overthrow... kings come and kings go." The man shrugged and rubbed a grubby hand under his nose. "I just want to know that I will get paid no matter what."

Anger flashed momentarily across Yolis' face, but his response was cool as ice. Had I not known better, I would have thought he was merely discussing business rather than what to do in the event of his own death. "If, by some ill wind, I should perish or otherwise be unable to fulfill our pact, I would advise you to make the terms of our deal known to your respective rulers and demand the same reward in exchange for a cessation of violence."

His eyes slid over the group, judging their reactions. Most were nodding, and the rest looked content. I realized a second too late that I was in the path of Yolis' traveling gaze. His face did not change, but my heart felt like it was trying to force its way up my throat. I rushed back to my room, praying to the Ascendants that Yolis would not exact further retribution because of my eavesdropping. My prayers went unheard or unheeded. I was alone, and there was no one to save me when Yolis came.

Terrors stalked me night and day. I had nightmares of Sophie's death, of my mother's death, and of monsters in the darkness. Eventually, I stopped sleeping very much at all. During the day, I lived an existence that should have been a horrible dream. I labored to maintain the façade of normalcy. I hid my bruises and cuts as best I could, and I tried to remember to smile and laugh at the appropriate times. Yolis still demanded information from me, so it was important I not offend the noblewomen. My performance gained me the knowledge I needed, but did not deceive Nahanni.

"What is going on, Lara?" she demanded bluntly.

It was a cold day near the end of winter, and Nahanni had invited me to her room for tea.

"Going on?" I echoed, and my voice seemed hollow. I imagined that my words were reverberating in the emptiness inside me. My rage, hate, and fear seemed to be fading, but nothing was returning to take their place. "What do you mean?" I sat down stiffly, folding my hands in my lap.

"That bruise right here." Nahanni touched her own cheek. "Where did you get it?"

My lips parted in surprise. The mark had faded so much that I did not think anyone would have noticed it. I felt like fleeing rather than answering her question. "I fell," I mumbled and stared at the floor.

Nahanni leaned forward and gently touched my knee. "Lara, is...is Yolis hitting you?"

"Yolis!" I nearly choked on the word. She could get me killed saying things like that. I looked up at her in desperation. "This has nothing to do with Yolis. Never say anything like that again. Not to anyone! Do you promise?"

She looked startled, and her eyes were wet with grief.

"Nahanni! Do you promise?"

She nodded.

"Thank you." I stood abruptly and hurried from the room.

Yolis was waiting for me in my chamber. He was standing before my table, running the feena penent bracelet that he had purchased so long ago through his fingers. I stopped at the doorway, dismayed by his presence.

"What have you learned today?" he demanded without looking up.

I edged my way into the room. "Everyone is very relieved you have been able to deal with the marauders that were terrorizing Caladore. No one suspects that the men are acting under your orders. In fact, they all agree that our neighboring countries are foolish not to take your aid."

"Good. We will celebrate our newly found peace with the ball this evening, and trust that my fellow sovereigns will soon join in our festivities." He took a few long strides toward me. I cowered, but did not retreat. Taking my wrist in his hand, he slipped the bracelet on. "Wear this tonight, and your necklace." His hand moved to rest on my hip and he pulled me hard against him. Hopeless tears blurred my vision. "Come now, Lara," he chided, and stooped to kiss me. "Just close your eyes and pretend I am Tren-Lore."

I closed my eyes but I did not imagine his rough embrace to be Tren-Lore's. Memories of Tren-Lore or Sophie or Namin, or anyone who had loved me, seemed to belong to another girl in another place. I no longer felt as though I was capable of being loved, or even of loving. Somewhere along the way, I had lost myself. What was left was like a cave, like stone wrapped around empty darkness.

Chapter Thirty-Three
Villains

My dress was a deep purple, and I wore the feena penent bracelet and necklace as Yolis had instructed. The servants piled my hair in heavy ringlets on top of my head, and I pinched my cheeks to give my pale face a blush of color.

"You are lucky that I find you beautiful," Yolis commented upon seeing me. He offered me his arm, and I reluctantly took it. "Shall we?"

I gave no answer. He did not expect one. Upon our arrival in the ballroom, I was immediately surrounded by a group of chattering noble ladies who mercifully swept me away from Yolis.

"Guess who has just returned?" Rose-Mary murmured to me as we all stood together near the northern wall. Before I could fathom a guess, she supplied me with the answer. "Prince Tren-Lore."

I nodded politely, but could not even bring myself to be excited by this news. My emotions were frozen.

Rose-Mary opened the fan she was carrying and flicked it back and forth. "My husband told me that the prince has been away fighting in lands far to the east. I heard stories of his battles." She shook her head at the eager expressions most of the ladies wore. "I will not tell them now. We can save them for tea tomorrow. Let me just say that he is rumored to be twice as deadly as even the most dangerous Sanysk that has ever lived. In the east they call him Jarin Yar Kryseth. It means Black Blade of Death."

"Why?" one of the younger ladies demanded, wrinkling her pretty little nose.

I was glad she had asked, for I too was curious in a vague sort of way.

"His sword is black, made of feena penent." She snapped her fan closed and tapped my wrist. The women leaned forward to look more closely. "Like Lara's jewelry. When he slew that hideous dragon at the last battle of the Renarn, the creature's blood ran into Venst and created the feena penent. The prince had it carved into a sword. Apparently it can cut through anything -- flesh, bone, or even armor."

Jizabelle clicked her tongue. "He should be here defending our neighboring countries. The bands of rogues are just getting more violent. My husband is leading a group of nobles to capture some bandits that have been roving on the Caladore-Nara Vit border."

I turned immediately to Jizabelle, Tren-Lore entirely forgotten. My pulse quickened. Stop talking, I silently willed her. Just stop talking. If I told Yolis what she had said, Lord Vanya was as good as dead. She continued to speak, however, and I could feel a slick of sweat wetting my back. I did not want to know about this. I took a step back, but stopped myself. Yolis would want me to stay and gain as much information as I could. If I did, and then told him what I knew...

I hurried away from the group. Slipping through the crowds of people, I headed for the door. I needed to be alone and away from the noise and the heat of so many bodies in such a close space. I needed room to think. When I reached the door, I slipped out and took a deep, calming breath. The air was cool and untainted by the ballroom's faint odor of sweat and perfume. I could not tell Yolis what I had heard. He would kill anyone who stood in the way of his plan. I would not be responsible for those deaths.

"Lara?" said a familiar voice. The tone was soft and the speaker near.

466

I turned, already knowing who I would find. Tren-Lore was the only person who could have moved with such silence and spoken my name with such kindness. We stared at one another without saying a word. Hope, something I had not felt in a long time, stirred within. Tren-Lore could save me. Tren-Lore could rescue me from Yolis.

A long sword hung at his side, and his tunic and pants were the gray of a Sanysk cloak. He looked at least ten years older than the last time I had seen him, and there was an unfamiliar coldness in his eyes. His silver bands wrapped around his throat. I unconsciously touched my own throat and felt a seasoned grief stir in the shadows of my spirit. Yolis had taken my Healer's ring from me. I no longer had the power to make the light of the Triad. I no longer had any power at all.

"I came to Caladore because I have a letter for you. I will be leaving right away."

It seemed as though he was reassuring me. Take me with you, my heart cried out.

Tren-Lore drew a weather-beaten piece of paper from a pocket in his tunic. He winced and tried to smooth the parchment. "It has seen better days, I fear." He sounded remarkably like Draows when he said this. "It is from Myste. He got married."

My hands shook as I took the proffered letter. I could barely hear what he was saying over the clamor in my mind. Tren-Lore could save me. Tren-Lore would know something was wrong and he would save me.

"Her name is Kalypceon," Tren-Lore continued. "We met her when...well, it explains it all in the letter." There was a moment of silence that stretched and grew until it felt like a towering force between us. "Anyway, how are you?" Tren-Lore asked finally. "I heard that you and Yolis were..." His voice trailed away and I could see the muscles in his jaw twitching. "I am happy for you."

Could he not see the faint outline of Yolis' fingers around my neck? Did he not know me well enough to know that something was terribly wrong? We had once been inseparable, morlan penent – one blood. This was not the Tren-Lore I knew. My Tren-Lore would never have exchanged these cold, false platitudes with me. The man standing before me was a Sanysk, he was Jarin Yar Kryseth. He would not be able to save me.

"Thank you," I said in a dead voice and brushed past him.

Tren-Lore let me leave without saying another word.

Once I reached the royal chambers, I requested a cup of tea. I sat in an overstuffed chair and tried to concentrate on Myste's letter.

My dearest Lara,

I hope this letter finds you well and that you did not try to maim Tren-Lore before he gave it to you. He told me what happened, and about you and Yolis but we can talk about that later. For now, I am writing to tell you some rather interesting news. I must have been mad to take up with these Sanysk. They are nothing but trouble, and while I like trouble, I do not relish being impaled and dying over the course of eight painful days.

But I digress. I had not intended to write you a letter about my likes (cooking, long walks, and manly hewing and hacking) or my dislikes (being impaled). I am really writing to tell you that I have gotten married and am currently basking in marital bliss. I apologize for not inviting you to the wedding – oh, sorry, my loving wife has just informed me, "It is not a wedding, you peat head, it is a Joining Ceremony." Anyway, I would have invited you to my Joining Ceremony if I could have.

Now brace yourself, Lara, this is where things get a little odd. During my travels with Tren-Lore and Draows, we became acquainted with some Elves. Somehow, in between the shooting and the threats, I managed to fall in love with one of them. Her name is Kalypceon. She is beautiful and brilliant and fabulous at putting me in my place. Tren-Lore thoroughly enjoys her. As you may or may not know, the Elves have very strict laws about outsiders. I just barely managed to convince them that my parents could come to our nuptials, and then I just barely managed to convince my parents that they should come.

I reread this paragraph several times. Not only had Myste gotten married, but he had married an Elf! I shook my head in wonderment. I had never even been sure that Elves were real. Obviously, they were!

The story behind all this, as you might have guessed, is entirely dull. No, I am just jesting. Tren-Lore and I had –

I jumped in fright as a door slammed somewhere in the royal chambers. Letter forgotten, I sat with muscles tensed, awaiting the predator I knew was coming. The quick footsteps in the hall told me Yolis was close. When he stalked into the room, I drew a small breath of surprise. Blood covered the front of his tunic, and he held a cloth to his nose.

"What happened?" I gasped. The paper in my hand crackled as my grip tightened about it.

"I was in a fight! What do you think happened?" He yanked open the drawer of the cabinet and rummaged through it. He whirled around, a clean cloth in hand. His face was a mess of blood and his eye was blackening. "Do something about this! Are you a Healer or not?"

No, I wanted to reply, you took my Healer's ring, remember? I stayed silent. With Yolis, that was generally the best response. Approaching him with the type of caution used with a wounded animal, I gently put my hand on his chin and titled his head back. Reaching up, I tried to help him put pressure on the bridge of his nose, but the movement was awkward as my hand was already holding Myste's letter. Yolis snarled in pain and jerked away from me. His arm came up, and for an instant I thought he was going to hit me. I squeezed my eyes shut, waiting for the blow. It never came. Instead he grabbed the paper from me, and when I opened my eyes, I found him looking at me with a kind of bemused expression.

"Never mind," he told me. "What would Tren-Lore think if he knew you were undoing all his hard work?" Turning, Yolis left me alone in the middle of the room, his blood all over my hands.

Λ Λ Λ

Nahanni glided into the dining room early one morning the next week. I was sitting at one end of the table, and Yolis was at the other. He was reading some papers Gormek had brought him, and I was pushing my breakfast around the plate. I did not have much of an appetite. We both looked up when she entered. Yolis grinned, and I tried to smile.

"Nahanni, darling, what brings you here?" He put his pages down. "You look radiant."

The princess gave him a dazzling smile that dimpled her cheeks and made her face glow. "Thank you. I came to say good morning and ask if Lara wished to accompany me to Cala. We are distributing bread to the poor."

Yolis nodded. "I am sure Lara would love to come with you."

He said it in a congenial voice, but I knew it was an order. He wanted me out of the royal chambers. Before the morning meal, Gormek had informed Yolis that he had reports on the progress of the hired parties. Yolis had declined to talk about it in my presence, and was eagerly disposing of me so that he could conduct his business without fear of being overheard. He really had no cause for concern. I tossed my napkin on the table and stood. I was uninterested in Yolis' plans. Each new bit of knowledge was like taking one step closer to the edge of a cliff. It could only bring me closer to death.

Nahanni tried to talk cheerfully as we rode down to Cala, but my morose silence proved to be too much for even the princess. Nahanni gave up trying to make conversation, and we rode on in silence. Once in Cala, she turned her attention to Mistress Jolie, a more receptive conversation partner. When we had given out the food, Jolie invited us back to her house for some soup.

"It will warm your insides," she chuckled, and patted me on the cheek. "It seems like your insides might need some warming."

I made no reply, but wrapped my cloak more tightly around myself. We trudged through the snowy streets of Cala, our breathing making smoke in the air before us. Soon we arrived at a large stone house that was much bigger and older than the houses that flanked it. The exterior was gloomy, with dark windows staring menacingly at the road.

The interior was a sharp contrast to the house's foreboding external appearance. The walls were made of a warm-colored wood, and it smelled like cooking meat and herbs. I was struck by the thought that this was the kind of place Sophie would have called home. Jolie led us down a long hall and into a kitchen that the kindly old woman certainly would have approved of. It was organized with obvious care and scrubbed clean. A large pot was boiling over the fire.

"Soup," Jolie pronounced. "Nahanni, the bowls are in that cupboard." She pointed up and to her left. "Lara, grab a handful of spoons from that drawer. We will need five settings. My husband and son should be coming in shortly."

As I went about setting the table, long fingers of scent beckoned to me. My stomach growled. "The soup smells wonderful," I told Jolie, just as noise from the other room announced the arrival of the rest of our group.

The men entered the kitchen, and while Nahanni exclaimed over the impressive height of Jolie's son, I stared at her husband in shock. He was one of the men Yolis had hired. I recognized his cleft chin and his calm expression immediately. Yolis had referred to him as the representative for Caladore.

"Here I am, forgetting my manners!" Jolie exclaimed. She slipped an arm around my waist. "This is Lara. Lara, this is my husband Nekadious and my son Arron. Nekadious is the finest carpenter in Cala, and young Arron is training to take his place someday." She beamed at them with genuine pleasure.

Perhaps she did not know of her husband's other profession, or maybe she did not want me to know. I bent my lips upward in a smile. "It is nice to meet you," I said, and could not help thinking that Nekadious looked slightly relieved.

The lunch tasted like something Sophie would have made, and the conversation was more pleasant than any I had heard in some time. Apparently, not only did villains laugh and joke with each other, but they had families and ate soup. The stories certainly had missed a few things. When the meal was finished, I convinced Jolie to let me do the dishes while she showed Nahanni the new quilt she was making. Washing the bowls and spoons was soothing. The kitchen was warm, and the task had the comfort of familiarity. I had just scrubbed my last dish when Nekadious appeared in the room. He came and stood next to me, and taking up a cloth, began to dry a bowl. Apparently villains dried dishes, too.

"She does not know," he said softly, "and she is happier not knowing. Thank you for being so discreet. I am in your debt." He set the bowl down on the counter and left.

* * *

I returned from Jolie's house feeling more at ease than I had been in some time. Yolis was in a good mood, also. The news he had received from Gormek must have been positive. Not wanting to do something to destroy this rare peace, I slipped into my room and sat quietly before the window, watching the evening approach. Just as the bruise of night had darkened the skin of the sky, I heard Gormek's voice coming from one of the outer chambers. It was too muffled to distinguish any words, but he seemed distressed. Yolis' voice replied. The clipped, hard words were followed by the sound of footsteps and a banging door.

I raised my eyebrows in puzzlement and listened hard for any further sound. There was none. Obviously the men had gone to deal with some issue. Exhaling slowly, I felt some of the tension leave my shoulders. I always felt anxious when Yolis was in the royal chambers. I never knew if his next action might be spurred by anger or ardor. Safe from both, I changed into my sleeping gown and crawled into bed. For once, slumber did not elude me. It came swiftly, but was banished even more quickly.

I awoke to a hand crushing my wrist and dragging me out of bed. I stumbled forward into the blackness of my room, and my knees hit the stone floor with a sharp crack.

Neither my mind nor my muscles were ready for this sudden movement. An utterance of fear and pain escaped my lips.

"Please, Yolis," I sobbed, but the voice that answered was not Yolis'.

"Get up," replied Gormek.

He yanked me forward so that my feet were under me once more. Someone else took hold of my other arm, and another set of hands put something around my neck. Immediately, I felt a rush of energy and knew, without looking, that it was my Healer's ring.

"We are here by order of his Highness, King Yolis," Gormek pronounced. "You are under arrest for the poisoning of the Lord Vanya and the Lady Jizabelle. You will pay for their deaths with your own life, Healer." He said the word 'Healer' like a foul swear. "In one month's time your throat is to be against the chopping block. Take her to the dungeon."

I was born swiftly down into the dungeons. I let them take me without protest. Even after being shoved into a cell with the slamming of the door still ringing in my ears, my shock was such that I could hardly comprehend what had just happened. I could see nothing in the inky blackness, but the stench in the air was enough to make me gag. Blindly, I reached out and my fingers met with the damp stone of a wall. I let myself sink to the ground. My knees protested in pain, but I did not have the strength to stand. The weight of the situation was too heavy for me to bear. No tears came to my eyes. My insides were frozen. Leaning my head back against the wall, I let the darkness devour me.

Chapter Thirty- Four
Solrium Vallent

I awoke the next day to a single shaft of light shining through a small grate in the low ceiling. The grate was scarcely the width of half my hand and about the length of my forearm, yet the sunshine coming through that tiny space was enough to destroy the absolute blackness that dwelt in the cell. I studied the faint, golden line of sunlight that spread across the dirt floor. Its shape reminded me of the dagger Tren-Lore had given me.

Would Tren-Lore come to save me if he heard of my imprisonment? His stony expression and dark gaze flashed into my memory. I felt certain that the Tren-Lore who might have tried to save me was gone. The man I had last met was a Sanysk through and through, and from what I understood of the modern Sanysk, they were not inclined to deeds of heroism without some kind of coin changing hands. Hopelessness descended, and I hardly noticed when night obliterated the small slice of light that had infiltrated the cell.

I drifted in and out of restless dreams. I stared into the darkness and waited. I waited for them to come and put an end to all of this. Someone brought me food and water each day, but I did not eat. My eyes fluttered open and I stared across the room at the shaft of sunlight that had returned again. I had seen it four or five times now. My body was drained of all energy. The nausea of hunger, had passed and a constant ache had taken its place. I lay listlessly in the grime and watched the dagger of light that lay upon the floor. I thought again of my dagger and pictured the keen blade and bold inscription. I traced the letters with my mind, and then parted my dry lips and said aloud, in a voice rough from disuse, "Solrium vallent."

The noise sounded strange in the silence of the dungeon.

"Self hero," I muttered as I remembered the night Tren-Lore had given me the dagger. "Solrium vallent means self hero."

I thought about this until the bleariness of my mind dragged me down into unconsciousness. I was awakened next by a voice that made me flinch.

"Good morning, darling," Yolis drawled in tones of sarcasm.

I opened my eyes slowly and I threw a hand up to shield myself from the bright light of the torch that Yolis was holding. I did not bother to move from where I lay on the dirt.

"I came to make sure that you understand the reason for your imprisonment," Yolis continued pleasantly.

I let my eyes settle upon the king of Caladore. He was dressed in his royal finery with perfectly groomed hair and face, but he had regained the dangerous look that had made me fear him in my youth. No, I thought blearily, not regained. That malice had always been there. It was just that, for a time, it had not been directed toward me.

"I know why," I said. My throat was so dry and sore it was difficult to talk. Jizabelle and Vanya had obviously gone through with their plan, and Yolis had assumed I would have heard court gossip about such a plot. He had seized the opportunity to rid himself of two problems. He poisoned the troublesome couple and blamed their death on me. All I could manage to say was, "You killed Jizabelle and Vanya, not me."

Yolis nodded congenially. "Quite right. However, that is not the reason you are here. I knew you would try to make me into the villain and blame me for what happened. In actuality, it was you who doomed yourself. If you had been even slightly worthy of trust..." He took an ominous step forward and I flinched. "If you had ever managed to forget about the gallant Tren-Lore and love me instead of him, you would not find yourself in this situation! Would you have questioned anything Tren-Lore said? Would you have tried to leave Tren-Lore? Would you have told *Tren-Lore* about Vanya's plan?"

"Yes," I said softly, "I would have told him."

Yolis kicked me viciously in the side, and I cried out in pain. "I know." He turned and stalked from the cell.

The slamming of the door sounded like the rumble of thunder. For an instant, even the ray of light on the floor was not enough to allow me sight. The torch had been too bright, and now my eyes were blind in the sudden darkness. I lay still. The pain in my body began to ebb, but the agony within me raged unabated. Yolis was right. I had done this to myself. Why had I let this happen? Why had I let him treat me so badly? Why had I been so stupid and taken up with him in the first place? Because, my mind answered, because you needed someone to save you, just like you need someone to save you now.

My hazy mind brushed against memories of stories I had heard when I was a child. I recalled the settings for some, the most exciting parts of others, but I recalled the villains and heroes in all of them. I said my favorite heroes' names aloud, tasting them in my mouth. Images from my own life meandered past my mind's eye.

"Solrium vallent," I muttered.

They were words of enchantment that seemed to put a tiny wedge in the door of possibility. Perhaps I did not have to lay here and wait for death. Perhaps I could save myself. Groaning with pain, I crawled forward until I lay beneath the shaft of light.

I imagined the sunlight seeping through my skin and gliding inside me. The layers of ice that had been building within began to melt. The water of this dissolving frost seeped from the corners of my eyes and ran down my cheeks. I wept for what had happened with Yolis, for the pain, the defilement, and the slow hollowing of my spirit. I wept for Tren-Lore, the loss of true friendship and love, and for what we had both become. My mind would not yet turn to Sophie and my mother. I had to grieve these other tragedies first, and then perhaps I could deal with those wounds. When my last tears dried, I felt as though the earth of my spirit was tentatively warming.

* * *

I paced my cell. Three steps forward, turn, and three steps back. It felt strange to feel the touch of soil against my bare feet again. I walked this short route daily, ever seeking a plan for escape. The shaft of light had come five more times. I had started eating again on the day Yolis came to see me. My mind and body had responded immediately to the nourishment. My thoughts became clearer as my body grew in strength. I was still unable, however, to think of a plan for escape.

"End this all!" I groaned and pressed my hands to my head. "Some hero I am. I cannot even think of a plan."

Rayn never had this problem. Plans had always come easily to him. I stretched my arms above my head and tried to loosen the developing kink in my back. My body's reaction to the tension was worsening daily. The longer I delayed escaping, the closer I came to feeling an axe against my neck. My fingertips brushed against the ceiling. It was cold metal rather than wet stone that met my touch. I leaned my head back and looked up at the grate. Light bathed my face.

Out of curiosity, I stood on the tips of my toes and looping my fingers into the grate, gave a tug. To my immense surprise, I felt it give slightly. I continued to pull until I fell backwards onto the floor. A shower of dust rained down upon me, but I victoriously held the piece of metal in my hands. I stared at the two rods of steel, riveted together at each end by crosspieces. I had a weapon. Now all I needed was the strength to wield it.

The guards brought food every second day. I accepted the stale bread and water gratefully, thanking them during the brief moment that existed between when they handed me the paltry fare and when the slot snapped shut again. I rationed what little food I was given and began recalling the exercises I had helped Tren-Lore practice. During my time with Yolis, my muscles had become weak and my endurance low. In the solitude of my cell, with the grate as my sword, I trained until I was too weary to stand anymore. Only then would I let myself rest. I would sit in one of the corners and eat slowly. I would turn my attention from matters of the body to matters of the mind. As I ingested the stale bread, I ingested memories. I chewed slowly upon the events of the past, swallowing them when they had been broken down into understandable pieces. Often, they had a different taste than the first time I had lived them.

It took some time before I did not choke on memories of Yolis. I hated him, and often just the thought of his violence was enough to make me retch. It was hard not to hate myself for turning to him. Yet, as I relived those bitter times, I could understand why I had been driven to it. The past could not be changed, but I could ensure that it would not happen again. I slowly began to forgive myself for my weakness. I did not know if I would ever forgive Yolis.

Memories of Tren-Lore were easier to swallow, but were certainly not without a bitter taste. In my mind, I revisited the day in the secret room when Tren-Lore had told us of his father's ultimatum. I had loved him so much then. I had made the decision to end our relationship so that he could see the fulfillment of his dreams. Yet, the last time I had seen him, he had been a harder, colder version of the boy I had befriended and the man I had loved. I wondered briefly how things would have turned out if we had resisted his father's ultimatum. It was an agonizing thought. So much had been lost that sometimes the pain felt unbearable; as though angry wounds festered within my body, oozing regret and sorrow. I came to understand, however, that acceptance was the only way to bind these injuries of the past.

This was not the only pain I was forced to endure. Each day I fought a new battle against my cold aching body, slow reactions, and battered ego. Perhaps the only good thing about my seclusion was that there was no one to witness my clumsy practices. I began to share the foul odor of my cell, and my sleeping gown was ripped and black with dirt. My hair was the tangled mass of a

Pandel's nest, and my skin felt gritty with old sweat and dust. In spite of my adversities, I was stronger in both body and spirit. Fond memories of my mother, of the adventures Tren-Lore and I had shared, and the love Sophie had consistently displayed sustained me and helped to keep dark thoughts at bay.

On the twenty-third day of my confinement I stood beneath the edge of light. It was fading as night approached, but I let its lingering touch warm my cheeks. My arms and legs remembered the old fighting forms I had known. I could move quickly and with force. I had a plan, and I was ready.

"I probably have never looked worse," I remarked to the sunlight, "but I certainly feel better."

My fingers went to the ring about my neck. I closed my hand around it, and then letting my grip relax, looked down at my palm. The thin scar was still visible through the grime that covered my hands. The verdant blush had returned to the silver of my ring. It was not the same green it had once been, but I could tell some life had returned to it.

"Soon," I told myself, and went to keep vigil at the door.

I was nervous and my ears strained for the sound of footfalls. The guard who brought my food would arrive soon and I intended to face him. I twisted my hand around the grate and swallowed hard. At least surprise was my weapon as well.

"Solrium vallent, solrium vallent," I repeated under my breath. "I can do this." Doubt filled me. Did I really have any chance of overcoming the guard? Was this plan born of desperation and destined to fail? If only there had been someone there to help me, to save me. I groaned. "Where are you, Tren-Lore?"

Not here, a voice within me replied, so grit your teeth and do this. You have no other choice. I could hear footsteps. They were coming nearer. I drew a ragged breath, and my muscles bunched into knots of fear. My heartbeat seemed to shake my whole body. The footfalls stopped. The guard was right outside!

The slot slid open and a burly arm extended inward, its hairy fingers offering a chunk of bread. It seemed that everything was moving slowly. The air felt thick as I drew the grate back and smashed it down across the man's wrist. He bellowed in pain and anger. I sprang forward and grabbed hold of his broken wrist. I pulled with all my weight, forcing him forward until the majority of his arm had been dragged through the slot.

"Take your keys and open the door," I told him, my voice quivering with fear.

The man was yelling someone's name.

Taking a deep, steadying breath, I recalled everything Namin had taught me about the bones in the arm and wrist. I began to carefully apply pressure. The man started to scream. It was a sound of torture and it made me sick. I lessened the pressure and repeated my demand, "Open this door right now, or the pain is about to get much worse."

This time I heard the jingling of keys and the click of a lock. I used the man's arm to pull the door open. He shuffled along with the door, moaning in pain.

"Ascendants forgive me," I muttered, and sharply twisted the man's broken wrist so that skin was the only thing keeping his hand attached to his arm. The guard let out one final gasp, and his arm slithered back through the slot. His body hit the floor with a loud thump. I could feel my stomach revolting, trying to force its way up my throat. I scrambled over the man's body and into the passageway, fleeing the horror of what I had done.

Another guard was rushing down the tunnel toward me, swinging his sword with the intent of slicing my chest open. Instinctually, I threw my arms up, the grate held in my white-knuckled grip. His sword met the hard steel of my crude weapon. The impact reverberated up my arms and tore painfully at my shoulders. He moved to strike again. I kicked at the side of his knee with my foot and heard the sound of tendons ripping from bone. He screamed in agony and staggered to one side. I swung my arm wide, catching him solidly in the side of the head with the metal grate. The guard dropped to the ground. He did not move again. I stooped, my stomach churning. My shaking fingers found his pulse, and relief steadied me slightly.

I looked about. There was no one else in the dim tunnel, but I did not doubt that they would be coming shortly. The fight had not been a silent one. I dropped the grate on the floor and almost felt regretful to leave it behind. It had served me well, but a sword would be of more use if I were in another conflict. I hefted the guard's weapon and began to run down the passageway. My mind was wild with random thoughts, and my body felt as though it was vibrating with feral energy. I had just fought my way out of my cell! It was like something from the *Rayn* books. What would Tren-Lore think if I ever got to tell him? I was climbing stairs now, taking them two at a time. At least I was going up. Imagine if Sophie could have heard about this, I thought to myself. What a tale she could have made of it! I took the last steps in a large bound and turned the corner to see a party of men – at least eight of them - standing at the end of the hall. I stared at them in horror and wondered numbly if I should turn and run or try to stay and fight.

"Put the sword down, *Healer*!" one of the guards shouted.

It was the way he said the word Healer. Reason evaporated, and I was left with burning anger. I would not run from him or any of his cursed men.

"End you," I growled from between gritted teeth and raised my sword in a ready position.

The man chuckled and strode forward. He had not even bothered to raise his sword. "Enough foolishness, woman," he snapped. He was close to me now. "Put down the weapon before I have to knock some sense into you."

There was no conscious thought. I felt as though my fury would rip me apart – would destroy me along with this hideous man. I lunged forward and caught the man under the chin with the tip of my sword. My hand was shaking. For an instant I wanted to drive the blade into his flesh. I wanted to silence the hatred that accompanied his use of the word Healer. I wanted to reclaim the power that had been beaten from me. I wanted....

The guard groaned in pain, and reason returned to me. I reduced the pressure on the blade. Blood stained the collar of the man's tunic. Meeting his eyes, I found that his gaze was shocked and more than a little afraid. He had not expected this. No one had expected that I might be capable of saving myself; no one, not even me.

"Tell your men to put down their weapons," I told him. My voice quavered, and I inwardly cursed this show of weakness.

He swallowed hard. I could see that the pulse in his throat was at least as fast as mine. "I cannot do that," he replied.

"Tell them!" I yelled at him, increasing pressure again. "Tell them to put down their weapons."

"Do as she says."

I jerked my eyes upward, past the guard before me. I knew who was speaking. I knew, and yet even as I beheld Tren-Lore, I could not fully believe it. His Sanysk bands were flashing in the darkness of the corridor, and deep within the black feena penent sword a storm of blue and purple swirled. There was a cry of surprise from the guards as they leapt about, tearing swords from scabbards. It was clear that none had been aware of Tren-Lore's presence until he had spoken.

"Your lives will be forfeited if you do not surrender," Tren-Lore warned grimly.

For a moment there was silence, and I watched in wonder as one of the men stooped and laid his sword upon the floor. "I will not fight a Sanysk," he murmured.

There was an abrupt growl of anger from the guard before me. Taking advantage of my distraction, he leapt backward, bellowing, "Fight, you cowards! Fight!"

He turned and charged toward Tren-Lore, spurring his companions to battle.

I gasped as two men lunged at Tren-Lore, swords leveled at his chest. Instead of bringing his sword up to block the stroke, the Sanysk slid to his knees, and in a blur of movement swung his blade through the first man's legs and up into the next guard's lower torso. The sound of splintering bone filled the jail. Blood splashed everywhere, and it looked as though the walls themselves were oozing gore. I watched in horror as the next guard aimed a low thrust at Tren-Lore. The young Sanysk kicked the blade aside, and in the instant the man's arms opened to leave his chest vulnerable, Tren-Lore ran him through. The guard behind him screamed and crumpled to a heap on the floor, a dagger protruding from his chest. I had not even seen Tren-Lore throw the small blade.

I hardly noticed three of the guards turn to run. My attention was upon Tren-Lore's face. It was without expression, lacking fear, remorse, or any kind of emotion. I was sure that those who faced in him battle saw, in that look, a chilling boredom, a knowledge that the Sanysk could kill them as easily as he could take his next breath. And while this was true, it was not the truth that I saw. I knew better. Tren-Lore only wore that expression when he was suffering great emotional pain.

The final guard, the very man who had been at my mercy only moments ago, was now demanding Tren-Lore's surrender in a shaking voice. Part of me wanted to laugh hysterically, but Tren-Lore remained impassive. Draped in Sanysk gray, his black sword at his side and his bands glowing with a near blinding light, he did not seem real. Tren-Lore had become the warrior from the legends we had heard as children. He was a force to match even Lord Rayn. For the first time in my life, I wished that he was only Tren-Lore and that I was only Lara, and together we had no grander dreams than that. The magic of our own ordinary stories would have seemed more than enough.

As though he could not stand Tren-Lore's calm patience a moment longer, the guard let forth a wild yell and swung his blade in a wide arch toward Tren-Lore. The Sanysk stepped to the side, and with a swiftness that defied the powers of vision, slammed his feena penent blade under the other man's hilt. The sword flew from the guard's grasp, and Tren-Lore caught it in his left hand. In the space of a breath, he had both weapons crossed at the man's throat, and then hot blood was gushing over my bare feet. I staggered away from the lifeless body on the floor.

I retched violently. My throat burned and my limbs shook. I tried to inhale deeply to calm myself, but the air reeked of blood. I gritted my teeth. After everything, this was no time to lose my self-control. Tren-Lore was here at last, and he going to help me escape. I righted myself and wiped my mouth with my grimy sleeve. Tren-Lore stooped and retrieved his dagger and then glanced up at me with an unreadable Sanysk expression. Our eyes met, and I held his gaze with steady determination.

"I am glad to see you," I told him earnestly.

His perfectly calm countenance was broken by the smile that creased his face. At that moment, he was just Tren-Lore, not the formidable Sanysk I had just seen in battle.

"I am glad to see you, too," he said, and then turned and strode down the corridor.

He still expects me to follow him, I thought in brief irritation. As I currently had no other choice, I matched my course and pace to his. He led me through a twisting maze of passages to a hall that ended in a ladder. The ladder stretched up to a trapdoor in the ceiling. Scaling the rungs with ease, Tren-Lore heaved the door open. A cold blast of fresh air rushed past my skin. The gust brought the smell of trees and earth and snow into the musty hall. I greedily sucked in the clean breath of the outside world. It had been so long since I had filled my lungs with anything other than stale, reeking air. Clambering after Tren-Lore, I emerged into the forest. Tren-Lore closed the door silently and kicked snow back over it.

I looked about the dark woods in shock. Was I really here? It seemed more likely that this was a cruel dream of freedom and I was still back in my cell, sleeping in the grime and stench, awaiting a sentence of death. Was it truly possible that the all-powerful Yolis had been thwarted? Were Tren-Lore and I really escaping from the dungeons of Caladore in the dead of night? I stared up into the sky. It was scattered with twinkling stars and a sliver of moon grinned down at us. So much light in the darkness, I marveled.

Tren-Lore took four paces forward, and putting his fingers to his lips, whistled quietly. The chill evening was quickly penetrating my dirt-stiffened gown, and I wrapped my arms around myself. My lips were shaking with cold, and my feet burned as though thousands of needles were piercing them. We would have to find shelter soon or - my thoughts were cut short by the sound of hooves crunching in the snow. The fear of discovery had crushed my stomach into a painful ball of tension, when a large black stallion cantered from the trees.

I gasped in relief. "Storm Wing!"

The stallion turned his head to me and gave a contentious snort.

"One and the same," Tren-Lore replied, patting the horse's neck, "and not too impressed about waiting in the cold. Climb up."

He offered me his hand, and I took it. His palms felt harder than I remembered. I mounted clumsily. It had been far too long since I had ridden.

"We are going to hide in the cottage tonight," Tren-Lore said as he unclasped his cloak and passed it to me.

I gratefully clutched the soft folds of cloth around my body. The material was light and yet it kept out the cold better than some of the winter cloaks I had owned. Tren-Lore leapt up behind me. Wrapping his arms around me, he took Storm Wings' reins and nudged the horse into a trot. It was a strange sensation to be this close to Tren-Lore again.

"So am I safe in presuming you did not really murder Lady Jizabelle and Lord Vanya?" Tren-Lore asked pleasantly.

I looked down at the ground. Guilt was filling me, swirling upward until I felt like I was drowning in it. My own plight had prevented me from thinking about Jizabelle and Vanya, but now that I was been granted temporary safety...

"I did not murder them with action," I said. My voice was so soft that I could barely even hear myself. "But my inaction did lead to their deaths."

I informed Tren-Lore of Yolis' plan to gain power in Caladore's neighboring countries, of Jizabelle and her husband's attempt to stop the rise of terror, and then of my final betrayal of Yolis. I rubbed tears from my eyes. I could feel mud streaking across my cheeks.

"It was not your fault, Lara." Tren-Lore's arms tightened around me slightly. "Adewus says that each battle holds within it an inherent choice between life and death. You must decide if you will be the one who survives, or your opponent. Choosing your own survival is always the right thing to do."

"I do not think that is true. It is not always right to choose life for yourself. I think if you always do that, you will end up dying another kind of death. It will just be slower and less apparent... and since when did you start quoting Adewus?"

Tren-Lore made no reply, and we returned to riding in silence. It was strange to be with Tren-Lore, to have his arms around me, and yet feel the distance that existed between us. We rode through the night in silence. I did not know what to say to him. I did not feel strong enough to withstand what Tren-Lore might tell me, and I was not prepared to give my experiences the strength of spoken word. Our journey to the cottage was a silent one, and when we arrived we had neither the comfort of warmth or company.

We did not light a fire or candles. If Yolis' men were looking for us, then stealth was our best defense. The dust lay where it was, the shutters remained closed. It seemed our presence was hardly felt by the house. We did not say much to each other, and retired to separate rooms and cold beds. As I slipped beneath Nahanni's sun quilt, I remembered how happy I had been the last time we had come here. I had fallen asleep in Tren-Lore's arms, and it had seemed as though nothing would ever go wrong. That night I fell asleep with uncertainty wrapped around me.

I was awakened by muffled cries. My eyes snapped open, but the rest of my body was paralyzed with fear. I was still in the dungeon – someone was screaming with the pain of torture. It had all been a dream. Tren-Lore had not come to save me. A sob of despair passed my lips, and I pulled my blankets over my face. The touch of the worn cloth against my cheek was like a brush of reality, and my pulse slowed. No, it had not been a dream. I *had* escaped with Tren-Lore's help, and now I was with him at the cottage.

I slowly forced my fingers to unclench the quilt fabric and looked around the room. The gray light of early morning was banishing the darkness, but the sound that had roused me continued. Tren-Lore was protesting something, in the loud, strangely indistinct, panic-filled voice of someone talking in their sleep. The floor was icy cold, and I winced with each step as I crept toward Tren-Lore's room.

He was lying upon his bed. The blankets had been kicked to the floor and one arm was thrown over his face, as though he was protecting his head. His other hand clutched his chest in a gesture of pain.

"I am sorry! I am sorry!" he was repeating again and again, his tone becoming increasingly frantic.

I hurried to his side and laid a hand on his shoulder. "Tren-Lore," I whispered, but he did not awaken. It felt as though the terror in his voice was seeping into me. I hated to see him like this. He was supposed to be the calm one, the one who knew what to do, the one who could take care of us both. "Tren-Lore, wake up!" I shook him.

He sat up with a start, grabbing my wrist and yanking my hand away from him. The fingers that wrapped around my skin were unnaturally hot, and the eyes that met mine were unfocused. "Lara?" he muttered as though surprised to see me.

"You were having a bad dream," I told him. It did not seem like an adequate response, but it was all I could think off. I tentatively withdrew my hand from his grasp.

He nodded and rubbed at his chest. "I have bad dreams all the time. Do you have any karhine?"

"Why?" I asked in bewilderment.

Tren-Lore lay back and pulled up his tunic to reveal three angry red scars running from his shoulder down across his muscular chest and stomach. It brought me pain just looking at them. There appeared to be an infection lingering beneath the partially healed wounds. Instinctively, I reached out and touched his chest. He stayed completely still, and in that moment of contact, several senses bombarded my mind. I could feel Tren-Lore's life force. It was weak, sapped by something that had been slowly draining his energy. His heartbeat was still strong, however, and quickened with my touch. My eyes flickered up to his face. His cheeks were flushed with fever, and his look...he had looked at me like that when we had been in love.

"The scars are from when I killed the dragon." He sounded as though he was daring me to say something. He wanted me to say something so he could justify what he had done – not to me, I thought, but to himself. "Did you hear about that?" he asked.

I laid a hand softly on his arm. It was the only comfort I could think to offer. I understood his pain, but I had no solution for it. "Yes, I heard about it," I replied.

"Dragon claws are poisonous, and the wounds are slow to heal."

"I never knew that," I said.

Tren-Lore grimaced. "It was never in any of the books I read, either. There are few people who actually fight dragons, and even fewer who live to tell about it. The poison in the claws prevents the injuries from healing completely. They always feel fresh. Karhine helps, though."

I patted the grimy sides of the sleeping gown I still wore. "Just your luck, I seem to have forgotten my karhine in my other dress." My teasing was rewarded with a slight smile from Tren-Lore. I found myself smiling back, a sliver of happiness appearing inside me. "I can get some, though," I reassured him. "It grows around here."

I left Tren-Lore's room, and after slipping my feet into his shoes and taking his cloak from the peg by the door, I shuffled out into the woods to search for karhine. I was thankful that the touches of spring had begun to melt some of the snow and reveal the foliage beneath winter's cloak. I spotted the leaves down by the brook. The ice had broken and the water flowed fast and black. Holding on to the side of the boat that had been pulled up on shore, I carefully scrambled down the bank and gathered the karhine. I returned to the cottage dirtier and colder than when I left, but with karhine in hand.

After filling a cup with snow, I chanced lighting a candle in order to dry the leaves over the small flame. It was a tedious process, but I hummed softly as I worked. It was a song Sophie had often hummed, and it reminded me of the kindly old woman. I wondered what she would have thought about everything that had happened. An image of Sophie shaking her head came unbidden to my mind. She would not have been happy with the choices I had made. When she had ... Suddenly, the flame blurred before me. The golden color became distorted as tears filled my eyes. The last time I had talked to her, she had told me that I was a remarkable girl. I certainly did not feel very remarkable now.

I removed the wine-colored leaves from the heat and crushed them as finely as I could before mixing them into the melted snow. I blinked to clear my vision and took the cup to Tren-Lore. He was asleep again. I laid my hand on his shoulder, and even through his tunic I could feel the heat of fever. I also became aware of some tainted part within Tren-Lore, some darkness that dwelled inside his body.

"Tren-Lore," I whispered softly.

He slowly opened his eyes and I offered him the cup. He tried to prop himself up on his elbows, but immediately fell back, his face strained with anguish. Hesitantly, I came to sit beside him on the bed. I rested his head in my lap, and slowly managed to help him drink the contents of the cup. Tren-Lore lay still with exhaustion. As the karhine began to take effect, his breathing grew more regular, and he appeared to slumber. I studied his peaceful face. It was easy to forget everything for just a moment. I let my sadness and fear wash away. It was just Tren-Lore and I as we had been in our youth. Love for him swelled within me. With a shaking hand, I reached down and gently stroked the hair back from his forehead. My finger ran with a reminiscent fondness down his temple. He moved his hand, and laid it on top of mine. For an instant, I reveled in his touch before abruptly pulling away as the past and present once more intruded upon my consciousness.

I rose from the bed. "Rest for a while, Tren-Lore."

"Tren," he grunted and rolled over, pulling the covers around his shoulders. "Everyone calls me Tren now."

Chapter Thirty-Five
Tren

I awoke to find bands of sunlight falling across my bed. The room was filled with the chill of winter. I slipped from bed, bringing Nahanni's sun quilt with me. Tren-Lore, Tren, I reminded myself, was sitting by the window when I emerged from the room. He was watching carefully through the cracks in the shutters.

"Good morning," he said without turning around.

"Good morning," I replied. My stomach felt like it was turning itself inside out. I was so hungry that it made me feel ill. "Is there anything to eat?"

Tren nodded. "It is in the kitchen waiting for you. I also melted some snow if you want to wash, and Nahanni should have some clothes in one of her trunks."

Tren's thoughtfulness made my throat feel tight. It was the first selfless act of kindness I had experience since Sophie had died. "Thank you," I said, and wandered into the kitchen.

There was a plate of dried meat sitting on the table. Next to this was a large bowl of murky water. Not even bothering to sit down, I eagerly consumed the food, tearing chunks off with my teeth, barely pausing to chew the salty meat. When I had finished eating, I found a cloth in the kitchen and carefully carried the bowl of water to Nahanni's room. I closed the door gently and set the bowl down. Rooting through the trunk at the end of Nahanni's bed, I found an old dress, stockings, and even a pair of her shoes.

I took a deep breath and pulled off my filthy sleeping gown. The air rushed over my naked body, and as I began to wash away the grime, the cold seemed to almost burn my skin. It had been so long since I had touched my body, since my body had been mine. I endured the pain until my skin was pink and clean. I dressed in Nahanni's clothes and went to sit by Tren. I was ready to talk.

"So," I began in a soft voice, "what were you doing in the east?"

Tren was quiet for a time, and then replied, "Do you want an honest answer?"

I nodded solemnly. I wanted to understand what had happened to my friend, what had turned Tren-Lore into Tren.

"Killing people for money...that is what being a Sanysk means now." Tren's voice was flat. "It is not like in the *Rayn* books. There is no glamour, no shining heroic actions."

"You came to save me," I replied. "That is pretty heroic."

He chuckled darkly. "You had things under control." We fell back into silence. "Why were you with Yolis, Lara?" Tren asked suddenly.

I could not find the words to answer his question. Tears started to spill down my cheeks and I angrily wiped them away. I had cried enough for Yolis. I did not want to cry over him any more. I raised my chin and Tren's storm blue eyes were there to meet my gaze. I took a deep, steadying breath. "When Sophie died, I felt like I needed someone to help me. You were with Areama." My voice hardened and Tren's steady gaze faltered. "Yolis was there, and certainly ready to take advantage of my weakness. By the time I realized what I had gotten myself into, it was too late."

"What did he do to you?" Tren demanded.

I shook my head. I did not want to revisit those memories.

The muscles in Tren's jaws were twitching. "I wish you had asked for help."

"You were gone, Tren," I replied. The shortened name felt strange in my mouth.

Tren and I did not speak again until evening returned. We were both sitting at the kitchen table chewing on more of the salted meat.

"So, what is our plan?" I asked between bites.

"I am not sure," Tren replied. He pushed the meat away from himself. "I cannot eat any more of this."

I blinked at him like an owl startled by daylight. "You...you are not sure?" Since we had escaped the dungeon, fear had been mounting within me. I knew Yolis would be hunting me, like darkness stalks the day. I knew too much, and if Yolis captured me, my death would be inevitable. My terror thus far had been held at bay by my faith that Tren-Lore – Tren – would know how to stop Yolis.

"It will not be long before his soldiers are here," Tren muttered with chilling certainty. "We need somewhere to hide that offers both permanence and safety." He reached out and began to absently sift through the smooth river rocks that rested in a bowl on the table. "We cannot seek refuge in Hemlizar, Renarn or Nara Vit. Since the turmoil began in those countries, they are about as safe as sleeping in a skeleth's den."

"As what?" I echoed, thinking perhaps I had misheard him.

"Skeleth," he repeated. "They are creatures from the east; sort of wolf-like, only ten times as dangerous. Perhaps we should return to the east." Tren stirred the rocks with his finger, and the small stones whispered softly, brushing against one another.

The sound was comforting somehow. It reminded me of summer, of solid earth and running water. A plan began to form in my mind, a plan so rebellious I could scarcely believe I had conceived of it. It was a plot more fitting to one of the bold heroes from my childhood stories. "We need to go to Cala!" I exclaimed. "We can take the boat down by the brook. It would be nearly impossible for Yolis' soldiers to track us along a route like that."

"Lara," Tren objected, "that is not the direction we want to go."

I was feeling warm with excitement. I gathered my knees up onto my chair and leaned across the table to Tren. "We cannot run from Yolis forever, and if you help me I think we can stop him."

Tren was regarding me cautiously. "How do you propose we do that?"

"All right," I began, "we need to take the boat to Cala. There is a man there named Nekadious who is involved in Yolis' scheme." I paused, realizing that Tren had not been fully informed of all the details concerning Yolis' nefarious plot. I filled him in as quickly as I could, and then continued to explain my plan. "We need to get in contact with Nekadious. I did him a favor once, so maybe he will be willing to help. The agreement Yolis had drawn up between himself and the men he hired should be more than enough to implicate Yolis."

Tren nodded and rubbed at his chin. "If the other rulers knew who was behind the recent chaos, I am sure they would be more than willing to help us force the crown from Yolis." Tren sighed. It was a sound of weariness. "I know most of them. They would grant me an audience."

* * *

"They are coming," Tren grunted as he shoved the boat out onto the water and leapt in. "It seems we are leaving just in time."

I nervously twisted the hem of my cloak. "How do you know?" I asked, and stared anxiously into the depths of the forest that were slipping past us. My heartbeat quickened as I imagined guards bursting through the trees.

"I can smell them on the wind," Tren informed me.

I laughed, and was nearly startled by the sound of my own delight. I had almost forgotten what sincere laughter felt like. "I missed you," I told him fondly. "No one else I know can smell other people on the wind."

Tren looked slightly indignant. "A group of horses, dogs, and soldiers has a very distinctive odor, Lara." He pulled his Sanysk cloak around himself.

"Do you think they will follow Storm Wing's trail?" I asked.

That morning, before the sun had even awoken, Tren had whispered words in his mount's ear. The charger had snorted a reply and set off into the woods. He was going to the Elves, Tren had told me. I had struggled to keep my mouth from hanging open in amazement. It was still hard to believe that the Elves were real, and harder yet to believe that Myste actually married one of them.

"They will follow Storm Wing's trail," he replied shortly. "For the time being, we are safe. Still, we should probably travel in silence."

I chewed on my lip for a moment. "What will happen if they follow Storm Wing all the way to the Elves?" I asked, forgetting to whisper.

Tren gave me a look that would have suited him better if he had been wielding his sword. "The Elvin forests are enchanted. Any person that enters unbidden forgets why they came and is suddenly overcome by the need to return to their home. Now, no more questions, Lara, we need to be quiet."

"But what if-"

"Lara!" Tren growled, his Sanysk bands flashing in the morning light. "I said, no more questions. We are traveling in silence."

The comment stung like salt in a wound. It was not like him to treat me with such disregard. Pressing my toes hard into the bottom of my shoes, I leaned toward him, my elbows on my knees. "Stop being such a Barlem!" I said from between gritted teeth. "Just because I teased you about being able to smell people does not mean you have to be so miserable. Remember teasing? Remember how we used to tease each other? Quit hiding behind this formidable Sanysk act and try being Tren-Lore for just a moment."

For an instant I thought I read surprise in his dark blue eyes, but the emotion was quickly replaced with a gaze as cool as the river water. I glared back at him. Let him sit there and brood. Let him wrap himself in his Sanysk ideals and rot from the inside out. I folded my arms over my chest and resolved to let him have his silence. I would not say another word to him.

It was not until the smaller stream joined its course with the powerful Venst, that sound rejoined our solemn company. Strong Aquara fingers had grasped the sides of the boat and were pulling it steadily toward a jagged pile of rocks in the middle of the river.

Tren took up the oars. "Well," he said cautiously, a small smile crooking his lips. "I suppose I had better start paddling."

I laughed in spite of myself. "Rowing, Tren-L...Tren. The word is rowing." We were both grinning now, and suddenly the sun seemed to have a little more warmth in its touch. Apparently, he did remember teasing.

"I am sorry, Lara," Tren said abruptly and heaved on the oars. "It has been a long time since I was with anyone who was not a member of the League. There is not any joking when you are with the Sanysk. You were right. I should try being myself, but..." He sliced the oars through the water. "When we were young, we both read all those stories about Rayn and the Sanysk and heroes. I wanted more than anything to be part of that. I promised myself that when I grew up, I would *be* one of those people. Now that I am, I have discovered there is a difference between being a hero and being a person. I am afraid I am lost in Sanyskhood."

I nodded. I understood losing yourself in the role of a person you wanted to be. Why was it never good enough to be yourself? Why had neither of us ever cared about our own stories? "At least you know enough to be afraid. If you are afraid, then you can fight to stop what is happening." I thought bitterly that if I had been less trusting, if my blindness to Yolis' true nature had not been so absolute, then perhaps I could have escaped him before it was too late. "You know, you were wonderful even before you were a Sanysk. You were a hero – you are a hero, just because *you* are *you*."

Our eyes met and to my surprise, the blue depths of his gaze had been darkened by tears. He smiled at me. "I always thought the same about you."

I looked away from him. "Be quiet," I told him, feeling a blush spread across my cheeks. The wind raked through my hair, but I did not heed its fretful touch. It was hard to believe that Tren had thought of me in that way, and yet... My mind drifted for a few moments. Perhaps it was not such a ridiculous idea. Perhaps there were many heroes that were not bound by the pages of books.

The current had returned our boat to the middle of the river, and Tren's skill as an oarsman was no longer needed. He leaned back against the bow and closed his eyes. Soon his chin dipped toward his chest and he slumbered. I watched him, pondering this new revelation and wondering absently if his Sanysk senses would alert him to danger even through the haze of sleep. We traveled until darkness fell and obscured the green and blue plated shore. With one elbow propped uncomfortably on the hard edge of the boat and my head supported on my palm, I slipped in and out of consciousness.

Out of the dimness, the image of two women appeared along the shore. They were standing in the shallow water, and they were calling to me, their words carried on the air. There were more words than I could ever hope to hear, but they surrounded me and cradled me in a bower of stories. I knew the tales as I knew my own breath. They were my mother's, Sophie's, Namin's, and Tren-Lore's. They came from a place of family, of love, and the bravery it takes to survive in the world. The women turned their faces to me. It was Sophie and my mother; their figures melded into one and the face looking back at me was my own. The woman raised her hand in a gesture of greeting and smiled. I waited for her words to fill me but all was silent. I blinked and she was gone.

There was pressure on my shoulder, and my experience told me pain was to follow. Yolis had made sure I associated pain with human contact. I recoiled instantly, shielding my head with my arms.

"Lara, easy, it is only me."

My eyes opened abruptly, and in a daze, I blinked slowly at Tren. I had been dreaming. My heartbeat slowed, and I struggled to gain an upright posture. My muscles screamed in angry protest, but I persisted. "Where are we?" I asked, kneading one of my shoulders. The scent of life was thick in my nostrils, and it was clear that this was a place of undisturbed earth and sleeping trees.

"The island we built our fort on," he told me, and leapt from the boat. His feet made no sound as he landed easily upon the shore. "We can sleep safely here tonight and keep traveling in the morning."

I teetered from the boat and climbed over the edge. I lost my balance, and for an instant my weight was thrown forward. My fingers brushed the ground. I was shocked to feel a jolt of energy. An image of my mother flashed before my eyes, and my arms tingled as the slumbering life force of the earth ran into my body. I could sense worms and roots and hibernating things. My ring was warm around my neck, and as I straightened, I beheld Tren bathed in the light of his glowing silver bands. He looked surprised, and then his expression faded back into the returning darkness.

"Well, well," he said, and then turned to move off into the forest.

I hesitated momentarily, surprised by what had just happened, and then followed him between the maze of towering trees. I was shaking with cold and fatigue by the time Tren slowed his pace. He stopped beneath a familiar circle of trees and stared up at the looming shadow of our old fort.

"I can hardly believe it is still standing," I murmured.

"Of course it is still standing!" Tren's voice was a mixture of indignation and amusement. He wasted no time in clambering into the fort, the trees groaning in protest as he made his assent.

"Is the floor still sol-"

My words were severed by a force that hit me from behind. I screamed, but the sound was cut short as my body hit the ground, the impact forcing the air from my lungs. I flailed wildly, fighting with a strength summoned by fear. Yolis was in my mind. I could taste him in my mouth, smell him in my nostrils, and feel his burning touch on my skin. There was the hiss of hard steel sliding from its sheath. To my right, I heard Tren land with a soft thud, and the light from his Sanysk bands flooded the clearing. There, standing above me was my attacker.

"Myste!" I exclaimed.

Chapter Thirty-Seven
Things Forgotten

"Tren," Myste laughed, "and Lara, too!"

Tren sheathed his sword and extended his hand to help me to my feet. The radiance of his bands had dwindled to a barely perceivable glow.

I brushed the dirt from my dress. My body was still shaking with adrenaline. "Hello, Myste."

"I am so sorry, Lara," he said and caught me in a hug. "I thought you were a bandit or some other treacherous beast of mankind."

"Why are you here?" Tren asked calmly, no glimmer of emotion showing in his voice.

"Here on the island or here in Caladore?" Myste inquired. Upon receiving icy silence as a response from his cousin, he answered both questions. "I was slightly concerned when Storm Wing arrived without you, and from what the Elves could gather, I knew there was serious trouble brewing. He is really a frightfully rude beast to talk to, Tren, you should teach him some manners. I came looking for you to see if there was something I could do to help. I was staying on the island to avoid a confrontation. I can no longer sleep peacefully in Caladore."

Tren nodded grimly and provided Myste the details of our adventures since we had escaped from the castle.

Myste clucked his tongue. "You never write any more, Tren. I worry, you know."

I laughed outright and a small smile crept upon Tren's face, softening the Sanysk hardness that had overtaken him since he had come to my defense.

"Do you expect to ever grow tired of irritating me?" Tren asked, clapping Myste on the back.

"No, I do not expect that will ever happen." Myste grinned.

I felt as though I could have taken that moment and wrapped it around me like a quilt. It was so comforting to be in the company of these two old friends. Their banter was almost as soothing as a cup of Sophie's berryroot cordial.

"Come on." Tren gestured up to the fort. "We are sleeping here tonight."

"Looks comfortable," Myste remarked sardonically. "That is all right, though. Lara and I will cuddle up together and keep warm."

It was foolish, but a giddy little spark of happiness ignited within me. It had been so long since anyone had flirted with me. Sincere or not, I appreciated the gesture. "What kind of talk is that?" I demanded. "You are a married man now, Myste."

"What is a little cuddling between friends?" Myste persisted teasingly.

I was not entirely sure, but I thought Tren glared briefly at his cousin before turning to clamber up into the fort once again. Myste slung an arm over my shoulder. My first instinct was to recoil, but I fought against it and allowed the heavy warmth of his arm to remain.

"I cannot wait for you to meet her, Lara. She is...she is...everything." I could tell he was smiling even in the dark.

* * *

The floor of the fort was covered in rotting leaves. As we scraped away the blanket of nature, we discovered rusted nails: long forgotten tokens from when Tren and I had still been interested in building our grand fortress. We had fought so many imaginary battles from this vantage point, high in the trees. I fingered one of the nails and allowed the corners of my mouth to turn upward in a wistful expression. When had all the pretending stopped? Perhaps it had not. I looked over at Tren, who was talking seriously with his cousin. Perhaps as we got older we pretended about different things: happiness, love, ourselves.

"Well, we should be very safe from bandits," Myste remarked cheerfully as he settled himself on the floor of the fort. "Unfortunately, we will probably be killed instantly when this old relic collapses under our weight."

"It is not going to collapse," Tren insisted indignantly, and turned the discussion away from the structural soundness of the fort to the details of Yolis' plan.

Myste whistled. "That is some devious plotting. It is hard to believe that I am even related to him. You know I will help you in any way I can," Myste promised.

"Thank you," Tren said simply.

Myste shrugged, and the men continued analyzing the details of the plan to thwart Yolis.

I struggled to stay awake and follow the conversation, but soon the wrappings of slumber held me in warm silence. When I awoke, cold had settled into my bones and the forest was as silent as a grave. My hands and feet ached from a painful lack of blood. I stirred and clumsily pushed myself to a sitting position, drawing my knees up to my chest.

"Lara?" Tren's voice whispered.

"Y...ye...yes?" I stuttered, through my chattering teeth.

Tren patted the boards beside him. The dull thud of wood sounded like a vague echo from somewhere far off. "Come here, you sound like you are freezing."

I hesitated a moment. I was not entirely comfortable with closeness and touch. It seemed an eternity since human sensation had come in any other form than abuse. Still, this was Tren, not Yolis. I crawled over the hard planks and settled beside him. He wrapped his arms around me and I huddled close to him. He was warm and smelled faintly of earth and leather. I could feel his life energy. Every time his heart beat, it washed upon me like lapping water. The last time he had held me like this, I had been dizzy with adrenaline, but now his touch was calming. I felt safer than I had in a very long time, safer than I had felt since Sophie had died.

When I awoke again, I was lying on my back with something digging into my left shoulder blade, my hip, and one of my thighs. Yet another truth of romantic adventures revealed, I thought wryly. I sat up and stretched, noting that both Tren and Myste were gone. "On the second day of his trip," I remarked out loud for my own amusement, "Lord Rayn could no longer ride his horse, as his bottom hurt too much from sleeping on the ground." I giggled and was startled when I heard laughter from below.

"What was that, Lara?" Tren called.

"Please watch your language, Lara," Myste added. "I find the word bottom very offensive."

I scrambled to the edge of the platform and looked down at Tren and Myste. They had meat cooking over a small campfire and were leaning against each other, laughing loudly. For an instant, Tren's Sanysk image disappeared in his mirth.

"End both of you," I replied, and carefully descended to join the merry group.

The meal of slightly burned rabbit, which apparently was entirely Tren's fault, tasted better than any food that had passed my lips since my days in the kitchen. We savored the juices of memory and jokes. We licked them off our sticky fingers, and the sustenance strengthened our flesh and spirit. I was alive. All around me I could feel the power of the forest, the interplay of growth and soft decay. A strong, steady life force emanated from Tren and Myste.

"Elves can see perfectly in the dark, and they think it is uproarious that I do not share this skill," Myste told us through a mouthful of meat. He wiped his lips with the back of his hand and swallowed. "So when Kalypceon and I got married, her father gave me-"

Out of the corner of my eye, I saw Tren straighten. "Quiet," he murmured, his voice commanding, but without the sharp Sanysk edge I had previously been cut with. Myste and I fell silent, and Tren listened for several moments. I strained to hear what he was hearing, but forest sounds overwhelmed me. "We have to leave," Tren informed us calmly as he kicked dirt over the fire. "Soldiers have just landed on the island and are coming this way."

My heart began to pound, and I swallowed hard. Tren caught my eye. "No matter what happens, we will be all right."

I nodded, but the gesture lacked the conviction I longed for. Stooping, I hefted a solid-looking piece of deadfall. I hoped I would not be forced to defend myself in that way. The images of the fight in the dungeon and the resulting gore were still so fresh in my mind that I could almost smell the sickly sweet scent of blond. Myste drew his sword. His face was pale with fear. Tren left his weapon sheathed.

We ran through the forest, forfeiting stealth for speed. Branches tore at my face and arms, and I ducked and dodged, weaving between deadfall. I sucked air into my lungs with greedy need, and my legs burned with exhaustion. The crunch of quick footfalls sounded behind me. Terror howled in my ears and snapped at my heels. They were getting closer! Finally, we burst onto the clear, soft soil of the island's shore. I hurled into the boat and slammed hard against the bottom. The impact reverberated up my body. With a grunting effort, Myste and Tren shoved the boat free of the thick mud that cradled it. They leapt in, and the current took hold just as a figure emerged from the forest.

The man's Sanysk cloak melted into the gray-green background of the trees. He drew a glittering sword and pointed it at our boat. A party of Caladore soldiers burst from the foliage behind him. Tren stood, and the two Sanysks stared at each other across the widening gulf of water. The man on the bank bowed slightly to Tren, and the young man returned the gesture.

"Who is it?" I asked in a voice strained with anxiety and bewilderment.

"Adewus, Head of the League," Tren replied softly. "Yolis must have paid him to capture us."

* * *

We arrived in Cala under the cover of darkness. The marketplace was deserted and we passed unseen through the shadowy streets. We stopped in the dark created by the looming sanctuary of Cala. The large windows in the building felt like eyes staring down at our huddled, whispering group.

"How do you get to Nekadious' house, Lara?" Tren asked in a hushed tone. His hood was up, and without his voice I could not anchor his figure in the gloom of night.

For a moment, my fear-tattered breathing was the only response I could muster. I desperately tried to think back. Nahanni and I had not come by this route. Without the aid of light and the leisure to wander, I knew I would not be able to find Nekadious' home.

"I do not know," I confessed. "I could probably find it in the light of day, though."

Myste brushed against my side. He was uneasy and kept glancing over his shoulder. The news that Adewus was tracking us had made him just as nervous as it had made me. "The sanctuary will be open," he whispered. "We could take refugee there for the night. It would be better than standing on the street waiting for Adewus to arrive."

I voiced my agreement with this plan, and Tren concurred. We moved swiftly up the stairs, pulled the heavy wooden doors open and slipped inside. It was cool and softly lit by torches that had been left burning. We settled in a nook by the front entrance. Exhaustion from our anxious journey soon brought an uneasy sleep. I do not know how long I slumbered, but I was awakened by a voice calling my name. I sat up abruptly.

Tren shifted slightly and mumbled, "What is it?"

"Nothing," I replied quietly.

I was not sure that this was true, however, but I felt no malevolence echoing within the heavy stone walls. My whole body remained tense with the effort of listening. Had the call been part of a dream? I felt compelled to move deeper into the sanctuary. Getting to my feet, I walked quietly down the grand hall, not looking for anything in particular. The door leading to the Temple of Eternity was ajar. I paused outside. My heartbeat had quickened, and I wiped my sweating palms on the sides of my dress. There was nothing to fear within the temple, I told myself. It would be empty. It had to be empty. I took a deep breath and slipped inside. I was not alone.

Memories stood on either side of me. They were shadows of my younger selves. Both gripped my hands tightly and led me toward a pallet near the front of the chamber. No body was visible, but the sense of grief was so palpable that I knew it was associated with my mother and Sophie. Sorrow burned at the back of my throat and tears blurred my vision. It had always been too painful to face the passing of my mother and Sophie, and so I had run from the truth for many years.

Tonight, the hands of memory were cold against my palms and the chill seeped deep into my body. I instinctively clutched at my ring, and warmness rushed through my fingers to counter the frost within my veins. Never had I been able to understand the exchange of energy within existence, the interplay between life and death.

"It is a Healer's job to give life, not to take away death," I told the younger versions of myself. My voice was firm. For the first time, I comprehended the meaning behind that expression. "They died," I whispered, and felt something within me crumble. Walls that had kept reality at bay were suddenly gone, and the truth smashed into my consciousness. It flowed over me with the power of a river. I was knocked to my knees, and grief was torn from me in ragged sobs.

I wept for the loss of my mothers. I wept for all the time I had spent hiding from their deaths. The walls had been so impenetrable that not even my own life had been able to reach me. My lungs were struggling to draw breath around the sorrow that clawed its way up my throat. Agony flooded over me as I lay sobbing before the pallet, my knees drawn to my chest, the stone floor cold against my face.

The torrent of emotions gradually diminished, until once again, calming silence was returned to the Temple of Eternity. I was alone. There were no figures of memory. There were no monsters in the darkness. There was only me: a Healer like my mother, with the knowledge and talent to give life and the strength to shoulder the onerous burden of scorn and ridicule. And a woman like Sophie, brave enough to traverse the chasm of pain caused by the death of a cherished one, yet resilient enough to live and love again. I fell asleep in the solitude of the temple and dreamed of baking bread and walking through fields filled with sunshine.

Tren found me in the morning. He did not ask why I was there. "Morning has broken," he told me. "We had best be off." As he had done many times before, Tren held out his hand to help me from the floor.

I silently thanked him for his quiet acceptance. I would not have been able to answer any questions he might have put to me. My revelations from the previous night were too intensely personal to be explained, but it appeared that Tren did not feel the need for explanations. He had never asked that of me. Since the moment I had arrived in Caladore, we had established a silent trust in one another. We had an inherent understanding that the wounds we suffered could not be healed by words or questions. Unwavering support was the only thing we could pledge to one another, and as Tren extended his hand to me in that dim chamber, he was offering me that same friendship again. I reached out and took it.

* * *

The market place was crowded. We kept our heads down, and matched the brisk steps of the busy people surrounding us. In the daylight, it was not as difficult to navigate the city but it was a challenge to avoid the Caladore soldiers prowling through the throngs of people. Just a little farther, I thought, attempting to loosen the grip of anxiety. "Left here," I muttered, and led the men around the corner. We came to an abrupt halt. I cursed softly.

It took but an instant to see Adewus standing in the middle of the street, talking to a man in a purple tunic. The crowd parted and passed around the Head of the League like the Aquara dividing to avoid rocks in their path. Adewus plucked at his Sanysk cloak and then gestured a hand's width above his own height. The man in purple shook his head. Adewus scowled at him and then turned, presumably to continue moving down the street. I spun around in hasty retreat, only to smash into Tren.

I could feel his strong grip steadying me. "Adewus is here!" I gasped into the rough cloth of Tren's tunic, but it was too late.

Adewus looked up and stopped abruptly as he beheld me, Myste and Tren.

"Ascendants help us," Myste whispered, and drew his sword. It shook slightly in his grip.

Tren's gaze was locked upon Adewus. Throwing back his cloak, Tren touched the bands around his neck and then pointed two fingers at Adewus. "Korcareth malisic."

The words leapt from vaults of recollection, and an image I had imagined countless times danced before my eyes. It was a scene from the fourth *Rayn* book. Rayn had touched his Sanysk bands and shouted the very same words. He had challenged the Head of the League, and the two men had fought to the death.

"Tren, no!" I cried, but Tren drew his sword. The blue and purple colors of the blade swirled and shifted like the clouds of a furious storm. A frightened cry rose from the people on the street as they jostled to get away from the angry Sanysk.

"Go to Nekadious' house," Tren ordered in a cold voice. His face was already a mask of unreadable expression.

"No," I replied instantly, though my voice quavered with fear. I would not leave Tren's side. I would not abandon him.

Tren's blue eyes flashed with anger. "Lara, there is nothing you can do here. Save yourself." Adewus mimicked the movements Tren had executed. The challenge was accepted, and neither Sanysk could retreat now. "Flee while you can."

I shook my head. "Morian penent," I murmured. In my mind I could envision the scar on his palm that matched the one on my own hand. I could feel the promise inherent in that mark.

For a brief moment, Tren's Sanysk stoicism cracked. His face became a mixture of gratitude, worry, and love. "Morian penent," he replied and gently brushed my cheek with his hand. "Thank you, Lara."

"She always was your weakness." Adewus' voice was like an animal's snarl, and it wrenched Tren's attention from me. "She nearly kept you from the League and now she will bring about your demise."

Tren walked confidently toward Adewus. There was no one left on the street except the two Sanysk, Myste and myself. "Money is not the only thing worth fighting for, Adewus. If you truly believed the ancient Sanysk doctrines, you would know that." Tren stopped at least fifteen paces from Adewus and pointed his sword at the ground. "Let us draw the circles."

Adewus laughed. It was a rancorous sound. "More archaic tradition, I see. I tried to rid you of those useless ideals, but Draows had already done his damage." Adewus drew two short swords from sheaths on his back and placed the tip of one to the dirt. The Sanysk began to walk, dragging their swords so they cut deep lines into the dusty earth. "Do you know how much your brother is paying me to capture you and that worthless woman?" He chuckled again. "Your own brother! What would the old doctrines say about that? I have told you before, Tren my boy, you can depend on money and your own skill... nothing else."

Myste leaned in close to me and I could feel the rapid pulse of his life energy. "What are they doing?" he asked.

Without taking my eyes off the two men, I began to explain. This part of the tradition had not been included in the *Rayn* books, but I had been present when Draows had explained it to Tren. "The rings represent the bands they wear. Adewus, as Head of the League, draws the outer circle. Neither can step outside that circle, or they have to forfeit their bands to the other Sanysk."

Myste nervously twisted his hands around the hilt of his sword. "How can they forfeit their bands? They do not come off unless...oh..." Color drained from his face as the bloody end to the fight became apparent.

"The challenger draws an inner circle for fighting. The Sanysk who steps outside must confine his movements to that space. It is a second chance, I guess. It gives you a few moments to regroup, because the other Sanysk has to return to the outer edge before the fight can begin again."

Myste cleared his throat. "But Tren is not drawing an inner circle. He is just tracing Adewus' line."

My eyes went directly to Tren's blade. Myste was right. Tren was giving up the safety of the inner ring. I curled my toes in my shoes. There was no calm left inside me. It had oozed out in the cold sweat that was trickling down my spine. Ascendants protect him, I prayed silently. I reached out and gripped Myste's hand. I did not know if he was shaking or if the tremors came from my own body.

Tren and Adewus had formed a complete circle and stood opposite one another, the heels of their feet just touching the ring they had cut into the ground. Their swords were ready. Suddenly, Adewus leapt forward, his blades flashing in the sun. Tren sidestepped him, and air hissed over his sword as he swung towards Adewus' back. Adewus turned and blocked. The weapons slid together, and then were free of one another again. The movement was so swift that it was hard to tell what was happening. They rained blow after blow upon each other. Adewus spoke to Tren in low, antagonistic tones, but apparently his verbal intimidation was of no use. Tren did not respond, and Adewus was slowly pushed toward the edge of the circle. I tightened my grip on Myste's hand and held my breath. Adewus' heel slid backwards in the dirt, inches closer to the line.

I saw the briefest flash of realization cross Adewus' leathery face. Tren was stronger and faster than he was. Adewus issued a startling cry, and in a sideways sweep driven forward by desperation and anger, he brought both of his swords to bear upon Tren. Adewus' first blade struck the feena penent of Tren's sword and shattered. Both men grunted with the impact. Adewus' second sword

509

glanced harmlessly off Tren's blade just as the young Sanysk delivered a sharp sidekick to Adewus' chest. The attack sent Adewus flying backwards. He landed heavily on his back, the line in the dirt running beneath his waist.

Myste bellowed in triumph and wrenched his hand from my grasp to throw his arms above his head in a gesture of victory. "He did it!" he shouted. "You did it, Tren!"

I could not cheer as Myste was doing. I felt uneasy. It was the impending gore, I told myself, and slowly raised my hand to my face, preparing to cover my eyes. I felt sick to my stomach. Tren was walking toward Adewus. The Sanysk had righted himself and was now kneeling, his naked sword glinting in the dirt a few feet away from him. He held his hands clasped behind his back and was looking up at Tren with an expression of hatred.

Tren stared down at Adewus with an impassive countenance. When he spoke, his voice was devoid of emotion. "In the name of the Ascendants who formed our brotherhood and forged our bands, I now claim both your rank and those symbols of our League as my own." Tren leveled his sword with Adewus' neck, and I shielded my eyes with my hand. I felt as though I was going to vomit at any moment. The muscles of my body tightened as I waited for the sounds of death. "May your spirit not be ended, but-"

Tren's voice was suddenly interrupted. He shouted out in pain and Myste's voice rose in outrage. I tore my hand away from my face. Adewus was on his feet again, sword regained and the broken hilt of his other blade in hand. Tren was gritting his teeth with his own sword now in his left hand. The knuckles and fingers of his right hand were reddened and swelling quickly.

"Adewus was holding that hilt behind his back. Just before Tren was about to strike, Adewus slammed it into Tren's hand," Myste explained in tones made loud by alarm.

"Ascendants preserve him," I murmured. Tren had never been as good with his left hand.

"You will have neither my rank nor my bands!" Adewus screamed in rage and lashed out at Tren, narrowly missing his head. "Who taught you that old speech? Draows?" He thrust forward, and Tren blocked and returned the attack. They battled back and forth, their blades blurring as though they were tearing the very air that surrounded them. If Tren's left hand had once been his weakness, it was no longer.

"Draows taught me to honor the traditions of our League." Tren's voice was barely audible over the sounds of the clashing swords.

"Then he taught you nothing! The traditions are dead." Their swords met and slid off one another with a sound that made me shudder. Adewus punched, and Tren blocked and then kicked forward, forcing Adewus to leap back. They circled one another tentatively, blades held at ready. "If you are one of us, then you honor death and your ability to bring it swiftly. That is what Draows taught you, even if he likes to conceal it with quaint tradition."

Adewus dove toward Tren. It looked as though he was thrusting low, but in an instant, he changed his attack and swept his blade in an arc parallel to the ground. I screamed as the tip of Adewus' sword nearly caught Tren in the face. He fell and rolled, coming up inches from Adewus. Leaping to his feet, he drove his sword upward, through Adewus' throat and then pulled it across.

I felt Adewus' life energy gush from him. It rushed forth to fill the space where we stood. The earth soaked him up. I could feel his heartbeat inside me, and then it was gone. I cried out in horror and without thinking, turned and ran. Myste was calling my name, but I did not stop until I was well away from the revolting sight of torn flesh and hot blood. Leaning against the cool stone of a building, I was startled by an entirely different feeling gently wrapping itself around me. For a moment, I felt a sensation akin to the warmth of sunshine upon my skin. It passed as quickly as it had come, but I was left with a strong sense of continuance. Adewus' life energy may have vanished, but his spirit had not been destroyed.

I heard the heavy trod of booted feet approaching. I turned to locate the source of the noise, and my stomach dropped as I beheld a contingent of Caladore soldiers being led by a man garbed in a Sanysk cloak. The Sanysk looked familiar, but I did not stop to ponder his visage. With my heart pounding, I turned and fled around the corner, only to hear a voice shout, "There she is!" The sounds of pursuit followed the cry.

I pushed my legs to move faster. The earth beneath my feet dissolved and in a moment, I was back at the bloody scene of Adewus' demise. Tren and Myste had sheathed their swords, but the expression upon my face and the haste of my arrival conjured a swift re-emergence of steel.

"They found us!" I was sucking hard for air that had been stolen more by fear than weariness.

Tren nodded, as though he had already surmised as much. He and Myste stepped forward to face the approaching soldiers. The eagerness of that first cry of recognition was certainly not reflected in their present countenance. A feeling of smug satisfaction tempered my fear. Their task would not be so easily completed with Tren and Myste standing in their path. The Sanysk signaled a halt. I frowned, perturbed by the feeling of familiarity gnawing at my stomach.

"Dayr," Tren said in quiet acknowledgement.

The sensation within me abruptly turned inside out, becoming one of horrified recognition. Yolis had hired Dayr, one of Tren's good friends, to hunt him down! Worse yet, Dayr had actually accepted.

Dayr said nothing for a moment. He was staring at the body of Adewus, and I could see the muscles in his jaw clenching and unclenching. I wondered if he realized Tren was now head of the League. Did Dayr comprehend how the situation had changed? He was no longer hunting someone who shared his rank. To challenge the Head of the League was to fight to the death.

"Hello, Tren," Dayr replied finally. His voice was raw with emotions I could not guess at. He inclined his head slightly. "I am sorry we have to meet again this way."

Was he sorry that he would have to fight Tren to the death, or that he was fighting him at all? I stared hard at Dayr, but could find no answer to my question. He also had mastered the unreadable expression of the Sanysk.

Myste glared at him. "If you are so sorry, then why did you take Yolis' tainted money?"

Dayr drew his sword with a slow weariness. The intervening years since our last meeting seemed to have passed over his face with the kindness of gravel grating upon skin. He looked haggard and old. "Why does a dragon have scales, Myste?" he asked. "We are what we are." Dayr paused and rubbed at his eyes. "Or have to be, I suppose."

A scowl formed upon my face at his explanation. It was not true. It was just some platitude Dayr used in order to reconcile the Sanysk ideals with his own conscience.

Dayr opened his mouth to speak, but Tren interrupted. "Save your formal warning, Dayr. I know you intend to fight me. It will be a death for both of us, though one may still be standing at the end of it all." He drove his sword into the ground and stepped back.

My lips parted in surprise. What was Tren saying? Was he actually surrendering? "Tren," I whispered desperately. "What are you doing? You could easily win!"

"I know," he said in a quiet voice and motioned to Myste to put his weapon down. Dayr advanced warily and collected the swords. "That is precisely why I do not wish to fight him," Tren continued. "You were right, Lara. It is time to try being Tren-Lore. If I do otherwise, I will not be able to live with myself."

"A fine time to decide that," I muttered as guards took hold of my wrists and tied them behind my back. Out of the corner of my eye, I thought I saw a flash of white. I turned to look but there was nothing; only the crumpled form of Adewus, his blood covering the earth beneath him, his severed neck naked without the silver bands of the Sanysk.

Chapter Thirty-Eight
The Storm

I only managed to get a brief glimpse of the cell Tren, Myste and I were shoved into. In the next instant, my vision was rendered useless by the kind of dark that would become no more penetrable with time. The ground was dirt and the walls solid stone. Beyond that, there was nothing more to note. I sank to the ground and leaned my back against the wall. I was trying hard to breathe calmly and restrain the tears and panic that were threatening.

"We have to get out of here!" My voice sounded shrill. Dayr's words surrounded me like the blackness of the cell.

"A message has been sent to King Yolis. You will be confined in Cala until he arrives, and then..." Dayr had been interrupted by a guard before he could finish the statement, but the conclusion to the sentence was clear.

I chewed on my lip, my toes curling and uncurling in my shoes. "Think of something Tren," I demanded. "Yolis is going to come and kill us all!"

Myste was cursing under his breath, and I could hear him shuffling from side to side. I could imagine him twisting the ring on his finger. I could imagine his terror, his desperate, guilty hope that Yolis' wrath would not extend to him, and his self-loathing for even letting the thought enter his head.

Tren's only reply was silence. In this darkness, his Sanysk quiet made him invisible.

"Tren!" I insisted. "Please!"

"I am sorry," he finally said.

The words reverberated through me, and I was suddenly filled with a ringing anger that deafened me. "Sorry?" I screamed at him. "Sorry!" Tears were stinging my eyes. The darkness was crushing my chest. "You are supposed to save us! You are supposed to save me!" My fingers clawed at the dirt in desperate spasms of panic. Hot tears burned my cheeks. I could feel earth pushing painfully up under my nails, and then another sensation-one of pulsing energy. I froze and explored the feeling until I was sure of what it was. I could follow the life power that was flowing through the thick roots my fingers had encountered. It wove through the floor of the cell, under the wall and up to a huge tree lulled to sleep by winter. I suddenly knew what I had to do. It would not be Tren who would save us, it would be me! I needed to channel my life energy into the roots and make them grow. I took a deep breath and relaxed my muscles. I had never been able to control my powers, but today that had to change.

Namin had once compared life energy to a storm. My first effort was no more than a gust that stirred the dusty corners of my being. It was certainly not a storm, but as my concentration increased, the wind grew and swirled. It wrapped twisting fingers of power around every bit of me, and for once, my guilt, my grief, and my desire to rewrite the past no longer quelled the winds. Memories of strength and dignity infused my spirit and whipped the winds of my life force into a roaring storm.

I let the hot, tingling energy flow through my fingers and into the roots of the tree. I felt warm and senseless, as though I was submerged in water whose surface glittered with sunlight. Conscious thoughts were swept away, and all I could feel was the tree. I could sense its stirring, responding to my caress of energy by slowly stretching forth to meet my touch. It grew. It pushed through earth and strained against rock, until finally, there was a deafening crack that wrenched me from my state of concentration. I was so startled I withdrew my life energy like a person snatching their hand from a flame.

Opening my eyes, I found that the darkness was now laced with ribbons of light. For a moment, I was confused. I reached down to find the roots once again, to regain the sensation of safety and warmth, but as I did I recalled why I had been channeling.

"The rocks broke! They broke!" Myste was shouting. "Why did they break?" I looked over to find Myste on his feet, looking as though he was about to begin running around in circles.

I clambered to my feet and turned to look. Two of the large stone blocks that met the floor had large cracks through them. "I did it," I murmured in wonder. I turned to look at Tren. He had a mysterious smile playing upon his lips. "I did it," I told him.

"I know," he replied, and bowed to me. "It is indeed a fortunate Sanysk who can call a Healer his friend."

It took only a few moment of frantic work to push the shattered rocks free, creating a hole big enough to escape through. We fled from our confinement, leaving Tren's sword, certain doom and a puzzling mystery for our captures to solve. As we ran, I could not help but smile. How would the guards explain this escape? We kept to the dark alleys and shadowed paths of the city. While this made our journey a longer one, it shrouded us from unfriendly eyes. I knew that I should have felt like a rabbit being pursued by a wolf, but that pulse-pounding fear was not aroused within me. I felt strong and powerful and capable of anything. I was not a creature to be hunted.

By the time we reached Nekadious' house, snow had begun to fall and cold was numbing my fingers and toes. I hurried to the door with Myste and Tren following behind. The three of us huddled close and I knocked, my cold knuckles smarting.

"End this," I muttered and brought my hand up to my mouth to press warm lips against the painful spot.

Myste was shivering beside me. He wrapped his cloak even tighter around himself and leaned back to look up at the shuttered windows. "Perhaps no one is home."

"No." Tren shook his head. "Someone is coming."

A few moments later, the door was opened a few inches and a man peered out at us. My heart gave an odd little jump. It was Nekadious! I recognized the cleft in his chin. "What can I..." His words faltered as recognition came upon him. He pointed his finger at me. "I know who you are," he murmured.

"Do you also remember that I once did you the favor of forgetting who *you* were?" I put my hand on the doorframe and leaned toward him. "Now I need a favor in return." My mind leapt to an odd thought. I had considered this man a villain, but now I was hoping to be in league with him.

He regarded me with a calm, appraising stare that revealed none of his thoughts. "Come in," he said finally, stepping back from the door. Nekadious led us to a small, book-filled room and quietly closed the door. "Please sit," he offered.

I could not help but peer at the books with an owl-like alertness, my neck twisting this way and that, endeavoring to see the titles that created the stacks of novels that lined the walls. Myste gently moved a particularly dusty pile from a chair and sat down. I chose a chair unoccupied by literature, and Tren remained standing.

Nekadious selected a seat by the window and crossed his arms over his chest. "Is this favor a request for concealment from the king?"

"In part." I tore my attention away from a book entitled *Lord Rayn: Fiction or Fact,* and concentrated upon Nekadious. "I also want the document Yolis gave to you when you agreed to create havoc in Caladore."

Nekadious squinted at me. "What do you intend to do with the document?"

"Just give us the docu-" Myste began angrily.

I interrupted him. "I trust that you will keep our secrets, as I intend to keep yours." Nekadious nodded, and I proceeded to describe the plan Tren and I had fashioned.

"I see," Nekadious said when I had finished. "You realize, however, that I stand to lose substantially if I help you."

"I will double whatever Yolis is giving you," Tren told him quietly.

Nekadious smiled for the first time since we had arrived. "Thank you, Prince Tren-Lore. If I am to be so handsomely compensated, then I see no need to continue the role I played for your brother. The side of good and honor is a better fit, anyway." Nekadious stood, rubbing his hands together. "Shall we go for dinner, then?"

I nodded eagerly, my hunger bounding forward in response to the call of food.

"We will tell my wife, Jolie, who you really are, though not the full reason for your presence here. Flight from a cruel and unjust king will be enough to win her silence and sympathy. She has yet to turn away someone in need."

Myste rose. "Would it help if we looked downtrodden?" His good spirits seemed to have risen with the assurance of Nekadious' help and the suggestion of food.

Nekadious scratched at his cheek, his expression one of contemplation. "Yes, that would probably help." His tone was as dry as old parchment, but laughter glinted in his brown eyes.

I felt some of the tension melt from my shoulders. Somehow, Nekadious' show of humor reaffirmed my trust in him. We would be safe here, at least for the time. We followed Nekadious out of the room.

"Are you sure your wife will have no allegiance to Yolis?" Tren asked. He pulled at the collar of his tunic so that his Sanysk bands were hidden.

"I am sure," Nekadious replied. "Jolie's politics are those of mercy, not power."

"She must be an extraordinary woman," Tren replied.

"She is much like your sister. Speaking of which..." Nekadious pushed open the door to the kitchen. Happy laughter and a voice I recognized immediately spilled out into the hall. Nahanni was here!

The reunion between the four of us was joyfully loud. We hugged each other wildly, laughing hysterically and talking simultaneously. Finally, Nahanni stamped her foot and declared, "How dare you do that to me!"

Tren rumpled her hair. "Do what to you?"

She slapped his hand away. "Leave me wondering what happened to the two of you. Not include me in all the fun!"

Myste snorted and wandered forward into the kitchen. "It was not that much fun." He sniffed the air. "Are you making natlus stew?" he asked Jolie, who, though still very confused, nodded. "I think it needs just a touch of spice."

The kindly-looking woman smiled uncertainly. "Oh. Well... I keep the spices over in that cupboard. Nekadious, what is going on?"

"You see, my love," Nekadious began. Throwing his arm around his wife's shoulders, he steered her from the room. I could hear them talking quietly in the next chamber.

Nahanni resumed her seat at the table and tucked her long blond hair behind her ears. "I would like to know the very same thing."

Tren and I sat with her, and between Myste's frequent exclamations over the depleted state of Jolie's spices, we filled Nahanni in on Yolis' plot and our own plan to stop him.

Nahanni thoughtfully twirled a piece of hair between her fingers and bit her lip. "I think," she said finally, "that your plan could be improved." A mischievous smile tugged at the corners of her lips. "What you do not know – what no one knows expect a select few – is that the rulers of Hemlizar, Nara Vit and Renarn are coming to Caladore. The rulers will arrive secretly in three days' time. Yolis is set to invite all the nobles and peasants of Caladore to a ceremony at the castle. They will witness the surrounding rulers pledge allegiance to Yolis as their overlord. In return, Yolis is supposed to give them the protection of Caladore. So..." Nahanni's cheeks flushed pink with excitement, making her look even more beautiful than she had a moment ago. "So I can sneak you into the castle and you can reveal Yolis' true plan to everyone."

Tren leaned back in his chair. "It will be dangerous."

"But when were you ever opposed to danger?" I interjected. He turned, and we grinned at each other.

At that moment, Jolie burst back into the room with Nekadious walking calmly behind her. "What a wicked man!" Jolie cried. "You need not worry. You can stay here as long as you need to."

* * *

Two days, I thought to myself. Not really such a long time to wait. I turned my attention back to the book I had spied the day before, but could not seem to concentrate on the words. My mind kept darting here and there, chasing one random thought after another. Someone rapped lightly upon the door, and my attention was at last directed towards a singular point.

"Yes?" I replied eagerly and shut the book. The ideas presented in the novel were really very fascinating, and the author made quite a case for Rayn as a fictional character of history, but if I was honest with myself, I had to admit that I was glad for some other type of amusement. Rayn no longer held much appeal.

Tren entered the room, cradling his hand carefully against his chest. The expression upon his face belonged more to a sheepish twelve-year-old rather than a grown man. "Lara, I was wondering if you could help me." He looked down at his right hand. "It is really bothering me."

"Come here," I said, patting the chair next to me. "I can have a look at it."

He came and sat, holding out his hand to me. It was swollen and bruised. The dark colors of blood beneath the skin reminded me of Yolis, and I felt a slight surge of dread. Perhaps two days was not long enough to wait before confronting him. No, another part of me interjected; the time for fleeing from my fears was over. "Right," I cleared my throat. "Can you move your fingers?"

He tried. The tips of his digits moved ever so slightly, and the muscles in his jaw clenched, but I was fairly sure that nothing was broken. With a confident, gentle touch, I caressed the top of his hand and allowed my mind to feel for any weakness in his life energy, any fracture that might indicate broken bones. There was nothing.

I smiled at him ruefully. "It is just swollen and bruised and probably very painful, but there is nothing here I can Heal. Get a bucket of snow from outside and put your hand in it for a while. The coldness should make it feel better."

"Are you sure it is not broken?" His voice sounded skeptical. I inclined my head, and he started to chuckle. "Not much of a tough Sanysk, am I?" I laughed along with him. "I do not think you are a very sympathetic Healer, either. I mean really, Lara, what kind of a cure is sticking your hand in a bucket of snow?"

I spent the rest of the day in Tren and Myste's company. Conversation and the discovery of a Questkon board made the time go much faster, but tension lurked beneath our conversations. That same anxiety found its way into all aspects of life. On the night before we were to leave for Caladore, it was so strong that it shattered the peace of sleep, and nightmares scurried through the fissures to fill my mind.

They were always the same images. I was yelling at Yolis with words that cracked and split with the heat of my fury. I raised my fists and tried to hit him, again and again, but I was not strong enough. He laughed at me. Raising his hand, he struck me hard in the face. I fell back with a cry of pain. Tren stepped forward, and wild hope filled me. Tren would be strong enough. He was a Sanysk. Yet, his hands were without a weapon and Yolis had a glittering sword. He grinned at his brother and then thrust the blade into Tren's chest. I struggled to scream, but could not make a sound. Tren collapsed. There was blood everywhere. I watched it gush from him. I was unable to do anything. I sat helplessly, terror paralyzing me as I watched Tren die.

After the third time this vision tormented me, I gave up sleep and sat by the window in my room watching the sky lighten. I tried not to think of the impending confrontation. Instead, I thought of what I would do after it was all over. Stay in the kitchen? Go and live with Namin? Travel? This idea appealed to me more than any other. I was struck with the desire to see more than just Caladore. Perhaps I would find Telnayis, the Healer school where my mother trained. Maybe I could be trained there as well. But first, I reminded myself, you have to get through today. Taking a deep breath, I rose from my chair and went to find Tren.

Tren and Myste were standing in the kitchen, strapping on the swords Nekadious had obtained. Neither was saying anything, but I could feel the weight of the dark words that must have been spoken only moments before. I looked to Tren, and his grim Sanysk expression confirmed my suspicions.

"What?" I demanded. Dread was blocking my throat and making it hard to breathe. I curled my hands into fists and felt dull pain as my nails dug into my skin.

"I want you to stay here," Tren informed me. I opened my mouth to protest, but he continued. "This plan is too dangerous. Even if we do manage to sneak into the castle, there is a good chance that a confrontation with Yolis will end in the death of one or all of us. There is no need to endanger everyone. I want to go alone."

"No!" I exclaimed. My passionate refusal sprung from my lips with the swiftness of reflex. It was true that I was terrified and nauseous at the thought of facing Yolis, but I refused to remain passive any longer. I would not wait while someone else went to fight my battles. I would not cower, as I once had, waiting for the monsters in the darkness to find me. "No, Tren, you are not going alone. I am coming with you. This issue is not up for discussion. Now get your things. I want to leave now."

I turned and strode from the room. I could hardly believe I had just made such a speech. Myste's voice was still audible as I walked down the hallway toward the door.

"Well, she told you," he chortled. "Put you right in your place."

I grinned and yanked open the front door, only to come face to face with Dayr. "Tren!" I screamed, and tried to slam the door shut, but it was too late. Dayr reached forward, grabbed me by the wrist, and yanked me into the street.

Chapter Thirty-Nine
The Sanysk Unite

"I am not going to hurt you," Dayr kept saying, but I struggled against him until the approach of someone I recognized lessened my alarm. It was Draows! Tren and Myste came thundering down the hall toward me.

"Let her go," said Tren and Draows at once. Both used the same tone - the verbal equivalent to the edge of a blade against your skin. Dayr looked from one to the other and obediently released my smarting wrist.

"Why are you all here?" Tren asked, and took another step from the house.

For a moment I stared at him in confusion, and then turned my attention back to the street where Tren's gaze rested. In the shadows of the street stood men garbed in Sanysk cloaks, nearly invisible but for their flashing bands. Slowly, they moved forward into the sunlight, drew their swords, and offered them hilt first to Tren.

Draows was the last to make this gesture. Slowly, he slid his blade from its battered sheath and held it toward Tren. "We have come in acknowledgment of the new Head of our honored League. We pledge our swords to you in times of battle, our voices to you in times of judgment, and our loyalty to you, keeper of the doctrine of the Sanysk."

Tears were blurring my vision. Tren had worked so hard to become a Sanysk but never, in any of our wildest fantasies, had we ever imagined that one day he might be Head of the League. I was so proud of him that had I not been surrounded by rough-looking Sanysk, I would have whooped with joy and hugged everyone there.

Draows came and stood next to Tren, who still seemed to be struggling to keep shock from showing on his face. "I believe this belongs to you," He handed Tren a bundle. Tren folded back the cloth to reveal his feena penent blade. "Dayr rescued it for you. He was the one who called for the brotherhood to convene," the old Sanysk told Tren quietly. "He spread the word that Yolis was about to have you executed. It was decided that if Yolis wanted to kill the new Head of the League, he would have to face the combined wrath of the brotherhood." Draows' weather-beaten face creased into a grin. "I must say, though, I am glad to find you well."

"I would not be so if Lara had not been there," Tren replied, and I could feel my cheeks grow hot with a pleased flush.

Draows laughed heartily. Catching me by the shoulder, he enveloped me in a hug. The familiar scent of horses and leather filled the air around me and I smiled into the cloth of his dusty tunic. "I always said it was a wise Sanysk who sought a Healer's friendship. Now," Draows said, releasing me from the embrace, "what is your plan?"

Tren considered the question for a moment. "I would like to change it, if I can invoke the rights of the old doctrine and ask for the League's assistance." He turned to the group of men and raised his voice. "I know the pledge you just spoke to me has become a tradition, rather than a binding oath, but here, in the face of a new peril, I am asking you to revive the Sanysk of old – the Sanysk that believed in those words and were indeed a League of brothers, rather than lone warriors pursuing their own ends."

A shiver ran up my spine as I listened to Tren's words. It was like a speech from a book, only this was real. He told the Sanysk of Yolis' plot, and then he told them of our plan to thwart the king. He had not yet explained how the Sanysk fit into the overall picture, but I was beginning to guess.

"First, I would ask you to stand shoulder to shoulder with me. Let us present ourselves as a united brotherhood and demand an audience with the current king of Caladore. Let us deliver the truth to our neighboring sovereigns. Next, I would call upon you to lend your strength and skill to stop the violence Yolis has caused. Our duty will be as established by the Ascendants of long ago: to conquer evil and restore peace. If we are united, there will be no one who can stand against us."

At the end of this speech I expected cheers or shouts of approval but Tren's words were greeted with silence. Trepidation stabbed me, but the pain was brief and healed instantly as I saw everyone in the group touch their bands and incline their heads. I smiled at myself. I had forgotten that we were dealing with Sanysk, and this response was probably the League's equivalent to fervent declarations of loyalty.

"We...I will do whatever you ask of me," Dayr said softly and stared at the ground. "I am ashamed of the way I acted. I will stand by your side until we have restored peace."

A murmur of agreement threaded through the crowd.

* * *

The guards at the gate stared in shock. The presence of one Sanysk was intimidating enough. To have thirty mounted Sanysk come riding into Caladore, swords drawn, bands flashing, and banners snapping in the wind, was an unparalleled sight.

The group drew rein before the massive gates, and Dayr called to the guards, "Prince Tren, Head of the League of the Sanysk, demands an audience with King Yolis."

Without a word of protest or question, the guards opened the gates and let the Sanysk through. The outer courtyard was filled with people, and the space thundered with the noise of so many voices. As we rode further into the courtyard, the noise began to melt into silence. It seemed that shock had robbed the people of their words.

"Seize them!" Yolis' voice commanded from the dais that had been erected against the inner courtyard's wall.

His demands had no effect. The guards remained still, unwilling or unable to respond to his orders. We continued riding until we had reached the grand stairs that lead up to the platform that Yolis and the other rulers sat upon. Yolis' gaze was upon Tren, and then slowly he turned to me. It was all I could do to meet his eyes. I felt as though I was going to retch at any moment. Why had I let him do what he had done? I was weak, I was foolish, I was – and suddenly a furious voice from within me interrupted. Why had *he* chosen to do those things? My emotional devastation had not been an invitation for agony; it had not been a silent plea to rob me of my free will! I lifted my chin and returned his gaze.

An expression I could not name flickered across Yolis' face and he looked quickly away. His focus was once again on his brother. "You have come, I presume, with some plan to destroy me." Yolis took a few steps toward Tren, and a ripple of verbal shock ran across the other rulers. "Have you thought about what this will mean?" Yolis demanded. "Have you considered what your life will be like if I am no longer king, and you have to take on those duties? When we were younger I thought you wanted the crown, but I have begun to suspect that this..." He gestured out at the Sanysk. "This was all you ever desired. And now you have it. Do you really want to give it up?"

Tren said nothing. The Sanysk behind him remained impassive, but I could feel tension crawling over my skin.

"Now see here, Yolis!" The king of Hemlizar barked, rising from his chair. "We did n-"

Yolis raised a silencing hand. "I am a ruler, and you are a Sanysk," he told Tren. "These roles are more than duties, my dear brother. They define and sculpt us into who we are. You can no more be a Sanysk- King than you could love your precious Lara and still have the ruthlessness it takes to be part of your League. If you do this to me, you will be giving up everything you worked for as a Sanysk."

Tren slowly looked up. "The roles we play do not have to define us," he said quietly. "You could have been so much more than a corrupt monarch. I am sorry for this, Yolis." Tren wheeled his horse about and brandished a paper from beneath his cloak. "I stand before you as Head of the League of the Sanysk and prince of Caladore. I have come to reveal the treachery that has been committed by King Yolis, and to offer my aid in restoring peace."

A cry of surprise rang through the crowd, and the other two rulers rose to stand beside the king of Hemlizar.

"The violence that has plagued your countries has been caused by men hired by King Yolis. This action was part of a more ambitious plot to gain power over you and your countrymen! The document I hold in my hands is a contract between him and one of these henchmen." Amidst the clamor of confusion that was sounding through the courtyard, Tren leapt from his horse and turned to the sovereigns behind him. "In the name of the Ascendants who formed our League, I pledge to you the strength of the Sanysk in quelling the chaos and restoring peace to your countries. It will be our honor to help you in any way we can." He smiled widely. It was the kind of smile I had not seen for many years. "It is an honor we have relinquished for far too long."

"Arrest the traitor!" I heard someone yell, and glancing about, found a regiment of guards marching toward Yolis.

I immediately looked to Yolis for his reaction, but discovered that he seemed oblivious to the situation. He was staring at Tren. His expression was one of unconcealed rage and hatred. He threw back his cloak and drew something from his belt. It glinted in the sun, and as he lifted it, I knew exactly what it was.

Before I could react, I heard Dayr's voice yelling, "Tren! Look out!" In the next instant, Dayr had spurred his horse forward, between Tren and his brother. The dagger struck Dayr in the shoulder. At least a dozen arrows were drawn back and pointed at Yolis, but Tren was shouting commands that Yolis was not to be harmed.

"Not to be harmed!" Yolis screamed, and wrenching a sword from his sheath, ran toward Tren. Tren drew his own sword only an instant before Yolis reached him. "You will have to kill me!" Yolis howled, and the blades clashed together. The impact seemed to have no effect upon Tren, but Yolis stumbled back under the force. He threw his arms wide open. "Kill me, Tren. Kill me or give me my crown!"

The sound of Yolis' voice made me shudder. "He has gone mad," I muttered in horror.

Tren shook his head and stepped out of ready position, his sword hanging in his left hand. He looked sadly at his brother. "Yolis, it does not have to be this way. Put down your sword. We can talk about it."

Yolis regarded his brother warily, and then to my surprise, he dropped his sword to the cobblestones and rubbed at his eyes. "You are right," he mumbled. "We can talk about it." He took a wavering step toward Tren. "We are brothers. It should not be like this."

Tren held out his hand, and Yolis reached for it. He pulled his brother to him in a rough hug. I stared at the bizarre scene unfolding before me. My stomach was twisting into knots of fear. Yolis was not to be trusted! Before I could react, Tren staggered away from his brother's embrace, a silver dagger protruding from his chest.

"Solrium vallent," Yolis screamed. "Who is going to save you now?"

Tren's face was shocked, uncomprehending. I had seen that face before. I had seen it years ago when the Renarn had attacked and Tren had killed for the first time. It was not supposed to be like this, he had muttered. There was something of that innocent boy left in the Sanysk that stood facing Yolis, something that had prevented Tren from truly believing his brother would harm him. Tren staggered backward, sweeping his own sword across Yolis' chest. Yolis fell to his knees, screaming in pain as he clutched at the gaping wound that had suddenly rent his flesh. I could feel hot, crimson energy spilling from Tren and Yolis.

I leapt from my horse and ran toward Tren. Time seemed to have slowed, and the only sound I could hear was the dull pulse of Tren's slowing heart. When I reached him, his face was already the hue of winter. I fell to my knees next to him and the warmth of his blood seeped through my dress and warmed my skin. My hands shook as I pulled the dagger from Tren's chest. The inscription, *Solrium Vallent*, glistened with blood. The wound it had made was mortal, and Tren's life energy ebbed.

"Fight, Tren," I whispered, and yanked the chain from around my neck. I slipped the ivy ring onto my finger, and it glowed with verdant brilliance.

I placed my fingers on Tren's wound and poured my life energy into it. I let the courtyard and all the curious onlookers dissolve. I knew only Tren. I sensed every gash and rent from which his life energy spilled. I knew every damaged fiber of his flesh, but I did not find the darkness I had felt within him that night in the cottage. The dragon's poison was gone. This was my last thought before the warmth and light of life enveloped both of us. I called forth every vestige of my power; I called upon my mother and the Ascendants. I fought to push more and more energy from myself. Weakness was overtaking me, and still Tren's life force was lessening. It was nothing more than the faintest of brushes upon my mind, and then it was gone.

Chapter Forty
The Healer Lara

Suddenly my life force was trapped within me. It would not leave my fingers and enter Tren's body. He had passed beyond the reach of my powers.

"Tren!" I screamed. "Tren-Lore!" I shook him as though I could somehow rouse him from death. "No!" I yelled, daring the Ascendants to challenge me. "No! I want him back."

My mind was more focused than it had ever been. Somewhere below the storm of my life energy lay a calm surface of power, undisturbed and undiscovered until this moment. I drew upon this source and felt my limbs fill with a power that had none of the rushing heat I was accustomed to. This force was sure and cool, like the earth beneath bare feet. I let it flow from my fingers and into Tren's body. I used it to batter against death. I fought on; wielding this new power even as stabs of pain erupted in my chest and air escaped me. As if from a great distance I heard a voice say, "You were his end."

My head snapped up, and I beheld Yolis upon the cobblestones beside me. He was bathed in a strange light, and the crimson life that was pooling around him glimmered with a beautiful luminescence. The light danced upon the surface of Yolis' blood and, enchanted, I reached out to touch it. As my fingertips brushed the strange radiance I knew at once what it was. It was Yolis' life energy. He was but moments from death, and the glowing around him was his life energy escaping.

Yolis laughed, and I met his gaze, only to find that even standing upon the brink of death had not humbled him. He took joy from his brother's death and my pain. I returned his smile, and with a sudden rush of cold power drew his life force from him. The glittering power that had been dancing upon his blood rushed into me, and his smile faltered as I summoned the remaining life force from his body. I met his unseeing gaze without fear, and then turned to Tren and directed the entirety of my power against the wall of death around him.

Each moment seemed to carry the weight of ages, and I felt as though every inch of my flesh was being pressed against freezing metal. All at once I felt the barricade between Tren and I crumble, and I could sense the fibers of Tren's life force knitting together. I could feel his flesh mending. Thousands of points of agony were piercing my skin, and the cold was unbearable. I tore my hands away from Tren and fell back in exhaustion, my body crashing to the ground. Unconsciousness overtook me.

I stirred as someone lifted me from the ground. My eyes fluttered open long enough for me to realize that Tren-Lore was holding me. His hair was rumpled and his eyes were the deep blue of a summer sky. He smiled down at me, and I tried to smile back, but could not.

"All hail the Healer Lara!" The call was thunderous with hundreds of joined voices. All around us, the Sanysk had dropped to their knees, and the cry was being echoed over and over again. "All hail the Healer Lara!"

I closed my eyes. I was unable to keep them open a moment longer. I felt Tren-Lore kiss my forehead and whisper, "I love you, Lara." After that, I remembered no more.

* * *

When I next awoke, I was surrounded by a soft golden light. My first thought was that perhaps this was what it was like to be dead. The aching of my body and the familiar ceiling of the castle of Caladore reassured me that

I was very much alive. I tried to move, but found the effort too taxing.

"Lara?" I heard the slight crumple of parchment, and then Tren-Lore was kneeling by my bedside.

I smiled at his weary face. "It is good to see you again, Tren-Lore – Tren," I quickly corrected myself. When had I begun thinking of him as Tren-Lore again?

He shifted the scroll of paper to his left hand and reached out to entwine his fingers with mine. The warmth of his touch seemed to ease some of my pain. "Tren-Lore," he said softly, "I like that name better."

"Me too," I replied. I closed my eyes again and rested for a moment. "What are you reading?" I asked him finally.

He chuckled, and I felt his weight shift as he rose from his knees and came to sit beside me on the bed. "One of the bards from Cala has written it. I think you might like it." He cleared his throat. "It is entitled, *The Healer Lara.*"

I laughed slightly, but the sound was weak. Sleep was already beckoning me. "What is it really called?" I asked.

"That is what it is really called," Tren-Lore told me. "Someone wrote a story about you."

"Imagine that," I mumbled, but I could not seem to locate true surprise through the haze of my weariness.

Tren-Lore's hand gently brushed against my cheek, and the bed shifted slightly as he stood. The words he had spoken after I had saved him floated across my misty mind.

"I love you, Tren-Lore," I whispered, though I did not know if my words were loud enough for him to here. "Morian penent."

The last thing I heard was Tren-Lore's quiet reply. "Morian penent, Lara."

When I awoke again, the sun was streaming into the room. Namin was sitting next to me, holding a tiny bottle filled with vile-smelling salts. Standing behind her, wearing identically ridiculously grins, were Tren-Lore, Draows, Myste, Nahanni, and Zander. I could not help but laugh. Nearly everyone I knew was crowded around my bed. Even Namin! I turned to her with a smile. "Why are you here?" I asked, pushing the bottle away.

Namin leaned forward to hug me. "Tren-Lore wrote me. Garidet, Aly and I came as quickly as we could." She gestured to a girl I had not noticed before. She was standing a little away from the group and bouncing a baby on her hip.

"Garidet!" I exclaimed, and the girl waved hesitantly at me. "And Aly? Your new baby, Namin?" Tears formed in my eyes. I could not believe that I had allowed Yolis to sever my ties with Namin. I had not even known the name of her new baby.

"Hello, Lara," Garidet said in a shy voice, and then blurted, "Mother is training me to be a Healer!"

Namin chuckled. "I certainly am, and she must take after you because she is learning as fast as I can teach her." Namin smiled fondly at me and gently cupped my cheek in her hand. "You gave us all a scare, my dear child. Do you know you have been asleep for nearly two weeks?"

I yawned and stretched. "I feel like I could sleep for another two."

Despite my weariness, I managed to stay up and talk with the group for a short while. Namin told me everything that was new in Karsalin, and Garidet bubbled with excitement about all she was learning.

"Mother says that I might be able to go to Telnayis for a year or two!" the young girl exclaimed. "Can you imagine, Lara?"

I actually could. There had been a time in my life when the last thing I would have ever considered was to have gone to the Healers' school. Now, the idea appealed to me immensely. I wanted to go to the school of my mother's stories. I wanted to discover more about what it was to be a Healer.

"Oh, Lara," Nahanni sighed contentedly. Her words returned my attention to the people around me. "You should have seen Tren-Lore's coronation! It was so beautiful, and Tren-Lore made a marvelous speech!"

"Oh, it was beautiful," Myste sighed with mock pleasure. "Especially the way Tren-Lore had his hair done. Very nice."

"Well, this roll-out-of-bed look does not just happen, you know," Tren-Lore said with a laugh.

Draows regarded the two cousins, and while his face remained unreadable, his amber eyes were warm with good humor. "You would be proud of him, Lara," he said, placing an arm around Tren-Lore's shoulders. "I feel certain that we will have the pleasure of reading many a book written about our new Head of the League."

"The brotherhood has been doing a good job restoring peace," Tren-Lore said, "but Caladore still has much healing to do. Yolis' reign did a great deal of damage." Grief was still fresh in Tren-Lore's voice and expression.

"He did many bad deeds," I said softly, "but I am sorry that it had to end that way."

"I am sorry too," Tren-Lore said. He was looking at the floor, and I did not think he was speaking to anyone in the room.

Nahanni wiped tears angrily from her face. "Why did you have to bring that up?" she asked her brother crossly. "Zander, tell Lara about how you heard them singing a song about her in a tavern."

Zander obliged, and our conversation turned once more to happier events. I soon found my eyes growing heavy. The call to sleep was as tantalizing as the song of the Pandel and Laowermings. It drew me quickly from my place in consciousness, and I wandered deep into the realm of dreams.

* * *

Spring had taken a firm hold on Caladore, and Tren-Lore had organized a huge party the likes of which Caladore had not seen since King Kiris had ruled. The gates of the castle were thrown open. Tents were erected within the outer courtyard, and the windows in the ballrooms and banquet halls were opened to let in the fresh air. The populous of Cala, the nobles, the Sanysk, and everyone else who passed Tren-Lore in the hall was invited to come and celebrate. Myste's wife Kalypceon even came, a group of Elves and the churlish Storm Wing in tow.

Tren-Lore insisted that the party was not for any purpose other than to have a good time. Myste and I howled when we heard about the dither this threw the nobles into. They could not comprehend a celebration without a specific reason for jovial behavior. Messengers were continually being sent to the castle inquiring after the occasion of the party.

"Just because I feel like it," Tren-Lore replied, and leaned back in his chair. "Has anyone seen where my crown has gotten to?"

Privately, however, Nahanni and I referred to it as the homecoming party. It seemed that the Caladore we had grown up in had finally been returned to us. Everyone was happier than they had been in many years, and the homecoming party reflected this lightened mood. There was lively music, dancing, and wonderful food everywhere you looked. I wondered vaguely how much turmoil the kitchen had been thrown into to create such a feast. Yet, as I surveyed the banquet hall, I knew that Sophie would have been proud of the result. The trials necessary to create such a party were well worth the struggle.

People were smiling and happily talking with one another. Even the Sanysk were enjoying themselves. Dayr, who had recovered fully from his wound, Draows who looked more jovial than I ever remembered him, and Tren-Lore were all standing together laughing.

I smiled across the table at Namin and Garidet. "I never thought I would see the day when a group of Sanysk would stand about joking with each other." I popped a piece of meat into my mouth and savored the taste.

"Are they usually serious?" Garidet asked. She craned her neck to catch a glimpse of a Sanysk in the crowd. Not everyone had chosen to come, but those in attendance appeared to be having a very good time.

"Serious!" Myste explained from his spot beside me. Snorting, he took a deep draft of ale and draped his arm around his beautiful wife's shoulder. "Positively grim is a more apt description." Myste winked at Garidet. "You should go ask Dayr to dance – teach him how to have *real* fun at a party."

Garidet blushed. Since she had been staying in Caladore, she had developed an innocent devotion to Dayr, which Nahanni and I often teased Dayr about.

Garidet looked at her mother, and Namin smiled warmly. "We should all dance."

Kalypceon laid a slender hand on Myste's arm. "That is a wonderful idea," she said in a lyrical voice.

I tossed my napkin down on the table. "I agree."

The eight of us had just finished dancing when I heard a familiar voice calling over the noise of the crowd.

"Lara! Oh, Lara! How lovely it is to see you!"

I turned and smiled as Flock made her way towards me. Leffeck followed behind. He was dressed as elaborately as ever, but he had grown a mustache, which he twirled around one finger as he stared contemptuously at everyone around him. I greeted Flock warmly, and Tren-Lore grinned wickedly as he slapped her stout little husband on the back.

"Leffeck!" he declared, "You are looking radiant, just radiant!"

Leffeck stumbled forward, and Flock grabbed his arm to steady him. Leffeck scowled at her and yanked his arm away. Turning to Tren-Lore and I, he bowed deeply. "Your Majesty. Reverent Healer."

I had been addressed by that title many times, but still could not help feeling a sense of shock. "It is nice to see you too, Leffeck." I turned to Flock. "How is everything?"

"Oh, wonderful," Flock exclaimed exuberantly, though it looked as if her smile would crack from her face and shatter on the floor.

She began telling me all her news, but before long the conversation turned back to memories of our childhood in the kitchen. By the time Flock left my side, I had a strong urge to return to that familiar setting. The only place that had ever truly been my home in the castle had been the small room Sophie and I had shared. I had not been there since the night she had died. I now had a great desire to go and see it.

When I arrived in the kitchen, I found that it had not changed. It looked identical to the first day I had seen it, except that it was deserted at the moment. Everyone who was not serving at the party had been given the night off. As I walked through the familiar chambers, I half expected to see Sophie come bustling towards me, or hear Flock's penetrating voice. I ran my hands over the smooth counters and fondly touched the backs of chairs that were tucked neatly against the table. Finally, I came to the room that Sophie and I had shared.

I opened the door with some trepidation, but the grief I had felt the last time I had been there did not come rushing back. A heavy coating of dust lay on the table and beds. Someone had taken the mirror. Other than that, the room looked as if it had been undisturbed. I sat on the end of my bed and closed my eyes, reliving pieces of the many memories I had made while I grew up there.

From out in the kitchen, I heard the sounds of footsteps, and then the scraping of a chair against the stone floor. I rose and went to investigate, shutting the door quietly behind me. Tren-Lore was sitting at the table.

"I thought I might find you here." He scratched absently at his rumpled hair and grinned at me. "All that talk about the past."

All that talk about the past, my mind echoed. It was time to start considering the future. I pulled out a chair across from him and sat down. We regarded each other in silence, and it seemed that visions from the past wound themselves about Tren-Lore like the arms of a lover. Impetuously, I shifted so that my knees were on my chair. I leaned forward across the table, and ignoring the confused look upon Tren-Lore's face, I kissed him. The instant our lips met, I felt the warmth of love course through my body. So many things had changed, and yet this beautiful, unbreakable bond remained.

As I drew away, Tren-Lore raised his eyebrows in question. I smiled at him and resumed my seat. It had always been that way with us. We understood one another as no one else ever had. The smile I had been wearing faltered. "I think I am going to leave Caladore. I do not know when I will be back. I might go to Telnayis."

Tren-Lore did not seem surprised. He nodded. "You might need this." From his belt, he drew the dagger he had given to me all those years ago. "Solrium vallent," he said.

"Solrium vallent," I repeated. I took the dagger from him and fondly traced the inscription on the hilt. When I looked up at Tren-Lore, tears were in my eyes. "When you first gave this to me, I could not understand what that meant, but now I do."

The next morning I called Tren-Lore, Myste, Nahanni, Zander, and Namin to join me in the courtyard. All my belongings were packed and stowed in Paence's saddlebags. I knew that I should have felt sad, but instead, I was filled with exhilaration. While I would miss everyone, I knew that I would have longed for their presence even if I had stayed in Caladore. Namin and Myste would be returning to their homes in a few days. Tren-Lore was only staying another week, and then he too would be gone with the Sanysk to continue to restore peace. Nahanni was to be left in charge, and the young woman was consumed with preparing for her role as steward of Caladore.

My good-byes were full of hugs and promises to write and come back to visit as often as I could. Nahanni wept a little, but assured me they were tears of happiness. Namin pressed me to her and murmured how proud she was of me, and how proud my mother and Sophie would have been. Myste warned me that traveling was a smelly business and to try to find as many nice inns as I could.

I hugged Tren-Lore the longest, ingraining in my memory the feel of his arms around me. There was scarcely a time in my life when he had not been present. Most of my memories included him in some way. He had been my first friend, my first love, and the one person I knew would remain with me until the end. How I would miss him! I stepped away and found that despite my elated mood, I was crying.

"I love you," Tren-Lore said as we broke apart from our fierce hug. "Morian penent."

"Morian penent," I replied, my voice feeling thick in my throat. I looked up into his familiar blue eyes and gently touched his cheek. "I love you, too."

Wiping at my eyes, I moved away from Tren-Lore and mounted Paence. "Farewell," I called as I turned Paence and nudged her into an easy trot.

Calls of parting followed me until I had ridden through the gates and onto the road. The only noise was the rhythmical pounding of Paence's hooves. They were like a drum in my ears. It was a rhythm that I had complete control over. The wind dried the dampness on my cheeks, and I inhaled a deep breath of spring air.

I camped that night by a small glade of trees. A stream ran through the middle of the grove. As I pulled my sleeping furs up around my chin and stared up into the vast sky, the sound of my soft weeping mingled with the song of the Aquara. I longed for Tren-Lore. I wept until sleep enfolded me in a soft embrace that quieted my mind.

I dreamed that I was back in the castle. I was wandering down the hallway that I had found on my first day at Caladore. Where tapestries had once hung, now stood only blank walls. The door to the balcony was ajar. I stepped through, expecting to find Tren-Lore on the other side, but instead found myself in an endless field. My mother was waiting for me. We walked hand in hand through fields of golden grass and she told me the old stories that I had loved.

"Mother," I asked, "will you tell me a new story now?"

She smiled down upon me, and her pink lips parted with a reply. "Perhaps you can tell me one of yours."

"All right," I consented, and began.

Printed in the United States
114902LV00005B/5/P